Sitti Djaoerah

SITTI DJAOERAH

A Novel
Of Colonial Indonesia

Sitti Djaoerah *(1927) by M.J. Soetan Hasoendoetan*
Translated and with an Introduction by Susan Rodgers

University of Wisconsin-Madison Center for Southeast Asian Studies
Monograph 15
1997

Library of Congress Catalogue Card No. 97–060978

ISBN (Cloth) 1–881261–20–4
ISBN (Paper) 1–881261–21–2

Published by the
University of Wisconsin-Madison
Center for Southeast Asian Studies
Madison, Wisconsin 53706 USA
Monograph Number 15
Volume Editor: Andrea Canfield

Telephone: (608) 265–5759
FAX: (608) 263–3735
Website www.wisc.edu/ctrseasia

Edited by Janet Opdyke
Designed by Andrea Canfield

Printed in the United States of America

Contents

Introduction

Djahoemarkar, who cracks open the past
Who breaks open all manner of sadness
Who opens wells of deep longing and loneliness
Who opens, too, the path to luck and joy.

These words are eulogies, derived from a form of Angkola Batak chant speech and epic narrative called *turiturian*, which was being eclipsed by the popularity of printed literature and Dutch-toned schoolbook learning by the time *Sitti Djaoerah*, the novel translated here and the source of these lines, was published in 1927. The loving inclusion of these phrases in this extraordinary Batak language, Dutch colonial-era, prose novel—indeed, their constant, playful reiteration with profuse variations throughout the narrative when the character Djahoemarkar is mentioned—made the book a sly, knowing, commentary text on this Sumatran society's cultural position in the 1920s between the sort of village oral culture that had fostered chanted epics and the sort of deep print literacy that yielded novels like this one.

Batak-language fiction of the 1920s and 1930s has generally been overshadowed by the more famous Indonesian-language novels of the same period such as Marah Rusli's *Sitti Nurbaya*, Abdul Muis's *Salah Asuhan*, Selasih's *Kalau Tak Untung*, and *Azab dan Sengsara* (the last, it happens, by the Angkola Batak author Merari Siregar but written in Indonesian). These "Generation of the 1920s" Indonesian novels have been well studied by Indonesian and foreign scholars and have even become part of the Indonesian public high school curriculum.[1] By contrast, it is not too much to assert that prewar Batak-language fiction, for non-Batak readers at least, is a lost literature today—an unfortunate circumstance on several fronts. *Sitti Djaoerah* (the title is the name of a young woman, Djahoemarkar's childhood friend and later his wife) is a largely unknown novel from the short-lived but incandescent and aesthetically quite breathtaking southern Batak fiction literature that thrived in the last two colonial decades in northern Sumatran towns such as Sibolga, Pematang Siantar, Sipirok, and Padangsidimpuan. Like the better-known Indonesian-language novels, the southern Batak works tended to be troubled love stories and journey novels about growing up and moving from an ethnic enclave society into the more cosmopolitan precincts of the Netherlands East Indies such as plantation-belt areas, commercial cities, and secondary school arenas. Within this small Batak fiction tradition (only a few titles ever appeared as books, but more works were published in serialized form in newspapers), *Sitti Djaoerah* stands out as the most fully accomplished work of art.[2] It was a resistance novel of sorts, in that it was a bold assertion by an indigenous author that Sumatra was not a Dutch colonial place in any final sense but a human terrain with Batak concerns and evaluative frameworks at its center. This novel was also a celebration of the Angkola Batak language, its profuse ritual oratory registers of speech, and its potential as a medium for a self-consciously modern print fiction. This, in an era when Dutch was the prestige language of the elite schools whose degrees many southern Batak were seeking and at a time when Malay (soon to be called Bahasa Indonesia) was rapidly becoming the canonical language of indigenous political resistance in the Indies. *Sitti Djaoerah* stands as a testament to Angkola Batak literary ingenuity in the face of all this.

This introduction to my English translation of *Sitti Djaoerah* (the first time the book has been translated into any language) is designed to help nonspecialist readers as well as long-time students of Indonesian literatures see some of the hidden political and ethnolinguistic dimensions of this unfamiliar text as they read the book for enjoyment. Indeed, my anthropological comments on *Sitti Djaoerah* notwithstanding, it should be remembered that this novel was clearly intended by its author, Soetan Hasoendoetan, to be a work of mass entertainment and popular literature for its first generation of Angkola fans. As the translator of this remarkable book, it is my hope that a good measure of the novel's social daring, but also its air of linguistic verve and fun, comes through in my English sentences, so that distant readers have a chance of understanding why many older Angkola Batak who read *Sitti Djaoerah* soon after it was first published look upon the work as the key record of who they are in Indonesia, who they were in the colonial Indies, and what sort of a past continues to shape the Angkola present, far away from the colonial Indies in modern-day Indonesia.

For many elderly readers in places like Sipirok and Padangsidimpuan (people in their seventies who I had the good fortune to interview during my ethnographic fieldwork on oratory, literacy, and literature issues beginning in 1974 in Sipirok), *Sitti Djaoerah* is not a lost novel at all. Most of these men and women, admittedly, had long misplaced their copies of the book until I came along and gave them photocopies of the original text, which is now in the National Library in Jakarta. However, they vividly remembered *Sitti Djaoerah* and its busy literary setting of local Angkola Batak– and Indonesian-language newspapers, verse novels in the same two languages, *adat* ('ancient customs') guidebooks, and locally authored schoolbooks. In southern Batak school towns, the reading public of students, teachers, booksellers, cloth merchant families, and newspaper people generally were fluent in both Angkola Batak and Indonesian. (Indonesian is the term I will use for colonial-era Malay, somewhat anachronistically. Promoted by Dutch officials as a language of pedagogy and commerce, Malay was adopted by early nationalists in 1928 as a language of unification, resistance to the Dutch, and interethnic communication. Indonesia has more than two hundred ethnic-language communities.) My elderly conversational partners talked to me at length about their memories of literature and oratory in the years before national independence; they were also voluble on the subject of the Angkola Batak language's standing in relation to Indonesian and Dutch, and on translation issues. I draw on those comments in this essay, along with my ethnographic fieldwork on ritual oratory in Sipirok (Soetan Hasoendoetan's hometown) and nearby villages.[3]

What I found, at base, about late colonial Angkola Batak–language fiction during my several stays in the Sipirok area and during my archival work in Jakarta and the Netherlands was that this is a fiction literature about history and social identity. An early chapter of *Sitti Djaoerah* is tellingly entitled "Taringot tu na Robian" ("About the Past"). Indeed, for both its elderly aficionados today and its first generation of readers in the 1920s and 1930s, *Sitti Djaoerah* is and was just that: a novel about Angkola Batak history and Angkola efforts to write imaginative history with precision, emotional seriousness, and artistic panache in a time of colonial domination and fragmentary nationalist Indonesian hopes.

JOURNEYS TO DELI

Sitti Djaoerah is a novel about several things at once: about novel writing itself in a time of colonial censorship and political control; about the Angkola oratorical world as it was coming to be apprehended in new ways in an age of print literacy; about Angkola social identity as that came to be a thinkable sort of concept in colonial Sumatra. Most obviously in terms of sheer story line, it is a novel about turn-of-the-century Angkola young people and their journeys to maturity as they emigrated from rural farm villages and highland market towns to Sumatra's east coast plantation belt, or Deli (see maps following this introduction). The novel concerns the period from approximately 1880 to 1925, which was, of course, the immediate past for the book's first generation of readers. Many of these people were themselves migrants to east Sumatra. The novel was also read and sold widely in rural Tapanuli. This was the Dutch colonial administration's geographical and administrative designation for Angkola's home area in the mountains. Tapanuli also extended into the Toba Batak region, to Angkola's northwest, while the southern part of Tapanuli covered the Mandailing region, which was situated along the Minangkabau border (another ethnic home region, with a different local language, closer in this case to Indonesian than the Batak languages are).

Angkola itself was sometimes dubbed Angkola-Sipirok by the Dutch, a usage that some local people adopted. Ethnic boundaries were inexact and changeable whatever the case, and, in fact, in Soetan Hasoendoetan's time in towns such as Sipirok local people sometimes identified themselves not as Angkola Batak but as members of much smaller chieftaincy leagues. For such people, Angkola apparently tended to be the term used to refer to residents of Angkola Jae and Angkola Julu, two large chieftaincy leagues located near the town of Padangsidimpuan. Ethnic designations are socially labile like this throughout all the Batak areas, and Angkola is certainly no exception.[4] Somewhat artificially, I use the word Angkola here to refer to the entire area between Mandailing and Toba. To render matters more complex, people in this southern Tapanuli region have long been skittish about claiming identity as Bataks, as that designation has overtones of "primitiveness" in east Sumatra among Malays living there. During the period *Sitti Djaoerah* covers, some southern Batak dropped their clan names so as not to be confused with "backward," pig-eating, pagan Bataks. Clan identity is consistently muted throughout *Sitti Djaoerah*.

Although it was manifestly about trips to Deli, *Sitti Djaoerah* was first published in Tapanuli in serialized form in the Angkola Batak–language newspaper

Poestaha in the port town and administrative capital of Sibolga. Today, Sibolga is a muggy, rather ramshackle trade town with no hint of its own newspaper (the city of Medan now dominates the north Sumatran mass media scene, and little Tapanuli towns have no local newspapers). However, in the two pre–World War II decades Sibolga was a major center of southern Batak literary life, with local publishing houses and several Toba and Angkola Batak and Indonesian-language newspapers. The word *poestaha* means 'ancient heirlooms', but the newspaper was (typically enough for this era of Batak journalism) a forward-thinking sort of weekly dominated by news of plantation crop prices, school policy issues, and political developments elsewhere in the Indies. Another staple topic was village *adat*, which had become "beset" by argument and tension (as newspaper feature writers reported) in a time of rapid social change—another prominent social assumption in the Sibolga journalism of the time.

Serialized novels such as *Sitti Djaoerah*, published as feuilletons, or continuing stories, from issue to issue, were used as circulation-boosting devices in almost all major Batak newspapers. Two years after its run in *Poestaha*, *Sitti Djaoerah* was issued in the form of a book by the Sibolga publisher Philemon bin Haroen.[5] The proprietor of this publishing house was a southern Batak man who had acquired his impressive-sounding, if improbable, Malay name in his travels through Minangkabau and central Tapanuli as a bookseller.

In this same period, Deli was undergoing such a boom in plantation construction that huge tracts of monocrop strips were being carved out of the old forest lands and *Sitti Djaoerah*'s author could mordantly but correctly refer to the east coast as "Deli het dollarland." To evoke this Deli world in print fiction, Soetan Hasoendoetan used Angkola Batak as the primary language in his novel, but he also made brief forays into Dutch, Malay, Toba Batak, and Mandailing Batak when his protagonists traveled to polyglot Deli or to ethnic worlds outside Angkola's home rural region. There are many of these in Sumatra, as well as five other Batak societies, and Soetan Hasoendoetan's characters are peripatetic.

Soetan Hasoendoetan writes that the rural hinterlands in Tapanuli were seen by many Angkola young people as constricted places where farmland was scarce and Dutch corvée labor demands were heavy and constant. Glittering Deli was seen as a place to build an Angkola future, but it also was construed as a troubled social arena where village morality could collapse and individual Angkola travelers could lose their way. It is the history of this migration out of the southern Batak highlands to Medan (Deli's city) and its expanses of tobacco and tea plantations that *Sitti Djaoerah*'s author sought to chronicle in the main, second part of his novel. The book is a socially panoramic one and operates in one main channel as a socially realistic record of Deli and Tapanuli worlds in flux, but Soetan Hasoendoetan also offered his readers a kind of poetic lament for the deep sadness that their particular migrational past held for Angkola individuals in terms of the Deli journey's many social, emotional, and aesthetic losses for both migrants and the villagers "left behind" in the highlands. It is this sort of "modern-day" and colonial Indies sadness that Soetan Hasoendoetan, ironically enough, indexed so often throughout the text with his use of affecting *turiturian* phrases like those quoted in the epigraph that opened this essay. When *turiturians* are performed as chants, and also here in this novel, these passages are designed to induce states of poignant sadness and feelings of loss. Soetan Hasoendoetan used this emotional register to tie his novel to Angkola chant traditions and give a distinctively Angkola Batak twist to novelistic prose.

Strongly influenced by the print world of newspapers and by nascent modern fiction traditions in Sumatra, Soetan Hasoendoetan wrote his "all manner of sadness" narrative in a transformed, purposely quite literate *turiturian* key. That is, he wrote a thoroughly Angkola novel that pointed toward both local Angkola oratory and cosmopolitan print; he tapped the Angkola Batak language's ritual speech registers *and* Deli's multilingual aesthetic and social richness and its complex print matrix of fiction and journalism. Along the way Soetan Hasoendoetan in effect invented the idea of the Angkola Batak novel as an art form distinct from the Indonesian-language novel. *Sitti Djaoerah* was his popular literature exemplar of this, for Soetan Hasoendoetan was certainly not a literary theorist in any formal sense. As we shall see, he wrote as a sideline to his basic job as head clerk on an east Sumatran tea plantation, and he operated largely independently of such prominent Sumatran writers and literary theorists as Armijn Pane and the novelists close to the publishing circles of Balai Pustaka, the colonial government's publishing house for "fine literature."[6]

Before discussing Soetan Hasoendoetan's own life story and *Sitti Djaoerah* as a text in more detail, we can look briefly at Sumatra's language world at the time he was writing his book and during the era he was invoking in his fiction.

LANGUAGE WORLDS IN COLLISION

For Soetan Hasoendoetan, the journey to Deli demanded a new narrative format for its description, with new timescapes and social vocabularies that went beyond the rhetorical capacities of the chanted epics. Soetan Hasoendoetan also found that chronicling young peoples' trips out of the highlands called for new perspectives on language and on interlinguistic worlds in multiethnic settings such as Sumatra's east coast. There, in Deli, languages such as Dutch, Malay, several varieties of Batak, Javanese (spoken by immigrant plantation laborers), and Minangkabau (spoken by merchant families and students from West Sumatra) were in daily contact with each other. All of these languages, and in some cases their special registers of oratory and printed discourse, mutually influenced each other as well as Deli residents' ideas about human speech in more general ways.

Deli, in fact, was classically heteroglossic, in Soetan Hasoendoetan's time, in a Bakhtinian sense. According to the Russian literary theorist Mikhail Bakhtin, whose work on languages in contact and the special status of the novel as a literary form is immensely helpful in looking at *Sitti Djaoerah* (Bakhtin 1990a; see also Bakhtin 1986; Holquist 1990a, 1990b; and Lodge 1990), periods of history when languages in effect ram into each other and compete for social space foster a specific type of language ideology. These language contact situations can also be spurs to a particular sort of literary creativity: novel writing. Bakhtin writes that languages in social contact encourage commentary about translation issues as well as interlinguistic parody. Within this, "languages and styles actively and mutually illuminate one another" (1990c: 76). Languages enter into a process of dialogization with each other, losing their inherent authoritativeness and comfortable believability for their speakers as they do so. Bakhtin goes on to specify the distinctive type of consciousness about language found in multilanguage worlds of the sort in which he is especially interested: the spoken and written universes of newly formed or just forming nations.

Along with other theorists of the novel, Bakhtin points out that this literary form's natural habitat is the time when old societies wash up on the shoals of nations. In the European case, "a multitude of different languages, cultures, and times [became] available . . . and this became a decisive factor in its life and thought" (1990b: 11). The European novel can be traced to a "very specific rupture in the history of European civilization: its emergence from a socially isolated and culturally deaf semi-patriarchal society, and its entrance into international and interlingual contacts and relationships" (1990b: 11): much the Deli situation, too.

Bakhtin spotlights the interrelationship between the novelistic world and the various types of discourse found in an author's wider culture. The latter might include various class-based registers of speech, different dialects, and the whole panoply of oral art practiced in the society (jokes, profanity, folktales, ritual speech routines, and highly authoritative forms such as epics). In Bakhtin's view, the novel voraciously consumes these oral forms. To change metaphors, the novel in effect playfully knocks the authoritative stuffing out of them. Thus, the novel's sense of scandal, play, and "newness." The same scandalous edge can be used in the novel to cut through the presumptions of different types of writing in the culture—and various social structural presumptions as well.

As soon as the novel appears as a type of writing in a society, it begins to ingest all other genres, subverting them to its own narrative aims of writing complete social worlds via a rhetorical strategy of having a culture's multiple streams of discourse interpenetrate. As letters, newspaper writing, advertising copy, schoolbook prose, folklore versions of oral tales, and so on become subsumed within the novel's imperial scope, they lose their self-sufficiency as distinct genres. For the novelist, they also become important for the commentary they can provide about each other. The dialogic discourse of the novel parallels—and comments on—the dialogic character of the larger language world that surrounds the novelist and readers. Critical perspectives deepen, and each form of writing, once distinct, now becomes a mere part of the fabric of the novel. Writers emerge as social and linguistic skeptics and critics, if not as outright parodists; thoughtful readers can follow them down these same paths.

Even the quickest glance at *Sitti Djaoerah* shows many of these Bakhtinian predictions in full flower. Moreover, in the hands of so adept a writer as Soetan Hasoendoetan, the novel could call into question the whole Dutch colonial adventure in Sumatra. In other words, a political carryover effect for the novel was possible. Soetan Hasoendoetan's book certainly does seem to have swallowed the language universe of 1920s Sumatra whole, for readers encounter a multitude of spoken and written forms as they make their way through the book. Each type of writing and oratory, too, has had its conceptual structure refocused away from its original canonical stylistic standards toward the narrative needs of telling *Sitti Djaoerah*'s protagonists' stories. *Sitti Djaoerah* is untidy and harlequin in character. Throughout, it makes its own rules: where all the other genres of writing and ritual speech that are portrayed in the book have a previous structure to which language would normally conform, this Batak work (like any novel) seeks to shape its form to utterance, lived speech, and language-in-the-world—to, in this case, Deli heteroglossia.

Not surprisingly, given his astute sense of language structure and the social life of speech and writing, Soetan Hasoendoetan focused a good deal of the aesthetic action of his novel on the ways in which various registers of the Angkola language (oratory, chants, courtship duels, and so on, but also such things as handwritten letters, printed books, and newspapers) bump into each other in his characters' lives and his narrative. Thinking about such linguistic complexity and the interaction between different levels of speech and writing is portrayed in *Sitti Djaoerah* as a most pleasurable thing, as something *tabo* ('delicious'), in the sense of something good to eat and savor. As we shall see, this was a consistently important idea for Soetan Hasoendoetan in his approach to language and writing.

Benedict Anderson's comments on national languages and commercial print capitalism and their link to nationalist ideology (as set out in his *Imagined Communities: Reflections on the Origins and Spread of Nationalism* [1983]) also helps us define this Angkola novel's specific sociolinguistic setting. Anderson asserts that nations can only be "imagined" if certain communications media and genres are available in a society. Mass literacy in a vernacular language "underneath" a more universalistic, elite language (such as Latin) is needed, he writes, to foster a specifically nationalist sense of peopleness. Further, a culture of widespread commercial print is necessary for the promulgation of secular nationalist ideas uniting people who have never met face to face and are imagined to live in secular, "clockable" time (all components necessary for the legitimation of nationalism, Anderson asserts).

Newspapers and their particular views of social time and space are also indispensable components of new nationalist ideologies and their spread, Anderson holds. He writes that the very act of reading the morning newspaper conjures up an image of many thousands of other persons similarly engaged, at that same time, reading their own papers. Such imagery allows the reader to accede to the notion that a large community exists, even if its members have no chance of meeting each other.

The literary genre of the novel itself works together with newspapers to foster the imagination of the sort of social landscapes and time frameworks crucial to the invention and promulgation of nationalism. Novels, like newspapers, posit a group of characters embedded in a "society" whose members move simultaneously through secular time. The novel's reader comes to see this "society" laid out in panoramic fashion, united by plotlines about social connections and ruptures. The act of novel reading itself engages the consumer of popular fiction in the larger, hidden endeavor of imagining new sorts of social communities like nations. For Soetan Hasoendoetan the people at issue in his work were not future citizens of some imagined independent Indonesian nation—that possibility is not even mentioned in *Sitti Djaoerah*—but members of a resilient, economically wily, Angkola Batak society stretching from Tapanuli to Deli. Readers invented themselves as members of this imagined community, in part at least, by consuming their Tapanuli novels and newspapers. As we shall see, these often tended to be rhetorical fraternal twins for both Angkola writers and readers.

SITTI DJAOERAH'S LITERARY SETTING

To capture a far-flung Angkola world in print, Soetan Hasoendoetan mined *turiturian* narrative for its aesthetic loveliness and emotional depth, but he also went on to draw upon European-influenced novelistic traditions, as these had been refracted into Sumatran print literature by the 1920s. Southern Batak and their ethnic neighbors rarely seemed to have read European novels directly, but they encountered the socially realistic novel via Indonesian-language fiction from the Generation of the 1920s books.[7]

Sitti Djaoerah's publication decade was a boom time for novel writing in several of Sumatra's societies, most prominently in West Sumatra. This was the same period in which modern fiction written in the Indonesian language first forcefully came onto the larger Netherlands East Indies scene. The government publishing house, Balai Pustaka, issued numerous titles directed at the growing numbers of eager Indonesian-language readers being produced by the secondary schools in many parts of Sumatra and Java. Some of these Balai Pustaka books were retellings of old folktales and chronicles, but the novels cut a higher profile in southern Tapanuli literary circles among writers and common readers both.[8] Angkola readers and writers such as Soetan Hasoendoetan (school graduates, basically, who lived in towns and cities as opposed to villages) were often fluent in Bahasa Indonesia, and they consumed the famous Balai Pustaka novels at a rapid clip. Also apparently quite popular with Indonesian-language readers in towns such as Sibolga at the time were crime stories and detective novels, which were often written by Indonesian Chinese, Minangkabau, or Acehnese writers.[9]

The higher-toned Balai Pustaka novels tended to chronicle the personal histories of fictional young people of village origin (or one generation removed from such) who find themselves thrust into morally problematic urban Indies situations (e.g., students attending Dutch-run schools with mixed race classmates or young schoolgirls forced into marriages with rich old merchants). Such turmoil-filled narratives were often couched in terms of unhappy love stories, in which young women in particular tended to find themselves suspended between village social expectations and Indies city dreams. Sumatran readers could recognize their own dilemmas in these stories, which were often written by southern Batak or Minangkabau authors as opposed to writers from elsewhere in the archipelago. In fact, the specific details of Minangkabau matrilineal descent and southern Batak marriage alliance often figure heavily in some of the more famous Balai Pustaka novels.[10]

About romantic love and therefore a touch scandalous, in some cases the Balai Pustaka novels cut close to the bone. Marah Rusli's *Sitti Nurbaya* concerned forced marriage and the emotional damage it could do to Sumatran young people, while Abdul Muis's *Salah Asuhan* ("Wrong Upbringing") dealt with young Minangkabau suspended between "village traditions" and the attractions of the Europeanized sector. Merari Siregar's *Azab dan Sengsara* related a tale of a young Sipirok girl whose father lost all the family money through gambling. This sudden loss of family status blocks her hopes of marrying her favorite, a boy of aristocratic background who had long been her childhood friend. Both protagonists are catapulted into disastrous lives in Deli, the young man forced into a marriage arranged by his parents for family alliance purposes and Mariamin, the young woman, consigned to an unhappy match with a much older man. (He gives her a venereal disease, and she dies an isolated death). Although ostensibly about domestic dramas and love troubles (to say the least in Mariamin's case), such novels obviously also nudged readers to think about larger losses connected with social change in a "Sumatra on the move."[11]

That Netherlands East Indies writers and readers of the period could draw on European novelistic traditions and transform them into print fiction meaningful in terms of their own situations was due in part to the popularity of schooling throughout southern Tapanuli during the previous fifty years. During this era many Angkola village and town families became obsessed with schoolbook learning and graduation rates, seen as their children's tickets out of farm life and into prestigious paid jobs in plantation offices, the school bureaucracy, or colonial government offices throughout Tapanuli and the *rantau*, the "regions beyond" the home ethnic areas in the highlands.[12] *Sitti Djaoerah* was both a product and a promoter of this overheated southern Batak school culture. It is no accident that the novel's hero, Djahoemarkar, begins his working life as an assistant teacher in an elementary school in Padangsidimpuan and that he meets his future wife, Sitti Djaoerah, in class. She is about twelve years old at the time, three or four years younger than her suitor, and is attending school against the wishes of her father, who thinks formal education for girls is a waste of time "since they'll only learn how to write love letters to boys."

Before print literacy in the Latin alphabet arrived in Tapanuli in the 1850s (it caught on in school classrooms by the 1880s), Angkola had long employed an old script syllabary. This had been used for runic purposes but also for some limited literary tasks. The Batak syllabary used in Angkola was probably derived from the Sanskrit-based writing systems of south Sumatran courts, and it may well have been known for hundreds of years in the southern Batak areas.[13] Village priest-diviners, or *datu*, were often fluent in the syllabary, but literacy in these old Batak letters may also have been fairly widespread among village young people at the time of earliest Dutch contact (the 1820s and 1830s). The Batak script was apparently used to record astrological knowledge, divination formulae, spells, and genealogical lore. However, parts of some *turiturian* narratives were also preserved on bark in folded bark books. Forms of entertaining speech such as courtship rhymes were also inscribed on lengths of bamboo. Literacy in the syllabary was not a school-based form, however, before European contact times, and the writing system was apparently used more to record oral forms than to develop a specifically literate, full-blown, imaginative literature of the sort typically fostered in commercial print.[14] That came to Tapanuli only with the Christian missions, the expansion of the public school system, and the lure of jobs in the Deli plantation sector, positions that demanded a knowledge of reading and writing the Latin alphabet.

Angkola also had a second writing system before the colonial schools arrived: the Arabic script. This had entered southern Tapanuli on a wave of conversions to Islam in the 1820s during the Padri Wars, when Minangkabau forces pushed northward into the Batak lands and converted significant numbers of villagers. Mystical brotherhoods, or *tarekat*, spread throughout Mandailing and Angkola in the wake of the Padris, and the rhythmic chanting of Qur'anic verses became an important, prestigious, ritual activity among converts. Rote memorization of oral chants and some rudimentary reading, or at least decoding knowledge, of Arabic holy texts became the center of Muslim piety for the new converts.[15] Arabic probably remained a runic script understood as a repository of ritual formulae and magical powers throughout southern Tapanuli for much of the century. Christian proselytization by the German Rhenish Mission followed in the 1850s.

Mission work began in Sipirok and the nearby villages of Parau Sorat and Bungabondar, which later became known as the homes of several generations of textbook authors. The Protestant mission brought Angkola its first European-style schools (Bible schools at first) as well as increasingly secular forms of literacy. The Rhenish Mission's efforts eventually resulted in the conversion of about 10 percent of the population around Sipirok to Protestantism, although most residents remained Muslim. (Today this is an area of unusually thoroughgoing monotheism, deriving from this early period.) Other Batak societies to the north (Toba, Dairi, Pakpak, Simelungun, and Karo) converted to the world religions after Christianity and Islam were already long established in the Sipirok and Padangsidimpuan areas. Soetan Hasoendoetan and all the southern Batak characters in his novel are Muslims; Batak Christianity is effectively invisible in the book.

In the Sipirok area the mission schools taught reading and writing in the old Batak script at first, during the 1850s and 1860s. A Batak script version of the New Testament had also been prepared by the mission for its work in Toba. However, by the 1880s the German and Dutch teachers and their first generation of Angkola teachers were converting many of their lessons into the Latin alphabet, which was also being used for hymnals. Many parishioners were still illiterate, so a church elder would read out each line of a hymn in a booming voice for the congregation to follow (in fact, this practice continues today in many village churches, long after literacy has become widespread). The Latin letters had also quickly become the main medium of instruction for southern Tapanuli's new, popular, public schools: primary schools in towns and larger villages, offering three grades of instruction in reading, writing, and figuring. By the turn of the century both religious and public elementary schools dotted the highlands, and Angkola and Mandailing (home of southern Tapanuli's first Kweekschool, or teacher training institute) had become centers of textbook authorship.

The next three decades saw the rapid rise of three other forms of print literacy in the Latin alphabet in Tapanuli, its outposts in Deli, and Tapanuli's capital Sibolga: newspaper publishing, folkloristic writing by indigenous authors, and Angkola Batak fiction. Some of this literature was written in the Angkola Batak language, while some was in Indonesian. Many writers with strong ties to the colonial school culture also spoke some Dutch, and phrases from that language often appeared in their work, although fiction and ancient customs folklore writing were generally either in Indonesian or Angkola Batak. Local newspapers were often written in a glorious mishmash of Indonesian and Angkola Batak, with Dutch and even English phrases thrown in for spice.

By the 1920s, Sipirok had become not just a school town but a writer's town, or at least a writer's hometown. Armijn Pane, author of the innovative 1942 Indonesian-language novel *Belenggu* ("Shackles") was born there, as was his dramatist-poet brother Sanusi. Both spent their careers in the *rantau*. The novelist Merari Siregar, *Azab dan Sengsara*'s author, came from Bungabondar, from a wealthy family educated in the Dutch-run schools. For these writers and their Angkola Batak and sometimes Indies-wide readerships (if they wrote in Indonesian), printed texts had come to work as media for imagining a "modern life" in the Netherlands East Indies.

As a Batak-language journey novel that was created in counterpoint to these much better known Indonesian-language novels of the 1920s, *Sitti Djaoerah* was also a book of huge sadness—for lost Tapanuli homes, Angkola pasts, and Angkola-language spoken universes from Tapanuli transplanted in time and space into plantation sector locales. However, along with this sadness and the book's many *turiturian*-like evocations of feelings of *lungun* (troubled sadness, isolated loneliness, poignant loss) in relation to the Angkola migration experience, *Sitti Djaoerah* also quite intentionally "opened a path to luck and joy," as the *turiturian* verse had it. *Sitti Djaoerah* did this exactly because it was a novel, and not some other form of printed literature, and because its author was enchanted with Balai Pustaka sorts of fiction and their writerly possibilities.

This is shown clearly in a short essay that Soetan Hasoendoetan wrote to introduce the first installment of *Sitti Djaoerah* when the novel began its run in the September 2, 1927, issue of *Poestaha*. In this page-one piece, Soetan Hasoendoetan tells his readers that he had been inspired to write this novel in the Angkola Batak language and not in Indonesian (which he of course knew) when he first read the many books being published by Balai Pustaka. Although he does not mention *Sitti Nurbaya* specifically, in all likelihood he had read it and probably several others. He begins his essay in the style of an *adat* orator, proferring elaborate apologies in advance for any deficiencies in speaking. He then goes on to note: "Indeed ... by now there have certainly been a very great number of books brought out by Balai Pustaka and read by the public, books written by smart and quite knowledgeable people who have afforded us much news about what has happened in the world. But, the majority of that news has been written in the languages of foreign places ..." This is a clear reference to Indonesian. At this point, Soetan Hasoendoetan goes on to remind his readers that their own good language is always their most beloved. He uses a food analogy, writing that, although rich Indian curries filled with exotic spices taste very good, Angkola home cooking is always the most delicious. Thus, will be, too, this local-language novel for speakers of Angkola Batak.

Sitti Djaoerah's narrative derives much of its attractiveness from a specific rhetorical circumstance: it omnivorously encompasses virtually all forms of Angkola ritual speech and written discourse, ranging from chants to curses, riddle speech, letters, and newspaper stories. All of these and even more types of oratory and Latin-alphabet print texts got stirred into *Sitti Djaoerah*'s delicious aesthetic of telling Deli lives in the "real world" of fictional near contemporaries of the book's readers. This linguistic scope gave a great exuberance to *Sitti Djaoerah*, both in its plot development and its views of language. Soetan Hasoendoetan had found the perfect literary medium for savoring Deli's (and the Deli journey's, and Tapanuli's) heteroglossic language experience.

THE TEXT AND ITS AUTHOR

Sitti Djaoerah was a lament but also a celebration of several types of exhilarating journeys. Some were in geographical space (toward Deli, toward paid jobs, and away from farm life and rural trading in such goods as resins and forest rubber). Other journeys were in biographical time (toward adulthood and often toward marriages based on love, not family dictates); yet other trips took place in linguistic experience (toward novels from oratory but also toward fully self-conscious fiction and away from folkloristic writing and standard schoolbook literacy). The latter path, toward novel writing as opposed to some simpler type of long prose work, was a trajectory that Soetan Hasoendoetan clearly saw as a positive and socially rewarding one.

The book's story line itself was strikingly optimistic. In sharp contrast to the plots of most of the Indonesian-language Balai Pustaka novels, *Sitti Djaoerah* chronicled migration biographies that ended happily. Whereas Balai Pustaka protagonists often either died or languished in forced marriages by the end of their stories, the characters in *Sitti Djaoerah* managed to hold on to both their core moral sensibilities and their home languages, in Deli, in adulthood. In fact, in this novel Angkola life and speech and even ritual oratory become transformed in cagey and creative ways in colonial contexts. This fosters considerable Deli prosperity for the book's Angkola protagonists. Djahoemarkar and Sitti Djaoerah thrive in Deli, and the novelist tells his readers that their secret of success is their deep Angkolaness. This is something that Soetan Hasoendoetan as novelist was very much in the process of inventing and imagining, in concert with his audience of literate sophisticates. In fact, *Sitti Djaoerah* and its ancillary texts in Angkola-language journalism and *adat* guidebook writing were working together at this time to foster notions of Angkola as a "society" having a "culture" in cosmopolitan Deli and Tapanuli within an Indies seen as being in social transition.

Sitti Djaoerah was part of an intertextual, cross-media ferment and as a consequence was a bounteous, thoughtful, and reflexive work on many fronts. It offers readers both a rousing good story (in fact, several rousing good stories) and an omnibus written evocation of every major genre of Angkola oratory. The book's characters, for instance, sometimes speak to each other in old courtship rhymes derived from village verbal duels—but they do this in a self-conscious, gamelike manner, playing at tradition. Ravishing cascades of mythic chant speech also break into the narrative. The phraseology of these chant interludes is exacting. Soetan Hasoendoetan adheres to extremely fine, high-oratory forms for his prose and verse passages related to the *turiturians*. *Sitti Djaoerah* includes two long chant passages, one in each part of the book. The first is arranged on the page in a verse format, while the latter is presented in prose. Individual *turiturian* phrases are worked right into the prose sentences. Sometimes the novelist urges readers to read his longer *turiturian* passages aloud or to chant them ("Dear Reader" is often addressed by the novelist in comradely fashion). Characters also tell each other folktales at frequent intervals in homes and schools. A few parts of the story line follow the logic and expository forms of oral folktales and *turiturian* epics.

But *turiturian* interludes are only part of *Sitti Djaoerah*. The author's vantage point is always that of print publishing, of fiction, not unreflective folkloristic writing. A prose format predominates. In fact, the original 457-page text had only 16 pages set in verse (although there are a number of song inserts and short verse passages such as those in which characters trade *pantuns*). The two parts of the book manage to encompass every prominent form of Angkola writing and print literature that had become popular in the culture by the 1920s. So, for instance, in addition to chant speech and folktales from the oral world (and some of their storytelling and aesthetic assumptions, as critiqued through literate frameworks), readers are given the texts of love letters, job notices, messages scratched on pieces of wooden furniture, and newspaper advertisements that the characters write to one another. Sometimes they lose track of each other's whereabouts and have to relocate themselves via the city weeklies. The Mandailing paper *Pertja Timoer*, published in Indonesian, comes to the rescue here (*Pertja Timoer* was a real newspaper). *Sitti Djaoerah* also includes journalistic accounts of village *adat* ceremonies, taken in one instance from a story that Soetan Hasoendoetan had published earlier in *Poestaha*. He modifies the newspaper article slightly to make it fit into his *Sitti Djaoerah* narrative, but he quite forthrightly informs his readers where the piece first appeared. This sort of thing obviously did not violate his standards of what constitutes proper novel writing.

Given this buzz of language activity, *Sitti Djaoerah*'s plot action and language play take place on several levels. The writer often mixes references to oratory, conversational speech, and printed literature in a single chapter, as he has his protagonists move between different social arenas, for example, from schoolroom to marketplace to a trip between a village and a town or a town and a forest. The first of the book's two long, mysterious, *turiturian* scenes takes place out in the deep woods, although late in the novel the second chant sequence occurs in an indelibly modern, Medan venue: the city's first makeshift airstrip, cleared for the metropolis's first visit by an airplane—flown by Tuan Chantelouq, a dashing French stunt pilot.

Sitti Djaoerah's mixture of linguistic registers and social landscapes is made more complex by the fact that the novel has two parts, in which the second essentially replays the plot structures of the first with new characters in new Sumatran settings. These are located the second time around more deeply in the *rantau* than was initially the case. This makes *Sitti Djaoerah* a considerably longer novel than the more familiar Indonesian-language novels of the 1920s.

A summary of some of *Sitti Djaoerah*'s plot action gives some indication of the book's attractions for its first readers. By the time the story begins, Dutch control was already well advanced in most Tapanuli mountain regions. Deli was well launched on its transformation into a get-rich-quick plantation belt for entrepreneurial Europeans, and European capital was turning the city of Medan into something of a colonial showpiece, with shining white civic buildings, trading company headquarters, and spacious tile-roofed residences. Angkola migrants hungered to see these wonders, Soetan Hasoendoetan tells his readers. The plantations themselves were rougher social arenas where isolated European families lived, wary of labor unrest and interethnic tensions among their native workers. *Sitti Djaoerah* begins far away from this, though, in Padangsidimpuan, southern Tapanuli's largest trading town. The narrative visits a few nearby villages and then strikes out toward Sipirok before wending its way through Toba to Medan and the Pangkalan Brandan port area. Another subplot veers off into Mandailing before the characters there also make their way to Deli.

Part 1 concerns the youth of Djahoemarkar's father and takes place entirely in Tapanuli. The focus of the story is on the adolescence, youthful misadventures, and eventual marriage of Pandingkar Moedo, Djahoemarkar's father, the "young martial arts battler." (Many of part 1's characters have names of this sort.) His own father dies in an epidemic and leaves a fortune in livestock and orchard lands to the boy and his mother. Pandingkar Moedo, who is about twelve years old when readers meet him, is a charming but irresolute youth who quickly links up with two weaselly young pals who push him into the local gambling dens of Padangsidimpuan. There he proceeds to rack up immense debts. The three boys fear that their creditors will find and beat them, but luckily they have recently set off into the forest to locate Raja Awaiting Battle, a great guru who teaches them the protective lore and martial arts they need to fend off enemies. The boys apprentice themselves to the guru, and he makes respectable martial arts practitioners of them. They learn some of the mystical arts for gaining invulnerability. Soon they attend a large *adat* ceremony in the aristocratic village of Batunadua and win a great deal of money at the gambling tables (this chapter gives Soetan Hasoendoetan the opportunity to insert his old newspaper article about the *adat* feast). The boys speedily fritter away their winnings. Soon they are forced to journey into the woods to gather forest rubber sap to sell in the market in order to make good on their debts. The forest is dark and mysterious. Pandingkar Moedo admits he does not know the lore of those-who-go-into-the-deep-woods (such matters as how to arrange oneself for sleep so as not to be attacked by tigers, how not to offend the forest spirits, how to talk to the trees, and so on). After a tiring day spent gathering sap, the three boys settle down around a campfire. One of Pandingkar Moedo's friends (both pals have

fighting cock titles, Rangga Balian and Rangga Poerik) volunteers to sing a *turiturian* chant to the others. This is what one does at night in the forest, he informs the
naive Pandingkar Moedo.

Drinking steamy mugs of strong gritty coffee, they listen to a long recitation
of a segment of a *turiturian* concerning a shadowy spirit woman living in a high
house on a cliff. She invites a passing human man to join her there. He does and
tumbles into the spirit world. The boy breaks off his recitation at this point, and he
and his compatriot drift off to sleep, but Pandingkar Moedo remains strangely troubled by the whole performance. His friends see the *turiturian* recital as an entertaining bit of nighttime amusement, but Pandingkar Moedo is not so sure: perhaps
just singing the words of the *turiturian* has served to break open the boundaries
between the everyday world and the spirit domain, he thinks to himself. Late that
night he sleepwalks out through the trees, imagining that he has fallen into the mystical realm of the chant and onto the strange shadow woman's plane of existence.

He does meet the odd spirit woman, who persuades him to cross over more
fully to her abode. Lost and shaken by his brush with the other world through the
chant, Pandingkar Moedo stumbles through the forest in a daze. He meets a magical tiger, which mauls and almost kills him. The beast stops at the last moment,
though, remembering that Pandingkar Moedo had thoughtfully removed a thorn
from his paw in a previous encounter (a typical *turiturian* plot twist). Pandingkar
Moedo finally comes back to his everyday senses and finds himself lying in a ditch
beside a road running alongside the forest, covered with mud and bleeding from all
the tiger scratches. A shopkeeper and rubber trader from Padangsidimpuan happens along this road in his high carriage. At this point in the novel the narrative
shifts to the socially realisitic plane for the duration of the story.

Recognizing Pandingkar Moedo as a family acquaintance (lucky coincidences
loom large in part 1), the merchant stops and insists that the young man climb into
the vehicle. This helpful fellow is named Awaiting Riches, and he soon becomes so
fond of Pandingkar Moedo that he takes the young man on as his junior business
partner, back in town.

Pandingkar Moedo's new job consists of daily trips to regional markets to buy
raw forest rubber for Awaiting Riches's brokerage firm in Padangsidimpuan. The
youth takes to stopping every market day at a fried bananas stand near the village
of Sihitang near the Mandailing border (all of these are real places). The propri-
etress sizes him up as a good marriage prospect for her teenage daughter, Si Taring.
The name means 'little girl' in a generic sense. In Mandailing families, the youngest
daughter goes by this tag until she is replaced with a younger sister who then takes
on the intimate nickname. (In Angkola, the youngest girl in the family is Si Butet.
Soetan Hasoendoetan is showing us Mandailing here.) Si Taring appears to be unin-
terested in Pandingkar Moedo, but she is actually quite smitten, as is he. They ban-
ter back and forth in sly courtship duels (pursued here in prose rather than the
rhymed verses of *martandang* ritualized courtship speech, which Soetan
Hasoendoetan uses in a parallel courtship scene in part 2). They eventually agree to
marry, although to grasp this point readers must be familiar with the extreme indi-
rectness, not to mention near perversity, of Angkola courtship speech. On the sur-

face of things the young pair seem more bent on insulting each other than on pursuing a marriage. Soon, Pandingkar Moedo's mother brings along the wife of Awaiting Riches to start the brideprice negotiations. An excruciatingly polite, roundabout social-visit scene follows, with much sharing of betel quid and exclamations about how delicious it all is (both the betel chewing and the *adat* talking about the brideprice amounts).[16] Si Taring keeps protesting that she does not want to marry this man, although of course she very much does.

The young couple marries, and soon "a little bird begins to sing": Si Taring shows the signs of early pregnancy. This phrase comes from *adat* oratory, from soul-firming ceremonies for babies. When their son, Djahoemarkar, is born, the couple's happiness grows. Before the infant is forty days old, however, Pandingkar Moedo's old sidekicks Rangga Poerik and Rangga Balian reappear. Pandingkar Moedo has brought them to trial (the colonial judicial system is a source of constant fascination throughout the novel) because they broke their solemn oath that no member of the trio would abandon the others, come what may. The judge decides that the boys are guilty and sentences them to jail.

The boys are angry, frustrated, and maliciously envious (a supremely important Angkola emotion) of Pandingkar Moedo's prosperous life. By the time they are released several years have passed and Pandingkar Moedo is a father. They wreak their revenge on him as he walks along the road, returning home from a market day in Sipirok and carrying a large bundle of cash. They jump him, steal his money, and throw a corrosive concoction of poison leaves into his eyes. He falls to the ground, rolling in agony. The poison has gutted his eyes. Somehow he manages to make his way home to Padangsidimpuan, where his boss, Awaiting Riches, is as distraught as Si Taring is about his condition. Pandingkar Moedo dies after a few days without seeing his infant son again. This is another vivid emotional point for Angkola readers, for seeing the face of a longed-for loved one is crucial to efforts to stave off overly strong feelings of *lungun*, or loss and pining.[17] Si Taring's *andung* (mourning laments) for her dead husband end the chapter, and readers must wait until part 2 to encounter her, her son, Awaiting Riches, and all the other main characters again.

Andung is an extremely affecting sort of sob-speech delivered by women at times of parting: from the dead at funerals, from children moving to the *rantau*, from daughters setting off on their wedding journeys. The *andung* passages that conclude part 1 are lexically precise, extended, and elaborate and seem designed to elicit sobs from readers. By the 1920s, *andung* was fading even in villages as a performance form, but it was still widely respected, and even loved, as an especially refined sort of speech known mostly to elderly women.[18]

Part 2 of the novel in effect replays Pandingkar Moedo's journey to maturity and marriage but this time on a wider Sumatran stage with a new pair of main characters: Djahoemarkar and Sitti Djaoerah (Awaiting Riches's daughter). They grow up in Padangsidimpuan, in shopkeeper circles, and then as teenagers migrate to Medan and plantation life. The new couple replaces the older one of part 1, so *Sitti Djaoerah* is obviously a pair of love stories as much as it is two tales of growing up. This made the book a piece of true mass literature by catching the wave of *Sitti*

Nurbaya's popularity and thus allying the story with the dominant thematic tradition of 1920s popular Sumatran fiction.

The second part of the novel relates the love story of the two Padangsidimpuan children from the time they meet in their Dutch-run (but Angkola-language) primary school, fall in love, vow to marry, and confront two major threats: a livestock plague that kills Djahoemarkar's family herds of water buffalo and the possibility of a forced marriage to a despicable old merchant for the girl (shades of *Sitti Nurbaya*). This man is called, appropriately enough, Sutan Hardwood, the Sutan Ashamed to Grow Old. He dispatches his present wife and child to the woman's home village while he pursues the lovely Sitti Djaoerah, then fourteen years old. Sitti Djaoerah and her mother run away from home and seek refuge in Mandailing on the eve of the arrival of the brideprice payments. Sitti Djaoerah's father, Awaiting Riches, had been hoping to gain a wealthy, high-status son-in-law and so had been pushing the marriage, all the while discouraging Sitti Djaoerah's profound love for Djahoemarkar.

Djahoemarkar, and then Sitti Djaoerah and her mother, take separate, dangerous paths to Deli, where Djahoemarkar seeks work on a dredging boat and then on a plantation. The dredging boat interlude gives Soetan Hasoendoetan the opportunity to provide his readers with a Malay-style fish story, in this case concerning a miraculous white crocodile. In Medan, all the parties eventually find each other, after several missed connections (the better to keep newspaper subscribers hooked on the story, probably). Soon the young people marry, have a son and daughter, and establish a permanent, successful, happy household as elite plantation employees. (They are definitely not coolie laborers. For southern Batak in this novel the latter status would be emblematic of abject failure in the trip to Deli.) Sitti Djaoerah occupies some of her time studying the Javanese language so as to get along more easily with her plantation neighbors, the coolies. At one point, during a labor dispute, she dresses up as a visiting Javanese prince who has purportedly been dispatched by the government to quell the threat of a strike by the misguided coolies. Djahoemarkar gets involved in workers' organizations and delivers public speeches about the benefits of buying shares in European concerns. The book ends with the airplane visit, followed by a clandestine journey—by car—for Djahoemarkar, Sitti Djaoerah, and her mother back to Padangsidimpuan to visit the graves of their grandparents. In other words, to *ziarah*, or to make a prayer visit to the grave, in a Muslim context. The party avoids seeing old Awaiting Riches, who has by now fallen on hard times.

A Deli man through and through, yet born in a Tapanuli village, Soetan Hasoendoetan led a life with undeniable parallels to some of *Sitti Djaoerah*'s plot action. He was a Muslim, a migrant, a plantation employee, a husband and father, an oratory aficionado, and a newspaperman. His career as a writer took place in tight counterpoint to larger trends in Sumatra's print worlds.

His full name was M.J. Soetan Hasoendoetan, which is an honorific title meaning Sutan Sun Sets in the West. As noted, he came originally from the Sipirok area, but he spent his adulthood in Deli as an amateur folklorist and newspaper freelancer. He was a member of the numerically rather small Sipahutar clan and never seems to have used this clan name in print. After several years of employment as a clerk in a European bank in Pematang Siantar (his first Deli job), Soetan Hasoendoetan went on to find even better work on a Dutch tea plantation located near the same city. He rose to the rank of Crani I, or head clerk, and stayed at that plantation for the rest of his working life. He wrote as an avocation, contributing occasional pieces on *adat* to Tapanuli newspapers and publishing several books: at least two novels, a long verse narrative, and a book version of a *turiturian*.

According to a 1989 interview I conducted with one of his daughters, the widow of a *camat*, or district administrator, Soetan Hasoendoetan was born in about the year 1890 in the village of Pagaranjulu, a few minutes walk from Sipirok. He attended elementary school for several years in Sipirok, in an Angkola Batak–language school. He married a local girl at about age eighteen, and they joined a small party of Sipirok people walking to Deli in 1908 in search of work. Soetan Hasoendoetan described their journey in an introductory essay he wrote for his *turiturian* book, a 1941 volume on the chant called the *turiturian* of Datoek Toeangkoe Toean Malim Leman. The book itself is quite remarkable for its print-oriented vision of *turiturians*: the chant is presented in sentences and paragraphs, shorn of many of the rhetorical flourishes that Soetan Hasoendoetan retains in *Sitti Djaoerah*'s excerpts from the same chant. In his introductory essay Soetan Hasoendoetan notes that the journey to Deli took nine walking days and they stopped along the way at the homes of southern Batak relatives and acquaintances. They had many luscious meals during these visits along the way (Soetan Hasoendoetan was fond of detailing gustatory experiences, and his characters munch on snacks with true Sumatran enthusiasm). The travelers walked to the east coast via Pangaribuan, not via Lake Toba. In the novel, Djahoemarkar walks to Deli via the lake, and Sitti Djaoerah and her mother take the more direct (but less scenic) Pangaribuan route.

According to Soetan Hasoendoetan's daughter, he wrote several other prose novels, including one entitled *Si Roente Simata Maridjen*. The family has no copies of these books, nor are these other novels apparently to be found in library collections in Jakarta, the Netherlands, or the United States. In 1925 Soetan Hasoendoetan published a verse narrative called *Nasotardago* ('that which comes in an unexpected manner'). This work is written in four-line verses and resembles *Sitti Djaoerah* somewhat in its story line, as it concerns a young man and woman who migrate to the *rantau*, where they navigate difficult passages to adulthood. *Nasotardago* later became a bone of contention between the families of Soetan Hasoendoetan and the Sipirok school principal and newspaperman Soetan Pangoerabaan Pane. The latter was the father of the Indonesian-language writers Armijn and Sanusi Pane. Both sides claimed that their writers had authored this verse book, and at one point in the 1950s (according to Soetan Hasoendoetan's daughter, who relished telling me this story) the Pane family actually arranged to have the narrative reprinted under Soetan Pangoerabaan's name. The national government's Ministry of Education and Culture compounded the mistake in 1979 by reissuing *Nasotardago*, again under the wrong name, in its regional literature series. Soetan Hasoendoetan's daughter was adamant on this point when we spoke in

1989: Soetan Pangoerabaan's faction had stolen her father's work. That sort of thing used to happen back then, she said sadly.

Soetan Hasoendoetan died in 1948, during the Indonesian Revolution, of natural causes. His novels and his *turiturian* book went out of print, and the memory of him as a writer faded as Indonesia as an independent nation came into being.

Soetan Hasoendoetan's village childhood and his Sipirok education provided him with ready access to important language building blocks, which he used in writing *Sitti Djaoerah*: the region's oratorical heritage and Sipirok's character as an important school town.

RITUAL ORATORY AND SCHOOLBOOK CULTURE

When Soetan Hasoendoetan was a child, Pagaranjulu was a tiny rice-farming settlement. Today the village is an unprepossessing jumble of small wooden houses abutting a few larger concrete structures. The latter are the fancier residences of émigré families living in Medan and Jakarta who wish to keep a toehold in their home village for those times when they need to return briefly to host an important *adat* ceremony. In the 1880s and 1890s, though, Pagaranjulu was famous as a center of fine oratory and *turiturian* recitations. This was so despite the village's diminutive size and its domination by the *harajaon*, or circles of ceremonial rajas, from Sipirok.

Oratory has a political base in southern Tapanuli. This part of Angkola has a few preeminent patrilineal clans: the Harahaps, Panes, Hasibuans, Pasaribus, a few Lubises and Nasutions, and, most importantly, the Siregars. The latter claim highest status as the founders of the triple *harajaon* kingdom that includes Sipirok. As is still the case today, in the late nineteenth century the lineages within each of these clans that could successfully claim "first son" status contributed a few high rajas to the councils of nobles for Sipirok, Baringin/Bungabondar, and Parau Sorat (the triple kingdom). When the Dutch arrived in force in the 1850s, pacifying the area in order to make Sipirok into a coffee depot in the state's new system of forced cash crop cultivation, certain lineages and rajas and their immediate households accepted Dutch sponsorship for their claims to most ancient geneaological status. These claims were often bogus, and other lineages resisted Dutch hegemony. By about 1880, however, colonial civil control of the area was complete and recalcitrant lineages had been ousted from power. Through the end of the century, those supposed high rajas who had gained command of the old rajaship councils amassed enough wealth through the coffee trade to style themselves grand aristocrats. They began holding splendid buffalo sacrifice feasts called *horjas* ('ceremonial undertakings'). In Sipirok and the nearby villages the favored rajas' families began to construct elaborate Malay-style wooden houses surrounded with gardens and orchards (such an image figures prominently in *Sitti Djaoerah*'s part 1). They contracted alliances through marriage with favored noble families in distant Mandailing and Padang Bolak.

Sipirok's most illustrious rajas were also awarded impressive letters of contract by the Dutch authorities, testifying to their geneaological claims. They served as members of boards of *adat* judges, who ruled on such matters as inheritance disputes. These prideful aristocrats also held many *horja* feasts, which provided the occasion for extravagant ritual speech-making sessions. These oratory congresses were strongly shaped by the colonial presence and Dutch systems of favoritism for certain lineages, although the high rajas endeavored to define their ritual speech-making sessions as integral parts of an "ancient Angkola heritage." Print literacy was soon to become a major venue for promoting such claims.

At the time of Soetan Hasoendoetan's childhood, this part of southern Tapanuli had intricate oratorical types of speech, many tied to the high rajas' political claims to hereditary elite status. These were the forms of ritual speech that Soetan Hasoendoetan drew on so luxuriantly in writing *Sitti Djaoerah*.

Elegant, verse-form, praise orations and blessing speeches (delivered at nighttime congresses of rajas called *alok-alok* sessions) were Sipirok's most spectacular ritual speeches at the time. In *alok-alok* visiting rajas who had come to a feast from as far away as Mandailing or Padang Bolak would gather in the host family's house to give their permission for the sacrifice of the water buffaloes, "the livestock of the rajas." Such types of ritual speech were accompanied in villages, and even in market towns, by extensive repertoires of *andung* laments. In these, most everyday words (*hand, head, leg,* and so on) had special, indirect, lament speech equivalents (Hand the Asker for Favors, Head the Bearer of Heavy Burdens, Leg the Swift Strider, etc.). There were also riddles, curses, courtship rhymes, and clan identification routines. In this last form of speech, called *martarombo*, speakers who had just met would quiz each other in verse about their respective clan and lineage origins and their families' patterns of marriage alliance in the past. Sipirok is rather famous in Tapanuli for its intense interest in *martarombo* queries of this sort. The practice may derive from the region's history of debt bondage and conflict. Some lineages had slave histories, having arrived as war captives of village founders or as debtors. A careful *martarombo* routine was thought useful in uncovering such origins, held to be tainted and shameful.

The Sipirok area also had a form of speech called *osong-osong*. This was a type of witty repartee traded between orators speaking for marriage alliance partners. *Osong-osong*, combative and fun, often concerned mock disputes over the size of brideprice payments to be levied for the marriages of the teenage daughters of the rajas who were hosting a *horja* ceremony. As is the case with the other Batak societies, Sipirok *adat* revolved around hierarchical relationships between "holy," high-status wife-giving houses and their ritually indebted, subordinate wife receivers, called "girl children" or *anakboru*. Much Sipirok high oratory, such as *osong-osong* speech, took the form of verbal duels between "high" and "low" marriage alliance partners jousting over their loving but tense relationships with each other.

The wife givers (*mora*, or 'wealthy', as the *adat* sobriquet terms it) would bestow their daughters as brides on the lower-status wife receivers. Accompanying the young women on their marriage journeys (in the ideal *adat*, at least, as this is portrayed in wedding oratory) were spiritual blessings, fertility blessings for the wife receivers, and sacred, "life-enhancing" textiles called *ulos*. Flowing back from wife receivers to wife givers would be brideprice payments in gold or cash as well as physical services such as help with the harvest and donations of cooking and food-serving aid for the wife givers when they staged their grand feasts. Praise orations by wife receivers for their wife givers and blessing speeches bestowed as gifts in the other direction were crucial parts of these marital exchanges. Oratory, in fact, was often talked about via an imagery of gift exchange, inflected for gender within Angkola's asymmetrical marriage alliance system.

Each wife-giving house and its larger lineage would have certain well-established wife-receiver houses (their *anakboru pusako*), and these people in turn would have their own *anakboru*. The marriage system (in the ideal, at least) was hierarchal and assymetrical in that a lineage that had given a daughter as a bride to another lineage was not supposed to get a young woman back from that same group. In practice, the thicket of marriage exchange alliances between prominent lineages of major clans was often convoluted. *Adat* speechifying in *horja* ceremonies was often useful in "fixing" such unorthodox exchange histories. In fact, the social efficacy of speech used in this way was explicitly recognized in Sipirok proverbs and verse routines. Throughout *Sitti Djaoerah*, Soetan Hasoendoetan drew on these points of local language ideology and on Sipirok's ritual speech repertoires in painting his Sumatran social landscapes.

Folktales (*hobar-kobaran*) and *turiturian* epics augmented these more overtly kin-based types of oratory in places like Sipirok and Pagaranjulu in the 1880s and 1890s. *Hobar-kobaran* were often folksy stories about resourceful animal heroes such as clever Si Landuk, or Mousedeer, who outwitted larger foes such as big, dumb elephants. There were also amusing tales about hunters, lovely young girls lost in the forest, generous-hearted rajas, and people turned into fishes (a common Sumatra-wide plot device also found in Malaysia). By contrast, the *turiturians* opened up mysterious vistas on realms that were clearly mythic. *Turiturians* usually concerned the troubled intercourse between strange denizens of an Upper Spirit Kingdom and the humans who find themselves on mystical, dangerous quests that take them into such sacred precincts. When sung at night on cold evenings around a village bonfire or in a *bale* (a tall-pillared village meeting house), *turiturians* were epic in length and narrative scope. In the 1880s and 1890s they were still being performed with some regularity in a few villages around Sipirok, although by the 1920s the chant was a dying genre as an oral form. Lasting seven nights and beginning with the sacrifice of a white goat (spilling its blood would "open the words of the *turi*"), these chants told much more intricate, elusive stories than did any other type of southern Batak oral art. They were the major shaping influence in the young Soetan Hasoendoetan's ritual speech world.

One famous southern Batak chant is the *turiturian* of Datoek Toeangkoe Toean Malim Leman. This was Soetan Hasoendoetan's favorite and the one he wrote down and transformed into a print version for his 1941 book. This is also the chant that weaves through *Sitti Djaoerah*. The oral version of this chant illustrates many features of the genre. (I was fortunate enough to tape-record a two-night version of this *turiturian* in 1976 in Sipirok, and I base my comments here on that performance and on interviews with the chanter and members of his audience: some

21

rajas and Sipirok schoolteachers and retirees who had heard I was arranging this special taping session.)

Like other Angkola *turiturians* Datoek Toeongkoe has strong ties to the epic traditions of Malay world states in Minangkabau, Aceh, and Palembang. The chant's story line has many correlates in the court epics of these societies and with the Putri Hijau and Malim Leman stories. The chant has numerous borrowed Minangkabau words and archaic Toba Batak phrases, all of which lend the narrative an air of ancientness, audience members told me in 1976. For these listeners, many *turituri-an* words and phrases remained opaque, but that just added mystical luster to the performance.

Oral versions of Datoek Toeangkoe sing of two aristocratic boys who set off into the deep woods on a quest to find a magic potion to cure their dying mother. The narrative begins with a droned low syllable and shortly breaks into words after a mysterious-sounding invocation of blessings addressed to ancestor spirits. Between sections of the narrative the chanter drones out his "Heeeeeee . . ." syllable once again, and when he feels it is time for a cigarette break he weaves that fact into his verses. In other words, there are many performance cues in oral *turiturians*.

The story line of this chant is both frightening and alluring, but present readers can savor it as they read the version offered in *Sitti Djaoerah*'s part 2. The story involves the hero's quest for a bride as he pursues his magical search for the potion. Datoek Toeangkoe's little brother dies of a mystical attack along the way, and the older boy is forced to leave him behind. The dead youngster comes back to life later in the narrative, reinvigorated by a few drops of magical oil, which his brother sprinkles on his body. Datoek Toeangkoe goes on to meet an old woman living a solitary existence in the forest. She urges him to court his mother's brother's daughter, the lovely offspring of a spirit raja of the Upper Continent (in Sipirok *adat*, a young man's ideal choice of a wife would be this cousin). Once a year the girl and her six sisters put on flying suits (their *baju bialal biulul*, a nonsense phrase spoken for aural effect) and descend from their sky world to earth (the human domain) to bathe in a sacred pool. "Steal her flying suit," the crone urges Datoek Toeangkoe, "and she will be forced to stay here on earth as your bride." The boy follows this plan, and the couple marries and has a son after the spirit girl extracts a promise from her husband never to tell any child of theirs that she is not a normal human being with a regular human lineage history. Such secret information would shame the family: the woman would be like a slave, unmoored in local clan pasts.

They have a small son, who is extremely naughty and unmanageable. At one point, after the child has purposely broken an heirloom plate he insisted on using as his dinner plate, his human grandmother shouts in exasperation that the child's mother is a spirit being, "so what can you expect from the likes of her son, after all?" Distraught at this revelation, the young mother steals back her flying suit from her husband while he is asleep and decides to go back to her father's abode in the sky. She leaves the earth by stages, going first to a coconut palm in the front yard, then to a distant field, then to a jutting rock that crashes through the "mouth of the sky" into the Upper Continent. As she arrives at each geographical point, she sings *andung* laments to say goodbye to her human family. Datoek Toeangkoe pursues her all the way to the Sky World; the family, and the two worlds, are eventually reunited.

Toward the end of their heyday, during the time of Soetan Hasoendoetan's childhood, all southern Batak *turiturians* had this type of compelling story line and "what happens next?" excitement. All the chants seem to have had the same ability to quickly engage listeners in a story and a set of characters about whom they become genuinely fond. The setting of the chant recitations was a key factor in their impact: near dawn both chanter and hearers are approaching exhaustion and the *turiturian* session takes on a trancelike air. Throughout the performance the chanter attempts repeatedly to "break open wells of sadness and longing," as he often reminds his listeners. They listen to the chant in order to grow sad and recall *na robian*, the past.

Replete with such lengthy narratives and story lines filled with critical illnesses among nobles, courtships, marriages, births, deaths, tragic departures, and joyful reunions, *turiturians* like Datoek Toeangkoe offered chanters the opportunity to include samples of most major types of orations found in local *adat* rituals. In any full-scale chant performance, an adept chanter would be sure to include long snatches of blessing speeches from weddings, laments from funerals, and the *alok-alok* praise speeches with which the rajas would regale each other in oratory congresses. There were also advice speeches for infants and brides, which would be inserted into characters' mouths at birth ceremonies and weddings in the story. And there would be great dollops of proverbs and riddles to make the *turi* performance more *tabo*, more delicious. Usually, too, there would be long samples of all the special registers of speech used in Angkola and Mandailing, for instance, samples from the language of curses, the language of the camphor gatherers out in the deep forest, and the language of love spells (what parts could be revealed in public, at least). All told, a complete *turiturian* would survey almost the full range of southern Batak high *adat* speech. Much of the chant's loveliness, in fact, came from the chanter's implicit promise to provide listeners with a solid taste of all the most beautiful and indirect types of special human speech that were set out in local *adat* or could be borrowed from other societies. Listening to *turiturians* as a child would have given Soetan Hasoendoetan a sense for both the great range of Angkola spoken forms and their aesthetic hold on audiences. He would also have been afforded a sort of protonovelistic model for storytelling in which this particular type of narrative both told a tale and described a rich oral language world in panoramic fashion.

Importantly, Soetan Hasoendoetan attended his Sipirok grade school at a time when these spoken and chanted narratives and verse routines were being thoroughly reexamined through the lens of print and the institutions of the formal classroom. Publishing was "editing" southern Batak views of *turiturians*, oratory, and images of speech in far-reaching ways. By 1914, in fact, Angkola and Mandailing readers had their first book version of a *turiturian*, in this case the chant of Raja Gorga of the Sky and Raja Suasa of the Earth, as compiled by the Mandailing raja Mangaradja Goenoeng Sorik Marapi ([1914] 1957). This particular chant book had been commissioned by the public school authorities as a Batak literature book for students in secondary school; the volume was so manifestly literate and scholarly that it came complete with a glossary of difficult words such as *andung* and *alok-alok* terms. Mangaradja Goenoeng translated these for his readers from indirect chant speech into everyday Mandailing Batak (a dialect very similar to Angkola Batak). Books of this type provided Soetan Hasoendoetan with the vantage point for using *turiturian* speech formats and storytelling conventions as component parts of his larger novelistic undertaking, all the while exploiting the chant speech for its great emotional depth.

Soetan Hasoendoetan used *turiturians* quite strategically, in fact, although it may be too much to claim that he formulated his overall aesthetic before he set to the task of writing his book. As he pushes his narrative along from part 1 to part 2 he first employs and then moves beyond a narrative strategy relying largely on constructing a pastiche of newspaper accounts of *adat* feasts, folktale inserts, and episodic, romancelike interludes. As he progresses through his chapters Soetan Hasoendoetan begins to lodge his major action increasingly on the socially realistic plane, and in part 2 both his long *turiturian* passage and his folktale inserts (still some of his favorite devices) are placed within deep conceptual brackets.

Other narrative techniques show Soetan Hasoendoetan puzzling his way through a sort of rough and ready theory of the novel fashioned in relation to *turiturian* narrative. In part 1, for instance, he often changes scenes by writing, essentially: "Now, that is enough of this scene. Let us switch to this other scene." This is the *turiturian* chanter's basic mode of telling a story. The technique is still used in part 2, but there multiple social worlds are united by an omniscient narrator for the reader's present-day consciousness as a fan of the book. Just as importantly, by the time Soetan Hasoendoetan works his way through part 2, his text's printed linguistic world has grown to encompass Angkola literate culture as well as virutally all of Angkola's oral heritage. All of this is set lavishly before the reader as an interactive linguistic world. For instance, Soetan Hasoendoetan has Sitti Djaoerah and Djahoemarkar write and read aloud handwritten letters that contain long passages of verse taken from *martandang* courtship duels.

The way Soetan Hasoendoetan treats names also shows his firm writer's hand as he deals with *turiturian* conventions and molds them to his novelistic purposes. In the performed oral chants the main characters tend to have long, playful, and often largely unintelligible sobriquets (e.g., Si Tapi Mombang Soero di Langit). Soetan Hasoendoetan gives some of *Sitti Djaoerah*'s characters "normal" names (Sitti Djaoerah itself is a common name for a Muslim girl) while giving others what might be called character names (Awaiting Riches, Sutan Hardwood). Djahoemarkar, though, gets a *turiturian* name of extraordinary beauty, a name that the novelist uses throughout part 2 to deepen the reading experience beyond the limits of regular secular prose. The *Dja* of the name is a diminutive of *raja*, while *hoemarkar* is an archaic grammatical construction of the Angkola Batak word *harkar*, meaning something that has been "opened up" in order to discover hidden things (*mangarkari* is one of the verb forms). In everyday conversational Angkola Batak, the use of an infix of this sort is normally found only in the simple comparative (*yellow* versus yellower, for instance: *gorsing* versus *gumorsing*). Use of such a construction with a word such as *harkar* denotes high ritual speech with a touch of ancient times about it. The name as a whole means something like Raja Opener of Many Hidden Things or Wonders, and it has a touch of intimacy and affection as well. The name is at once an honorific title and a fond nickname, a convention reminiscent of *turiturian* names.

Coined especially for this novel, Djahoemarkar is clearly no ordinary name but a sort of miniature *turiturian* experience. Every time readers encounter the young man's name the reading experience for that fleeting moment "breaks open deep wells of sadness and longing" in reference to the sadness of Djahoemarkar's early infancy (when his father died) and his mother's grief during that period. In the story, after Djahoemarkar's father, Pandingkar Moedo, dies in the poison leaves attack, the baby's mother finds that she does not have the heart to give her infant a name. However, she does tell some neighbor women and girls who crowd into the house each afternoon that seeing her baby's face "breaks open" her grief and longing for her dead husband. Soetan Hasoendoetan opens the first chapter of part 2 with this situation, in fact. There, Taring cries out:

"If only, if only his father was still alive and drawing breath! I don't really want to give him a name right away, but all my friends keep asking me about it, about what unlucky Little Boy's name is, but what name can I tell them? So, kind women friends, please, please don't keep asking me, all of you. Asking me his name just reopens all my feelings of sadness and pain. But it recalls more than those emotions, too: asking me his name also reopens my feelings of deep longing and loneliness for his father," she said, wiping her tears.

She'd always answer like this if anyone would ask her her child's name, and eventually people stopped asking when they came to the house. They would just say: "Let me take Good-Hearted Little Dad here on my lap for a second, he who reopens memories of the past, he who reopens feelings of deep longing and loneliness, he who reopens feelings of sadness and pain." The more time passed, the more people began to like saying "He who reopens feelings of deep longing and loneliness."

The nickname stuck and became the baby's name. Many times later in the book, at the mention of Djahoemarkar's name, this longer series of loss and longing phrases come tumbling out in Soetan Hasoendoetan's sentences, drawing readers more deeply into Taring's pain and memory but also more deeply into the wellsprings of affection that Djahoemarkar's other, later admirers have for him. Readers are drawn into the intimate circle in the process. Very importantly, the novelist marshals this channel of fond emotions in two directions: toward lovely old ritual-speech turns of phrase such as this one and toward the Deli experiences of Djahoemarkar's adulthood. Readers come to yearn for a distinctively Angkola "tradition" (mediated largely through oratory and chant usage of this sort) but also for distinctively Angkola modes of life in east Sumatra, where Djahoemarkar eventually resides. Notice that Djahoemarkar does not seek to change his name once he migrates to his adult life on the tobacco plantation. He and Sitti Djaoerah still speak Angkola Batak with each other, and Djahoemarkar often entertains his wife by reciting oratory passages or snatches of *turiturians*. In the front room of their house on the plantation, Djahoemarkar paints some homilies from *adat* oratory in big

Latin letters all around the top of the wall. He wants things both ways, as does Soetan Hasoendoetan's imagined reader.

Along with this play of words is an important conceptual shift, again in relation to *turiturian* speech and in this case the reader's critical distance from its veracity. In part 1 readers are given to understand that human characters interact with shadowy beings who have definitely supernatural characteristics. These supernaturals, or at least part-supernaturals (such as Pandingkar Moedo's two undependable sidekicks, Rangga Poerik and Rangga Balian, who are sometimes rather like evil sprites), are presented as actors in this early part of the novel.

The spirit woman of part 1's *turiturian* recital is also a supernatural character, an overt one in this case. Speaking to Pandingkar Moedo in a spirit voice, she draws him temporarily out of human life and into her forest domain (a sequence presented in verse). In part 2, though, the perspective changes: the one long *turiturian* passage is written out in prose, and spirit beings have been "demoted" in legitimacy to the status of "characters in *turiturians*" that the protagonists recite to each other for their entertainment (in this case, during the car ride to the airfield to fly into the clouds with Tuan Chantelouq).

Early southern Batak schoolbook writing set the philosophical stage for this print literacy view of ritual speech, and language in general, and for Soetan Hasoendoetan's particular type of critical reader.

Not surprisingly, book publishing in Tapanuli first centered around school needs and mission priorities and remained mostly in the hands of the colonial government and the church throughout the 1860s and 1870s. Textbook publishing was especially dominant during this period, although church publications (hymnals, almanacs, and the New Testament) were also important in introducing printed materials to otherwise somewhat isolated mountain villages far from Sipirok. Even in this early period, southern Batak schoolteachers and principals were beginning to write their own primers and folktale collections in the Angkola Batak language for school use.[19] At first such books appeared in the old Batak script, as had also been the case with some of the early Bible translations. By the 1870s, though, textbook publishing was shifting to the Latin alphabet and the Batak writing system had begun its long descent into the status of a special subject in the school curriculum (where it languishes today). *Sitti Djaoerah* was published in the Latin alphabet with no insertions of Batak letters.

One of the most influential nineteenth-century schoolbooks published in the Latin alphabet was the Mandailing schoolmaster Willem Iskandar's elementary school reader *Si Boeloes-Boeloes, Si Roemboek-Roemboek* (1872). This book was used as a primer throughout Angkola and Mandailing. Containing a hidden critique of colonial rule, this small anthology of reading selections consisted of a series of elegant renditions of folktales, verse songs, four-line verse narratives, and dramatic dialogues between children (this last format was probably based on Dutch models). The collection also includes odes to Mandailing's great scenic beauty. Generations of southern Batak children learned to read with the help of *Si Boeloes-Boeloes*; Soetan Hasoendoetan himself surely would have used the text in class. Willem

Iskandar's lyrical evocations of Mandailing's mountain scenery became a rallying point for southern Batak local pride. The school authorities were apparently oblivious to this situation at first, and they financed many reprintings of the book, but by 1933 they deemed *Si Boeloes-Boeloes* a seditious text. It was banned in that year.[20]

Other, almost equally superb, children's primers and folklore collections appeared in print over the next twenty-five years. Some of these books fostered a certain rather secular and even ethnographic attitude toward the "old spoken ways." These important works included the Sipirok school principal Soetan Martoea Radja's classic *Doea Sadjoli* ("Two Walking Together," 1917) and *Ranteomas* ("Golden Chain," 1919). These two books have their child characters appreciating Angkola's old oral heritage as literate sophisticates, ones who doubt the claims to truth of the old folktales and oral routines they read about in school. In a typical chapter in *Doea Sadjoli*, for instance, the child characters visit the office of Pak Camat, the district administrator. They ask him for a story, so he tells them a fable about the miraculous origin of a mountain lake located in the hills near Bungabondar. This is an actual lake, the book's young readers would realize. In the olden days, the children hear, an old woman wanted to enjoy the sight of a beautiful bride in her full wedding finery. However, since there was no village wedding in the offing anytime soon, the old lady grabbed her cat and dressed the animal up in a tiny version of Sipirok's bridal costume, a red *songket* sarong, crossed scarves on the chest, and a miniature gold spangled headdress. But, "Those Not Seen" (the ancestral spirits) were offended by this mixture of human and beastly attributes and sent a huge thunderbolt crashing toward the village to instantly destroy the old woman and her anomalously attired cat. Lake Marsabut came into being as a result, as the huge crater filled up with water. In the school anthology, one chapter consists of this tale framed by the visit to Pak Camat's office. The next chapter presents the child characters of the book discussing the story with Pak Camat. Entertained, but skeptical, the youngsters decide that mountain lakes do not really come into being in this way but it is pleasant to hear the old fables anyway. They chide Pak Camat for implying that the old tales should be taken at face value. In such scenes, small Angkola schoolchildren were presented to their young readers as acutely discerning critics of village life and language ways.

Books like these, in concert with the subtle *Si Boeloes-Boeloes*, prepared the way for unusually reflective fiction and also made for uncommonly skeptical observers of language, starting in the grade school years.

TAPANULI NEWSPAPERS AND *ADAT* GUIDEBOOKS

Journalism encouraged similar views and also set the stage for Soetan Hasoendoetan's work. By this same period, quite small towns such as Sipirok sported their own newspapers. Prominent weekly or biweekly southern Batak newspapers included *Soeara Ra'jat*, *Soeara Sini*, *Poestaha*, *Soeara Tapanoeli*, *Oetoesan*, *Partoengkoan*, and *Pertjetoeran*. As noted, language use was complex. Some of these papers' stories were in Indonesian, some were in Angkola Batak, and many used the occasional foreign phrase. All these newspapers, though, tended to have the same run of stories: items on cash crop prices and government agricultural policy, editorial pieces on such topics as the place of *adat* in modern life, the changing role of women (particularly with regard to raising children who would do well in school), and the proper role of the old hereditary *adat* chiefs in the Tapanuli of the present day. Poems and prose renditions of clan geneaologies and *turiturian*s were also published in these newspapers along with serialized prose novels and long verse narratives. The latter were apparently quite popular and were sometimes reprinted as books. These verse narratives were often love stories, composed as a combination of clan identification riddles and courtship duels along with more loosely structured narrative passages. There was also a large Indonesian-language literature of verse narratives tied to Malay and Minangkabau literature. The newspapers also offered school graduation news, updates on the scholastic and employment achievements of the sons of aristocratic southern Tapanuli families, crime news (a good deal of this), accounts of *adat* feasts, and, as noted, political news from elsewhere in the Indies. By the 1930s, the share of space devoted to the last topic had grown in many cases. Discussions of nationalism in the Indies and elsewhere in Asia as well as updates on the development of political parties often appeared on the front page. Censorship by the colonial government was constant, and Tapanuli newspapers often had their publishing permits revoked. They folded and reopened under new titles with regularity.[21]

The issue of *Poestaha* in which *Sitti Djaoerah* first appeared had a typical mix of news and feature stories that framed *Sitti Djaoerah*'s publication within a bustling Sumatran social world. There was an item on a new rice mill in Bungabondar and a story about local officials (town *demang*s) to whom the colonial government had awarded gold, silver, or bronze stars for meritorious service. There was also a long piece on "forest in the Bataklands," an article that pursued a forest management tack. The paper's advertisements that day solicited interest in gasoline from Standard Oil of "Nuew Jork, Amerika," in small Tapanuli hotels, in Goodrich tires, and in apparently miraculously efficacious Chinese medicinal potions. *Poestaha* in general had a busy tripartite focus: parochial southern Tapanuli concerns, often relating to *adat* and ritual speech; Deli coast plantation issues and related Tapanuli economic matters; and Indonesian nationalism, usually set within a broad Asian framework. The occasional story on European politics would also appear in *Poestaha*, along with amusing items on such things as crime in America, used as fillers.

Adat guidebooks with samplers of ritual orations were another important type of print literature for southern Batak writers and audiences during Soetan Hasoendoetan's young adulthood. An early *adat* guide by a Sipirok *adat* "expert" (a print literacy convention in itself) was H. Soetan Paroehoem Pane's *Adat Batak II* (*Dibagasan Siriaon*). This small volume, published in Pematang Siantar in 1922, consisted of sample *adat* orations but also a jaunty narrative about a family's difficult migration to Deli. *Adat Batak* was thus a kind of almost-novel in the guise of a ritual speech handbook.[22]

Sipirok had its own folklorist extraordinaire in the 1920s and 1930s: the aforementioned Soetan Pangoerabaan Pane (whose family contested the ownership of *Nasotardago* with Soetan Hasoendoetan's family). The editor of *Poestaha*, Soetan Pangoerabaan was a manifestly indefatigable newspaper reporter, publisher, printer, textbook author, Muslim pamphleteer, poet, lexicographer, and—perhaps not surprising by now—Angkola-language novelist. Soetan Pangoerabaan's varied oeuvre included one main novel, called *Tolbok Haleon* ("Famine Time," referring to the period directly before the new rice harvest).[23] This was a journey-to-Deli novel first published in 1917 and then reissued several times during the 1930s by Soetan Pangoerabaan's own publishing house in Sipirok (Soetan P was this establishment's name). This book was written in Angkola Batak, but some of his small pamphlets on language use and Islam were at least partly in Indonesian. A social geography book, intended for school use, was entirely in that language (1934).

Soetan Hasoendoetan drew on all these oratorical and print formats in composing *Sitti Djaoerah* as a record of the Tapanuli and Deli language worlds and historical experience. In the process, he contested Dutch claims to hegemony in Sumatra.

Writing Angkola in the Dutch Imperial Domain

In *Culture and Imperialism* (1993) Edward Said urges observers to remember the colonial setting that shaped the writing of familiar nineteenth-century British novels such as Jane Austen's *Mansfield Park*. This situation was somewhat hidden from the novelists themselves as well as from these books' European common readers and ensuing generations of literary critics. In Said's view, the Austen, Dickens, or even Conrad novel was part and parcel of the European colonial enterprise in the Caribbean, Africa, and Asia. As a partner in the ideology of European conquest and capitalist exploitation of these regions, the nineteenth-century realistic novel systematically hid the larger structures of oppression that surrounded the small social class worlds that authors such as Jane Austen were so adept at describing and skewering. But, Said also notes, the "empire wrote back" and continues to do so, constructing and recalling colonial reality in very different, critically non-European ways. Novels such as Chinua Achebe's *Things Fall Apart* (1959) and James Ngugi's (now Ngugi wa Thiongo) *The River Between* can be seen as instances of resistance literature of this angry, humorous, politically insightful sort. James C. Scott points to much the same phenomenon in his *Domination and the Arts of Resistance: Hidden Transcripts* (1990): colonized indigenous peoples produced a stream of "offstage" jokes and parodies of their colonizers and sometimes constructed entire alternative artistic worlds hidden from them.

Sitti Djaoerah can be read, in this light, as a text on an Angkola Batak world as an Angkola Batak author defined it for Angkola readers in the Netherlands East Indies. Soetan Hasoendoetan "writes back" to the colonial state in a gentle but nonetheless powerful way. He obviously wrote his novel during a period when oral registers of Angkola speech such as epic chants, ritual oratory, and verbal duels between marriage alliance partners were coming into competition with written and printed Angkola works, with Bahasa Indonesia's expanding world of print, and with Dutch. Soetan Hasoendoetan did not despair at this political and linguistic circumstance but seems in fact to have written his novel as a sort of guide for readers on how to maintain their pride in the Angkola language as the proper center of their imaginative worlds. In making this implicit argument about language, Soetan Hasoendoetan also charts a way for readers to think about the larger journeys to the *rantau*, to life in the Indies. In such transitions, his story implies, not only the Angkola language but Angkola as a society and conceptual world must remain for prudent readers the center of their lives if they are to survive the Indies experience.

The migration trope here is key to Soetan Hasoendoetan's larger social message. The novel traces its characters' journeys to Deli in terms of both their turns of mind and their physical trips out of the rice-farming Tapanuli highlands to east coast plantations and Medan rooming houses. As the narrative works its desultory way along, the main characters "migrate toward" more cosmopolitan ways of apprehending the social world than had been the case "back in Tapanuli"—back, that is, in the Batak home regions where inherited *adat* had dominated village life and social position was largely determined by a family's relationship to the village founder lineages of the old patrilineal clans.

In *Sitti Djaoerah* characters find that city life and plantation work in Deli bring modes of social interaction largely unknown in village Tapanuli. In the city of Medan, Angkola clerks in the big Dutch *maatschappy* (trading corporations) find themselves working alongside Malay and Javanese employees, whereas highland villagers live in a largely Angkola world. Sipirok and Padangsidimpuan migrants, too, find that they have to use Bahasa Indonesia to communicate with these foreign peoples, whereas at home in the southern Tapanuli mountains the Angkola Batak language is understood by all. Such use of Indonesian turns "foreigner peoples" into a common community of Indies "natives" vis-à-vis their Dutch overseers.

Late in part 2, Mandailing migrants to Medan working as cloth merchants discover that Muslim traders' associations there boosted their profits and protected sales more than did any of the old pronouncements of *adat* about the inheritance and management of family wealth. By the end of the book, too, the main characters have begun to attend such things as political meetings—a far cry from the nighttime oratory congresses convened by *adat* chiefs in Tapanuli and directed toward unseen audiences of ancestors as well as human listeners.

Sitti Djaoerah's readers discover that city life and plantation work in Deli do indeed bring many wondrous innovations of communication and travel. These contrast greatly with the ritual oratory routines, footpath trips, and cart rides of the mountain villages and towns. The fictional new migrants discover Medan's huge print culture, and by the end of the book the central characters are tooling around town in a motor car and going to airplane exhibitions. By the time the book's readers have traversed the long text they, too, have gained a distanced perspective from which to view "old home ways." These they now inevitably see from the vantage point of plantation belt society and in light of political visions of "the modern Indies" fostered in multiethnic urban settings.

In this situation it is a measure of *Sitti Djaoerah*'s strength as a piece of fiction that "tradition" is not portrayed in the book's pages in an unreflective, nostalgic vein. Some of the 1920s *adat* guidebook literature and its related newspaper accounts of old village ways, so called, did tend to pursue a saccharine approach to presenting a southern Batak heritage to readers. In such literature, *adat* tended to emerge as quaint old customs and village ways presented as valuable but rather out of date. In the folkloristic works on old oral literature, too, the fact that a hereditary class of wealthy nobles dominates village society is portrayed as just. In *Sitti Djaoerah*, by contrast, Tapanuli society and issues of village heritage are presented in more critical tones. In the novel, that is, rajas bicker and jockey for status, currying favor with the colonial administrators; they exploit their commoners, who in turn complain about and mock the great aristocrats. And, as we have seen, ritual speech for its part is not trivialized at all in *Sitti Djaoerah* but is offered to readers in much of its full lexical and even grammatical complexity.

It is also a testament to *Sitti Djaoerah*'s power as a piece of fiction that the novelist goes far beyond a clichéd treatment of his journey-to-Deli theme. Contrasts between village ways and village locales (on the one hand) and urban life, modern times, and Deli places (on the other) are staples of everyday southern Batak conversation even today. It has apparently been such ever since Angkola and Mandailing villagers and townspeople first began to migrate to east Sumatra in significant numbers at the turn of the century. Of course, Soetan Hasoendoetan plays on these thematic contrasts in pursuing his journey trope, but he often throws the whole enterprise of village Tapanuli/plantation belt distinctions into serious question. He rarely allows his Angkola readers to remain comfortable with Angkola common knowledge about "tradition" or with any major social change theme.

In fact, in Soetan Hasoendoetan's narrative Tapanuli itself emerges as a creation of colonial times. At frequent turns in his story "the modern Indies" penetrates deep into rural Batak lands. Privileged Batak schoolchildren there are taught a Dutch curriculum and learn to conform to Dutch classroom etiquette. Corvée labor demands by the colonial administration in the most rural precincts of Tapanuli turn out to be a major cause of family migration to Deli. In Soetan Hasoendoetan's prose large trading towns like Padangsidimpuan have architectural styles first made popular in Deli, as well as garrisons of soldiers, Dutch judges, and a Dutch resident (chief administrator). Padangsidimpuan's marketplace is alive with trading activity structured by villagers' knowing and crafty relations with the Sumatran plantation economy.

Soetan Hasoendoetan's rural Tapanuli fictional characters, in other words, are not simple peasants tilling rice fields but astute, politically savvy residents of the Indies. They are schoolteachers drawing salaries from the state, for instance, who urge their pupils to strive for salaried work in government offices or on plantations. They are shopkeepers who stock Western-style clothing alongside big piles of Bugis sarongs (in southern Tapanuli these patterned shiny cloths connoted luxury wear and noble status, and everyone with the cash to spare would try to buy one). And it should be remembered that Soetan Hasoendoetan's characters are also small-time traders in forest rubber, coffee, benzoin, and camphor, out to make a fast profit in a pressured colonial economy.

Soetan Hasoendoetan's Deli is similarly nuanced in sociological terms. Angkola ethnic enclave communities thrive there; *adat* feasts abound on the plantations. In fact, sometimes these ceremonies are more elaborate there than they are in the home villages, although readers learn that the Deli *horjas*, or ritual feasts, take a different form than the rural ones do. Readers are also reminded that Angkola-language conversational speech and ethnic-language newspapers flourish in Medan alongside Indonesian and Dutch usage and periodicals. Angkola lineage mates help each other get jobs in publishers' offices and on plantations, while marriage alliance partners draw on Tapanuli *adat* ties to foster Deli career moves. In other words, Sumatran social worlds interpenetrate in Soetan Hasoendoetan's prose in various promising ways. The journey to Deli and toward increasing engagement with the colonial state takes place in Tapanuli towns just as it does along the roads that lead out of the highlands. Old village worlds are undergoing seismic tremors everywhere in *Sitti Djaoerah*'s large social purview.

All the linguistic and social journeys that Soetan Hasoendoetan evokes in *Sitti Djaoerah* carry political freight. When Sipirok young people like Soetan Hasoendoetan walked to Deli they inevitably passed deeper and deeper into the bureaucratic precincts and economic structures of the colonial state. As Tapanuli young people grew up they became more and more enmeshed in the systems of evaluation used in the colonial schools and job markets. And, as readers of Sumatra's 1920s world of Indonesian, Dutch, and Batak texts discovered, the old logic and aesthetic standards of village ritual oratory were often relativized and in some cases trivialized in the wider literate world beyond village Tapanuli. Soetan Hasoendoetan wrote his book as a bulwark against the more destructive tendencies of these processes.

It must be admitted that the book is hardly revolutionary in tone. In fact, the novel's few Dutch characters are presented in rather flattering ways, and in the chapters on plantation life Soetan Hasoendoetan reveals forthright class prejudices in favor of the clerks and overseers and against the coolie laborers. However, on another level, *Sitti Djaoerah* nevertheless represents a defiant denial of the very importance of Dutch culture in Sumatra. The novelist largely ignores the Dutch claim that they are in charge on the island. On every conceptual level, *Sitti Djaoerah* has a Batak world at its center, not a European one. Angkola Batak persons, *adat*, social locales, foods, standards of female beauty, speech forms, written genres, and hopes for the future operate as the active subjects and creative themes of the narrative, not as objects of Dutch evaluation or European economic or political interest. *Sitti Djaoerah*'s heroes, heroines, rogues, and onlookers recognize that they live under a colonial administration and are caught up in a plantation economy, but they construct meaningful personal lives and ethnic universes within those frameworks nonetheless. They milk their structures of oppression in a variety of inventive, exploitative ways. And, as the narrator of their stories, Soetan Hasoendoetan wrote so linguistically complex a book that the Dutch in Sumatra at the time had little hope of even reading it. Few if any Dutch civil servants or employees of businesses in the 1920s and 1930s were fluent in the full range of Angkola oratory genres that Soetan Hasoendoetan brings to his novel. Some civil authorities, teacher training institute headmasters, and missionaries were fluent in conversational Angkola, but few controlled the high oratory and *turiturian* chant speech so central to *Sitti Djaoerah*. By writing so elusive and oblique a novel, Soetan Hasoendoetan produced a celebratory in-group text on surviving the Indies and the journey to Deli.

It is ironic that Soetan Hasoendoetan's courageous narrative became a virtually lost novel in the Indonesian national era and that prewar southern Batak fiction in itself has largely disappeared from the sight of literary scholars both in Indonesia and abroad. This is probably not a politically innocent situation: in the national era Angkola Batak oratory has been surrounded by the national culture of Indonesian printed texts, and, while today spoken, conversational Angkola Batak survives in sturdy fashion in rural Tapanuli homes and marketplaces, the ritual speeches are acquiring the status of "old speech ways" known mostly to the village elderly. Southern Batak writers have been among the most prominent novelists in national times (consider only Mochtar Lubis, from a Mandailing family), but to an overwhelming extent their works have been written in Indonesian.[24]

Why should this be so, since Angkola Batak in Soetan Hasoendoetan's hands proved to be so subtle a tool for writing fiction? George Quinn discusses a related literature and power situation that can help us answer this question in his essay "The Case of the Invisible Literature: Power, Scholarship, and Contemporary Javanese Writing" (1983). In appreciatively examining the large body of twentieth-century Javanese-language popular fiction, Quinn asks why these works have remained largely hidden from view in mainstream Indonesian literary scholarship and in the Indonesian popular consciousness as well. A consistent denigration of the importance of ethnic- language literature in favor of Indonesian-language prose may be at work both in Indonesia and in scholarly circles overseas, Quinn writes. Notions that Javanese-language works must necessarily be old-fashioned, hidebound, and parochial also seem to be crucial parts of Indonesian nationalistic discourse, where Bahasa Indonesia emerges as, supposedly, the only language in the country that can deal with modern lives and social change issues. Quinn recognizes that this construction of Javanese is artificial and urges his readers to ask what the plot lines, imagery, and characters in Javanese novels may be "about" in a deeper political sense than would be evident from a superficial reading of these popular works. Javanese culture's place in the national state, he asserts, may be the real subject at hand; a true mass literature such as Javanese popular fiction presents an implicit critique of nationalist literary canons, their standard literary critical interpretations, and the heroic images of Indonesia per se that stand behind these aesthetic judgments. Strong ethnic arts traditions, which cannot be tightly supervised by the national state, may be subject to pressures from the national culture to keep them invisible or at least consign them to the realm of the past.[25]

A similar dynamic may be at work in the "forgetting" of *Sitti Djaoerah* in national times. As we have seen, after his death knowledge of Soetan Hasoendoetan as a novelist quickly disappeared. Soetan Hasoendoetan's work is not mentioned in any survey of twentieth-century Indonesian fiction. His service in 1919 as the Pematang Siantar local editor for the Sibolga newspaper *Tapian na Oeli* is mentioned briefly in Mohamad Said's valuable historical study *Sejarah Pers di Sumatera*

Utara (1976: 92, "History of the Press in North Sumatra"). Mohamad Said, a Mandailing man and himself a former newspaper editor, briefly describes this Siantar paper but does not provide biographical details about Soetan Hasoendoetan.

But, in the face of this collapse of southern Batak local language fiction and *Sitti Djaoerah*'s disappearance, some of Soetan Hasoendoetan's elderly contemporaries and near contemporaries have not forgotten his contributions. My Angkola Batak language teacher, G. W. Siregar, who was born in the mid-1890s (he died in 1980), read *Sitti Djaoerah* while serving as an elementary schoolteacher in a Dutch-language Hollandse Inlandse School in the late 1920s. In the 1950s, once he went to teach in one of Sipirok's middle schools, Bapak G. W. taught the Angkola Batak language and its literature to thirteen and fourteen year olds using such texts as Mangaradja Goenoeng Sorik Marapi's *Turiturian ni Radja Gorga di Langit*. This was the sort of textbook approved by the school authorities. All the while, though, he loved *Sitti Djaoerah* and considered it the most complete repository of "genuine Angkola" language use ever set down in print. Therefore, he made the novel my reader for advanced sessions of language study in 1974 and 1975 when I first did fieldwork in Sipirok. For years Bapak G. W. had been without his own copy of the novel (old books that don't get lost in Sipirok tend to be eaten by mice), but in 1974 one of his former middle school students (who was by then a school principal in Padang, West Sumatra) sent him a partial photocopy of the text to use in teaching me Angkola Batak. The rest of the text had somehow gotten lost, but Bapak G. W. was delighted to have what remained (pages 70 to 255) for our lessons and for his own enjoyment. The former student had heard through the Angkola grapevine that Bapak G. W. was teaching an American anthropology graduate student to speak Angkola. Since we did not have the book's title page we had no way of knowing that Bapak G. W. was mistaken in recalling that the title of the novel was *Tolbok Haleon*, which, of course, was the book written by Soetan Pangoerabaan. We persisted in this mistake for several years; I even published an article on Batak fiction using the wrong citation for the book (1981b)—luckily, unbeknownst to Soetan Hasoendoetan's family.

Knowing only the wrong title I had no luck in finding a complete copy of *Sitti Djaoerah* over the next several years in libraries in Jakarta, the Netherlands, and the United States, although both *Nasotardago* and Soetan Hasoendoetan's 1941 *turiturian* book proved to be easy to locate. The actual *Tolbok Haleon* was readily accessible, too, both in its original form in the library of the Koninklijke Instituut voor Taal- Land- en Volkenkunde in Leiden and in its reissued version in the Ministry of Education and Culture's local literatures series.

None of this helped me find a complete copy of *Sitti Djaoerah*. Finally, in 1986, while sifting through the "Ss" on another research task in the old card catalogue in the National Library in Jakarta, I came upon an entry for *Sitti Djaoerah: Padan Djandji na Togo*e ("Sitti Djaoerah: The Vow"). (The vow here apparently refers to two things: the promise that Pandingkar Moedo and his two sidekicks made in part 1 to always work together as a team and Djahoemarkar and Sitti Djaoerah's secret oath, taken as teenagers, to marry. The actual Angkola Batak phrase is not simply "the vow" but something closer to "the firm oath-promise," an almost sacred vow.) I cried out happily upon discovering the text, especially since it turned out that the library's copy was a complete one and in good condition. I made multiple photocopies for Sipirok local-language literature fans whom I knew, but unfortunately Bapak G. W. had died by this time. Later, after a ceremonial *adat* chief named Ompu Raja Doli Siregar with whom I often worked had introduced me to Soetan Hasoendoetan's daughter, I arranged to have another round of photocopies made for the family (*Sitti Djaoerah* had also been lost to them). A lecture I gave in 1992 about *Sitti Djaoerah* as resistance literature to a large Medan audience of Batak writers and students of literature resulted in another set of donated photocopies of the book, since no one seemed to have a copy of their own but many coveted one.

Perhaps this English translation of *Sitti Djaoerah* will help bring this protean book back into the spotlight a bit. I hope this translation project will also lead to the reissuance of the novel in the Angkola Batak language for present-day *rantau* and Tapanuli readers.

A Note on the Translation

When Bapak G. W. and I were first reading *Sitti Djaoerah* together in 1975 as part of my language lessons, we agreed that Soetan Hasoendoetan's vision of the novel as a text that would encompass many registers of Angkola Batak as well as Malay proverbs and extended interludes written in Toba Batak and Mandailing Batak made the book consistently *rame-rame*: fun to read, boisterous, and crowded with event. Since my translation of the novel has moved from this complex, multivoiced, Deli and Tapanuli language world toward that of a single language, English, some of this *rame-rame* quality has, sadly, been lost. As a translator, though, I have fought this tendency by several means.

Most central to my translation strategy has been an effort to try to preserve some of the *tabo* (delicious to savor) quality of the novel in my English version. Much of the text's delectability for Angkola readers seems to me to come from the narrative's many rapid shifts among different registers of Angkola Batak and sometimes from one Sumatran language to another, for instance, from Angkola Batak to Toba or from Angkola to Mandailing. Such switches occur during Djahoemarkar's trip through the Toba lands to Deli, when he is accompanied by a series of market sellers from various language areas. When the men get deep into Toba and encounter a tricky Toba bridge watchman who tries to swindle them out of some money (for so-called bridge-crossing fees), Soetan Hasoendoetan warns his readers in one of his occasional footnotes that he is going to switch the entire narrative over to the Toba Batak language for the duration of that part of the story. Toba Batak is lexically quite close to Angkola Batak, and so reading this part of the novel was not much of a strain for Soetan Hasoendoetan's first audience—in fact, the story gets tastier with the switch in dialects. Soetan Hasoendoetan does not stop with Toba Batak in this part of the book, though: when Djahoemarkar decides to trick the Toba trickster back and put a spell on the old man's daughter, causing her to fall ill, Djahoemarkar's curse and the ritual formula he uses later to heal the girl are both executed in an hilarious mixture of Angkola Batak, Toba Batak, and garbled Arabic. And, as noted, in many places in the novel Soetan Hasoendoetan uses high oratory phrases or snippets of *turiturian* speech in the midst of his regular Angkola sentences. In other instances, he inserts long passages of difficult *turiturian* narrative and then switches back to conversationally paced dialogues or regular Angkola storytelling prose of one sort or another. In one case, late in the book, an entire chapter is written in the Mandailing dialect of Batak, during a time when Sitti Djaoerah and her mother are hiding in Panyabungan, on the run from the threat of the girl's forced marriage to old Sutan Hardwood. When the travelers finally get to Medan and seek each other out, important conversations in newspaper offices take place in part in Bahasa Indonesia. The protagonists also use that language for the classified advertisements they place to find each other.

To handle such thorny Sumatran linguistic complexities I have strived to avoid writing an English version executed in a single register. For Soetan Hasoendoetan's occasional outright shifts between entire dialects of Batak, I have had to compromise and simply flag these switches by means of footnotes, for shifts between different regional variants of English seemed to strike an artificial note. Other situations were easier to handle. The novelist mixes slangy conversational Angkola Batak with schoolbook prose, newspaper-style writing, and, of course, written evocations of many types of spoken Angkola oratory and genres such as folktales. In such cases I have aimed for a certain bumpy quality in my translation by using a variety of English styles on a single page if Soetan Hasoendoetan has done that, too.

Whenever Soetan Hasoendoetan inserts a Malay proverb into one of his Angkola sentences, I make this fact clear (as, indeed, the novelist himself tends to do by using phrases such as "for as it says in the Malay proverb . . ."). When the text switches from conversational Angkola Batak into more esoteric ritual speech registers, I have tried where possible to retain the exact wording of the oratory as well as some of its poetic quality. This has sometimes resulted in newly minted English phrases such as "Dusky Dark Evening" as opposed to just "evening." This is a technique the great Dutch (actually, Dutch-Indonesian) nineteenth-century linguist H. N. Van der Tuuk advocated, as he explained when describing his translation strategy for Toba ritual oratory in *A Grammar of Toba Batak* ([1864, 1867] 1971: xlviii–xlix). Whenever a phrase of this sort appears my readers should assume that it has ties to ritual language and that Soetan Hasoendoetan was using such special phraseology intentionally. I have made many translation compromises, even so, in order to write a text that reads well in English. When an oratory image has been lost in the main text I try to allude to it in endnotes, which I base on my ethnographic fieldwork on contemporary Sipirok ritual oratory.

Verse inserts in the original text have been translated as such and arranged as verse on the page, as Soetan Hasoendoetan did with his Angkola text. Wherever it was typographically possible I included the original Angkola Batak verses alongside my English translation for speech forms such as courtship rhymes. English readers thus have a chance to appreciate Angkola Batak's considerable alliterative potential.

Elusive but crucial phrases such as the wordplay associated with Djahoemarkar's lovely name have also been retained in their metaphorically explicit form.

Angkola Batak oral interaction between all persons is predicated on proper *tutur*, or kin term usage. All acquaintances must be assigned appropriate kin terms of address and reference, for instance, father's older brother, marriageable son of father's sister, younger lineage mate, and so on. When two strangers meet for the first time, the vital *martutur* session, mentioned above, should ensue. This is the mannerly question and answer routine pursued so that the pair of speakers might "discover" (anthropologists would say construct) their proper kin term relationship. Much of the dialogue in *Sitti Djaoerah* assumes such a reliance on Angkola kin term usage as a normal part of human social interaction; the novelist also assumes that his readers share his kin term world. So, since kin terms are so intimately connected to the semantic texture of the book, I have taken care to retain and translate them with some social structural exactness, although they are most definitely quite foreign to the English-language kin term world. (E.g., the Angkola word for "mother" is *inang*, and daughters and sons often address their mothers in formal usage as Inang. But the mother in this case would also address her daughter as Inang. A similar reciprocal use of terms holds between fathers and their sons and grandparents and their grandchildren.) Kin term usage between potentially marriageable young people, and between members of wife-giving houses and their wife receivers, is especially elaborate and painstaking. Sometimes a character's choice of one kin term over another potentially applicable one conveys important messages about their relationship. Thus, my rather rough and ready kin term translation strategy here, for I felt I had to avoid "over-Englishifying" this part of the text. When an Angkola kin term is first used in the text, I translate it as literally as possible, and often add an endnote as well, explaining matters more fully. I also often retain the original Angkola kin term in the first sentence in which the word is initially used. I have had to coin some new usages here to evoke the Angkola marriage alliance world. For instance, I use "clan brother" and "clan sister" (or sometimes "brother" and "sister") to denote *ibotos*: men and women within a single clan segment who may not marry according to *adat*. In contrast to this relationship of respect between clan siblings there is the raucously intimate (but sometimes also maddeningly indirect) joking relationship that holds between men and the women they can marry: their mother's brother's daughters, their "daughters of our wife givers." These speakers call each other *kahanggi*, members of a single lineage. It is doubtless confusing to many English speakers to find that Angkola speakers consider young women to be members of their husbands' lineages, even before marriage. (These young women "carry" their husbands' lineages as their own. These young women are *anakboru*: girl-children, members of a wife-receiving group in their fathers' lineages, just as their husbands and their husbands' brothers are.) Obviously I had to use kin terms different from the regular English sibling terms, so I have employed "older lineage companion" and "younger lineage companion" in this instance. Men within a *kahanggi* lineage sort themselves out according to age this way, as do the potential brides from their *mora*, or wife-giving, houses. Some Angkola kin term assumptions simply had to be dropped in my English translation (e.g., the way mothers call their daughters Inang); such losses of meaning I have tried to flag through footnotes and endnotes.

Soetan Hasoendoetan was unabashedly fond of *andung* lament phraseology and, of course, *turiturian* speech. When he relies on such forms of oratory in the text I have marked this practice, whenever I can, through fidelity to the original lyrical phrasing and by adding endnotes. Occasionally a strange phrase on a page must be immediately explained to English-language readers to forestall confusion. For this, I have used footnotes. Very occasionally Soetan Hasoendoetan himself writes a footnote on a page, usually to tell "Dear Reader" to be sure to sing or chant a verse passage aloud, a recommendation I leave to my readers' discretion. At other times Soetan Hasoendoetan tells his readers in a footnote that he is switching dialects. I have indicated the novelist's footnotes by rendering them in italics.

Sitti Djaoerah, sadly enough, is fully intelligible to few Angkola Batak readers today, since Soetan Hasoendoetan drew so heavily on esoteric ritual speech forms that have now fallen very far from popularity. Today, in New Order Indonesia, Angkola *adat* oratory has faded in the face of Indonesian linguistic as well as political hegemony. In villages around Sipirok and Padangsidimpuan, very few adults know more than a few phrases of *andung* sob-speech; fewer still can recite *turiturians*. Most villagers under the age of forty, in fact, have never heard a *turiturian* chant. Only the most prominent rajas are adept at the *alok-alok* oratory used in the buffalo sacrifice feasts of merit, and apparently no adolescent knows more than a few snatches of the old courtship rhymes that figure so heavily in the love stories of *Sitti Djaoerah*. Given this situation, and because the available Angkola dictionaries do not chart the whole language by any means,[26] as the book's translator I found that I had to do most of the final translation work in the Sipirok county district, working directly with raja *adat* orators there. I was fortunate to be able to spend a period of eight months in 1992, supported by a Fulbright research grant, checking every line of the translation with Baginda Hasudungan Siregar, a raja from the village of Bungabondar (I stayed in a house next to Merari Siregar's old lineage home, it happens). For these eight months Baginda Hasudungan and I would work together on the text in the afternoons when he had returned from his job at Bungabondar's middle school, where he was a teacher and the assistant principal. I would translate each page as best I could and work through several rewrites on my own. Then I would underline any problematic passage in the text and Baginda Hasudungan would translate it into Indonesian, recording his painstaking work onto the lined pages of small school notebooks we would buy. We would then go over his notes at length, speaking Angkola or Indonesian as the situation dictated. We taped these discussion sessions, and I have relied on those cassettes as well as our notes in preparing the final translation.

Baginda Hasudungan was a remarkable colleague for me in doing this difficult translation. Now in his mid-fifties and newly retired from the public schools, we met in 1974 during my initial fieldwork in Sipirok. At that time his star was just beginning to rise in regional *adat* oratory circles. Today he is Sipirok's finest orator, other rajas have told me; he is often summoned to *horja* feasts throughout this part of South Tapanuli to deliver not only expert *alok-alok* speeches but the much more difficult *osong-osong* verbal duels. Baginda Hasudungan and I, it happens, are "companions of a single teacher," too, as oratory-influenced speech would put it. My Angkola language teacher, Bapak G. W., was Baginda Hasudungan's instructor at Middle School No. 2 in Sipirok in the late 1950s. When Bapak G. W. and our raja *adat* mentor, Ompu Raja Doli Siregar, arranged a special session at my house in 1976 to tape-record a *turiturian*, Baginda Hasudungan was the first person Bapak G. W. insisted on inviting. After I had transcribed the words of the *turiturian* into a typescript and Bapak G. W. and I found that we could not puzzle out all of the chant's images by ourselves, we went to Baginda Hasudungan for translation advice. He consulted some of his raja friends and a few other chanters and helped us navigate our way through that 1976 verion of *Datoek Toeangkoe*. He has continued to take this active fieldworker's role in all of our later collaborations.

Baginda Hasudungan and I often smiled at the old-style spelling conventions used in *Sitti Djaoerah*. In modern-day Indonesian and Angkola Batak prose and verse, the old *oe* has become *u*, *tj* has become *c*, and *dj* appears as *j*. In my translation I have retained the old spelling style for personal names of characters in the novel and for colonial-era Batak writers' names, so that usage would be consistent with the hero's and heroine's names and with the author's own. However, when a word such as *sutan* is used as a noun, I rely on the new spelling conventions. Place names and nouns (*horja*, for instance) also appear in the new spelling.

Given Soetan Hasoendoetan's aesthetic ambitions and the sheer enormity of the Sumatran linguistic landscapes he sought to portray, *Sitti Djaoerah* ultimately can probably never be fully translated, although, as many researchers have noted, the novel as a literary form tends to be the most translatable genre across distant language spaces. I hope some of that claim proves true here.

NOTES

1. See, for instance, A. Teeuw, *Modern Indonesian Literature* (1967); C. W. Watson, "The Sociology of the Indonesian Novel, 1920–1955" (1972); and C. W. Watson's essay "Some Preliminary Remarks on the Antecedents of Modern Indonesian Literature" (1971). See also Alberta Joy Freidus, *Sumatran Contributions to the Development of Indonesian Literature, 1920–1942* (1977); Harry G. Aveling, "*Sitti Nurbaya*: Some Reconsiderations, with a Comment by Taufik Abdullah" (1970); Anthony H. Johns, "Genesis of a Modern Literature" (1963); and Anthony H. Johns, "The Novel as a Guide to Indonesian Social History" (1959). Among many other titles, the Indonesian scholarship includes Umar Junus's *Perkembangan Novel-Novel Indonesia* (1974); Ajip Rosidi's *Kapankah Kesusasteraan Indonesia Lahir? Berserta Sepilihan Karangan Lainnya* (1964); and Ahmad Sabaruddin's *Pengantar Sastera Indonesia* (1960). For comparative work on Indonesian poetry of the same period, see Keith Foulcher's "Perceptions of Modernity and the Sense of the Past: Indonesian Poetry in the 1920s" (1977). Foulcher's equally perceptive essay "Literature, Cultural Politics, and the Indonesian Revolution" (1993) is valuable in calling for close attention to the intellectual culture of the 1930s as a backdrop to the study of the Generation of '45 writers. Unfamiliar local-language works such as *Sitti Djaoerah* would suggest that regional literatures of the 1920s should be brought into the same scope of research.

2. The main prose novels in the Angkola Batak language in the 1920s and 1930s were *Sitti Djaoerah* and Soetan Pangoerabaan's *Tolbok Haleon*. Soetan Hasoendoetan's lost novel *Siroente Simata Maridjen* may also be an important work. Two Angkola-language *adat* ('ancient custom') guidebooks also take a literary form similar to that of the novels: Soetan Paroehoem Pane's *Adat Batak II: Di Bagason Siriaon* (1922) and A. N. Loebis's *Harondoek Parmanoan* (ca. 1934). Both of these books follow journey-to-Deli themes. A related work is Soetan Kabidoen's *Parsorminan: Barita di Loeat Mandailing* (ca. 1936). Verse narratives, published as booklets, often took journey themes as well (e.g., Soetan Hasoendoetan's own *Nasotardago*). Some of these were written in Indonesian (e.g., M. D. E. Panggebean's *Pantun Melajoe* (ca. 1930) and Anak Moeda's [obviously a pseudonym] *Sjair Penggoda Gadis* [ca. 1925]). Other verse booklets were written in Angkola Batak (e.g., Toean Mangaradja Alom Sari's *Si Tapi Ranting Malina* [1931, still a warmly remembered work today among the elderly in Sipirok and Padangsidimpuan]).

3. The portion of my work most directly related to the sort of ritual oratory Soetan Hasoendoetan drew on in writing *Sitti Djaoerah* includes "Angkola Batak Kinship through Its Oral Literature" (1978, a dissertation that includes translated samples of several types of oratory); "Advice to the Newlyweds: Sipirok Batak Wedding Speeches—*Adat* or Art?" (1979a); "A Modern Batak *Horja*: Innovation in Sipirok *Adat* Ceremonial" (1979b, a piece that includes sample *alok-alok* orations); "Blessing Shawls: The Social Meaning of Sipirok Batak *Ulos*" (1981, an essay that includes *pangupa* reading speeches); "Political Oratory in a Modernizing Southern Batak Homeland" (1983, on *alok-alok* speeches); and "Symbolic Patterning in Angkola Batak *Adat* Ritual" (1985, on oratory in a dance context). On social change and the transition to print literacy issues, see "Orality, Literacy, and Batak Concepts of Marriage Alliance" (1984); "Batak Tape Cassette Kinship: Constructing Kinship through the Indonesian National Mass Media" (1986); "A Sumatran Antiquarian Writes His Culture" (1990a); "The Ethnic Culture Page in Medan Journalism" (1991a); and "Batak Heritage and Indonesian State: Print Literacy and the Construction of Ethnic Cultures in

Indonesia" (1993). On *Sitti Djaoerah* specifically, see "Imagining Tradition, Imagining Modernity: A Southern Batak Novel from the 1920s" (1991b). For comparative context on a Toba writer and his vision of the past (in this case the 1920s and 1930s), see *Telling Lives, Telling History: Autobiography and Historical Imagination in Modern Indonesia* (1995), which concerns the Sumatran childhood memoirs of the Toba author P. Pospos and the Minangkabau writer Muhamad Radjab. My Sipirok fieldwork began with July 1974 to February 1977 ethnographic research on ritual oratory, first in town and then in a village nearby. Two shorter visits to conduct research on the same topic followed in 1980 and 1986–87. The work concentrating most directly on southern Batak print literature and *Sitti Djaoerah* as a text to be translated came in June through August of 1989 and January through August of 1992, as is discussed in the "Note on the Translation."

4. This is a pattern found in many highland Southeast Asian societies, as E. R. Leach famously pointed out in *Political Systems of Highland Burma* (1954). For a good discussion of changing Karo ethnic identity in east Sumatran contexts in the 1970s, see Richard Kipp, "Fictive Kinship and Changing Ethnicity among Karo and Toba Migrants" (1983). Rita Smith Kipp's *Dissociated Identities: Religion, Ethnicity, and Class in an Indonesian Society* (1993) deals expertly with Karo identity in rural Sumatra and the Jakarta diaspora. Also on Karo identity vis-à-vis the national state and monotheism, see Mary M. Steedly's *Hanging without a Rope: Narrative Experience in Colonial and Post-colonial Karoland* (1993). On closely related issues in Kalimantan, analyzed from a critical feminist perspective, see Anna Lowenhaupt Tsing's *In the Realm of the Diamond Queen: Marginality in an Out-of-the-Way Place* (1993). For an astute political economy study of Deli plantation society, see anthropologist Ann Stoler's *Capitalism and Confrontation in Sumatra's Plantation Belt: 1870–1979* (1985). A basic source is also Clark Cunningham's "The Post-War Migration of the Toba Bataks to East Sumatra" (1958), which focuses on the period following 1945.

5. There were a number of book-publishing houses in southern Tapanuli in the 1920s and 1930s, most prominent among them Soetan Pangoerabaan's Tapiannaoeli firm, Philemon bin Haroen's publishing house, Soetan Pangoerabaan's small Sipirok printing house (usually just called "St. P"), and the Padangsidimpuan firm Partopan. None of these continued after the Revolution. In the national era the most influential and largest publishers of Angkola-language works were Medan's Islamiyah and Padangsidimpuan's Pustaka Timur, which is still in operation (although it is turning increasingly to textbook publishing).

6. Useful historical studies of Balai Pustaka include A. Teeuw's "The Impact of Balai Pustaka on Modern Indonesian Literature" (1972) and G. W. J. Drewes's "Balai Pustaka and Its Antecedents" (1981).

7. I base this claim on interviews in 1974 and 1975 with my Angkola Batak language teacher Bapak G. W. Siregar and his circle of elderly male and female friends. This group was composed of retired schoolteachers for the most part, along with a few shopkeepers, retired government clerks, and a tailor.

8. This situation is certainly not limited to Angkola. In both P. Pospos's *Aku dan Toba* (1950) and Muhamad Radjab's *Semasa Kecil di Kampung* (1950), the remembered children, growing up in the 1920s and 1930s in Toba and Minangkabau villages and towns, recall loving the Balai Pustaka novels and checking large numbers of them out of their local lending libraries.

9. In the late 1920s and 1930s, southern Batak authors were also publishing pulp fiction of this sort—in Indonesian. Typical examples were Emnast's (i.e., M. Nasution's) *Pembalasan* (1940) and Sjamsoeddin Nasoetion's *Keris Poesaka* (ca. 1930). Some of these were probably retellings of the story lines of other books. Other paperbacks were love stories (e.g., D. I. Loebis's *Dalarn Katjauan Pertjintaan* [ca. 1935]; A. A. Siregar's *Gagalnja Kewadjiban*

Lantaran Doea Soempah [ca. 1930]; and U. Siregar's *Tjinta Membawa Korban* [1936]). This last love story, a potboiler, concerns a man who two-times his wife and eventually is eaten by a big fish in retribution. Siregar wrote his book while incarcerated in Balikpapan, Kalimantan, for political activities.

Writers from other ethnic societies authored pulp fiction to which southern Batak consumers likely had access, at least in Deli. Some of these titles were by Indonesian Chinese (e.g., So Chuan Hong and Njoo Tjiong Sing's *Tjerita Penghidoepan Manoesia, atawa Satoe Gadis jang terdjeroemoes dalem geloembang pertjintaan* [1919, from a publishing house in Surabaya]). Other books were by non-Batak Sumatran writers (e.g., Joesoef Sou'yb's *Bibir jang Mengandoeng Ratjoen* [1939] and Si Kontet's *Diantara Dua Peti Mati* [1940], both of which were from Medan; Decha's *Tragedie Dilajar Pergerakan* [1939, published in Padang]; and S. Oesmany's *Dr. Chung* [from Medan]). Two Indonesian-language novels directly concerned with Batak migration and social change issues were Tamar Djaja's *Samora, Gadis Toba* (ca. 1930) and D. I. Loebis's *Lily van Angkola* (ca. 1925). Loebis was a southern Batak, judging by his clan name, but Tamar Djaja's background is unknown. Despite the Dutch air to *Lily van Angkola*'s title, the book is written in Bahasa Indonesia.

10. For instance, an early chapter of Rusli's *Sitti Nurbaya* has a middle-aged, aristocratic brother and sister arguing about the man's financial responsibilities toward his sister's daughter versus his wife and son (a stereotypical dispute in matrilineal Minangkabau).

11. This image of an Indies ethnic society "on the move" was certainly not limited to Batak social thought. See Takashi Shiraishi's *An Age in Motion: Popular Radicalism in Java: 1912–1926* (1990), especially the sections on popular print literature and newswriting.

12. Toba was also "school mad" in late colonial times, something evident from P. Pospos's childhood memoir *Aku dan Toba* (1950). See my *Telling Lives, Telling History* for a discussion of Batak views on formal schooling.

13. In South Tapanuli today, government-published middle school textbooks are available as lesson books for learning the old script. The major collections of Batak script texts inscribed on bark are in the Netherlands, in large part thanks to the efforts of the remarkable linguist H. N. Van der Tuuk. He assembled large collections of texts from Angkola and Mandailing from his research posts near Barus and Sibolga in the 1850s. Since he encouraged his Batak informants not only to bring him texts but to write down everything in their oral heritage, his influence could well have been a sizable one along the interface of talk and text. Van der Tuuk left his collection to the University of Leiden. The Tropen Museum in Amsterdam and the Museum voor Volkenkunde in Leiden also have large collections of bark books. Jakarta's National Museum and Medan's provincial museum also have considerable holdings on bark, wood, and bamboo. For a recent discussion of the history of the script, see Uli Kozok's "Bark, Bones, and Bamboo: Batak Traditions of Sumatra" (1996). For general context, see Joel Kuipers and Ray McDermott, "Insular Southeast Asian Scripts" (1996).

14. There is an extensive historical, anthropological, psychological, and literary-critical literature on the social-organizational and ideational consequences of the transition from oral culture, to script literacy, to commercial print literacy (a bumpy trajectory, it often turns out). Major works on other societies particularly useful for looking at Batak literacy issues include Walter Ong's *Orality and Literacy* (1982); Jack Goody's *The Domestication of the Savage Mind* (1977); Goody's *The Logic of Writing and the Organization of Society* (1986); Alfred B. Lord's classic *The Singer of Tales* (1965); Michael Stubb's *Language and Literacy: The Sociolinguistics of Reading and Writing* (1980); Brian Street's *Literacy in Theory and Practice* (1984); R. A. Hougton's *Scottish Literacy and Scottish Identity* (1985); and Sylvia

Scribner and Michael Cole's *The Psychology of Literacy* (1981). In the specific Indonesian context, Mary Zurbuchen's *The Language of Balinese Shadow Theater* (1987) provides a rich case study of the ways in which oral performance styles, script literacy, and (to a lesser extent) print interact. See also Nancy K. Florida's *Writing the Past, Inscribing the Future* (1995); John Bowen's *Sumatran Politics and Poetics: Gayo History, 1900–1989* (1991); James Siegel's *Shadow and Sound: The History of a Sumatran People* (1979); and chapter 2 ("Writing Subjects, Writing Authorities") of John Pemberton's *On the Subject of "Java"* (1994). All of these studies are particularly insightful about the politics of writing and speech. The essays in A. L. Becker's edited volume, *Writing on the Tongue* (1989), on the translation dilemmas of Indonesian "texts" of various sorts, also offer illuminating discussions of orality-script and occasionally print situations (see also Becker's valuable *Beyond Translation: Essays toward a Modern Philology* [1995]).

15. Lance Castles's doctoral dissertation, "The Political Life of a Sumatran Residency: Tapanuli, 1915–1940" (1972) examines both the Muslim proselytization and the Christian missionary history of the Sipirok area. His bibliography is excellent. Castles's essay "Statelessness and State-Forming Tendencies among the Batak before Colonial Rule" (1975) goes on to put the *harajaon adat* chieftaincy structure in a useful "development of the state" perspective. For an early Christian missionary's report of the Sipirok field, see Gerrit van Asselt, *Achttien Jaren onder de Bataks* (1905); see also A. Schreiber, *Ein Besuch auf Sumatra* (1877). On the pioneer missionary to Toba, see J. H. Hemmers's *L. I. Nommensen, de Apostel der Batakkers* (1935). For an anthropological discussion of Christian missions in Karo, to the north, see Rita Smith Kipp's *The Early Years of a Dutch Colonial Mission* (1990).

16. Soetan Hasoendoetan knew very well that his readers would be familiar with two crucial parts of local wedding *adat*: the initial-visit scene, between the two lineages to be united by the forthcoming marriage, and the oratorically demanding *kobar boru* session, in which the various brideprice payments are haggled over and finally settled and paid. It could be that reading such sections of the novel gave the Angkola an artistic format for subjectively reconstructing their kinship world (see Geertz 1972 for a productive framework here).

17. Emotions in the southern Batak cultures have not been extensively studied, unfortunately. One valuable start, related to emotions and gong music, is ethnomusicologist Margaret Kartomi's "'Lovely When Heard from Afar': Mandailing Ideas of Musical Beauty" (1981). A promising anthropological framework for exploring the social construction of emotion in this part of Sumatra is provided in the essays (on other parts of the world) in Catherine A. Lutz and Lila Abu-Lughod's edited volume *Language and the Politics of Emotion* (1990).

18. For a sample of *andung* as performed recently, see Rodgers 1990b. In the 1990s, most brides only sob wordlessly and mourners gathered around a corpse only gasp out a few *andung* phrases before swtiching to crying per se. For comparative material on women's lament speech from eastern Indonesia, see Joel Kuipers's "Talking about Troubles: Gender Differences in Weyewa Speech Use" (1986) and his book *Power in Performance: The Creation of Textual Authority in Weyewa Ritual Speech* (1990). For another excellent discussion of women's laments and issues of subordination and domination, see Janet Hoskins's "Why Do Ladies Sing the Blues? Indigo Dyeing, Cloth Production, and Gender Symbolism in Kodi" (1989).

19. Beyond the major classics *Si Boeloes-Boeloes*, *Doea Sadjoli*, and *Ranteomas*, other important classroom primers and anthologies were Radja Bagindo's *On Ma Barita Tingon Binatan-Bintang bahatna Lima Poeloe Ragam* (1868), *On Ma Soerat Tongononkon* (1893), and a primer that the Sipirok school principal Soetan Martoewa Radja wrote with Toba schoolman and folklorist Arsenius Loembantobing, *Soeloesoeloe: Boekoe Sidjahaan ni*

angka anak sikola metmet (1921). Other important schoolbooks in the Angkola Batak language in the 1920s included Radja Goenoeng's *Moetik* series (1923), P. Siregar and Soetan Kinali's *Barita na denggan-denggan* (1926), and Dja Parlagoetan's *Parsanggoelan* (1929). Typical of the Indonesian-language readers used during that decade in the area was *Serba-Neka: Kitab Batjaan jang pertama Bagi Moerid Sekolah Melajoe* (1923). In the 1930s, Dja Parlagoetan's books were reprinted many times, augmented with others such as Moehammad Kasim's *Doea Oeli: Boekoe Basaon* (1936). The Dutch school offical J. G. Dammerboer also authored schoolbooks for southern Batak pupils, including his much-used *Singgolom: Boekoe Basaon* (1931). He and his colleague Dr. A. Schreiber also published numerous scholarly works on Angkola literature. S. Nasution's *Sejarah Pendidikan Indonesia* (1983) has an extensive bibliography of sources dealing with the introduction of schools to this area.

20. Basyral Harahap's edited version, *Si Boeloes-Boeloes* (1987), provides useful historical information on the book's past as well as Willem Iskander's biography.

21. See Ahmat B. Adam's *The Vernacular Press and the Emergence of Modern Indonesian Consciousness, 1855–1913* (1995) for the Indies-wide context of local Batak journalism far from Medan. His bibliography is especially good.

22. Some of this local folkloristic writing seems to have been strongly influenced by Dutch scholarly models, as was the Toba ancient history literature as well. For instance, C. A. van Ophuijsen, perhaps the preeminent Dutch folklorist of Angkola and Mandailing oral traditions, published his rich *Bataksche Teksten* (*Mandailingsch Dialect*) in 1914. This book was apparently well known to Angkola and Mandailing schoolmasters, who seem to have used it as a model for some of their own work. In Toba, Dutch scholarly practices and ideas of what constitutes a folk culture are also evident in some of the work of the tireless Arsenius Loembantobing (in such volumes as *Doea Toeritoerian na masa di Halak Batak* [1919] and his rather ethnographically toned *Pingkiran ni Halak Batak Sipelebegoe taringot toe Tondi ni Djolma Doeng Mati* [1920]). Loembantobing was a Christian and tended to report Toba "ancient beliefs" through a stern monotheistic filter.

23. Soetan Pangoerabaan's works include, among others, *Tolbok Haleon* (1933), *Roekoen Bersoetji* (1933), *Roekoen Iman dohot Roekoen Islam* (1933), *Parpadanan* (1935), *Nai Marlangga* (1933), *Ampang Limo Bapole* (1936), *Adat* (1933), *Singgorit I: Boekoe Basaon* (1930), *Na Mongkol* (1931), *Anggota* (1935), and the extraordinary social geography text, written in Indonesian, *Mentjapai Doenia Baroe* (1934). In this volume Soetan Pangoerabaan presents young readers with an Asia-focused history of recent colonial times.

24. There is a considerable amount of Angkola Batak-language writing being done today on *adat* antiquarian themes (guidebooks for how to conduct an *adat* funeral or wedding, for instance). Typical of this large literature is Ch. Sutan Tinggi Barani Perkasa Alam's *Mangampar Ruji/Mangkobar Boru* (1978). In my "A Sumatran Antiquarian Writes His Culture" (1990a) I discuss a number of titles along this line. There has been one novel-like piece of writing published recently in Angkola Batak: Abdul Rahman Ritonga's *Turian ni Hak Sipirok Banggo* (1986). The book is an odd combination of personal memoir, family history, novel, and *turiturian* sampler. There is one other Angkola Batak–language novel in the post-Revolution period: Abu Arab Siagian's *Magodang Aek Marali Tapian* (1955), about Sibolga families during the Revolution. Abu Arab's other works are verse narratives such as his locally fondly regarded *Pisang Maralohon Duri* (ca. 1955). Verse narratives are still being written and published in Angkola (two typical ones are M. Harahap's fine *Anak Pangun Sandean* and Daulat Ritonga's *Na Lambok Marlidung* [1986]). In the 1980s the Indonesian government's Ministry of Education and Culture sponsored several local liter-

atures series for public libraries throughout the country, although these titles tended to be inaccessible to the general public since the books were often stockpiled in ministry offices. The South Tapanuli series included reprints of folktales first collected in colonial times. Today the provincial government also sponsors the publication of tourist magazines such as *Majalah Budaya Batak dan Pariwisata* in Medan.

25. Rita Smith Kipp writes in *Dissociated Identities* (1994) that the national government today is in effect attempting to transform some ethnic cultures into showpiece cultures suitable for touristic consumption (of course, politically trivialized and partially controlled in the process). Hoskins's "The Headhunter as Hero" (1987) discusses another aspect of this hegemonic process and local resistance to it: local efforts to write a people's history in the context of the national state's own history-writing apparatus.

26. The main dictionary is still H. J. Eggink's *Angkola- en Mandailing- Bataksch/Nederlandsch Woordenboek* (1936). This is a good basic source, but it does not delve exhaustively into oratory. A newer Angkola-Indonesian dictionary is much sketchier: Ahmad Samin Siregar's *Kamus Bahasa Angkola/Mandailing Indonesia*, published in the national government's local languages series in 1977. This dictionary was compiled using a fieldwork technique of simply recording all the words used in a few regions over a short period of time. *Adat* oratory was apparently not encountered by the researchers, although many Indonesian loanwords certainly were.

REFERENCES CITED

Achebe, Chinua. 1959. *Things Fall Apart.* London: McDowell, Obolensky.

Adam, Ahmat, B. 1995. *The Vernacular Press and the Emergence of Modern Indonesian Consciousness* (1855–1913). Ithaca: Cornell University, Southeast Asia Program.

Anak Moeda. ca. 1925. *Sjair Penggoda Gadis.* Sibolga: Marah Hanin Zoon.

Anderson, Benedict. 1983. *Imagined Communities: Reflections on the Origin and Spread of Nationalism.* London: Verso.

Asselt, Gerrit van. 1905. *Achttien Jaren onder der Bataks.* Rotterdam: D. A. Daamen.

Aveling, Harry G. 1970. "Sitti Nurbaya: Some Reconsiderations, with a Comment by Taufik Abdullah." *Bijdragen tot de Taal- Land- en Volkenkunde* 126 (1970): 228–45.

Bakhtin, M. M. 1986. *Speech Genres and Other Late Essays.* Translated by Vern W. McGee, edited by Caryl Emerson and Michael Holquist. Austin: University of Texas Press.

———. [1981] 1990a. *The Dialogic Imagination: Four Essays.* Translated by Caryl Emerson and Michael Holquist, edited by Michael Holquist. Austin: University of Texas Press.

———. 1990b. "Epic and Novel." In Bakhtin 1990a: 3–40.

———. 1990c. "From the Prehistory of Novelistic Discourse." In Bakhtin 1990a: 41–83.

———. 1990d. "Forms of Time and of the Chronotope in the Novel." In Bakhtin 1990a: 84–258.

———. 1990e. "Discourse in the Novel." In Bakhtin 1990a: 259–422.

Becker, A. L., ed. 1989. *Writing on the Tongue.* Michigan Papers on South and Southeast Asia, no. 33. Ann Arbor: Center for South and Southeast Asian Studies, University of Michigan.

———. 1995. *Beyond Translation: Essays toward a Modern Philology.* Ann Arbor: University of Michigan Press.

Bowen, John. 1991. *Sumatran Politics and Poetics: Gayo History, 1900–1989.* New Haven: Yale University Press.

Castles, Lance. 1972. "The Political Life of a Sumatran Residency: Tapanuli, 1915–1940." Ph.D. diss., Yale University, Department of History.

———. 1975. "Statelessness and State-Forming Tendencies among the Batak before Colonial Rule." In *Pre-colonial State Systems in Southeast Asia,* edited by A. Reid and Lance Castles. Pp. 67–76. Kuala Lumpur: Malaysian Branch of the Royal Asiatic Society.

Cunningham, Clark. 1958. *The Post-War Migration of the Toba-Bataks to East Sumatra.* Cultural Reports, no. 5. New Haven: Yale University, Program in Southeast Asian Studies.

Dalimunthe, Drs. H. 1981. *Mangordang dohot Mamuro.* Jakarta: Proyek Penerbitan Buku Sastra Indonesia dan Daerah.

Dammerboer, J. G. 1931. *Singgolom: Boekoe Basaon.* Batavia: Landsdrukkerij.

Davis, Lennard. 1983. *Factual Fictions: The Origins of the English Novel.* New York: Columbia University Press.

Decha. 1939. *Tragedie Dilajar Pergerakan.* Padang: Roman Indonesia.

Dja Parlagoetan. 1929. *Parsanggoelan.* Batavia: Lands Drukkerij.

Drewes, G. W. J. 1981. "Balai Pustaka and Its Antecedents." *Archipel* 13:97–104.

Eggink, H. J. 1936. *Angkola- en Mandailing- Bataksch/Nederlandsch Woordenboek.* Bandung: A. C. Nix.

Emnast [M. Nasution]. 1940. *Pembalasan.* Medan: Doenia Pengalaman.

Florida, Nancy K. 1995. *Writing the Past, Inscribing the Future: History as Prophecy in Colonial Java.* Durham: Duke University Press.

Freidus, Alberta Joy. 1977. *Sumatran Contributions to the Development of Indonesian Literature, 1920–1942*. Asian Studies at Hawaii Monographs, no. 19. Honolulu: University of Hawaii Press.

Foulcher, Keith. 1977. "Perceptions of Modernity and the Sense of the Past: Indonesian Poetry in the 1920s." *Indonesia* 23 (April): 39–58.

———. 1993. "Literature, Cultural Politics, and the Indonesian Revolution." In *Text/Politics in Island Southeast Asia*, edited by D. M. Roskies. Ohio University Monographs in International Studies, Southeast Asia Series, no. 91. Pp. 221–56. Athens: Ohio University Press.

Geertz, Clifford. [1972] 1973. "Deep Play: Notes on the Balinese Cockfight." In *The Interpretation of Cultures*. Pp. 412–54. New York: Basic Books. Originally published in *Daedalus* 101 (1972): 1–37.

Goody, Jack. 1978. *The Domestication of the Savage Mind*. Cambridge: Cambridge University Press.

———. 1986. *The Logic of Writing and the Organisation of Society*. Cambridge: Cambridge University Press.

Harahap, Basyral Hamidy. 1987. *Willem Iskander, Si Bulus-Bulus Si Rumbuk-Rumbuk*. Edited and translated into Indonesian by Basyral H. Harahap. Jakarta: Puisi Indonesia.

Harahap, M. ca. 1976. *Anak Pangun Sandean*. Padangsidimpuan: n.p.

Harahap, Parada. 1925. *Tjoba Dapatkan! . . .* Weltevreden: Bintang Hindia.

Hemmers, J. H. 1935. *L. I. Nommensen, de Apostel der Batakkers*. The Hague: J. N. Voorhoeve.

Holquist, Michael. 1990a. *Dialogism: Bakhtin and His World*. London: Routledge.

———. 1990b. Introduction to *The Dialogic Imagination*, by M. M. Bakhtin. In Bakhtin 1990a: xv–xxxiv.

Hoskins, Janet. 1987. "The Headhunter as Hero: Local Traditions and Their Reinterpretation as National History." *American Ethnologist* 14 (4): 605–22.

———. 1989. "Why Do Ladies Sing the Blues? Indigo Dyeing, Cloth Production, and Gender Symbolism in Kodi." In *Cloth and Human Experience*, edited by Annette Weiner and Jane Schneider. Pp. 142–73. Washington, D.C.: Smithsonian Institution Press.

Hougton, R. A. 1985. *Scottish Literacy and the Scottish Identity*. Cambridge: Cambridge University Press.

Hunter, J. Paul. 1990. *Before Novels: The Cultural Contexts of Eighteenth Century English Fiction*. New York and London: W. W. Norton.

Johns, Anthony. 1959. "The Novel as a Guide to Indonesian Social History." *Bijdragen tot de Taal- Land- en Volkenkunde* 115:232–48.

———. 1963. "Genesis of a Modern Literature." In *Indonesia*, edited by Ruth McVey. Pp. 410–37. New Haven: Human Relations Area Files Press.

Junus, Umar. 1974. *Perkembangan Novel-Novel Indonesia*. Kuala Lumpur: Penerbit Universiti Malaya.

Kartomi, Margaret. 1981. "'Lovely When Heard from Afar': Mandailing Ideas of Musical Beauty." In *Five Essays on the Indonesian Arts*, edited by Margaret Kartomi. Pp. 1–16. Clayton, Vic.: Monash University Press.

Kipp, Richard. 1983. "Fictive Kinship and Changing Ethnicity among Karo and Toba Migrants." In *Beyond Samosir: Recent Studies of the Batak Peoples of Sumatra*, edited by Rita Smith Kipp and Richard Kipp. Pp. 147–55. Ohio University Monographs in International Studies, Southeast Asia Series, no. 62. Athens: Ohio University Press.

Kipp, Rita Smith. 1990. *The Early Years of a Dutch Colonial Mission: The Karo Field*. Ann Arbor: University of Michigan Press.

————. 1994. *Dissociated Identities: Ethnicity, Religion, and Class in an Indonesian Society.* Ann Arbor: University of Michigan Press.

Kozok, Uli. 1996. "Bark, Bones, and Bamboo: Batak Traditions of Sumatra." In *Illuminations: The Writing Traditions of Indonesia.* Pp. 231–46. New York and Tokyo: Weatherhill.

Kuipers, Joel. 1986. "Talking about Troubles: Gender Differences in Weyewa Speech Use." *American Ethnologist* 13 (3): 448–62.

————. 1990. *Power in Performance: The Creation of Textual Authority in Weyewa Ritual Speech.* Philadelphia: University of Pennsylvania Press.

Kuipers, Joel, and Ray McDermott. 1996. "Insular Southeast Asian Scripts." In *The World's Writing Systems*, edited by Peter T. Daniels and William Bright. Pp. 474–84. New York and Oxford: Oxford University Press.

Leach, E. R. 1954. *Political Systems of Highland Burma.* Boston: Beacon.

Lodge, David. 1990. *After Bakhtin: Essays on Fiction and Criticism.* London and New York: Routledge.

Loebis, A. N. ca. 1934. *Harondoek Parmanoan.* Medan: Handel Mij. Indische Drukkerij Medan.

Loebis, D. I. ca. 1925. *Lily van Angkola.* Medan: Pertjatimoer.

————. ca. 1935. *Dalam Katjauan Pertjintaan.* Sibolga: Tapiannaoeli.

Loembantobing, Arsenius. 1919. *Doea Toeritoerian na masa di Halak Batak. Batavia: Lands Drukkerij.*

————. 1920. *Pingkiran ni Halak Batak Sipelebegoe taringot toe Tondi ni Djolma Doeng Mati.* Leiden: S. C. van Doesburgh.

Lord, Alfred B. 1965. *The Singer of Tales.* Cambridge: Harvard University Press.

Lutz, Catherine A., and Lila Abu-Lughod, eds. 1990. *Language and the Politics of Emotion.* Cambridge: Cambridge University Press.

Majalah Budaya Batak dan Pariwisata. Medan.

Mangaradja Alom Sari, Toean K. 1931. *Si Tapi Ranting Malina.* Sibolga: Tapiannaoeli.

Mangaradja Goenoeng Sorik Marapi. [1914] 1957. *Turiturian ni Radja Gorga di Langit dohot Radja Suasa di Portibi.* Originally published, Sibolga: Tapiannaoeli.

Mgr. Ihoetan. 1926. *Riwayat Tanah Wakaf Bagnsa Mandailing.* Medan: Sjarikat Tapanoeli.

Moehammad Kasim. 1936. *Doea Oeli: Boekoe Basaon.* Batavia: Lands Drukkerij.

Mohammad Said, H. 1976. *Sejarah Pers di Sumatra Utara dengan masyarakat yang dicerminkannya* (1885–1942). Medan: Percetakan Waspada.

Muis, Abdul. 1928. *Salah Asuhan.* Jakarta: Balai Pustaka.

Nasution, Prof. Dr. S. 1983. *Sejarah Pendidikan Indonesia.* Bandung: Jemmars.

Nasution, Sjamsoeddin. ca. 1930. *Keris Poesaka.* Padang: Ps. Malintang.

Ngugi wa Thiongo. 1965. *The River Between.* London: Heinemann.

Oesmany, S. ca.1925. *Dr. Chung.* Medan: Doenia Pengalaman.

On Ma Soerat Tongononkon. 1893. Batavia: Lands Drukkerij.

Ong, Walter. 1982. *Orality and Literacy: The Technologizing of the Word.* New York: Methuen.

van Ophuijsen, Ch. A. 1914. *Bataksche Teksten (Mandailingsch Dialect).* Leiden: S. C. van Doesburgh.

Pane, Armijn. [1942] 1961. *Belenggu.* 5th ed. Jakarta: Pustaka Rakyat.

Pane, H. Soetan Pane Paroehoem. 1922. *Adat Batak II: Di Bagasan Siriaon.* Pematang Siantar: n.p.

Panggabean, M. D. E. ca. 1930. *Pantun Melajoe.* Sibolga: Marah Hanin & Zoon.

Pemberton, John. 1994. *On the Subject of "Java."* Ithaca: Cornell University Press.

Pospos, P. 1950. *Aku dan Toba.* Jakarta: Balai Pustaka.

Quinn, George. 1983. "The Case of the Invisible Literature: Power, Scholarship, and Contemporary Javanese Writing." *Indonesia* 35 (April): 1–36.

Radja Bagindo. 1868. *On Ma Barita tingon Binatang-Bintang bahatna Lima Poeloe Pitoe Ragam.* Batavia: Lands Drukkerij.

Radja Goenoeng. 1923. *Moetik III.* Batavia: De-Unie Weltevreden.

Radjab, Muhamad. 1950. *Semasa Kecil di Kampung.* Jakarta: Balai Pustaka.

Reid, Anthony, and Jennifer Brewster, eds. 1983. *Slavery, Bondage, and Dependency in Southeast Asia.* New York: St. Martin's.

Ritonga, Abdul Rahman. 1986. *Turiturian ni Hak Sipirok Banggo.* Medan: Jenggal-Jepput.

Ritonga, Daulat [Baginda Guru]. 1986. "Na Lambok Marlidung." Manuscript.

Rodgers, Susan. 1978. "Angkola Batak Kinship through Its Oral Literature." Ph.D. diss., Department of Anthropology, University of Chicago.

———. 1979a. "Advice to the Newlyweds: Sipirok Batak Wedding Speeches—*Adat* or Art?" In *Art, Ritual, and Society in Indonesia,* edited by Edward M. Bruner and Judith Becker. Ohio University Monographs in International Studies, Southeast Asia Series, no. 53. Athens: Ohio University Press. Pp. 30–61.

———. 1979b. "A Modern Batak *Horja*: Innovation in Sipirok Adat Ceremonial." Indonesia 27 (April): 103–28.

———. 1981a. "Blessing Shawls: The Social Meaning of Sipirok Batak *Ulos*." In *Indonesian Textiles: Irene Emery Roundtable on Museum Textiles,* edited by M. Gittinger. Pp. 96–115. Washington, D.C.: Textile Museum.

———. 1981b. "A Batak Literature of Modernization. " *Indonesia 31* (April): 137–61.

———. 1983. "Political Oratory in a Modernizing Southern Batak Homeland." In *Beyond Samosir: Recent Studies of the Batak Peoples of Sumatra,* edited by Rita Smith Kipp and Richard Kipp. Pp. 21–52. Ohio University Monographs in International Studies, Southeast Asia Series, no. 62. Athens: Ohio University Press.

———. 1984. "Orality, Literacy, and Batak Concepts of Marriage Alliance." *Journal of Anthropological Research* 40 (3): 433–50.

———. 1985. "Symbolic Patterning in Angkola Batak *Adat* Ritual" Journal of *Asian Studies* 44 (4): 765–78.

———. 1986. "Batak Tape Cassette Kinship: Constructing Kinship through the Indonesian National Mass Media." *American Ethnologist* 13 (1): 23–42.

———. 1990a. "A Sumatran Antiquarian Writes His Culture." *Steward Journal of Anthropology* 17 (1–2): 99–120. Reprinted in *Anthropology and Literature,* edited by Paul Benson. Urbana: University of 1Illinois Press, 1993.

———. 1990b. "The Symbolic Representation of Women in a Changing Batak Culture." In *Power and Difference: Gender in Island Southeast Asia,* edited by Jane M. Atkinson and Shelly Errington. Pp. 307–44. Palo Alto: Stanford University Press.

———. 1991a. "The Ethnic Culture Page in Medan Journalism." *Indonesia* 51 (April): 83–104.

———. 1991b. "Imagining Tradition, Imagining Modernity: A Southern Batak Novel from the 1920s." *Bijdragen tot de Taal- Land- en Volkenkunde* 147 (2–3): 273–97.

———. 1993. "Batak Heritage and Indonesian State: Print Literacy and the Construction of Ethnic Cultures in Indonesia." In *Ethnicity and the State,* edited by Judith Toland. Pp. 147–76. Volumes in Political Anthropology, no. 9. New Brunswick, N.J.: Transactions.

———. 1995. *Telling Lives, Telling History: Autobiography and Historical Imagination in Modern Indonesia.* Berkeley: University of California Press.

Rosidi, Ajip. 1964. *Kapankah Kesusasteraan Indonesia Lahir? Beserta Sepilihan Karangan Lainja.* Jakarta: Bhratara.

Rusli, Marah. 1922. *Sitti Nurbaya*. Weltevreden: Balai Pustaka.
Sabaruddin, Ahmad. 1960. *Pengantar Sastera Indonesia*. Medan: Penerbit Saiful.
Said, Edward. 1993. *Culture and Imperialism*. New York: Knopf.
Schreiber, August. 1877. *Ein Besuch auf Sumatra*. Barmen: Rheinische Missions-Gesellschaft.
Scott, James C. 1990. *Domination and the Arts of Resistance: Hidden Transcripts*. New Haven: Yale University Press.
Scribner, Sylvia, and Michael Cole. 1981. *The Psychology of Literacy*. Cambridge: Harvard University Press.
Selasih. 1933. *Kalau Tak Untung*. Jakarta: Balai Pustaka.
Serba-Neka: Kitab Batjaan jang Pertama Bagi Moerid Sekolah Melajoe. 1923. Leiden: P. W. M. Trap.
Shiraishi, Takashi. 1990. *An Age in Motion: Popular Radicalism in Java, 1912–1926*. Ithaca: Cornell University Press.
Siagian, Abu Arab. 1955. *Magodang Aek Marali Tapian*. Padangsidimpuan: Pustaka Timur.
———. *Pisang Maralohon Duri*. Padangsidimpuan: Pustaka Timur.
Siegel, James. 1979. *Shadow and Sound: The Historical Thought of a Sumatran People*. Chicago: University of Chicago Press.
Si Kontet. 1940. *Diantara Dua Peti Mati*. Medan: Antara.
Siregar, A. A. ca. 1930. *Gagalnja Kewadjiban Lantaran Doea Soempah*. Pematang Siantar: Moechtar Nst.
Siregar, Ahmad Samin. 1977. *Kamus Bahasa Angkola/Mandailing Indonesia*. Jakarta: Pusat Pembinaan dan Pengembangan Bahasa, Departmen Pendidikan dan Kebudayaan.
Siregar, Merari. [1927] 1958. *Azab dan Sengsara: Kissah Kehidupan Seorang Anak Gadis*. Jakarta: Balai Pustaka.
Siregar, Ph., and Soetan Kinali. 1926. *Barita na Denggandenggan*. Batavia: Lands Drukkerij.
Siregar, U. 1936. *Tjinta Membawa Korban*. Balikpapan: Tan Siang Tjay.
So Chuan Hong and Njoo Tjiong Sing. 1919. *Tjerita Pengidoepan-Manoesia, atawa Satoe Gadis jang terdjeroemoes dalem geloembang pertjintaan*. Surabaya: Thetenghoey Buitenzorg.
Soetan Hasoendoetan, M. J. 1925. *Nasotardago*. Rpt., 1979. Jakarta: Departmen Pendidikan dan Kebudayaan, Proyek Penerbitan Buku Bahasa dan Sastra Daerah.
——— 1927. *Sitti Djaoerah: Padan Djandji na Togoe*. Sibolga: Philemon bin Haroen.
——— 1941. *Datoek Toeongkoe Adji Malim Leman: Toeritoerian ni Halak na Robi Ingotingoton ni Halak Sannari*. Pematang Siantar: Sjarif Siantar.
Sotean Kabidoen. ca. 1936. *Parsorminan, Barita di Loeat Mandailing*. Sibolga: Tapiannaoeli.
Soetan Martoewa Radja. [1917] 1968. *Dua Sadjoli I/II*. Rpt., Medan: Islamiyah.
———. [1919] 1922. *Ranteomas*. Batavia: De Volharding.
Soetan Martoewa Radja and Arsenius Loembantobing. 1921. *Soeloesoeloe: Boekoe Sidjahaan ni Angka Anak Sikola Metmet*. Batavia: Lands Drukkerij.
Soetan Pangoerabaan [Pane]. 1930. *Singgorit I: Boekoe Basaon*. Padangsidimpuan: Partopan.
———. 1931. *Na Mongkol*. Padangsidimpuan: Partopan.
———. [1933a] 1937. *Tolbok Haleon*. Medan: Handel Mij. Indische Drukkerij.
———. 1933b. *Roekoen Bersoetji, Roekoen Soembajang sanga Roekoen Toloe Bolas na niboeat sian Kitab Islam*. Sibolga: Soetan Pangoerabaan.
———. 1933c. *Roekoen Iman dohot Roekoen Islam*. Sibolga: Soetan Pangoerabaan.
———. 1933d. *Nai Marlangga, 2*. Sibolga: Soetan Pangoerabaan.
———. 1934. *Mentjapai Doenia Baroe*. Sipirok: Soetan Pangoerabaan.
———. 1935a. *Anggota*. Sipirok: Peroesahaan Indonesia.
———. 1935b. *Parpadanan*. Sipirok: Peroesahaan Indonesia.

————. 1936. *Ampang Limo Bapole: Toeritoerian.* Padangsidimpuan: Partopan.

————. 1937. Adat. Sipirok: Soetan Pangoerabaan.

Sou'yb, Soesoef. 1939. *Bibir jang Mengandoeng Ratjoen.* Medan: Bibliotheek Hidoep.

Steedly, Mary M. 1993. *Hanging without a Rope: Narrative Experience in Colonial and Post-colonial Karoland.* Princeton: Princeton University Press.

Stoler, Ann L. 1985. *Capitalism and Confrontation in Sumatra's Plantation Belt, 1870–1979.* New Haven: Yale University Press.

Street, Brian. 1980. *Literacy in Theory and Practice.* Cambridge: Cambridge University Press.

Stubbs, Michael. 1980. *Language and Literacy: The Sociolinguistics of Reading and Writing.* London: Routledge and Kegan Paul.

Sutan Tinggi Barani Perkasa Alam, Ch. 1978. *Mangampar Ruji/Mangkobar Boru.* Padangsidimpuan: n.p.

Tamar Djaja. 1930. *Samora, Gadis Toba.* Fort de Kock: Penjiaran Ilmoe.

Teeuw, A. 1967. *Modern Indonesian Literature.* 2 vols. KITLV Translation Series, no. 10. The Hague: Martinus Nijhoff.

————. 1972. "The Impact of Balai Pustaka on Modern Indonesian Literature." *Bulletin of the School of Oriental and African Studies* 1 (1972): 111–27.

Tsing, Anna Lowenhaupt. 1993. *In the Realm of the Diamond Queen: Marginality in an Out-of-the-Way Place.* Princeton: Princeton University Press.

Van der Tuuk, H. N. [1864, 1867] 1971. *A Grammar of Toba Batak.* Translated by Jeune Scott-Kimball. KITLV Translation Series, no. 13. Translation of *Tobasche Spraakunst.* The Hague: Martinus Nijhoff.

Vergouwen, J. C. [1933] 1964. *The Social Organisation and Customary Law of the Toba Bataks of Northern Sumatra.* Translated by Jeune Scott-Kimball. KITLV Translation Series, no. 7. Translation of *Het Rechtsleven der Toba Batak.* The Hague: Martinus Nijhoff.

Watson, C. W. 1971. "Some Preliminary Remarks on the Antecedents of Modern Indonesian Literature." *Bijdragen tot de Taal- Land- en Volkenkunde* 127:417–33.

————. 1972. "The Sociology of the Indonesian Novel, 1920–1955." M.A. thesis, University of Hull.

Watt, Ian. 1957. *The Rise of the Novel.* London: Chatto and Windes.

Willem Iskander. 1872. *Si Boeloes-Boeloes Si Roemboek-Roemboek.* Batavia: Lands Drukkerij. 1976 ed., Jakarta: PT Campusiana. 1978 ed., Padangsidimpuan: Pustaka Timur.

Williams, Raymond. 1973. *The Country and the City.* Oxford: Oxford University Press.

Zurbuchen, Mary. 1987. *The Language of Balinese Shadow Theater.* Princeton: Princeton University Press.

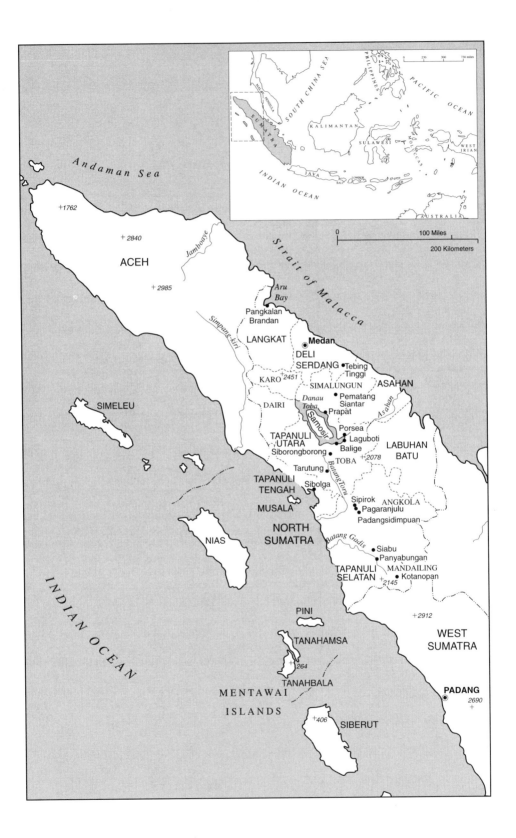

Andaman Sea

+1762

+2840

ACEH

+2985

Jamboaye

Simpang-kiri

Strait of Malacca

Aru
Bay

Pangkalan
Brandan

LANGKAT

●Medan

DELI
SERDANG

●Tebing
Tinggi

KARO +2451

SIMALUNGUN

ASAHAN

DAIRI

*Danau
Toba*

●Pematang
Siantar
●Prapat

Asahan

Samosir

Porsea

●Laguboti
●Balige

LABUHAN
BATU

TAPANULI
UTARA

Siborongborong ●

●TOBA +2078

Tarutung ●

Batang Toru

TAPANULI
TENGAH

Sibolga ●

MUSALA

Sipirok ●

ANGKOLA

●Pagaranjulu

Padangsidimpuan

NORTH
SUMATRA

SIMELEU

NIAS

INDIAN OCEAN

Batang Gadis

●Siabu
●Panyabungan

TAPANULI
SELATAN

MANDAILING

+2145

●Kotanopan

+2912

WEST
SUMATRA

PINI

TANAHMSA

+264

TANAHBALA

MENTAWAI

ISLANDS

+406 SIBERUT

PADANG

2690
+

0   100 Miles
0   200 Kilometers

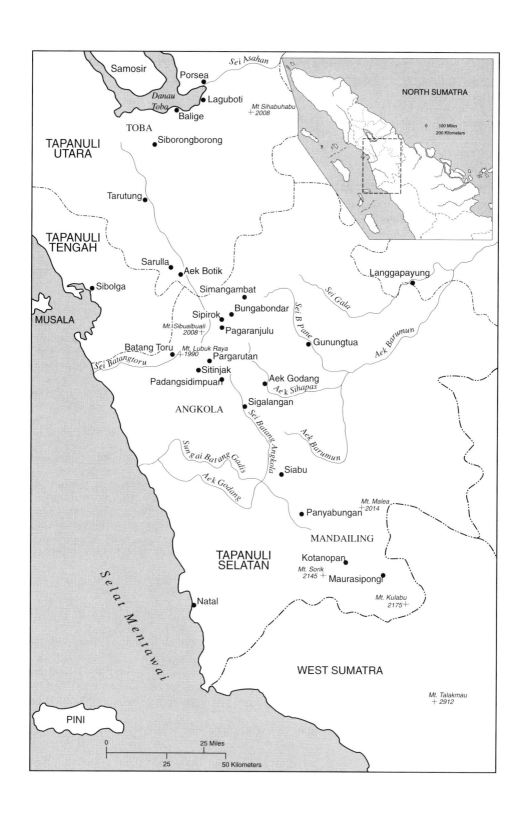

Samosir

Sei Asahan

Porsea

Danau Toba

Laguboti

Balige

TOBA

Mt Sihabuhabu +2008

NORTH SUMATRA

100 Miles
200 Kilometers

TAPANULI UTARA

Siborongborong

Tarutung

TAPANULI TENGAH

Sarulla

Aek Botik

Langgapayung

Sibolga

Simangambat

Sei Gala

MUSALA

Sipirok

Bungabondar

Mt. Sibualbuali 2008 +

Pagaranjulu

Sei B Pane

Gunungtua

Aek Barumun

Batang Toru

Mt. Lubuk Raya +1990

Pargarutan

Sei Batangtoru

Sitinjak

Padangsidimpuan

Aek Godang

Aek Sihapas

ANGKOLA

Sigalangan

Sei Batang Angkola

Aek Barumun

Sungai Batang Gadis

Siabu

Aek Godang

Mt. Malea +2014

Panyabungan

MANDAILING

Selat Mentawai

TAPANULI SELATAN

Kotanopan

Mt. Sorik 2145 +

Maurasipongi

Mt. Kulabu 2175 +

Natal

WEST SUMATRA

Mt. Talakmau + 2912

PINI

0   25 Miles

25   50 Kilometers

PART ONE

1

Padangsidimpuan

Padangsidimpuan—that was the capital of the Residency of Tapiannauli and the place, too, where Tuan Besar, his honor the resident, had his administrative seat for all the Tapiannauli Domain. The town was part of the government district of Losungbatu, which was located in the old Losungbatu Domain (in 1906, though, the Tapiannauli Residency's capital was moved to Sibolga).[1]

The realm's climate was oppressively hot,[2] and thus it was no wonder that a variety of severe illnesses beset people, especially bad fevers and malaria. Nonetheless, the town and its penumbra of small villages boasted quite fertile land. Crops thrived, and these afforded abundant food for the populace.[3] The area's produce included coconuts, pineapples, glowing yellow *lanseh* fruits, sweet-smelling mangoes, the even more fragrant *ambasang* mangoes, hairy red *rambutan* fruits,[4] and more and more. But coconuts were the basic wellspring of life there, for Lord Commoner, for the populace at large.

Besides the crops just mentioned there were also wide, fertile expanses of green rice paddy lands. These regularly yielded a solid crop that served as the public's staple food and basic source of income. After all, it was their rice paddy land that provided residents with cash for shopping. Some folks even had surplus rice to sell in the market, and since the town was surrounded by spacious grazing lands lots of people living there and in the nearby small villages also raised such livestock as cattle, water buffalo, goats, and so on.

The town of Padangsidimpuan was also well known, in the past, as the origin point from which all the countryside roads fanned out. The town was also the starting point for measuring the milestones. In Padangsidimpuan, in the past, these would start there with zero (0) and then they'd branch out along all the various roads that led out of town. There were three main forks the road took, the first going to Sibolga and the second leading to Greater Mandailing, Mandailing Julu, and on to Ulu and Pakantan. At Pakantan this particular road bent toward the Natal River, taking a shortcut through the mountains to lead down to the coastal town of Natal. After that, at Muarasipongi, it branched off toward Rao and also beyond that to Bukittinggi and Padang.[5] However, at that time buffalo carts and horse carriages could not traverse those particular two routes. The third fork in the main road went on to Sipirok and from there into the Toba Domain. However, once this road got past the village of Pargarutan, on the way to Sipirok, another route appeared, this one leading to Padang Bolak.[6] Since the road from Natal pushing inland into Mandailing was hard to traverse—and since the seas were rough around Natal's harbor—it was exceedingly difficult to transport goods into the interior of Mandailing. The road to Rao, moreover, could not yet be used for transporting merchandise. So goods from Padang and Penang had to enter Tapiannauli via the port at Sibolga. From there they'd be carried by cart and wagon on to Padangsidimpuan.

Once the merchandise arrived there, it would finally get divided up and the goods would go coursing out along the various roads just mentioned.

Given all this it is clear that Padangsidimpuan was not simply the capital of Tapiannauli; it was also quite a crucial trade center.

In addition to being a governmental capital, a trade center, and the origin point for the network of roads that made the region bustle with activity, Padangsidimpuan was a military post for soldiers, not to mention for Dutchmen with big titles such as Captain, Lieutenant, or Officer.[7] It was a main post as well for who knows how many overseers, or whatever word it was that people used back then to mean "the Resident for Road Construction."

The same was true, in the grand name department, for the people at the Office for Mountain Lands and for the various minor supervisors, or menteris,[8] who oversaw all the land surveying for Tapiannauli. All of these very fine offices employed huge numbers of people, all of whom drew salaries—people such as clerks, menteris, work gang overseers, and, of course, their coolies.

Chinese merchants and other folks from that country had come in, too, and opened big stores all around the main marketplace in P. Sidimpuan. Why, those sorts of stores even lined the road to Sibolga, and they were found along the other routes as well.

In addition, in the past there were some secondary schools—and even some Dutch schools.[9] These were the pride and joy of the realm—it pleased folks to gaze upon busy crowds of diligent young schoolchildren busily going about their lessons.

On the town's outer limits, but in its center as well, our beneficent God had seen fit to provide people with two large rivers, flowing down from the slopes of Mount Lubuk Raya. These were the Ayumi River and the White River. The Ayumi River was the one that separated the main marketplace from the Other-Side Market.[10] There was a big bridge over this river, connecting the road to Mandailing to the road to Sipirok. There was also a kind of hanging bridge upstream that served as a shortcut to Sipirok. But vehicles could not be used over this route; it was only for people walking on foot. The White River flowed in from the western edge of town, or in that vicinity at least, and you'd have to cross this body of water going to or from Sibolga. There was a big iron bridge there, too.

Starting at their headwaters, set deep in the upper slopes of Mount Lubuk Raya, these two watercourses were put to constant good use, irrigating wide expanses of paddy fields. The rivers served as rich fishing territories, too, for the entire populace. As it flowed downstream the White River moved through heavy jungle, but the Ayumi River coursed through thickly populated Angkola Jae. Once it got there it was called the Angkola River. At Sihitang Village, there was a big bridge spanning it, and as you entered Greater Mandailing there was another, even larger one, at Saromatinggi. From there the river spread out like a huge naga dragon-serpent,[11] undulating through the big marshes in Greater Mandailing. Finally, it met the Young Girl River, which came in from Mandailing Julu. This river's headwaters were set far back in the slopes of distant Mount Kulabu. Once it had joined with the

Young Girl River the two streams got renamed, becoming the Singkuang River. And, because the river banks were rather narrow downstream, when heavy rain fell in Mandailing Julu and in Angkola the marshlands in Greater Mandailing would flood. Clever types said it must be those wide marshes that bred those many mosquitoes and brought on the terrifying malaria.

But, to return to what we said before, it surely is evident to all of us that these two rivers (the White and the Ayumi) definitely did considerable good for the people living nearby, despite everything. The waters cooled the climate a bit, making things healthier for the native inhabitants. Without those rivers, in fact, no one could have lived in that area.

About the Past[1]

As we explained in chapter 1, the thing that made Padangsidimpuan such a prosperous and bustling town was the variety of work to which people there could set their hands. Rickety old wooden bridges were being replaced with iron ones; potholed roads were being repaired and resurfaced. Each such job meant work for many people: for those who would cart the lumber, those who would fetch all the heavy loads of sand, those who would serve as coolies. And the same was true with untold other job opportunities. Similarly as well with the Office of Mountain Lands: it always needed people to work as overseers or coolies who could be taken out into the forests to survey the mountains throughout the Residency. Houses and offices for the government officials were also constantly being built, so carpenters and other good craftsmen found much work. And when you looked toward the main marketplace it would be jam-packed with merchants erecting new shops. Because so many jobs opened up at the same time in the town people flocked in from Toba, Sipirok, Padang Bolak, Mandailing, and Daret (that is, from Padang).[2] Each person sought a job appropriate to his skills:[3] those who knew how to write tried to get hired as scribes, those who were good with their hands tried to find work as craftsmen, and Mr. Thick-Calves, for his part, sought a job as a work gang overseer.[4] And those without any skill at all just became coolies.

When the bell at the soldiers' barracks would ring at six in the morning the whole populace[5] would come pouring out of their houses, setting their hands to their different tasks. The *tuans* would boss their overseers about and twirl their moustaches, while the work gang overseers themselves would order the coolies about and wave their canes in the air, saying: "Pick that up! Here, hold this! Hoist that up on your shoulders! Put that down! Take hold of this!" And if the coolies were the slightest bit slow in doing any of this the foreman's voice would boom out and his eyes would grow huge with anger. Some overseers would get so mad that their jawbones would crunch together fearsomely, making a terrible noise; the coolies would tremble in fright and despair. The clerks would all point their hands this way and that as they divided up the workers and told them in which direction to go. As in "To Sihitang, to the big stone pool for catching fish in the river over there" or "To the bridge over the Rungkare Stream . . ." That would be all you would hear.

Now, a while ago, at 4 A.M., Little Girl's Mom[6] was busy, scurrying around the kitchen baking dozens of tiny cakes so that she would have plenty of delicacies to sell at the marketplace once it got light. After all, early morning was the time when merchandise moved the fastest, when you could sell it to people on their way to work. As soon as it got light all of them would be lining up along the street. Why, even the coolies would throng in to ask for their favorite foods. "Wrap me up some rounds of sticky rice and some *rendang* spiced meat chunks!" "Listen, I'll have a rice cake and a Bugis treat." "A slice of layer cake for me, all right?" "I'll take an *onde-onde* sugar snack," they'd all say.[7]

The hawkers would only return home after the crowds had thinned, to count up their profits. They'd all be chuckling on their way back home, too, for it had indeed turned out to be pretty sweet to rake in all those payments, for selling all those cakes. And having drowsy eyes as a result of getting up so very early wasn't really such a problem. There was only one young girl, almost a teenager now, in fact, who was walking along, disconsolate. She had forgotten to get paid for selling two big cakes to one of the overseers, a big cocky guy she could usually trust pretty well. He was already way off in the distance when she remembered that he hadn't paid her yet. So she kept mulling over what to say to her mother so that the woman wouldn't get mad at her. After all, her mother had counted out exactly how many cakes she had to sell when she first left the house.

Folks walking home were taken aback to see the girl behaving like this, so sad and all. They asked her what was wrong, and she replied: "But someone ran off without paying me for two big cakes! How can I make up for that money so our Mother won't be mad at me?" she said, wiping away her tears.[8] "Oh, now, listen, don't you worry—you just let me explain things to her, you hear?" someone said, luckily. Only at that point did she feel a bit mollified. And off she went back home.

The later it got, the longer it got, the more Padangsidimpuan prospered and bustled.[9] Everyone going home to their rural villages would take back the news about how very crowded and busy the town was and how easy it was to make a living there.[10] And how easy it was to acquire money—just so long as you were willing to work hard.

Dear Reader[11] . . . when a land gets more prosperous and crowded, more and more untoward things begin to happen and occur there, for, after all, it is not just genuine jobseekers who flock to the spot, no, not at all. . . . No, it's like swallows swooping down on a burgeoning rice field full of grain. People's desires, thoughts, and behavior follow that pattern, too: the bad mixes with the good and everyone crowds in for a try. So Toba folks came to town to find their pals, while Sipirok folks came looking for their friends; Padang Bolak people came seeking their buddies, and Mandailing folks sought their chums, while Daret people from Minangkabau came looking for their companions of a single island.[12]

When all of these various ethnic peoples would step out of their homes to go to work, why, it would look like a swarm of tree ants milling out of their tree nest. And then, when they went home again at night, it was like huge masses of ground ants marching along in columns, returning to their anthills.[13] Once it got to be Dusky Dark Evening everyone would set off toward their various activities.[14] Some, to be frank, would just go strolling around the main marketplace, while others would go look at the soldiers playing games over at their barracks. And others, it must be admitted, would just go gambling. And then maybe someone who did not want to go anyplace at all would just roll himself up in his rattan mat and fall asleep on the spot, seeking solace from exhaustion.

What everyone did in pursuing their various pleasures need not be related at any length—enough, simply, to say that it was like a herd of deer set loose in the middle of Padang, there was so much activity going on.

If someone should come up to them and tell them to stop doing what they were doing, people would shoot right back: "Hey, listen, don't tell me not to do it! Don't hassle me, all right? Don't you know what's what around here? Listen, we work for the Resident of Road Construction." Or for Tuan Mountain Lands. And on hearing that people would be afraid to bother them anymore, for villagers thought you weren't allowed to hassle anyone who was in good with the Dutch. Oh, friends: what stupidity.

And so, because people kept doing excessive things and kept forgetting their manners, public standards and behavior declined sharply. Many people simply forgot all about their birth villages—why, some even forgot the very path back to those settlements. Consequently, many of these young folks (who were small-time market sellers or worked in the shops) became the town gamblers and the local juvenile delinquents. They took to disturbing the good townspeople's peace and that of the residents of the small villages nearby.

Folks would say . . . why, gambling just has to be the most wonderful and delicious occupation in the world! But if your luck should turn bad, like a hollowed out gingerroot, well, things can go sour on you pretty quickly. When a guy is winning he's like a king (although, admittedly, a king minus a populace), but when he starts losing things can swiftly go to pot on him. He no longer cares where he sleeps, he loses all shame, he loses all self-respect, not to mention social reserve. He does nothing all day but chase around after possible gambling partners, not caring how he might make a cent to put some food in the Middle Continent (in his belly, that is). For, as it says in the Toba song:

Tanduk ni lombu	Cows horns, Cows horns,
Tanduk ni lombu lepe	Cows horns pointing earthward
Hancit ma na tarbeang	Turned-down cow horns,
Tanggal au ba lae	How hard to be chained in shackles
Muda monang marjuji	Oh, brother-in-law, please free me from my cage, my jail,
Sude halak mandok lae	When you're winning, well,
Tai muda talu marjuji	Then everyone calls you dear brother-in-law, I guess,
Sude halak mamursik.	But when you're on the losing end—
	Well, everyone just spits on you.

The more intense the gambling got in town the more thefts occurred, and folks in town and in the little surrounding villages would often find themselves saying: "Last night somebody made off with fifty of my coconuts, can you imagine!" while others would declare: "But my chicken's disappeared!" And somebody else would complain: "Someone's made off with all the fish in the bamboo trap I left between the stone walls out in the river! And I think he got a really huge carp because there's a fish scale left in there that's as big as a mouse ear."

Eventually, virtually everyone got robbed. The burglaries and violent muggings got to be everyday occurrences, taking place at all hours, even in the early evenings. Eventually, it got so that people were afraid to venture out of their houses if there was news of a robbery, for the criminals would go after anybody, at any time. They would do anything to get their way—they'd even mug a person carrying money if he was standing on the banks of the Ayumi in plain sight if they thought they could make off with a haul.

And, if a guy didn't turn over his money, they'd beat the tar out of him. Over at the Torop rest stop, near the camphor-collecting spot, out on the road to Pargarutan, and over at the Sihitang Bridge, too—well, every day word would come that a thief had made off with a person's entire bundle of money. It is beyond telling how many folks walking along carrying their goods by pack horse coming from Sipirok got themselves robbed in the big camphor forest. The thieves would just swoop down on them from the right side of the road. The same would be true of men guiding the slow buffalo carts along near the Toropan rest stop.

The more the police increased their surveillance activities and the more frequently the rows of soldiers (for their part) went marching smartly about on guard duty, well, the cleverer and more energetic the criminals themselves became in pursuing their nefarious ends. It got to be extremely difficult to catch them. Oftentimes they would stage big attractive parties to draw people in—huge big festivities! Real blowouts—and then they'd arrange for a gambling session to be held out in back, inside a little shed. Well, needless to say, gambling thrived.

Word of people fighting and beating each other on the shoulders and head with sticks of firewood flowed ceaselessly from these gambling dens. Men fought with knives, and even sabers, in addition to simply having fistfights or beating on each other with clubs. Folks trembled at word of all this. Gamblers were arrested in droves and thrown in prison—but, well, that just became a badge of honor for them. They'd say, come on, look, if you stay home in the village like a chump there's no chance you'll ever get to dine on duck eggs and thick curries whipped up from fine imported fish brought all the way from Siam—But! Ah ha, if you get into *jail*, well! Then every such thing will come to you free. And that was why the jailhouse was always packed with gamblers.

Young Martial Arts
Battler

People still remember, I would think, that in the past it was common for folks to drive carts or ride horses into Padangsidimpuan to sell goods or to go bartering. This was also true of people who lived right there in town: they'd go on toward the center by cart or by horse. Why, look, over there . . . over near the Other-Side Market, on the right side of the road if you're going to Sipirok (and on the left side if you're going to Mandailing)—There it is! A fine, big house standing beneath a thick ring of verdant coconut palms, palm trees hanging heavy with rounded fruit—a large, solid house surrounded by sweet mango trees and even sweeter *ambasang* mangoes, by glossy yellow lanseh trees, by *rambutan* shrubs hung with bunches of their hairy red fruit, and by thickets of abundant pineapple bushes. The house was four entire armspans wide and three armspans (plus two elbow-to-middle-fingertip lengths) deep. It had a proud peaked roof and four stout houseposts, one at each corner, while its walls were made of strong, thick, casuarina planks and its roof of tin.[1] At the front of the house there was an office-entryway, stretching all the way across the front of the home. And this porch had two big glass windows extending across its front with two additional windows on each side. All of these panels were neatly set into their frames in carefully matched pairs. The kitchen angled out a bit at the back of the house, and behind the home, beyond that good abundant orchard just mentioned, there was a capacious pond well stocked with a variety of fine food fish: *halu, lampan, siroken, gabus,* and *tingkalang* along with all manner of tiny minnows that just happened to live in the pool anyway. Surrounding this pond was a wide expanse of fertile green rice paddy, and between the orchard and the paddy land was a corral for water buffalo—and there were, oh, about ten fat buffalo cows grazing and gamboling about in a nearby field. And all of the things just mentioned were, indeed, the property of the householder.

Considering the beauty and size of the house's surroundings, the reader of this story will surely understand that the person who owned this home was not just anyone but was definitely a member of the very wealthy class.

But even though he enjoyed all this wealth and prosperity there is no claiming that he lived long on this earth to savor his riches, for when one's predestined Hour of Death arrives who is one to contest it?[2] And so, too, it can be said that at a certain juncture of time not ever to be forgotten a great, disastrous epidemic came to Padangsidimpuan, one that resulted in many, many people rushing to their graves. With no advance warning whatsoever the man who owned the house was taken with a dire illness and soon drew his last breath. He was wrenched away from his companion of a single house, from his dear wife, and so, too, taken away from that fine strapping son of his, his only child—who at the time was just entering adolescence. Left behind in death, too, was all that wealth, left behind here upon the earth.

The pain a person feels when she is torn from the man she ladles rice for,[3] that is the pain, too, that a child feels when he is wrenched away from his beloved father. But we must not speak of that at any length here in this story, for if we dwell on that it would be just like people who part a thick stand of bamboo with their two hands to peep in or who break open the shy swallow's nest—no, it would be like someone breaking open deep wells of sadness, opening up immense stockpiles of grief, making us sad beyond bearing. We'll get to that a bit later, anyway.[4]

And as for that bereaved child left behind by the deceased, well, he was just shooting up like a beanstalk. He was stoutly built, robust, and positively glowing with health. Even though he lived in a muggy town he enjoyed a hearty constitution. From the time he was very small he was always a quick-moving little guy, so his parents named him Pandingkar Moedo, or Young Martial Arts Battler.[5] At first this was just a sort of nickname his father would call him, but because the little kid's body and soul really did confirm his name people kept calling him that.

Now Pandingkar Moedo has been left behind by his father in death and is living with his good-hearted mother, his soft-spoken mother, his mother so adept at salving the pain of her only child.[6] So, even though she was a widow now, the pain of missing her long-time sweet companion would not disappear from her heart. Beyond that, though, their life was not really much harder than that of other people. Before, in the past, people did not feel any great need to make their children go to school. After all, at that time folks still had enough money to take care of their basic living expenses and didn't need to go out and get a formal education to get a job. Then, too, there were folks who said that there was no use for schooling because going to school only made children become too full of themselves.

So, because of such ideas his parent did not send Pandingkar Moedo to school anymore. He was left pretty much to his own devices. After all, what did he possibly lack in the way of goods or wealth? The money his father had left him was enough to keep him happy and pay for all his needs as he gadded about town, buying stuff both upriver and down.[7]

As we related above, as time passed Padangsidimpuan had become more and more crowded, bustling, and prosperous, and more young kids began to work there, selling merchandise of one sort or another on the street. And more crimes were being committed at every turn. A clear demonstration that he was not getting any moral instruction from a school was the fact that Pandingkar Moedo began to join with the other kids in these small-time buying and selling activities—and these were the very same juvenile delinquents who were bringing pain and problems to the populace.

Two peddler kids sidled up to Pandingkar Moedo one time and asked to become his faithful retainers.[8] They knew well enough that he was a scion of a wealthy family. Oh, these two fellows were good enough to him at first. They'd always faithfully execute whatever little tasks their boss and mentor happened to give them. For instance, they took good care of the orchard, the rice land, and the livestock at P. Moedo's house, and afterward they'd take their pay and put it nicely in its proper safekeeping place. Every Monday, market day in Padangsidimpuan, they'd sell coconuts to the merchants and horseback peddlers coming into town from Sipirok. They'd sell at least five hundred per market day. Oftentimes the cash profits would reach twelve and fifteen rupiah per sale per coconut. They would give a portion of all this money to their parents; another portion of it they would use to buy glasses of hot coffee at the rice stalls, on the edge of the main marketplace.

While they were drinking coffee over at the stall they'd hear all sorts of rumors and gossip from the other market boys, who were there drinking their coffee, too. After they'd finished their drinks they'd go striding cockily through the town, and then they'd all end up (eventually) over at the gambling dens out behind the jailhouse.

The more often Pandingkar Moedo would sit there in the rice stall with his faithful followers, each little thing the circle of market boys would say entered deeply into his heart. The same was true for his two young minions, but because they were just gofers they didn't come right out and say what they thought. They held back a bit: whatever Pandingkar Moedo declared, well, that would be their statement, too.

Pandingkar Moedo named those two followers of his Rangga Poerik and Rangga Balian or Fighting Cock Bubbling Like the Rice-Cooking Water and Fighting Cock Out on the Ramparts. He named them according to the sorts of things they did. Rangga Poerik's character was as follows: if he was angry or being hassled in a fistfight or an argument he'd be so furious he would snarl and snap. He'd jump this way, he'd bound that way, and then he'd proclaim: "You can't box with me! You can't beat me up! I can withstand any force or resistance!" he would say. Often enough he'd take to boxing with a banana tree trunk, calling out to it: "All *right*! Who dares to come up against me? Let him try—that'll just give me a chance to twirl him in the air and fix him good." And his eyes would go as round and big as potatoes.

Seeing this, people who didn't know his true character would actually believe what he was saying. And, if someone happened to dispute what he was claiming and stood up to him, he would sing right out: "All right, come right over so I can hoist you up over my head! And, listen, if this ground down here had fruit tree trunks planted in it, I'd be hauling them out of the earth right now and throwing them over my head, you can just bet!"

But all of this was only a bit of arrogance: once he was through jumping about he'd be as sweet tempered as a horse being tickled. In fact, he was like the water in the pot when you're cooking rice—when it is bubble-boiling sprinkles of water jump off its surface in a pretty fearsome way, but once it's cooled down its surface is smooth, hard, and calm like a big block of starch.

And as for Rangga Balian's character, he was just like a poisonous snake (that is, a *dari* snake) that lies sleeping in the grass. He didn't have much to say, he would only speak one or two words, and he would work diligently without pausing for breaks. But if anyone did something the least bit unfriendly to Pandingkar Moedo he'd be right on the mark, ready to spring in his enemy's face. Once it was clear that the other guy was at fault, without saying a single word, he would land a few boxing blows on the guy and give him a big kick or two in the jaw, K.O.ing him in a flash. And the guy wouldn't be able to emit so much as a feeble little strangled peep. So, all told, Pandingkar Moedo felt he could place a good deal of faith in the guy.

Clearly, Pandingkar Moedo was protected by two friends who could stand up for themselves. Consequently, if Pandingkar Moedo should happen to run into some enemy who was likely to be frightened of being snarled and snapped at, he'd let Rangga Poerik loose on him. Alternatively, if they happened to meet an enemy who wasn't afraid of anything, he'd sic Rangga Balian on him, that is, the Fighting Cock Who Never Runs Home in the Face of Resistance, if he's leaning forward he's leaning forward to the fore to do battle.

Well, suffice it to say, his enemies would be better off being long dead and long since turned into bony skeletons than they would be being alive and having to confront Rangga Balian's terrifying, immense, angry eyes.

Once the gambling demon had taken ahold of the hearts and imaginations of Pandingkar Moedo and his two faithful retainers there was no restraining them. They went parading about, to and fro, seeking sparring partners. The only thing that would send them home was if they got beaten themselves. And, of course, Pandingkar Moedo's mother would always be waiting for them back home, and their food would be all ready for them, and they wouldn't have to buy anything at all. Needless to add, back at the house there were all those coconuts growing in the yard for cooking curries and all those plump fish swimming in the stock pond. In short, the only thing the house and lands could not provide for them was their salt. After eating their meal, they'd go lounge around in that fine glassed-in front porch—and promptly fall asleep.

When the gambling demon first took hold of Pandingkar Moedo, he would still attend to the garden when it needed weeding. He would still try to keep track of a buffalo in the herd if it happened to wander off into the fields. But, once the gambler's rulebook had worked its way further and further into his heart, morning to night he forgot to pay attention to the abundant property his father had bequeathed to him. For their part, his two faithful minions also neglected the estate. After all, if the boss is slack and lazy, his dependents will be, too. Fortunately, his mother (although now middle-aged) was still quite energetic and diligent at overseeing their fortune. If that had not been the case, I suspect that the entire property would have fallen into ruin as quickly as a suit of bark-cloth clothing wears out and falls off in tatters. But, then, you have to ask, how much strength does a mere woman have? They're afraid sometimes just to step down out of the house: dusk itself spooks them.[9]

When Pandingkar Moedo was over at the gambling den he would witness all manner of goings on. And, if one of the gamblers should happen to suffer a large loss, a fight would break out, bringing shame to everyone. They wouldn't just box with their forearms, either, or merely kick each other on the shins; often the fighters would draw blood.

Seeing what had happened there Pandingkar Moedo would shudder. He would say to himself: "People who tangle with gambling are really selling their souls. And, you know, with my luck I'd always be on the paying end." But he would also be advised that going down the gambling path constituted no problem at all, none whatsoever. Then a voice inside him would tell him to stop this sort of activity forthwith.

Finally, he asked Rangga Poerik and Rangga Balian what they felt in their hearts about all of this. He himself was befuddled. What Rangga Poerik and Rangga Balian said was that that sort of sentiment about quitting gambling was really the best sort of stand *possible*: "Ideally, you see—but one certainly should not give up an activity just because you're afraid. For, after all, gambling was the very finest sort of entertainment for young people who are out to have themselves a good time, most especially if it involves becoming famous and renowned and strutting around town as the big winner after a big game. You can look down on everyone that way, you know. And, look, as for being afraid, sometimes when you see what happens over in the gambling dens, well, okay, being afraid is normal enough. No problem. But listen: all that fighting is just a sign that those fighters are real men. Macho! It's proof that they can stand up for themselves and defend themselves. C'mon, they're just growing boys—and luckily their inner selves are growing firmer and more inviolable in the process.[10] So, if Boss is still bothered by what happens over in the dens, let's go take lessons from a great teacher who can help us learn to defend ourselves. That way, if we should happen to find ourselves in trouble, we shall be well prepared. Because, you know, in our life endeavors we must confront four major things: first, finding a compatible spouse; second, seeking good luck; third, dealing with bad luck; and, fourth, confronting death itself. So, see, it's simply best that we set off in search of this great guru," they declared.

"Well, just where can we find such a fierce and fearless guru, one who has more to offer than the fighting knowledge possessed by the men we've seen so often in the gambling dens?" asked Pandingkar Moedo, albeit now with some small hint of hope and happiness.

"But, Boss, right over there! . . . in Sihitang Village. His name is Dja Mananti Porang, Raja Awaiting Battle. Believe us, he is a tough one. He can stand being clubbed and cudgeled, he can repel knife attacks, he can withstand being tossed in the water, he can take being laid out on rattan mats to dry in the sun like rice grains or coffee beans—well, better put, he can stand up to anything. A-*ny*-thing! However, he's usually not any too pleased about giving an audience to people he has not been formally introduced to."

"Hmmm, well, so, what sort of plan can we make to find your fierce, fearless friend and talk to him?" asked Pandingkar Moedo.

"Oh, well, that's easy!" came back Rangga Poerik and Rangga Balian, "because as it happens at the moment he's just running a little coffee stall over in Sihitang. He doesn't have any other work at hand, so he'll have no excuse to refuse to honor your request. Just so long, hmmm, as we can get together a modest little teacher's fee for him. He's sort of an old guy, but his wife's a young one."

"Well, if that's the case, let's just set off and take some lessons from him! And as for his teacher's fee, look, that can be arranged. No problem! If we don't happen to have any cash right now, c'mon, let's just go sell a water buffalo cow. Easy, right? But all three of us will have to take lessons together, as a group. Otherwise folks hereabouts will start ridiculing us. After all, I never ask you to do very much for me, do I?" said Pandingkar Moedo happily, with great hopes now that everything would turn out well.

"As you will, Boss. But you should know that this man is not just a great expert in the knowledge of this earthly realm; he also commands knowledge of the Sacred World Hereafter. In short, he has everything from crude to refined knowledge under his control and at his command—and absolutely no one can touch him.[11] He is invulnerable. However, if we are going to have any kind of success taking lessons from him we're going to have to prepare a proper practice arena for our martial arts exercises. And when we're out there in the courtyard arena practicing away we'll have to go at it for real, you know, because the spot will be guarded by a bunch of tigers. Once we've got a bit of martial arts experience under our belts this guru is sure to send his big tigers after us, you can bet. But no one has to end up getting totally mangled as a result; as long as no one harbors any evil intentions things should be okay."

So, one day, when very few people happened to be going to Sihitang Village, off they set toward the place, pretending to be simply taking a little stroll, maybe just to catch sight of Raja Awaiting Battle's fine countenance.

All along the road Pandingkar Moedo kept changing his mind again and again, mulling over the good points and then the bad points of the plan. Sometimes he'd say to himself: "Once I have succeeded in becoming an *adult* Martial Arts Battler, well, *then* you can bet I'll get to go around the countryside all the time searching for enemies to fight in every nook and cranny."

He knew he'd be leaving his normal, good-hearted, well-intentioned activities behind, never to undertake them anymore—"and I guess, as a result, my mother will get pretty mad at me." So that slowed him down a bit. But a moment or two afterward he would be saying to himself: "It's what you have in your mind, as plans, that really gets things accomplished here on earth. That is true for as long as you draw breath." So the upshot of all this was that they eventually *did* arrive at Raja Awaiting Battle's place over in Sihitang. Eventually.

When they got there, they went straight to Raja Awaiting Battle's coffee stall. But they just found his wife there, busy hawking glasses of hot coffee. To recover from their exhausting trip they asked her to serve up three mugs full, complete with sticky rice treats. After they'd finished their drinks and snacks they set to chatting about the camphor-gathering spot.

"Now where might you be going, you fine young fellows?" asked Boroe Soeti (Raja Awaiting Battle's wife).[12]

"Oh, well, wherever. You know, Angkang, Older Lineage Companion,[13] we're just strolling around, dissipating our discontent. It makes us feel worse just hanging around the house. There's nothing to do and nothing to be gained there," said Pandingkar Moedo.

"Now, look, don't you go addressing me as Older Lineage Companion, as Angkang! After all, your father here in this house is so old he's already walking around with a cane, for goodness sake! So, it's best that you simply call me Mother, all right? That way you won't go using two separate kin term practices with us, and when you finally *do* encounter your Father, in a bit, you'll be saying 'Father' to him. And then, too, what do you mean when you say 'dissipate your discontent'? However could young fellows like you have anything to feel bad about?"

"Ha, ha, well, that's how it often goes: joy replaces sorrow upon the earth, I guess. But why did you go and marry such a decrepit old guy? From the looks of your figure you're pretty young," joked Pandingkar Moedo.

"Well, if you go and fall in love with an old guy, that's the one you want, I guess! And, look, he might be old, but, as they say, hmm, 'The older the coconut, the more oil it has.'"

"Ha, ha . . . yeah, well, I guess that's about right! So, just where *is* Father at the moment? We'd like to shake his hand and maybe make his acquaintance—so that no one will be able to say we don't pay proper respect to our elders," said Pandingkar Moedo.

"He's just left to go fishing, so you'll have to wait a bit for him to come back. Hopefully, he'll catch a big carp and you'll be able to help eat it," said the woman.

"All right," they said. Not long afterward along came Raja Awaiting Battle, his rattan satchel stuffed with fish. "*Bassss. . . !*" the satchel said as he set it down in the kitchen. He commented: "You just see to these curry fixings, Boroe Soeti, so they don't go bad on us."

"I'm coming, I'm coming," said Boroe Soeti, "but you should know that three sons of yours have arrived for a visit and they've been waiting here a very long time. All through the morning, in fact."

"Oh, and who are they, do you figure? Come up into the house," said Raja Awaiting Battle, setting out his tobacco supplies.[14] And the young fellows went right up into the house and proffered their tobacco to him, going on to shake his hand.

Just as a means of starting the conversation Pandingkar Moedo said, "Well, you've really been hard at it, catching fish, haven't you, Honored Father? How far upriver did you get, coming home so late in the day on us here?"

"Oh, child, as far as fish go, they were pretty easy to catch all right! I'll allow that! Why, this morning I'd just throw my line in two or three times and they'd bite immediately—and two or three of them would be on the line at once. So these curry fixings came easy enough, maybe because of your visit. What made me late was that I had a big carp in my trap out there in the bend of the river near the deep whirlpool. I saw him very clearly, swimming downriver. So I followed him. And then a big turtle bit onto my hook, too, and the carp went and escaped into the whirlpool. And, I thought, *now* what should I do? If I pull in my line I'll lose the other one. So I thought I'd just see if I could get the turtle to submerge himself in the water, but, of course, that didn't gain me much because he was used to swimming underwater. But at least I wasn't getting bitten by him, and so I played with him a bit and egged him on, and finally I just wore him out. I eased the net carefully over to the side of the sandy bank and then I beat that turtle with a stick till he died—but I couldn't catch sight of the silly carp anymore! And I was getting pretty hungry by then," said Raja Awaiting Battle, sneering a bit as he drew in his cigarette smoke.

"Wow! . . . you sure had a time of it, didn't you? I would love to have seen it," the young fellows said.[15]

"Yes, indeed," said Raja Awaiting Battle, gazing toward the kitchen. Boroe Soeti understood her *tuan*'s glance and a moment later she swept into the front room with steaming bowls of rice and curry. The rice was delicious, luxurious Sipahantan rice, while the curry was made of firm-fleshed carp and all manner of boiled vegetables.[16] These had been mixed and strongly seasoned with a condiment made of tiny salt fish and red pepper sauce. Talk about delicious! Your mouth would start to water just catching sight of the little gobs of grease on top of the curry there.

Once all of the food had been set out in front of them Boroe Soeti chimed in from the kitchen: "You children just dig in, now, and help yourself to our poor papaya leaf curry—I'll bet you're real hungry. Even if we don't have any fine curry to offer you, and even though it certainly won't taste very good, well, after all, what is to be done? You have to understand, you have come to the household of very poor folks like me, so this is the best we can manage."[17]

"Well, come on, what are we waiting for, children? Let's just say, 'Bismillah' as our blessing for our meal and dig in! . . . Hmmm, well, just as long as our luck holds out I guess we'll keep having a little bit of something to eat, whatever the case. When there's nothing about the house to make a fancy curry of, what can you expect after all?" said Raja Awaiting Battle.

So they set to eating their "nothing." Because it had gotten so late in the day and their bellies were so terribly empty (since they hadn't eaten since early morning) the food that Boroe Soeti had given them tasted extremely good. Just extraordinarily good. "This woman's cooking is *amazing*," they said to themselves.

Once they had finished their meal the tobacco was put out on trays there in the main room and they all set to smoking. Once everyone was content and had had a chance to sit and chat, they finally declared why they had come. "Well, Honored Father, it is like this, the reason we have come here. We are just young people and surely when we go on a journey to someone else's village oftentimes we encounter serious difficulties, being attacked or bothered or slandered by folks as we walk along on our peaceable way. So because of this if perhaps our Honored Father might just take pity on us we hope with the deepest fervent hope possible that Honored Father might teach us some good self-defense techniques we could use to protect ourselves from attack. So that our inner selves might be hard and firm as we proceed along on our peaceful journeys, you understand," said Pandingkar Moedo.

Raja Awaiting Battle glanced upward and said, "Oh. . . . So, you have come here to take lessons, have you now? If that is the case, well, all right, fine, but since I really do not have very much esoteric lore in my possession, exactly what am I supposed to teach you? I am only at the very first level of expertise, you should know; I only have enough knowledge to defend myself. So how am I going to know what to say to you?"

"Well, whatever Honored Father decides to say to us and teach us we certainly will not object to it, just so long as Honored Father has love and kindness in his heart for us," they declared.

"Well, you know, it's a real difficult thing . . ." said Raja Awaiting Battle, mentally jacking up the price of his store of knowledge while glancing sideways at the boys' faces to see whether or not they meant business.

Not too long afterward he piped up: "What I would have to teach you and your friends would be a very difficult and dangerous body of knowledge because you aren't old enough to control it yet and use it properly. And, to tell the truth, I am not bold enough to break the oath given to me very specially by my own guru, the guru who taught all this to me."

"Oh well, listen . . . if it's a case of not wanting to go against your own guru's oath in order to give us your secret knowledge, it won't be a problem if you don't teach us *everything*, will it? Look, it will be fine if you just send us kind of in the right general direction! To go seek the knowledge, you see!" said Pandingkar Moedo.

"So, well, what exactly is it that you are seeking?"

"Well, hmmm, I guess you'll have to teach us pretty much everything, for Father knows how fierce people tend to be nowadays. So . . . well, in short, just make sure the people we have to fight do not know more secret lore than we do, I guess," said Pandingkar Moedo.

"Perhaps you don't understand. You're going to go picking fights all over this domain?[18] What would be the use of that? After all, you and your pals must take care and use your lore-knowledge in just the right way. If they are going to use it to harass people in their own land I have no desire whatsoever to teach such lore to them. I am, after all, a normal human being with fully normal sentiments of sympathy. Live and let live is what I say."

"Oh, be assured, Honored Father, this knowledge will not go toward evil ends. As for us, we are well aware of the Dangerous Path toward Disappearance,[19] the Path toward Self-Destruction that could come from all of this. But, look, as Father himself has as much as admitted, there will surely be some good use for all this knowledge later on. And what is so wrong with laying in a stock of umbrellas before it rains?" asked Pandingkar Moedo.

"Well, if that's the case, all right then, if you agree that what I teach you and your friends will not be used for evil purposes! But first you must prepare whatever small gifts and offerings might be proper to have in readiness, according to the customs of people who take lessons from gurus. And then we'll also need to ask blessings from the guru of my guru. Then I'll come to the marketplace to meet you, Monday of next week." said Raja Awaiting Battle.

"Oh, whatever Father needs to prepare beforehand just go ahead and prepare it, for actually we have never worked with a guru before. We hope to simply follow along and do whatever Father tells us and that way we'll know how to prepare everything," they said.

"Well, all right then. . . . According to the usual plan, we'll need a grilled chicken, a folded quid of betel leaves, and a length of pure white cloth, along with a few mantras."

"However many mantras Father may need to say just go right ahead and say them. You determine the number. After all, we wouldn't want to come in conflict with our guru's oaths, would we?"

"Look, I don't know how many there are! However many there might happen to be, all right! Just as long as they're said with Allah's blessing. Later, once you've seen what's going to be taught, you'll understand all this. But once we get to the point of actually going into the practice arena in the village courtyard you are going to have to take it seriously, you know. You can't go halfway or truly evil things will happen. . . . So let me tell you this: before coming over here always steal a look at my housetop to see if there's smoke from your Mother's cooking fire. That way you'll see if you have an invitation to come in or not. If you do not see any smoke, well, then, I guess you'll just have to make do and borrow a meal of rice and a pinch of salt from someone. Behave this way or our work together will surely go awry," said Raja Awaiting Battle.

"Yes, yes . . . rest assured that we understand, Honored Father."

"Well, indeed, then, we'll just go on home now, but let's not any of us go altering our promises to each other, all right? Father must really and truly come to meet us Monday in the market. We'll come out and welcome you at the edge of town so we can show you exactly where we live."

"Fine, fine . . ." said Raja Awaiting Battle. And they all shook hands, and the young people set off for home.

All along the way they discussed how they should best go about dealing with their guru so that they would be certain of securing his most powerful blessings. All the way home they weighed various strategies for this great undertaking, but unfortunately they were talking so much that they walked right past the turnoff to their house.

Once they finally did get home Pandingkar Moedo's mother welcomed them, saying, "Now, *where* exactly is it you've come home from? Did you forget that you'd be hungry? Come and eat or the rice'll get cold."

"Where have we come from, Mother? . . . Um, well, we just went out for a walk, see. You're mad because we were wrong not to let you know where we were going early this morning. We didn't know we'd end up walking this far." He said this so his mother wouldn't feel she had done all that work for nothing. After all, she had cooked all that food. Then, of course, they ate their meal.

While they were eating Pandingkar Moedo said to his mother: "We went in search of a guru over in Sihitang and what this guru, Raja Awaiting Battle, said was that our visit was a very good thing, indeed, and that he will teach us self-defense techniques. To keep ourselves safe from Dangers, you see. Because, after all, the more time passes the more crowded this land gets and the more people's behavior becomes arrogant and arch, and so, if one doesn't know such things as the arts of self-defense, people will take you for a fool. They'll take advantage of you constantly. So, Mother, do you maybe have some money you could slip us, some cash that we could use to pay our guru?"

"Ah . . . now why exactly do you and your pals need to learn how to fight and fence? Unless maybe you've done something to make people mad at you, hmm? If you run around fighting you'll just bother people. And this money we're supposed to shell out? Wouldn't we just be frittering it away? Why, I have to really and truly economize just to get together the least little bit of cash, and even after all that one doesn't have any money to speak of. Don't you recall the Malay saying? 'Watching your money carefully is the basic building block of wealth, while neglecting your funds and spending foolishly brings only debt.' Now, tell me, isn't that the truth?"

"But, look, this is self-*defense*, Mother! What's wrong with that? And we need the exercise, to keep us healthy. That's not frittering money away, is it? And besides, Mother, it is not good to be too stingy about doing things for yourself. We wouldn't want folks to go around referring to you as Djahontiplonong, Raja Selfish and Stingy,[20] would we?"

"So, okay, how does this Raja Selfish and Stingy behave exactly, for you to want to use him as a proverb?"

"Well, Mother, just listen so that we can hear what is happening, so that we can witness what is occurring.[21] Apparently you don't know what is happening right here in our own land, much less in the Lands above the Winds.[22] Well, all right, just pay close attention while I relate the story," said Pandingkar Moedo.

"All right," said his mother, settling herself into a better position.

Raja Selfish and Stingy lived in the main part of town and he had thousands and thousands of rupiah bills. His fortune was so large, in fact, that even he didn't know how big it was. But his clothing! Talk about stingy. Well, he would not even consider buying anything that cost the least little bit of money. He wouldn't consent to put it on if it was made of anything more expensive than plain old unbleached cotton. And his wooden clogs were about ten years old, I'd guess, and crummy looking. They'd had been repaired so many times that they had more staples in them than they had wood. In fact, the staples made them weigh about half a kilo per foot. It half killed him to walk with them. Now, apparently because he was so very stingy, the good God who gives us our money grew angry with him. Well, one time on a certain Friday before people went in to pray at the main mosque it started to rain very, very hard. Upon hearing the rain falling the imam in the mosque began to make his scripture recitals longer and longer. Normally it would have been a simple matter of saying the Halataka and the Sabbihis, the usual verses for a Friday, but because of the rain the imam droned out the Ammajatasa, too. The heavy rain caused flooding, and many people's shoes (which they had left outside the mosque) were washed away. Among the clogs were those of Raja Selfish and Stingy. His shoes disappeared downstream into the White River. They got caught up in the fishing gear and nets of a young wife[23] who happened to be out netting minnows in the river. The clogs were carried down past two bends in the river, totally tangled in the woman's fishnet. She was furious, for her minnows' skins and scales were torn by the nails sticking out of the shoes. Once the net had floated into a quiet spot she was able to retrieve it. Back in the village she showed it to the neighbors who lived on both sides of her house, asking who might own these clogs. The answer came back: "Good grief, those are Raja Selfish and Stingy's shoes. Quick, go lodge a complaint about him with the judge and press charges. He needs to be punished; he's just too stingy for words," they all declared. Once she came before the judge the woman recounted all the hardships she had suffered because Raja Selfish and Stingy's shoes had rammed into her net. Upon hearing the woman's complaint and examining Raja Selfish and Stingy's clogs most carefully, the judge shuddered in surprise.

"You, court clerk!" called the judge.

"It's me, at your service! . . . Your slave awaits."[24]

"Go summon Raja Selfish and Stingy so that his case may be tried. Someone has been placed in danger and undergone difficulties because of his shoes."

"Yes, sir, my lord, honored Tuan,"[25] said the court clerk. And off he set to find Raja Selfish and Stingy at the main mosque, for that's where he would surely be, searching the grounds for his clogs.

Before the court clerk got there it appears that Raja Selfish and Stingy had been scrambling all over the grounds looking for his missing possessions. Totally tuckered out from the shoe hunt, but still not finding them, a plan occurred to him: he would initiate a court case so that the person who had stolen his clogs would be brought to justice and get stuck with a big fine.

But with no advance warning along came the judge's clerk, who declared: "The judge says for you to come right over to the court."

"What does the judge need me for? I am in the midst of searching for something someone stole from me. However, our esteemed court clerk, since you just happen to have come at an opportune time, let me simply report to you officially that someone stole my wooden shoes while I was at Friday prayer services in the mosque."

"You just come answer to the judge first—you can look for your shoes later," said the court clerk.

"Well, all right," said Raja Selfish and Stingy. Then he walked to the judge's chambers.

Once he was there, the judge asked him whether his shoes might possibly have disappeared, how they might have disappeared, and what they looked like.

"Oh, I have suffered such a loss, our esteemed Tuan. As a matter of fact I have totally exhausted myself searching for those clogs. My Lord, who do you suppose stole them? I surely trust that Tuan will punish that person severely, because I have had to expend entirely too much energy searching for them," said Raja Selfish and Stingy, hope stirring now in his heart.

"I wouldn't know about any thief who might have taken your shoes, but this woman here has complained to me that while she was netting fish in a muddy eddy in the White River your shoes came along in the water and struck her net. It forthwith vanished and sped two entire riverbends downstream. The nails in the clogs tore all the mesh. And all the fish she had just caught disappeared downstream. With the net. *And* she got injured falling onto the rocks after tripping over your clogs," said the judge.

"But *she's* the woman who's been giving me so much grief, my Lord, my esteemed Tuan! Apparently, *she* is the thief! Punishment is called for here," said Raja Selfish and Stingy.

"No, it is not proper to punish someone over your pair of shoes, especially since the sight of those filthy old things throws all the womenfolk into a fright.

Rather, it is entirely fitting that you be fined five florins. And, after you've paid that, give this woman a ringgit to pay for the medicine she needs for her injuries as well as some cash for the fish she lost. And then, for her other losses, such as her fishnet and all the food inside, see to it that you pay her four coins. If you fail to do this you will be jailed," said the judge.

"Hoi . . . ," cried Raja Selfish and Stingy. "I am the one who has suffered a theft, yet I am the one who gets fined! That's far too steep a punishment, far too much suffering for your humble servant here," he said, expelling long breaths but also peeling some bills from a roll of cash. People who saw the scene said that he was leafing through hundred-florin notes, then fifty-florin ones, then twenty-five florins, and finally five-florin notes, the smallest denomination he happened to have. In fact, he had so many bills folded up in his wallet that he didn't know where the different ones were. Once the judge caught sight of how much money the man had, he said: "So, apparently you have a good deal of money there. Well, then! We'll increase your fine from five florins to twenty-five."

"Ah, that would just finish me off, our Lord, our Tuan," he said, forking over the fine anyway. So that is the story about stingy sorts of people, about that sort of folks. The upshot is that their big fortunes just get reduced through fines. "Now, Mother, didn't you enjoy this story about people and their big fortunes?" asked Pandingkar Moedo, ending his tale.

"Oh, my . . . if that's how these things go, I'd be better off having no money at all! After all, it's clear from your story that his fortune caused him to incur those fines."

"All right, all right, so don't hinder me in my efforts to get some self-defense training. Don't be stingy in paying our teaching fees—and don't wrinkle your forehead if you have to give my guru a hearty meal when he comes calling. In fact, properly speaking, you'll have to give him so much food that he will have to take the surplus home in little leaf packages. If that is not the case, he won't be happy eating in our house. You should know, Mother, that we ate a meal in the guru's house when we were there, and the curry that Boroe Soeti cooked for us (that is, the guru's wife) was so good, well, in my entire life I have never tasted such delicious food. I don't know where that woman learned to cook like that. I have sampled all the different foods in the rice stalls at the marketplace, but not one of those meals comes close to the tastiness of Boroe Soeti's curry. Ah, that my future wife should be able to cook like that," exclaimed Pandingkar Moedo.

"What time of day did you eat?"

"Oh, going on 11 o'clock . . ."

"Well, all right then, that makes sense. . . . I know who taught her how to cook. I believe that Guru Raja Awaiting Battle's good wife must be a graduate of a certain cooking school in Egypt," said his mother.

"There's a cooking school in the land of Egypt, Mother? Hmm, maybe Boroe Soeti did go there—although I don't think she ever went to Mecca," said Pandingkar Moedo, somewhat taken aback.

"Well, then, if you don't believe all this, you just listen while I tell you a story so that you won't go astray in your thinking later."

"Fine," said her child . . . and they all listened to the story.

"Well, in the past there lived a very rich merchant in the land of Egypt. Because he had so much wealth his main activity was issuing complaints and recriminations. He had already married a large number of brides. But he had not as yet found any of their cooking very tasty. Oftentimes one of these women would set to work cooking a meal in the kitchen, and he would divorce her straightaway, after just one try—all because she didn't know how to cook. He was afraid to hire a cook because he feared being poisoned, and if he died that great fortune of his would be wasted. So finally he got engaged to a woman who actually sported a diploma, she was such an expert cook. Those skilled at telling tales[26] said she was such a great cook that she could take an old log and cook it up in a handful of spices and you'd have a more delicious meal than if she had used a big carp for her curry. This woman came complete with references, all saying that she was guaranteed to bring this merchant total satisfaction in the kitchen.

So, he went ahead and married this woman who was such a fine cook. Well, once they were living together in the same house the woman employed all sorts of fancy cooking techniques and tricks for preparing the merchant's food, but none of it really came out as he had dreamed it would. Even though the food was well creamed and curried the merchant simply did not find it tasty. So he felt really bad about the whole situation. Considering all the trouble he had gone to, well, he nearly lost hope of ever finding real happiness here on earth.

One day, when the merchant went out walking to try to ease his regret and hurt feelings, he happened upon a farmer, a thick-calfed, big-bicepped guy, a really strapping fellow. After they had shaken hands and exchanged tobacco in greeting, they got to chatting about the merchant's walk and what he happened to be thinking about. The upshot was that the merchant declared that he had nearly given up hope because apparently his fate was to never locate a bride who could cook. "I've married a whole string of brides, but there hasn't been one who made me happy. So what do you say? Might you know a woman who can cook to fulfill my desires? I don't care one way or the other about her face or her figure—what will make me happy is if she can *just cook*," said the merchant.

"Well, there is someone like that, someone who went to the same school my wife did, in fact. I can say with confidence that she's a really fine cook because in all the long time my wife and I have been a couple cooking together I've always found it to be simply delicious. Simply de-lic-ious. And it has always made me robust and healthy and full and satisfied. Just look: look at how big my biceps and how thick my calf muscles are. See? So if this woman I'm talking about becomes your wife you'll be real happy, too. She's an even better cook than my wife is," said the man. "Please just eat your midday meal right here with us, so the two of us can eat together and put my claims to a quick test. I'll tell her, this other woman, to cook our meal, so you can taste just how good the food they learned to cook is."

"Well, fine," said the merchant. So the man told his wife to put the rice on the fire. He told his wife to just make the curry out of regular old boiled mixed vegetables with a bit of hot pepper sauce thrown in and maybe a dash of fish sauce. "Now look, okay, at least remember to make it smooth and soft," the guy said to his wife.

While the woman was busy cooking the man took the merchant out for a walk around his garden lands while they were waiting for the rice to cook. They looked at all the plants that happened to be growing there. They hiked around the garden until they were completely worn out—and about to die of hunger. It was well after the noon hour when they returned to the house. When they got there they washed up, and then they finally ate.

Well, soooo . . . , because they were so tired and their bellies were so hungry, the guy just stuffed down great big handfuls of that simple boiled vegetable curry and its hot pepper sauce. He dumped big gobs of the red pepper sauce onto his vegetables and stuffed away. "I've found her!" cried the merchant. "Here they are just cooking plain old boiled vegetables for us, this younger lineage companion is,[27] and look, it's already this delicious. Just think how great it would taste with some real cow's fat and butter and Indian spices. That sure would go down easy, would it not?"

Once they had finished eating the merchant felt tired and he nodded off to sleep. His snores went *do-hur, do-hurr;* he was so sound asleep that he had no idea what might be occupying the sky above him.

After a moment he woke up and said: "They really are great cooks! Let's go ask this woman to become my bride right now. I surely won't regret making *her* my wife," said the merchant.

The other man piped up and said: "Well, my friend, Master Merchant, you listen here! I cannot give this woman to you. But, just so you will know, if you force yourself to go outdoors and get tired, and if, say, you go on a long walk once a day, then your food will taste good to you! All this time you've never been willing to go out and get good and tired. You just sit around keeping an eye on your big fortune and waiting for folks to come up to you and say 'Yes,' 'Yes,' 'Yes.' That's why you haven't been hungry; it was because you were exhausted that the food tasted so good."

"You know, I think you are right," said the merchant. "Beginning today I shall consider you my close lineage mate,[28] for you have shown me the path to true happiness. Because of this, you mustn't stay here on this poor little farm! Bring your whole household to my town so that we can live close together. I shall provide for all of your needs. I'll even present you with a portion of my great fortune as a means of setting you up in your own household near me. But, of course, you will not be allowed to leave my side, you hear?"

"Well, fine, if you would be so kind," said the man. And from that day forward they all lived happily ever after.

"*So,* my dear son,* that's the story about the good cook. You were just like that this morning. Boroe Soeti's rice and curry hit the spot with you because you were so tired and it had been so long since your morning meal," said his mother.

"Well, I guess you're right, Mother. . . . That could have been the case, I suppose. But why did you never tell us that story before?"

"Son, I told you this one because *you* told me a story first!"

"Well, that's okay, I suppose. So, look, this big undertaking I'm going to start

---

*Dear Amang. Amang is the kin term children use to address their fathers. Fathers and mothers also employ this word in addressing their sons.

with the guru is going to leave me bone tired. So the right thing would be for you to get dressed up in good clothes and go meet him, you know. This Sunday the guru is coming, and you're going to have to be respectful to him," said Pandingkar Moedo.

While waiting for Sunday to come, the three boys scrambled around crazily, arranging everything they would need for the guru's arrival. And their mother did the same: she had to run around and do everything her son ordered so that no one would say they weren't offering the proper measure of respect to the man who was coming to pay them such a fine visit.

Pandingkar Moedo needed each and every one of the seven days of the week to prepare. Seven days felt like seven years. Every few moments he'd say: "This week sure is *long*. Maybe someone's captured the sun and made it hang still in the sky." "Well, all right," said Rangga Poerik and Rangga Balian. "Now who might be expert enough to climb into the sky and set the sun free? Mount Naggar Jati already lies in ruins, so what peak can serve as our stairway to heaven?"[29] they joked. "If someone had really stopped the sun in the sky there wouldn't be twenty-four hours in a day and night. But, look, everything is just as it normally is. . . . Look at the clock on the wall over there; it's still working, you see. And the same is true of the watch we got from Hennemann's down in Sibolga, the one with a money-back guarantee (at this time there was no Hennemann's in Padangsidimpuan). Or at least it had better be working, the amount of money our late Father paid for it. . . . You must be patient. So what if it takes a long time? Just so we get there safely. After all, the mountain's not going to run off even if we chase after it," they said.

"Yeah, yeah, you're right," said Pandingkar Moedo, somewhat shamefacedly.

The second hand of the clock on the wall kept right on ticking those sixty seconds per minute, and the minutes in each hour kept on adding up to sixty, and the hours kept chiming along at twenty-four per day, and so, once the twenty-four hours had gone by seven times, finally the Sunday Pandingkar Moedo was hoping for came along.

Everything was laid out in readiness: the grilled chicken, the yellow ceremonial rice, the fold of betel quid, and so on and so forth.

"Yes, well, I guess everything is in order. You all go out and greet the fine guru so that he gets his proper measure of respect," said his mother.

The guru arrived in the evening, so that no one would know about it, no one but them.

With only a little daylight left they set out to greet him with considerable fanfare. They met him with slow and elegant ceremonial dances out there in the middle of the road. They greeted him formally, shook his hand, and escorted him in a courtly manner back to Pandingkar Moedo's house.[30]

"Now, you go fetch a prayer mat and some washing water, please, so we can say our prayers. It's getting on toward the time for evening prayers, and, you know, we'd better earn some religious merit to bail our souls out in the Hereafter," said Raja Awaiting Battle, coughing a bit.

"All right, you guys hurry up and fetch all that," said Pandingkar Moedo.

While Raja Awaiting Battle was saying his prayers their Mother came in from the kitchen and whispered something in her son's ear: "Is your guru a theologian or something? He's so fluent at saying the Fatiha formulas and reading the verses of the Holy Koran that he must be quite learned in religion. I think maybe we could have him read some special prayers in memory of your late father."

"No kidding. . . . *Sure* this man is special! He can read the Koran from here to Eternity, for sure. If you want him to read some verses for our beloved Dad he'll go right ahead and send the readings on their way toward the soul of the dear late departed one."[31]

Raja Awaiting Battle heard their words in passing and proceeded to draw out even more elaborately the Arabic syllables that he was muttering his way through as he wiled away the time, waiting for the evening prayers.

After he had finished saying his *isa* evening prayers the meal was set before him; they all ate heartily. After that there were betel and tobacco to pass around, and then they went on to chat a bit, to help the day fade deeper into night. At that point Pandingkar Moedo's mother interrupted to say: "Perhaps Guru would offer these readings and direct them to the proper, exalted place for which they are intended."

"With God's will," said the guru, reading his readings. . . .

By nine o'clock things had gotten quiet and still. No one was about now. Rangga Poerik and Rangga Balian stepped out of the house to check that no one was listening from underneath the floorboards. Once they had determined that nothing was down there they came back up into the house, carrying a tray. On it were laid out the mound of yellow rice, the grilled chicken, the fold of betel quid, the length of special cloth, and various and sundry other things.

Once everything was in order Raja Awaiting Battle arranged himself on the floor in a comfortable position. Pandingkar Moedo spoke up: "Well, indeed, then . . . this is the reason we have called Honored Father to come here. Seeing our abject poverty, we are here seeking better luck. . . . If Honored Father might possibly see fit to instruct us in the martial arts and their associated mantras, we would be most grateful. That is exactly what we related to Father last Sunday in Sihitang. So, indeed . . . because you would be such a great guru for us we have our hearts set on asking you to come to our aid and have gone ahead and summoned you here. If our mode of greeting is lacking in any way, I surely hope that Honored Father will forgive it. It is only because we can claim so little expert knowledge in these matters. Here, in front of you, we have set out what we have to offer as a poor means of asking blessings of the guru. Indeed, we certainly do not have enough to make a full offering here or to truly fulfill Father's needs, but you should take this as a first small payment toward our later, fuller contributions, which we shall make in full accord with tradition and law.[32] So here we have only what we are able to present this evening. If our lessons come to their good completion and everything attains its proper end—well, at that point we shall fulfill the needs and wants of the body and soul of the Guru Who Has Gurus," said Pandingkar Moedo.

Raja Awaiting Battle responded: "Now, according to strict family and lineage ties it is not really fitting, what you have set here before me. But, then, it is really all right since you said the aim of all this is to pay respect to the 'guru of my guru.'

Hopefully, all will go well and come to a good conclusion and you will get your heart's fond desire. So, let me formally accept your presentations,"[33] said Raja Awaiting Battle.

Once Raja Awaiting Battle had accepted the guru's fees he told them: "Let us eat this repast together, so that we might receive its blessings together . . ." "All right then!" they answered as a group, quickly laying into the grilled chicken and dividing up the big mound of yellow rice. And, although Raja Awaiting Battle was an old man, he was adept enough at shoveling in the yellow rice and gobbling up the grilled chicken bones. His pupils, for their part, also tucked into the food and grabbed it in big handfuls.

Once the grilled chicken had been packed away Raja Awaiting Battle said to them: "So, this evening we shall start the lessons in a small way, partaking of the protective blessings afforded us by this fine repast. This is all in the way of a little beginning, like performing the first hand moves of karate with all their exact rules and regulations—so that our good plans will indeed come to fruition."

And so, that very evening he began to instruct them in how they should do the martial arts strides, how they should stand in the various self-defense poses, and so on and so forth. Deep into the night they finally stopped, and Raja Awaiting Battle said: "Tomorrow we must move our scene of operations out to the edge of the garden lands. That way we can say all the protective spells so that people won't get maliciously jealous."[34]

"Fine!" they all said. And since their eyelids were slipping down demanding sleep they decided to just take a bit of rest. They all slept there together, that one night.

At dawn they went out to the clearing near the garden lands and set to cutting off all the tree stumps and underbrush so that they wouldn't get wounded by thorns and stickers as they thrashed about in there both day and night. The fighting ground was three fathoms across, and Raja Awaiting Battle spit his saliva around him to form a protective circle. In that way they constructed a little boundary line around the playing arena to guard against other folks casting malicious, jealous glances at them. They only commenced their studies after the playing arena and its various efficacious mystical guardrails were in readiness. Then the only sounds to be heard in the martial arts arena became: Punch! Kick! Gotcha! Return punch! Forearm block! Pow! And then, a moment later, *rup-rap-rapak* went the sounds of their blows till the very ground shook as they flailed and thumped about.

Once the guru had finished instructing them in punching and kicking and fancy footwork and so on and so forth all of them felt as if they were kneaded lumps of dough. The guru himself just looked on from the sidelines.

And this is how they carried on, for three full months, with Pandingkar Moedo's mother also knocking herself out cooking for them day and night. After the guru had finished teaching them all the martial arts, the self-defense moves, and the protective mantras, he sent Pandingkar Moedo off with a final verse reading from the Koran. But to Pandingkar Moedo's two loyal minions he just gave some very rough lessons and lore that didn't really amount to much. And as a final exam Raja Awaiting Battle tested Pandingkar Moedo's powers of self-defense by setting a big tiger loose on him. Word has it that Pandingkar Moedo and the tiger fought and battled and tussled and tangled for a full day, a full night. However, the tiger's jaw and claws had been locked shut through the aid of a convenient magical spell, so Pandingkar Moedo could not be thrown on his back upon the ground. And no matter how strongly the tiger fought Pandingkar Moedo always defeated him.

Finally the tiger ran off in defeat toward the edge of the fighting arena, making pitiful little *ngius-ngius* sounds, with Pandingkar Moedo attacking him: "All right, you, go ahead and croak!—That's what you get for trying to tangle with the Black Haired One," he called out.[35]

"Well, now, what do you know? Just look at that," said Raja Awaiting Battle as he watched the tiger limp off.

The battlefield was totally demolished and trampled. . . . "Well, that other big Martial Arts Battler has hightailed it off into the forest, I guess. It was pretty hard work, but I finally did cast him back, all right!"

"Well, that was very good, indeed. Now I shall declare you independent of me and able to stand on your own. Don't let yourself feel that you lack anything in the way of martial arts techniques or knowledge. And if you should forget anything just come back to Sihitang to get it straight," said Raja Awaiting Battle.

As Raja Awaiting Battle was going home, they did not forget to grill another chicken and present him with yet another mound of yellow rice as his teacher's fee. The present writer does not know all that they gave him, but people say that Pandingkar Moedo stuffed a sack of money into the guru's pocket.

From that day onward Pandingkar Moedo would always call the guru "Father." For his part, the guru considered Pandingkar Moedo to be his son. And so they became like close lineage mates who frequently exchanged friendly visits. And, as for Boroe Soeti herself, she would stop by Pandingkar Moedo's house every so often, when she came into Sidimpuan on market day, either to eat a meal there or at the very least to take some betel.

The Great Horja
in Batunadua*

"Burrr . . ." said the voice of the huge cannon, a full seven times, making the ground itself shake.[1] Its boom echoed over on Mount Lubuk Raya, making all the Commoner Lords in the foothill country in Angkola Julu and Angkola Jae start in surprise. And the Eight *Adat* Domains All Around[2] shook in sympathy with the boom of the cannon fire and everyone exclaimed: "What in the world has happened here in this land and valley?"[3] Suddenly from Batunadua the news came: a great *horja* ceremony was beginning, to celebrate the *besluit* of the Honored Old Leaf of the Tree of Life, Patoean Soripada.[4] For the government had promoted this revered gentleman to the post of district chief of Batunadua. People said, news had it, that this ceremony of the rajas would last a full seven days and seven nights. Word was that a variety of games would be held there, too, and gambling would be allowed during the whole period. And all the important nobles would come: the rajas, the high aristocrats, the great *sutans*, the high *orangkayas*, the oratory adepts who knew how to take the correct measure of things (that is, the respected *anakboru* wife receivers of the host family—the wife receivers who knew how to subtract what is in excess supply, who knew how to add something when fair quantities were lacking).[5] And all the great rajas came, the ones from Angkola Julu and Angkola Jae and from the domains of Mandailing, Sipirok, Padangbolak, Batangtoru, and all the way from Sibolga. And as soon as the general populace heard news of the ceremony they all flocked into the village as well. Most especially the big gamblers. They had not even been formally invited to the ceremony with a presentation of betel quid: no, they just showed up, ready for action.[6]

When the people flooding into the ceremony were still a long way off they already appeared pleased and happy, for they knew they would soon be seeing the ritual banners flying over the great gathering. That is, they'd be seeing the merry red ant flags calling folks to attend the ceremony and the jaunty centipede flags, which showed that the host family was overflowing with *kahanggi* lineage mates. And there'd be wondrous golden yellow flags of the nobles, too, and many other banners all flapping gaily in the wind. And as people got closer and closer to the village they

---

*This story has actually already appeared in the newspaper Poestaha—that is, the story about the great horja celebrating the change of Patoean Soripada's honorary title to Daoelat Patoean Soripada. But after that story was published, we received some clarifying information about this feast: that is, that the ceremony was really about Patoean Soripada receiving the official Dutch besluit title to becoming the village head of Batunadua. I ask that the readershall forgive this change, for I myself did not personally witness this horja feast. —THE WRITER

began to see the festive rattan fringes hanging from the tops of the village gates. The *tabu* drums boomed out incessantly, the *tawak-tawak* cymbals clanged nonstop, and the nine *gordang* drums sounded their deep resonating booms continuously, while the voice of the *gondang* gong ensemble itself moaned gently, like a lullaby sung to a baby.[7]

An indescribable number of people poured in for the ceremony. The folks who were formally receiving the guests all had their set places, determined according to their home villages. That way it would be easy to give everyone their food in an orderly manner and find them a place to sleep. So, as soon as the dinner bell would sound everyone would go back to their designated house to be fed. And so every day toward Dusky Dark Evening[8] great crowds of people would be walking hither and yon in the village, going back and forth between their houses and the ceremony. And in the wide rice fields in back of the Great House a profusion of lamps had been lit; it was like an all-night fair.[9]

And, of course, that was where all the gamblers gathered to make a fast buck. The rajas, the high aristocrats, the *ambtenaren* civil servants, and the village elders all gathered in the Great House where the ceremony was centered, while the religious teachers, the *lobes*, and the *haji* pilgrims all went over to the mosque.[10] The *tuans* from Sidimpuan strode back and forth, simply looking at all the goings on.[11]

And that is how it all went for the first six days of the ceremony, but the night before the seventh day was even more festive and busy. On that night all the major invitees who had been called to the ceremony gathered to hold their formal *alok-alok* oratory congress, for the next day had been designated the eye of the ceremony, its main, core day and the ritual's heart.[12]

Once all the rajas, aristocrats, government civil servants, and elders had finished their meals in the Great House (as had the little clumps of commoners, too) the ceremonial betel quid was finally presented to all the rajas, nobles, and village elders. This betel quid announced the Revered Old Leaf on the Tree of Life Patoean Soripada's intention in holding this great feast and having the climax fall on the next day. He did this in order to turn over the core ceremonial work to the high aristocrats; they were the proper ones to take charge, he averred. For, according to customary *adat*, great ceremonial undertakings of crucial importance had to be surrendered to the good supervision of the aristocrats and the village elders. The family hosting the ceremony would thenceforth remain as mere followers of orders from on high, much like malleable banana tree trunks—and just like white threads that could be turned either black or yellow depending on the dictates of their betters.[13]

Well, we do not have to go into much detail about this custom, for we are not here to study *adat*, after all. Suffice it to say that the high aristocrats accepted Patoean Soripada's request with good grace and agreed to supervise, manage, and measure out the activities of this immense ceremonial undertaking. Finally they formally and officially gave their permission to hold the ritual; they were all in agreement on this. After these speeches the host family spoke up once again: "Well, indeed, since now all the rajas, high aristocrats, and village elders are quite in agreement with the good request of the Revered Old Leaf on the Tree of Life Patoean Soripada, we would like to say thank you for all your good ceremonial work here.

And now, since we happen to see here some of the noisemakers of our honored ancestors, we think it only fitting that these instruments be tuned up and struck! That way the rajas, high nobles, and village elders will be afforded the chance to glide through some refined *tortor* dances out there in the wide public arena before us."[14] Thus declared the host family.

"Oh, fine, fine," said all the nobles as a group, and the deep *gondang* gongs were struck for the dancing. That night it was incredibly fun, busy, and boisterous there inside the walls of the Great House, for the nobles and the village elders were all taking their set turns, dancing their elegant slow and gliding *tortor* dances.

In accord with venerated custom the host household of course danced first. . . . And so the second that the Little Squirrel *Gondang* gongs were struck (or, as folks used to say in the past age, the Salempong Jau Simelungun gongs were beaten), the revered Patoean Soripada and his close lineage mates stood up and danced, protected and supported from the rear by a reverent circle of their wife receivers.[15] Just as soon as the Revered Respected Aristocrat had bent his leg to make his first gentle dance moves, the *onang-onang* singer[16] began to call out the lyrics:

Iden den iden . . .	*Iden den iden . . .*
Didenden iden ke iden	*Didenden iden ke iden*
Iden den ni Patuani	The *den-den* steps of the revered Patoean
Patuan Soripada i	Of great Patoean Soripada there
Soripada oloan i	Soripada, who all say yes to and revere
Kepala Kuria Batunadua i	The Kuria Chief of Batunadua
Didenden iden keiden	*Didenden iden keiden*
Didandan idan ke idan	*Didandan idan ke idan*
Didandan ni do Patuan I	It's the Exalted One who's plaiting it all together
Parsegar caluk kanan i	Who wears the ceremonial headcovering, its tie
Parbagas simargomgom i	slanted to the right[17]
Parsaba habangan onggang i	Owner of the house that holds its occupants in a
Parrayat na pitu torluk i	magical, firm, protective fist
Parhorba batu ni pasir i	Who owns rice fields broad as the birds can fly
Parlumbu tuktuhan longa i	Who commands large populaces in seven entire
Parhata na so juaon i	areas
	Who owns as many buffalo as the beach has grains
Didenden iden ke iden.	of sand
	Who owns as many cattle as the tree's nest has ants
	Who delivers speeches no one can deny
	Di denden iden ke iden.

"*Horas . . .* ," everyone said together,[18] for the revered aristocrat had finished dancing now and he had turned the floor over to his close lineage mates. And then the others on down the roster all took their turns at the *tortor* dances, matters finally concluding with the *anakboru* wife receivers. Only after this whole roster of troops had danced did the *hula-hula* holy wife givers contribute their own blessing *tortor*.

Dear Reader, as we all know, according to *adat*, if the *hula-hula* of the cere-mony's host family are going to *tortor* dance they cannot just be ordered to do so, like that, without any more to-do. And you can't just throw them a sarong and hope they'll put it on and start dancing. No, the wife givers are the Sun in the Sky for the host household, the ones they revere and most deeply respect.[19] So, because of this, the host household has to carefully present them with a special fold of betel quid and ask them gently to perform their kind and beneficent *tortor* dances. And the host household has to offer them gentle, mellifluous orations, too, to praise and cajole them sweetly. Now, normally the details of all this vary according to what *adat* domain you happen to be in. Consequently, so that the present writer will not make some serious mistake, it is best to consult the experts about such matters, for I am not terribly adept at *adat* lore. But, just to give it a try and do our best, let us add a bit here about this important subject.

Now, as for the main *hula-hula*, holy wife givers for Batunadua folks, well, they hail from the city of Siantar, from Baringin Mountain, and from Sipirok. At this particular time, in the ceremony at issue here, sitting in the place of honor, lined up along the front wall of the main room of the Great House, were the most revered noblemen Djagoenoeng Mandailing from the city of Siantar, Patoen Diatas from Gunung Baringin, and Soetan Radja Amas Moeda from Sipirok.[20] And, since the host household's holy wife givers were going to *tortor* dance now, some unfurled betel leaves were laid out in a tray in front of them along with some of the ceremo-nial heirloom clothing of the rajas and the wealthy nobles. This clothing consisted of the black bowler hat with gold braid, worn by the men, and a dagger wrapped in a good sarong cloth. After this was nicely laid out and the Batunadua elders and nobles had taken their seats, speeches finally were made.

Well, indeed, then, . . . this, then, is what we see, our good rajas, our honored rajas from the city of Siantar, and Patuan there from Gunung Baringin, and the kind *sutan* from Sipirok. Now that we have presented all that is necessary to the nobles, let us say that a while ago, as pertains to this *horja* ceremony, along with our betel quid, which we offer here to you, our revered *mora*, holy wife givers, as our invitation betel offering to you we say: we use this to invite you to be fleet of foot enough to glide through the countryside to come here to attend our *horja* ceremony in the village of Batunadua.[21] And we did, thank-fully, get our wish, and here you are, indeed, and you have had the time to come to our ceremony—and good luck and prosperity consequently has arrived with you here in our Great House! And so, indeed, what we say here, our good rajas . . . we once again present betel quid to all of you along with the fine ceremonial clothing of the nobles, for here are folded before you lovely, rich-threaded sarong cloths. And, now, why would this be? Why, the *tondi* souls and bodies of those of us who occupy this Great House miss you so very much, that is why![22] We need you to come for a visit, so that you might see your way clear to glide elegantly over the countryside toward us, toward our public dancing arena, toward our wide-welcoming dancing spot—to convey *tua* magic power blessings and luck to those of us who live here in this Great House.[23]

So said the rajas and village elders of Batunadua.

And the rajas from the city of Siantar, from Gunung Baringin, and from Sipirok answered these good words, declaring:

Indeed, then, . . . we accept your offering of betel quid set out here before us, we do indeed, and we also accept your good words to us. All of this strikes us as being quite in accord with *adat*. . . . Now, according to what is said in the Age of Religion,[24] one is not allowed to lift one's arms in *tortor* dance gestures out in the public dance arena. But how could that be true? For your betel invitation has been presented to us—betel quid that follows *adat* and law—so our hands cannot be said to be too heavy for dancing, nor our feet too weighted down for fine *tortor* striding. No, we simply must head for the dance arena and convey magic power blessings and luck, the luck and blessings your hearts so much desire from us.

And then the whole assembly shouted their agreement to all this, calling out "*horas*" three times over.[25]

Once the three revered noblemen had gotten ready and donned their *ulos* cloaks, their ceremonial raja's costumes, and their heavy, fringed, shoulder cloaks for dancing, the deep *gondang* gongs were struck—hesitantly at first and then stronger and stronger—and the three revered nobles proceeded slowly to *tortor* dance, protected and supported by a ring of their loyal *anakboru* wife receivers circling around them on the outside. And the singer followed along and said:

Iden den iden . . .	*Iden den iden . . .*
Didenden idenden iden	*Denden'd*, indeed, *idenden iden*
Didenden ni Sutan Radjo Amasi	Soetan Radjo Amas's dance steps
Kepala Kuria Sipirok na soli i	The district chief of Sipirok the beautiful
Dolok na so gakgahon i	The revered magic mountain at which we may not stare
Liung na so tungkiron i	The valley whose depths we may not plumb
Parbagas silengkung dolok i	The owner of the grand Minang-style Great House
Parbagas sitolu bungkulan i	The owner of the fine three-ridged house
Parsopo godang, sopo lauti	The owner of the village meeting hall
Parmasodjit Sori alam dunia i	The owner of the grand Sori Alam Dunia mosque
Iden den iden ke den . . .	*Iden den iden ke den . . .*
Paranjung so malo anjung i	The owner of the house with many annexes, yet no relaxation time in which to use them
Paralaman silangse utang i	The owner of the courtyard where all come to pay their many debts
Utangan sala madenggan i	All those many, many debts
Pardjambur sitare bohi i	The owner of the rice stall, providing generous meals to all who need them
Partataring na so mintopi	The owner of the kitchen hearth whose fires never sputter out
Parrayat ratus marribu i	The one with hundreds and thousands of followers
Parsaba habangan onggang i	The owner of rice fields as broad as the birds can fly
Parkudo sitahop razoki i	The owner of the luck-bringing horses
Didandan idan ke idan.	*Didandan idan ke idan.*

These fine lyrics were answered by a guy from Mandailing (who employed a Mandailing tune as he sang):

Jado . . . jado le . . .	Raja, Raja, Our Great Sutan

O . . . Dolok Sorik Marapi na godang	O, great immense Sorik Marapi Mountain
O . . . haruaya na godang parsilaungan	O, great protective noble banyan tree,
nir na bolak ale . . . parkolipan	enfolding your followers in its pleated trunk
Jado . . . jado le	Whose deep tree trunk's folds protect us safely deep within
O . . . Raja godang panusunan	
	Raja, Raja
	O great honored, revered, common raja over all of us . . .

And this guy had no more than paused a moment when the first one came back and sang:

Iden . . . iden iden . . .	*Iden . . . iden iden . . .*
Didenden ni na uli bulung	Noble Ancestral Leaf on the Tree of Life
Pareme usang do marusangi	The one whose rice stocks never run out
Parjegang na bubur on i	The one whose corn is so abundant it rots
Parpining na rorondar i	in the granaries
Parlancat na rurusan i	The one whose areca nuts are beyond
Parhorbo jangan dipadang i	counting
	The one whose glossy yellow lanseh fruits
Iden den iden ke iden . . .	tumble down in floods of abundance
	The one with herds of fat buffalo out in
	the wide grazing fields all around
	Iden den iden ke iden . . .

"*Horas . . . !*" they all cried, finally bringing their *tortor* dance to an end. And the songs kept answering each other, back and forth like that, for as long as people danced, with all the grateful hands of the *anakboru* wife receivers gladly receiving the generous *tua* magic power blessings and prosperity wishes of their *mora*, their holy wife givers . . .

After the honored noblemen had finished their *tortor* dances, the honorific titles were awarded to the aristocrats and also to the womenfolk and the pretty adolescent girls, the *bujing-bujings*.[26] Everyone was having an immensely good time, the rajas and the government civil servants dancing in the protective circle behind the pretty girls. The village young people, the Younger Leaves on the Tree of Life, didn't get to go inside the house that night and dance, but they weren't put out, for they'd been well occupied those previous six nights with many amusing activities and good, heavy, ceremonial work.[27] They were always scurrying back and forth, taking care of all the folks who had to be fed—all those hundreds and thousands of guests had kept them hopping! And the dancers were just as busy, not pausing till dawn. Actually it was almost morning before the rajas and the government employees noticed that they were feeling kind of wan, pale, and worn out. Their bodies ached, and so the gong ensemble paused finally and the big round gongs were carefully stored away in their rattan cases.

But it was no more than 5 A.M.—the little sugar palm shoots were just now opening up and unfurling in the first light of dawn[28]—when the drums were beat once again, the small gongs thumped out their *do-bur, do-bur* sounds, and the Nine Gordang Drums thumped out their earth-shaking message. And, even though everyone was extremely sleepy, no one could really get any rest since things were still so much fun and crowded and noisy. So off everyone set to the bathing spot to cool off, while others went to the Whirlpool Filled with Boulders to massage their aching arms, over at the Ayumi River.[29] And after they were refreshed they came back to the ceremony.

Once it got to be full morning, folks looked toward the courtyard in front of the Great House, and what did they see but a profusion of royal parasols of office: there were yellow umbrellas of office of the high nobles and star-bedecked parasols of the high born. It was all quite a splendid sight. And the long ceremonial spears were guarding the courtyard on the right and the left, and the brave *ulubalangs*,[30] all outfitted in their red costumes, were striding back and forth, guarding the roadway grandly from dangers and harm. For a very great many people were flocking in to the ceremony from their homes, some coming from Sidimpuan, some coming from the nearby villages. Some were on foot, some were in pony carriages—they just streamed in unceasingly. And the Commoner Lords from the home village, serving as the hosts for the ceremony, had all streamed out of their houses, with their eyes squeezed together in very serious expressions, ready to take up their separate tasks for the ceremony. The womenfolk set to boiling the rice and cooking the curry to feed those hundreds and thousands of male attendees. Once the grain of life and the curries were done, the men were offered their meal. Not a single one was left out, nor did anyone go hungry. And that was because the host household took great care to strike the dinner gong and call everyone to eat. Once all the rajas, the nobles, the government employees, the village elders, and the Commoner Lords had eaten their meals, they got properly dressed in ceremonial garb—for they were going out in grand formal procession to greet the Big Tuan of Tapanuli in the middle of the main highway.[31]

"*Burrrrrr* . . . ," said the voice of the cannon booming out, announcing that the general populace was now ready to stride into the main road to await the arrival of the honored Revered One. And the *ulubalangs* by now were sweeping back and forth, clearing a safe, protected passage for him. Once the rajas, the nobles, the government employees, and the village elders were all lined up in good order along the roadway, the womenfolk filed out of the ceremonial house. Following them were the pretty maidens and the *doli-dolis*, the dashing youths. By now there was an immense crowd of people out there in the courtyard, and it was perfectly lovely what with all the parasols bobbing about (some belonging to the nobles, but some, too, just held by the pretty young girls). Out there, out in the courtyard, there were shiny silk parasols and satin ones threaded lightly with gold, ah yes—with yellow-yellowest, glittering bridewealth gold.[32] The gold threads extended down to the fringe, waving there in the wind, a sight so lovely it almost blinded you.

"*Burrrrr* . . ." said the voice of the deep reverberating cannon once again, telling folks that the procession should move out to greet the Revered One. The sun was already rising in the sky, and it was getting on toward 9 A.M.[33] The Calling in the Invitees Gongs were sounding and resonating in the air, summoning family and friends to the site, and the hairs on the back of one's neck stood up upon hearing the sound. Everyone with any experience and expertise in the dance arena simply could not restrain him or herself from going out there and joining in when they heard the reverberating voice of the gong ensemble. After all, it was the adept Djaraiten (from Sipirok) who was playing the gongs, the Gongs that Made Women's Hairbuns Shake and Tremble. And the girls' feet would trip up and down, teased and bothered by the fast pace of the gongs. And the crowd's feet swept back and forth in sympathy with the music and the sweeping, strong beat of the girls' dance. And the *onang-onang* singer called out:

Oi on . . . ma da ibana	And there she is, she
Sitaring na lomloman on	The sweet, dark-faced one
Na lomlom so ni agongan on	The dark-faced one who got that way without
Bako ma sikandulo on	black ashes
	The descendant of Sikandulo here
Na gomos mangan gulo on	
Na engjeng na djarodjo on	The girl with the big sweet tooth
Na djarodjo markoum on	The spoiled little brat, never afraid of a thing, bold
Oi on male baya ibana	as brass
	The one who's never afraid or shy of interacting
	with close family, never, never
Abit na lomlom na imbaroan on	Ah, she's hungry now, hankering for snacks
Na ditongos ni tulang nia on	
Tulang nia sudagar Padang on	Wearing her brand new black sarong
Na olo marbere on	The one her *tulang*, her good mother's brother, has
	sent her
Tattai tolo ale taring	Her *tulang*, the great merchant from Padang[34]
Lambat simbur ko ale magodang	The one who's so good to his *bere*, his sister's child
So ro hamu tu hamian	
Tumopot sianak namborumu	Sail along a cape in your little boat, Taring, Little Girl[35]
	May you grow up strong but slow
Bayo na duldal doli i	So that you can come over our way
Haholongan ni amana i	So that you can come and see your *anak namboru*,
Ima Si Konong dolidoli	your father's sister's son
Sikonong baya bako na jogi	
	That dashing young *doli-doli* deep in adolescence
Amporik taruan mama i	The most beloved one of his Dad
Anak na endjeng oloan i	Descendant of Si Konong, that dashing, cocky
Na so tarpodom borngin i	*doli-doli*
Na gonan mandoli pado mangani	Descendant of Si Konong, the good-looking, fresh-
	faced one
Tumbur ni latong baliani	
Nagatal so mandoiti	Little sparrow eating his tiny meal
Bayo sigaya pariki	The spoiled, overindulged, beloved young son
Parroha na so taranjui	The one we have so hard a time getting to fall asleep
	Who'd rather go swaggering about than eat a meal
	The tiny shoots of the itchy plant, right outside the
	village
	It makes you itch without being stung
	The guy who's always hanging around in back of
	the house, whispering courtship verses
	The one whose fancy and favor we cannot ensnare.

"*Hurrrrrr*," shouted everyone exuberantly upon hearing this wonderful song by the *onang-onang* adept. "Oh, do it again," begged a certain young wife from Kampung Tobu, for all this singing and dancing had made her cast her thoughts back to her freer, younger days. The fellow had broken open all those feelings of deep longing and loneliness for her, once again, and she felt poignantly troubled.[36]

"Ah, no, that's enough, that's enough! Look, we can already see the flags and banners of the *ulubalangs* who've gone out to greet Big Tuan. The Revered One must be getting close by now, so we'd better all line up," said a serious-thinking, mature man in front of the crowd—a guy with some years on him.

"Oh, what's the harm in it, it's just a way to pass the time," said the woman, but she said that in a rather hidden way, so that no one would know how much she had been affected by the song and how much it had awakened feelings of longing and loss in her.

In the prearranged spot, all of the nobles, the rajas, the village elders, the womenfolk, and the Commoner Lords were lined up according to their station in life, waiting for the Revered One. As soon as the royal carriage appeared (the Revered One's fine vehicle) the gongs rang out. Not too long afterward the Revered One did indeed arrive. He stepped down out of his carriage and began to *tortor* dance immediately, all the while accepting betel quid from people who presented it to him from a ceremonial beaded purse.

After he had taken the betel he proceeded to walk around, shaded by a fine royal parasol and accompanied by a gong ensemble from behind. He walked along very slowly, accompanied by his followers: the rajas, the nobles, the village elders, and the Commoner Lords. And then, when the Revered One finally arrived at the Great House, the atmosphere had become extraordinarily noisy and loud, since the drums, the cymbals, and the Nine Drums *Gordang* were all sounding at once in a shattering tumult of sound. The great hullabaloo was augmented by the boom of the cannon—the sound shook the earth and echoed and reverberated all the way to Mount Lubuk Raya. The loudness made one tremble and quake. As the Revered One was stepping up into the Great House he was again greeted by people doing elegant *tortor* dances, and once he finally got inside he was seated in a place of honor, in a chair bedecked with flowers and padded with lovely folded sarong cloths.[37] Once he and his followers were comfortably settled (and so, too, the rajas, the government employees, and the nobles) people began to do *tortor* dances again and play various sorts of games. These included martial arts entertainments, mock war dances, and so on. People just wore themselves out.

Once all the food was cooked (for Big Tuan, the rajas, the nobles, the government employees, and the Commoner Lords) it was ladled out to everyone, as it was getting on toward noon. When all was in readiness the Revered One ate his meal inside the Great House, accompanied by the various *tuans* he had brought with him and the rajas, nobles, and government employees. And the general public was also fed, in their separate outlying houses all around the village, according to which *adat* domains they happened to come from. Speeches were given after the meal in the Great House and the other residences. The first ones to speak organized everything in an orderly fashion.

Someone from the main host household[38] would say: "In the name of the respected Old Leaf on the Tree of Life Patoean Soripada, first we would like to express our sincere thanks to the Revered One, Big Tuan, Resident of Tapanuli, and also to the other *tuans*, to the rajas, the nobles, and the government employees, who have all kindly seen fit to stride forth with legs the gliders, to walk along proudly swinging arms the askers for favors,[39] to come here to the village of Batunadua. And why would that be? Why, it is because Big Tuan Resident has kindly seen fit to promote the Old Leaf on the Tree of Life Patoean Soripada to the rank of *kuria* chief of Batunadua. We have gathered everyone together in this Great House to ask that the Old Leaf on the Tree of Life might enjoy a long and prosperous life as he accepts this new position, that he might govern successfully, and that his populace might prosper and be happy as he cares for them assiduously, like someone holding and protecting something firmly and safely in his fist.[40] And so, too, may the Dutch royal house continue to remain safe and prosperous. That, then, is what we have to say," declared the speech maker.

And then a response to this came from Tuan Controleur of Sidimpuan, who acted as the representative of Tuan Besar.[41] He spoke as follows.

In the name of the Old Leaf on the Tree of Life, the most highly revered Big Tuan, Resident of Tapanuli, please allow me to say a few formal words to the fine Patuan here as well as to all the occupants of this splendid Great House. Let me also address the rajas, the nobles, and the government employees. Well, then, indeed. . . . In line with what *adat* custom tells us, but also in the careful estimation of the Tuan Besar, Resident of Tapanuli, the Patuan here is the exactly appropriate man to rule over this rajaship. And so we respectfully ask God that the Patuan may be granted a happy and long life as he governs the district of Batunadua, may all his populace be happy and satisfied, may our government progress, may the Dutch royal house continue to grow stronger and more powerful. That, then, is our speech . . .

"*Horas. . . . horas . . . horas . . .* "

Now, Dear Reader, let us drop this subject and turn to another: that of the events in the gambling dens.[42] Just as most folks were having a noisy, boisterous time doing all those *tortor* dances, so, too, others were revelling in gambling activities out there: in playing dominoes, betting on fighting cocks, playing dice, playing cards, and engaging in sundry other sorts of games.[43] Dozens and dozens of folks were out there hawking snacks, cakes, drinks, and so on.

Many of these folks had come from Sidimpuan especially for the occasion, in fact. The main marketplace in town was almost deserted, word had it. One of the gamblers happened to be a visitor from Siulangaling. He was called The Victor, Who Always Wins and Defeats Everybody. If anybody happened to beat him at a game he'd invite them into the fencing arena for a good fight. And if he hadn't lost yet he wouldn't let the other guy rake in his winnings. This guy was not simply a great gambler—no, he was also a renowned and accomplished martial arts battler who knew all the swift and clever moves out there in the public arena. He was a sly one! Word had it that he had never lost at gambling, not once. Nope, he'd just rake in the profits, nonstop. That's why he was called The Victor, Who Always Wins and Defeats Everybody.

Now, throughout this great ceremony The Victor, Who Always Wins and Defeats Everybody, had been gambling constantly with Pandingkar Moedo out in the back rice fields, playing card games, and when they tired of that, dice, and after dice, domino-cards, and so on and so forth. They'd take turns winning, then losing, then winning again, and so on. Sometimes all the winnings would be piled in front of Pandingkar Moedo, and then a moment later the pile would move to the The Victor's side. And this went on for the full seven days and seven nights. They had wagered as many coins as there were grains of sand at the beach; they had bet as many bills as there were *biobio*-creeper leaves drying out in the noonday sun.

As it got on toward midday on the day of the eye of the *horja*, when folks were delivering their blessing speeches to Patuan inside the Great House, things were also working up to a climax out in the gambling field. Who was going to lose and who was going to win was about to be determined once and for all. Pandingkar Moedo had all the winnings laid out in a big pile in front of him, and a number of large-denomination bills were already stuffed in the pockets of Rangga Poerik and Rangga Balian, who were sitting by Pandingkar Moedo's side. And The Victor, Who Always Wins and Defeats Everybody, had long since pawned a lot of valuable goods to Pandingkar Moedo. These things were piled in a little heap in front of him. Rangga Poerik was beside himself with joy; expensive Tuban cigarettes hung from his lips, one smoke after another. The smoke from these cigarettes drifted upward in large clouds like the smoke from a newly cut swidden being burned in the fields. His hands kept dealing out the cards; his words made less and less sense. Often he'd say: "But, no matter what he does, he seems to win! Come on, the *horja*'s about to break up, and when that happens the gambling session will be over, too, you know." And, as for Rangga Balian, he kept his head down so that no one would see how delighted he was at the ongoing victory. For a long time he had thought to himself: "Winning or losing at gambling is not based on the amount of time you put into it. If your luck turns bad you can lose big. In fact, you can lose your shirt." So because he knew this he kept careful watch on how it was going to come out.

Well, things had gone so far downhill now that The Victor was only able to pay off his debts in IOU notes. He had taken some of the *kowa* notes and written "f.10" on them.* But, no matter how hard he tried and no matter what strategy he used, he couldn't seem to reverse his luck. He just kept racking up more and more debts. So after a moment he heaved a huge sigh, stood up, and shifted his belt around so they would get a glimpse of what he had hidden there: a long knife. And Pandingkar Moedo for his part heaved an equally big sigh and showed that he also had quite a big knife hidden in his waistband behind his back. Now The Victor did not have anything left to bet, and consequently Pandingkar Moedo declared: "Well, okay, Victor, Who Always Wins and Defeats Everybody, pay what you owe me, 'cause the *horja* is coming to a close here. Pay up all your notes, you got it?"

"*Ngir . . .*" sounded out as these words crashed uncomfortably on The Victor's ears. He declared: "Well, I may have lost here on the gambling mat but it cannot be said that I've lost in the fighting arena! Step outside! Let's just finish this game in the

---

*That is, ten florins.

middle of the courtyard! And whoever loses the match will have to pay all the losses, and whoever wins, ha! It will be winner take all. That's how we'll know who's a real man."

"All right, Guru!" said Pandingkar Moedo. He told somebody to go tell the *ulubalang* so that the latter could inform the raja of what was going to occur and they would strike up the *gondang* gongs once again—for The Victor, Who Always Wins and Defeats Everybody, from Siulangaling, was going to do battle with Pandingkar Moedo, he of the Other-Side Market, all to determine who would win the big gambling match.

"Well, that's agreeable enough," said the *ulubalang*, and off he went to inform the raja. And the raja said: "If that's what's happening let me go inform the most Revered One." And once the news had gotten to Big Tuan, all of the rajas, the nobles, and the government employees were quite surprised to hear of this turn of events. And so they quickly finished the blessing speeches for Patuan with the cheer "Heb . . . heb . . . Hurra . . ." three times. The most revered Big Tuan and all the rajas forthwith emerged from the interior of the Great House and stood on the glassed-in front porch to get a good view.

As soon as the word got around that The Victor, Who Always Wins and Defeats Everybody, was going to hold a fencing contest, great hordes of people began to swarm into the courtyard. They were all demanding: "So who's going to fight him?" And the answer came back: "Why, Pandingkar Moedo from the Other-Side Market." Now, apparently there amid the crowd watching the *horja* was Pandingkar Moedo's mother, and just as soon as she heard the news about the fight she dashed back to the rice fields and caught hold of her son. She said: "Now, don't you go fighting him. . . . He'll dice you into tiny little pieces if you start fencing with him out there in the martial arts arena! It won't faze him at all if he goes and kills you. Give him his gambling winnings, all right? I didn't raise you on gambling winnings, you know."

Pandingkar Moedo answered: "Oh, go on back home, what are you doing here? You're just embarrassing me. If I die, well, then there's nothing to be done about it. But look, I'll stuff some big black stones in my shirt to protect my chest from his blows and he won't be able to do anything to me, Mother, you can be sure. I'll just stand there safely and watch him try to hit me. After all, aren't I the brave, tough, young son to whom you gave birth, here upon this earth?"

"Ah, don't be so sure, Son. If anything bad happens to you, don't think that I'm just going to pack off to my home village.[44] No, indeed, I'll be throwing myself in the Ayumi River so that we can die together," said his mother with a worried sigh.

The crowd had poured into the courtyard by now, especially once they had heard that this could well be a fight to the death. About half of the crowd said: "Pandingkar Moedo really shouldn't try to fight The Victor 'cause he won't be able to withstand his dastardly stratagems. He'll die like a dog out there—and him an only child, too!" But the other half of the crowd said: "Oh, but even the smallest, most innocuous-looking stream can cause a person to drown, you know. So maybe The Victor should just watch out . . ." As soon as Pandingkar Moedo and The Victor, Who Always Wins and Defeats Everybody, arrived in the fighting arena in the courtyard, the *ulubalang* in his smart red jacket began to stride back and forth. Holding a long spear in his hand, he declared: "All right, stand back, stand back, give them room . . ." Onlookers were crowded under the houses, standing between the house-posts, and clutching all the coconut palms. Why, even the mango and orange trees were loaded down with people. Once everyone had claimed a spot, the gondang gongs were struck and the two martial arts combatants strode forward into the arena. A shout went up: "*Hurrrrr . . .*" And all those hundreds and thousands of people cheered.

As has long since become *adat* custom for martial arts combatants, at the start of a contest the men always have to shake hands and make their formal apologies to each other in case anything excessive happens. And then they go on back to their respective corners. "Come on, let's shout and urge them on!" the crowd exclaimed again to fire up the contestants. "*Hurrr. . . .*" everyone shouted.

And it appeared that The Victor, Who Always Wins and Defeats Everybody, had emerged from the sidelines and was paying his respects to Big Tuan, the rajas, and the Commoner Lords. Then he unleashed a dazzling series of dance moves: slicing the air like a combatant, swooping low like a ritual dancer, and whirling about with elegant turns. As his hands spun through the air he sounded like a top whizzing. "Ha . . ." said the crowd, "how could anyone stand up to somebody like that? Pandingkar Moedo had better just give him back his IOUs so things don't get really embarrassing," said the crowd.

But when folks looked toward Pandingkar Moedo he was just smiling slightly as he made his first few dance moves to pay his respects to Big Tuan and the rajas and the Commoner Lords. When the crowd saw that it gave them pause. They declared: "Well, I guess I don't know which one's a cock and which one's a hen. They both look pretty macho." And then Pandingkar Moedo strode forward with a few mature-looking, fearsome combat steps—they quite demonstrated his strength. Folks trembled at the sight. When the dances and the fencing steps had drawn to a close a voice rang out: "Okay, confront each other!" And The Victor, Who Always Wins and Defeats Everybody, sprang into the center of the arena like a tiger about to pounce on a deer. But once he had landed—"*Tak!*" said the feet of Pandingkar Moedo, like a cat bounding off into the dusky darkness.

All right, then, let's see what the audience members were doing. . . . After the two combatants began to fight no one emitted a peep. The only sound was the deep boom of the war *gondang*, which shook the earth in reverberating jolts and made as if to say: "Push him . . . pressure him. . . ." It scared you just to hear all this. When the combatants made a move the audience members made the same move, till finally they got backaches from all the swaying back and forth.

They got more worn out than the fighters! And, as for all those people up there on the rooftops and hanging from all the trees: if they had made the least false move they would have tumbled down off their perches like ripe *durian* fruit falling out of the tree branches.

"Now, careful, careful . . ." said Raja Awaiting Battle from beyond the sidelines. He had been intending to return home, but once he got word of the contest and heard that Pandingkar Moedo was fixing to fight The Victor, Who Always Wins and

Defeats Everybody, he hurried back to the courtyard to watch. Pandingkar Moedo's spirits lifted considerably upon hearing his teacher's voice, and he jumped right back into the fray, going nose to nose with The Victor.

"*Ba-he . . .*" said the Victor. "*Gap . . . !*" said a blow from Pandingkar Moedo. "*Tap!*" and then The Victor caught Pandingkar Moedo and was about to double him over, but because Pandingkar Moedo leaped out of the way so quickly he was able to wiggle out of The Victor's grasp—especially since he was as slippery as the eels in the back rice paddies. And they kept throwing kicks and jumping and bounding out of each other's way like that. It went on and on and on with the onlookers panting and trembling at the spectacle.

After a quarter hour of this, Pandingkar Moedo thought to himself: "Well, I'm going to have to employ some special tactics to defeat *this* guy, that's clear." He thought back to the way David had managed to defeat Goliath in the ancient war that the Israelis had waged in Palestine. "It's going to take some sort of extraordinary stratagem to vanquish this guy, what with how he's as big and strong as a coral tree whose roots are sucking up the river water."

A plan occurred to him just as they were tussling again in the middle of the arena. "Hey, tough guy!" he called to The Victor, raising his fists as if he were going to box with him. The Victor tried to defend himself from these blows, but all the while he was thinking haughtily: "Ah, just as soon as we get close I'll double him over, and that will do him in for keeps." But at that Pandingkar Moedo reached down to the ground quickly and got a bit of sand between his fingers. And then he swung his arm around and tossed the grains straight into The Victor's eyes. He made sure the crowd had no idea what was going on. Some of the sand found its mark, and The Victor was immediately blinded, greatly discomfited by having something strike his eyes. The hand he had been going to use to strike Pandingkar Moedo he had to use to rub his stinging eyes, and at just that moment Pandingkar Moedo thrust a vicious kick toward The Victor's armpit, rendering him helpless. "*Ngek . . .*" was the sound everyone heard, and The Victor, Who Always Wins and Defeats Everybody, flopped down in a heap on the ground, unconscious. A knockout!

"Hurrrrr!" shouted the crowd, and the loud cheer echoed and reverberated, it was so very strong. It sounded as if the very Judgment Day had arrived! Pandingkar Moedo was lifted aloft on people's shoulders, carried up onto the front porch office of the Great House, and taken to a spot in front of the Revered One, Big Tuan. The Revered One delivered a congratulatory speech and wished him much health and safety. . . . And the rajas and the government civil servants did the same, pushing Manila cigars upon Pandingkar Moedo as appreciative gifts, they were so delighted at seeing how macho and tough he had been in defeating that great, fearsome fighter.

And as for The Victor, Who Always Wins and Defeats Everybody, after he regained consciousness he ran off and hid, not even aware that he had left his fine Minang-style headpiece behind on the ground in the courtyard. He just hightailed it to the main road and went off to hide in the big rocks at the bend in the stream. He thought maybe he'd wait for his students to come along before he left the arena, but no: shame forced him to slink away.

And, as for Pandingkar Moedo, once he stepped down out of the Great House the whole crowd came up en masse to congratulate him. And he shook so many hands that his right hand began to smell like an old buffalo horn.

With the fencing match over the ceremonial feast drew to a close. Word was put out that the gambling mats should be rolled up. And everyone went on home: the rajas, the government employees, the Commoner Lords. Pandingkar Moedo, his mother, and Raja Awaiting Battle and his aides de camp also went home, back to the Other-Side Market, carrying Pandingkar Moedo's winnings, his incalculably large take, from the great fighting arena. The journey home was happy and bright. Rangga Poerik kept turning his hand back and forth and saying: "That guy didn't get enough of what was coming to him. If I had been fighting him I would have beat him like a little toad on the ground. And he thought we were going to be afraid of him! Sure! Right! Ha! I could swallow seven of him."

Once they got back to the house they presented a soul-firming hot meal to Pandingkar Moedo composed of a boiled egg and a mound of piping hot rice.[45] This was to ensure that his *tondi* soul and his body would be able to absorb this great victory safely. As Raja Awaiting Battle and Boroe Soeti were leaving to go home to Sihitang, Pandingkar Moedo slipped a little change purse into Boroe Soeti's betel case, saying: "May you be *horas*, safe, sound, and secure as you proceed on your journey.[46] And be sure to come back here in two or three days so we can all share a good, hot luck-meal, and so we'll be able to ask blessings of our gurus."

Beginning with that *horja* ceremony out in Batunadua, Pandingkar Moedo grew quite famous throughout the Angkola domain and all the surrounding regions. And folks began to call him Pandingkar Moedo the Terrible, the Fighter Who Withstands All Affronts and Challenges, and the Incomparable Big Gambler. He wasn't afraid of anything or anyone now. Everyone would sink down in submission when he happened to pass by in the main marketplace. In fact, no one would emit so much as a feeble "*nguk-nguk*" sound when he passed.

And that is how the *horja* ceremony ended, so the story goes, but, of course, if there have been excesses or inadequacies in the telling please do forgive me. I fully acknowledge that I have spiced up this tale a bit here and there—but what's the harm in that? After all, spices spark up the food.

A Sideline Income

Dear Reader . . . let us go down a somewhat different fork in the road, to follow the story about the people who were going home from the makeshift gambling den out at the *horja* feast we talked about in chapter 4, so that we can bring this story to its proper conclusion. We're not the sort to spend our time going back to the beginning of a story all the time, but we should repeat what happened once the gambling was over at the great convocation of aristocrats so that we can see how it all came out.

Apparently many folks got hooked on gambling just by standing around the edge of the games. In fact, some of these people had never even seen a pair of dice before. A number of young husbands and youths, both being sort of dumb, went out to the rice fields where the dens were. All of the peddler boys and regular gamblers from the main marketplace (in P. Sidimpuan) had gathered out there, and frankly you really couldn't tell the gambling den hangers-on from the pious *malims*, the Muslim leaders. Anyone at all was subject to being lured out into the rice paddies in the hope of making a killing. Consequently some guys would get cajoled into joining in, as we've just mentioned. When the gambling was going on at the noblemen's feast sometimes their buddies would say: "Come on and try it, pal! Maybe you'll get lucky, too, and get a bunch of ringgits back."

However . . . good people, what can be said? High hopes came to nothing. The entire contents of their pockets were paid out in the fierce give and take of the wagers. Or they simply set all their cash down on the dice mat in a meek, mild manner and then proceeded to lose it all. Often losers would be stunned, simply struck dumb, but then sometimes they would get furious and go right on to wager their inherited rice paddies no less.[1] They would lose some winnings they had acquired early on; sometimes, in fact, they'd even lose the very funds with which they had started. The *adat* of gamblers says that if you are winning then you must seek new opponents and if you are losing you must seek loans. You can't just put your losses on the tab.

Many of the guys with cash on hand to loan would keep shaking the dice box, offering loans to any and all gambling partners—just as long as there was someone to wager with them. In just a moment's time several long lengths of rice paddy land would fall into the other fellow's hands. And someone else would throw a parcel of rice paddy down on the dice mat as a wager, and then he'd go and up that bet to a whole tiered bank of rice paddies. Some would even put up their family heirlooms as bets.[2]

As soon as the *horja* feast got under way, the gambling would start, too. That was the bitterest time for the men who had been led astray by the gambling demon because if their wives found out, well, they'd have a big fight for sure. Because of this some men would just go crazy and run away—they would simply never go back home to their villages. Others would just wander around aimlessly in the marketplace in Sidimpuan, homeless.

The pain that young wives felt when their husbands left them and ran off like this is beyond telling. Similarly the pain they felt in harvesting rice fields that had been given to someone else to settle a gambling debt.

In the village house yards, children's voices could be heard, singing a little song in the Toba style.

Tona ni dianang	An oath said to Mother
Dihot poda ni daamang	A promise to my Dad:
Indang na langkalangka	"Never shall I walk
Na laho tu parjujian	Toward the gambling den."
Na hancit da inang	It is a bitter feeling, Mother,
Na talu sian pardujian	When you lose at gambling.
Targade bajubaju	You're forced to sell all your clothes
Dohot ulos sibunian	And even the *ulos* blanket in which you wrap
	yourself.
Soro ni aringki	
Jala sambor ni nipingki	It's just my destiny,
Hamagoan ni tondingki	My fate for dreams to remain unfulfilled,
Hasudaan ni untungki	The loss of my very soul,
	My good luck: all laid to ruin.
Jalang amanta hai	
Mangandungi ma dainang	Shake my hand in farewell, Father,
Dibahen hauma nami	Mother is singing mourning laments,
Nunga side diparjujian.	For our garden land
	Has all been lost to gambling debts.
Amanta so niida	
Inanta sai manginongi	Our father is no longer to be seen,
Manyarihon na suada	Our mother is sitting there musing sadly,
Amanta pe so olo muli.	Mulling over what is not there in the fields,
	And Father just keeps on not coming home.

And many other things reached people's ears: often folks would be missing a chicken or a duck from the rice fields. The culprit unknown. People who had lost at gambling had no shame, none.

Now, Dear Reader, we shall shift over to Pandingkar Moedo and see what was going on with him once he had returned home from the *horja* feast. Well, at that time he had gained lots of gambling winnings; his martial arts expertise, too, had grown in fame both upriver and down. He couldn't be bothered by anyone at all, no one in the entire domain. When he would go over to the gambling dens he always insisted on winning, and if he didn't win he would plunder all the money lying on the dice mat. People never wanted to gamble with him now, since he'd always manage to find fault with them one way or another. If they lost to him he'd swing a punch at them, and if they won he'd hurl abuse at them.

When he would go to the main marketplace he found no one there worthy of his respect. He'd always be wearing fancier clothes than normal, clothes such as a silk shirt cut in a dashing style with the sleeves about a whole yard long. His sarong would be a rich *palekat* brocade from India, a "shrimp" brand one, at twenty-five florins a throw.[3] Or if his sarong wasn't of that type then it'd be an elegant *morong* brocade, at thirty rupiah, while his trousers would be slick Chinese-style ones. Ten florins a pair. And the fancy ceremonial headdress, which, of course, he wore, would have to be made of satin and cost seven and a half florins. His smokes would always be Manila cigars. All of this made people most wary and respectful of him.

Dear Reader, even in situations like this, even if one's fortune might be as big as Mount Lubuk Raya, if you do not keep a careful account of your treasure it will disappear with some speed. Particularly if you're not adding to it all the time. Well, that was how it was with Pandingkar Moedo and his wealth. Within a year all of the winnings from the games at the noblemen's *horja* feast were totally gone. But his lifestyle remained on the same high plane. In fact, it got more excessive as time went on.

The thieves in town got bolder and bolder, and every day folks would come to the courthouse to lodge complaints. However, no one ever knew with any certainty just who the thieves might be. People were not able to press a case without evidence, but there certainly was a strong feeling that those peddler boys out at the market were pulling off these robberies. Most of the really serious rumors whispered: "It must be Pandingkar Moedo's two followers, those gofer soldier boys of his. Look at how rich a life he's leading, yet those three don't have any obvious means of support." Even though Pandingkar Moedo was the son of a wealthy father his excessive behavior made folks suspect him of the crimes. In light of his behavior, the authorities and the chief judge undertook an investigation, so that peace and order might return to the country. Not knowing that such revered elders were looking into the matter, he would go gallivanting around even more than before, every evening, always taking care to determine where there was the most action.

What was happening and what was being quietly whispered eventually came to the notice of Pandingkar Moedo. A voice inside said: "Ah, if I'm arrested my mother will be very, very ashamed. She might even fall ill from worrying over me."[4] So he summoned Rangga Poerik and Rangga Balian so they could all decide on a strategy to deal with the public accusations. "Well, the chief judge is involved now, so I guess the crimes occurring in this land are pretty serious. We haven't had anything to do with them but we've been gravely insulted anyway: the general populace is going around accusing us of committing the crimes. Given that, what do you think we should do? If it was only a matter of the police I wouldn't be too worried, for after all I haven't done anything wrong. However, the fact that the chief judge is involved has me scared. This is not only because of his harsh policy in chasing criminals but also because of how big a *tuan* he is. Don't you folks recall what happened out at the Dutch plantation over near Lubuk Raya?"

"Well, the coolies from Nias Island went on a rampage, refusing to work.[5] They were armed with knives and Atjehmese machetes. So, the danger was very grave. The court clerk and the judge immediately arrived to investigate. They threatened them and ordered them all back to work, but no one would listen. The Niassians were so fierce that no one would go near them, to the spot where they were. After it was clear that cajoling them wouldn't do any good they tried sending in about a dozen soldiers armed with rifles and swords. They were all lined up like they were going to war. Their drum went "*dorom-dorom*"; their oboes[6] went "*torot-torot*"; everyone sang out "*Woorwartsmarsch!*"—but the Niassians did not retreat an inch. The soldiers even let loose a salvo (that is, they shot their rifles in the air), but the Niassians didn't care. They didn't believe those devils' rifles had any harmful bullets in them.

Then along came the controleur and his troops under the command of his lieutenant—but the Niassians still weren't afraid. They had never had to confront soldiers before. Nonetheless, since the government knew how really ignorant they were (and since the government troops really didn't enjoy shedding their own blood over something perfectly stupid), they planned to merely scare them. After all, if they shot off their rifles people would probably die without a real order to shoot ever having been issued.

Once news of the Niassians' stubbornness reached the ears of the illustrious chief judge he immediately dressed to go out and take a careful look at the disturbance.

"No, now don't you go over there," said his wife. "Why, even the soldiers don't have the force to fight these Niassians."

"Ah, so you're afraid, are you? Do you think those Niassians are a big herd of tigers or something? If they are human beings then surely we shall be able to make friends with them."

"Yes, well . . . I'm always being accused of being bossy and telling you what to do, but you really don't have to go over there," she said.

"Oh, now, honestly! . . . You really are scared, aren't you? C'mon now, how many times in a month is there a full moon? Once, right? This thing is as certain and safe as that. Here's a Malay proverb that we must keep in mind: 'Before it is one's appointed Hour of Death, don't go and die.' So, now, listen, what is there to be afraid of? When one's appointed hour of death has come the Angel of Death will always be able to seek you out even if you hide inside an iron box. So screw up your courage; there is nothing whatsoever to fear. If you spot a fire don't go fanning the flames, just fetch some water to cool it off. So, off I go!" said the illustrious man, bounding into his horse-drawn buggy.

Once the illustrious judge had arrived at the Lubuk Raya plantation all the soldiers rose to their feet out of respect for him. He saluted them back smartly.

"Well, what should we do, Sutan? What exactly can we do here to calm down this big commotion? If we use force, there'll be bloodshed. So, if the good Sutan has a better plan, let us put it into action!"

"Call the soldiers back from their front lines so that I can go in," said the chief judge.

"But won't that be dangerous, Sutan? Do not take this situation lightly, Sutan—these Niassians are really fierce. Nothing will be accomplished easily here."

"With faith in God nothing untoward will happen. Just do not allow anyone to follow me in."

"All right, then, go ahead," said the commander, ordering his soldiers to pull back.

"*Gap . . . gap . . . !*" went the shoes of the illustrious judge as he walked toward the Niassians, his forehead clear and untroubled.[7] Once he got near the terrifying men he said: "*Horas. . . .* Now what exactly has happened to make you people cause such an uproar?"

"*Horas*, our Lord," said the Niassians, bowing down to the illustrious judge. The chief judge immediately thrust out his hand to shake their leader's hand and asked if they could go find a better place to talk.

After that the illustrious elder said: "Well, please lay down your weapons first so that we might resolve this case. Look, I have just returned from a trip to Sibolga, and I haven't even had a chance to eat a meal today. However, once I heard that there was some difficulty here I immediately came over. Now, you must not fear; whatever is bothering you you must tell me about it frankly. We are not interested in going to war with you. Come here so I can write down whatever wrong the plantation owner might have done. If he is at fault we shall punish him."[8]

Once the Niassians had so much as heard what the illustrious elder had to say they immediately bowed down in respect to him and threw all their weapons on the ground. After that, the illustrious elder told them once more: "Now, when you folks go back to work tomorrow don't be afraid. I shall make sure you are paid today's wages. If the *tuan* doesn't pay them I shall punish him in court."

"Our . . . our Raja, we gratefully acknowledge what you say. However, please do not punish us for our wrongdoings, for we are ignorant people and we did not know how to complain about what the *tuan* does."

"Yes," said the chief judge. "If this happens again you must simply come and see me first."

Upon seeing the illustrious elder's expertise at winning over the angry crowd and making them bow down their heads in respect, all the soldiers and their lieutenant *tuans* were simply astounded. "Ah . . . that *sutan* certainly has a great deal of *tua* magical blessing power and luck, doesn't he?" they all said.

Once all the Niassians' weapons were rounded up the chief judge went back to where the other powerful *tuans* were standing. "So, let us go on home, Tuans. I have removed the troublemakers' wasp sting. There's no need to keep watch over them, for they have promised me that they will not do anything inappropriate. A Niassian's promise cannot be broken, after all. Simply put, they think it's better to croak than to break a solemn vow."

"All right, then," said the powerful *tuans*, going on to thank the chief judge profusely. With that, they all returned home. On their way there the soldiers praised the illustrious elder's cleverness.

When Big Tuan himself got the news that the disturbance out at Lubuk Raya had been pacified without any blood being spilt he immediately called the capable and powerful chief judge to his office. Once he arrived the *tuan* told him, "Thank you" and said that our government would remember his good service in the future.

"Now, this is the sort of thing I am afraid of around here, in this land," said Pandingkar Moedo, ending his story. "Nowadays it seems that you have to act like this and behave as the chief judge did if you are to figure out how to resolve such situations. Well, indeed, let us simply give thanks to God and ask that He point us in the right direction so that matters might be resolved appropriately."

Dear Reader . . . we need not relate how the story about what happened at the Lubuk Raya plantation eventually came out, for revealing this much was just a way for us to keep Pandingkar Moedo's own story moving along. So, it is best that we get back to where we were going.

"All right," said Pandingkar Moedo. "If we can't come up with a good acceptable way to get the money we need, troublemakers will hate and resent us. So, what do you think we should do? Come to think of it, I've never actually worked at a real job. Since being born into this world and seeing first light I have always just lived off the farm my late father left me."

Rangga Poerik and Rangga Balian answered: "Look, there is a good way for us to deflect people's accusations. And it's also an easy way to get some money, although it's hard to gather the stuff we'll need because there is so very, very much of it. Over there, over near Simincak Peak: there is so much valuable forest rubber sap there that even blind people would be able to find it. And there are loads of gutta percha, too. That will fetch a pretty price. But no one is bold enough to go get it because that mountain peak is inhabited by Evil Ones, by *begus.**

"Where's Simincak Peak? And look, as for those *begu* spirits, you don't have to be afraid of them. After all, haven't we finished a full set of lessons with the great guru? We now have sufficient protective charms in our armory to confront any such situation," said Pandingkar Moedo happily.

"Well, the peak's nearby. Over there—you know, the hills thrusting out toward Pargarutan on the way downhill toward Padang Bolak. From the higher ground there you can see this peak. It's the bald-looking one, the one with the sheer rock face. It's the one called Seven Maidens Mountain. That's because, storytellers say, in the far distant past seven young girls from Pargarutan went out there one time to play since the view from the mountain in the direction of Pargarutan is so lovely. The Sipirok country can be seen from there, too, and the far distant Padang Bolak domain. However, by evening the girls had not returned home. Folks searched for them endlessly, and people back in the village beat the deep gongs for them to call them back home, but they never did return. Now they are just words in this story—made into the name of the mountain. That's so no one will ever forget them."

According to the beliefs of folks in the far distant past (and even today) Simincak Peak was the home of the raja of the *jin* demons—the raja of all those hundreds and thousands of *jins*.† And, according to what all the sorcerer *datu*9 could secretly see in there, that mountain was the very location of the village of the *jin* population's district chief. And he was the one whose kingdom was always fighting with the raja of the *jins* of Mount Sibualbuali and the raja of Mount Lubuk Raya. The ones who lived on the slopes of Mount Sipipison and on the other mountains were just these big rajas' outlying, subservient lands. And the ones over in the

Begus are small, sometimes human-form, evil spirits who have villages of their own beyond the edges of human settlement. Sometimes they infest bewitched persons, causing madness.

†*Jins* are demons, too—an Arabic usage common in Muslim southern Batak areas.

direction of Mandailing's Mount Sorik Marapi were much the same. And it wasn't just *jins* who lived on Simincak Peak—no, the mountain had big corrals full of tigers, too, and huge forest snakes. And that's why people can't go gathering rubber sap there," said Rangga Poerik and Rangga Balian.

"Oh . . ." said Pandingkar Moedo, nodding his head. "Well, I don't know how to go about striking off into the forest to gather resins yet, you know. But when it comes to confronting *jins*, *begus*, tigers, and forest snakes we don't have anything to fear. Because, listen, if you get near them you just have to give them what they very most like to eat and then you can easily make friends with them. They'll start behaving like family right away. Then they'll be pretty easy to deal with, all right. *But*, you must not go dealing with them in a careless, slovenly way. That's definitely not a good thing to do, not even with unrefined rough beings (that is, with us human beings). And most especially that's not a good thing to do with invisible beings (that is, with *jins*). So how do you think we should go about gathering that forest rubber?"

"Look, you're the one whose wishes we shall respect, Boss. Whatever road you say to follow, that is where we will go, even to the grave. But, look, once we've been there on the mountain for a week we'll have hundreds and thousands of rupiahs' worth of resin. We'll get so much we won't be able to carry all of it away. Boss, don't worry about how we'll go about finding and gathering all the resin. Rest assured, we have long since been in possession of such special knowledge, of such a special technique."[10]

"Well, if we really intend to set off on this journey, then we must swear an oath to each other," said Pandingkar Moedo.

"So, what's our oath?"

"We must swear an oath, we must make a promise before God, that we will be of a single death and of a single life. If we get our trunks chopped off we'll fall to the ground together, if we get dunked in the drink we'll all get soaked together, if our heads pop up out of the water we'll all float as a group, if we head upward we'll all ascend together, if we go down we'll all descend at once, if we fall in the stream we must all drift downstream together, if we catch fire we'll *all* get singed, and if we head upstream, ah, it's upstream for the whole lot of us![11] And if we go downstream then it's downstream for the group, and if we get lucky we shall all share in the profits; if we lose, we'll just share the same fate," said Pandingkar Moedo.

"Gosh . . . it's almost as if you were trying to find out where we stand with you, Boss, even though we've been together all this long time. Was there ever a time, Boss, when we tried making excuses when you asked us to do something? But, look, okay then, and with God as our witness, we shall never deviate from this promise. Even if a windstorm should come that cannot be shut out of the house or if rain should fall that cannot be stopped by leaf umbrellas, yes! No matter what, we shall indeed be of a single life, of a single death, from this world into eternity.[12] If we must stay out there in the forest we'll just stay out there together, and if we should manage to get back home then it's home we'll go together. Let us get our journey under way so that folks won't keep accusing us of bad things."

"How much money for provisions should we take along, so that my dear old mother can start getting it ready for us?" asked Pandingkar Moedo.

"Enough for one week, to start with, because by that time we'll know what sort of luck we're having, one way or the other," said Rangga Poerik and Rangga Balian.

"Fine," said Pandingkar Moedo, going on to call his parent so that they could tell her all about the oath they had just sworn.

When his mother came in, they explained the lay of the land: about how folks were going around making false accusations about them. "So, because of all this, we have decided to go gathering sap out at Simincak Peak. So, Mother, go get some money ready for all of our provisions, okay? Enough for a whole week—and throw in some hot pepper sauce, too, so we'll have something to put on our rice when we're out there in the forest."

"Oh, good Lord! So now you're going to go gathering forest rubber? What next? You haven't even learned how to use a machete yet. Are you sure you're not just going mountain climbing? If you have that much strength and energy why don't you just set to work weeding the garden around here? I'll guarantee you will get ten to twenty rupiah a month for doing that. Now, just look: see how many coconuts are bunched together up there in the palm? But, of course, it would be beneath you to shake them down, wouldn't it?" said his mother.

"Oh, Mother! That's women's work. Men are ashamed to make money gathering coconuts. So you just go do all that work of shaking them down from the trees for us, please, and get together the provisions money, okay? Or just go ask Raja Helpful to have his monkey climb up there into the palm and whack all the nuts down. Don't delay our journey any more! Hurry up and get everything I've asked for ready, so that we can get under way. After all, we might have to stay in the forest for a whole week, who knows? If God affords us good fortune we won't just get dozens of rupiah but *hundreds* of them once we've sold the sap for a neat profit. Folks like Rangga Poerik and Rangga Balian are used to sap gathering out in the forest, see, so I've put them in charge of this undertaking. I'm just kind of their work gang overseer here—but I'm also there to protect them from the great dangers of the forest. In fact, please note that that is one of the many good uses to which we are putting our guru's martial arts lessons."

"Well, son, if that's what you want, let me get right to work filling your orders."

And so, once everything was in readiness, one fine day they set off to gather forest rubber out at Simincak Peak. They carted along all their provisions and their tools and equipment for resin gathering such as machetes, a sharp knife, and so on and so forth.

That day, just as the sun set in the west they arrived at Simincak Peak. They approached it from Morang (or, put another way, Panampua). From there they went up hill and down dale and penetrated the deep forest. As soon as they got there they constructed a little lean-to—a rest stop lean-to out in the dry field, a hasty lean-to without wooden walls, a flimsy lean-to without a fence around it, a poor lean-to without a leafy top.[13]

Dear Reader . . . constructing a little shelter in the forest had to be done according to strict rules, so that The One Who Owns the Forest, Raja Tiger, would not get too angry. You were not allowed to build your lean-to on the rock face of the mountain, for that was where Tiger had his customary path; that was where he would habitually walk along his way at night. Seven peaks, seven valleys, that was the domain guarded by Raja of the Forest. And similarly one was not allowed to build a lean-to beside Tiger's customary path through the woods, nor was one allowed to approach the clumps of bushes where he normally landed as he bounded around. That would be taboo. According to the orders from the Datu Sorcerer in Charge of the Forest, in order to maintain an air of safety, one must not construct a shelter in Tiger's forbidden zone, if, that is, your shelter wasn't carefully placed down along the folds of the mountain.

In addition to that, one must take care to build one's shelter near a river source so that it will not be difficult to fetch water. And your lean-tos weren't allowed to have walls all the way around them—you could only have three sides. If you enclosed it all around that would violate another one of the Raja of the Forest's taboos. Once the shelter was finished you'd bank up the fire, tossing on some stout logs so you'd keep warm, for the deep forest was much colder than the village. Often people who came from hot areas would feel that being in the forest was like being stuck under water in a river, it was so chilly. So you wouldn't be able to sleep in the forest unless you had a good fire going.

Once they had finished cooking their evening meal and eating it they decided to go to sleep, as they were worn out from their full day's journey. As they were drifting off to sleep they tried to divine any orders the guru might have had for them. And after that they mulled over some advice of the sort the respected elders of the past would convey to young people. After all, Pandingkar Moedo had never been in the deep forest before.

There were many taboos to observe when sleeping in the forest. If you slept on your back, facing upward, a huge snake would come and swallow you up. But if you slept with one leg sticking up and bent at the knee a tiger would get it. And you would also be a tiger's prey if you happened to move into the central part of the shelter. Because of all this, when you slept you would have to cock one leg up and stretch the other one out straight. If you could not manage that then it was better to sleep with your body aslant with one arm on top and one beneath—but don't lie on your back whatever you do! Only after you had fulfilled all the sacred orders could you go to sleep.

Even though they were sleeping on the hard ground they had only one thick mat beneath them and bunches of leaves as pillows. But they slept very soundly and did not stir until daybreak. In fact, it was morning prayer time before they actually awakened. They reached down and felt their bodies: ah, they were as stiff as banana trunks. They looked at their blankets: ah, they were soaked with heavy dew. If it had not been for the fire they had stoked they might well have died, way out there in the nighttime cold.

Once it was dawn and the Sun That Warms and Dries the World had arisen they set to cooking their rice and curry. They ate their meal and then struck their flintstones to light their hand-rolled cigarettes. They drew a puff or two. After that they decided to push on into the forest. That day, they determined, they would only search for the forest rubber and the gutta percha sap and mark the stands of trees carefully with small signs so that they could go back to gather it when they had more time. As they did this they took pains to remind each other not to forget any of the *adat* rules or orders for people who were going into the forest so that they would not go astray and get lost in the middle of the jungle. Because of this they would mark every step they took with a little rattan strip on both the left and the right sides. Or they would cut little notches in the trees near the paths they used so there'd be signs they could use to find their way back again. Mere footprints would have disappeared in the rain. Even though they were deep in the forest, dark fog could roll in and they would not realize that it was evening already. But if there were rattan markers you couldn't get lost, for there would be some obvious signs out there in the middle of the forest. As they walked through the woods they moved three abreast, not one after the other, so that they would not all be making their separate signs. And walking like this they figured they'd spot more rubber and gutta percha.

As we related at the beginning of this story, Simincak Peak was so full or resin and sap trees that even blind people could gather the stuff with ease. However, if you did not know how to walk along in the forest gathering these saps you might just go and disappear forever. If not that, at least you'd be led astray by the evil ones who owned the forest, that is, by the *begus*.

But if the trees loomed up right there in front of you you wouldn't have to work very hard at finding the stuff, to tell the truth. Rubber and gutta percha would just sort of appear before your eyes. On that day they spent their time combing the countryside for those forest rubber and gutta percha trees. They found a good number, too. So they left little marks so that they could find the stuff again on the second day. As it got on toward evening they went back to the lean-to. Nothing had gone wrong; they had located a great abundance of the trees.

"Why, I've put down marks for twenty copper rubber plants and ten gutta percha plants," Pandingkar Moedo said.

"As for me . . . I've got twenty-five banyan rubber plants and ten copper rubber plants—and ten gutta percha trees to boot," said Rangga Poerik.

"Well, listen, as for me, I didn't even keep count. But I know I put down lots and lots of signs," said Rangga Balian.

"Well, if that's the case then all has gone pretty well, hasn't it? Look, what do you say we cook our meal? I'm so hungry my belly is folded over on itself like little leaf bundles," said Pandingkar Moedo.

"All right," said Rangga Poerik and Rangga Balian, setting to work with the cookpots, lighting the fire, and fixing the coffee. The cassava was no more than barely cooked when the rice was ladled out onto their makeshift leaf plates; they all set to eating. Because their bellies were so empty and because they were so worn out from their work that day they scooped up big handfuls of rice and stuffed them into their mouths without worrying about how hot it might be. It was lucky they weren't using big gourds as their curry base or a stem would have pierced their livers for sure! They didn't have the patience to let their food cool down even a little.

After eating they smoked a bit, suffused with a sense of total contentment. Halfway through smoking Pandingkar Moedo spoke up: "Being in the forest is so great! The food tastes so delicious out here—why, it tastes as good as what Boroe Soeti fixed us that time out in Sihitang!"

"Yeah . . . I guess that's about right. But there's something even more delicious when you're out here like this, half lost in the forest, getting ready to go to sleep. That is to say, hearing a lovely song, one that happens to really hit home with you. Its beauty will stun you! You'll feel it so strongly you won't know whether it's day or night. All your fears disappear; you totally forget cares and troubles," said Rangga Poerik.

"Now, whatever are you talking about? You sure have great stores of knowledge in you, don't you?" said Pandingkar Moedo.

"According to the *adat* of people going into the forest, once they've finished their evening meal they must chant *turiturian* stories*—very lovely ones, too, ones that bring joy to the Public the Two and the Three. And these chants also bring joy to the evil spirits deep in the forest. But, you know, these *turiturians* must be truly lovely, good ones—especially the ones about the spirit goddesses of the Upper Continent Above, about the ghostly ones, and about the invisible people," said Rangga Poerik.

"Well, if you know one of these stories then just tell it to us, good friend Rangga Balian. Pass me that pot of boiling water once more, and make the coffee tasty, too, so that Rangga Poerik can get to singing *turiturians*," said Pandingkar Moedo.

"Let me fix the coffee so that Rangga Balian can chant *turiturian* stories: he's the real *datu* of that!" said Rangga Poerik.

"Ha, ha. . . . Come on! I don't know about that!" said Rangga Balian.

"Oh, come on, do it! Apparently you're really good at telling *turiturian* stories. Where did you hide that fact all this time?" asked Pandingkar Moedo.

"Ah, come on, my friend Rangga Poerik, you have to help me out here—when it's a matter of trying to do what you're not expert at. But look, don't you guys make fun of my voice 'cause you're well aware that I have the voice of a rice pounder banging away out in the paddies!"

"All right, then . . . let's begin. We shall begin the words of the *turiturian* story," said Rangga Poerik from his spot down on the ground.†

Then, indeed. . . . Friend, Ompung, first Origin Rice of the land who inhabits the
    valleys of this mountain
I pay my respects ten times, ten times I pay my respects to you.
As I prepare to offer the sacred words of this *turiturian*.
Yes . . . the words of this *turi* story are numerous indeed.

Oh, may you not be startled or surprised, Friend Ompung
At hearing this unlovely, imperfect voice
If you are startled or surprised
May that only bring magic luck powers and prosperity to us all.

*Extended mythic chants, sung slowly in a droned style.
†*Dear Reader, when reading this* turiturian *I kindly ask that it be sung out loud as if it were a real* turi *rendition, so that it sounds fittingly lovely.*

Oh, it is not us, Ompung,
Who show off our huge biceps
Nor brace our legs to display our rock-hard calf muscles.

We only come here on this visit to foster good luck
Since those of us without it suffer so severely
That is why we have come here to the deep forest like this.
Ois . . . the words of this *turi* story are numerous, indeed.

Oh, the spokes of the spinning wheel
Have been whittled down from strips of bamboo.
My mind is afflicted with pain.
I look with dismay upriver and down.

Indeed . . . numerous are the words of the turi story.
Oh, please listen, Ompung of Magic Powers
To the voice of the three of us, all on our journey together
While we are here together in the deep forest
Resting underneath the leaf-topped lean-to.

Underneath the field hut made of fence stakes
The makeshift field hut casually thrown together
The field hut not protected by a fence
The field hut so rickety that it has no ceiling.

Yes, yes, indeed . . . my good close friends . . .

So let us start, then, and let us get small sections
Of the tree source of the *turiturian.*
Let us commence and begin
The words of this *turiturian.*

Ois . . . and this is what it is fitting to say
Concerning the great raja, Raja Oloan
The raja and *datuk* whose house walls are solid gold
The raja with huge stores of wealth
But whose fate in having *babere*, in having sister's sons, is quite different
   from the norm.

The raja who lives in the ocean dark with banks of flowers
In the odd, queer locale, as odd as the *sampilpil* wood
The raja who lives in the Simarapi-api confluence of the rivers
The great and wealthy raja of all the wealthiest people
The great raja whose pronouncements must be followed
The raja possessing divine inspiration.

Now, as for this great raja . . .
The raja and *datuk* whose house walls are solid gold
According to the words of folks in the past
That this poor body here had a chance to hear.

He had a daughter did this raja
A lovely girl with all nine lovelinesses
The much-loved favorite of her father and mother
Well spoken to all her family and lineage mates.

This was Sitapi Dajang Maromboen Boelan
A girl of extraordinary prettiness
To whom no other could compare
If it's a matter of that era of the past.

Now, it happened that one fine time
Down she descended to the Lower Continent.
She caught sight of her perfect match
Her son-of-*namboru*, her father's sister's child.

Son of Siradja Manisia, humankind's raja,
A surpassingly handsome leaf on the tree of life
To whom no other could compare
According to what all people said.

Yes, indeed . . . numerous are the words of this *turi* story.

When he was out courting around the countryside
Looking for his perfect intended
The one who's smart and very clever
The one you could have walk on in front of you, who'll also happily follow along behind.

At such a time as this
Their eyes met along the way
Their glances, which glistened like sunlight in the early evening,
The dreamed-of one was found.
As soon as their eyes met they laughed
And said as one, Oh . . . my friend to grow up with, apparently!

Up spoke the son of Radja Manisia
Going on to inquire and ask
Now what land exactly do you come from?
And may I perhaps talk with you?

Might you possibly want to be my *tondi* soul mate
My friend of a single fate and outcome
And live here on this earth
And be the one to whom I surrender my feelings of pain and suffering?

For I have searched for so long a time
Coursing over all the Eight Village Domains
But only now have I found you
And I rejoice at living.

Yes . . . friend, the son of my *namboru*, the son of my father's sister,
Son of Radja Manisia
It's only that I have come down here
But not really for any set purpose.

If you should have some love in your heart
For this physical body, for me,
I shall say yes to you at every moment
And I shall surely not just look for brideprice gold.

But there is something that scares me a little.
It concerns our father and mother.

Maybe they won't allow me
To be given in marriage to the son of Radja Manisia.

My dear father Datoek Mardingding Sere, Radja Golden Walls
He whose words may not be refused
If he, say, does not give me as a bride
Then exactly what shall we do?

Perhaps a great disaster
Will come to this fair valley
And that could you ever withstand
And serve as the guardian of my body here?

And, of course, along came the son of her father's sister
The nephew of our father
That raja who had dozens and dozens of followers
Surely he will not wage war on us.
If you remain firm in our consensus
Surely he will not refuse us.
You just have to say at every opportunity
That you have to be his *babere*, his sister's son, the husband of his daughter.

Yes, indeed . . . numerous indeed are the words of this *turi* story.

Well, yes, indeed, my good friend, companion . . .
Regarding now the great raja
The great raja from Pinang Haluang
The raja with abundant riches
The raja with sufficient yea-sayers
He resides at the base of Big Mountain

He was the sister's son of Datoek Golden House Walls
And he was the perfect fitting companion with whom to grow up
For Sitapi Dajang Maromboen Boelan
And he was going to arrive with brideprice gold
To fetch in marriage his *boru tulang*, his true intended, his own mother's brother's
    daughter
To make her his companion in life's sufferings.

He was the son of the raja's sister, the raja's good clan sister
The son of Boedjing Nai Badak Badjingkal
Good Mother Pleasure-Seeking Nanny Goat
The one who's used to folks saying yes to her
The clever, wise, and smart one
The one who has never encountered fighting words.

Now as for the great raja, Radja Pinang Haloeang
His face and visage were quite different
From the normal run of living humans.
His face thrust forward like a bear's big muzzle
Though he had the body of a man
Surely he was not like the Public the Two and the Three.

And this was the man who was the fiancé
Of Sitapi Dajang Maromboen Boelan
A man who surely was not fitting

To become her companion in sharing life's fate.

And that was why she came on this courtship journey
To the Lower Continent where humans live
Searching for her life's companion
To become her son of father's sister.

Once she had met him
Met the son of Radja Manisia
She was even more determined
To contest her father's decision.

And as for her view of Radja Manisia
He was happy to approve.
Even though her father and mother had forbidden it
They weren't willing to object.

Yes . . . numerous, indeed, are the words of this *turi* story.

And now my friend and good companion
As for the good sister of the great raja
She went off to see the girl who was engaged to them
To make her the spouse of her good son.

Once she arrived at her brother's house
She bowed her head in deep respect to him
Saying to her virtuous *mora* wife provider
She would like to ask for her *parumaen* in marriage, for her own good brother's
     daughter, her son's intended.

Since my son is all grown up now
That great raja, Radja Pinang Haloeang
Residing at the foot of Big Mountain
I would like to fetch my *parumaen* for him
Sitapi Dajang Maromboen Boelan
To come and live in our Great House.

Yes . . . my good friend, Ito . . . my good clan sister
What you say here is fine and perfect.
You're not pretending to be dumb
As you come asking for your daughter-in-law.

He called in his daughter
Sitapi Dajang Maromboen Boelan
To come before her good *namboru*, her good father's sister,
Who endured such deep sufferings.

Once the fine girl had taken her seat
The raja unleashed his tongue.
Now, as for why your father's sister has come here:
She's come to request her intended daughter-in-law in marriage.

Yes . . . good little friend, little mother Bujing!
Tapi Dajang Maromboen Boelan
Please listen well . . . little mother Bujing!
I will not repeat these words.

Would you be willing, daughter . . .
Would you be willing, good young daughter
To marry your son of father's sister?
To marry Radja Pinang Haloeang
The raja who lives at Big Mountain
The well-respected, wealthy raja
Who lives in the magnificent Great House
And become his companion on to old age?

I pay my deep respects . . . my father . . .
Father Datoek Golden House Walls
But I cannot agree to do it . . . Father, my good Father
To marry Radja Pinang Haloeang.

Better for me, rather than doing such a thing
Better that I take a *langge* plant rather than a *langgoyu* one.
I cannot agree to that request.
Far better that I die rather than live if it's a matter of saying yes!

My deep respects to you . . . my young daughter
Please, please agree to what your father's sister has requested.
It's not that this will cause you great, unusual suffering
To go and marry your father's sister's son, you know.

Please, daughter, do not
Do not, good daughter
Go altering all the measuring tools and tapes
Here in this valley domain.

It is far better that you simply set off on your marriage journey, girl.
You can come back often to visit us.
Please traverse your fitting marriage journey.

And may you not, young daughter
Fan the flames of war
Nor strike together the flintstones
Divorcing yourself from your close family.

If that raja should grow angry on the morrow
That is, my good nephew—
The great raja from Big Mountain
How could I possibly answer him, My daughter?
I have no power nor energy.
Surely he will contest all this with sharpened spears.

My deep respect, my friend, good Father,
Father Datoek Golden House Walls
I simply cannot say yes, Father,
And marry my father's sister's son there.

And if he should come here
Like a great strong wind we have no walls to defend ourselves against
Like a fierce rain for which we have no umbrellas
Devastating everything in his wake
I will just go and ask aid and succor
And recruit my friends to help me wage war.

Oh . . . please don't, please don't, Father
Better than enjoying great stockpiles of yellow-yellowest, glittering brideprice gold
Which overflows all its containers.
Far better, father,
That you defend your daughter's interests
So my fate is not so much worse
than that of all the public.
Well, indeed, good friend . . . my clan sister
Said Datoek Golden House Walls
Speaking to his sister
So that you will go inform my nephew.

Now, as for what your intended daughter-in-law has to say
She cannot give words of argument.
Please do not be sick at heart, sister
We do not mean anything bad by this.

His clan sister was somewhat put out by this
And home she went to Big Mountain straightaway.
And she related the story to her son
What his mother's brother's daughter had had to say, what his mother's brother's
    daughter had declared.

Once the raja had heard this
The raja from Pinang Haloeang
What his dear mother's brother's daughter had had to say
He cried and sobbed and shouted Father! Mother! in despair.

He called in all his people
The seven huge groups from downstream
The seven huge groups from upstream, too
So that on the morrow they could set off
Fully armed with weapons and war spears
To go wage war to contest that shaming action.

That shame as heavy as the huge sky above
That shame as weighty as the earth below
So that we can snuff them out like little mosquitoes
So that we are not insulted.

And now, good friend, companion . . .
As for the daughter of the raja
Off she went on a journey, swinging her hands elegantly
To confer with the son of Radja Manisia.

She went down to the Lower Continent
To the Sorrowful Suffering Rest Spot in the deep forest
To say that her father's sister had come on her visit
To tell all this to the medicine for her love longings.

So that he would quickly get dressed and be ready
To confront the arrival of enemies
So that we can banish and chase away all of them
So that our thoughts do not weigh heavily.

Well, then, indeed, daughter of my wife givers!

My companion as I grow to adulthood
Let me call together my own populace
And lead them into battle, on toward the fighting arena.

My people, who know all the martial arts kicks and tricks
Who never retreat in the face of the enemy
Whether it be evening or daytime
The people who have no fear of bullets.

To put the matter briefly
Here came all the people led by the raja
From the base of Big Mountain
Like flocks of hunted sparrows
Spreading out across the countryside
Announcing the onset of a huge war.

Once he had so much as seen all that
The great Radja Manisia—
Straight up to his enemy did he fly
Followed by all his people.

A crashing-big-river-boulders war ensued
A real hack-them-to-pieces battle
And all those who could be taken captive
Were thrown right in the clink.

The war went on and on and on
Daytime, mid-nighttime, too
The warfare progressed.
Enemies were beaten, pummeled, flipped upside-down.

For seven nights and seven days
The war lasted out in the fields.
The enemies ran off helter-skelter
Back to the base of that big mountain of theirs.

As if they had stepped on live embers
Thrown in there by Radja Manisia
They could not evade him.
They all surrendered in shame.

Once the warriors had finished their fighting
Along came Radja Manisia.
Up he went to the old raja
To introduce himself to the revered nobleman.

And along came the old man's daughter
Sitapi Dajang Maromboen Boelan.
Now, here, Father, is my father's sister's son
The one I want as my dear marriage companion.

The friend and companion to this body
The one who can grow old with me
The one who can become your daughter's husband
The one who is just my age and size.

And then, too, he's invincible and strong
A firm tree trunk who can't be split with a wedge
A great raja with many followers and wide domains of land
A raja who knows all the gambling tricks and moves.

Well, then, good friend, companion, little daughter!
Declared Datoek Golden House Walls
Go ahead and marry, daughter
My dearest sister's son.
Go ahead and set off on your journey, young daughter.
I go along to order you off toward your marriage.
Here is the one who will become your protector
Who will be your father's sister's son.

And they held a great *horja* celebration with blessing-conveying foods.
They all celebrated festively
And they increased in wealth, prosperity, descendants, and plump infants strapped to
    their sides
And all grew in health at every instant.

And little bark shavings grow
Along with all the soft grasses.
May sons be born to you and daughters, too
And may absolutely nothing come to plague you.

"So, my friends, that is the *turiturian* of Si Tapi Dajang Maromboen Boelan," said Rangga Balian, going on to say: "Now you just bring me a cup of that great coffee, Rangga Poerik, for I don't want to nod off to sleep here."

"Ha, ha . . . I guess my senses sort of slipped away from me there for a moment," said Rangga Poerik, passing around another cup for each of them.

"Ah, may you suffer death at an early age, Rangga Balian! So it seems you did have that sort of talk in you!" said Pandingkar Moedo, sipping his delicious coffee.

Now it was deep at night, so they decided to go off to sleep. After just one or two moments their eyelids drooped and they each fell sound asleep. Rangga Poerik and Rangga Balian did not particularly take the words of the *turiturian* to heart, for they knew that that was the sort of lesson that you tended to get when you were out in the middle of the forest. But Pandingkar Moedo found himself greatly troubled by its words—it was as if what had been related in the *turiturian* story was really *true*. And because of this the lovely visage of the beautiful girl still appeared in front of his eyes and if he so much as squeezed his eyelids together the faintest bit the shadowy image of Sitapi Dajang Maromboen Boelan would loom up before him, and it would be as if she were saying:

Malalum batu ni dapdap	The *dapdap* fruit is ripe.
Namalamun so ra matonggi	But, though ripe, it will not sweeten.
Dao dope hamu hutatap	I saw you only from afar
Madung tama upa ni tondi.	But it seems you're already the perfect balm
	for my *tondi* soul.

"Allah, God above . . ." Pandingkar Moedo's eyes latched onto her image, gazing intently at her. He was deeply shaken, no longer able to make a sound. But his inner self mulled over the question: "Is this a girl born of human beings? Or a girl of the unseen ones? One who might send sleepers into a daze? But they're usually not all that willing to treat you like family way out here in the middle of the forest."

"Ah," said his inner self, going on to say: "I guess all that's just our fate out here in the deep of night." And then he shut his eyes tightly, trying to sleep. As they were shutting the girl's lovely visage appeared again. "Goodbye then, good-hearted, handsome Older Lineage Companion,"* she said as she went away. Pandingkar Moedo followed the girl with his gaze until she completely disappeared from sight. He felt downcast and deeply disappointed, and without his knowing it a young man's *ungut-ungut* lament song escaped him.

Ulang ale manjaring loba	Now, don't go netting bees
Tu Sialang Gonting Barumun	Out at Sialang Gonting Barumun.
Ulang ale manggotap roha	Now don't go losing hope
Ulang diarjeng halalungun.	And don't suffer deep, deep longings.[14]

Rangga Poerik was startled to hear someone singing low-toned, sad *togol* courtship laments like this.[15] He thought that the songs must be coming from someone lost out in the dark, someone who might be approaching their lean-to to rest for a while. For his part Rangga Balian didn't hear him, for his snores were going upriver and down, up hill and down dale. He was really conked out! But once Rangga Poerik found that Pandingkar Moedo himself was doing the singing he woke him up and cried: "Hey . . . whatever made you sing out your loneliness in the middle of the night like that?"

"Eh," said Pandingkar Moedo, going on to ask: "What do you see around here that could frighten you?"

"Oh, so you were just dreaming, then. Well, let's just all go back to sleep." And from then on till daylight they did not awaken.

Once it was light and the world-drying sun had risen once more they set to cooking their meal. They fixed rice and curry and spooned it out onto big, broad, areca palm leaves and used these as plates. On finishing their meal they smoked a bit. "Well, okay, let's set off. . . . Let's everyone gather up his gear so we can go get that sap we marked yesterday." Once they had arrived at the forest rubber spot they all started working on the tree trunks, gathering the sap, with Rangga Poerik and Rangga Balian teaching Pandingkar Moedo how to do it. They cut bracelet-shaped cuts on the lower parts of the tree trunks and then gathered the sap from the indentations. As soon as they arrived at a field they would make a couple of trial cuts on the trunks to show Pandingkar Moedo how to do it. They didn't allow him to gather the sap yet, for they weren't sure he was expert enough for that. Once they had cut a gash in that first trunk and seen that the sap was really good (not to mention quite plentiful), Pandingkar Moedo spoke up: "Gosh, it sure is easy enough! You two keep gathering the sap and let me go on up the hill a bit to locate some more trees."

"Fine, fine," said Rangga Poerik and Rangga Balian. "But don't go too far or you'll get lost."

---

*Angkang: the appelation girlfriends use with boyfriends, suggesting that they are companions of a single lineage (i.e., future spouses).

"Yeah, yeah, all right, all right," said Pandingkar Moedo.

But once they had split up Pandingkar Moedo no longer knew what was allowed and what was taboo there in the deep forest. For the apparition he had seen in the nighttime dream still appeared before him. "Oh, maybe this is where she went last night! I must follow her there." That is what his innermost self kept repeating, going on to lament in an *ungut-ungut* song:

Sarindan hupopoi	The little parasites I clean all off,
Sarung ni raut hubarbari	I whittle on a wooden knife handle
Tu ginjang husigei	I climb up the coconut palm by little footholds
Taripat laut hulayari.	I sail over the far ocean, looking for my
	mysterious chant girl.

Since his inner self was now so totally scattered in pieces he was seeing more and more strange things.[16] Apparently the Evil One had infested him out there in the forest, and the spirit had worked a little game so that he would see the girl from last night's *turi* chant sitting up there in the window of a high-gabled, swoop-backed house, just taking in the fresh air, combing back her luxuriant, lustrous, black hair. She gazed at him as if to wave a greeting and said: "So, where might you be going, my good friend, you who are all alone on your fine journey?"

"Ah," said Pandingkar Moedo, "how can I get over there to you? Where is there a hanging footbridge over this deep chasm, which I might use to cross over and go up into your fine house? If you perhaps have any feelings of loving kindness toward me, help pull me up there with a rope."

"Ha, ha," laughed the girl from her perch in the window, going on to say: "Well, if you so desire it, come on up! I'll be waiting for you!"

So Pandingkar Moedo climbed up the footbridge. But this sheer rock face could not normally be traversed by regular human beings since it was extraordinarily slippery. However, since he was already sort of friends with her he bounded right up into the house.

It was getting late in the day, and Pandingkar Moedo had not returned to the work site. Rangga Poerik and Rangga Balian waited a moment more, but he still did not come. Since Pandingkar Moedo had apparently disappeared they went in search of him, following his footprints, to discover where he might have gone. "Allah, my God . . ."

And they saw: he was suspended on a tiny footbridge over a canyon like a silly civet cat that had completely taken leave of its senses! And he was calling out "Hello, hello, hello, Little Lineage Companion . . ."

Well, this was pretty serious. . . . And they said to themselves: "What in the world could have made him climb up onto that hanging bridge?" They muttered the magic protective phrases they had studied to guard people from evil ones and *jin* spirits. They took hold of a rope (a stout piece of rattan really) so that they would have something to hold onto as they edged their way across the hanging bridge toward him. They caught hold of him and immediately sprinkled him with dew from big handfuls of fresh green forest leaves. Then they carried him back down to the ground.

They asked him where in the world he had been going. To their surprise, Pandingkar Moedo answered them with the words: "Why, toward that one over there. That is the one I have to have . . . that beautiful girl over there. Look! There she is, she's still waving at us." They looked over at the side of the cliff but could not see a thing. Consequently they felt sure that Pandingkar Moedo had been bewitched by the Daughter of the Jins out there in the deep forest. So they gently took him by the forearm and escorted him back to their lean-to. There they tried all sorts of endeavors to persuade the beings who had stupefied Pandingkar Moedo out in the forest to vanish from his sight.[17] But what was to be done after all? . . . He did not get any better. His body remained as hot as fire; when they looked into his eyes, they were red, like newly plucked ground cherry fruits.

"Ah, such rotten luck! We haven't gathered any of our forest rubber yet and our Boss has already gotten himself infested with *begus*. This is *not* how we dreamed things would turn out. . . . Well, look, so, what should we do?" asked Rangga Poerik. "What if we don't succeed in collecting any sap? Or what if we do but we can't carry it home, if our invalid here doesn't get any better—or even gets worse on us?"

"I think it's best that we just carry him home because if something bad happens to him out here in the forest then people will blame us for everything. So we should stash away all of our tools so they'll be safe and set off on our way," said Rangga Balian.

Once they had stashed away all the equipment and things they really didn't need to carry with them they set off into the deep darkness there in the middle of the night. When Pandingkar Moedo was feeling strong enough to walk they would push and pull him along; when he could not make it by himself they would carry him between them.

And this is how they proceeded along in that deep dark night. It was about midnight when they arrived at Bobak Lake. The darkness grew deeper, since drop-sprinkling rain had rolled in. Every few seconds a stunning lightning bolt would crash down from the sky as if flung from a boomerang. And just as soon as the lighting flash had disappeared, "*Ra-tang!* . . ." would say the voice of the great thunder, as if it were fixing to split the earth in two. When they came to the land sloping upward toward Hapoeran (that's the name of a slight rise in the terrain as you go upward toward the Panompuan folks' rice fields) huge hailstones started to pelt down. They had no umbrella nor even a little field hut in the paddies under which to hide. A moment later it was "*Ra-bas!* . . ." And then, well, to tell the truth, "*Ngaum!*" would say something in the forest.

"*Ngaum!*" in fact, said the voice of a very huge and very fierce tiger, leaping out from the foliage and landing right in front of them. You'd look at his eyes: they were like burning fires.

"Oh, brother, do we ever need a magic charm now," said Rangga Balian. . . .[18]

"Yeah, *right*, you take a look at that tiger's eyes! How could we ever protect ourselves against that? His mouth is already gaping open, and his fangs are all hanging out. Even our sick one is starting to speak again because of all this. And rain is pouring down—things do seem to have closed in on us a bit here!" said Rangga Poerik.

"Look, this is just a trial, sent by God, to make us all the braver," said Rangga Balian, pulling the shawl a bit tighter around their sick one's shoulders.

"Oh, where's my mother? I am going to die here for sure! Now that tiger is standing *right there* in the middle of the road!" said Rangga Poerik.

"Let's back up a bit here. . . . Now, all right, all right, don't be afraid," said Rangga Balian.

"What I say is, we'd better make a quick decision. We can't be bound by our oath-promise if it means we actually have to *die*. Come on, let's just leave the sick one behind," said Rangga Poerik.

"Good grief! Don't say that sort of thing. Remember our oath! Haven't we all pledged to be of a single life, of a single death?" answered Rangga Balian—although in his inner self, frankly, he agreed with the notion of simply leaving Pandingkar Moedo behind and taking right off.

"Yeah—but we can't always manage to follow our sacred oaths, you know. It's true, we love him as if we all shared the same skin, but don't forget: as great as one's love for one's friend might be one still must give oneself a little bit of an edge. And why would I say such a thing? Well, look, if he gets eaten by the tiger then we'll still be alive to carry the unhappy news back to the village. Otherwise we'll never get home to Sidempuan," said Rangga Poerik.

Rangga Balian tried as hard as he could to screw up his inner stores of courage, to take issue with these words, but in the end he just fell into agreement with them, and the two decided to leave Pandingkar Moedo behind. That tiger was bounding closer and closer to them all the time. Louder and louder they could hear his crashing, as he landed heavily as he approached.

So they hot-footed it off into the black darkness, the one of them pulling the other down the path.

So Pandingkar Moedo was lying there abandoned in the middle of the road, with the hard rain drumming down on him, with that big tiger sizing him up with considerable eagerness. Pandingkar Moedo was so sick that he didn't even know what happened to be hanging in the sky above him. He could barely move his jaws to take a breath—in fact, he was just about fixing to croak. And as for the tiger, well, he didn't really want to eat Pandingkar Moedo but just to bat him back and forth and maybe turn him over and over and roll him around a bit. And so, after he was through with all of that, he firmly licked Pandingkar Moedo's body up and down and then he went back into the forest. So that left Pandingkar Moedo lying there like a piece of garbage, sprawled out on the ground, his clothes totally soaked from the downpour. To look at his body you'd think there wasn't an inch left clear of mosquito bites.

Once it got to be daylight Pandingkar Moedo woke up with a start and looked around with wonder at where he was. He was no longer safely under the lean-to: why, here he was, right out in the middle of the highway that cut through the forest. And when he looked around for his companions neither of them was to be seen, and surrounding him in a big busy circle were the pawprints of a furious tiger.

"Oh . . . I guess I had the world's closest call last night! Where are my buddies? Well, maybe the tiger has gobbled them up," said Pandingkar Moedo. Once the heat from the sun had warmed him a bit and he felt somewhat stronger, his sight cleared and he could see again. Apparently, the hailstones and the tiger pawprints had served as healing potions for his body, rather like those always-effective *jamus** that hail from Jambi.

All his ailments had now healed, and he felt only a bit soft and woozy. He thought for a moment about what could have brought him there. "Oh! . . . Apparently my companions took great pains to take care of me and carry me out of the forest on their backs, but—since they've got a touch of craziness to them (and the tiger would have been enough to have caused that)—well, I guess we all got worked over pretty well by the Raja of the Forest last night. Now, it's sure amazing how firm our sacred oath remained, once death itself loomed—what, did they think they could hide from the Angel of Death in a box and save their souls?

"But when one befriends people who are a bit thoughtless and cowardly one has to put up with a lot, I suppose," he said to himself, fashioning himself a walking stick and proceeding to hobble along the road. His thirst and hunger knew no bounds, but who could he complain to about that? After all, there was not a single house in sight along the road. No one was even passing by. There in the middle of the road he did happen to see a person's footprint, though. In fact, it looked rather like a *frightened* person's footprint.

"I'll bet that was them, dashing away in fear. When you look at their faces, you know, you'd think they were men, but their hearts sure show them to be women." He sped up, hoping that they'd be waiting for him at the fork in the road, the one that headed off toward Sipirok. Or maybe they'd come walking out of the forest at any moment to see what was happening there on the road. But his fond hopes came to nothing, for Raja Sun was already high overhead and no image of anyone at all passed by on the highway.

Very carefully he checked out the possibility of there being someone on the Sipirok road. But there was no one. "Ah," he said to himself, drawing in a long breath, rather without hope: "Those two guys have run off on me."

Without any warning . . . "*Hor!*" said a pony carriage coming from Sipirok. When he got a look at the person in the carriage he felt as if he knew him somehow. "Oh, right, today is Friday, yesterday was Thursday, which is market day in Sipirok. So this must be a Sidimpuan merchant in this carriage going home to Sidimpuan."

"Now, who exactly is in that carriage?" the Reader wonders, I should think. Well, you surely are going to find out who that fellow might turn out to be.

Well, look, okay, so that we don't all grow too anxious and bothered, it is perhaps best that we clarify matters immediately. The man in the carriage was the merchant Awaiting-Riches, an important rubber dealer from Sidimpuan. And for his part, too, this man had been taking a careful look at the guy hobbling along the road very slowly and painfully. The closer the merchant got to the fellow the more he felt in his inner self that he might know him. So he slowed the carriage down as he came to the spot where the man was going along all by himself. And, amazingly enough—

Jamus are restorative potions made from herbs and ground forest substances.

why, it was none other than—it was no different from—why, look, it was someone he knew!

"Good heavens. . . . It's you, Pandingkar Moedo, isn't it? Where on earth could you be coming from this early in the morning, all bent over a walking cane like this? Lord, you're as weak and pale as an invalid, and your clothes are all caked with mud. . . . Whatever happened to you last night?" asked Awaiting Riches anxiously, stepping down from the carriage.

"Ah . . . nothing really happened to me one way or the other, but when it's your appointed time to die what can you do. . . ?"

"Well, what happened?" asked Awaiting Riches.

"I'm really a bit ashamed to relate the story, for no matter how it's put it'll seem like I'm at fault. I feel as though I spit upward and it came back and smacked me on the forehead. So maybe the only thing left for me to do is cultivate patience," said Pandingkar Moedo in a rather pathetic voice.

"Well, in that case you just get on into the carriage here so that we can proceed to Sidimpuan together. If you try to progress the way you're creeping along now it will take you two or three days to get there. You don't even have any medicine to heal your ailments. When bad luck befalls you, things get worse and worse, don't they?"

"Thank you for your help! But you go on ahead. Let me just hobble along the road here—I guess I'll get there when I arrive."

"Ah, don't you worry about the cost of the carriage ride! I've already paid Raja Carriage Driver, now isn't that so!?" he asked the guy leading the horse along the way.

"And, even if you're not paying a cent for the ride wouldn't I have stopped for Pandingkar Moedo anyway? Why, I'd stop even for some nonacquaintance if he was having this much difficulty! So, come on, let's go," said Raja Carriage Driver, helping Pandingkar Moedo along the road toward the carriage.

"Alhamdulillah. . . . I feel like I'm being aided across the Final Sirotholmustakim Bridge into the World Hereafter,* I feel so lousy," said Pandingkar Moedo, finally finding a seat in the carriage. "Ah," he went on to say, sucking in his spit because his throat was so parched from thirst and hunger.

Awaiting Riches immediately understood that Pandingkar Moedo was thirsty and hungry, not to mention exhausted from lack of sleep. So he told Raja Carriage Driver to make the horse's hoofbeats speed up. Once they had arrived at Malim Maradjo's rice stall beside the Sitorbisan River, Awaiting Riches said, "Let's stop awhile!" And he ordered up some hot coffee and a plate of rice from the rice stall keeper. "All right now! Be sure to put lots of sugar into that coffee, and let's make it venison curry from Padang Bolak that you spoon over the rice!"

"All right," said the proprietor, seeing to the food that the toke† had ordered.And here came Malim Maradjo's underling bringing in the food, and Awaiting Riches asked Pandingkar Moedo: "Are you sure you don't want some of

---

*A common reference in Muslim Sumatra.

†The shopkeeper. This term was often addressed specifically to Chinese shopkeepers in Sumatra, but here the word is used in a more general sense.

this Green Fish curry? It's real sweet and good. . . . And let's put in some cucumber tree fruit to add a bit of tartness. Come on, take three cans full of rice so you'll get enough to eat here. It's not as if we're people who've never met before and have to hold back when they eat with each other," said Awaiting Riches.

"Oh . . . Raja Carriage Driver, you come on in, too, so we can all eat. Take the harness off the horse and get him out of the heat."

"Well, all right—but Shopkeeper should go first while I take the harness off the horse," said Raja Carriage Driver, leading the horse to the rice field in front of the rice stall to graze.

"Hurry up! Your food's already laid out on the table and it'll get cold if you don't watch out."

"So, let's say Bismillah and dig right in, friends," said Awaiting Riches.

"Yes. . . . I'll just drink this coffee first, my throat's so dry," said Pandingkar Moedo, sipping the sugared coffee carefully.

Then Raja Carriage Driver came in and sat with them. When he had just so much as poured a tiny bit of the soup from the tart-tasting fish stew onto his rice he immediately grabbed a big scoop of it and tossed it slickly down his throat. He polished it off with only one or two cursory chews.

"Now, *this* is the reason I keep coming back to Angkola here, even if the horse cart trade isn't all that good over here! It's sure better than hiring myself out as a coolie up in Toba! Because, over there, when you're in a food stall up there, why, they just take a handful of some ferns and peel the skins off a bit and pretend to make a decent curry out of that. And when they actually *do* have fish in the curry it's always saltier than sea salt," he said, scooping up the rice quick as lightning from his coconut shell.

"Ha, ha . . . it's all that salty, is it? You say the fish is saltier than sea salt?" asked the rice stall owner, chuckling to himself.

"Yeah, that's really how it is over there, and if you don't believe it just consider: starting from Raja Rattan's rice stall at the Simajambu River and going on up the road to Hobal's Dad's rice stall there at Onan Sarulla, *all* their curries are like that. Look, if you eat their food and then you start sweating and then you get out in the sun and dry off, you'll start to feel the little grains of salt all along your back."

"Oh, brother . . . Oh, Lord," said Pandingkar Moedo, and all the other people in the rice stall laughed uproariously, too.

"Well, then, do you feel a bit better now, Pandingkar Moedo? asked Awaiting Riches.

"I do, yes, yes . . . for Raja Carriage Driver has certainly made my food taste better. Seeing him shovel in the rice by the great handful I've wanted to eat more, too. I do feel better. Now I can see the housepost quite clearly, whereas before, wow! I couldn't see farther than the distance to the yoke on the carriage horse."

"Well, then, let's just harness up our old horse, Raja Carriage Driver. It's already getting on in the day," said Awaiting Riches.

"It's all ready, Shopkeeper. Let's set off."

"Let's go, then, Pandingkar Moedo," said the shopkeeper, stepping into the carriage.

Raja Carriage Driver gave the horse a tiny tap with the whip and off he trotted, *pak-pak, pak-pak, pak-pak,* pulling the cart behind him. Once they got past Pargarutan, Awaiting Riches spoke up: "Well, as for me, Pandingkar Moedo, I admit to still being a bit hazy about what could have left you wandering about, bent over like that, on the road to Padang Bolak. As if you'd lost your companions, you know? Try explaining it a bit to us."

"Ah, I'm embarrassed to tell you about it. But if you must know what happened then so be it," said Pandingkar Moedo.

"Well, a while back . . . the three of us decided to go gathering rubber sap out at Simincak Peak. Word has it that there's so much there that even blind folks can gather it up without much trouble. Well, to tell the truth, I was a bit worried, since I had never done that sort of work before, gathering forest rubber. However, since I was sure that Rangga Poerik and Rangga Balian would help me—they had assured me that they did this sort of thing all the time—I went along with the plan. Our oath to each other was: we would always be of a single death, of a single life. And we made that oath even firmer with a sacred promise that no matter what might happen none of us would leave a companion behind. Once we got to Simincak Peak, we saw all that forest rubber, and right away we started to gather it. In just one day we got about half a shoulder load. And that was high-quality sap, too. Apparently, however, if one is beset with bad luck, one can't just pick what's going to happen, for on the second night I came down with a bad chill and fever. So, they were taking me home, and they left all the sap and our provisions behind. Apparently, once we arrived at Lake Bobak a great hailstorm rolled in—and a big tiger tried to capture me. But I didn't really know a thing about any of this, for I was unconscious from the fever. Apparently, they were so afraid when they saw the tiger that they abandoned me and ran off—and where they went I don't know. I only saw their footprints, leading this way. The hard wind and the tiger's fearsome cry became a healing charm, a good luck protective amulet for me, cooling my soul. For by dawn I was all right again. I felt no more illness in my body. I investigated the spot where I was, and it appeared that I had been rolled over and over by that tiger the whole night long. Golly, it sure was lucky I knew that tiger beforehand! If that hadn't been the case, I think he would have torn me in two. I looked at my clothes and saw that they were all damp and caked with mud.

"Ra-*pak!* . . ." said the carriage wheels. "Oh Lord, we're all going to die!" said the shopkeeper. "Why are you driving on the edge of the road like that, Raja Carriage Driver? What are you thinking?"

"Oh, hey, sorry, sorry—it's just that listening to Pandingkar Moedo's story made me lose my head."

"Well, look, just be careful, will you, so we don't tip over and land in the ditch. But, you know, you're right: this story really is something," said the shopkeeper. "The pair of them should be punished, you know. If we should happen to meet up with them, let's turn them right over to the authorities, for people who break faith with others must be punished under law in accordance with the official statutes. Such people are just like murderers. Really, your story quite shocks me. . . . And, now, just what exactly made you say you were already somewhat acquainted with this tiger?" asked Awaiting Riches.

"Oh, well . . . a while back, when I was taking lessons from a guru, I happened to confront that particular tiger. That's why I said I knew him, for I saw from his pawprint that one of his toes was wider than normal. I had noticed that when we were fighting. So, once he realized that I was the fellow in trouble he applied magical medical potions to me. If that had not been the case how could I ever have recovered from such a severe illness in just one night?" asked Pandingkar Moedo.

"Oh . . . so that's how your travels went, did they? At least now you understand people's ways of thinking a bit better, don't you? Now you're not so naive. Why, those two guys, even though they've been your followers for years and years, once hardship came they sure didn't keep their promises, did they? Well, look, no use fretting over it! If you're on the lookout to make a few pennies let's just the two of us go into business together, selling merchandise at the markets, all right? For at the moment I happen to be looking for someone to help me conduct my business and make it grow. If God affords us good fortune, this business can truly expand and prosper," declared the shopkeeper.

"Thank you, Shopkeeper, thank you, indeed! Indeed! If you want to befriend me, then I want to befriend you back ten times as much," said Pandingkar Moedo.

About three o'clock in the afternoon they arrived in Sidimpuan, and Awaiting Riches took Pandingkar Moedo to his house straightaway. Sighs and regrets issued copiously from Pandingkar Moedo's mother at seeing her only child's sufferings. Her only child—just the one leaf's worth of him!—well, what she felt was beyond words. She did not know how to thank Awaiting Riches enough for delivering Pandingkar Moedo from his many difficulties, especially when she heard that they had decided to go into business together.

So, once they had welcomed Pandingkar Moedo back with a ceremonial meal of health-securing rice and a hard-boiled egg, to firm up his soul and keep him safe from dangers, Awaiting Riches headed for home in the main marketplace.[19]

6

*From Bad to Worse**

Once Pandingkar Moedo was feeling a bit healthier and had recovered, he did go on over to the main marketplace to find Awaiting Riches and begin his new job, the one they had discussed. When Pandingkar Moedo was still far off in the distance Awaiting Riches was already waving a hearty greeting. The shopkeeper's wife hurried to warm up the coffee. "So, you're feeling better, then?"

"Hopefully so—and thanks to your prayers, I do feel fine. My strength has come back just like before," said Pandingkar Moedo.

Not too long afterward along came Awaiting Riches's wife, his dear house companion, bringing coffee into the central room of the house and going on to say: "Drink your coffee, Younger Lineage Companion,[1] so you'll keep feeling good. And is our Mother well, over there on the other side of town?"

"Oh yes, she's just fine," said Pandingkar Moedo.

"Good, good! Now you be sure to tell them to come over to the house when they come on market day so we can get to know each other," said Awaiting Riches's wife.

Starting on that day, they worked together as a team, selling merchandise at the market. Pandingkar Moedo would slip a little bit of the money his Mother had sent to him into the till to add a little to their capital and also so that Awaiting Riches would believe he was serious about being in commerce.

"Ah, come on, your mother doesn't really have to fork out the pennies in her change purse to help us: we have enough capital already. If we're lucky we'll only have to use the profits that I already have right here to advance our business. But, all right, so that our business will prosper, I'll take the money anyway! After all, change purse funds that come from our own parents always bring luck," said Awaiting Riches, accepting the money.

At first Awaiting Riches taught Pandingkar Moedo all about the politics of selling things: about calculating a price and bargaining back and forth like kids playing tug of war. "If someone comes to bargain about some piece of merchandise that you have to sell, you have to look first at his face to see if he's really determined to buy this thing. If he is, you can stretch things out a bit, to jack up the price, til you snare him with all this talking back and forth. But if he's not really taken with the piece of merchandise, well, you have to have lots of smart martial arts moves so that he somehow accepts the price anyway. In short, one must have a thousand little strategies for selling your merchandise, as well as a good sense for what's in your sparring partner's heart."

---

*Literally, the chapter title reads "If You Have Luck as Bad as an Empty Gingerroot, That's Not All! Fungus Will Attack Your Salt Supplies, Too." This is a well-known proverb.

"Oh . . . so that's why the buyer is so often like a fish caught in a basket trap. Merchants really do have to have superior strategies, don't they?"

"You bet . . ." said Awaiting Riches.

The shopkeepers would work late into the day; their enterprise prospered. They eventually had agents in all of the little domains surrounding Sidimpuan. When it was market day in Sipirok they would go over there, and the same would be the case if it was market day in Sitinjak, Sigalangan, Saromatinggi on the way to Siabu in Panyabungan, and in Gunung Tua Batangonang (in Padang Bolak). Pandingkar Moedo had to learn the business first, and then they began to divide the job of going around to the markets in all the villages just mentioned.

Since their profits were so good and abundant, their enterprise became quite well known, even famous, all over Angkola and well into the surrounding domains. Birds will always flock to the trees that are full of fruit, after all, and after such creatures have consumed their fill they'll sit on a branch, preen their feathers, and break into song. We humans are like that, too: wherever there's a prosperous way of life to be seen, that's where people will flock. And so it was that veritable multitudes of people brought their goods into Awaiting Riches's shop. The shopowners would always weigh the goods and then hand over the money they owed without the least hesitation. People liked that, all right. There was never any delay in getting your money! The owners of the merchandise just sold would chuckle happily to themselves, and Awaiting Riches and Pandingkar Moedo would simply rake in their profits.

One time, when there was a bit of free time from work, when the sun hung straight overhead, when it beat down intensely, everyone was just sitting around the shop sort of thinking about going over to the White River to wash. Noon prayers were approaching. "*Taktakuwak koooooook . . .*" said the voice of the teenage rooster sunning himself as he perched on a branch of a sweet cucumber tree. "*Ke-rook!*" said the voice of his hen, answering him. The sound's loneliness struck deep hidden chords in the heart.

At such times, Awaiting Riches's dear wife would come close to the shopkeeper, yawning sleepily, and after sitting down next to him she would joke: "Today certainly is hot—and there aren't many folks around, are there? It makes you feel lonely; it opens up feelings of deep suffering and pain."

"Ha ha ha, now whatever could be making you lonely, since Shopkeeper's right here beside you," asked Pandingkar Moedo.

"Oh, friend. . . . It is not because of that that I talk about deep loneliness and pain, but it's at times when I remember the past and think of the places where I used to play as a girl and of my parents—all because the young roosters out in the gardens beyond the village always used to sound just like that."[2]

"So, even a chicken's squawk can make you feel lonely, it seems? And open up deep stores of pain and suffering? That's that's just weird," said Pandingkar Moedo.

"Oh, I'd say differently, my friend. May I be very frank? Is that all right?" asked the shopkeeper's wife.

"Well, there's nothing wrong with that," they all declared, getting ready to listen.

"Now, it's clear that you've already set your feet upon the ground in all the little outlying domains around here by this time. Didn't you maybe see something that might turn out to be a good plaything?"[3]

"*Tor!*" went that message as it sped straight toward Pandingkar Moedo's heart—for he knew very well what the shopkeeper's wife meant with her words. However, he didn't show that he knew. He only said the following: "Now, what sort of plaything or playmate might you be talking about? Is it a thing, or an animal, or maybe an article of clothing?"

"Some of them are that . . . but, to tell the truth, I am talking about a plaything for the heart, about someone who's good at making you happy, someone who brings you joy,"[4] said the shopkeeper's wife.

Pandingkar Moedo found that these words made electric contact with his heart.[5] Nevertheless, he kept pretending that he didn't know what she was talking about. So, he said: "It's really hard to follow what you're saying. I do not know the meaning of your words, maybe because I'm so ignorant. . . . Shopkeeper, what do Older Lineage Companion's words mean?"

"Ah, you know their intention well enough. And you can bet she'll be able to tell you a lot about it, too," said the shopkeeper.

"Now, look, I have a handsome rooster already outfitted with plaited leg-rings for cockfighting—haven't you folks maybe seen a youngish hen who can become his good companion of a single roosting place?"

"But, golly, you're talking about so many chickens they're hard to keep up with. We can just buy one at the market, can't we, and be done with it?" asked Pandingkar Moedo.

"Yeah, but even though there are lots of them there, many don't make good, tame, domestic chickens around the house yard, for one reason or another," said the shopkeeper's wife.

"But I've gotten away from what your older lineage companion was saying to you, Pandingkar Moedo. She is actually telling you to go get married, to become a full adult, according to *adat*.[6] And that's a good thing, too. You will enjoy traversing the passage to adulthood. The real meaning of the "plaything for the heart" she was talking about is a girl. So what do you say? Have you perhaps spied someone's pretty daughter here near the main marketplace or in any of the small villages we have happened to visit?" asked the shopkeeper.

"You, you sure know a lot of things! You said 'a hen,' but you meant a girl. But girls for brides can be hard to find, you know—at least, ones who are willing to get married."

"Oh, the marketplace is full of girls. In fact, you can have your choice of pretty faces. Whatever type you might want, she's available: shopkeepers' daughters, *malims'* daughters, salaried folks' daughters, rich folks' daughters—well, there are lots and lots of each type. And you can have your choice of faces, too. There are pretty ones, and snooty, stuck-up ones, and fetching cute ones, and lively, energetic ones, a few real genuine knockouts, and some pretty, dark-faced ones and light-faced, good-looking girls who are about as white as kapok trees. And then there are even some of those light buff-colored ones everyone's always talking about these days. Why, there are even ones so white that the water can be seen going down their throats when they swallow.[7] In short, you can pretty much have your pick," said the shopkeeper's wife.

"Ha ha ha . . ." said Pandingkar Moedo, "but who is going to want me, seeing as I haven't even got a thin rattan mat to my name?"

"Now, just as long as you are willing! And as for rattan mats, well, look, if there are two of you in the house to share meals then isn't that two people to share in great good fortune, too? And if there happen to be three to be fed, well, that's three to enjoy all that good luck and good living! So, what are you afraid of? Look, if no girl in the marketplace happens to have struck your fancy then just keep an eye out when you're on your market rounds. *Surely* you can find her, no matter what type it is you want. But, remember:

Muda boru sian Sipirok	Now, as for girls from Sipirok
Na torkis jana na marroha	They're robust and sensible
Na basa na malo marorot	Polite and adept at caring for little kids
Na pantun tu dongan tu hula	Well mannered to friends and relations.
Muda boru sian Sitindjak	Now, as for girls from Sitinjak
Na malo mangatur manggana	They're adept at organizing things and getting
Na rama maradopkon halak	projects under way
Na olo tu hatuananna	Friendly, too, with folks
	Not to mention agreeable to their good *tuans*.
Muda boru kan Goenoengtoea	Now as for girls from Gunungtua
Na bajan mangalage hata	They're adept at joining words together
Bahat do i maroban tua	And that, of course, brings great good fortune
Muda na dung disolon mata	If they're the ones who've caught your eye.
Muda boru kan Pargaroetan	Now, as for girls from Pargarutan
Na pantun maradopkon	They're well mannered to friends
Denggan ma tu manuk pautan	*Very* good to their young cocks.*
Dongan sapinggan sapanganan	Her pal of a single dinner plate and drink.
Muda boru kan Sigalangan	Now, as for girls from Sigalangan
Nada adjaran be marroha	They sure don't need any extra instruction
Tama ma dongan sajalangan	They're friendly to all comers
Na olo di ganop hatiha	Saying "yes" at every moment.
Muda boru sian Siaboe	Now, as for girls from Siabu
Sadiahon hian tintin langkitang	You'd better get a little snail ring ready
Manyammanyam ni na marbaju	A tiny plaything for the girls old enough now
Baen patorkiskon pamatang.	to wear *kebaya* jackets
	A toy to make their bodies grow robust.

"Ha ha ha, oh, wow . . ." they all laughed merrily at the words of the shop-keeper's wife's song.

Pandingkar Moedo put in the last word: "Ah . . . no, my friend . . . my heart doesn't feel right agreeing yet to what you're asking. Maybe it's better that I just concentrate

---

Author's note. That means friendly toward Pandingkar Moedo.

on earning a living before I go getting married and all. Come on, let's go say our prayers. It's getting on toward noon."

"Yes, saying your prayers is a good idea. After all, that's the money you pay to get into heaven, isn't it? But you keep talking over what we've been discussing," said the shopkeeper's wife as she left.

Pandingkar Moedo set on off for the White River. After he had finished bathing there he went to the main mosque to say his prayers. Once he had bowed his head and paid respect to God, he pronounced the holy syllables: "Astagafiru'llah . . ." and the words of the shopkeeper's wife really began to strike home with him. He meditated quietly, saying, "Astagafiru'llah." Then he went on to say: "All right, then, but I really don't want any of the girls from here in town. Even if they are sweet and good natured, even if they have teeth as white as the shining trout flickering lightly in the rushing river."

Now let us switch to his weighty efforts to search for a soul mate fit to be the companion with whom he'll grow old.

In all the various domains that he happened to visit he had never really paid attention to the behavior of people's daughters, for it had never seriously occurred to him that he was going to take a bride. So, given this, a notion occurred to him: he should keep a close eye on the faces and behavior among the young unmarried girls, among the maidens in all the small realms that he normally visited for business. As the proverb says: "If you hurry you'll stub your toe on a rock, but if you go slow you'll surely get what you're waiting for."

Trying to locate a companion to grow old with is just like that: a difficult proposition. For if you move too fast and are in too much of a hurry you'll live to regret it.

Now, all of you members of the general public[8] who are reading this story: surely all of you know that Pandingkar Moedo was quite famous and renowned, especially after he won the sparring contest at the feast of merit in Batunadua. He had definitely entered the ranks of the famous, but he was also highly accomplished in the sorcery arts and in spell casting and spell removing, as well as in the courtship arts of Young Leaves on the Tree of Life.[9] Now normally, of course, he didn't use this knowledge in his everyday life, but when you need something, well, you use it! What Awaiting Riches's wife had told him was truly affecting. It had struck home with him, but he didn't yet know in what direction his feet should point in order to find his true love, to find the one to become his companion into old age.

Finally, he went to consult with the *datu*-diviner, who endeavored to construct a special augury knife, a power knife that had no handle. This he spun around in a circle. Whatever direction the divination advice indicated, that is exactly where he would go.

Once the handleless knife had come to a stop he noted the direction in which it was pointed: toward Angkola Jae. "Well, fine, in that case, if that's what's to be, that will be for the best, I am sure."

One fine day, none other than Sigalangan market day, he traveled there to contact the forest rubber agents and the forest product brokers in order to buy his goods from them. After he'd obtained his merchandise he looked around for any girls who might be likely soul companions. So, he thought, he'd be able to accomplish two things at once, kill two birds with one stone, or, as the saying goes, by eating red ground cherry stew he would not only get his belly full but would succeed in killing all the worms in there, too. Or, as another saying goes, you swing your axe once and two trees fall; you take a single swipe at the *sandurut* plant and you cut down two at once.

That morning, as he pulled the buggy along, the horse's steps were different from normal. Usually the creature was unruly, but today he ran along so smoothly that he was sort of swinging you in a baby sling. Pandingkar Moedo didn't pay much attention to that—"Oh, he must have eaten a bunch of especially tasty grass last evening," he said to himself. Trot-trot, trot-trot, trot-trot.

Look, over there . . . near Sigalangan, over to the right side, as you're approaching the village: why, there's a stretch of garden land and in the garden a rich stand of yellow corn. The garden belonged to Djaimbaran, a hard-working and industrious man, still robust in his middle years. At the edge of this garden he had constructed a little stall for selling fried bananas and boiled corn on the cob, the rich produce from the garden. On market days he'd have the water boiling for coffee, too, to sell as an accompaniment for the fried bananas and boiled corn. The little stall had a good solid shape as well as a floor made of neatly split bamboo. The side facing the road didn't have a wall, so that the people who stopped there would have a good view. Djaimbaran's wife was clever and well scrubbed as well as well spoken and adept at conversing with the general public.[10] This woman always wore a black sarong and a neat reddish jacket, while on her head she would wear a lovely, delicate, rectangular scarf. All who caught sight of her would praise her neatness and good looks.

One fine morning, the woman had just set the fried bananas and the pounded rice flour on her sales table. She had laid out the boiled corncobs there, too, while they were still steaming hot. Without any warning, "*Jo-bos!*" said Pandingkar Moedo's buggy from up the road. When they'd arrived at the food stall the horse came to a sudden halt. Now, Pandingkar Moedo had not *asked* the horse to stop there, but because he had Pandingkar Moedo decided to stop, too. And then, too, he was attracted by the luscious smell of all that hot steaming corn. Since Mr. Middle Continent—that is, his belly—was asking to be fed he decided to stop there for some hot coffee.

"Maybe you people could give me a mug of coffee and some of the snacks that go with it," said Pandingkar Moedo, sitting down in the bamboo stall.

"Well, all right," said the woman, going on to fill his order.

As she was getting his coffee ready Pandingkar Moedo's eyes gazed constantly around him, noting how extremely clean and orderly the stall owner looked. He was quite taken aback to note how happy and good-natured she seemed.

"Well, I guess it's a case of, 'Be mannerly to life, uncivil to death?'" said Pandingkar Moedo to himself. He went on to say, out loud: "And what might your clan be so that I might know the appropriate kin term of address to use with you?"

"Now, whyever would you want to know that?" asked the woman, surprised.

"Well, so that I'll know how I stand with you," said Pandingkar Moedo.

"Heh, heh . . . well, all right. As for my clan, it's Batubara, but the one who took me for his wife is from the Dalimunte clan," said the woman.

"Well, indeed, then! Fellow family member, that's just fine, for that means that I can call you Nantulang, my potential wife's mother, my mother's brother's wife, according to polite kin term talk."[11]

"Fine, then, but I don't have any daughter yet, so why are you calling me Mother's Brother's Wife?"

"But surely I'm just following proper polite kin term talk standards! It doesn't just have to be because of a daughter that I call you Mother's Brother's Wife, does it? Let's go ahead and employ that usage, no matter what," said Pandingkar Moedo, sipping his coffee.

Once he had finished folks walking to market started to come by. He asked the woman's permission to leave. "Well, just take my mug here, Mother's Brother's Wife. I have to take my leave of you—I suspect people are milling around the marketplace by now."

"All right, Bere,"* said the woman.

After Pandingkar Moedo had gone far off in the distance she washed his mug and took the money the fellow had left her. When she toted up the cost of the coffee and fried bananas she found that that was exactly the sum she had asked him for when he had finished his coffee. "Ah, my . . . that fellow is adept at figuring out what is in my thoughts, isn't he? I would suspect he is a good friendly sort."

When he arrived at the marketplace Pandingkar Moedo set about going hither and yon buying up forest rubber, gutta percha, climber rubber, and so on. "Weigh this," "Pay for that," "Haul that over to the cart" was all that was heard from the very large number of folks buying and selling merchandise. When the sun had risen directly overhead, Pandingkar Moedo went home to Sidimpuan, for he had already loaded all the goods he had bought into his cart. Because he had forgotten the good cheer and kindheartedness of the woman he had called his potential wife's mother he did not stop again at their food stall on the way home. He was already far past it when he remembered them. "Ah, on the next market day I shall go drink coffee there again at the fried food stall," he said to himself. And the woman herself didn't give much thought to the man who had passed by, for folks were besieging her with orders for fried bananas and boiled corn. But from that day on, whenever it got to be market day in Sigalangan, Pandingkar Moedo would stop there in the morning to have coffee.

If close family comes to visit, well, you do get a bit bold and brave and forward with them. If folks are already acquainted with each other, hesitancy and embarrassment vanish. And so it was that sometimes while he was sitting there drinking his coffee the woman would ask him questions. "Well, Husband's Sister's Son, what exactly is your reason for coming back here to visit each and every market day?"

"Ah, you know, Mother's Brother's Wife—I sort of work in commerce, you know. Just always on the lookout to buy rubber and gutta percha and products like that, to sell in Sibolga."

*Husband's sister's child, potential son-in-law.

"Oh my, indeed, well now. . . . That's nice, Nephew. It doesn't really matter much how we make our living now, does it?" But the woman decided to start paying very close attention to the commerce in which the man was engaged. Was he perhaps just a minor sort of merchant or maybe a very rich and major one? So whenever Pandingkar Moedo would go off to the market she would put her clothes on and go there, too—and she would keep a close watch on what sort of thing he was selling and with whom he dealt. And this would continue until he was ready to go home.

When she got to the market she would immediately set to seeing exactly what this young man was selling and what sort of commerce he practiced.

"Why, folks are really thronging around him to sell him their forest rubber, aren't they?" And just as soon as they'd agreed on the price Pandingkar Moedo would pay out the money. The forest rubber, gutta percha, and the strips of rattan, too, would be layered in thick piles on his cart, but the young man would still be busy weighing goods on his scale and paying the price for his purchases. From her hiding place the woman figured that he was raking in not just hundreds but thousands of rupiah.

"Oh . . . this man really is something. He is most definitely not just any merchant. If he is not married yet, well, then it is best that he be presented with a bride, a well-mannered and soft-spoken one, I should think. Now, hmmmm, it makes one wonder. Do you think he would take to little Taring (for that was the name of her daughter)? But, indeed, since they are really still so young they shouldn't be getting into that sort of thing, I guess. Ah, but I sure wish he was one's actual, very own nephew. *Then* I'd be pretty happy, I must say," said the woman to herself as she stole glances at him out of the corner of her eye.

And from that spot she sidled over to the stall where Pandingkar Moedo was selling his goods. Pretending not to do it on purpose she insinuated herself into the midst of the crowd milling around there and she ran smack into him.

"Oh! Are you out shopping, Mother's Brother's Wife?" asked Pandingkar Moedo, a bit embarrassed since the woman had come upon him so suddenly.

"Ha ha . . . no, not that. One's nephew is certainly being thronged by people here. No, I'm just browsing, looking for a few cheap betel leaves to buy. And what are you shopping for here?"

"But, Mother's Brother's Wife, all this—forest rubber, gutta percha, rattan. What can folks do, after all, if they want to go into commerce and they don't have any capital? They just sort of have to sun-dry a little tough buffalo hide to have something to hawk at the market, I suppose."

"Yes, that's true, Nephew, people do support themselves with different sorts of commerce, although everybody is after the same thing, I guess: a bit of money. Now you go ahead and finish, Nephew, and I'll just be going on back home. Your mother's brother, your good Tulang,* will get angry if I'm late."

All the way home, along the road, the woman's thoughts kept turning over and over: "Is this man still a youngster or does he have a wife? What strategy can I

---

*Your mother's brother, the father of your potential wife.

use to find out for sure? Perhaps it's best that I quiz him when he comes by so I'll know for sure if he's a kid or an adult with a wife already." When she got back to her garden she set to work as she always did, waiting for Pandingkar Moedo to pass by. Once the sun was directly overhead, Pandingkar Moedo did indeed set off toward home from the market. When he reached the front awning of the fried snacks stand he said: "Well, here I am, Mother's Brother's Wife . . . !"

"Oh, gee, well. . . . Do stop in for a while, Nephew, and have some coffee. My, you look hot today. There's still lots of daylight left, so there's no danger of night overtaking you later, on your journey home."

"Oh, perhaps another time, Mother's Brother's Wife. Don't worry, I'll be coming back by here again."

"Well, fine, Nephew. But now be sure to take along two or three cobs of corn as little gifts to my grandchild back at your house. Just say the word and we'll get them ready. Even though this is all I have to send him or her, what can you do, after all, when you're just poor folks?"

"Ha, ha. . . . No need to do that, Mother's Brother's Wife. You don't have any little grandchild yet—and, in fact, your daughter is still living in her father's house![12] So who would I give your little treats to?"

"God Above . . . I must ask forgiveness of you, Nephew. Now, don't think I was teasing you. I'm really a good-hearted sort. But, Nephew, maybe I could give these to your parents, do you think? I've already shucked this corn."

"Ah, well, who am I to refuse a windfall? Just bring them over here," said Pandingkar Moedo enthusiastically.

Once he had gone home the woman set to thinking some more: "Since this fellow is still an unmarried young man I think it would be a real fine idea to give him a good look at Si Taring. Maybe their hearts would meet, who knows? Maybe they would hit it off. But how to do that? If I make Taring stand here and fry bananas like she was somebody else's daughter it would be as if I were putting their daughter on display for sale and ignoring mine. After all, you always have to jack up the price a bit; you have to be as clever as the otter hiding in the stream, hiding what you need to, showing only what you must. Well, all right, then. . . . After all, I was once a young girl myself, and I know how to hook men's gazes on a line and reel them in. So, let me just find a way to snare his heart a bit."

One day turned into the next, and seven days passed. It was market day in Sigalangan again, and as usual Pandingkar Moedo showed up. So near daybreak the woman walked into her banana garden and gathered up some fruit, and then she set quickly to cooking up her stocks of fritters. Without Taring knowing it, the woman snitched her headscarf (which had delicate lace all along one edge) and tied it to the top of Pandingkar Moedo's usual chair. It was no more than eight in the morning when Pandingkar Moedo's horse and buggy came by and stopped at the fried fruit stall.

"So, is our coffee ready, Mother's Brother's Wife?" he asked, coming into the stand.

"Gracious me. . . . So, you're here, are you, Nephew? Take a seat so I can hurry this coffee along. I'll bet you're thirsty, aren't you?" asked the woman, patting him gently as she spoke. Once everything was ready she said: "Now, drink your coffee, Nephew, so the bananas don't get cold. Fried bananas taste better when they're piping hot. And look, the corn I'm roasting is done, too. Would you like to have some, Bere? That's just the thing for a fine young man like you."

"Well, okay, bring some here, Mother's Brother's Wife. It sure smells great."

While Pandingkar Moedo was gnawing so hard on the corn that his teeth got loose, he happened to cast his eyes upward and he saw the scarf. "Eh . . . do these folks have an adolescent daughter, then? Where have they been hiding her all this time? I'll bet it's their daughter who owns this scarf; she's pretty and good hearted, too, I'll bet, because kids are always chips off the old block." Pandingkar Moedo was not paying much attention to the coffee, fried bananas, or corn on the cob, since his eyes remained fastened on that lacy scarf.

All the while the woman stole glances at Pandingkar Moedo as he was looking at the scarf. But he didn't notice that his gaze was being spied on.

"Well, here's this cup to wash, Mother's Brother's Wife. It's getting on in the day, and the marketplace must be getting crowded."

"All right, Nephew, you go on along. People will be getting bored having to stand around and wait for you."

Then she thought to herself: "All right, now what plan shall I follow when Pandingkar Moedo comes back here once the market is over? I'll have to come up with a particularly subtle bird trap to snare this fellow. I'm afraid he'll get away before he locks his gaze on Taring."

When the sun was setting in the west Pandingkar Moedo came back from the market. He had taken the notion to stop there a while in order to determine once and for all who owned that scarf. For, if it belonged to someone who actually lived there, it wasn't really very nice for the scarf to just be tied to a chair, was it?

When the woman had no more than caught sight of Pandingkar Moedo arriving she bustled around, muttering angrily to herself, pretending that she didn't know anyone was coming. And just what did she say?

"Lord, she tells me to buy her the weirdest things. . . . Nothing's ever pretty enough for her. . . . Or else it's not fancy and *refined* enough to suit her tastes. She's always asking: 'Oh, where did you get *that*?!' And me as impoverished as I am."

"Golly. . . . What's made you so angry, Mother's Brother's Wife?"

"Astagafiroellah. . . . Oh, you've dropped in, have you, Nephew? Have a seat. Oh me, oh my, there's just no dealing with her, if it's not one thing she wants it's another. And I think, oh, please, don't let folks find out that I don't have the resources to support her demands, but now here you are, hearing what I said. Honestly . . ."

"Well, what's wrong?!" asked Pandingkar Moedo.

"Oih, it's your Younger Lineage Companion, your *anggi*.* Here she is asking for a ton of fancy things, even though she knows very well that I am getting on in years here. Every market day she wants to buy a new set of clothes—and here we are, living in abject poverty."

---

*Men call their potential wives *anggi*—their companions of a single *kahanggi*.

"Ha ha. . . . But, Mother's Brother's Wife, that's the sort of wages parents have to pay. I was a child once, and I sure didn't know or care anything about the fact that my parents didn't have any money to hold in their hands."

"But, Nephew, why do you say 'the sort of wages parents have to pay' when it's the child who is going about asking for all these kinds of things?"

"Yes, that's certainly true, Mother's Brother's Wife. Our parents have raised and supported us all that time, and we won't ever be able to repay that. For once they've paid out wages like that to their children—that is, once they've gotten them all married—why, they're not supporting them anymore, are they? Now we have to support our own sons and daughters. And if we find that a difficult task, why, that's exactly how our parents felt trying to raise us. That's why I say the wages parents pay to their children do not really yield the children any profit. Rather, it all gets passed on to their grandchildren. Aren't the sons and daughters a person has replacements for his and her own father and mother? For, after all, we call our children Father and Mother when we speak to them every day.[13]

"Well, Nephew, what else is there to say? . . . You're right, you're right. In fact, I find all you say quite compatible, I do, when I think it over. God is merciful, after all," the woman said.

Once Pandingkar Moedo finished his coffee he got ready to go home. The woman did not neglect to say "May you be safe and healthy as you go along your way, Horas!"

"Now, next week, on the next market day, what can I do to show off Si Taring to him?! I think it's best that I have that child cut the kernels off the corn out in back of the coffee stall while I do the frying. And then when Pandingkar Moedo gets ready to leave I'll have Taring bring a bucket of water into the stall. That way he can't miss her. And he'll realize right away that I have a lovely, young, unmarried daughter." Her daughter and Pandingkar Moedo knew nothing of her plans and schemes.

Next market day, Pandingkar Moedo returned. Straightaway he stopped at the fried food stall. For her part, Taring was indeed shucking kernels off the corn behind the little building. Pandingkar Moedo had no more than sat down when a glass of coffee arrived, as it usually did. Behind the stall there were rustles and rumbles. Pandingkar Moedo thought that it must be his honored mother's brother,[14] harvesting corn back there. But with no advance warning Taring herself spoke: "Is this enough corn to fix, Mother?" Her mother pretended not to hear Taring's voice, making like she was fully occupied at the frying pan.

But in reality her eyes were sneaking little glances at Pandingkar Moedo, as he himself was glancing at her daughter.

When Pandingkar Moedo heard a human voice out there he immediately looked back toward the garden and saw Taring, shucking the corn. But she was not looking at him. Pandingkar Moedo was surprised and rather taken aback for a moment, for he thought back to the *manyang* spot out in the deep forest when they were all out at Simincak Peak. Her face looked exactly like the lovely visage of the girl he had seen then. He wiped his forehead and thought: "Maybe an evil one is going to come and carry me away again." But his mother's brother's wife spoke up: "No, that's enough corn, daughter. If we need more later we'll get it then."

"Well, then, should I go on back home to the village?"

"Yes . . . but bring back two more bamboo containers full of water if you could when you come back so that we'll have some more hot water for cooking."

"All right," said Taring as she went on off.

Pandingkar Moedo stole a glance at her, and the girl received this with a smiling laugh, a small shy one.

"Well, I'll just be on my way, Mother's Brother's Wife. You see to this glass. I suppose my buddies are already waiting for me at the market."

"Fine, Nephew . . ."

Once he had reached the road he quickly jumped into his buggy and the horse set off. His eyes did not neglect to look back at the cornfield. And, apparently, the girl was there at the edge of the field, looking studiously at him, too. But her mother didn't know this.

"Well, yes, indeed, girl! I believe you *are* the right one to be my companion in joyful times on this earth . . ." said Pandingkar Moedo as he went on off to the marketplace.

As promised, once Pandingkar Moedo's work was finished at the market he set off for home, and most certainly he did stop by the fried food stall again—and there was the girl carrying in the two containers of water. "Where should I put this water, Mother? I'm going to go back home right away."

"Put it over there, girl, and go on home. I'll put it away myself later."

"Ah, she sure is going home in a hurry," said Pandingkar Moedo to himself. Then he asked, "Is this the younger lineage companion that you were mad at about the clothes?"

"Yes, Nephew. She's got entirely too many wants and requests. She has no shame anymore. As this girl's mother I really suffer when I see how much better other people's daughters behave at the market, buying and selling things so nicely and politely."

"Oh, is that so, Mother's Brother's Wife? But it's just because she's still thinking like a child. Once she's been properly instructed, her embarrassing behavior will quickly disappear."

"One hopes so, Nephew, but what is to be done with her? She doesn't want to go out of the house like other people's daughters. If she's spending the day sewing or embroidering or cooking she never wants to budge. Everything has to be attended to there first, she'll say to herself.[15] Why, nothing else even occurs to her."

"Oh . . . so that's the way it is, is it?" said Pandingkar Moedo to himself. After drinking his coffee he asked leave to go on home.

"Well, all right, Nephew. Godspeed," said the woman.

Once Pandingkar Moedo had gone Taring asked her mother who that fellow was and why had he come there. "And why do you call him 'my own nephew'? Is it because you're trying to be family with everyone here during the roast corn season or because there really has been some family relationship for a long time?"[16]

"Oh my . . . you are the clever one, aren't you? If some man calls you Mother's Brother's Wife then surely you'll call him Nephew back, won't you? And if that fellow is a merchant from Sidimpuan and he comes to the area buying merchandise each and every market day, what's there to ask questions about?"

"Oh, shoot. . . . Aren't I even allowed to *ask* so I'll know if he's family or just some acquaintance?" asked her daughter, for this fellow had attracted her—especially when she heard that he was a merchant from Sidimpuan.

And, as for Pandingkar Moedo, there was no telling what his thoughts were. It was as if the visage of that radiant young woman flickered like a mysterious shadow in front of his eyes. He said to himself: "So, it *was* real, what I saw out there at Simincak Peak. Now, how can I get them to give me that girl so I can traverse the road to adulthood? When I think of how her parent has conducted herself over this long period of time I feel certain that woman would be happy to be family, but what can I do so that that girl herself wants to become my friend in joyful times, my companion in the daylight hours of life?" Pandingkar Moedo wasn't paying a bit of attention to all the twists and turns in the road between Sigalangan and Sidimpuan as he drove along. Thinking about the girl who had taken his fancy, it was as if all his bodily sufferings lifted off him. By the time he got back home he wasn't even aware that today had been market day in Sigalangan. It was only after he realized that fact that it occurred to him that he had just come from a big market.

Waiting for the next market day was an even longer proposition than usual. He didn't know what to do with himself as he stood behind the counter in the store. Often he'd just lie on his back and conk out, like someone who is deeply heartsick. Awaiting Riches was well aware of this behavior, but he surely didn't know what had brought it on. He tried all sorts of stratagems to cheer up Pandingkar Moedo. Nothing worked. So he suspected that this fellow was suffering an attack of deep loneliness and longing.

When it got to be market day in Sigalangan, Pandingkar Moedo put on his good clothes, and no later than 4 A.M. (the time for the dawn prayers) he hitched the horse to the buggy and off he set. The horse's tiredness disappeared upon starting off, but to Pandingkar Moedo the journey was still taking too much time. Thanks to the horse's swiftness the sun had not even risen two punting-pole lengths in the sky when they arrived at Sigalangan.

His mother's brother's wife was ready and waiting for his arrival, but she pretended that she had overslept. She pretended that daylight had overtaken her unexpectedly. Everything was scattered around the food stall in disorder. As soon as the buggy pulled up she rushed out and greeted him there in the road. "Now, why have you gotten here so *soon*, Nephew? The fire's not even lit yet. Ah . . . perhaps you're thirsty? Yes, of course you are. . . . Have a seat so I can get the water boiling for the coffee," the woman said, taking hold of him gently.

"Now, don't go getting things under way too soon, Mother's Brother's Wife. The day's still young. Just let me sit here and dry off the sweat for a moment. I got here this early because I think the horse was scared by something. I think maybe he was spooked by a tiger, I don't know." Pandingkar Moedo's eyes did nothing but gaze toward the stand of corn, hoping to see the girl he missed so much standing there again. But with a heavy heart he just sighed, like someone who is very tired. His mother's brother's wife understood what his sidelong glance meant, but she didn't show it. She kept this knowledge stored inside her, for she figured this guy was already hurting enough from lovesickness and longing.

Once the coffee was set in front of Pandingkar Moedo, she said: "Drink your coffee, Nephew, the day'll get late on you, and in a moment I have to leave for the market to buy some salt."[17]

"Then who is going to look after the goods here in the stall? Won't all that money disappear, what with people always coming in and out?"

"My thoughts exactly, Nephew, but you know I can't always be here. If my child is willing sometimes she'll keep watch at the coffee stall. I always wait until there aren't many customers."

"Well, just what is it you need to buy at the market? If it's only salt let me get some for you so you won't have to pay out any cash," said Pandingkar Moedo, groping about for a way to help her on her trip.

"'Buying salt' is just what it's called, Nephew. What I'm really after are the various things your little younger lineage companion needs. And that will cause me to be sort of late getting back." (What the woman really intended here was to explain that her daughter would be the one to sell the fries at the stall, and if Pandingkar Moedo wanted to chat with her there'd be nothing to rush the woman home from the market.)

"Oh ... *good*," thought Pandingkar Moedo, "I'll delegate someone to buy forest rubber at the market, and I'll rush back to the stall and chat up Taring. That way I'll know if she's willing to be friends with me or not."

So once he'd finished his coffee he set off for the market. And he did indeed get lots of forest rubber and gutta percha there. When any of these goods were placed on the scales he would pay up immediately. Even when the merchandise was not of a very high quality, he didn't care, he'd just add it to his store of goods anyway so that he could complete his transactions as quickly as possible. After only two hours of dealing goods he packed up his scales, slung his rubber and gutta percha on his back, and lifted it all into the cart so he could set off. As he was leaving he cast his gaze around the marketplace to see if his *nantulang* really was out shopping. He *thought* he saw her standing by a clothing store, but she was sort of half-visible and half-hidden. Once he finally saw her clearly and knew definitely that she was at the market, Pandingkar Moedo went on his way.

"Why are you doing everything in such a rush, Boss? All this lifting makes me nervous, I tell you."

"Okay, now, look, if anybody comes along selling forest saps, you just go ahead and buy them. Here's the money. Put it into the cart so I can examine it later in Sidimpuan. Let's settle everything up by letter since surely you trust me, Djaloemidang" (for this was Pandingkar Moedo's trusted helper).

"All right, but don't you go complaining about this later," said Djahaposan, loading the goods on top of the buggy.

"*Sirrr* ..." said the buggy's wheels. "*Pak, pak, katipak ... katipak*," said the horse's hooves, carrying Pandingkar Moedo swiftly on his way. Not long afterward they arrived at the fried food stall, and, indeed, the only ones there were Si Taring and her little sister, who was just about the age to begin decking herself out in jewelry and colored ribbons.[18]

"Why has Older Lineage Companion come back so soon?" asked Si Taring shyly. She hadn't been able to leave the stall since Pandingkar Moedo had come up so suddenly.

"Ah . . . I thought I was coming down with a fever a while ago, you see, and I was afraid I might faint right there in the marketplace. Where's our mom? And what gives with you watching the stall all by yourself?"

"Ha ha . . . she's gone shopping, of course," said Taring, gazing at the road.

"Well, then, before she comes back, give me some of those welcoming sweets."

Taring kept quiet, but her eyes were observing Pandingkar Moedo nonstop.

"So, when are you going to take the journey to adulthood and get married, Taring? Our mom said earlier this morning that you've already lifted your feet to set off on your journey. If that's the truth, tell me, so that I can go into hock at the nearest clothing store and buy you a wedding present."

Taring's brow darkened with embarrassment, for she thought what Pandingkar Moedo said was really nice. A moment later she said: "But who would I marry? Is it allowed, then, that only the boy gets what he wants, even if he doesn't strike my fancy? And, in addition to that, I really don't want to get married yet. I'm not of age yet, really, so what in the world would make me want to become someone who has to go around taking other people's orders?"[19]

"But, little friend, she said you were being married to a man who drew a salary. And I thought to myself, oh, well, that's a fitting enough partner for you to go get married to all right," said Pandingkar Moedo.

"Well, that's how parents are. What made them agree to a request that I be married off to somebody I surely don't know! Do you imagine somebody like me would sell well to a man who draws a salary?[20] Huh! That'll be the day," said Taring hotly.

"Wow! . . . Don't get mad! Angry people grow old too soon. If you don't want to go along with what they plan you don't have to, do you? But please accept this small gift of clothing so that you'll have lots of finery to wear."

"I don't really like clothes," said Taring, lashing out at the frying pan with her spoon.

"Taring," said Pandingkar Moedo, starting in again. "Look, if you don't want to do what your mother orders, would you possibly be willing to have a poor man? And a villager to boot? A guy who doesn't draw a salary? And one who surely is no descendant of wealthy nobles? If you'd be willing to do such a thing, let me point him out to you."

Taring moved about softly, unperturbed now, for now she knew that Pandingkar Moedo loved her. So she answered his words immediately: "What sort of man are you talking about, Older Lineage Companion? Maybe he's a mean sort who'd sell me to the Red Tobaman."[21]

"Ah, now, joking aside, Younger Lineage Companion, I know very well that you wouldn't see anything in a guy like that. For, look, you've not even seen his face; you don't know from what class of society he comes. Why, you don't even know if he's got any money. In short, you wouldn't see anything in a man like that. So in order to avoid embarrassment I'll go no further with my plans here."

"But what's the harm in it?" asked Taring. "If we strike each other's fancy, then it's not too important to keep our eyes fixed on the brideprice gold, is it? Why, it's not really necessary to take wealth or social class into account, for don't you know the song that goes:

Salaksalak na mata	Ripe, ripe snake fruit
Ima salak na tumonggi	That's the snake fruit that's the sweetest.
Muda dung disolong mata	If someone's struck your fancy
I ma halak na jumogi.	He's the one who's surely the handsomest.

"Yeah, right, but with someone like you here, Younger Lineage Companion, and I don't say this to flatter you—at the very least you'd have to be married off to an assistant schoolteacher or maybe a clerk."

"Oh . . . do *you* find me pretty? Me, with my hair not even pulled back in a bun," said Taring with some embarrassment.

"As for me, Younger Lineage Companion, what I say is that no one is prettier upon the surface of the earth. If, say, you would see fit to say yes to the guy we were just discussing I don't think his joy could be measured."

"Ha ha ha. . . . I'll give it a try, then, Older Lineage Companion! You just bring that fellow here so I can take a look at him. Once I've seen him then I can make up my mind one way or the other. If he suits me then you could say straightaway:

Juguk mangkail sulum	You squat down to catch minnows
Jongjong mangkail simarderadera	But you stand up to catch tiny river fish, too.
Muda panombo ni lungung	If you're lovesick
Bulung botik mardai mera.	Even papaya leaves taste like golden carp.

"Here comes our mom," said Pandingkar Moedo, leaning weakly against the wall, like someone sick with a fever. Taring understood what he was doing, and she walked outside and began to examine the big cornstalks, which were overflowing with ears.

"Goodness gracious. . . . What made you decide to come back from the market so soon, Nephew?" asked Taring's mother, happily, for the two she had introduced seemed to have some sort of relationship going.

"Hoooi. . . . I've come down with a high fever, Mother's Brother's Wife! I thought that you'd be here, so I rushed back to ask for a mug of coffee, but look what has happened. . . . When I got here it was as if I were a bother to this child who's minding the stall. I think she's put out at me for being here. Why, I've had to ask for my coffee two times . . ."

"Lailahaillalla Muhamadorrosullah. . . . Why did you not take care of your older lineage companion, with his bad fever? Don't you know how to set out coffee mugs anymore? Oh Lord, this girl doesn't have a smidgen of manners or politeness left in her! She's just getting wilder and wilder," said the girl's mother.

"Hmm, this fellow's really good at hiding little crabs inside folded emblic leaves, at keeping secrets. He's just letting me be the target of her anger, so the old one doesn't find out we were talking. Oh well, so be it," said Taring to herself.

"Now that you've arrived, Mother's Brother's Wife, let me push off, for I am feeling a bit better. Maybe the fever'll just disappear on my way home."

"But why don't you just spend the night here, Nephew? Maybe the fever will strike you again while you're on your journey and you'll fall off your buggy. Now, that would certainly make things difficult."

"That's not really necessary, Mother's Brother's Wife. My parent back in Sidimpuan will get mad, and that will just give her something else to worry about."

"Yes, indeed, Nephew. . . . Do as you wish. If you think it won't bother you then you'd better go right on home."

Once "giddyap" had been said to the horse Pandingkar Moedo made ready to go on his way, but as he was fixing to climb up into the seat it occurred to him that he had left something behind. It seemed that if it wasn't his market scales it was his socks. It got so that he kept going back and forth to the coffee stall constantly. Now what, the reader asks, could be the meaning of this?

Yes, indeed . . . he just wanted to fall under Taring's gaze one more time, so that she'd remember him after he left. And then after she'd had one more glimpse of him he'd go back and catch her laughing face one more time so there'd be something for his *tondi* soul to hold onto. For if Taring so much as smiled that would bring his soul an hour of bliss.

"*Kek*," said Pandingkar Moedo, flicking the horse with the whip. Right away Old Red set off carrying the buggy swiftly upriver. About half a milestone away he thought back to the girl and looked back: apparently Taring was standing there by the side of the garden waving a white handkerchief at him. Pandingkar Moedo's heart broke, as if it were coming loose from its bindings. That is how he felt when he thought about this girl, his medicine for his love longings. But what was to be done? The sun was beginning to sink behind Mount Lubuk Raya—and if it hadn't been for that he would have gone back and got her right there.

"Come back again. If you're going to become my soul partner, my wife, we shall meet again next market day." So on he went back to his home village. Once he had arrived at the house he was exhausted, like someone worn out from running hard.

Now joy showed on Pandingkar Moedo's face. But, as for his *work*, well: whatever he'd lay his hands on he would drop immediately. His thoughts kept flying back to the cornfield. Awaiting Riches was able to see his behavior quite clearly but did not bother him about it. What had happened he related to his wife: "I think Pandingkar Moedo is hiding a secret. That's what's caused his current behavior. Now listen, okay? You just go observe what he does when I go off to say my prayers at the mosque."

"All right!" said the woman, getting her secret hiding place in good order. She called "Come on, let's go to the baths," to her neighbor so as not to give away her real intentions.

"Let's take turns reciting the prayers," said Awaiting Riches to Pandingkar Moedo.

"All right. I'll take the first turn watching the store. I can see you've already gotten ready to go on down to the baths, to prepare for saying your prayers."

Awaiting Riches had no sooner left the store than Pandingkar Moedo threw himself into the easy chair they used as a napping place out in the front part of the shop. He seemed about ready to cry. He looked back and forth and saw no one passing by. It was quite lonely. So he unleashed a dirge, in the Mandailing style.

Sajari urat ni bira	Little caladium root the size of a finger
Dua jara urat nin antaladan	And two fingers' worth of drop-tongue root
Sadari inda huida	If I don't see you for a single day
Dua ari mardandi mangan.	I go on a hunger strike for two.
Tintin hupartintin	Whatever it takes to make a ring, I use
Golang hupargolanggolang	And so, too, with my bracelet
Muda ho anggi tumbuk ni nipi	If you're the one, Little Lineage Mate, who's
Na menek hupagodang-hupagodang.	found in a dream
	Then whatever auspicious dream it takes, I'll
	help you to grow up fast.
Muda buruk bajungki	
Angkon na hubalong-hubalong	If my clothes should fall apart
Muda tumbuk ni rohangki	I shall surely have to mend them.
Angkon na huoban-oban.	If you're my dream companion
	Then surely I'll have to take you along with me.
Sugari hodong gabe pahu	
Timbako ni Gunung Tua	If only the spine of the sugar palm branch
Sugari ho anggi di au	could become a fern
Tilako manjadi tua.	Tobacco hails from Gunung Tua.
	If you'd just be mine
Marumbak ma rambutan	Bad luck'd turn to good.
Marumbak tu bona ni unte	
Paidar marutang sambutan	Lushly grow the rambutan fruits
Sodang dapot siboru munte.	And lushly thrive the orange trees.
	May my hopes be fulfilled
	Just so long as I get that Boroe Moente.

"Oh, Allah Above, so it is true after all: he's having a loneliness attack. If that's the case it's best that we just continue listening to find out where this girl he's longing for lives, so that they can be seated before the village elders as soon as possible. Let's not let them be beset by loneliness for *too* long a period!"

When Awaiting Riches returned Pandingkar Moedo got ready to go and say his midday prayers. Once Pandingkar Moedo was in the distance the shopkeeper's wife greeted her husband with a laugh, saying: "It's *true*, they're really in love, their eyes have met. And I could hear from his song that their hearts have really been pierced by love's arrow. You had only just left the house when he turned on his *sitogol* songs.[22] When a young swain sings young men's songs like

Sajari urat ni bira	Little caladium root the size of a finger
Dua jari urat ni antaladan	And two fingers' worth of drop-tongue root
Sadari inda huida	If I don't see you for a single day
Dua ari mardandi mangan.	I go on a hunger strike for two.

well, his loneliness and pain are pretty darn serious, I'd say."

"Ha ha. . . . So it appears you know such songs yourself, do you?" said Awaiting Riches.

"Oh, come on, I'm not really a very good singer. It's just that I listened carefully to what he was saying. Look, he repeated one song two or three times!"

One day replaced the next, and then it was market day in Sigalangan. It was just daybreak when Pandingkar Moedo began to get ready to go to the market. "Careful now, Old Red," he cried as he jumped up into the buggy and the horse began to pull the vehicle along quite lustily. The horse didn't stop a single time all the way to Sigalangan; he took every turn in the road with dispatch.

From far off Pandingkar Moedo had already examined things very carefully to see if the girl was there, but as he got to the fried food stall he wasn't any too hopeful, even though his *nantulang* came out right away to greet him. From the way his face and eyes looked it was clear that he was not too hopeful that the girl herself would come out to welcome him. So he said: "I'll just be off, Mother's Brother's Wife. I'm pressed for time on this trip. I'm behind a bit in my accounts since I had that fever last market day. If there's time I'll stop here on the way back."

"Oh my . . . but the day's still young, Nephew! Nobody's at the market this early. You must drink some coffee first." At that moment, Taring called from the middle of the garden: "Oh . . . Mother! Are a hundred ears of corn enough?" As soon as he heard Taring's voice his face cleared, and he said: "I think you may be right, Mother's Brother's Wife. Nobody's at the market yet, for I see that the food stall at the bridge over there is still shut tight."

"Yes, indeed, would I ever lie to you?"

Rather heavily Pandingkar Moedo climbed down from the buggy, his face now covered with smiles. "Here, Mother's Brother's Wife, come and get what I've brought you from my parent or I'm going to forget."

"What is that, Bere?" asked the good wife as she opened the package. It appeared to be a bunch of snake fruits, which Pandingkar Moedo himself had picked from the snake fruit bushes in back of their house.

"Oh my, Nephew. . . . Where did you get these snake fruits? Do you know, I've been craving some of these for the longest time, but I haven't been able to get any. I even asked the cart man there to go find some for me in the snake bushes out in Sihepengan Forest, but he didn't bring even a handful back. I didn't get even one taste. But, oh, these are so scrumptious, sweet, tart, good and juicy. You just give one of these a whack and it opens right up. They smell so good, and they taste sweet as sugar. Ah, and it is only now that my longing for snake fruits has been satisfied. Here, Taring, do you want one? Give some to your little sister. Save two branches full for your father; maybe he'll want some later."

Taring kept silent, but her little sister came up and went first. She put the snake fruits in front of the girl.

The good wife kept exclaiming about how delicious the fruits were. All the while, her hands were never still, setting coffee in front of Pandingkar Moedo. "Drink some coffee, Nephew, to rid you of your evening chill."

"*Sep*" said the coffee as he drank it, but his eyes kept stealing sly glances at Taring. His gaze was always received with love. Her mother saw what was happening very clearly, but she pretended not to know so the young people wouldn't have any interference. Not long afterward the good wife said: "Oh, I am certainly the forgetful one here, what do you think? Would Taring be brave enough to go over to the bathing spring by herself to fetch my prayer beads for me? I left them there accidently a while ago."

"I'm scared to. That's an awfully lonely spot without very many people around," said Taring.

"Oh, forgetful folks like me always have much to lament. Oh well, now I'll have to go and leave you here drinking your coffee. That's certainly not very polite."

"Don't worry, Mother's Brother's Wife! Go on ahead and fetch them. You're still far too prim and polite around me," said Pandingkar Moedo.

"Well, Nephew, forgive me, then. I shall run fast so the beads won't get snatched by the little kids who are out there cutting back the grass."

When the good wife had gone a short distance, Pandingkar Moedo's thoughts hurled round and round. With a trembling voice he said to Taring: "So, Taring, are you actually going to go through with it and embark on your marriage journey? If you do go off to get married here's a store-bought length of cloth for you from me, a sign that you call me Older Lineage Companion."

"Now, you just make things so hard and painful. Wherever would I go? No one talks to me. What would people see in me anyway? My face isn't worth much, I don't have any good manners worth mentioning, and that sure is true of my social class, too! You just want to keep mocking and insulting me," said Taring, tears running down her face like tiny beads falling off the thread as girls sew the ceremonial betel purses.

What could have caused this, the public asks, I should not wonder! Oh . . . but the tears here flowed because of longing, loneliness, and love—all suffered for so long a time by this girl as she went from week to week between his visits.

"Well, then, if you don't want to do as your mother has ordered, might you want to go marry that guy I was talking to you about? If so, I'll bring him here next market day. If I'm busy with something I'll have someone else accompany him. But whoever comes, I'm the one who ordered him to come here. I very much hope that there will be love in your heart for this man."[23]

"If he strikes my fancy, if he suits my way of thinking, of course I shall say yes to the man. But, friend, what if he looks just great but turns out to be quite another proposition altogether? What then? I'll just send him right home, you know."

"Fine . . . let me leave then, since people are probably already milling around the market in droves. They'll be getting pretty bored standing there waiting so long for me to get there."

Dear Reader!!! Where do you think the garden's owner has gone? Off to fetch her prayer beads or off to a secret hiding place to listen in on the young people's talk?

She had not really left her prayer beads behind. She had actually snuck away beneath the stalks of corn, listening to what transpired between the two of them.

Once she found out, once she heard clearly that the one loved the other, she was limitlessly delighted. She had gotten what she wanted! Pandingkar Moedo had no more than begun to step into the buggy when she let out a great racket from the edge of the garden: "Laila haillalla. . . . You are leaving, Nephew? I've been away too long? You're angry? Well, what can you say about this child, the way she's always such a 'fraidy cat' about everything."

"No, indeed, Mother's Brother's Wife, not at all. It's not because I had given up hope of your coming back and not because of anger. I'm just leaving because so many people must have flocked into the marketplace by now."

"Well, all right, Nephew. Just as long as it's not because I took so long getting back. Someone had already come along and cut back the grass there, so I had a hard time looking for the beads."

Pandingkar Moedo had barely arrived at the marketplace when all the agents descended on him, taking out their wares. Merchandise was weighed, and however much weight it showed on the scale that is exactly how much he would pay. That very second.

Once all these goods and implements were piled on top of the cart, back he went to his mother's brother's wife's fried food stall. He wasn't really very thirsty, but he asked for a mug of coffee anyway so that he'd have a reason to sit down. "Where's Taring?" he said to himself. He sharpened his sight and made his hearing more acute, all to see if she might be in the stand of corn, cutting down ears. He got tired searching for her, but not so much as her shadow was visible. He asked his mother's brother's wife's permission to leave and go on home to Sidimpuan. "Now, good Mother's Brother's Wife, try not to go too far away this week because, you see, our parent is going to come here on a little visit. She got what you sent her, and she was so moved by your gift that she has decided to come and visit you. But you know how it is: 'There's been too much weeding work to do out in the hillside rice paddies.' But sometime this week I think she'll be able to come after all. I've already gone and hired somebody to help out with the brush clearing. I just couldn't stand seeing her all bent over like that, toiling away out in the paddy field."

"Fine, Nephew, I'm longing to meet her, too, but what is to be done? The rain falls down hard, the horse's water trough gets full, the heart's avid, but the legs remain stiff and immobile, don't they? I guess it just goes to show that we don't have enough money to go gallivanting around the countryside paying visits!"

"Well, then, may hindrances remain far away and may your longings for each other be assuaged. So, I take my leave of you then. May you remain safe and healthy, may I myself stay hale and hearty,"[24] said Pandingkar Moedo, bounding up onto the seat of the buggy. His horse Old Red had no more than set off briskly when, without warning, Taring appeared in front of his eyes by the side of the road, carrying firewood. He was limitlessly happy. He immediately jumped down and asked: "What are you doing carrying firewood? Aren't you getting ready to leave for your wedding?"

"Oh, go on, can't you find anyone but me to insult?" responded Taring, laughing.[25]

"Ha ha. . . . Well, look, when we come bringing you that man don't you go changing your mind!"

"All right. . . . But just so long as you yourself don't behave toward your friends as Raja Mousedeer does toward his: always leading them off into the little mountain valleys where they get totally lost."[26]

"Now, rest assured, when you see me coming you'll have no reason to complain."

"And where exactly is this fellow from?" asked Taring.

"Let's just say he's a stranger to the village, someone you have to size up first. You have to do that before you get to know them well, don't you?" asked Pandingkar Moedo.

"Well, okay—you just come and I'll be waiting."

"Couldn't we maybe shake hands on this to show that we've made a promise?" asked Pandingkar Moedo.

Taring kept quiet, but words were visible on her lips: "Well, if you want to, what's the harm?" Pandingkar Moedo had barely put his hand out when Taring took it firmly. Pandingkar Moedo didn't say a thing to accompany the handshake, but it felt as if his body had been wafted up to the Highest Heaven. All because their hands had touched.

A moment later Pandingkar Moedo said: "Let me go off then. May we both be hale and hearty, safe and sound. Till we meet again, then."

Once they had separated Old Red galloped off nonstop to Sihitang.

All this long while, if Pandingkar Moedo was going in that direction anyway (up toward the river source) he would always stop at Awaiting Riches's house in Sihitang to bring them little food gifts. If it wasn't a flatfish as wide as a drying tray it would be a carp as big as half your chest. And it was like that today. But this time Boroe Soeti saw something different in Pandingkar Moedo's face, for deep happiness was pictured there. Once he had offered the little gift he said: "Could you maybe go somewhere with my mother next market day? She's going to go to Sigalangan, visiting."

"And what would the need for that be? My friend, is there a pretty one there who might become my *parumaen*?"*

"No, indeed, Inang Tobang! She's just going visiting because she misses them. Because all this time that I've been traveling back and forth out there there's been a woman who is always sending gifts back home with me. She owns the fried food stand by the side of the road. They knew each other when they were girls. That's why they have to see each other."

"Now who is she exactly? I know almost everyone in that village," said Boroe Soeti.

"Right, that's the thing to ask, so you won't be like someone who's never heard of folks. Ask what the kin term usage is before you go to meet somebody, right? Well, that woman who has the big garden as you come into the village, that's her."

Parumaen ('daughter-in-law'): recall that Boroe Soeti uses the term Amang with Pandingkar Moedo, considering him her son. Inang Tobang in the next line has the connotation of Father's Older Brother's Wife.

"Oh. . . . But I know her! Make them come over from Sidimpuan real fast so that we can get a move on here. But, you know, I'm really not able to walk all the way over there. We'll have to pay for a horse carriage," said Boroe Soeti.

"Fine, fine. Would I make you walk? My doing that would be as impossible as getting oil from a stone," said Pandingkar Moedo.

Once he arrived in Sidimpuan he went straight to the store to find the shop-keeper. He told him how much merchandise he had bought at the market. Then he went home to the Other-Side Market. His mother greeted him upon his arrival: "Have something to eat, son! You're probably hungry. Why are you always getting home so late in the day recently?"

"I went to the main market in Sidimpuan first, Mother," said Pandingkar Moedo, stuffing in his rice by the handful. As he was eating he began to talk to his mother, bit by bit, and he told her a little more each time.

"Mother, both you and that Older Lineage Companion, Awaiting Riches's wife, have been urging me to take a wife for a long time now. All this while I was never ready to accept what you said, though. It just wouldn't sink in, I guess. But that was because I hadn't seen anyone nice, anyone who'd make me a good com-panion for a lifetime. But now, during the time I've been working as a merchant, I do happen to have seen a girl with a beautiful face, a girl whose words are medicine to the mind, whose social class is appropriate, too—and whose figure, frankly, is first class.[27] I've known her mother for a long time. They've been calling me *bere* all this time because I always stop to have coffee there in the mornings. But I've only just seen their daughter for the first time this month. It seems they've been hiding her. I tried striking up a conversation with the girl—and she was really easy to get to know. Now it seems we've promised each other that I'll tell you to go over there and begin the marriage negotiations. I don't know if her mother wants to be fami-ly with us or not, but, just observing the way they think, I would say that they do want to become family. A while ago I told Father's Older Brother's Wife out in Sihitang that she'll have to accompany you on your journey, and she's willing. In fact, she already knows my mother's brother's wife; she says the woman is a well-respected person in Sigalangan. So get everything ready to go and ask for a bride for the household. But you'll have to be clever, for it could be fairly said of the girl's mother that she's the sort who is adept at digging planting holes in the ground, the type who can always keenly measure out the lay of the mountain lands.[28] She'll know all about your plans and schemes for the brideprice negotiations beforehand. If you see that she's ready to accept things then go ahead and negotiate the bride-price. If not, well, look: at least make friends with her. I'll tell Awaiting Riches's wife about all this tomorrow, and she'll want to help. She's the one who's always telling me to take a wife, after all—she more than anyone. So, all three of you will have to share a carriage, I guess. But in negotiating with my *nantulang* you'll have to be cagey and adept at give and take."

"Oh my. . . . Well, if that's how things are, then fine, son. It's been fun getting presents from them all this long while. But even more now. My goodness, to get a bride to boot! I do believe I'll sleep more soundly now," said Pandingkar Moedo's parent.

When the news reached Awaiting Riches's wife she got dressed right away and readied all the appropriate gifts to take along: First-Acquaintance Presents; then, second, gifts to determine the other party's thoughts; and, third, gifts to assuage suffering.[29] Once everything was ready and upon a certain fine day, on the day determined as auspicious by the *datu*-diviner, on the day when good things can be had,[30] they all set off for Sigalangan to meet the woman whose name they did not yet know.

What did they chat about during their trip along the road? None other than how they could come up with a crafty plan so that their intention to ask for a bride would not be known. For if the general populace found out about it there'd be words that would divide people and their negotiation sessions might not go well.

"Now, don't be worried about that. I've been over to that area lots of times on visits, and, besides, our trip looks like a regular friendship visit. Look, we're not bringing along Brideprice-Negotiation Cooked Rice, which, of course, they'd be able to observe quite easily. And neither are we carrying the Brideprice-Negotiation Beaded Purse for Betel Leaves, are we?[31] It just looks like we're paying a friendly little visit to people we happen to know. They won't have the slightest suspicion that we're going to ask for a bride," said Boroe Soeti.

"Well, okay, you just arrange things so they don't get wind of what's really going on.

"Oh, Dear Woman-Friend, we must have faith and trust in you to do the good hard work here, to figure out what to do. I've had folks come to me to ask for a bride—but as for determining their intentions about a bride's willingness to come to *us*, honestly, I'm no expert! But really, just consider: if you take care to be precise in how you answer their inquiries, well! They can't wiggle away! They're like a fish snared in a trap—they're just ripe for reeling in," said the shopkeeper's good wife.

Now, if I'm to be the one who's leading the way, well, what I say is that we shall have to employ an inescapable trap to catch that girl's father and mother. The girl herself'll be easier to snare."

"Look, now, there's a cornfield. Dear Woman-Friend, is that the garden land we're looking for?" asked Pandingkar Moedo's mother.

"Yes, that's it, all right. And they're at home, too."

The woman was tying up some broken stalks that had been knocked over by the wind the night before.

"Well, whatever do you know . . . " said Boroe Soeti from the road.

"Oh my, is that you, Boroe Soeti? Where are you going? Please do stop for a bit. And who are your companions?" she said, asking them to stop.

"Yes, . . . everybody get down out of the carriage so we can stop for a moment," said Boroe Soeti. "This is Pandingkar Moedo's mother—Pandingkar Moedo, the good, well-spoken young man, you know—and the other one is Awaiting Riches's wife—Awaiting Riches, the great merchant in Sidimpuan, of course. They're the ones who've asked me to go visiting and take a little look at the pretty scenery around here. Because, after all, you folks have been sending gifts back and forth all this time but you haven't even met each other."

"Yes, indeed. . . . So apparently you are my *eda*, my husband's sister," said Taring's mother, going out to greet them on the highway.

"That's right, it's me, Eda—the one who's been lonesome for you all this time. But for reasons of poverty it's only now that I've been able to come and visit you," said Pandingkar Moedo's mother.

"Well, that's just fine, my husband's sister. Please have some betel quid for starters," said the woman, offering the betel tin.

"Take out our own betel leaves, Boroe Soeti, so that Eda can have some, too."

"Heh, heh, heh, I forgot! I missed you so much that I forgot to offer betel."

"*Tje-kep, tje-kep,*" went the sound of the women chewing betel. Not long afterward Pandingkar Moedo's mother spoke up: "My, my, my, your betel quid certainly is delicious. Why, it's just scrumptious, and the soda is all nice and crumbly. The gambir leaves really hit the spot, too, I must say. And the areca nut's just right, not making you dizzy and drunk at all. Oooh, it just sharpens the vision, my, my, my."

"Yes, indeed, my husband's sister, this is betel quid from Saromatinggi. That's where my betel is always from, and our soda's from Siabu. If they're not from there I just don't find that they taste very good, Eda," said Taring's mother.

"I guess that you find your betel tasteless and boring. We just grabbed some tiny, mildewed leaves since we were in a rush. And our soda's the sort that's still clumped together because we didn't have enough firewood to properly roast the snails. And our gambir leaves aren't dry enough, and our areca nut's unripe. And our tobacco is just Stringy Tobacco, but at least its name is A String to Draw Friends into a Single Agreement."[32]

"Not at all . . . Eda. Though it might lack something in looks, it hits the spot in taste. And I'm happy to chew it, for betel quid given by long-missed friends is always tastier than the normal sort. But, may I say something else? Since this is the first time you have come to visit we shall just have to go back to the village! Though there won't be anything there but well water and fern greens to eat, for me to be happy we must share a meal and you must meet your good clan brother. Imagine how he'd regret it if he heard you'd come but never got to meet him."

"Oh . . . that's not necessary, Eda. Let's save that for another trip. We haven't brought anything with us—what would be our reason for sitting down and talking and listening, after all?—even though we said we've been missing you and longing to see you," said Pandingkar Moedo's mother. But to herself she said, "Oh, *good.*"

"Well, you certainly are the experts here. Indeed, then, whatever you wish. But your brother is not the sort of man to put on a big show, and since you're only passing through on a little visit how could he possibly wish for presents from you? If you don't have any gifts in the rattan satchel over your shoulder, then it'll have to be gifts of words that we share!" said Taring's mother.

"So, what do you say, Boroe Soeti, what do you say to what our *eda* has proposed?" Will our prayers be fulfilled, do you think?"

"Oh, let's do see if we can agree. . . . What do you say, Maen?* Are we able to

---

*An affectionate form of *parumaen.*

go on back to the village with them for a bit before going on our way?" asked Boroe Soeti of Awaiting Riches's wife.

"Well, if that is the decision reached by the entire congress then who are we to refuse it?"

"Ah, that's the way! Daughter, come here so I can get back to the village," said Taring's mother. Moving along quite happily, she took a shortcut and arrived at the house quickly in order to roll out the sitting mats and say to her daughter: "Oh . . . Taring! Sweep out the middle section of the house; our wife receivers have come for a visit. After that get to cooking, and make it delicious, too. We don't want your father to be ashamed."

"*Tor*," said Taring's heart, as she asked: "Who are these wife receivers of ours? And where are they from to throw you into such a dither?"

"Why, it's your father's sister, Pandingkar Moedo's mother, along with Boroe Soeti and Awaiting Riches's wife—Awaiting Riches, that is, the much-discussed one in Sidimpuan, you know."

Taring had no more than heard these words when she immediately unrolled the good mats on the floor. Then she got out the lace curtains and set to scurrying around, working furiously. She had absolutely no idea how to properly welcome *anakboru* wife receivers to the village.

When the women in the carriage were still some ways away they caught sight of the girl, crocheting lace and seated at the double window. "Over there, friend, there's our kinswoman's daughter, our brother's wife's girl. And how very fitting, to find her crocheting and not walking about hither and yon. It's rare that you find such behavior as this.[33] Why, yes, yes, indeed! And, you know, her face is like a spirit's visage, she is so lovely. No wonder Pandingkar Moedo is attracted to her," said the shopkeeper's wife.

At that very moment Taring's mother called them from up in the house: "Come up, . . . even though one is poor, and one's house is no more than a sparrow's nest, and what we offer you to sit on is no more than a rotted old mat." Taring stoodup and greeted the women: "Come up, Namboru. I would guess that you're tired, Sidimpuan is so very far from here."

They were taken aback to see the girl's face and to hear how very friendly and cheerful she was. Once they were inside the house and sitting in the middle room Taring scrambled out and set to work, cooking furiously in the kitchen.

"Now, where's our *iboto*, our good brother, so that we may shake his hand?" asked Pandingkar Moedo's mother.

"Oh—hey you!! Come on in here, into the center of the house! Your lineage sisters long to catch sight of you."

"Good Lord, when did you get here, Sister? I can tell you, it's lucky that I didn't leave the village," the man said merrily.

"We came at ten o'clock, but we talked a long while out at the garden, for our original plan was just to stop there, after all. Now, Ito, we haven't brought you a thing. Don't be put out with us, body and soul: we really didn't know we'd be meeting you."

"Ah . . . what would you need to bring, Sister? Just to see your face makes me feel as if I've been fed and given drink. It's good health that we ask from our God, after all."

"That's certainly so," said Boroe Soeti, passing around betel quid in a silver tin. Djaimbaran accepted the tin and took some of the betel to eat.

After they had chatted for a moment or two, Taring came in from the kitchen to say: "It's noon already, Mom. You must take everyone to pray so that we can eat."

"Is the rice ready?"

"Everything's cooked and put away in the cupboard. You all go off to pray; you'll be hungrier after noon."

And what did they chat about there in the middle of the house? It was none other than how happy they were to have met and to have had the chance to get to know each other. All other talk was kept hidden away inside them.

As for Taring, she had not been told anything formally about her *anakboru's* arrival, but she already knew the score. Now she knew for sure that it was Pandingkar Moedo himself who wanted her. And she? Why, she wanted no other man. Just him. That's why she was cooking so furiously for the *anakboru's* visit.

When the prayer sayers had returned Taring carried all the dishes of food into the center of the house and arranged the plates on the floor in good order. Each wife receiver got a plate and a cup. The dishes of water for washing their hands were placed on the right, the extra helpings of rice and the curries were placed in the middle above the plates, and the drinking cups were set to the left. When everything was set out correctly Taring's mother called out: "Let's dish up these poor shameful papaya leaves, Eda. Everyone's hungry, I see."

"But where's my clan brother going? Oh, come on, let's do eat together. Aren't we all lonesome for each other? He can go sit at the front of the house, while we sit on this side."

"Now, isn't that the truth, Taring's Father? Your sister says we all have to eat together. Come on in."[34]

"Your words are certainly welcome ones for me," said Djaimbaran, sitting down.

Once he was settled Pandingkar Moedo's mother winked at Boroe Soeti so that she'd get out the Brideprice-Negotiation Cooked Rice that they'd brought along. "Oh, good grief, where is it? I must look inside our rattan satchel and take the rice packets out." Before they'd come, they had arranged all the curries in the satchel with the rice and had packed everything into portable carrying cases.

"So you have come bringing rice, my husband's sister? You certainly *must* be lonesome for us," said Taring's mother, setting the *new* rice and curries in front of her husband. At that point, they all ate together. No one was embarrassed or shy, not the father and mother of the girl, nor Taring, nor the *anakborus* from Sidimpuan. Once everyone had eaten Taring put away the plates and dishes in the kitchen. And she perked up her ears sharply to catch just what it was these wife receivers were after.

"We've eaten our fill, so here's our betel quid, which we present to you," said Boroe Soeti, passing it around in an ornate gold tin.

"Oh my . . . and what new sort of betel is this? After all, I already had betel just a little while ago," Djaimbaran said, accepting the tin by touching it gently on its top. Then Boroe Soeti presented the tin to Taring's mother. "I'm happily stuffed from all the food you brought, and now I've accepted your gift of betel, too. So, what exactly are the words of your betel?" asked Djaimbaran.

"Yes, Clan Brother, though the food we brought may not have been very tasty, may it serve to fatten you up, nonetheless, one would certainly say. . . . But, indeed, so that one might not hide behind one's index finger, nor hunker down secretly behind the second finger, as for our meeting here, it is best that we not hide any of our messages from each other any more than the rice in the cookpot can hide its presence. The path that has led us here to visit you, accompanied as we are by Pandingkar Moedo's mother and Awaiting Riches's wife: Oh, we come lamenting our pain and suffering to you—but, indeed, when we consider our abject state of poverty we are not really bold enough to deliver fine speeches to you. But, indeed, as the adept speech makers say, when close family come visiting boldness for making speeches arrives, too! So, indeed, Clan Brother! If you have any pity or love for us, we come here asking for a strong cane[35] from you, so that there'll be someone to take good care of my younger lineage companion's son, for she herself is getting quite old," said Boroe Soeti.

Djaimbaran answered them, facing his rice spooner: "So what is to be said? What is to be noted? Why don't you just go ahead and answer their speech, for you know I'm not very good at orations."

"Ha ha ha. . . . I feel quite oppressed and hemmed in from all sides to be asked to think over all you've said, for when I consider this child, she's still so very young, so very, very young. She doesn't really have her wits about her yet. If we say 'there's nothing there,' well, there's nothing to say, that would be as if we weren't happy to receive your visit. Well, indeed, Eda, if you still wish such a thing, even given this situation, then it'll have to be you, Taring's Father, who responds to their words."

"Well, indeed, then, Clan Sister, it is not as if we are simply dismissing your request. No, no, let us think it over for a week and then ask your *parumaen*, your brother's young daughter, if it sets well with her that we accept your request, for surely it is better that we are all of a single agreement here and that no one is forced to do anything, so that heavy regrets won't come later. Next week you shall get the news one way or the other," said Djaimbaran.

"That's just fine, Brother! Surely that is for the best. But surely Ito knows that we don't have the resources to keep traveling here every other second, so would there be anything wrong with perhaps coming to an agreement now? After all, we don't want our speeches crisscrossing haphazardly, nor would we want people to come and say things that might serve to cut us apart from you. You understand the way people think. So, Ito, don't go saying that we aren't close to our family. After all, here we all are, along with my brother's little daughter. This is the place where things are in perfect agreement. Then we can order the village elders to come here and present whatever brideprice wealth we can get together. If all these fine discussions are stored in tight little rice packets for too long a time, why, a pair of the world's sharpest English scissors will surely come and cut us apart, so that our fond wishes will all come to naught."

"Ah, it is as if I am being forced to eat *sisungkot kola* areca nut, Clan Sister! If you eat it, your father dies; but if you don't, your mother dies. So, indeed, what do you say, Taring's Mom?" inquired Djaimbaran.

"Oh my, how can I know what to say? It is as if I don't know what to declare, this whole thing is all so good. But, my husband's sister, even though you are trying to make these discussions easier, what if Taring herself does not say yes later on? Wouldn't your visit then come to nothing? Because of that, it's best that we urge her on a bit and encourage her."

"As for the exact words of the agreement, Brother's Wife, we do not come searching for a knife tip (the end of the blade) in a machete handle. Why, in fact, our trip here has been very painful for us, for if we do not bring back good news great feelings of regret will ensue. Because of that let us keep trying to find some way to make a decision that will carry us toward a good resolution."

Dear Reader! So that he could collect his thoughts, the speech making paused for a moment, while Djaimbaran smoked a cigarette and the womenfolk chewed some betel. But what of Taring? Hearing what the Sidimpuan people had to say her joy grew boundless. "So Pandingkar Moedo *does* love me! So it was only playacting that he'd send a man here asking to marry me. The guy is really good at trying to sell you a hundred for a thousand it appears. As for me, if Father and Mother order me to go to him I won't have to think *that* over for very long! If he says, 'now,' then now it is, I'm ready and willing. If it's 'tomorrow,' then tomorrow it is. In short, whenever he gives me the order that's when I'll say yes." But after a moment her happiness turned to pain when she heard her father's words as they twisted and turned. As if he would actually turn down the Sidimpuan people's request! Straightaway her forehead crumpled into wrinkles, like the face of a person stunned by the fearsome roar of a tiger. Her hands began to tremble; the tiger's muzzle sprang forward and took on a four-sided shape. His muzzle kept thrusting and his maw turned elliptical, and she got more and more like a frightened cockatoo. "The Sidimpuan folks' speeches were so fine and friendly, why did you keep making your responses so twisty-turny? I am going to break all of these plates and dishes if you don't consent to what they ask," she said, pummeling the dishpan with her fists. But even as she was fixing to break all the dishes to pieces she softened her blows a bit so that the sound wouldn't be heard out in the central room. A moment later, she said to herself: "If you won't let me go with that man I'll follow him anyway, next market day. Come on, there's nothing left to make speeches about. Do you think I'm going to keep on being your obedient yea-saying servant around here till I get old and decrepit? You have provoked me this time—well, good-*bye*! If they turn around and go back home because of the nasty way you're behaving, well, next market day I'll run away and marry him. I'll just take off with him."

"So what is to be done, kind clan brother? Don't go saying that we're moving too fast but think about our visit carefully, for we have come here without a man to accompany us, you understand. If you might happen to have any love in your heart for us we hope to get good news, so that our steps will be light and carefree as we go back home upriver. But if we just go home, and that's that, we'll feel like the axe that's pierced the hardwood tree and has been rebuffed by the trunk's toughness."

"Hah, heh . . . let's do this, so that all of us are happy: since your brother's little girl happens to be here let's call her in and ask her what she thinks. By following such a plan, you'll see our turn of mind quite clearly. Now, isn't that the way to do it, Taring's Mom?" asked Djaimbaran.

That's . . . it!" said the woman, calling Taring from the kitchen.

"What do you need me for?" inquired Taring with an untroubled, pure face, her feet diligently rushing, one after the other, carrying her into the central room. Once she was seated on the floor, her mother spoke: "Now, Taring, your father's sister over here has come from Sidimpuan, and I thought they were just paying us a friendly visit, but it appears they have asked your father for a cane over the slippery spots, for a torch to light their way in the darkness. We said, of course, that we'd like to think it over for a week, but they don't have the patience for that. Moreover, daughter, all this long while I have noticed that you don't seem to care very much for our *babere*.* So I'm puzzled as to what has caused them to come here to see if you want to be his bride. Frankly, I didn't think he saw anything in you, either. So, girl, even though you're not really interested in him and, in fact, basically wouldn't give him the time of day, their marriage speeches have been presented to us. So, daughter, should your father assent to your father's sister's request speeches? Or are you still looking at our nephew hatefully?"

Taring bowed her head, as if she needed to think over her answer carefully and quietly, but inside her thoughts already said: "Yes, Mirthful and Generous Ompung, may your *tondi* soul stuff protect me and keep me so that I can marry that man, that potion for my lovesickness, that medicine for my mind, that boon companion for my *tondi* soul!"

But, as a first bargaining chip sort of thing to say, she declared: "Well, I am not really willing to marry their son. He's too stuck up. Once we met on the big road, and he absolutely pelted me with the stink of his fancy scented soap—it just made me want to throw up. And, more than that, he's always making fun of my fried bananas. There hasn't been a single time when I could give him what he wants. So if you go selling me to that market man the only thing I'll get out of it is a bunch of pain and misery. As for *you*, well, I already know that as long as you can get loads and loads of gleaming brideprice gold you don't care a thing about my future sufferings and tribulations. Now, that is what I really feel," said Taring.

"Well, Sister, now you've heard how stuck up your brother's girl is. But what can I do? That's why we asked for a week more. Now, what am I supposed to say to you? This youngster tends to be *very* frank."

Awaiting Riches's wife spoke up: "Oh, my little woman-friend, you are so shortsighted. If a young man causes you pain, now, that's simply a sign of love, isn't it? And you say he pelted you with the smell of his scented soap? Well, isn't that just giving you love, too? Honestly, of course it gets pitch dark at midnight! Why, it seems just yesterday that I was a young girl myself, and I tell you if I had been given the <u>chance to be friends with someone who behaved the way Pandingkar Moedo</u>

*Our *babere*: an especially intimate form of *bere* ('husband's sister's child'), our very own *bere*.

does—well, that would have been pretty sweet water to drink, for *sure*! So, my friend, if it is only a matter of that don't you be afraid. It's no problem, I can guarantee it: if he doesn't treat you as he promises I shall be the one to deal with him, believe me!"

"Maybe you're trying to trick me," said Taring, happily.

"Astagafiruncing, by the cat's whiskers! Now do you *believe* what I'm telling you, Younger Lineage Companion? Isn't she something else?"

"Indeed, then, Father and Mother, if that is what you tell me to do then that is the pronouncement I shall follow," said Taring, who then disappeared into the kitchen, feeling that she had been securely caught, body and soul, in a happy trap.

"So, Clan Brother, I feel as if my brother's girl has said yes. What do you say?"

"Ah, but you know what these yesses from little children mean. She'll say yes when she's right there next to you, but she'll forget she said it once you've left. She's never been punished for saying yes to anyone before, so why would she find doing it all that difficult?"

"Well, let me just slip into the kitchen and find out what gives," said Boroe Soeti, going in search of Taring. "Now, Maen, as a sign that we truly mean what we say, here's a lovely batik cloth that Pandingkar Moedo sends you. It'll be your cloth to dream on.[36] Now, what can you give me to take back to Pandingkar Moedo?"

"But I don't own a single thing of my own, Father's Sister. What could I possibly give anyone?" said Taring, draping her hand over Boroe Soeti's shoulder and hanging there.

"Here, right there on your finger," said Boroe Soeti.

"Oh, don't say that, Friend, good Father's Sister: that's so awful looking. What use would anyone have for that?"

"The ugliest of my ugly things, the best of my best things. Those things go along with the words of the song:

Tintin huptintin	This little ring I make into a ring
Golang hupargolang-hupargolang	This bracelet I use as a bracelet.
Muda dung tumbuk di nipi	Once you've dreamed an auspicious dream
Na menek hupagodang.	about someone
	Then, although he's still a little kid, you'll
	just have to help him grow up fast.

So said Boroe Soeti as she took the small ring off Taring's ring finger. It was a simple, solid gold band.

"Oh, you're a hard one to deal with, Father's Sister. This little thing will only show how poor I am. It's better that we use something else."

"Not at all, girl—this one's the best."

After that Pandingkar Moedo's mother said: "Well, then, Clan Brother, what would be a fitting time for us to come to fetch my brother's daughter as a bride? Let's not turn the mats wrong side out, all right? We wouldn't want folks to mock us, now would we?"

"Oh goodness, it's as if you've given us some hot peppers to put in our mouths and our lips get burnt. I think we should take some time to think, without pressure, and then you could come. What do we have to fear from what people might say, for, after all, we've already made our good promises to each other," said Taring's mother.

"Well, there's really no way things are going to come to a halt, you know, but it's just better to get things under way quickly so that luck will flow in all the swifter!"

"Well, all right, if that's how it is then have the village elders come from where you live—but what is to be done about the brideprice gold? What I think is that the sums should be negotiated and settled upon before you come to fetch your *parumean*, your son's wife," said Djaimbaran.[37]

"As a sign that we mean what we say, let me present you with 150 rupiah as a first payment. When I come here again to fetch my son's wife, rest assured, I shall add to it. And, over the next two to three days I shall have the village elders bring these negotiations to a more advanced stage. So now, Brother, I feel what we have been discussing here has come to an end, so let us go back home so that folks back in the village will get this good news and be glad. Little ants and big ants, Brother, good luck flowing in like swarms of ants, as the saying goes—may you be hale and hearty always and forever, may all your wishes be fulfilled." Once everyone had asked and received permission to leave, back they went to Sidimpuan. As they progressed along the road they were boundlessly happy, chatting along, praising the girl's father and mother and the girl's own prettiness. In short, they averred, she was as pretty as anyone in all of Angkola Julu. Because they were chatting so animatedly and having such a good time the trip between Sigalangan and Sidimpuan felt like a journey of no more than two stone kilometer markers.

In Sihitang, Boroe Soeti stayed, and the others went on to Sidimpuan. When they arrived at the Other-Side Market they found Pandingkar Moedo waiting. From the laughter on their faces Pandingkar Moedo could see that they were bringing good news. But he didn't immediately get to the point and ask them about that. Rather he asked: "Why are you back so late in the day? I was about to come after you. I thought maybe that guy's horse was getting lazy." But, then, because he couldn't hold back, he went on to ask: "How did it go with the ones you went to meet? Is there maybe some hope?"

"Be of good cheer, Son. Just ask your Older Lineage Mate and you'll find out exactly what happened," said his mother.

Up spoke Awaiting Riches's wife: "Well, you *got* the one you're lovesick for, Younger Lineage Companion. Here, take this ring and dream on it. Use it tonight to dream of what is to be in the future, so that your mind rests easier. But really, my friend, you're the real expert here at finding a life companion: the moment one lays eyes on that girl one cannot help but be attracted to her."

As soon as the ring was placed in Pandingkar Moedo's hand, Awaiting Riches's wife asked leave to go on home, as it was getting late in the evening. "All right," they said, and Pandingkar Moedo's mother escorted her as far as the *kinari* tree. At home Awaiting Riches's wife related all they had done that day and how they were planning to bring the brideprice negotiations to an end so that they could fetch the girl as soon as possible. "We're just waiting for an auspicious day so we can order our departure."

"Well, how did the girl strike you? She wouldn't be an embarrassment, say, if we brought her here to the Center of the Ceremonial Dance Arena? Folks wouldn't scorn and ridicule us? We wouldn't want them to say 'If you take too much time picking out your stalk of sugarcane, you won't get a sweet one.'"

"Ha, ha, no matter where you might bring that girl there will be no regrets what-*so*-ever! She's not deficient in the least little thing," declared the shopkeeper's wife.

"Well, well and good, if that's the case. We'll just divine an auspicious day so that our negotiations won't be postponed too long."

Once an auspicious day had been determined the village elders were ordered to go to Sigalangan to further advance the marriage negotiations. And after that the womenfolk came and fetched Taring. Regarding the brideprice negotiation session, there's no need for us to discuss that at length here: enough to say simply that it did not depart from *adat* in the least, neither in the direction of too little nor in the direction of too much money paid out. They simply did what was customary in *adat*. When the brideprice negotiations were over, only then did they come to her place of residence to fetch the bride. Once they had done this and various other things of such and such a use in *adat*, out stepped the girl to embark on her marriage journey, with her father's sister fetching her and carrying her back to Padang Sidimpuan. There she was asked where she was going, so as to make her intentions clear and definite for all to witness. And Taring answered in good form: "I'm embarking on my journey to adulthood; I am going to marry Pandingkar Moedo, to find him in his house."[38]

As they were arranging for the pair to sit down formally in front of the Council of Village Elders, they came to a decision to marry them according to the full *adat*, with a buffalo sacrifice and a full gong ensemble. But, since at that time it was difficult to celebrate the arrival of a bride with formal gong music if the families weren't from the wealthiest class, they couldn't arrange all that. Pandingkar Moedo could be said to be of the middle class; moreover, he mixed every day with the *malims*. So the public clamored for a *fakir*-style wedding, a Muslim one. That is, they would celebrate the event by simply singing songs of the Prophet's miraculous birth, to the accompaniment of drums. So they called in all the religious teachers, who beat their prayer drums and recited their sacred phrases. They called in all the gurus from the entire Angkola Domain and from the surrounding foothill country: eventually this whole group decided to hold the wedding in the drum and birth-story style.

On the determined day, the drummer gurus came in from Angkolu Julu and Angkola Jae to join the ones in the marketplace. After everyone had gathered in Pandingkar Moedo's house, they counted their drums; there were a full thirty of them it seemed. So, clearly, there were also as many as that number of *dikir* ritual drummer-gurus, too, all gathered together: most impressive. People from the vicinity of the house came over, too, and visited, and watched, and helped out with the work.

Once the evening prayers were over, all the invitees gathered and were duly given a hearty meal, as was, of course, only fitting. All the young girls were hard at work keeping the coffee glasses filled, shucking sugarcane, cooking gingerroot, and so on.

After the meal there were speeches about the reason for holding the ceremony. The decisions were turned over to the rajas, the nobles, and the gurus. Then everyone traded speeches, back and forth, saying that they were all certainly of a single decision, of a single agreement. The prayers chanted from the prayer books began, then they had a short intermission, then they started singing *ollolo* songs, as if they were going out to greet a great prophet.

Everyone stood up at this. Then everyone sat down. Then they started to tap the drums lightly and chant the phrases from the prayer books, starting with "Assala. . . ." It was as if he was creating good fortune powers by chanting this way, that guru, Guru Lila. He was the one to start things off, softly, softly . . . the guru saying: Maule . . . i . . . assa . . . la . . . Allahum . . . a muale . . ." And "*reng, reng*," went the drums, as well as "*bur . . . bur . . .*" The drums sounded as if they were moaning softly, going *dering-dering, dering-dering*. And to look upon the gold rings on the young people's fingers, all turned to the left, with their faces turned in that direction too, and with the girls sitting there in pairs, their eyes turned toward the front of the meeting room: Lailahaillallah—well, it might have been called a simple, pious, *fakir*-style wedding, but the end result was that all the young folks got to flirting anyway.

After the "Assala" part they went on to the second stage. It started out softly, but eventually the drumbeats speeded up furiously. The beats and the prayers moved on to another verse, and then it was the turn of Djanapen's folks from Angkola Julu. That fellow had to be lit with a torch so folks could see him, his face was so black from the sun. And then his eyes: they were like the black eyes of a ghost bird. But his voice! It was absolutely lovely, beyond all telling. According to the ones knowledgeable about such things, he had one of the Prophet David's own secret charms in his possession—the very charm that made Sitti Fatimah burst into tears when she so much as thought of it. I would hazard to guess that folks started to ask themselves: "*Where* did Djanapen get those verses of his?" Ah, but it was impossible to say. "Alamokot"—well, of course, most people know that one. That must be a magic potion! everyone said. So Djanapen started again, from the beginning: "Ala . . . almukot . . . da . . . me . . . hellllel . . ." "That's it!" . . . "Fa . . . aaather! Aya rodian . . . Allah our God . . ." The houseful of people fell silent; it was as if you could hear a tiny colored bead drop. Even those asleep were shocked awake by everyone's silence, listening to this man's voice. It was as if even the horses outside were listening carefully to what was happening there in the house. When the drum went "*do-reng*" the crowd muttered: "Allah our God, the greatness of God." And it continued like that, with people taking turns all through the night, straight through until dawn.

Once it got light Pandingkar Moedo was formally married according to Islamic law, in accord with the usual practice. And after that they offered a meal to the rajas, the gurus, and the *fakirs*. And the general crowd was fed, too; everyone got full and happy. The ceremony was over; Pandingkar Moedo now sat among the mature men of the village as a married man. Everyone who had come to the ceremony remained hale and hearty all the way back to their homes.

Once they were actually married, Pandingkar Moedo was limitlessly happy at finding himself together with his companion in his own house. And Taring was the same: she had no regrets about coming to marry Pandingkar Moedo. To the contrary she felt extremely lucky to have her beloved—and not to have been forced into it, either. One can clearly read from this the fact that it is good for children to get married by their own consent. Because they were in good, firm agreement with each other, one never heard arguments issuing from that house. Rather, they always attracted great public affection, and so they were a good example to anyone who came to observe them. Pandingkar Moedo's parent, for her part, was indescribably happy to have a married son and a good daughter-in-law right there in the house. It was as if she had both sons and daughters now.

If a person is happy he or she will work with great diligence at making a living. Pandingkar Moedo and his wife were just like that. They never tired of setting off for the store every day to find Awaiting Riches and his wife. Their compatibility was represented by a saying: Together they rise to the sky, together they descend to the earth, like the bobbin-shaped top of the crown ginger plant, its knobby fruits all clustered together. Their business prospered, and their profits were not inconsiderable.[39]

Now, Dear Reader, let us turn for a moment to Rangga Poerik and Rangga Balian after they abandoned Pandingkar Moedo by Lake Bobak, out at the Hapuran resting spot, out in the deep forest. We do this to see what happened. Well, it appears that these two guys were just like two birds newly sprung from their comfortable cage, out on their own for the first time, not knowing how to find anything to eat for themselves. Because, after all, as we related in the beginning, back when they had themselves a boss and protector they had never lacked for a thing. If they were hungry they'd be fed till they were stuffed; if they were thirsty they'd be given ample drink. If their clothing fell into tatters it was Pandingkar Moedo who would feel ashamed. Once they were separated from Pandingkar Moedo they were total losses at finding something to put into their Middle Continents. Sometimes they'd behave like a couple of wild tigers, in fact: if they happened to catch a deer they would gorge themselves till they got sick. But if they were down on their luck and didn't catch anything they'd find a baby cricket and maybe roll it around in the dust before eating it, just to have a bit of curry to scoop into their mouths.

The news of Pandingkar Moedo's great good fortune echoed and reechoed throughout the countryside, and word reached their ears, too. So they took a notion to snare him as their beneficent boss-protector once again. But how could they manage to get close to him again? There seemed to be no way—after all, they were seriously in the wrong for defaulting on their promise. So they started hurling accusations back and forth. "It's all because of you, Rangga Poerik, that we're in this fix, you know," said Rangga Balian.

"Well, true, but why did you go and do what I did when you saw that I was doing the wrong thing? If you'd stuck to your guns and told me not to break the promise then I surely wouldn't have run off," said Rangga Poerik.

One time, off they set, walking fast and flashing by, around the mountain twists and turns,[40] off on a journey to discover whether or not Pandingkar Moedo was wealthy. But apparently for all this long while the police had been spying on them, deeming them legally culpable for what they had done. So they had no more than shown their faces for an instant when they were wrapped in two pairs of strong arms and arrested. They were put in jail to await their verdict in court.

On the appointed day their trial opened in public court. Pandingkar Moedo was called as the first witness before the session, and he explained exactly what they had done to him. Pandingkar Moedo related everything, from the beginning of their trip to collect resins, to the firm oath-promise that none was allowed to forget, to the oath they were never allowed to change. "But, when I was very sick and in great pain, and rain and hail were pelting down on me, and, moreover, a huge tiger was gnawing on me, they upped and left me in the middle of the road. For that, well, when I mull over what they did, I find I have simply lost all faith and trust in them. They're no more than murderers," said Pandingkar Moedo.

"Do you have any other complaints?" asked the judge.

"No, your Honor, our Lordship."

Rangga Poerik was called to the stand, and he was asked: "What is your name? How old are you? In what village were you born? And just what sort of work do you do?"

"My name, our Lordship, is Rangga Poerik, and I am twelve years old. My village is Sialogo; my job till a while ago was loyal servant and faithful retainer of Pandingkar Moedo. Nowadays, though, I am just a poor beggar."

"Why did you run away and leave Pandingkar Moedo in the middle of the road when he was so sick, when you had promised to remain together for as long as you lived, to be of a single life, of a single death?"

"Yes, indeed, your Honor, our Lordship, as for me myself, I did hold firmly to the words of our oath, though I happened to already be in the jaws of a tiger who was fixing to swallow me, there in the falling hail, there in the deep darkness. Given all that, I still tried to be brave, but, our Lordship, your Honor, what could I do? Though the heart was sufficiently brave, the feet wanted to flee. If I am in the wrong then I should be punished: make me Pandingkar Moedo's faithful retainer once more, please, please."

"Hey, heh, heh, you are the clever talker, aren't you?" said the judge, turning then to Rangga Balian.

Asking Rangga Balian the same questions, the judge inquired: "As for you, Rangga Balian, why did you leave Pandingkar Moedo in the middle of the road when he was so sick and beset by hailstones and deep darkness—and with a big tiger after him to boot?"

"As for me . . . our Raja, with regard to what you ask, your Honor, our Raja, all of this is surely true. Indeed, my love for Pandingkar Moedo cannot be measured. I feel that I love him more than I love myself. If I go fishing, your Honor, and I catch a big river fish, I will give some to Pandingkar Moedo before I eat any myself. But, your Honor, when it becomes a matter of living or actually *dying*, I have to admit that I have an onion skin's worth more love for myself than I have for him. Because this tiger was so close, and closing in, it occurred to me, your Honor, that we were actually fixing to *die*—to croak right there in the middle of the road. And that is why I picked up my feet and ran. I had endured what could not be endured."

"Ho, ho, ho . . . so, you are equally clever at answering questions, are you? But now your guilt is evident—as people who cause others to lose faith in them, as folks who betray friends. You are to be punished by being jailed for three months, though not in full convicts' chains. Look, you'll have free food and free clothing just like any other jailbird. And your work will be to dig loads of sand from the riverbeds in Angkola Jae."

"*Tak* . . ." said the desk as the president of the court session thumped it with a gavel, the sign that the verdict was final and immutable.

After the two guys had been sentenced Pandingkar Moedo felt happier, for what they had done had been gnawing at him. Now all that disappeared.

The days went by and the months followed in their turn, and people began to notice all the small signs: the birds sang out their glad news, that the wife of Pandingkar Moedo was going to have a child. At this, there was no measuring Pandingkar Moedo's joy nor that of his parent.[41]

The days came, the months passed, the year coursed on, and a child was born there in the womb.[42] And there, under water, it could be seen that it was a boy, a big, strong, healthy one, and handsome, too. But, as he was coming out onto this earth, his trip was made back end first, with his right hand holding a gift.[43] Seeing this child's manner of birth, happiness was mixed with pain for that pair of house sharers, for, according to the prophecy of the *datu*-diviner, if a child is born in the breech position, his father will die, if not his mother, and if not them then the child itself. But if the child carries a gift in its hand then that child will go on to live a lucky life and have an easy time of it, making a good living.

One day, about a month after the child was born, the shopkeeper called over Pandingkar Moedo and said: "Younger Lineage Mate . . . look, I know you don't really have the time, since our child has just arrived, but because I'm down with a fever I must ask you to go to Sipirok and make the collections from our creditors, for I have an agreement with them that I'll go into the mountains (that is, to Sipirok) on Thursday, two days from now. But you can come back right away so they won't get to missing you too much at home. If we don't go on that particular day they'll have the excuse of waiting another month to pay."

Pandingkar Moedo found it very difficult to agree with these words, but in light of the promise the shopkeeper had made to the creditors he went to Sipirok that Wednesday. Once it was daylight, that is, on Thursday (market day in Sipirok), all the creditors started to crowd in, paying the money they owed. According to the folks who told the story, Pandingkar Moedo received as much as two thousand rupiah. As soon as he had collected all the money he did not wait for Friday but started right back home on Thursday. He did not take a horse carriage, since at that time it was harder to go by carriage than it was simply to walk because of all the rocks in the road. There were stones as big as a person's head. The carriage wheels would be pummeled by the ricocheting rocks.

Now we'll switch over to Rangga Poerik and Rangga Balian—and to their thoughts after they got out of the clink! Oh——it was like a fire deep inside a pile of dry rice husks: smoke might not have been visible, but a fire was burning down deep inside, nonetheless. So they kept a careful watch on where Pandingkar Moedo might be going, so that they could exact their revenge and assuage their malicious jealousy—the malicious jealousy that kept gnawing away at them.

"If we don't fight him with brute force then we shall fight him with subtle strategies. We shall use all manner of secret fighting knowledge on him," they thought to themselves. So, once they found out that Pandingkar Moedo had gone to Sipirok that Wednesday, they went to the dark forest to watch him go by and way-lay him there. Beginning on Thursday morning they awaited Pandingkar Moedo's arrival. Their intention was: if he didn't die they would always live in fear of him. Why, even though they were alive they still didn't have any orderly, dependable way of getting food to eat every day.

Well, Pandingkar Moedo was rushing along on his journey, virtually running, he was going so fast. He climbed into the hills again, getting into Angkola at noon. When he got to the three emblic plants there he looked toward the Pargarutan Valley and tears flowed down his cheeks. He thought back again to Simincak Peak, for over to his left there it was . . . looming over the domain of Padang Bolak. And in the Pargarutan Valley, people's villages were rather evenly spread out, one from another, there were so many of them there. The villages followed the main road and were very easy to see because of the coconut palms growing along the road in each settlement. He paused for a bit, thinking about his little boy who had just been born—the child had been asleep when he left him. A moment later he let out a long breath as he lifted his feet and set off on his way again. He walked along once more, going upward toward Djatabaen's hot and cold drinks stand. He had two glasses of fresh palm toddy there since he was very thirsty. After he'd paid for the toddy he moved on. At Malim Maradjo's rice stall he stopped for a quick meal, and then he set off again, driving himself to exhaustion. About three in the afternoon he got to the clearing in the woods where the horse carts stopped to pick up the sap. His chest was heaving up and down painfully, he was so tired. But because he missed his new-born child so much he forced himself onward.

As he was climbing into the resin forest, he had the two thousand rupiah in a satchel slung over his shoulder, for he couldn't stuff all the bills and coins into his pockets. He had no more than reached the turn when Rangga Poerik sprung on him in a flying tackle. It was to little avail, though, since he was able to kick Rangga Poerik savagely in the chest (although the youngster was quite close to him) and toss him to the side of the road, about five fathoms away. Rangga Balian said: "I am willing to die at the hands of an enemy in order to make you acknowledge defeat." But he hadn't finished saying these words when Pandingkar Moedo lashed out and punched him on the chest with six flying blows. "What *is* this?"

"Are you just now seeing that it's me, Pandingkar Moedo?"

But what was to be done? Pride goeth before a fall: he was afraid they'd be overheard fighting like that by people passing by, so he jumped the two guys by the side of the road. At that moment apparently Rangga Poerik had already regained consciousness, but he played dead out of fright. And, even though Pandingkar Moedo's attack had made him hurt all over, Rangga Poerik opened his pocket and without Pandingkar Moedo suspecting it he suddenly took out a big handful of stun poison, which had been ground together with hot peppers and itching poisonous leaves. He threw all of this right into Pandingkar Moedo's eyes. Pandingkar Moedo fell down and began to thrash his legs back and forth in pain. He splashed what water he could scoop up into his eyes, which had now been gutted by the itchy, stinging, poison leaves. The pain and the itch was beyond all telling, and he dropped all the money in the package and forgot all about it. For, after all, if you look straight at the bright sun for just a moment and are blinded the whole earth is dark—but how much worse it is to have poison leaves thrown into your eyes.

As Pandingkar Moedo was lying prone on the ground Rangga Poerik snatched the money away, and they ran off. Where they ran to no one knows, to this day. People think they ran off to Tamuse Jungle. That was a village the Dutchman had not yet subdued, near the White Land,[44] over by Kampar. As for Pandingkar Moedo, after he could see a bit more clearly he looked around for his money and found that it was gone. And he discovered that the two guys had absconded, too. That made him fall to wiping away his tears again, thinking about all the money that was gone, all those thousands of rupiah.

When he got back to the house he was sobbing even harder, for his eyes were hurting more and more now. The shopkeeper was told that Pandingkar Moedo had been attacked by robbers at night and that his eyes had been gutted by poison leaves. Hearing this, the shopkeeper cried so hard that there's no telling of it. But what could be done? For as time went on Pandingkar Moedo's illness continued to worsen. He was given all sorts of medicine, but his eyes just got worse. He was even taken to Tuan Docter, to the Dutch doctor, but he got even worse than before.

His mother and his wife were now very fearful, indeed, when they considered his state, for his eyes looked as if they were going to pop out. He groaned so much in pain that no one in the household could sleep at all. At times, when Pandingkar Moedo felt a little better, his wife would tell him: "Look at Uncok and see how big he's gotten. He's sprouting up like a cucumber, isn't he?[45] Please, please get better—so we can have his *ompung* give him a name and so we can call in a *malim*. Look! Look! You're the only one who can make him laugh."

"Oh. . . . my son . . . my little boy, what am I to think? Please, please, Allah, my God, make this terrible illness abate," he said, breathing very heavily.

Hearing this his wife and his mother grew despondent. Whenever they looked at Pandingkar Moedo's eyes they would both start to sob. In a moment, Pandingkar Moedo took his son onto his lap and started to weep very hard. "You must be sure to love this child very much, for I feel I am going to die."

Recalling the *datu*-diviner's prophecy they became even more fearful. So they sent word to his mother's brother and his mother's brother's wife in Sigalangan, and to Awaiting Riches and Boroe Soeti, for all of them to come as soon as possible.

The shopkeeper had tried all sorts of things by this point, such as bringing in a *datu*, but the sickness just kept getting worse. The shopkeeper kept saying: "If you'll only get well again I'll give you anything you want. You just have to ask for it and I'll buy it. As for the money that disappeared, don't you worry about that. With God's sacred help I shall certainly not hold that against your account. Hopefully, if you can get better real fast we'll quickly make some money to replace it all."

But all this did no good. So, one night, since his illness was so very severe, Pandingkar Moedo came to the end of his life. He breathed his last living breath, this Young Leaf on the Tree of Life—he died surrounded by lineage companions, in front of his mother, his wife, and his son, he of the unhappy requests to his father. The reader can well imagine what sort of sobs and cries the occupants of the house moaned out, for a death like this one took a man before his time. A short bit of Taring's *andung* mourning wails, *andung* laments that people can never forget, will indicate this immense suffering.[46] I ask forgiveness of the public if there be mistakes, shortcomings, or excesses here.

"Oh——Father——Mother, oh——Dear Older Lineage Companion, whom I never imagined would die, apparently you have had the heart to leave us, to leave my body here, to abandon our unlucky little son! Apparently you went ahead and asked to leave, asked to leave us behind! Oh, I lament that request! You left us with a feeling of mourning greater than others have ever borne, hi-hi-hi—I lament, I lament——Father, Mother, oh, perhaps it is best that your life companion simply follow you to the grave, taking along our unlucky little son, so we're all together in the grave. Oh, that is my mournful request! Oh, what are we to do, I ask? For your life companion's eyes are like the eyes of a horse who's lost his race, never daring to raise his head to people again, that's how this solitary person's eyes are now, shifting from side to side, blankly watching people go about their normal work, gazing at them but always thinking and mulling over my life companion and his death request, his plea to die, which carried him off to his grave. Oh——Father, oh, Mother, oh—— It is only my life companion's death request that has left me destitute here in the midst of other people happily going about their work, Oh—— If your hand outstretched to me has already died I do not have the strength of will to continue drawing life's breath. Oh—— It is better that I just follow along behind you to the grave. Oh—— My husband, how am I to think of our little son, whose good fortune has been so very short-lived? If people sit there eating their meals, his gaze rises and falls to watch them put food in their mouths, yet he has no food himself, and his gaze is like the gaze of Meow-Meower, Hip-Hopper in the Kitchen, waiting there on the floor for people to drop table scraps for him to eat. Our son is like someone carried into the center of a big grassy field where the vicious birds will swallow him up, his fate none other than that, the fate of our unlucky little son, Oh, Mother—— Oh, my mother, who once gave birth to her little daughter, hai——"

Everyone in the house was crying now, on hearing Taring's mourning wails. People's good advice speeches simply rolled off her without sinking in. A moment later, her little son slid off her lap onto the floor: she did not even know he had fallen. By about dawn the coffin had been built, other things that had to be done for the burial were all in order, and the late Pandingkar Moedo was escorted to the grave. At Pandingkar Moedo's final steps out of the house, Taring's sobs and those of his parent and lineage mates could not be described. Even his little son joined in and cried in a soft, moaning voice, as if he knew that this was the day of his final separation from his father.

When everyone had returned from the ceremony all of them gave advice speeches to Taring and his mother as well as to the whole family. They told them to

be diligent and patient in the face of their loss as they went about the work of raising this little child—for, after all, he was Pandingkar Moedo's little replacement. He
would assuage their feelings of deep longing and loneliness and would surely bring
stores of patience to the people left behind in life by the death. If Taring just kept
going on and on in her pain and sadness that could not possibly come to any good.
It is best to simply have patience, so that they could pray and give aid to the one
who's died as evidence of their love. But if they persisted in this suffering and pain
it would bring ruin. And, it won't just be you who will go to your grave but the little one you're responsible for, too, they told her. Now, he did not simply die and then
his body disappeared—no, not at all. Rather, if we have the proper measure of piety,
we shall surely all meet him again in the Afterworld. So, because of that, it is better
just to read more of those prayer verses out loud so as to bring patience to the living and make the departed rest easier in their graves. After the *kenduri* meal and
prayer session was over, all the family members went home. Only the very close ones
stayed behind, to give advice and tell of good examples to follow, so that they would
have patience in the face of the death. And people's advice was not summarily tossed
aside by the late Pandingkar Moedo's parent and wife. Rather, they took it to heart.
So their pain lessened a bit. Only at that point did they become somewhat aware of
people's advice to them, and they offered heartfelt thanks to everyone who had
made them rest a bit easier.

PART TWO

7

Djahoemarkar

Na mangarkari na robian	The one who opens up the past
Na mangarkari sude ni na dangol	Who breaks open all manner of sadness
Na mangarkari halalungun	Who opens wells of deep longing and loneliness
Na mangerkari dalan tu parsaulion.	Who opens, too, the path to luck and joy.

In a certain house standing to the right of the Other-Side Market if you're on the road to Sipirok (and standing on the left of the road if you're going on to the Mandailing land) sat a woman enveloped in sadness, musing dejectedly, wiping away her tears. Her teardrops fell one after another onto the child she was holding on her lap in a cloth sling. What could have caused this? It all resulted from Pandingkar Moedo's death, which we talked about in part 1 of this book. Even though family and lineage mates kept coming to visit and help her bear her grief, her pain remained clearly etched on her face. While she did not dismiss her visitors' good advice and heartfelt commands to cheer up, she had not taken them to heart, either. It was as if all that good advice just slid off her; none of it penetrated to reach her real feelings. But since she did have some small store of patience in her heart her pain eventually began to subside a bit.

As more and more days went by, unlucky little Uncok* grew larger and larger, just like a cucumber sprouting. He was a healthy, sturdy, fast-growing kid. If Taring were sitting in the front office of the house, musing sadly, the birds in the orange trees surrounding the house would often burst into lively song. They'd be singing from sheer happiness, and after a moment they'd hop from one branch to another. All the sad memories would come rushing back to the woman, and she would think about the man to whom she had surrendered her *tondi* soul. Her pain and sadness would increase when she remembered him like this. At such a time, Little Boy would free himself from the safe resting spot at her breast where he was nursing and, "he he . . . he he . . . ," the child's voice would ring out brightly, greeting his mother in her sadness and pain. Once Taring noticed such a thing occurring she would kiss her son tenderly. She felt that her beloved child's laughter was true balm to her heart. As more days went by and more months passed the child did more and more of these small charming things and so became an adept assuager of his mother's pain and longing. A proof of that was the fact that her deep sadness began to disappear little by little from Taring's heart.

Sweet Uncok was already able to sit up a bit, but Taring still had not had the heart to give the child a name. Everyone just kept calling him Little Boy. When the young wives from next door and all the nearby houses came over to the house,

---

*An affectionate term of reference and address, often used in family circles, meaning "littlest boy in the family."

they'd ask Taring what her good-hearted, sweet Little Boy's name was, but her tears would always splash down her cheeks when she tried to answer her friends' questions. "If only, if only his father was still drawing his life breath! I don't really want to give him a name right away, but all my friends keep asking me about it, about unlucky Little Boy's name, but what name can I offer them? So, kind women friends,[1] please, please, don't keep asking me, all of you. Please, asking me his name just reopens all my feelings of sadness and pain. But it recalls more than those emotions, too: asking me his name also reopens my feelings of deep longing and loneliness for his father," she said, wiping away tears.

She'd always answer like this when anyone asked her her child's name, and eventually people did not ask her what the child's name was when they came to the house. They'd just say: "Let me take Good Hearted Little Dad here on my lap for a second, he who reopens memories of the past, he who reopens feelings of deep longing and loneliness, he who reopens feelings of sadness and pain.[2] The later it got, the more people began to *like* saying "he who reopens feelings of deep longing and loneliness." So, for his name they'd just call him "He Who Reopens Feelings of Deep Longing and Loneliness." Eventually people added a few embellishments here and there, and his name became Djahoemarkar, "Raja Who Reopens Deep Feelings of" this and that.

Dear Reader, if people like to say a certain name (even if in the beginning it was just a playful nickname), eventually it will develop into a good, usable name. That is how this child's name was treated, till finally it became his permanent name. When the adolescent girls from that same row of houses would come over to visit or share some snacks, they'd always ask Taring if they could take Little Boy onto their laps. They'd be so happy playing with him there that they would forget he was an orphan who had lost a parent while still very small. Straightaway they would burst into *ijeng-ijeng* songs:*

Ijeng . . . ijeng ijeng . . . C'mon, let's sing *ijeng* songs. . . . Djahoemarkar, too, *ijeng-ijeng*, Djahoemarkar, he who reopens memories of the past, the one who reopens feelings of deep longing and loneliness. . . . Ois. . . . May you grow up fast and get real big so there'll be medicine for the mind and something to cure our feelings of deep longing and loneliness . . . *ijeng*, my little pal, *ijeng ijeng* Djahoemarkar . . .

"Oh, you'll all die young for saying such things, my little women-friends," said Taring to the girls. "If only you had not reopened all those inconsolable feelings of pain and sadness for me! Just when I can finally see a brighter day you go and open up all those painful emotions again."

"Allah, our God. . . . Honestly, I didn't know I was saying all *that* in my song, good Older Lineage Companion! I only did it because I was so happy to see this good-hearted little guy," said the girl, laughing merrily, and after that they all went to sit under the overhanging branches of the fruit trees and munch on ripe rose apples and red *rambutan* lychees.

We can shorten the story a bit here, so that we don't go on too long about Taring's pain and sadness. From day to day, from month to month, from year to year: Djahoemarkar is now seven years old.

Ijeng-ijeng are playful, "teasing" songs sung by children and young people.

The bigger Djahoemarkar got the more his size and shape made people take great delight in looking at him. He had a sturdy, healthy body, his face was handsome, his mind was good, and his manner of speaking was soft and well modulated.[3] One time Taring got to thinking about how she should bring this only child up and what sort of life he should have. Since he was quick, shrewd, and already knew how to count, she was sure that her only child was very smart. After she had thought it over and weighed the options it occurred to her that this child should be sent to school. After all, cleverness and knowledge are the greatest heirloom treasures on earth and ones you can never exhaust, either. Inherited property, silver, yellow-yellowest, glittering gold,[4] and such are things that can be lost if you are not careful in keeping a close watch over them. So . . . even though a person might have only one plot of rice paddy land and one tiny little colored bead to his or her name, if they have intelligence and knowledge the world will never be a harsh place. Rather, it will serve as a beneficent, fortunate arena, providing him or her a rich livelihood. So, with that in mind, she was very certain and determined that she should put her single little leaf, her only child, into school.

Everyone in the houses in the row nearby told her not to put her child in school, for was he not a dear, cherished only child? And, after all, they had lots of inherited property, didn't they? So whatever was the use of putting him in school? If he was smart in school later on he'd just go and get a salaried job and ignore the house and garden land he had inherited, not to mention their wide expanses of rice paddy land. Now, what benefit could possibly come from that? But Taring did not pay them any mind; she was just as determined as ever to put her child into school.

When it got to be the Fasting Month, schools would usually open ten days afterward. That was also the time when new students would register. Dozens and dozens of people came from upriver and down, bringing their children to be enrolled in school. For her part Si Taring surely did not forget to take her son to school. And out of all the children who crowded into school it was only Djahoemarkar who had a glowingly healthy body. Seventy-five percent of the other children had some sort of illness, such as continual fevers or a tendency to waste away and keep losing weight—all signs that they weren't cared for very well.[5]

Taring didn't have to wait very long before the schoolmaster called her in and had her bring Djahoemarkar before him. After he had written down the boy's name name and home village, the teacher patted Djahoemarkar softly on the head because he liked him so much. As he did this he said to Taring: "You go on home—your child is safely enrolled in school now."

"Thank you, your Honor, our Lordship, I truly hope that my child will behave himself, for he is the only child left behind after his father died. His father was sort of the root under this little cucumber, making him grow. Because of that I hand him over to you, so that he might become a child who serves a useful purpose—though if he *also* turns out to be the sort of person who can easily adapt himself to all manner of new social situations, well, that would be all right, too." Her tears were already gathering in puddles at receiving this sign of affection from the guru.

"Then let us join together in asking God that what you request will indeed come to pass," said the schoolmaster, patting Djahoemarkar gently on the shoulder.

Then he took him by the hand, led him into the schoolhouse, and put him in the first-grade class.

Since he was healthy and strong Djahoemarkar was ready and willing to go to school every day rather than stay home. Moreover, the lessons that the teacher fed him slipped down real easily. And so he came to be called a smart child, an apt pupil, one who was easy to teach. At the end of the year, when the list of absences was examined, he had attended school 100 percent of the time, while many of the other children had reneged many times on their promise to go to school regularly. Why, sometimes between 25 and 50 percent of them would not be there. This resulted in a large number not being promoted to the next class.

Each Fasting Month, at each school, there would be a ceremony to present prizes to the good students (based on their accomplishments). Some would receive pencils, some would get penholders, some would get handkerchiefs, others would get socks, a few would get clocks, and some would even get a luxurious, shiny sarong. Well, as for Djahoemarkar, he got a batik hat worth five florins, a knife from France, a writing tablet, *and* a pencil.

We cannot describe how happy he was to get these prizes. Suffice it to say that he felt as though he had received a lump of gold as big as a horse's head.[6] So the long walk home that day didn't bother him in the least; he couldn't wait to show the presents to his mother.

As soon as he got home he showed his mother and his grandmother* all the prizes he had won, and their joy was ten times greater than his own. The prizes the child had received clearly demonstrated that the boy had gotten more learning than had all those other children. When school opened again Djahoemarkar moved up a class from his first level. But lots of the other children did not get promoted. Some of them stayed in one grade for three years but *still* did not get promoted. Eventually they were turned out of school.

From what we have related above it is quite clear that the fundamental building blocks underlying hardworking habits and clear thinking are none other than a healthy body and a happy mind. Because of this, for the Dutch, good health is worth more than great landed wealth and inherited treasure here on this earth. They're not like some people, who think that silver and gold are more valuable than physical health. Such folks would rather die than let a coin slip out of their money sack to buy themselves some medicine, it seems. A person who values property over his life is like someone who prefers death to life, actually, and what comes of that except that folks fall all over each other rushing to get the money he leaves behind when he dies. The writer of this story, in fact, has often encountered people who want to get very rich, very quickly. Such a person is never willing to buy medicine to make his body healthy. Ah, but as for what he eats, well, he must have exactly what he wants, he says! One time such a person ordered his wife to buy a big golden carp cooked in a thick curry sauce, with fern greens and a bit of torch ginger to boot as its tart condiment. The curry was so rich that it was positively viscous, and the rice, of course, had to be Sipahantan Rice, the most delicious of all life grains. After it was prepared his rice spooner presented the food to the guy. "Fine," he said, putting it in

*His grandmother—the late Pandingkar Moedo's mother.

front of him, but after he had tried a little bit none of it budged from his plate: he had lost all desire to eat. Well, what is to be said? In the end it is only healthy people who can really eat their fill. Indeed, what is the use of property if not to satisfy your body's needs? For that reason, friend, if we are going to progress and live happy lives we have to satisfy our physical body's needs and keep ourselves healthy.

We can clearly see the difference here by comparing Djahoemarkar with the physically unhealthy children: they got left far behind in their school accomplishments.

As for Djahoemarkar, he who reopens memories of the past, he who reopens feelings of sadness and pain, he who reopens feelings of deep longing and loneliness, as the years added up his storehouse of knowledge did the same. He also shot up in size and stature. His sturdy body and his clothing's cleanliness both added to the healthy glow on his face, pleasing everyone who caught sight of him. Everything about him served as good examples of things people loved.

His mother—the one who was adept at figuring out other people's thoughts, who was expert at ordering words, who knew her manners and followed rules[7]— never tired of teaching her son all the fine etiquette and behavior a person should exhibit in public, such as how to use the correct kin terms[8] and how to pay respect to family and friends. His mother would often teach him about this. He was taught how to talk to people and how to follow all the rules of speech when talking to the rajas, when talking to the government employees, when talking to schoolteachers, and when talking to the respected elders.[9] He was adept at speaking politely, taking careful account of everyone's position relative to his own.

His mother saw to it that he had the right kind of clothing and that he wore it in the correct way. And so, even though he might be wearing normal clothing, he still served as an example of how to dress to anyone who might happen to observe him, for his outfits always fit exactly. He never wore a shirt that was not tailored to order for him. His way of walking and the length of his strides were calm and consistent, not at all like the way a water buffalo in the rice field shuffles along, shaking his big head lumpily from side to side. Rather, he was always calm, collected, and quiet, with his eyes fixed straight ahead. If he had to turn his head then he would turn it by turning his whole body.[10]

And so, because his behavior was inlaid with silver and his manner of speaking was gilded with gold,[11] everyone around him loved him dearly. And as a consequence no one hindered his way as he would walk along upriver and down. Wherever he would go he would always find friendly acquaintances there; wherever he sat down he would always find family and lineage mates reposing there as well. And because of that he improved his manners still more, for he could already clearly see the value of polite, respectful behavior in his daily life.

By the fifth year of school Djahoemarkar was already in Class Five, right on schedule. All his teachers at school liked him a great deal and were always delighted to see him. The teacher who had him in class would never be stingy with his teaching skills, not with this child. As the boy demonstrated his high intelligence more and more the teachers would start to bring out all sorts of knowledge that they had not been able to teach in years. After Djahoemarkar had learned it they would just stash it back in its hiding place again. Whatever the teacher bestowed on him in their lessons Djahoemarkar would immediately soak up and store in his heart, never to be forgotten.

One time, when the Fasting Month was approaching, his teacher quizzed the child to see what he thought about continuing on for further schooling. How far did he want to go? He was already in the fifth grade. Should he go just that far, or should he go on?!

"As far as I can see, your Honor, I'd like to be in school next year, for I am still very young and have not yet stored up all the knowledge that you've been teaching me. I can't be sure yet that it will stay with me forever and ever. If you're young in body you are young in mind, too, and I'm afraid everything in my heart is still immature and inexperienced. Why, sometimes I still don't know the value of very expensive things. So, because of all that, yes, I *would* like to continue my schooling next year."

The teacher shook his head as he explained. "Well, frankly, you now have as much knowledge as can possibly be packed in there. Even if you study very diligently, I will not be able to add anything more to it; in fact, if we add something new it may well ruin your brain. Djahoemarkar, a schoolteacher's mode of teaching is not the same as that of Lobe Malang, you know.[12] Your pal there is just interested in gaining a fancy high position in life and impressive titles. And your friend would never stoop to bother himself with teaching little kids who are so young their umbilical cords haven't been cut yet—little kids who can't tell what it is they're being taught."

"Why (the teacher continued), if you tell them the world is round like a chicken's egg and that it revolves once every day and night, it's a foregone conclusion that they won't believe you, for they'll say: if the world is round then what's used to suspend it? And if it turns around why doesn't the water in the ocean fall off when the ocean's pointing downward? And, for that matter, why are we still standing here? We're *sure* we've never walked upside-down. But they can come to understand all this once they know that the earth has the same nature as a big magnet, attracting things to itself, and once they know that because of the slow speed at which the earth revolves no one here on the surface feels it moving. After all, it's twenty-four hours from Masjrik to Magrib."

"Lobe Malang says that the earth is laid out flat like a rattan floor mat and that it's held up by who knows how many water buffalos and how many cows. According to him if a wasp happens to sting one of these cows or buffaloes the whole thing can suffer an earthquake. That sort of thing kids accept. And then, too, Lobe Malang's always teaching adult prayer lessons to very small children. It's true that the kids learn the verses right away, but oftentimes, because they don't really take in the meanings of the phrases, your friend there is making things too easy for them. He'll even teach children words that one is not allowed to pronounce. That's all because there is no real step-by-step order to what is being taught. We can take as an example a small child who is being fed mashed food that his mother has just chewed for him.* We give him some banana: he's willing enough to eat it and in fact finds it

---

*Toddlers were fed masticated food as a kind of baby food.

quite tasty. So, we give him more and more of it, but because his stomach can't take such food yet he gets sick. His belly swells up, his eyes get yellow, and he doesn't do anything but cry, for his belly is full of sickness.

"Now who do you think is at fault there? Surely it's the one who gave him the food in the first place. . . ! Lobe Malang's like that. It gets to the point that I've seen him teach the 'Twenty Attributes of God' to children who are just learning to recite their Arabic prayers. But you more properly should be giving that sort of teaching to people who already have their wits about them. No matter how old he is, if he can't really take something in it should not be taught to him. Ideally he should be a full twenty years old before he knows how to recite the Arabic verse from *alip* to *ba* to. . . . Yeah, and from there on to the end! If it's done that way people won't misunderstand things, for by then a person has already analyzed God's work with His servants, he's already thought about the One who created things and about what has been so wonderfully created. True enough, Lobe Malang does have a lot of students who can recite well, but there aren't many who really grasp what it is they're saying. So, many, many young pupils misunderstand things. If something is said the wrong way, folks will say the kid's touched in the head or has lost his memory, even though it's really the teacher's own fault for trying to teach people who shouldn't be the target of such advanced lessons in the first place.

"And one additional thing: Lobe Malang often reads the Holy Book with a big crowd gathered around him, and among the folks who are there are people who have never heard the words of the Book before or who have never learned how to do their recitations. But at the same time there are folks there who have studied with a teacher many, many times. So, if you jumble people who know a lot with people who only know a little in the same Koranic reading session it's certainly not going to come out very well because their levels of understanding differ. The words in the Koran go by levels, with some harder than the others. People who've just begun to study with teachers use the easy parts of the Holy Book, and from there they go higher, and finally they get lessons in accordance with the teacher's own level of knowledge. If that is done, you won't have folks misunderstanding the verses they recite.

"Europeans, as you have noticed here in this school, teach according to different grade levels. If a person hasn't learned the lessons in first grade then he can't go on to second grade, and the same thing holds true from second grade to third and so on to the end. For each class there are special reading materials. The higher the grade the more mature the words are in the readers (in the reading books). From folktales to stories, from stories to *turiturian* epics, so it goes from easier to harder. In school two or three people a week are asked to recite. Recitals in the first grade aren't the same as those in second grade, and the same thing is true of the other grades, too. Often in first grade the recital will be about Raja Mousedeer asking for betel quid from the daughter of the great nobles, but in fifth grade it'll be Hakayat Bachtiar or Si Miskin.[13] So, because each grade gets its appropriate reader, there aren't any schoolchildren who misread things, as there are with Lobe Malang's pupils. In more advanced schools the lessons get more advanced, too; what is taught there simply cannot be taught in the first grade because that class of students is not the proper target audience. So, Djahoemarkar, that's the way we do things here in this school," said the teacher.

"Well then, your Honor, I would like to advance my studies to the next year so that I'll get more knowledge inside me. After that it'll be up to you to determine the proper place for me and what I know. You must be the one I turn to for that decision, so that all our efforts to educate me don't just disappear."[14]

"Well, if that is the case, fine. Indeed, I have had some hope that you might take the entrance exam for Bukittinggi* next year, but if you go there who will assuage your mother's feelings of deep longing and loneliness? You're a beloved only child. So that you won't have to stray far from her side we shall make you an assistant teacher. How about that? You can still come and take lessons from me or the other teachers; that'll just be to make your store of knowledge more complete. Your family will have enough to pay your school fees for you; it is said that you're from a wealthy background. After a year you can take the entrance tests. If you pass I'll still ask you to remain in Sidimpuan but as a Kweekeling, a Kweekschool student. If that comes to pass you will be able to rest easy and so will your parent. So, don't worry, rest easy, so that nothing hinders you along the road you shall traverse."

---

*For the elite teacher-training institute, or Kweekschool, in West Sumatra.

Sitti Djaoerah[1]

After Pandingkar Moedo had breathed his last life's breath Awaiting Riches looked at the world with downcast eyes and bowed head, like a horse who has lost a match out in the fighting arena. For, beyond losing thousands of rupiah he had lost his beloved, trusted associate. If one estimates the progress of the business and its profits after the loss of Pandingkar Moedo, it must be admitted that it fell off considerably. It can be fairly said, in fact, that the shopkeeper felt knocked aslant after his trusted associate's departure. He thought about Pandingkar Moedo night and day, and if he felt bad he would go over to the Other-Side Market to visit with Pandingkar Moedo's son and wife. Each time he went, he would take along little gifts; when he got ready to leave, he would leave behind some money for the unlucky little child's expenses, for, when he thought about it, he was the child's father now.

In the beginning he had no hesitation about going to the late Pandingkar Moedo's house, but as more days passed he went only if his wife went, too, for he felt as if there was a sort of barrier there when he came to show his love for the child. Actually, in his mind there were no bad intentions whatsoever and he continued to feel love toward everyone Pandingkar Moedo had left behind, but because Pandingkar Moedo's widow was young and she had only one child he was afraid people would gossip about all his trips to the house. Because of such feelings, as time went by, he went there less and less frequently. Why, sometimes it would be a week or even a month before he would visit. Then a month became a year, and eventually it was as if he didn't remember them at all.

We cannot fault Awaiting Riches for this. Rather, we should praise him for taking care that no vicious gossip was directed at Pandingkar Moedo's widow. Rather than have people see bad things it is better to just snap off those feelings of deep longing, at least until the orphaned child grows up. But, truthfully, if one were to open Awaiting Riches's heart one would find nothing as big as a quarter section of a hairtip that was less than polite and respectful toward the residents of that house. Nonetheless, since it is the nature of humanity to spread gossip, he reined in his feelings of deep longing and love for Uncok.[2]

Now let's look at Awaiting Riches's fate. It had already been about six years since he had married, since he had gone to sit among the adult men of the settlement, but he still had not had any good fortune—that is, he did not yet have any children. He and his wife were just as they were when they first married: no kids, just the two of them. Without letup, day and night, he asked for Almighty generous God's love and pity—the God who created the sky and the earth, the God who arranged for food to be placed in our bellies, the God who separated our fingers—

that He might have love and pity enough to give them a little gift to firm up the soul—that is, to give them golden hairpins to decorate his rice spooner's glossy plump hairbun: to give them sons and daughters.[3]

If people really mean what they say when they request something like this, God will not be all that stingy. Rather, he will graciously and richly bestow all that is elegantly requested. And now, indeed, the birds were singing out their joyful news about Awaiting Riches's rice spooner as a sign that she was going to have a child. Awaiting Riches's joy at seeing his wife in such a state of good health could not be measured with a rod nor weighed on a scale. His wife was the same way, for now she had great good fortune and shining luck powers safely in her hand.[4]

The months passed, the year turned, and the day came. A child was born in the womb, and it could be seen there in that sea that it was a girl, a healthy fine girl, with a good strong body and a very pretty face. When the baby had been wrapped in swaddling clothes Awaiting Riches took it right on his lap to show that, however much he had loved his wife all this time, now that her hairbun had a golden pin in it he loved her twice as much.

As soon as family and lineage mates had heard the news they all came crowding in to greet the baby, each of them bringing along small leaf packages of rice and curry.[5] Awaiting Riches's clan sisters* brought long lengths of cloth in which to hold the newborn, while the *hula-hula* holy wife givers brought a cloth baby sling so the child would have a tight wrapper for her body and soul.[6] When she gets bigger later on, she'll have to come over to her mother's brother's house so they can buy her a fancy scarf and a length of lacy jacket cloth all the way from Paris. Awaiting Riches's clan sisters all offered enthusiastic prayers to God, as if giving prayers to their holy wife givers. They prayed that the child would be healthy and cool souled, that she would grow bigger quickly, and that once she was grown, they prayed, she wouldn't go and marry someone from *outside* but would marry one of their very own sons, someone in the family.[7] The very variety of their speeches demonstrated their joy. After everyone had eaten their fill they all returned to their houses.

When the child was forty days old the general family and lineage mates were called in once more, along with the *hula-hula* wife givers and all their good friends.[8] They were called to Awaiting Riches's house for the purpose of giving the newborn a name. With great joy and happiness everyone rushed to come to the fine ceremony. Once all the *hula-hula* and good friends were gathered a ritual speaker grabbed hold of the rattan tray with its big mound of ceremonial rice and condiments. This mound of food was Butet's food to firm up her soul.† The rice was ready, the curry was there, all the perfect foods were made even more perfect so that Little Girl could be celebrated and given firm soul protection, as she was given a name. Awaiting Riches had asked that Little Girl's name be SITTI DJAOERAH.[9] The whole family readily agreed to that. No one said it was not a perfect name—ah, on the contrary, all said it was just *fine*.

---

*That is, his sisters.
†Si Butet ("Littlest Girl in the Family"): the feminine equivalent of Si Uncok. In Mandailing usage, the name is Si Taring.

To go back in the story a bit, Awaiting Riches had not forgotten Djahoemarkar's mother, nor his grandmother, at the arrival of his child. The same thing was also true at the time of the naming ceremony. They did attend, but to tell the truth they didn't behave as they had in the past. They weren't bold enough to speak to Awaiting Riches or his wife, for both of them felt that a sort of barrier was in the way. Djahoemarkar was five years old by now and could walk swiftly; his body was strong and healthy. To look at his face you would think he was a spirit child, he was so handsome. His manner of speaking was fluent and lovely to hear; he was fearless and bold. Whoever saw that child grew happy at the sight.[10]

When Taring and her *namboru** were sitting beside Awaiting Riches's wife they got to chatting about how much they had missed each other and they asked themselves what had caused them to visit so infrequently. Every one of them was crying, but what was to be done, after all, if that was their destiny from God!

As Djahoemarkar's mother was sitting there, chatting with Awaiting Riches's wife, Djahoemarkar never budged from Sitti Djaoerah's side. Every moment or so he'd give her a kiss, and if she'd cry he would caress her face, trying to comfort her. The adults' joy was no small thing as they observed the two children. Their happiness was a sort of sign that all the old pain and suffering had disappeared and the dead had come back to life.[11]

After the *horja* ceremony all the family, and lineage mates, the *anakboru* wife receivers, and the *hula-hula* wife givers returned to their respective villages. Djahoemarkar and his mother and *ompung* went home, too, to the Other-Side Market. Along the road, Djahoemarkar did nothing but talk about Sitti Djaoerah. He kept asking: "How about if we ask for Sitti Djaoerah, Mother, so I'll have a little *anggi*, a little younger lineage companion?"

What he said went straight to Taring's heart, for she couldn't figure out what made her son love Sitti Djaoerah so much. She just told him: "Once Sitti Djaoerah gets big let's ask her mother if she can come over so you'll have a playmate. Right now they can't give her to you since you're not big enough to carry her in a sling."[12]

"But I can carry her, Mother! C'mon, I'm strong enough. If she cries I'll rock her and sing her lullabies."

"But, Oppung, what will be your lullaby?"

"Oh, that's easy, Oppung:†

Buah manggis, buah Kadongdong	Mango fruits and *kadongdong* fruits,
Kaluo menangis torus kugendong	If you start crying I'll tuck you into a baby sling.[13]

Thus Djahoemarkar said, for it was as if Sitti Djaoerah was right there in front of him.

"Well, that's good, Ompung," said his grandmother, laughing. But Taring just lowered her head, as if she were musing, remembering her husband who had rushed on to his grave.

---

*Si Taring's *namboru* is the late Pandingkar Moedo's mother. A woman's *namboru* is her husband's mother, her father's sister.
†The reciprocal usage for grandparents and grandchildren used here is a fancy, intimate, unusual spelling. The regular usage is *ompung*.

Djahoemarkar's chatting made the road from the main marketplace to the Other-Side Market seem very short. Once they got back to the house they wiped off the sweat. After that day, they did not visit back and forth until Djahoemarkar was in school. Except for the one time he went there, to the center of town, Djahoemarkar never visited the main marketplace again. Who they saw there and where the house was he did not remember. He didn't even retain any memory images[14] of them. As a result he was not aware that some friends of his late father lived over there. Awaiting Riches was the same way: after Djahoemarkar came to his house that one time he never saw him again. As a result, even when Djahoemarkar walked in front of him, he did not recognize him. But he did love to see that particular child pass by on his way to school, as he was so healthy and good looking and sounded so friendly when he spoke. And he was very adept at using the right kin terms. But whose child he was he did not know.

In the past, once a week, teachers would hold games for the schoolchildren to help them work up a good sweat and make them tired. When the bell rang in the middle of the marketplace, the children would line up in rows like soldiers going off to war. At such times, when the children ran around shouting happily in the middle of the road, everyone would get a real kick out of seeing them. They were so healthy and hearty looking and were walking along so merrily. Women would exclaim, "Ois, Ois," as they watched the children out there giggling. When Djahoemarkar was in the third grade, Sitti Djaoerah was seven years old. She'd grown as fast as a dart out of a blowgun. After all, it's the nature of little girls to grow up faster than boys. When the children would file by in rows in front of Awaiting Riches's store, she loved it—especially when she saw that there was a girl out there. She wanted to be there, too, but what she should do to accomplish that she did not know. So she just had to stand there and enjoy watching them.

Because the schoolchildren filed around the marketplace in rows like that so often, Djahoemarkar got to know all the town's side roads. When he was out playing he'd walk wherever he wanted. Maybe one child would have some money and they'd buy some food in the market. Some would buy slices of layer cake, some would buy roasted peanuts, others would buy candy. They'd wear themselves out playing down under people's houses, down between the houseposts, shaded by the big awnings.

Djahoemarkar was not one to stay out in the hot sun. If he was tired after walking around a while he would seek some shade under the awnings of the stores. That way he would not bump his head playing under the houses.

Awaiting Riches's store had a big front stoop. That was a good place to sit and rest, as folks came to buy things. So if no customer happened to be sitting there Djahoemarkar loved to play there. The shopkeeper and householder and his wife loved to see that child, and they liked to give him snacks. People'll say that oftentimes, in fact, Awaiting Riches would buy a whole big basketful of salted peanuts from Kie A Tak in Sidimpuan and divide them up among all the children who'd come to the house.[15] At such times Sitti Djaoerah would be as happy as she could be. Even if she wasn't particularly interested in snacking she would still ask for her share from her father. Once she had the nuts she would give them to the other children, but she loved to give them to Djahoemarkar the most.

There was no estimating how happy the shopkeeper was at seeing all these children crowd around noisily. After everyone was full he'd strike up a conversation with one or the other of them, especially with Djahoemarkar (who was so good at talking). Whose child this was he did not know. It did not occur to him to ask, either. And so it went, like that, till they got to know Djahoemarkar, he who reopens feelings of deep longing and loneliness. If the shopkeeper happened not to be there himself his wife and Sitti Djaoerah would be there to chat with him. Once they began to talk they'd never tire of listening to Sitti Djaoerah chat away, she was so expert at saying things. Finally, Djahoemarkar asked the shopkeeper's wife: "Why don't you put this child in school? After all, lots of people's daughters are in school. If you put her in school I'll take good care of her."

"But what's the use of putting girls in school? Cooking rice and making curries are the only things women do, aren't they? If she needs some other skill, like crocheting lace or embroidering, she can be taught that at home," said Nandjaoerah.*

"But there's a lot of use to it: so that she'll be a smart person and can learn how to recite from the Koran easily; because they teach the letters in school, and the roots of those letters are the same as the ones in the Koran. And, then, when she's out buying things, she'll know how to count her change and figure the cost of something. She won't be tricked by somebody at the market."

"Oh . . . but how much money do wives have anyway? And what's so hard about buying hot peppers and everyday vegetables, or Siam fish for that matter. You just go over to the vegetable stand in the cornfield, after all," said Nandjaoerah.

"But, *that's* the reason! You have to know how much change is coming to you so you can do things quickly. If you have to use corn kernels to count your money it'll get to be pretty late in the day on you. But if you have some school knowledge you'll know how to do all that with ease. If you have ten cents and you use it to buy two big vegetables you'll know how to subtract the sums: twelve pitis minus four pitis leaves eight pitis, or two benggol and one big coin. Or five cents and a big coin. That way you're able to go home quickly because, after all, doesn't that time you save count for something, too?"

"Well, all right, all right, it certainly does. So, Djaoerah, does Inang† want to go to school to learn how to change money?" asked her mother.

"Sure I do! . . . But Djahoemarkar will have to be there in school with me," said Sitti Djaoerah.

"Of course, we can't be in the same grade, since I'm already in the third grade and people who've just started school have to begin with first grade. When you're in school the teacher always keeps a good eye on you—and you should know that you're not allowed to pinch each other. You can't jostle and play with each other too often, either. Whoever's misbehaving will get punished by the teacher. Your punishment will be to stand in front of all the schoolchildren with one foot on the other

---

*A teknonym, "Djaoerah's mother."
†Inang is used reciprocally between mothers and daughters.

knee and your arms outstretched. If you don't ask for mercy you'll just have to keep doing that. So studying is really the only thing allowed there, but when it's recess you're allowed to go out and have fun. You can play but not pinch. But at recess, don't worry, I'll watch out for you so nobody bothers you."

"All right, all right, if that's how it is then I guess I do want to go," said Sitti Djaoerah.

Not long afterward Awaiting Riches came home. The woman told the shop-keeper what they had been chatting about, and what the child had said went straight to the shopkeeper's mind: he readily agreed to it. Next day he took Sitti Djaoerah to school, and the teacher enrolled her without the slightest problem.

Everything Djahoemarkar had promised about taking care of Sitti Djaoerah he did. When Sitti Djaoerah was going to school he'd pick her up at the market-place, and when she'd go home he'd escort her, and then he'd go on back to the Other-Side Market.

From a day to a week and a week to a month and a month to a year, Djahoemarkar's knowledge continued to increase: he went from the lowest grade to the highest. Sitti Djaoerah also made good progress. After Djahoemarkar had been in the fifth grade for two years and Sitti Djaoerah was in the fourth grade, she heard that Djahoemarkar was going to graduate. She felt very bad, for she would have no one to take her back and forth to school.

In chapter 7 we related how Djahoemarkar was not sent to Bukittinggi to take the examination to enter the teacher training school but rather he was going to become an assistant teacher right there in the local school. What the teacher had promised him worked as a balm to Sitti Djaoerah's anxious thoughts. He told her: "Younger Lineage Companion, Djaoerah, I've graduated from school now and the schoolmaster says I'm to become an assistant teacher after the next Hari Raya, the holiday ending the Fasting Month. But what can I do to make sure this really comes off and succeeds? I'm a poor person and assistant teachers do not draw salaries, but their clothing and conduct have to be respectable and good looking. When I think it over I don't believe I can meet those requirements."

"So you have to wear trousers and not shorts if you're an assistant teacher?" asked Sitti Djaoerah.

"No, indeed . . . but you do have to have two or three suits of clothes cut in the dashing Daret style like Minangkabau folks,[16] since if one suit's being ironed and one is being worn you have to have another one stored away in the cabinet in case you get caught in the rain, y'see. Or you have to have some clothes ready in case Tuan Inspecteur[17] comes to school. Then, too, you have to have two pairs of pants from the store, one with stripes down the side. In addition to that you have to have a sarong cloth that's good and smooth and really sort of expensive, and then shoes, too, and a *kupia* cap and a good cloth headdress.[18] When I count up the cost of all this stuff I know that my mother will not be able to buy it."

"Ha . . . ha ha, if an assistant teacher's clothes are as fancy as Older Lineage Companion says they are, I can just see you now as you stand before the school-children—I'll bet you'll really be a sight to see," said Sitti Djaoerah merrily.

"Well, yeah, right, but what's to be done? Rules are rules and it's my fate to have to follow them, as it says in the words of the song,

Dipalu gordang sambilan	The Nine Drums are struck
Matapor ogung ni Singali	The gongs snap in two in Singali.
Diroha giot tu ginjang	One wants to jump up in the air
Disundati dapot ni ari.	But you meet with obstacles when you try."

Djahoemarkar said, drawing in his breath.

"Un-bel-lievable! But you have lots of money, don't you? And who's our mother? And is our father still alive?"

"No, there's really no money at all, and, in fact, the schoolmaster has already given us a cut rate on tuition. My mother is still alive, but my father died when I was only forty days old, and to tell the truth his death was the sort to keep the living feeling despondent. When he was coming home from Sipirok in the past, you see, carrying a great deal of money, he was jumped by robbers at night out in the precious resins forest and the robbers threw poison leaves in his eyes. And so he couldn't see—the pain was awful. You know how eyes are. If you just look at the sun too long they hurt a lot, and much more so, what with poison leaves and itchy stuff. And that's what killed him, leaving me in poverty like this," said Djahoemarkar, pitying himself mightily.

"That is really *awful*, my friend. But if you don't become an assistant schoolteacher, won't you have to leave school entirely? And then who will look out for me? If that happens I'll leave school, too! I just won't graduate."

"Well, all right, but what can be done?... Whether it comes to pass or not, I guess we'll just see after Hari Raya," said Djahoemarkar.

"Let's go on home," they said, and they went back to their respective villages.[19]

When Sitti Djaoerah got home she told her mother everything they'd discussed and about how she'd feel so bad if she didn't have a friend in whom to put her trust. "Mother, what if we just help Djahoemarkar buy those clothes so he can be an assistant teacher? If he's still at school then there'll still be someone to watch out for me. I even think he'd have the nerve to be my own teacher. And if we don't help him he'll leave school for sure, they're so poor. His father died because he was jumped by robbers when he was only forty days old and 'cause of that there's only his mother to make a living for them and buy his clothes and give him his tuition money and all."

Only when Nandjaoerah heard that did she realize that this child must be the son of the late Pandingkar Moedo, the one they used to know. She started in surprise. Without being aware of it tears began to course down her cheeks upon hearing what Sitti Djaoerah had said.

"Why are you crying, Mother? Gosh, you sure cry easy! Why do your tears flow when you hear such a thing? What did I say?" asked Sitti Djaoerah, wiping away her own tears, for she had started in, too, out of pity for the unhappy fate of Djahoemarkar, he who reopens feelings of sadness and pain, he who reopens memories of the past, he who reopens feelings of deep longing and loneliness.

"Oh my, now, daughter, it's nothing, it's nothing—I'm just thinking about the past. It's only now that I realize who that child is: why, he must be the son of the late Pandingkar Moedo, someone we knew well, your father's business partner in this store. Because there's been so much work we haven't been able to go and see them over in the Other-Side Market for I don't know how many years. But all this is really a stroke of luck, you know. When your father finds out he'll be overjoyed; he'll feel as if Pandingkar Moedo himself has come back to life. Why, all this time he liked that child, but he didn't know whose son he was."

"If that's the case, Mother, let's do help him out so he can get to be an assistant teacher. If he passes the exam he'll get to be a teacher, and there'll be someone to help his mother. And, in addition to that, if he's still at school there'll be a companion for me and someone to take me home so no one will bother me along the road. He's really a good person, Mother! If people hassle me he'll fight 'em off. And when I leave school he's still watching out for me. He won't go home to their village before I have arrived at the front steps of our house."

"Well, yes, I agree . . . it's because his mother is so good hearted and generous and good at following *adat* and laws," said Nandjaoerah.

"Here comes Father from the mosque. Mother, ask him if he'll help Djahoemarkar, so that I'm happy at school."

"Ha ha. . . . Oh——Father," said Sitti Djaoerah.

"Come here! There's some good news this child has brought home from school," said Nandjaoerah.

"What news does she have now? Sitti Djaoerah just keeps learning more and more things it seems. If the teacher so much as tells her a story about a shy man off she'll go and get acquainted with him in nothing flat," said Awaiting Riches.

"No . . . no, this is different. . . . I think maybe we've done something to offend Those Not Seen."*

"Now what . . ." said Awaiting Riches.

"That child who's always coming over here, the one who's so good looking, the sturdily built one who's such a good talker, who's such a speech maker, who's good at coming to a meeting of the minds, well, apparently he's not just some stranger's child—he's our *own* little kid! It seems he is Pandingkar Moedo's son. He's gotten this big already, and we're only now realizing it. I'll bet his late father's *tondi* soul is a bit put out with us by now, I do! So, according to what our daughter here says, he'll graduate from school after this coming Fasting Month and he'll become an assistant teacher since he's so smart and generous hearted and nice to the little children. He's the same way with people in general. Why, haven't you noticed what he's like in all this time? Is there anything at all lacking in that child's behavior?"

"But what is to be done? . . . When he took Sitti Djaoerah home just now he told her he didn't have the clothing he needs to become an assistant teacher because before he passes the exam he can't draw a salary. And if he fails to become an assistant teacher because he doesn't have any clothes Sitti Djaoerah herself doesn't want

---

Na so niida: the *begus*, the Evil Ones.

to go to school anymore—that's because he's the only child willing to help our daughter walk to and from school. So what do you say? Can we help the child out so people won't suspect that he's the son of poor folks?"

"Ah . . . so he's really the son of the late Pandingkar Moedo? Well, look, why would I not want to help him? Why, I'd even be willing to make him my own son. All this property, half of it would be his!—just so long as he's willing to become an assistant teacher. And, as for his clothing, he'll have it, everything he asks for! Bring him here tomorrow so we can place an order for the clothes, and I'll aver his father is the one who owns this house," said Awaiting Riches.

"But if Father only buys him a ready-made shirt from a shop that really won't do any good, you know. He has to have pants, a sarong, and shoes and all, because if the *tuan* sees that the least little thing is wrong with his clothes he'll lower his grade."

"All right, all right, daughter . . . as long as you keep going to school we'll help this child. But haven't I just said that I'd even want him as my son because I remember my love for his late father and how very good he was?"

Sitti Djaoerah was immeasurably happy to find out that her father and mother loved Djahoemarkar: she was positively merry. What caused her to love that child so much is not known; it can simply be said that it was God's destiny.

Once it got to be daylight, Nandjaoerah, accompanied by her daughter, went to the Other-Side Market to visit Taring and her generous-hearted son—and also to find out for herself if what Sitti Djaoerah had said was true.

"Let's buy these little Bugis cakes and layer cakes, Inang, so we'll have something to take Djahoemarkar," said Sitti Djaoerah.

"All right, let's do, and let's buy lots so we'll have something to eat when we're visiting with his grandmother and mother."

Along the road Sitti Djaoerah kept chattering away, all about how pleased she was that her father was willing to help Djahoemarkar get to be an assistant teacher. When they reached the Batang Angkola Bridge (over the Ayumi River), Sitti Djaoerah asked her mother if she knew which house was Djahoemarkar's folks' place.

"Now, of course, I know that. Why not? We used to come here a lot when his father was alive. Why, I even went along to Sigalangan to help fetch his mother as a bride."

"Well, good grief, then why haven't we ever come here? And why haven't they come to our house?"

Once Djahoemarkar caught sight of Sitti Djaoerah and her mother, he called out: "Well, where are you going, Djaoerah?"

Taring was surprised to hear Djahoemarkar ask this so she ran in from the kitchen to catch a look at the girl who'd come. When she saw Awaiting Riches's wife she rushed out to greet her heartily. ". . . Oh, do come right up into the house, Older Lineage Companion. Even though the one who owns this house is no longer alive, his replacement's here all right. Oh, gracious, why has it been such a long time since you came to visit us? Please don't be peeved at me, either. I just haven't had a break from work in all this time, trying to make a living for this child. You know, after working myself to the bone in the rice fields I have to go and chop down under-brush in the garden and then I have to go cut away the grasses choking the rice field *and* work in the fields from the time the grains first fill their cases till harvest time—and then once the rice has been carried back to the village the sweet grass is chok-ing out the vegetables in the garden and I have to work on that. It's like that day in and day out, without a minute's pause in an hour. So I must ask forgiveness of Older Lineage Companion," said Taring.

"Oh, listen, Younger Lineage Companion, I am not put out at you nor at our *namboru.* Look, I'm the one at fault for never coming to visit you. And if it wasn't for our daughter here we would still be neglecting you, for you know coming here often sometimes just serves to reopen feelings of deep sadness and pain, for, when I see you and your son, I always think of the dear departed and memories of the past come rushing back. Look... every day our son Djahoemarkar comes over to escort our daughter to school, but we had no idea whose child he was. We were quite in awe of him, you know—this child was so good and so well behaved and generous hearted. So, it seems that Almighty God has made it our destiny that we would take a notion to come here on a visit. I'll tell you why: Sitti Djaoerah burst into tears telling us how Djahoemarkar had graduated but was going to quit school entirely this coming Fasting Month. Even though the two of them loved being in school together! And, Sitti Djaoerah said, the teacher had told Djahoemarkar that he would be made an assistant teacher after Hari Raya. But he didn't have much faith that it would really happen since he didn't have any decent clothes to wear to school. It seems he told Sitti Djaoerah how he felt, and because of her love for him (given his help all this time) she told me about their conversation, all about his pain and suf-fering at being left an orphan, about how his father had met his unfortunate, trag-ic end. And as soon as our daughter finished her tale of course I immediately thought of you here. Even after I heard her story I held it back at first. Finally, though, I told your *angkang.** Once he heard it he sighed deeply, for it was as if we had been greatly in the wrong all this time. Not finding out, you know, exactly who that child was. And, he's already gotten so big! And here we were, striking up con-versations with him every day, but we didn't know who he was," she said. "So that is what made your older lineage companion send me over here, to talk about the sets of clothes that have Djahoemarkar so worried. According to your Angkang, and if Djahoemarkar agrees, of course, he'll make sure the boy has enough clothes.[20] If what the guru says is true about him being promoted and needing nice clothes, well, then, of course, we'll help out. Now, listen, just bring him over to the market tomor-row so that the clothes can be ordered. That way things won't get too rushed at Hari Raya."

"Astagafiroellah.... Aren't the ways of God diverse and wonderful? Making it our destiny for you to come here on this visit. Honestly, he has not said a single word about any of this to me nor to his grandmother, and then he goes and tells Sitti Djaoerah more than he tells me! But, whatever the case, it is surely God's work."

While the two children's parents were busy chatting Djahoemarkar and Sitti Djaoerah had gone out to climb up the rose apple tree. They had not the slightest

*Angkang ('older lineage companion'): that is, Awaiting Riches. Both women call him Angkang.

care about what their mothers were discussing—not even a needle tip's worth! They were just indescribably happy whenever they were together.

Not long afterward: "So, you've come on a visit without warning, have you? . . ." said Taring's father's sister, coming in from the kitchen with hot coffee and steaming *katupe* cakes* (the ones she had planned sell at the market that morning). "Do drink some coffee, Maen. These taste better while they're hot, you know."

"Oh my, I must beg your pardon, Father's Sister—we had so much to chat about that I forgot to ask after you. And apparently you were back in the kitchen? Oh, aren't you the single-minded one, keeping to your cooking like that? Why didn't you come right in here?"

"I was going to come in, but what could I do? The frying pan was still on the fire, and I was afraid they'd burn if I left them. Now, you don't have to go playing up to me, girl who might marry my son. Come on, let's eat, so our feelings of deep longing might be healed a bit."

"Oh, Djahoemarkar, call your younger lineage companion, Son, so we can eat these cakes," said Taring from the double windows.

"'Rah . . . (which is to say, Djaoerah) come on, let's go and have some cupcakes!" said Djahoemarkar.

Once they got in the house Djahoemarkar grabbed a cake and gave it to Sitti Djaoerah.

"Oh. . . . Mother, where are those cakes we just bought? Come on, why didn't you give them to Djahoemarkar? You said they were for him! Oh, c'mon . . . what's wrong with you? Honestly . . . we buy gift food and it never gets to the one for whom it's intended."

"Now, not at all, it's just that it's been such delicious fun chatting like this. So here, take these, please, Apa,"† said Nandjaoerah, putting the cakes into Djahoemarkar's hand. After that Nandjaoerah went on to say: "Now, only eat a few of these cakes. Here, we certainly brought a lot of food. We should leave them some of their cakes to sell, you know! So they'll have a bit of salt money."

"Now, not at all. Everyone should just take exactly what they want. Don't hold back."

"Eat some more, potential daughter-in-law. . . . After all, you don't come over here very often. Not every bit of effort has to go toward making money, you know. And, after all, these are your good luck foods. If I had cooked them real early this morning I would have sold them already at the market. But that's not how it came out, is it?"

"Why, exactly, have they come to our house, grandmother?" asked Djahoemarkar, whispering.

"But don't you know they're close family?" she replied.

"No, Grandmother. But Sitti Djaoerah and I are together in school every day, and that's how I know her. It's not because I know her family."

"But Sitti Djaoerah's father, Little Grandchild, was your father's very close friend. They were merchants together. We're very close family to them."

*These are moist cakes made of a coconut milk base.
*Apa ('little dad'): a joking, intimate form of the Malay word *bapak* 'father', which southern Batak speakers use interchangeably with their own word, *amang*.

"Oh, well, that makes sense. . . . I have to admit, I am always real happy to be over at their house. All this time they've been giving me snacks and stuff, but I didn't know they were family."

"What does Djahoemarkar say, Father's Sister?" asked Nandjaoerah.

"He says he didn't know your reason for coming here. Now, isn't that child stupid?"

"Ohhhhh—but we are, too, Father's Sister. We didn't know whose child he was all this time. Every day we'd get into conversations with him, but we didn't know that Djahoemarkar would be this big by now. So we didn't think to find out whose child he was."

Tired from talking, tired from cake munching, and what with the day getting later, too, Nandjaoerah asked permission for them to go home to the main marketplace, "for at noon I have to cook the shopkeeper's meal, you know."

"But let's just eat our midday meal right here, Little Daughter-in-Law. Here, I'll get to cooking. Surely our child here would be pleased to fill up on a good rice meal right here."

"Oh, but that's not necessary, Father's Sister. Let's do that on another visit. This Hari Raya we'll come here to visit and have a meal then. Look, we can make a good repast of simple boiled vegetables with our rice. I see you have lots of squash and papaya leaves around here, and green beans, and some onions and young hot peppers. If you throw all those together I'll bet they'd be tasty enough, Father's Sister."

"Yes, Daughter-in-Law, I'll put some aside for you, but it won't bother us a bit if you eat here with us."

"Now, you don't need to go playing up to us, Father's Sister. Your child here will think we've lost our way, for we promised to come here just for a moment or so."

"Ah . . . I wouldn't know about that. Here, take some of these cakes along with you so she'll have something to carry home. It'll be a little present for you, my friend," said Djahoemarkar's grandmother.

"Well, that'll be all right, Father's Sister, but it doesn't have to be a lot."

After everything was stored away they decided to go home. "Come, escort us home, Djahoemarkar," said Sitti Djaoerah.

"Oh, come on, there're so many people about, what do you have to fear?" said Djahoemarkar.

"But just so it'll be more fun and noisier along the way," said Sitti Djaoerah.

"So, what do you say, Djahoemarkar—let's escort them home," said Taring, taking Nandjaoerah's packages in the cloth sling and putting them up on top of her head. They chatted all along the road as they walked along, and they weren't even aware of it when they reached the big *kwini* tree. Once they got there Taring and Djahoemarkar went home.

The next morning, as they had promised, Taring and Djahoemarkar came on over to the store. As soon as they arrived Awaiting Riches kissed them soundly. "Now why didn't you say right away that you were the late departed's son, Little Friend? I'll bet his soul is angry at me for sure! Well, listen, don't be peeved: as for your clothes I'll make sure you have quite enough. Here, let's go have them ordered and sewn, so you won't have to worry about becoming an assistant schoolteacher," said Awaiting Riches.

"Don't we have to buy shoes, too, Father?" said Sitti Djaoerah from behind.

"We'll buy everything, don't you worry. The both of you are our children," said the shopkeeper.

"Ah, that's the way!" said Sitti Djaoerah, grinning a bit, she was so happy.

Once they got to the tailor's house the craftsman measured Djahoemarkar to determine his size, asking how many sets of clothes he was supposed to make.

"Make two suits in white, one in yellow, and one more in brown."

"Fine. A market week from now you can pick them up here," said the tailor.

"What about the sarongs and trousers?" asked Sitti Djaoerah.

"But here are lots and lots of fine sarong cloths, what do you have to worry about? Everything'll be perfect," said the shopkeeper.

At mealtime they ate their food, and after that Djahoemarkar's folks asked permission to go back home—Djahoemarkar who reopens memories of the past, who reopens memories of pain and sadness, who reopens feelings of longing and loneliness. "Can't we escort them home, Mother?" asked Sitti Djaoerah.

"Oh, sweetie, that's not necessary. We're not afraid, girl," said Taring.

9

Assistant
Schoolteacher

A week after the clothing had been ordered Djahoemarkar and his mother went to the main marketplace once again to see Awaiting Riches at home. On their arrival the shopkeeper greeted them warmly and said: "Well, well, so you've come to see us, Djahoemarkar? All right, then, let's just go and see about those clothes of yours over at the tailor's."

When they got to the Daret man's* shop they inquired whether the clothes were ready. "The brown suit needs one more buttonhole, but all the others are ready. Try them on to see if they fit, so if they need some alterations we can make them," said the tailor.

"Fine, fine, go ahead and finish the last buttonhole," said Awaiting Riches, helping Djahoemarkar to slip into one of the finished shirts. "Ha—it fits perfectly. Not the least bit off! The hem length, the size: it all fits you to a T. There aren't even any wrinkles."

"Well, of course: it's a made-to-order suit, isn't it? But if you see anything wrong with it we'll make alterations," said the tailor.

"There's not a thing to complain about, I must say. Fold them up so we can get on home. Here's the money for the clothes, and may this child always be safe and healthy wearing them," said Awaiting Riches.

"Happy wearing, then! And thanks, you know, for the payment for the clothes," said the tailor.

"We ask your kind permission, Tailor, to go on home," said the shopkeeper, taking Djahoemarkar by the hand.

Once they got back to the house along came Sitti Djaoerah, who said: "So did the tailor sew them right, Father? Djahoemarkar, you don't want clothes that are tight or baggy, like suits you buy ready-made in a store, you know."

"Allah . . . but of course we tried them on. What are you worried about?" said the shopkeeper.

"Put them on, Djahoemarkar, so we can take a look," said Sitti Djaoerah, calling her mother and Djahoemarkar's mother from the kitchen.

They rushed in and found the child wearing the white shirt. "Oh my, that fits just perfectly," said the two mothers, laughing.

"Yes, indeed. He looks quite the young man, I must say," said Sitti Djaoerah, moving closer to him.

---

*The tailor must have been from Daret, from Minangkabau in West Sumatra, near Padang.

"Well, at least the tailor didn't skimp on cloth or anything. But let's have them ironed so that they will look really good for Hari Raya," said the shopkeeper.

"That's the way, Father. . . . But where are the sarongs? And the pants, and the shoes? If you didn't have them made as a whole set of clothes with these, the coat measurements will be off, believe me," said Sitti Djaoerah.

They all laughed uproariously at this comment. "Well, all right, you go pick them out so you'll be satisfied, 'cause you're so much better at it than we are," said Awaiting Riches, opening the doors to the clothes closet.

"All right, I can do it . . . but don't be mad if I have to pick expensive ones. After all, you only have us two children to take care of . . .'"

"*Tap!*" And out she pulled two pairs of pants at five rupiah apiece and two striped sarongs at three ringgit apiece. Merrily: "These'll go well with your shirts. Do you like these, Djahoemarkar?" said Sitti Djaoerah.

"Ha, ha . . . I don't know which ones are good, and I really don't know cheap from expensive. They look good enough to me as long as they're *new*. It's the folks who look at them who'll be able to tell the good-looking ones from the bad, not me," said Djahoemarkar, lowering his own importance a peg. But, deep inside, he really didn't want Sitti Djaoerah to put the clothes she had picked out back into the cabinet.

"This one: do you like this?" asked Sitti Djaoerah, giving him a sarong.

"Now, that's enough, that's enough. You just work hard in school, Djahoemarkar, and next year on Hari Raya if you pass the exam you can have any clothes you want. If they can't be found here in Sidimpuan we'll order them all the way from Padang."

"Oh, all right . . . but if I don't get promoted to the next class you still have to feed me my midday meal! And if Djahoemarkar doesn't pass the exam, I'll go and snap him on the ear with my fingers."

"All right, all right, we'll be waiting for that," they said, playing along with the children lightheartedly.

"It's getting late in the day, so we'll be getting on home. This evening, I think, we'll do a ritual hairwashing with limes because we're going to visit the grave of the late departed,"* said Taring.

"Oh, come on now, don't go home till you've had a meal with us, what do you say? Tomorrow or after that, if you miss us, we won't be able to share a meal together, for we'll be fasting by then. We'll only be able to eat together after Hari Raya. And, I ask you to be sure to come over here as fast as possible so we can all share the Hari Raya holiday together."

"Of course, of course. . . . So, Djahoemarkar, are you hungry, Son?" asked Taring. "I'm not all that hungry yet, but if Amantua's† asked us we'd better not refuse.

"As for visiting the grave, we can go later this evening."

---

*This is an important Fasting Month practice throughout Muslim parts of Sumatra. Lime hair rinses prepare one to intercede with the dead.
†Father's Older Brother, a term of particular affection reserved for older men one considers to be within one's *kahanggi*.

"Well, then let me help you cook this rice so things will be ready sooner. It might rain by midday, because normally it pours and your head gets drenched when you do the ceremonial hairwashing for the Fasting Month," said Taring.

While waiting for the rice to cook Awaiting Riches and Djahoemarkar chatted about the assistant schoolteacher job and whether or not there was a good chance he'd get it.

"We'll just have to increase our prayers to God. . . . And let's not go and make fools of ourselves in all this, either. The teacher says they're all real confident about sending me into the examination arena. So if the teachers are confident then a person can be, too. After all, they're the ones who'd know if you have enough material in you or not, I guess," said Djahoemarkar.

"We'll just hope to God that your luck will not turn bad and that you will get what you seek," said the shopkeeper.

Right then Sitti Djaoerah came up to them, saying: "So you're going to start fasting tomorrow, Djahoemarkar? If you are, tell me, why? What exactly are your intentions in doing that? Maybe it's something some friend of yours wants? After all, things can be gold on the outside yet silver beneath—keeping a fast yet eating a meal at midday, tricking the cooks and all."

"One could lie like that to God? Or eat meals in secret!!? That would make the sin all the greater," said Djahoemarkar piously.

"Well, when I was fasting one time, I thought, if one happens to sin what can you do? I went over to the White River with Mother at noon one time, and I jumped into the deep eddy in the stream and I was pulled right under the water and I gulped down all the water I possibly could," said Sitti Djaoerah.

"Well, hmm, then why are you always so anxious to break the fast with the evening meal if you're not really fasting in the first place?" asked Awaiting Riches.

"But, Amang, you're always changing your story: if you give me a plate of rice of *course* I'm going to grab hold of it."

"My, my . . . if that's how it is maybe you shouldn't fast at all. Maybe I'd eat the food that I didn't give to you? Since you're still little you don't really have to fast. But if you do you'll get a large reward in heaven," said the shopkeeper.

"Oh, what are you talking about? You're just making noise. Come on in so we can eat. They need to get home," said the shopkeeper's wife.

"It's because Sitti Djaoerah knows so much," said the shopkeeper, coming into the middle room, for the food was already stacked on the table.

"Let's share this good meal," they all declared, passing the dishes around. And they ate their fill.

When they were finished Sitti Djaoerah said: "Eat up, Djahoemarkar. Tomorrow when you think about eating you'll regret not finishing all this now."

"Well, after all, fasting means suffering some hunger, you know. If you feel full, fasting wouldn't amount to much," said Djahoemarkar, as he polished off the rest of his meal.

Once they'd finished eating Djahoemarkar's folks went back to the main marketplace. All along the road Taring kept asking about the assistant schoolteacher job and whether or not he needed anything else for it.

"Now that I'm all set for clothes I'll take that exam no matter what."

When they got back to the house they were tired and hot from eating such a big meal. After about an hour, Djahoemarkar said: "Come on, Mother, let's go *ziarah* out to the cemetery to pay our respects to the dead. It'll get too late on us if we don't leave now."

"Fine," said Taring, getting a bamboo container for the lime water. When they got out to the late Pandingkar Moedo's grave they sprinkled it with the water and recited their readings, as people normally did. Then they went home. Lots of people were crowded along the Ayumi River, washing their hair with the water they had carried from the cemetery. We don't have to say a great deal about the Fasting Month here since we'll be relating material about that in chapter 10. Now we'll say no more than what's needed for the moment.

So—as it was approaching Hari Raya, Djahoemarkar and his mother went to fetch the clothing over at the main marketplace. When they got there Sitti Djaoerah greeted them straightaway with: "All the clothes have been ironed and they're just as slick as can be and the fine cotton shirts are shiny and smooth and as white as a hummingbird's egg. So, which set of clothes will you wear on Hari Raya?" asked Sitti Djaoerah.

"It doesn't matter, whatever's presentable, I guess. I don't want to put on particularly nice clothes for Hari Raya. Everybody's always wearing brand new clothes then, but if you don't take the new suits out of the cabinet for one or two weeks then they've got more style," said Djahoemarkar, for, after all, it was just the two of them chatting there.

"Yeah. . . . I guess I can see that. But just so you'll know, even if folks knock themselves out trying to get new clothes right before Hari Raya that's only because they want to celebrate the holiday the right way. You've got everything backward, like a chicken's hind claw," said Sitti Djaoerah.

"All right, all right, I'll put them on then. But I won't do it willingly. If I wear, say, the Chinese jacket and the drill pants and the striped sarong and the Padang cap, will that be enough for you for Hari Raya?"

"That will be quite enough, but you folks just make sure to come over here early enough on Hari Raya so that the *onde-onde* sugar cakes aren't all gone. And, as for the Indian doughnuts, I won't eat any so that there'll be some for you," declared Sitti Djaoerah.

"Oh, we'll come early, and even if there's some delay it's no problem if the goodies get polished off first. After all, I've stood it for a whole month, fasting like this. One little cake won't bother me one way or the other," said Djahoemarkar.

Not long afterward his mother came in from the kitchen to call him to start for home, for the glaring heat had abated a bit. After Djahoemarkar had shaken hands with the shopkeeper they went home to the Other-Side Market. It was getting on toward evening, and they felt their fasting hunger more sharply. In fact, Djahoemarkar sometimes felt his great fasting efforts were simply going to break down. There were two more hours of daylight left before evening; Djahoemarkar felt that this period passed like two whole years. So he went off and read some holy verses to keep his mind off the situation. It got to be past six, and he was still singing away. His mother had to call him again and again before he knew it was time to break the fast.

"Oh my gosh . . . so it's already evening prayer time? Alhamdulillah, hopefully the fast for this year is *over*," he said, taking a good-sized handful of his breaking-the-fast dinner. Once he had broken the fast, he went off to pray, and then he ate yet another meal.

There were big crowds of people at the Ratib Mosque, chanting prayers and swinging their heads forcefully from side to side in rhythm with the verses. After doing that they'd all read holy verses to the beat of the drum, and then they'd go amuse themselves with one thing or the other, waiting for daybreak. But Djahoemarkar just kept reading and reciting holy verses as a way to give alms to his late, departed father. Once people thinned out in the mosque he finally went to sleep. He slept so soundly and was so very tired that it got to be near daylight before he woke up. The cannon at the Great Mosque called out, "*Do——Burrrrr*," announcing that the Fasting Month had turned into the first of Sawal. It was Aiddilfitiri, the great day of celebration, the glorious holiday. Once the cannon sounded, rifle shots could be heard from all directions, and gongs resounded from all the small villages. Energetic children leapt from their beds to eat, and then they went and asked their parents for new clothes.[1] Once it was full daylight, everyone came outside. The children were leaping and hopping about, running in all directions, absolutely tireless in their glee.

Once Taring had stored her little leaf packets of gift rice safely away in their rattan satchel, she called out, "Father's Sister, come on, let's go over to the main marketplace. Get ready, Djahoemarkar, or the shopkeeper'll be kept waiting. We promised to eat there this morning, you know."

"Well, everything's put away, so let's go," said her father's sister.

Djahoemarkar came out of the house, too, and off they went. Once they got to Awaiting Riches's house they all started shaking hands, asking forgiveness of each other—saying that they must forgive each other if any offense had been committed, physically or spiritually, internally or externally, any time here on this earth or in the Afterworld.[2] And after that they ate their food.

They had an unimaginably huge amount of provisions. Over there was the gift rice in its little leaf packets, topped with a tangy curry of minnows and shrimp, and over there were chicken curry, meat curry, soup, spicy fat potato pancakes, boiled greens, and on and on and on. You'd fill up just looking at it all. What a spread!

"Well, let's say, 'Bismillah' and just dig in," said Awaiting Riches. And they shared the fine meal till they all were totally stuffed. No one felt the slightest lack of anything. After that, they all set off to visit their relatives, their teachers, and so on, and after that they stayed at home and received their own complement of guests. It continued on like that until evening, without letup. Sitti Djaoerah and Djahoemarkar never got a rest from keeping their visitors' coffee glasses filled.

Once it was five o'clock they asked permission to leave and start on their own visiting rounds. "All right," said the shopkeeper, calling a horse carriage so that they'd have a vehicle to carry them around the center of town. They went home only after they were totally worn out.

"Let's go home! After all, there's no one there to watch the house," said Taring.

"All right, just take this carriage, then," said the shopkeeper, paying the fee.

This is enough about Hari Raya—in later chapters we shall expand on it, never fear. Now we'll just go on to the job that Djahoemarkar's about to get, so we can see how all that came out. Normally, ten days after Hari Raya the children would all go back to school. On the first day they'd also register the new students. Children would flock in huge numbers from all directions to enroll. However, not every child in those great crowds of potential pupils would be accepted, as there weren't really enough places. So, whichever ones were the most appropriate to enroll would get first dibs on the scarce spots, while the others would go home in disappointment.

The children who would progress would follow their lessons: they'd go on from first grade to second grade, from second grade to third grade, from third grade to fourth grade, and from fourth grade to fifth grade, while the dumb ones would stay behind a year. Djahoemarkar did pass the exam, and he became an assistant teacher; Sitti Djaoerah, for her part, went on to fifth grade.

That day, even though it was called "the first day of school," no one really had any lessons. This was normal since the children were still being registered, seats were still being found for them, and the benches were still being cleaned off. Moreover, all the excitement of Hari Raya was still going on. So all told you could say that the whole schoolhouse full of folks was just waiting for one o'clock to roll around that day. Djahoemarkar was pretty much just mimicking whatever the teachers did, as they went from one class to another.

"Oh . . . Djahoemarkar, my good friend, could you please be the one to tell the fifth grade some stories as a way to greet the children who've just been promoted?" asked the schoolmaster.

Djahoemarkar stood up in front, still in his normal old clothes since he hadn't taken his tailor-made clothes out of the cabinet yet. "Now, everybody please be quiet and listen to this tale, for starting today Djahoemarkar is the assistant teacher. You must respect him as you would a regular teacher, so that your studies will proceed well," said the teacher.

"In the past, back before,"[3] said Djahoemarkar, beginning the story, "there happened to be a raja named Djamartoea Mamora, Raja Lucky and Wealthy. Now, this great raja had seven daughters, each one slightly shorter than the next—a real staircase set of girls![4] Now, the youngest daughter was incredibly, unusually, unbelievably pretty, and her mode of behavior and thoughts were just the same: totally, indescribably, extraordinarily pretty. She was respectful and friendly to the public and always in accord with what her father and mother told her. As a result the old raja just loved his youngest daughter all the more. He made sure that she had the best food and the nicest clothes, too."

"Seeing the raja's way of thinking the six older sisters got their feelings hurt every time they thought of her. As a result, they waxed maliciously jealous of their little sister. They'd complain about her quite often to their father, saying that she was stuck up, and ugly, and ill-mannered to the public—'And so, because of that, people do not think very highly of our kingdom anymore!' But their father did not listen to any of that, for he saw easily enough that they were just angry and peeved at their little sister."

"Once upon a time this great raja became very seriously ill. According to the *datu*-sorcerer, the raja would have to eat a fish netted by his daughters in order to get well.[5] As a result the raja told his daughters to go netting fish in the river near that village of theirs, 'and whoever gets the most fish will become my favorite daughter. But whoever doesn't get any, well, that fact shall be a sign to me that she doesn't want me to live. As a consequence, I shall exile her from this Great House forthwith.'"

"'All right, Father,' they declared, all together, and they set about deciding how to deceive their little sister once they got to the fishing hole at the river."

"Once they were out there they started to dip their nets into the water. Whenever the youngest sister would get some minnows she'd show them to one of her older sisters and ask: 'What sort of fish are these, Older Sister?'"

"'Nope, nope, they're no good. They're just garbage. Just toss them over to the riverbank so you don't waste your time,' her older sisters would say. As soon as their little sister had tossed them over her older sisters would race each other to scoop up these same fish. Their nets never caught any fish, but their youngest sister's net would no more than touch the water when it would absolutely teem with fish."

"The rattan satchels of the six older sisters were soon full since they had gotten the unlucky young girl's entire catch. Her own satchel didn't have a single thing in it. 'Unhappy fate! All of you have full satchels, but I don't even have a little pinch yet. My luck is *so* bad,' said the child."

"'You just keep on netting away, Little Sister, you're sure to start getting some,' they said. The child was already starting to feel chilly. She came over to the river's edge, carrying her catch, which consisted this time of a tiny crayfish about as big as the tip of a red sugar palm fiber. "'Oh. . . . Older Sister, what is this in my net?'"

"'Ah, now, that's what you've been looking for, Little Sister. Put him in your satchel so we can all go home,' they said."

"When they got to the village they laid out their catch. They all had lots and lots of fish. 'Well, as for me, Father, I only caught this one crayfish,' said his youngest daughter."

"'Yeah, well, that's because she never wanted to get right in the water, because she's so *pretty*. She'd just keep to the riverbanks, and, of course, what could you hope to catch there? Why, it was even hard for *us* to catch anything, though we'd bravely plunge right into the deep parts,' they all said in concert. Well, as a result, the raja did not have to think very long before he grew angry and exiled the child from the house."

"The hurt feelings and pain of this unhappy, unlucky girl ran deep. She cried and lamented and sang *andung* mourning wails, but all this did her no good whatsoever. She still wasn't allowed to keep on living in the Great House. So off she went to live in a little field hut out in the middle of the rice paddies, bearing her unhappy fate and accompanied by her tiny crayfish. Once she got to the field hut she made him a little pool in front of the structure."

"Her six older sisters could not have cared less about their little sister's unfortunate suffering. For her food, they arranged to have the spoiled, hard crusts of rice from the bottom of the cookpot taken out to her. These were the crusts that had been picked over beforehand. Whenever the packet of rice arrived the girl would open it up and see that the grain was spoiled. Her tears would flow down her cheeks, drop by drop, to see the food her older sisters had seen fit to give her. But what could be done? Body and soul, she needed feeding! She wiped away her teardrops, went over to the crayfish's little pool, and said:

Crayfish—crayfish—crayfish,
A tiny fingerful for you, a fingerful for me,
Of the rice crusts provided by my older sisters.

"'*Sarrrrr* . . .' said the voice of the rice. It had not so much as gotten into the water when the crayfish sped over and caught it. However many rice grains she scattered over the water that was exactly how many new little crayfishes the crayfish produced. 'Well, all *right!*' the girl exclaimed to herself, working quickly to enlarge the width of the pool. Wherever drops of water touched the land, those spots immediately became part of the pool. And it went on like this every day until the pool was as wide as the ocean as far as the eye could see. The fish inside were numberless. There weren't only crayfish in the pool but every sort of fine food fish as well. And, as for that tiny little crustacean, he had gone on to become a huge glistening Sihatirangga carp with big golden scales that gleamed and glittered yellow in the sun. He was the raja of all those hundreds and thousands of fish. The child sold a portion of these many fish so she'd have something to live on because her father's rice sometimes wouldn't come for two days on end. Because the fish tasted so good people crowded in to get them, and it got so she couldn't keep track of all her sales."

"One time, in the evening, when it was getting dark and cloudy, a wind sprang up from that wide pond. It brought a cold wind to the sacred flower grove of those noble-born girls, the grove where they dressed their hairbuns. Her six older sisters were out there playing merrily, chasing each other about in the middle of the prosperous garden lands. They were joking and carrying on, they were so happy. Once they got tired they went and sat down on a bench that had been placed underneath a big spreading banyan tree. As they happened to gaze around in both directions they were shocked to see a wide pond, and so, too, they were amazed to note the great crowds of people coming in and carrying away fish from the pond."

"'Oh . . . girlfriends! What sort of evil one is our little sister? Just look how wide that pond is and how many people have crowded into her field hut.' Well, no one knew quite what to say about that. They were nonplussed, in shock, each one saying her piece, stunned. Not one of them was brave enough to tell their father, or anyone else, what they had seen."

"When it was evening they all went once again to the sacred flower grove to find out exactly what it was they had seen that day. Maybe they had seen wrong, they thought. They had only been sitting on their spying bench for a moment when a comely young man appeared on his way to their little sister's field hut. He was in search of betel quid."

"Frightened, the girl who owned the hut said to the fellow: 'My respects to you, good kinsman, but don't come here to my modest field hut; that will come to nothing, for I am a girl who has been cast out of her home, a girl who has no *adat*, who follows no law, a girl who serves no useful purpose for her father and mother. If you're seeking betel quid in greeting, go ask it of the raja's daughters. After all, they are your correct and fitting partners.'"

"'Yes, indeed, Daughter of our Raja, but if you order me to go off in the direction of those raja's daughters it will look as if you are being stingy with your betel quid. So that my wishes might be fulfilled, please, I would very much like for you youself to give me one folded package of betel quid.'"

"'Well, if that's the case, don't be peeved. Since I am a most unfortunate person who has no *adat* and knows no laws I do not have a metal tin in which to keep my betel. So you'll have to take it directly from my right hand,' said the girl."[6]

"'No problem, just as long as you give it happily,' said the fellow, accepting the betel."

"After he'd chewed betel he said thank you and asked permission to go home."

"The young girl was very, very surprised, for she had turned her back for just a moment, and now she looked and the fellow wasn't there anymore. Where he went she did not know. But, patiently, she carefully stored away everything that had happened deep down inside herself—just like you keep steaming hot food safe inside your rattan satchel, folded away in its tight little banana-leaf packets."

"At dawn the next day here comes the fellow again, seeking out the girl to ask for cooked rice. With compassionate, sympathetic words, the girl told him to ask the raja's daughters for some, for she herself had no food, just spoiled rice crusts that folks had left behind. 'It is not very fitting to give rice like *that* to a son of rajas.' But, no matter what she said, the fellow simply did not want to go to the Great House to see the daughters of rajas. He wanted the girl's rice, none other."

"'Well, indeed, then, Son of the Great Raja, may you not say that I lack respect for men who come visiting, but, as I have already told you, since this is the sort of rice I have, this is what I must give you. It's not that I'm being stingy or anything.' The fellow accepted the rice politely and ate it. Once he had finished eating he returned home to the pond and went back to being a huge golden Sihatirangga carp, with glistening golden yellow scales."

"As the fellow was leaving it seems that the girl caught a glimpse of where he was going. Once she had seen clearly that the fellow was actually a huge Sihatirangga fish there was no telling how pleased she was. 'Well, then, indeed! Apparently the huge Sihatirangga fish is a human being. That is great good luck! If you'd like to share my unhappy fate as my partner I would surely be pleased—so that I can have a pal with whom to divvy up the mosquitoes here in my little field hut,' the girl said to herself. She hid that secret deep inside her thoughts."

"One time, when the fellow had returned to the field hut and they were happily chatting away, her six older sisters caught sight of them there from their vantage point in the sacred flower grove. 'Oh. . . . Girl who absolutely doesn't know her place! Girl who doesn't know her numerical order in the family!' they all complained, trying to think of a clever way to make her look bad so that the fellow would come over and ask *them* for betel. They all rushed over there, and once they got to the field hut they yelled at the girl and asked themselves: 'However did she catch that son of the rajas and get him to ask for betel quid from *her*?'"

"'My heartfelt respects to you, Older Sisters. I told him and told him not to come to this field hut, and I pointed out the path to Father's house so that he would go there and ask you for betel, but he just wanted to come here and bother me. Look, Older Sisters, dear Angkangs, if he comes here again I won't let him stay. Let me wear myself out escorting him to our Father's house, so that he might ask all of you for betel.'"

"'Yeah, yeah, all right, all right. . . . You'd really have the gumption to do that? You don't know your own fate or place, you dummy,' they all said, purposely trying to pick a fight with their little sister."

"Now, it could be said that the raja fell very ill once again. And, according to the considered opinion of the *datu*-sorcerer: 'The raja has a craving for a huge *mera* fish, a great huge carp. If he does not get that *mera* I think the raja will just go and die this time. *But*, if he gets the carp it will bring him back to life.' Because of this, the raja ordered his six daughters to go out once more and net fish. And if they did not catch that fish they would not be allowed to return to the village. With considerable pain and sadness out they strode to the big river and purposefully tried to net that fish. But what was to be done? No matter how tired they got casting their nets into the water they found it hard even to get a little bass as large as a finger. Why, it fact, they couldn't even get a minnow as big as a hair tip to swim into their nets. Their fingers were water-wrinkled and their bodies were shivering with cold from being immersed in the water for so long, but they still hadn't found the fish that their father craved. Finally they went to their little sister to ask her help, so she'd give them one of the fishes from the pond to use as their sick father's food. The unlucky girl took their request well, and she told them to go right into the pond and take as many fish as they could carry."

"Seeing how many fish were in the pond and how very big the carp were, they had great hopes of getting the fish their father craved. But once they'd swung their nets into the pond they were left peeved and angry, for they scooped up mere hopes, no fish. Though there were so many fish in there that even a blind person could catch some, not a single one went into their nets. After they got worn out from casting their nets into the water and not getting the *mera*, no matter what, they looked at each other and asked: 'So, now what do we do? We've caught the chills but not that fish we're seeking. We can't just go back home.' This situation was far different from simple fright. They were terrified now that maybe their sick father had gone and died on them. But, no matter what idea or plan they thought up, nothing came to anything, for if you borrow some water from somebody you'd better be sure to pay them back in water, too."[7]

"Just then the handsome young man came along to ask the girl who owned the pond for some betel, but the girl said to him fearfully: 'You must ask my older sisters, the daughters of rajas, for your betel, all right? They're the appropriate ones. As for me, I am just a contemptible, humble, very small person. So, please, please, don't come here.'"

"Well, as for her six older sisters, their mouths were absolutely hanging open to see this gorgeous aristocrat. But the man wasn't willing to say a single word to them. Because their thoughts went blank and they forgot everything when they caught sight of his handsome face, they also forgot about catching the big carp and the fact that people back in the village were awaiting their arrival."

"Once the villagers came to a common consensus they went searching for the girls beyond the perimeter of the village. When they came upon them they escorted them to the raja and asked them why they hadn't brought the big fish back to the house."

"'But we couldn't catch him, Father, because a man kept bothering us. Indeed, there were so many fish that a blind person could catch them, but wherever we'd go that man would follow and bother us. This man's residence is over there in your unfortunate daughter's field hut. That's because she's tending to him over there, like, like a head of livestock! And the only work that guy ever does is hang around and wait for his food.'"

"'Bring her here so that I may punish her,' ordered the raja."

"So the suffering, mournful girl was fetched and brought before the raja. Once she was there in front of the raja, she was asked why she was behaving in so haughty a manner and why she should not be punished, there in that realm. And why did she keep that fine aristocrat with her, like a head of livestock?"

"'But, Friend Father, there's no man in my hut! Who would want to come there? If someone bothered my older sisters at the river, how should I know about that? Why, I never budge from the field hut.'"

"'Well, look, since they were not able to catch the special big carp for me to eat, then you shall go look for him. If you catch him, you'll be my daughter again and you shall live here in the Great House,' said the raja."

"'As for that, Father, if you love me I shall indeed give it a try. Order someone to go with me so that there'll be someone to carry the big carp back. But, as for coming back to the Great House, that's not really necessary, Father, for you're always unhappy and dissatisfied with me. Out in the field hut in the rice paddies I find I am content. I'm happy enough living off the rice crusts my older sisters send.'"

"Off the girl went, accompanied by some dashing spearsmen. These servants had been summoned by the raja."

"Once they got to the field hut, the men were very surprised to see how wide the pond was and how many fish were in it. The girl swung her net in the water just one time and a huge carp popped in. He was as big as half a person's chest. She swung her net again and a double armload of big *mera* fish floundered in the net, wriggling around. There were so many of them that they were piled up in heaps."

"'Carry these on back to the village and give them to my father so that he will get well again. If this isn't enough, come back and get some more tomorrow,' said the girl."

"'Yes, Daughter of Nobles,' said the servants, and off they went, getting tireder and tireder as they went along because they had to carry so very many fish. Once they got to the house they gave the fish to the noble wife, so that she could cook them up right away as the raja's food. When the raja saw the carp, he didn't even have to eat them: his heavy illness healed right away. He became healthy and cool souled; his body regained its former strength. After the carp were cooked, the raja ate them. He gave a portion of them to the people in the house. There was so much fish that folks had to protest, 'no more, oh, no more!'"

"Once the raja had finished eating, and the people had too, he ordered them to go to the field hut in the rice paddies and fetch his daughter home to the Great House. Off went the whole Council of Village Elders, the womenfolk, and all the adolescent girls of the village to fetch the girl back home. Once they got to the field hut in the rice paddies they delivered the raja's order, saying that she must return forthwith to the Great House."

"'Now you all just go back home. I am not willing to go back to the village unless my six older sisters bend down and serve as my stair steps as I walk up into the house, you hear? For they tricked me and caused me to get no fish in my net when we were all out netting in the river. They scooped up every fish I caught and tricked me into handing them all over to them—yet those were actually good food fish.'"

"The unhappy, mournful girl's story was related to the raja. Once he heard the story he immediately issued an order that his six daughters should be arrested and laid out there on the house steps so that the little sister they had tricked would have something to trod upon as she ascended into the house."

"The ones who had gone to fetch the girl were ordered out again, and they announced to her that her request had been fulfilled. They were very shocked to see a handsome and well-mannered young man sitting next to the daughter of the raja. It seems that before they came to get her the fellow had broken out of the huge Sihatirangga fish's scaly coat. He had told her (as he emerged from his scales) that he was a Son of a Raja, a nobleman who had fallen victim to a curse and had become a fish. 'But now you have freed me from my suffering and I surrender myself to you,' said the man. 'However happy you are at my helping you, why, I am ten times happier than that at what you have done for me. If you turn yourself over to me, I shall turn myself over to you as well—along with all this property,' said the girl. So off they went to the village together, with a *gondang* gong ensemble following them from behind. Once they got to the village they ascended the stairs into the Great House, using her six older sisters as places to trod upon. In the house, the daughter of the raja showed the fellow to her father, and they were wed. They were transformed into mature adults, according to all the strictures of *adat*. And on that same day they were presented to the Council of Rajas as the replacement for the old raja. And, as for the six older sisters, once they had asked for mercy they were set free, even though they had committed great and considerable sins. And all this became a path to luck and prosperity for their little sister. The pair stayed firm willed and hard souled, justly governing that kingly realm. The residents of the Great House prospered, and the new raja became old and wise."

"*Now*, that's the sort of thing that happens to people who cultivate patience," said Djahoemarkar, concluding the tale.

"Very *nice* . . ." said Sitti Djaoerah, clapping her hands, while the other children just sat there, thinking seriously to themselves with their heads bowed. They wanted to hear more of the tale since they had not gotten enough; they had not yet had their fill.[8] However, since it was now one o'clock, school let out for the day. As they were going home, the teacher said to Djahoemarkar how pleased he was to hear that tale and to witness Djahoemarkar's fine mode of presenting it to the children. "Now, tomorrow shape up your clothes a bit, so that the kids will respect you a bit more, all right?"

On the second day, once the sun had risen in the sky and it was nearing nine o'clock, the children came streaming toward the lesson house[9] from upriver and down. Among all those children was a rather large person in everyday clothes (but well-sewn ones, admittedly), wearing a fine sarong folded around his waist. In his hand he held a book with a green cover, while a small notebook and pencil were slipped into his pocket. He went quietly to the lesson house. A girl who had just been promoted to the fifth grade stood leaning against the housepost on the school's porch, looking at the children as they arrived. But the only one she gazed at was this neatly attired fellow. Though she saw that the young man was well dressed, perfectly turned out, and well behaved, her forehead darkened a bit, for she had not expected him to look quite like that. Once the children had gathered the bell rang—*teng-teng!*—telling everyone to go inside.

"Djahoemarkar . . ." said the schoolmaster. A young man with a quick body, nice clothes, and a clean face came up to the teacher and paid his respects.

"Now you must begin your lessons, but which grade would you like to teach?"

"Whichever grade you advise me to take on, Your Honor. I am like a soft-trunked banana tree, and whatever direction you send me in, that is the way I will bend," said Djahoemarkar.

"Well, then, you will start with the third grade. That will get you off to a flying start," said the teacher.

"Fine, Your Honor."

Once all the children had come to order, each teacher's pupils began to study their appropriate lessons, according to the lesson plans (that is, the official roster of studies). This hung from the wall of the school. When it was time for recess the children came out of the schoolhouse. Djahoemarkar went out, too, and watched them run back and forth as they played. He kept a good watch over them so they wouldn't fight.

"Djahoemarkar," said a girl, standing by a rose apple tree in the schoolyard.

"Now what do you want of me, Djaoerah. . . . Is somebody bothering you?"

"No, Kind Friend, not at all. Just come over here," said Sitti Djaoerah. When Djahoemarkar was by the girl's side, she said: "Here you've become an assistant teacher, but your clothes look like regular old everyday ones. Why didn't you put on the tailor-made ones?" asked the girl, laughing a little.

"Oh, I want to do it this way first, Friend. If I take those new clothes right out of the cabinet immediately, folks will call me Raja Striding Proudly Upriver and Down.[10] It's not just houseposts that have notches cut into them for the cross beams: people have to set some limits, too, you know. So it's better to do things slowly, so folks don't get too shook up. As the Malay *pantun* says: 'No matter if it takes a long while, just so you arrive safely.' And: 'Never fear, we'll get our fair share after all is said and done.' Now wouldn't you say that's true?"

"Oh, graaaaaaa-cious. . . . You sure have lots and lots of things to say! But, look, the clothes are all paid for, you know. What do you have to be worried about?" asked Sitti Djaoerah with some embarrassment and shyness.

"Come on, let's go to school. Tomorrow or the next day or on the third day or the fourth I'll take them all out one by one. Once the full set is out then you'll see how good it looks. Me, I just wear them; it's other folks who'll know whether they look good or not."

"Well, all right, I'll wait to see what you will eventually look like," said Sitti Djaoerah.

And Djahoemarkar did wear the tailor-made clothes in just that way as he went from day to day. If he wore his new shirt one day, he'd wear an old sarong with it. If he wore the new striped sarong he would wear old pants with it. If he wore the black pants, an old shirt would be teamed with it. Because of this folks did not realize that he was wearing new clothes.

One day he reached the point of wearing the full set of new clothes, but folks weren't exactly bug-eyed by then to catch sight of him. At recess Sitti Djaoerah came over to Djahoemarkar's class, a smile on her face.

"Now I've seen the fellow I was talking about. The clothes look just great. Let's go over to the house so Father can take a look at you," said the girl.

"Ah, we'll be late. . . . Let's just do that when we're going home. It's better that we go over and stand under the big overhanging branches of that tree by the side of the road so we can catch a cool breeze. That'll keep us healthy," said Djahoemarkar.

"All right, let's go," said Sitti Djaoerah.

Because they were used to being together and because people knew they were like brother and sister folks didn't see anything amiss when they walked through the marketplace together.[11]

At a big stand of bamboo, they stopped for a moment, since it was pleasant standing there under the overhanging leaves with the cool wind blowing gently on them.

"Do you know what sort of bamboo this is, Djaoerah?" asked Djahoemarkar.

"So there's another name for bamboo, for this bamboo?"

"There's no other name, but the end parts of the phrase are different: there is big bamboo, *sorik* bamboo, Chinese bamboo, *poring* bamboo, *sorik* bamboo, *lomang* bamboo for making steamed sticky rice sweets in long bamboo tubes, and thorny bamboo of our ancestors used for writing their cries and laments. The bamboo in front of us here is named big bamboo, and it is the beginning of a little song that goes:

Madungdung bulu godang	The big bamboo bends earthward
Mangalaungi na mandurung	Sheltering the fish netters.
Simbur hamu magodang	May you grow quickly to adulthood
Anso adong ubat ni lungun.	So there's medicine for my lovesickness.

"Ha, ha . . . so plants can be made into songs, can they?" said Sitti Djaoerah happily, for this was the first time she had heard talk like this coming from Djahoemarkar.

"Why not . . . ?!"

"Well, then, what is that tree over there with the red buds?"

"That's called *simartulan*," said Djahoemarkar.

"It would be nice if song lyrics could be made from that," said Sitti Djaoerah.

"All right:

Ummolat simartulan	Greater the *simartulan* tree
Sian dangka ni simartolu	From the branch of the *simartolu*
Ummolat paruntungan	Greater my unhappy fate
Sian dongan na dua tolu.	From that of all other people.

"Oh, indeed . . . that fern over there, that would make a good song lyric."

"All right:

Sangjongkal dope pahu	The fern is just a handspan high
Madung ditinggang pangaritan	A lathe for bamboo has fallen on it.
Sangjongkal dope au	I am just a handspan high.
Madung ditinggang parkancitan.	Pain and suffering have fallen on me.

"That orange tree over there, how is that made into a song?"

Madubu unte tonggi	A sweet orange falls off the tree
Na mata painte malamun	Unripe still, unready to eat.
Madabu holso ditondi	An oath falls into the soul.
Iba markancit mangan minum.	I hurt just to eat and drink.

"The stalks of those rushes over there, how might they be made into a song?"

Ditampul bona ni tolong	Chop down the *tolong* rushes.
Marumbak tu bona ni pisang	They fall back into the banana tree.
Sapola pola na manolong	If you lend help
Ulang dilanglang pangusayang.	Don't let your love go for nothing.

"Can a garden be made into a song?"

Muda kobun parpisangan	If it's a banana orchard
Buntu buntu parkacangan	It's on the hills around the bean farm.
Muda kobul pangidoan	If my request be fulfilled
Ho . . . do . . . donganku sapanganon.	You . . . then . . . be my partner of a dinner plate.

"Can a jacket be made into a song?"

Gari tarbaen songon batu	If only the path was made of stones
Manangkok tu adian batang	We could go up to the clearing.
Gari targaen songon baju	If only you were like my jacket
Ulang sirang sian pamatang.	You wouldn't be separated from my body.

"Ye-es in-*deed*! What about a banana peel?"

Gari prodangku taparpoda	If only my scythe we'd use as a scythe
Sarisir lambak ni pisang	The lining of my banana skin.
Gari rohangku taparroha	If only my heart got its wish
Satapak so jadi sirang.	So much as a footprint's distance we would not be separated.

"And what, then, might be the song out of a scarf?"

Basaen ragi dua	A two-colored scarf
Undung-undung tu sikola	Protecting you from sunbeams on the way to school.
Muda rap muda rap hita na dua	If the two of us would only be together
Lupa au di na suada.	I would totally forget my poverty.

"I'll bet *sanggar* grass cannot be made into a song, can it?"
"Why not? That's the best one of all."
"How does it go?"

Sanggar na mait-ait	Field grasses that blow
I ma na padungdungdung-dungkon	That's what bends down on itself, double.
Muda dung padais dais	If you barely touch me
I ma na palungunlungunkon.	That's what makes me long for you.

"Golly . . . now, apparently that was a good one, too! Well, can you make a song out of a *tandiang* tree fern?"
"You bet, and here's how that song goes:

Tandiang boti losa	*Tandiang* fern, *losa* fern
Boti lancat boti tarutung	Lanseh fruits, not to mention durians
Marnyiang boti loja	Losing weight and getting weary
Boti diarjeng namalungan.	Not to mention beset by longing and loneliness.

And another one would go:

Tandiang marrompu ijuk	*Tandiang* fern, satchel handle woven of palm fiber.
Pangitean tu sidohodoho	We'll use that as our little bridge to Sidohodoho Village.
Marnyiang markondur sibuk	We're wasting away and getting skinny
Hape na malungun di hodo.	Apparently from pining for you.

"Oh, goodness, have *mercy*! What's next?!"
"Ah, listen, that's enough, pal, okay? We have to get to school. Later I'll tell you some more," said Djahoemarkar.
"Oh, come on, one more! If you tell me just one more then we can get to school and I really, really, really won't ask for any extra ones," said Sitti Djaoerah.
"Ah, that makes things real weird! If I say another one, now don't you burst out laughing! I'm a poor person here—how could I go and become a comedian on us?"
"Just *one*. I won't laugh too hard."
"Well, look . . . have a listen."

"All right, good Older Lineage Companion."

Tandiang sipapan allehe	*Tandiang* tree ferns as house walls
Disoksok ni . . .	At the river source of . . .
Da oyallehe aek poeli	Of, of Aek Poeli.
Marnyiang pamatang allehe	My body's wasting away
Pa toenda ni . . .	Because of . . .
Da oyallehe bujing-bujing.	All because of a *bujing-bujing*.

"Ha . . . ha . . . oh, wow . . . you are really something here, pal," said Sitti Djaoerah.

By now . . . Djahoemarkar was already sixteen years old and could be said to be a cocky, dashing, adolescent young man. Sitti Djaoerah for her part was only thirteen, but because of the way she had shot up so quickly, even though she wasn't really old enough in strict years she could actually be said to be a blooming, budding, teenage *bujing-bujing*. Following Djahoemarkar's joking words in his songs, a path opened between them, allowing the pair to declare their deep longing for each other. As a result, beginning on that day their love for each other made contact, just like two magnets. But neither one was bold enough to say so. It was like the character of unripe fruit: the more you keep it sealed inside a tight covering the riper the fruit will get. Well, we shall just have to await developments.

Hari Raya in
Padangsidimpuan

It is the same for all people here on this earth: everyone will have a certain day designated as their major holiday. That is, they will have a glorious New Year's Day. But, since folks follow different religions their New Years are not quite the same. The Europeans and those who embrace Christianity celebrate January 1 every year, while the Indians celebrate Bulan Api, or Taipoesam. The Chinese, for their part, celebrate their own distinctive New Year's Day: that is, the All Night Fair (Tsapjigu). People who profess Islam celebrate 1 Sawal, which falls at the end of the Fasting Month. That day is not really New Year's Day, for, according to the way the Arabic months are calculated, 1 Muharram is the real beginning of the new year. Before Islam and Christianity came to this realm, folks did not celebrate Hari Raya or New Year's Day. But, of course, they did know how to calculate the months and days. They'd say, Sipaha-One, Sipaha-Two, Sipaha-Three . . . all the way to Li and Hurung. And the days had names: Day One was Adittia, Day Two was Suma, and then there were Anggara, Muda, Boraspati, Singkora . . . and all the various others.* So, one would ask, which major holiday did our ancient *ompungs* see fit to celebrate?

Let us simply reveal a bit of knowledge about the distant past so that our children will have a way to remember it in the future.

Well, as for the day that was celebrated as a major holiday by our ancient *ompungs* in the distant past: it was Harvest Day, actually. What they would call Eating the Year's Head. Once the grain harvest was safely in the storehouses, they would all bring prestations of rice to the raja's house along with chickens, some fish that they had caught in nets, some *tuak* or palm wine, and various other things. And everyone would have to gather there in the raja's house before the womenfolk would start boiling the rice and cooking the curries. And, of course, the nubile *bujing-bujings* and the dashing *doli-dolis* would all be adjusting their festive leafy crowns on their heads by this point. These crowns would consist of *hapias* leaves, Swedish begonia, *game-game*, Boston fern, wool flower, en so forth.† All the menfolk and the village elders would gather in the central room of the Great House and publicly announce how much rice and so forth each household had harvested.

Once the speeches were over, the official decision would be reached: the ritual drums would be struck, and the two small wait-a-minute gongs would be rung. The girls would *tortor* dance, carefully protected and guarded from behind (that is,

---

*These are the old Batak days, in which system there was a name for each day of the month.
†"En so forth," in Dutch, in the original.

with *ayap-ayapi* dances) by the youths.[1] All this would go according to who should properly be dancing with whom.

The rice would be cooked, the curries would be done, and the general public, the Two and the Three, would get to eat their fill. After everyone was full, the gong and drum ensemble would ring out again, going on for days and days at a time. They would only return to their work when everyone was thoroughly tuckered out from all the celebrating. Now, I am not just telling tales here: I had the opportunity to see such goings on myself in the Simelungun Land in 1909. This sort of thing still goes on among people who live out in the boondocks.

But let us return now to what we were saying about the Muslims' great Hari Raya festival, which took place in Padangsidimpuan. It was conducted according to Islam's Five Rukun, that is, according to the basic principles of the Muslim religion.

1. The faithful should declare that they believe in the two articles of faith.*
2. They should say their prayers five times each day and night.
3. They should fast during Ramadan.
4. They should give alms to the poor if their rice harvest is sufficient to the task.
5. They should go on the *haj* to Mecca if they have the financial resources.

"Same social level, same feelings," as the saying has it. But, to tell the truth, we should not misinterpret this sentence, which, of course, says that all human beings are equally the humble servants of God and that one person does not differ from another. Thinking about that contention can ruin our minds, it is so difficult a point. We should explain this assertion a bit so that we will have some small chance of understanding it.

All of us, all together, must give hearty support to this religion, which God handed down to the prophets and the Prophet handed down to us. That means that the raja, the wealthy nobles, the rich people, the prosperous folks, the poor, the suffering and destitute, the have-nots, the strong, the weak, absolutely all of us, have been ordered to bow down before God, to avoid the things he has tabooed, and to carry out the things he commands us to do. No one is an exception when it comes to bearing these burdens. During the month of Ramadan the entire Muslim populace, the entire *ummat* of the Prophet Mohammad S.W.A., are ordered to keep the fast. That is, the whole lot of them simply join together in bearing the heavy burden of hunger and thirst. The raja will be no different here from the general populace, nor are the wealthy nobles different from the destitute, nor are the strong from the weak. All of them must carry out these dictates. And it is not simply their bellies and throats that suffer hunger and thirst but also their eyes, ears, feelings, and so on: all their senses join in the fast. However, if they find they cannot sustain a total fast then they should at least try for a partial one.

A great many people misunderstand the fasting endeavor. They think it is an immensely stupid thing to do, which only serves to hurt people. But whoever wants to keep the fast will surely reap God's blessings. That is how He gives his love to his beloved humans. This is because whenever a raja might happen to feel severe hunger

---

*That Allah is the only God and that Mohammad is his Prophet.

214

and thirst he will be experiencing the suffering of the poor people who do not get enough to eat because they do not have enough money. And it is at that time that the rich show their love for the poor, for they realize how much the latter are suffering. They feel sympathy toward them since they have not been able to eat a meal, and the rich feel pity for the weak and powerless. And during the same Fasting Month the poor people witness God's great power, as he forces the rajas to bow down to him along with the wealthy nobles, the rich people, the powerful, and so on. They are not forced to do this; they are not threatened at spearpoint. Rather, they bow their heads down of their own accord to carry out God's commands and the Prophet's orders. They willingly bear the pain of hunger and thirst.

At such times the Prophet Mohammad's entire human following feels itself to be on exactly the same level. Now, it is not really that everyone is equally rich, poor, tall, or large, and that there are no differences between people. The five fingers on our hands are not equally long, we must admit. Could this earth's residents be exactly equal, either? Indeed, the real sense of equality is just as we have set it out above.

In 1918, the World War in the Land above the Winds* drew to a close. In that same year various *syarikat* associations (now only dreams) sprang up with considerable frequency.[2] And it would often happen that clever folks would announce in *vergaderings* (read this, *perhadering*) or the newspapers that all human beings should ideally be considered to be exactly the same and to exist on the same level.[3] And then they would go on to explain this, saying that all human beings are equally God's humble servants, none different from the others. And they'd assert that no one is excepted from this. The wise ones just teach the dumb ones; the rich must give their inherited wealth to the poor; the haves must help out the destitute. That way, everyone exists on exactly the same level, like an even-topped stand of milkwort.

And because such clever folks as these pulled the wool over the eyes of the poorer classes many folks fell into grave misunderstandings. Some were even emboldened to do illegal things to the rajas. But surely it is quite clear to us: that raja, why, he is the earthly replacement for the Prophet whom God has given to us in this world. Things have been arranged so that not everyone becomes a raja. A person won't become a raja unless he has been so designated by God—and that's true even if he happens to be the descendant of nobles, the offspring of the great raja.

As an example, consider the crown prince of the German kaiser, and the Rumanian kaiser, and so on. So it is probably best that we keep the above-mentioned verse hidden deep down inside us and not go trying to explicate the meaning of the notion of "same level, same feelings," and "all on the same level, all sharing the same feelings."

Now we shall switch once again to that Hari Raya holiday in Padangsidimpuan, all right? After a full month sustaining great hunger and thirst, our God provides a wonderful holy day, a great and glorious special holiday, that is, the first of Sawal. On that fine day all of Muhammad's followers receive their pay for what wonderful deeds the Prophet has wrought here on the earth. All join together

---

*In Europe.

in receiving these blessings: the destitute, the impoverished, the rich, the raja himself—all celebrate with great joy and festiveness.

On that certain important day all the most delicious foods are brought out along with all the sweetest drinks.

On that day all the people show their deep respect for the raja and their gurus. On that special day folks really enjoy themselves, and they do whatever they like. But they also remember their close relatives down in the grave. In the special Hari Raya sermon people receive instructions about how they might properly have fun and enjoy a good time. They should not have a good time simply by sporting fancy new clothes or wearing loads of yellow-yellowest, glittering gold. And they *also* should not only rejoice by playing the *gondang* gongs and displaying their prowess at the martial arts. No, not at all: the sermon instucts them not to overstep the bounds of law. *Adat*, religion, law: we can fairly say that all these go together as a single roadway leading us on toward goodness. That is why, even though some folks will say that certain *adat* practices in certain domains might run counter to religion, well, we just let that pass. For, after all, *adat* was here before religion was.[4] And the same is true of the laws (that is, the official rules): they cannot contravene *adat*, which was in existence in this realm beforehand, before law arrived. But it is true that eventually, in the future, what gets followed must be the best choice of the three. So that means that if we witness a certain realm really putting on a huge, festive celebration for Hari Raya we should not immediately fault them for it and say that it goes against religious law. Probably that sort of thing had long since been established as *adat* custom in that realm.

In Padangsidimpuan, Hari Raya was indescribably crowded, fun, and festive. The Commoner Lords, the general public, would stride upriver and down, sweeping gallantly back and forth across the countryside, wearing the very finest clothing possible. The best time was when it got near the evening and all the horse carriages would roll out in a long twisting procession as far as the eye could see. They'd sweep upriver, they'd sweep downriver—what a fine sight! They would keep this up, too, for a whole week. An incredible, kaleidoscopic, changing array of sights could be seen as you sat there in these carriages. No one could begin to describe it.

However, even though folks had certainly been celebrating with great gusto for that entire seven-day, seven-night period, Hari Raya was never officially over until folks had flocked out to the village of Sihitang to formally draw the holiday to a close. That procession and journey to that destination had become firmly established as *adat* for Padangsidmipuan folks, every year. When they could grab a little free time, all of the government employees, the village elders, and the general public would convene a meeting and decide to formally "close the holiday." With that decision having been made and all parties being in accord, they would amass the necessary money to buy all the goods needed for this particular festive undertaking. Because it had all been established as *adat* custom, the people did not feel it at all burdensome to donate the contents of their pockets to the effort. Everyone happily chipped in whatever they might be able to afford. After the sum of money had been totaled up, it would appear that they had enough to buy a cow to sacrifice for the festive meal. That way, there would be enough to eat a big meal out there in Sihitang

Village. And there'd also be enough money for the Indian curry spices, the special drinks, and so on that they would need out there.

On the designated day (normally a Sunday) all the residents of the main marketplace would be boisterously busy. They would put on all their fancy clothes and take out their games and toys. Every single surrey and two-wheeled carriage would be rolled out. All the budding, blooming maidens would come outside, while the cocky young guys would go swaggering about in both directions and the Commoner Lords would stride back and forth ebulliently. Why, even the young girls whose parents normally kept them locked up safely in their houses would come out. And they'd compete to see who had the prettiest clothes.

As soon as the first rays of dawn would appear all the pony carts and carriages would gather together in a great roundup of vehicles, all of them absolutely jam-packed with blooming young girls and dashing, cocky, young guys—not to mention young and old government employees, religion teachers, *haji* pilgrims, and *lobes*.

Earlier that morning four or five big buffalo carts full of food supplies had already set off, complete with frying pans, spoons, cups, trivets, and salt. After the vehicles had gathered in a big group they would course around the marketplace once before setting off to make sure to get word to anybody in danger of being left behind. The big gongs would be beaten, and the smaller gongs would sound; the drums would go "*do-cap, do-cap*"; the violas would go "*iot-iot*"; the flute songs would rise and fall and undulate through the air. And you would look over at the blooming girls, and they would be pushing and pulling on their accordions as the dashing youths crooned Kambang Barus songs.* Everyone would totally blank out all memory of their dire poverty at that moment! People who had been feeling poorly the night before would leap from their sickbeds; their chills would disappear, with joy replacing illness. And after they had circled the marketplace they would cross over the Batang Ayumi Bridge and head toward . . . the Other-Side Market.

Dear Reader, let these festivities take a little break here while we switch to the young Djahoemarkar and the blooming, budding Sitti Djaoerah to see what is happening with them while folks are busy making up their minds to go and close the Hari Raya holiday once and for all. In chapter 9 I noted that the love between the two of them was like two magnets making contact but that neither one was bold enough to say so out loud. Even though Djahoemarkar had not reached the end of his carefree teenage years, God had decreed that his feelings were now those of a young man. And the same was true of Sitti Djaoerah: even though she was only thirteen or fourteen years old she was already experiencing deep love-longings for that young man since they were attracted to each other like a pair of magnets. So as soon as they heard that folks were going out to Sihitang to bring Hari Raya to a close they knew they had to go along and join in the fun. But devising a strategy for getting there was something of a challenge.

With a succession of sad sighs, Djahoemarkar said: "Well, what I think is, even though I want to go, I don't know how I can. How could I ever just take off and play? You know how little wealth our good mother has—how little salt money we can

---

*Another west coast Sumatran style influenced by Minangkabau music.

claim! Going off and having a good time with you folks would just add extra expenses!"

"Well, so, what do you think? I'll pay our expenses to go out there, okay? I'll tell Mother to let us come along with her and to have your mother come along, too. That way all four of us can share a carriage," said Sitti Djaoerah.

"There won't be any obstacle to that, you think?"

"Folks who know the score won't be put out to see us, although people who don't understand will think we're up to something bad. Because, after all, Little Lineage Mate, I'm a *doli-doli* and you're a lovely, blooming girl, a pretty *bujing-bujing*. How could we get away with being together in public, being together the way we've always been before? Here in town, it's no real problem, but outside this city, well, it doesn't look so good," said Djahoemarkar.[5]

"Oh my . . . you sure know a lot, I must say. If a person is accompanied on a trip by her mother, for heaven's sake, no one can take it the wrong way. And, no matter what you do, water flowing downhill will always fan out in little rivulets: people will always gossip, you can't stop them. You just have to mind your own affairs. As it says in the song, after all:

Soban niba diparsoban	One goes out and collects firewood.
Ulang iba marsoban laklak	Just don't go collecting bark for kindling.
Roha niba diparoha	Just mind your own business.
Inda da iba ro di halak.	No reason to answer to other folks.

Thus said Sitti Djaoerah with a little chicken smile and a tiny goat kid's laugh.

"Well, if that's what you think, okay, I suppose. Let's just get everything we need ready beforehand for the special day. And then as you're setting off come by our house and fetch us so we can all go together from there. But don't let on to the old folks that we've made a promise about all this, all right? Pretend you don't know anything about my planning this with you, so no one will smell food in the banana-leaf packets. You've got to remember the words to the song:

Tjiok-tjiok manuk hotoran	Peep, peep, go the baby chicks
Dilombang ni Sunge Durian	Nearby the Durian River.
Iboto dihatoropan	You're my *iboto* in public
Boru tulang dihabunian.	But my *boru tulang* in secret.*

"Ah, that's the way, Kakanda!" said Sitti Djaoerah happily, very glad, indeed, to hear what Djahoemarkar, who reopens deep feelings of love and longing, had said.

"Well, if that's how it is, let's both of us go home," said Djahoemarkar, standing up.

"All right . . . but have we had our Hari Raya handshake?" said Sitti Djaoerah.

"Nope, not yet! But, I say, even though we may not have had our formal handshake I have already forgiven you any internal or external offenses against me that you may have committed, here in this world or, of course, as regards the hereafter."

---

*You're my clan sister in public but my eligible mother's brother's daughter in secret. Kakanda, in the next line, is an affectionate, teasing form of the Malay word for Angkang.

"Ah . . . but, come on, we really do have to shake hands to make those apologies stick, pal!" said Sitti Djaoerah.

"Well, okay," said Djahoemarkar, thrusting out his hand. This was the first time they had ever shaken hands, and it was a handshake of deep longing and desire. When their hands made contact their joy was boundless; they felt as if they were walking up the staircase to High Heaven. "So, *horas*, and good health to both of us . . ." they said, for they were incapable of saying anything more.

When Sitti Djaoerah got home she went straight to her mother to tell her everything she had heard about people's plans for officially drawing the Hari Raya holiday to a fitting close. "Everyone's decided to go out to Sihitang, so let's go, too, Mother, okay? Otherwise we'll just have to sit here and listen to folks tell us how much fun they had out there."

"I've already said as much to your father, but it seems he can't come along or no one would be here to watch the store. And we don't have anyone to take along as our companion; everyone else has already gone in together to charter their carriages. I really don't know who can accompany us out there. So once your father said he couldn't go I decided I wouldn't be going either."

"But I know someone who can go with us, Mother! My Inanguda* over in the Other-Side Market! Let's ask her and Djahoemarkar, and that way no one will be able to hassle us on our journey. All right? C'mon!"

"Ah . . . she wouldn't want to go. She's too preoccupied with her poverty and suffering for that," said her mother.

"Oh, she'll want to go, she will. I'll go do the cajoling, okay? Come on, let's go. You go put in our order for a carriage. But, you know, we'll have to be the ones to pay for the carriage so they'll be willing to go, okay? If we ask them to help us pay, what would they use for money?" said Sitti Djaoerah.

"Well, just as long as they're willing to go I wouldn't begrudge them the cost of the carriage, now would I? Even though money's hard to come by, let me go ask for a very nice looking cart and a dashing sort of horse," said Nandjaoerah.

"All right, Mother," said Sitti Djaoerah, with considerable hope now.

The aforementioned Sunday arrived. Sitti Djaoerah got all dudded up. She took her very fanciest clothes out of the cabinet and sprinkled herself with flowery-smelling fragrant oils—their sweet scent floated out in clouds. Her hair was looped around her head like the petals of the coconut flower. And the hair of that blooming, budding girl was like the swept-back wing of the male staghorn beetle bird. When she stood in front of the wide mirror and looked at the reflection of the person there she was quite taken aback. It hadn't occurred to her that she was a teenager yet—she'd thought she was still a little kid. She looked behind her, though, and there sure wasn't anybody else standing there. So, she figured, well, I guess I *am* a *bujing-bujing* now! And then she thought: "Oh . . . I'll bet when Djahoemarkar catches sight of me he'll be surprised. He'll be happy enough to see me coming, that's for sure!!! Now what kind of outfit will he be wearing? Maybe a bark-cloth jacket? Ha! A bark-cloth jacket to go with his elegant Pekalongan sarong cloth,

*Inanguda ('father's younger brother's wife'): Djahoemarkar's mother. Sitti Djaoerah is being sly here, treating Djahoemarkar as an unmarriageable cousin, for public purposes.

maybe? And maybe he'll have his Padang *kupiah* cap cocked on his head at an angle? Ha, ha, ha. . . . Well, if he shows up in that sort of outfit he'll look pretty darn good, I'd say. It'll make for a fine sight if we walk across the Sihitang Bridge arm in arm. Golly, that would make him positively, absolutely take leave of his senses, I'll bet," said the girl, thinking hard.

"Come on, Djaoerah, let's not be last in line. After all, we have to stop awhile at the Other-Side Market and pick them up," said her mother.

"All right, Mother. I'm already dressed. Here, hand me my purse so I'll have something to hold."

"Don't you want to take along this pink silk parasol? You don't want to get overheated, now. What will you use as your parasol?" asked her mother.

"All right, all right, Mother. . . . I almost forgot. Give it here," said Sitti Djaoerah, setting off.[6]

"Now be careful and keep your horse in line, Djakoemango," said Sitti Djaoerah to the carriage man.

"Don't you fret: we'll trot along to Sihitang nonstop, never fear. I fed this good hearty striped horse a whole nosebag full of juicy Sipahantan rice to give him the strength to climb these mountain roads. He won't go sliding back downhill, don't you worry!" said the driver, giving his horse a tap with the crop, and "*sir-rrrrrrrrrrrrrrrrrr*" said the cart's wheels, and "*pak-pak-pak-pak-katipak*" said the horse's hooves.

"Oh, urge him on so he goes even faster," thought Sitti Djaoerah, drawing in her breath.

Once they got to the Other-Side Market Nandjaoerah told him to stop for a moment at Djahoemarkar's house. "Fine," said the driver, turning his horse in toward the structure.

Once Taring (that is, Djahoemarkar's mother) caught sight of Nandjaoerah she started in surprise and asked: "Now where in the world are you going, Older Lineage Companion? Maybe you're going on over to Sihitang with the rest of them to finish off Hari Raya with a flourish?

"Yep, sure are . . . but it seems your Older Lineage Mate can't see his way clear to come along. I had thought that I wouldn't go either, but this young child just kept badgering me. So, Good Woman-Friend . . . could you maybe come along so we won't have to go by ourselves?"

"Oh my goodness:

Pasundur-pasundur bulu	Parting the thick stand of bamboo with
ma da ho Angkang	your hands
Manyarsar asar ni sipagol	And breaking open the caterpillar pupa bird's
Pasunggul-pasunggul lungun	little nest
ma da ho Angkang	You do break open deep wells of longing
Mangarkari sude ne na dangol.	and loneliness, Angkang
	And open up all manner of sadness.

Thus said Taring with tears at the edges of her eyes.

"Oh . . . now, now, come on, you have to find ways to amuse yourself so you don't keep wallowing in pain, you know! If you just keep mulling over what's happened in the past how can you ever clear your thoughts and rest easy? Come on, get dressed, get dressed, let's go."

"So where will Djahoemarkar go?"

"What if he goes along with us so we'll have some companionship? There'll be big crowds there, and maybe we'll get into a dispute with somebody, who knows? Maybe somebody'll want to deal with us roughly, like bondswomen, you never know," said Sitti Djaoerah.[7]

"I don't know, maybe he's already run off over to Sihitang," said Taring.

"Oh, I don't think he's gone yet. I believe I saw him carrying his hoe out toward the back garden," said his *ompung* from inside the house.

"Come on, let's look, Grandmother. Let's go call him. We've got to have a man along: folks are always so nasty, you know, likely to do bad things to us," said Sitti Djaoerah.

"If he's hard at work on his hoeing there's no way he'll want to go along with us. But come on, let's try anyway. He has matured considerably in the way he thinks now that he's an assistant schoolteacher," said his grandmother.

From far away Sitti Djaoerah could already see Djahoemarkar hard at work swinging his hoe through the air, chopping back the thick sweet grass covering the ground. Djahoemarkar noted their arrival out of the corner of his eye, but he pretended not to know anything. He made out like he was working away as hard as he could.

"Boo! Surprised you, I'll bet. That'll make you straighten up your back," said Sitti Djaoerah from behind.

"Now, who in the world are you . . ." said Djahoemarkar to the girl, pretending to strike at her with his hoe.

"Now, you be careful, Older Lineage Mate. . . . Don't you go hitting your friends," said Sitti Djaoerah.

"Ah, you took me by surprise. C'mon, I wouldn't hit you with my hoe. I don't want to get exiled to prison in the Celebes," said Djahoemarkar.

"Well then, c'mon, let's go over to Sihitang! There's our cart, all ready and waiting. Have you forgotten the promise we made?"

"No, I remember it all right, but don't forget Raja Mousedeer's customary little strategem."

"Oh . . . *even* so! You're such a Sibiobio type, I swear, always talking in riddles,"* said Sitti Djaoerah.

"Ha, ha . . . all right, all right, let's get a move on."

When they got back to Djahoemarkar's house everyone burst into loud shouts of laughter at the sight of the young man's clothes. They would not have recognized him if they hadn't known who it was beforehand.

"Now, come on, Little Dad, get dressed on the double so we can leave for Sihitang," said Nandjaoerah.[8]

"Oh me, you just go on by yourself, Respected Mother. I was having a good

---

*Raja Mousedeer, of Sumatran and Malay folktale fame, is always hiding his true intentions cleverly behind sly ruses. Sibiobio folks are reputed to speak in riddles and veiled allusions.

time hoeing up all the sweet grass, and here I've got just a little bit more to do on my section. Tomorrow I'll be too lazy to finish the job."

"But, but . . . what about us, over in Sihitang later on? What if some nasty person tries to hassle us? What then? Who'll protect us?"

"But who's going to be nasty to you? Come on, get serious. The Hari Raya month is an unusually good-hearted month, isn't it? Folks tend to behave themselves, right? Go on, set on off on your journey, so I can get back to my hoeing," he said. But inside, everything seemed to be going too slowly for his liking. He wanted to set off as soon as possible. Of course, he didn't have a cent to pay his own way, and by going with them everything would be free. "Hooos," said his breath as he sucked in the sweet smell of perfume, wafting softly from Sitti Djaoerah's clothing. It was like the fragrance of the storied angels up in heaven.

"Oh, c'mon," said Djahoemarkar's voice. "I've only got a bit more here to do. There'll be lots of folks over there to help look out for you. Why do I have to go, too? Good grief!"

"Oh, honestly, this is *Hari Raya*, c'mon now! Why do you want to go to work today? Get dressed so we can get a move on or else Djakoemango will get tired of waiting for us. Look at how much fun we'll have. Listen to all the gong and viola music, and the harmonicas, and the drums! Those sounds just sort of carry one along—it's as if your body were flying through the air," said Sitti Djaoerah.

"Oih, it's all settled then, Son. Let's go—hurry up and change your clothes," said his mother.

With extremely heavy footsteps (purposely heavy, of course) Djahoemarkar made a show of not wanting to go so that no one would suspect their secret plan. Finally, he did manage to stand up and go into the house. Once inside, he carefully put on a crummy old Chinese-style shirt and an old sarong with holes in it. And he kept on the old beat-up trousers he had worn out in the garden. He threw this ensemble together, any which way, so as to make it clear that he did *not* want to go to Sihitang.

As soon as he appeared in the doorway Sitti Djaoerah's spirits plummeted. She glanced sharply at Djahoemarkar, opened her mouth a bit, and then pursed her lips. Those small gestures meant: "Listen, you, change those clothes immediately and put on that made-to-order suit. Don't be an embarrassment to us and all living human beings. I swear, don't you know this is the Hari Raya holiday?"

"Now, really, do try to go fix yourself up a bit," said Nandjaoerah to Djahoemarkar.

"Yes, really. You may say you don't have a change of clothes, but do give it a try anyway. *Immediately*, you hear?" said Si Taring, too, from the front yard.

"Oh, you guys are always hassling me. What do you want me to wear? You won't be happy with the clothes I pick out anyway," he said, going into his bedroom.

Now, it happened that the clothes he changed into now had all been very carefully laid out in readiness so that he just had to step into them.

Maybe four minutes later he swept out of the house, very neatly done up. He was wearing just the sort of outfit Sitti Djaoerah had hoped for: a Padang-style hat tilted jauntily to the right, a pair of Betawi shoes turned up at the tips (black as burnt driftwood, too), and in his hand a plaited rattan cane. He looked quite the aristocrat. As soon as he got to the front steps he had the nerve to sing out: "Well, come on, let's get a move on if you're so anxious to get going." He was smiling a bit at Sitti Djaoerah and glancing at her secretly with a look laden with love, as if to say, "Let's go."

"Now, that's the way, Apa. Don't you look the perfect dashing young man," said Nandjaoerah.

Looking relieved and happy now, Sitti Djaoerah smiled a tiny smile and tried not to laugh. Her cheeks were round and full like a Maria mango; they blushed red and glowed brightly, like ripe, pink rose apples ripening in the noonday sun. This reddish glow picked up the rosy hue in some little bumps on her forehead, and this red radiance simply intensified the sunlight on her face. Consequently, the girl simply glowed with prettiness.[9]

"So, let's go," they all said at once, setting off toward Djakoemango's carriage. "Let me sit in the front, and you three sit in the back, okay?" said Djahoemarkar.

"Well, all right," but then up popped Sitti Djaoerah, who said, "Let me sit in the middle. I'm afraid I'll fall off." Actually she was making sure that she'd be sitting right behind Djahoemarkar. Once everybody had taken their seats, Djakoemango called out "Giddyup!" and he quickly guided their carriage into the middle of the throng of pony carts. There were about twenty carriages in front of them and about that many behind. After all those vehicles had lined up they pulled slowly out of the Other-Side Market and headed off toward Sihitang. Each bamboo flute was carrying its own tune, and all told it just took your breath away.

And the gold jewelry! Yellow-yellowest, glittering gold shone brightly in the sunlight, whether it be in twinkling gold braids looped over girls' thick black hair-buns or in the form of heavy, round, gold necklaces and bracelets. The ornaments came in all possible varieties.[10]

And, as for the youthful Djahoemarkar, he who reopens deep stores of longing, he just sat there quietly thinking of God's great bounty in providing them with this scene. He paid no attention whatsoever to the occasional girl who would try to steal a look from him. He was so blissful that it was as if he was at the All Night Fair in Seventh Heaven.[11] And when a breeze would bring a whiff of Sitti Djaoerah's floral perfume in his direction his eyes would become even more blissful and sleepy, if that was possible. He was absolutely unaware that the carriage had gone pretty far by this time. In fact, he was shocked when they got to Sihitang. It was only the noise of folks getting down from their carriages that brought him to his senses.

Once people had climbed down from their carriages they all put their hands to their separate tasks. Some put up cooking stalls, some got the hearthstone tripods ready, some set to grinding red peppers with their mortars and pestles, some butchered the slaughtered livestock, while others chopped the meat into little cubes. The womenfolk were unbelievably busy, clanking all their rice pots and frying pans around: it was simply beyond description. Folks started their games only after the food preparations were well in hand. Some danced and sang "Siasam Payah Buanyutan" songs while others beat time with the drums. Others beat the *gondang* gongs, *tortor* danced, or slunk around exhibiting martial arts moves. Of course, some folks went over to the edge of the festivities and started gambling. Some went over to the Angkola River and splashed around, and so on and so forth.

Nandjaoerah, Taring, and their two kids were left to wonder where they would stop their carriage. "Oh, come on, let's go over to Father's Sister's house, over to Boroe Soeti's," said Djahoemarkar's mother.

"Oh, right, okay. So it appears we do have some family here, after all, and a place to drop in on. You know, I had totally forgotten that," said Nandjaoerah.

"So, good friend Djakoemango, take us over to Awaiting Battle's house. That's where we'll stop."

"Sounds good," said the driver.

When they got to the awning of the house they stopped, and the four of them got down from the carriage and called out: "Oh . . . Father's Sister! Are you here?!!

"Now who in the world is that? Come in, come in, here I am," said Boroe Soeti as she opened the door to the house. "Oh, my goodness, so you've come for a visit have you, my son's potential wife? Oh, yes indeed, yes indeed, so you still remember me, do you? How very nice. Come into the house, you all look overheated. Now, who are your two friends here?"

"But it's Djahoemarkar, of course, your sweet grandchild, the one who lost his father when he was still a baby. And the other child is Sitti Djaoerah, our daughter from this Older Lineage Companion here," meaning Nandjaoerah. All this, of course, was what Taring said.

"Alhamdulillah hirobbilalamin: oh, you've gotten so big! Oh, yes indeed," she said, rubbing each of the two kids gently on the chin. "So this is your boy, Grandmother? And this is your blooming girl, Good Woman-Friend???" she kept saying, she was so happy. "Have a seat so I can at least fetch some cold water for you to drink. Whatever will I be able to offer you to eat and drink, for I'm just as poor as I ever was. And then, too, my poor body's just as unexceptional as ever—not too plump, not too skinny—just a stalk of corn struggling and straggling along in a bit of unfertile soil, you know!" she said, bustling off toward the kitchen.

Once Boroe Soeti had set all the coffee glasses and the fancy sweet treats in front of them, she said: "Well, let's have some good hot coffee to whet your whistle. It's pretty far from Sidimpuan, after all."

And the snacks were nothing less than lavish Hari Raya cakes and sweetmeats. This quite took them aback. "Father's Sister, why do you still have Hari Raya cakes left at this late date? It's long after the holiday."[12]

"Oh, my son's wife, it's like that every year; we always have to have lots of holiday cakes on hand. Your father's sister's husband's great pack of students is always pouring in for Hari Raya from distant locales. That's been *adat* for us for a long time now. Right now, in fact, your father's sister's husband hasn't come back from his fishing hole, but when he gets back, the whole lot of them, him and his whole crew of students, will all expect to eat here. So I'll have to cook something, even if it's only poor old boiled *ampapaga* leaves, you know. Oh gracious . . . you're probably still under the impression that we're doing all right by ourselves here. Well, we aren't! After the late lamented Pandingkar Moedo passed away we didn't have anyone left to help us out financially. So, look, Amang Djahoemarkar: you've just got to grow up real fast so us old folks'll have someone to depend on, okay?" said Boroe Soeti.

"Well, one hopes so. He is an assistant schoolteacher, you know," said Si Taring.

"Oh, yes, yes, yes. Oh, Grandparent Who Is Filled with Luck Powers, may you succeed in attaining what you seek in life!* And my, my, don't the two of them make a nice-looking pair," said Boroe Soeti.

They all lowered their heads at this comment, for Boroe Soeti had put her finger on what they were all thinking. So they didn't say very much about that.

After they'd finished their coffee Sitti Djaoerah got up and went over to look toward the banks of the Angkola River. "Oh . . . Mother! Look how much fun people are having! And how many things they have to do. Here, give me my umbrella so I can go take a look, okay?" But they were having such a fine time chewing betel with Boroe Soeti that they didn't seem to hear what Sitti Djaoerah had to say. Not long afterward they happened to look out the window, and there was Sitti Djaoerah stationed right in the middle of the crowd.

"Oh, good Lord, she *is* the wildest girl. . . . Go fetch her back, Djahoemarkar," said Nandjaoerah.

"What are you worried about? She's safe enough out there with all those other young girls," said Djahoemarkar. But, in fact, he was ready to go leaping out there after Sitti Djaoerah.

"Oh, now, isn't she just going to go running after people—make sure you don't let her wander far from you, all right?"

"Well, all right, I'll go call her back home," said Djahoemarkar, going out the door.

As soon as he got out on the main road he started twirling his rattan walking stick and his Betawi shoes went clickety-clack on the roadbed—and the eyes of the whole crowd of young girls turned right toward him. They pinched each other and whispered to their friends: "Who's that good-looking young guy? He sure is a good dresser—pretty handsome, too! For sure, I think that guy would cure my lovesickness if he'd just return my glances," said one of them, while a few others just sucked in their breath, so taken aback that they didn't know what to say. Nor did they know who the fellow was or where he might be from.

"'Rah. . . . Why are you so wild, honestly?! Our Mom's already put out with you. Come here, come here. You can see everything that's going on from here; there's no need to go plunging into the crowd," said Djahoemarkar.

"Can you?" said Sitti Djaoerah, walking back over to the road.

Once she got there the two of them stood there and looked at the crowd. Both of their foreheads glowed red and ruddy in the heat, and that made them even handsomer, especially since they were standing there side by side as if posing for a photograph. The light reflected softly off the pink silk parasol onto their faces, which made them even better looking to the crowd. Everyone who caught sight of them drew in their breath: they looked as fine as a matched pair of male and female

---

*Exclamations of this sort, designed to secure luck, are common statements made by old people to youngsters.

ducks bobbing along atop a lake surrounded by *tolong* high reeds under the *sitarak* boughs.

When they had had enough of standing there they walked over to the Sihitang Bridge to watch the people swimming in the river and playing along the sandy banks of the Angkola River. As they walked people's eyes followed them, especially the eyes of the young guys and girls.

Something in particular caught Sitti Djaoerah's attention amid the goings on: a bird, a black one with some splashes of white on its wings. Sitti Djaoerah was struck by the fact that this bird didn't want to budge from the riverbank no matter how many folks were crowded around. Rather, the creature simply increased his activities because of all the people there and started flying from branch to branch even more energetically. So Sitti Djaoerah asked Djahoemarkar what sort of bird it was.

"So you don't know its name? It's a *pincala* bird. Lots of thoughts spring from that one!" said Djahoemarkar.

"Could you make a song out of the bird's name, do you think? If you can, tell me how good hearted the little bird is by making a real good song out of his name."

"Ah, all you talk about is songs," said Djahoemarkar with a laugh.

"Yeah, well, what do you expect? Didn't we come here to have fun?"

"The only song I know from this bird's name is a real long one—so maybe you won't like it," said Djahoemarkar.

"It's okay if it's long. Go ahead, tell me what it is. So I can hear it."

"Well, okay, listen then.

Itottojto	*Itottojto*
Itottot the pincala bird	Itottot, the *pincala* bird
Iboto impol ni mata	My sister, my *iboto*, apple of my eye
Iboto na so dongan samarga	My sister who really isn't a clan sister at all
Na tama dongan tu saba	Who's a good companion to go out to the
Na tupa dongan tu roba	rice fields
Na pade ubat ni roha	A good friend to go out to the half-cleared
Na so dompang hata ni bada	dry field
	Wonderful mind-medicine, balm for
Ois . . . habangkon au da pidong pincala	my thoughts
Tu tonga tombak urung-urung	Who never utters words of argument.
Tu dolok ni Lenggahar	
Tu rura ni Panyabungan	Ois . . . off flies the *pincala* bird
	Flying off to the deep jungle
Ois . . . sarihon au da ibotku	To the mountain at Lenggarhara
Iboto impol ni mata	To the valley of Panyabungan
Ulang diardjeng halalungun	
Ho do na sumalung roha	Ois . . . I think of my dear clan sister
Na tupa dongan sapanganan.	My *iboto*, apple of my eye.
	May I not be beset by loneliness and longing.
	You're the one to assuage my thoughts
	The one most appropriate as my friend of a
	single dinner plate.

"Ha, ha, good grief! And it keeps going downhill and getting more pitiful by the minute! I guess I'd better let up and end it right there," said Djahoemarkar, looking over at Sitti Djaoerah. She responded to his glance with love, and that response clearly meant: "I love you very much."

It was getting on toward noon, and the rice and curries were done by now. They were spooned out onto the banana-leaf plates, although, of course, some people did get to eat on real porcelain plates, truth be told. Those were the rajas, the government employees, the gurus, and the *haji* pilgrims.

"Well, let's just give our hunger free rein here, what with all this rice and curry," said Raja Throat. "Even the pesky little bacteria will get a good meal today, I'd say," said Raja Finger Bowl. "Here, look, pass me that dish, would you, so I can get a cup of that soup before anybody else can. I'm hot as anything from all this cooking," said Djahapogan, dipping his big spoon into the cookpot. "Ah, but if folks see us snitching an early bite they'll get mad," said Malim Shy and Embarrassed from behind them.

"Get everything ready so we can say 'Bismillah' and get to eating," said the master of ceremonies, and then everyone dug in with gusto. There was so much food they finally had to say, "Enough, Enough!"

Some of the naughtier young girls began to talk in proverbs and rhymes and giggled: "C'mon girls, let's finish up all this rice and curry so the good-looking guys are left with just soup bones and rice crusts from the bottom of the pot."

Djahoemarkar and Sitti Djaoerah did not join in all the feasting, but they certainly heard what the girls were saying. They weren't eating with the rest of the crowd because they had promised to have their meal at Boroe Soeti's. The latter went over to the common kitchen and asked for a washbasin full of Indian curry and a lot of Padang-style *rendang* spicy meat chunks and various other curries. She wasn't able to leave her house to come to the festivities since she was expecting so many men for a meal.

People weren't hesitant to give her what she asked for, either, since everyone knew her to be such a good-hearted, generous, and friendly woman.

While the big crowd was still occupied with its meal Djahoemarkar and Sitti Djaoerah came back to Boroe Soeti's house from the bridge. Along the roadway, near the place where all the girls were crowded around, there grew a half-dead old banyan tree. Its lower trunk had masses of mushrooms on it. Sitti Djaoerah was surprised to see this amazing sight, so she stopped to look. "Look at all those mushrooms on that banyan tree," she said to Djahoemarkar.

"Golly, you didn't know that mushrooms grow on banyans?"

"Nope, the only thing I know is how to eat 'em. I did that once. . . . Where they come from and how they grow, I have no idea," said Sitti Djaoerah.

"But that's what it says in the riddle: 'What living thing comes from the dead?'" said Djahoemarkar.

"Oh my, is that so? Hmmmm. So maybe you can make a song out of that?"

"Why not?" said Djahoemarkar.

"Okay, so how does it go?"

"Just have a listen."

Tubu ma dan tabo   The yummy mushrooms flourish

Di ginjang ni dan halihi   Atop the hawk mushrooms.
Muda panganon na tabo   If you've got some yummy food
Mata pe so marpanailu.   You sure don't want to share it!

"Ohhh, wow! That's pretty good, I have to admit," said Sitti Djaoerah.

The girls who were sitting there eating their meal heard every word. They had a hard time choking down their rice and meat. Some of them just stopped eating in midstream, embarrassed to hear the young guy's song. And Djahoemarkar and the blooming, budding girl (rather, that fine matched pair of ducks) just kept gliding on toward Boroe Soeti's house.

Once they got there it occurred to them that their feet were blistered from all that walking and their bellies were growling from hunger.

"You two certainly have a lot of staying power, going without food for this long time. Weren't you starved out there?" asked Nandjaoerah.

"Ha, ha, it was because people were doing so many great things to see," they said.

All of a sudden Awaiting Battle arrived, and he called out: "Well, let's have a handshake, Ompung! You've certainly gotten big, haven't you? If we had met in the middle of the road I surely wouldn't have known you. After all, I never have any time to come into town and visit you. Boroe Soeti, get that rice on, you hear? And wrap this carp up in leaves and get it on the fire, okay? Just throw some chopped onions and red peppers on it, maybe that'll be enough, with a mess of ketchup on top. A fish like that will be our antidote for all those sweet Hari Raya cakes."

"Okay, okay, everything's in order," said Boroe Soeti, hauling out the rice, curry, and grilled fish.

"Come on, let's all eat together instead of separately so it won't take so long. Folks will want to go on back home soon and the roads will be crowded," said Nandjaoerah. And so they ate, and the rice tasted incredibly delicious. Why, they didn't know, but Boroe Soeti always did endeavor to feed people when they were ravenous. That way she could maintain her reputation for always serving great rice.

Well, whatever the case, they all stuffed themselves and emitted deep, long sighs after they'd finished. Full, for sure! The women and the two young people were as pleased as could be to accept the blessing words of Boroe Soeti and Awaiting Riches after their good meal. Their bodies and *tondi* souls had certainly been well fed they felt.

The sun was starting to go down, so folks started thinking about going home. The carriages started to line up in a long row once again, headed this time toward Padang Sidimpuan. Once everyone had taken their seats on their vehicles they all set off slowly, but the carriages were no longer lined up in good order as they had been earlier in the morning. No, everyone just sort of started running and trying to get in front of one another. Djahoemarkar, Sitti Djaoerah, and their parents sped along, trying not to careen into the other carriages, all the way home to the Other-Side Market. They let Djahoemarkar and his mother off there, while Sitti Djaoerah and her mother continued on toward their house. Everyone arrived safely, without mishap, as was also true of all the people in the big crowd.

The Firm Oath

Sutan Hardwood, the Sutan Ashamed to Grow Old, that is what people called a certain gentleman of high social position living at that time in Padangsidimpuan. Now, people in this domain did have considerable respect for the *sutan*, but even though it was true that the gray hairs grew thick on his head the situation was as folks nowadays would put it: he's zinc roofed, true, but young at heart![1] The *sutan* himself was of the opinion that his body might be getting on in years but his manner of thinking certainly had not changed a whit from his youth. As the Malays say: old, old is the coconut; the older it gets the oilier it is. Consequently, his manner of dress and behavior remained quite cocky and dashing. At the time of the final festive meal concluding the Hari Raya celebrations (just mentioned), the good *sutan* was one of the ones sponsoring the feast. He was in Seventh Heaven on this occasion, in fact, because of all the blooming, budding girls upon whom he was able to feast his eyes. The second he arrived in Sihitang he set to scurrying hither and yon, pouring glasses of lemonade, purportedly for the whole population in attendance at the festival, but in actuality he was paying very special attention indeed to the spot where all the girls were gathered. He carted snacks and drinks to them nonstop. It got so that the girls began to burp gently, they were so full.

When Sitti Djaoerah and Djahoemarkar walked to the Sihitang Bridge the *sutan* caught sight of the pair. He noticed that they were walking abreast like a couple of matched ducks in the stream. True, they weren't actually walking arm in arm in the Dutch manner, but to his eyes it looked as though they were trying to play *tuan* anyway. They looked quite splendid, he had to admit, especially with the lace fringe on the parasol waving them along so merrily. The moment he caught sight of the pair the girl took his heart. And his feet were suddenly no longer quite so assiduous in running back and forth fetching snacks and drinks for the other girls.

What was hidden in his heart let us not yet plumb, but rather, like an augurer, we can say the following. He was thinking: "Oh, this young guy is sitting in the catbird's seat?[2] Who *is* he? Here I am, a man of high social station, yet even I can't go about like that." And his gaze followed the youthful pair. His eyes grew large as saucers as he stared at them; the whites of his eyes flashed white and shiny like the upturned belly of a silver river fish.

A moment later he thumped himself on the chest and said: "Oh,[3] that fellow is really putting on airs, you know. I know he's just an assistant schoolteacher. So, what does that fine young girl see in him?"

This shows the pridefulness of some folks of high social standing. Apparently they imagine that it is high social status that makes one person feel attracted to another. They don't know that love will be directed toward whoever happens to take your fancy. As it says in the words of the song:

Salak-salak na mata	Ripe, ripe snakefruits
Ima salak na tumonggi	Those are the snakefruits that are the sweetest.
Muda dung disolong mata	If someone's caught your fancy
Ima halak na jumogi.	That's the one who's by far the prettiest.

Why, even if a noble-born girl (a very pretty, fresh-faced one to boot) is engaged by her family to a man of high social position, oftentimes she'll take it into her head to go off and marry some simple villager if he's the one who's caught her eye.

But the *sutan* gave such matters very little thought. He was sure that his onions smelled sweeter than anyone else's. So, he waxed maliciously jealous of the happy pair and plotted revenge. He kept saying to himself: "I must subdue this assistant schoolteacher and render him helpless. I am just going to have to snatch this blooming girl out from under you, fella!" I'll use my influence with her father, that's the ticket. Normally, after all, if someone of high social standing comes asking for a girl's hand in marriage he'll get her just like that. And as for Little Boy's Mom,* well, I'll just order her to go home to her father's village for two or three months. I'll say I've divorced her so that the girl will be willing to have me. And that will put an end to it, won't it? So, just wait for what's coming to you, assistant schoolteacher. *I* am going to be the one to escort that girl by the arm through the marketplace, just you wait. Now, then, what is the best way to turn her fancy to me?" The *sutan* ceaselessly tried to think of some tactic to get the girl under his sway—and so, too, to control her father.

During the evenings he'd take a little stroll around town. To rest a bit afterward he would mosey over to Awaiting Riches's place and engage the shopkeeper in friendly conversation. He would always eventually get around to buying something, maybe a shirt, maybe a length of calico. The next day he would repeat the procedure until he got to be on quite friendly terms with Awaiting Riches. Every time he came into the shop he would steal a glance at Sitti Djaoerah out of the corner of his eye if she happened to be there. But her eyes smoldered silently if she caught sight of the *sutan*. "Oh,[4] worse luck" (he would say to himself), "here I am, a person of very high social position, and this girl won't pay the least bit of attention to me. Now that's a stupid way to behave! Maybe she thinks she's be better off marrying someone who doesn't even draw a salary yet—and someone from a poverty-stricken family to boot. But oh, yes, you just wait and see what's coming to you."

Once the friendship between the *sutan* and Awaiting Riches had deepened, the *sutan* began to go on about all the things Malim Most Hopeful had taught him about religion, that is, all about the religious laws for parents of young adolescent daughters and about the taboos specified in the Holy Book.[5]

"Who exactly *is* this Malim Most Hopeful you keep talking about, my respected friend? I would wager his recitations are quite well advanced. And his religious knowledge is doubtless quite deep, too. I'm sure that is so because I find that lots of what the *sutan* says really does hit the mark with me."

---

*That is, his own wife (referred to here by a teknonym).

"He's from over near Natal,* you know. And if I didn't think what he said was true would I be following his advice? Would I submit to his instructions? No way. Especially not given the fact that there are so many other mature and experienced religious teachers available for us to choose from right here in the main part of town. But, I must say, none of them seem very convincing to me," said the *sutan*.

"Well, let's see if he might be willing to come over here sometimes so that I can study religion with him. Then I'd have someone to explain things to me," said Awaiting Riches.

"If you wish to be instructed by a religious guru, of course, he will be most pleased to come. He is in the business of spreading religion in this domain, after all. But, actually, people usually go to him . . ."

"Indeed, then, I must ask forgiveness of you, Respected Sir. If the *malim* might have the time let's just ask him to come here. There's no chance at all that I can go to him, for I don't have the opportunity. Just look at me here, running this store all by myself," said Awaiting Riches.

"Well, then, in that case I shall just tell the fellow to come. Maybe you don't believe everything I've told you, if it's just my stories."

"No, no, I believe absolutely everything you say, Respected Sir, but certainly the lessons will become clearer still if the good *malim* himself shows up."

"If that is your considered opinion, Respected Sir, I shall simply tell him to come." But before the *malim* set off for Awaiting Riches's house Sutan Hardwood made sure to instruct him carefully so that he would be adept at insinuating a sub-tle needle into the shopkeeper's heart. Once they had begun studying the Holy Books they would skip directly to the parts concerned with knowledge of women. "After we've got him under our sway with all these religious laws then we'll broach our real subject, right? And that way we shall get exactly what we seek."

"If we reach our goal, Malim, you shall have a free choice of thank-you gifts from me, rest assured," said Sutan Hardwood.

"Great." And so the next morning Malim Most Hopeful went over to Awaiting Riches's store. The proprietor greeted his arrival in the friendliest possible way; he then offered modest refreshments. When the small meal was over tobacco supplies were laid out before them. Both had a smoke. And what the *malim* said at the end of almost every utterance was nothing less than the sorts of Arabic words that the gurus would normally recite such as Lahawala walaquattabillah . . . , masa Allah, Alhamdulillah, and so on and so forth. That way, folks would be more likely to believe what he said.

After they'd finished a cigarette or two they broke open the Holy Books, first those concerned with all the necessary religious laws and then those listing the com-mandments and the various forbidden acts. They discussed all the problems that occurred when one read the holy texts in mistaken ways, and they also discussed sins. If a person misrecites the verses of the Holy Koran he can really compound his sin, that's for sure.

"Often I hear folks say the following, especially when they're mad at some-thing and maybe haven't gotten something they craved: 'Laila. . . .' However! You

---

*A coastal town in Mandailing reputed throughout Tapanuli to be a place of esoteric, dangerous knowledge.

should know that such an utterance *really* says 'There is no God.' *But*, if one says 'Laila haillallah,' *that* means 'There is no God but Allah.' And please note how tiny the difference is between the two readings."

"Oh . . . true, true, true, Guru! So apparently the sentence 'Lailah' means that there is no God. Now, do you hear that, Sitti Djaoerah's Mom? You're always finishing what you say with 'Laila.' So, stop it, all right, so you don't go and commit some big sin," said the shopkeeper.

And that's the sort of thing the *malim* would go on about from day to day. After he had corrected the shopkeeper's mode of recitation, he veered into a new topic. "Well, look, now we have studied our lessons about the dangers of misreading certain verses and sentences. But we have left out some very important laws, crucial ones even: the laws governing the lives of married couples. These are about things that are extremely wrong according to the Syariah law. Many women who happen to be woefully underinstructed in religion commit great sins against their *tuans*, you know. Why, sometimes women even try to lord it over their husbands, the ones for whom they spoon rice! And lots of them refuse to heed what the ones to whom they should say yes tell them to do. And then, on the man's side, many of them fail to support the household sufficiently. Or they consider a woman to be just someone to obey their dictates. Now, if you don't know the religious laws pertaining to this sort of thing it can lead you to the very gates of hell."

"In our society" (he went on), "there are many forbidden behaviors that women are most definitely not allowed to do, such as: showing their faces to men who are not their husbands or conversing in a friendly way with them. Why, in the land of Arabia—which, of course, is the place of Kaabahitullah and the sacred origin land of the Muslim religion—it is taboo for a woman to interact publicly with a man who is not her husband, her father, or her clan brother. And because of this rule it is most fitting that we conform ourselves to that law, too, so that no tiny, tiny sin occurs! Now, the very greatest sins pertain to your virginal unmarried girls (to *bujing-bujings*). As for *them*: Well! No one but their intended husbands are allowed to see and be seen by them. And it's not just in Arabia that that rule holds. No, the very same is true in the parts of Malaya now converted to Islam. And they really keep that rule quite strictly. Consequently, once a girl is twelve years old she has to be penned up in the house so that great sins do not occur. For, with adolescent girls and young boys along about fourteen or fifteen years old, well, they're like a flint and a flintstone: put them together and they'll ignite. And, moreover, according to the Syariah, you must not teach young girls any sort of knowledge except how to recite the Holy Koran and the religious laws—and how to work in the kitchen, of course, and how to take care of all the folks in the household. Learning the Dutch letters is taboo for young girls—only the most holy Arabic letters are to be allowed. And you have to take careful precautions beforehand so that great sins do not occur, so that you will not have serious, serious regrets later," said Malim Most Hopeful.

Awaiting Riches took all of this in and believed it implicitly. Why, for as long as he had been on this earth this was the first time he had ever heard that the Holy Book said such things. So he praised the *malim*'s great expertise to the skies.

"Oh, now it makes sense that Sutan Hardwood submitted to this fellow's will," he said to himself.

After Malim Most Hopeful had gone on home, Awaiting Riches told the woman of the house what the guy had explained to him from the Holy Books. And he told her all about the rules they should begin following so as to be freed from the occasion of sin.

The woman answered: "All of those religious laws Malim Most Hopeful talked about are true enough, and, I'll admit, folks who live in Arabia and Malaya do conform to such rules. That's because all the work in those lands is turned over to the menfolk; it's only inside the house that women have to do anything. And we womenfolk are delighted to hear of it, too. Hearing about all those religious laws just bouys up our spirits. But don't you forget that here, where we live, here in our own society, we can't do things like they do in Arabia or Malaya. That's because here the work is divided between the men and the women. For instance, consider the work out in the rice fields: beginning with the heavy hoeing of the dry fields and the breaking up of the big clumps of earth into smaller pieces, and then on to the planting, why, that's the work of the menfolk. But cutting away the grasses and weeds and all the tasks associated with that, that's the work of us women. Then, when it gets to be time to cut down the ripe rice stalks, and stamp on the sheaves to shake the grain loose, and then take the chaff off the kernels and get the harvest back to the village, why, *everybody* helps out with that. And the same holds true of work in the gardens. Beginning with slashing the little trees and underbrush in the fields, and cutting down the big trees and burning off the swidden, and then going through the field again and gathering up any leftover ground cover and burning it all off, well, that's men's work. But the women help with the planting, and then, too, to women devolve the tasks of weeding the garden and bringing in the produce—but everybody goes together to carry it back to the village. And, why, some folks even go together and share the work tasks all along if they agree to do so. Stamping down the sheaves of grain, fetching water in long bamboo tubes, gathering firewood for the hearth, watching the children, keeping an eye on the house, and cooking the rice meals—well, that's women's work whatever the case.

So if women worked only inside the house how in the world could the man hope to make a living for the whole household? And that's why there is no way we can follow the customs they use over in those other lands. The way we do things here is pretty good, I'd say. Tasks are divided up nicely, and the work comes out even. So, when you examine the real situation, you'll see that our own rules are right on target.

And then, too, the situation here with young adolescent girls can hardly be compared with that in Arabia or Malaya. After all, around here all children, both boys and girls, have to pitch in and help their parents as soon as they are able. In Arabia, the rich just sit there and get richer while the poor serve as slaves, going around doing the bidding of the rich. Things aren't like that anymore around here, though. And we certainly can't pen up our adolescent daughters inside our houses like they do in Arabia and Malaya. After all, different fields, different grasshoppers. Here in our domain, too, if you have an adolescent daughter, you do have to watch her carefully, but, since it's been established as *adat* custom here that girls are given their freedom to practice ritual courtship talk with boys, such interaction is not sinful. Why, if folks don't come courting your daughter that's a sign of misfortune for you, too. Because, as young people trade courtship rhymes and courtship play, that's where they observe each other's behavior and find out how well the other person speaks and conducts himself. You can tell whether the other person follows *adat* that way. This is true for both boys and girls. And ritual courtship is also a time for folks to gauge the love one party may or may not have for the other. True, this island of Sumatra is getting along in years, but not once has anyone seriously chastised folks who go courtship rhyming or girls who receive such attention. There is simply nothing there, nothing there that violates good conduct, good standards of pleasant speech, and *adat*. And, even if one does very occasionally hear of some problem, that's not a problem with the *adat* of courtship per se but a failing of the ones who try to carry out the practices—a failing of folks who depart from polite social behavior.

In your own books, doesn't it say that religious law is not allowed to alter practices that have been made customary *adat* in a certain area? And the same thing is true for governmental law. That always follows *adat*, too. So, all this means that the advice your *malim* gave you simply can't be followed," concluded Nandjaoerah.

On hearing the woman's explanation, Awaiting Riches felt himself growing sympathetic with that stand, too, for he felt that everything his rice spooner had said was certainly true. So he didn't really know *what* he should uphold: religious law or *adat* law. He was in a quandary.

When Malim Most Hopeful came to Awaiting Riches's house again, with his Holy Book in tow, the shopkeeper told him about the woman's explanation of things. Hearing this the *malim* despaired, but he said: "Now, all right, what she said is true enough. But all of that is nothing more—nothing more!—than a matter of worldly desires and wants, that is, a matter of laws that exist outside the sacred Holy Book. And, moreover, to be truly in accord with good Islamic law, it is only fitting that one follows Islamic law to remain a genuine Muslim. One must not tell God riddles, nor respond with riddles to the laws that he has passed down to us! No, those fine laws are exactly what we must follow. Whoever does not follow such laws will find himself struck down by them.[6] And the result of this? Fiery hell! Here, *this* is the Holy Book, which God passed down to the Prophet. Who would dare to deviate from it in any way? If one veers away from this holy text one is deviating from one's Islamic faith, believe you me!"

"Well, hmmmm, that's certainly so," said Awaiting Riches to himself. And so he made up his mind to follow the words of the Holy Book.

Once the *malim* had left, Awaiting Riches told Nandjaoerah that not a single word of her explanation could be found anywhere in the Holy Book, and, because of that sad fact, what the good *malim* had said was certainly truer than what *she* had said. And because of that Sitti Djaoerah should be taken out of school. For it is a very sinful thing to teach girls the Dutch letters. "At this time in her life she needs to be penned up inside the house so that she will not be visible to men who do not happen to be her intended husband."

"Oh, for heaven's sake. . . . Won't that mean that the child's studies will have come to absolutely nothing, that they will have been a total waste? A child's school lessons that go this way and that in chaotic fashion are exactly the same thing as a *lobe* who hasn't sufficiently studied the holy verses: things come to no good in the end since he hasn't paid careful enough attention to what he knows. Now, surely it is best to let her graduate from school first. After all, she can hardly be said to be a full-grown budding girl yet (that is, a *bujing-bujing*)," declared the woman.

"But all of that is totally sinful, totally sinful! Everything you say is nothing more than a matter of worldly desires. Because of this, this child must be taken right out of school," averred the shopkeeper.

Nandjaoerah's great sadness at taking her daughter out of school can hardly be put into words here. But, since she could not go against what her *tuan* told her to do she conformed.

As usual, once it got on toward one o'clock in the afternoon, Sitti Djaoerah came home from school. Before she got there her mother thought hard, trying to find some way to tell the girl her father's words so that she wouldn't be too surprised and shaken.[7] After Sitti Djaoerah got back to the house her mother called her into the kitchen to tell her the shopkeeper's orders.

"Now, my daughter, Djaoerah, in conformity with the religious law, your father says you must leave school. Now, you should know, I did speak very strongly against this, saying that you should go ahead and graduate first, but your father will not allow it. It's because he's so caught up these days with listening to the words of the Holy Book."

On hearing this, Sitti Djaoerah's sadness was beyond telling, especially when she heard that she must now be kept caged in the house as a Penned Up Young Girl. She stamped her feet and threw herself on the floor: "I don't *want* to leave school! I want things to stay the way they are. Listen, if they all go to hell, too, then I won't feel bad about doing the same thing! Inang, oh Inang . . . what is to become of me?" What made her complain like this was, of course, nothing other than her fear that her meetings with Djahoemarkar would now have to cease. Why, when she couldn't see him on Sundays, when there was no school, even that made her feel they had been parted for three whole years. So she began crying silently to herself in a dispirited, exhausted way. Maybe in this way, she thought, she could convince her mother to cajole her father into keeping her in school until she graduated.

Her mother told Awaiting Riches what the girl had had to say, but that came to precisely nothing.

The next morning, Sitti Djaoerah was not allowed to go to school. The shopkeeper himself went to the school and told the teacher that Sitti Djaoerah was going to end her education because she had to stay at home in the house given that her age was now fourteen years.

"Ah . . ." said the schoolmaster: "You're demanding this far too early in the game, far too early. I would say, let her stay until after the next Fasting Month. If that can be arranged we can give her enough lessons by then so that she'll graduate."

"Thank you, Our Lord, Your Honor, but let's just have it cease at this point. She's got enough knowledge in her for a girl," said Awaiting Riches.

"Well, there is nothing to be done, then. If you are that determined to take the child out of school, then that's that," said the schoolmaster, going on to issue Sitti Djaoerah's exit letter.

When Djahoemarkar heard that Sitti Djaoerah had left school he felt as though the world had narrowed around him in a terrible way. He felt cramped, closed in, and unbearably sad. He knew very well that the domains of the world were wide and expansive and divided into five huge rajaships: America, Australia, Europe, Africa, and Asia. According to geography, he well knew, the island of Sumatra was just a little pile of rocks. But now he felt the very earth to be tiny and cramped—a sign that Sitti Djaoerah had left school. He mulled over everything that had happened with a heavy heart. "God has no mercy if I am not able to see Sitti Djaoerah every day, if I cannot visit her every day at the store like I always do. Why, she's like my little sister here in this worldly existence, here in this external world."[8]

Well, whatever the case, it can be fairly said that after Sitti Djaoerah quit school during every recess Djahoemarkar would go over to Awaiting Riches's house, just like before. He found he could still go to their place despite what had happened. He would just keep going into the kitchen, like before. He would ask them for one thing or another: if it wasn't cooked rice, it would be a glass of drinking water, and so on and so forth.

Since his *adat* and manner of speaking were so very fine, it turned out that the shopkeeper did not object to him being there. The man just took him in as if he were his own womb-child. Whatever Djahoemarkar might lack, the shopkeeper would provide for him. All told, Djahoemarkar was not particularly lonesome for Sitti Djaoerah, for they found they could talk together every day. They just could not walk hand in hand or trade kitchenchat.[9]

Now, Sutan Hardwood saw how they were behaving. So a nasty idea occurred to him: one day he ordered his spokesman to go and tell Djahoemarkar that the shopkeeper would no longer countenance him coming around to visit in the shop. And if he continued to try to come there he would be ordered to be beaten to death.

When Djahoemarkar heard this news, he was deeply hurt. "Oh, Lord . . . what a stroke of bad luck! So now I can no longer meet my sweet, well-spoken Younger Lineage Companion? What exactly have I done wrong? Why are they mad at me? Is it just because some liar has slandered me? Oh, my God, Allah, please explain things to the shopkeeper so that he won't lose his love and sympathy for me, for me, this suffering, unlucky soul."

But, afraid of being told such things, he quite stubbornly decided not to go around to the store anymore. This went on for months and months. His loneliness and pain cannot be *turi-turi*-chanted here, nor in fact can Sitti Djaoerah's own pain. But what could be said? Large obstacles stood in their way. If they said they missed each other as much as they did, that might result in an even greater sin.

The shopkeeper was surprised that Djahoemarkar no longer paid personal visits to the store. So was his wife, but she said: "You know, I think Djahoemarkar's heart is broken because Sitti Djaoerah has been pulled out of school. And that is a great shame, too—the way he worked so hard, escorting her to and from her classes, and then suddenly to have her yanked out, and now she won't even graduate. Such a pity."

But no word at all came from him. Sitti Djaoerah for her part was deeply hurt. Day in and day out she would mull over the fact that her studies had been cut short so abruptly and she was not going to graduate. She even tried to study by herself, but that didn't work because she did not have anyone to teach her.

"Well, look, this is what the law says, so what can you do?" declared the shopkeeper.

And so eventually a thought occurred to Djahoemarkar: maybe he could try to meet with Sitti Djaoerah. He could no longer stand the way he missed her; he longed for her deeply. So he sent her a letter via a little school kid.[10] The child was not to let on to anyone what was going on; if he did Djahoemarkar would have him thrown out of school. The letter's words ran as follows.

Sweet, well-spoken Younger Lineage Companion,
Sitti Djaoerah

Given that an unexpected stroke of bad luck has prevented us from meeting every day (since your parent has had such a change of heart about me, it seems), I ask you, if, indeed, you have any love and pity for me, please come to the White River to meet me tomorrow at noon prayer time. I'll be standing there fishing, but that will be just a ruse, so we'll be able to chat. I shall be able to tell you what has been happening all this long while. However, if you go along with them and have nothing in your heart for me then I shall just climb up the hanging tree and pull tight my suicide rope, letting my body hang parallel to the tree trunk until my life is over.[11] But, listen, I will be waiting for you tomorrow there at the water's edge. You just be there hiding a bit in the folds of the big coconut palm, the one that bends down toward the fishing hole. That way I think my strategy for meeting you should work. Do respond to this letter quickly.

A big basketful of my best regards,
Wg. Djahoemarkar.*

Sitti Djaoerah read the letter the moment she got it. She was delighted—absolutely blissful—to hear the words of Djahoemarkar's letter. "Oh——so slander has caused all this! And he hasn't stopped liking me, after all," she cried, fetching paper and ink to pen a response to his letter.

To Djahoemarkar,
medicine for my longings and loneliness
and the one I surrender my *tondi* soul to in P.S.

I have indeed received your letter, my friend, and very thankfully, too. I am in full agreement with everything you say and rest assured I shall be there. But don't you be even a second late. You have to be at the river at one o'clock sharp, for I can't tell you how much I miss you. I cannot begin to explain it now. But what made you give up on me? When did I ever offend you? When did my father and mother do so? They are also very surprised, trying to figure out what is going on with you.

Now, don't you go changing your plans, all right? . . .
Ten buffalo cartloads of kind regards,
Wg. Sitti Djaoerah

---

*Wg.: an abbreviation for "signed by" in Dutch.

After the letter was folded and put into its envelope, the little kid acting as dispatcher was sent off to school, carrying this communiqué to Djahoemarkar.

He read it right away, immediately upon receipt. When he had read the letter and thought about its words, he was taken aback. "Why, apparently the shopkeeper is *not* mad at me. That's very clear. And it's all because of some liar's mean-hearted slanders. Tomorrow I'll tell Sitti Djaoerah everything that has happened," he said, putting the letter safely into his shirt pocket.

Once it got light, and then when school finally let out, he went right home to the Other-Side Market and got dressed as a person going fishing. He got a pole and a net and walked along the edge of the marketplace until he reached the White River.

His mother saw what he was doing but didn't question him. After all, Djahoemarkar often did that sort of thing.

Once he got to the river he fished for a bit downstream from the big mosque. Then he slowly worked his way upriver. As he waded through the current his steps leaned forward, and he kept hooking fish without hardly trying. Not long afterward he reached the coconut palm where they had promised to meet. Sitti Djaoerah, it seemed, was already waiting there. She had seen Djahoemarkar from far away, but because he was so scruffy looking she did not immediately think it was him, that it was Djahoemarkar, who reopens deep wells of longing and loneliness. She didn't try hailing him, for she was afraid it might be someone else. Because so many fish had snapped up his bait Djahoemarkar was behaving as if he'd forgotten their promise. The moment when her heart leapt at catching sight of him standing there fishing was also the moment when she got peeved at the guy—for Djahoemarkar surely seemed more interested in fishing than in meeting her.

But that was not really the case. Djahoemarkar's eyes kept glancing toward the coconut palm, trying to see where Sitti Djaoerah might be, but because she was hidden behind the folds of the big trunk she wasn't immediately visible. But once he caught sight of Sitti Djaoerah he jumped right onto land and caught hold of her hand. What happened at that moment was nothing other than weeping, they had missed each other so much. Their joy was indescribable. "Now," said Djahoemarkar, "you stand over there near the coconut palm while I fish, and I'll talk to you from the water so folks won't know."

Djahoemarkar jumped into the water again and cast his line into the deep eddy, and whenever a fish took his bait he wouldn't pay any attention. His left hand held the fishing line and kept it taut while he faced Sitti Djaoerah, standing there on land. That way they could chat unimpeded.

So Djahoemarkar said: "I know very well and very clearly that we have been victimized by someone's malicious jealousy. That is why we haven't been able to see each other much. And if we had met folks would have hated me."

"But now, as long as we do love each other faithfully here in this world and on into the hereafter, if luck wills it, we shall be able to keep on meeting in the future. What I ask of you, Djaoerah, is this: if you really and truly love me, let us take a firm oath-promise, one that we will not be allowed to change."

"What sort of vow, kind friend? And, as for my love for you, surely I don't have to keep telling you. Just suffice it to say that the love you have for me, why, I have ten times that amount for you. So whatever promise you propose, of course I shall go along with it," said Sitti Djaoerah, wiping back her teardrops.

"Well then, I ask you to make a certain promise.[12] If I don't get married then you must not get married either, all right? And if you don't get married then I shall not take a wife. One fine day, when folks come asking for you as a bride, that is exactly when I shall ask my family to go asking for a bride for me. The very night that you set off on your marriage journey as a bride to some folks' house—that is the night when a bride must arrive in my home for me. When you are formally seated as a bride in front of the Council of Village Elders, that is the time when I will receive the council's blessings for my marriage. I say this so that neither one of us will suffer any hard feelings. If it is predestined fate that you marry someone else and I don't get a bride for myself, how do you think I will feel, to be left behind that way and all? And it would be the same for you. If fate predestines that some stone-blind person wants this body, however will you deal with your hurt feelings and complaints? So because of all this I ask that we both agree to marry, to become mature adults, in the very same hour. If you are happy following the dictates of the one you spoon rice for I shall also be happy having my rice spooner say yes to me. That way there will be no hard feelings. Now, what do you think?" asked Djahoemarkar.

"Well, golly, it's real hard to understand what you are saying, my friend. How would you know any of that anyway? When someone comes to ask for me as a bride, you will go reading the heart and intentions of a girl as a bride for you, you say? How would you know that I have to be in someone's house as a bride for them just when a bride comes over to your house? And what did you mean when you said that I should be made a mature adult so you can at the very same time receive the blessings of the Council of Village Elders? Since I don't understand I guess I don't know how to respond to what you've said. So, so that we don't hide behind the tree trunk folds of our index fingers, nor play hide and seek behind our second fingers, please tell me straight out what you have in mind.[13] But before you say it you should know that I'll agree to whatever promise you propose, so that there will be no possible way that we can hurt each other's feelings, see," declared Sitti Djaoerah.

"Well, all right, then, what I ask of you is that you yourself become my companion to maturity. As I live, you shall live, as I am happy, you shall be happy. In short, I say that we must be of a single endeavor, of a single shared body from this world on into the hereafter. And if that is not to be the case tell me beforehand so I can hang myself from this tree right here."

"Alhamdulillah . . . that is exactly what I have been asking God for, day and night! Now that you've gone and said it I feel so much more at ease, I can tell you! Now I understand what you are saying, for this way it all works out right! If I go off to get married, then you will have a bride arrive for you; I arrive, and you receive a bride—um, now what have I left out from all you said?"

"Well, look, if it's like that, let's just shake hands on it, to firm up our promise. But you remember! When we make this vow, we're not standing in front of God.

And we are absolutely not allowed to change our minds. If we cannot be together in this world then we shall be in the hereafter."

"Yes," said Sitti Djaoerah, firmly shaking Djahoemarkar's hand up and down to solidify the promise.

But, while these two young persons were talking, what was happening off to the side, the Reader might well ask. Just listen diligently, and we shall explain it to you.

Now, as for Sutan Hardwood, the Sutan Ashamed to Grow Old, it seems he quite resembled a chicken that has her eye fixed on a big pile of rice being sun dried on rattan mats out in front of the house. He was watching Sitti Djaoerah's every move at every instant. So when the *sutan* was on his way to the main mosque he saw the man fishing in the river. Rather taken aback, he observed this guy carefully. He noticed that he was turned, facing land, for about half an hour. "Now, what's this character doing? He's surely fishing in a funny way," commented the *sutan*, going over to spy on him from a closer vantage point. He moved upriver and down, searching for a spot. After he got a really good look he could see that there was a girl there; she was young, entering her teenage years. She was standing under the coconut palm with her bicolor scarf shading her head gently like a parasol. She was chatting back and forth with this guy. "Oh . . . these young kids are pretty clever, huh?" said the *sutan*, looking closer to see who this girl was. Apparently she was none other than the girl who had his heart in such a dither. "Well, all right, then, well and good! So here is a means of getting this girl married real quick!" He forgot about going to the mosque to pray but instead went straight to the store to find Awaiting Riches and tell him about what he had seen. Upon arriving at the store he immediately declared: "Come quick! Come and see your daughter out courting by the riverbank. You've only got the one daughter, and you can't even keep an eye on her."

Angry now, Awaiting Riches and his wife went to see what their daughter was up to out at the coconut palm along the banks of the White River. And they saw that it was true: one of them was in the river and one was standing under the coconut palm. But it seemed as if they were talking along quite nicely, not violating *adat* or any conventions.

"Go tell your daughter to get herself home immediately or I shall roast her over a spit. *This* is what you get for sending that child to school," said Awaiting Riches.

Trying to remain patient, the woman did not respond to her husband's words but rather went quietly over to her daughter on the riverbank. When she got there she asked Sitti Djaoerah what they were doing.

Djahoemarkar answered: "What could we be doing, Respected Mother? I was fishing and Sitti Djaoerah came up to bathe. I saw her, and she said: 'Give me some of those fish.' And at that point I threw a few of them onto the riverbank toward her. I think there were about ten of 'em. Count them, Djaoerah," he said.

Even though this was a ruse there did happen to be some fish laid out there on the ground alongside Sitti Djaoerah.

"I told her to go right home, but she wanted to watch me fish. So I took pity on her, Good Mother, not wanting anyone to bother her," said Djahoemarkar.

Hearing this, Nandjaoerah was very happy and relieved. She took them home, and when they got there she said to the shopkeeper: "Now, look, it seems that Djahoemarkar was just keeping her company out there on the river. He happened to be fishing, and Sitti Djaoerah came along to watch, and since he is so fond of her he tossed some fish up onto the bank for her. It was only because Sitti Djaoerah was having such a good time watching him cast his line into the water that she stopped there for so long a time. Why do you go listening to what folks tell you? Whatever was wrong with what these two were doing? After all, do you imagine you have any children besides these?"

"Oh . . . so that's what it was. I thought maybe it was someone else, that's why I got so hot and angry. Well, just get to fixing the curry, I guess, so we can eat," said the shopkeeper.

"Well, all right, it's true that we have to be careful," said the woman, going on to tell Sitti Djaoerah and Djahoemarkar to prepare the fish so they could get them on the fire. "Sitti Djaoerah can do the frying, Good Mother, and I'll gut them," said Djahoemarkar. Their joy at meeting each other and then actually being able to work in the kitchen together was so intense that its heat could not have been measured with a thermometer—rest assured it was some few degrees hotter than normal. Suffice it to say that they felt as good as if they had happened upon a lump of gold as big as a horse's head. So doing all that cooking hardly wore them out; they thrived on the effort. Once all the rice and fish curry was done they spooned it onto plates and carried it into the central room.

As they were leaving the kitchen Sitti Djaoerah separated out a big carp to give to Djahoemarkar: "Well, here's your salary for doing all that fishing."

"Oh, if so, then where's yours for watching me fish?" asked Djahoemarkar.

"Oh, later, later, but bite me off a little piece and that will be my share," said Sitti Djaoerah.

"Yeah, all right, I'll leave you lots of fish so you'll have enough food to make you grow up real fast," said Djahoemarkar.[14]

After they had finished eating Djahoemarkar went home to the Other-Side Market, carrying packets of rice and fish for his mother. As he was leaving, Sitti Djaoerah said, "deli . . ." and Djahoemarkar came back with, ". . . cious," and so if you put those two words together they made "delicious"!

12

Sitti Djaoerah Runs Away from Home

After Sutan Hardwood, the Sutan Ashamed to Grow Old, had informed on Sitti Djaoerah he did not simply go on to pray in the mosque. He didn't know how big a sin it was to miss prayers on purpose, but he felt it was considerably more expedient to pay a visit to Malim Most Hopeful at his house. For now he had found a good way to pressure Sitti Djaoerah into getting married on the double.

"If the *malim* is any good at predicting the future that girl simply must fall into my hands—for I think it's likely that Awaiting Riches will want to force his girl to get married so that she won't learn things she should not know according to the laws of religion."

As soon as he encountered the *malim* he said: "Malim, go dredge up some words from the Holy Book for Awaiting Riches and his wife,[1] especially some verses about folks with young maiden daughters in their houses (that is, with *bujing-bujing*s at home). Once your recitations find their mark, we'll have a rope around her neck as if we were lassoing a water buffalo. You know, I came upon their daughter courting along the banks of the White River—and as soon as I saw that I told Awaiting Riches right away, and he rushed right out to the river to witness the whole scene. I'd say he's beaten that child with a cane, for his face was already turning red just to see her there on the riverbank. So, just remember: when the waters are swirling with mud that's when you can catch minnows. Indeed, you must go and give some Holy Book lessons to the shopkeeper, just please don't let on that I told you about what happened. Once he believes everything about the difficulties people get into when they have young maiden girls in their houses, I'll order Djapartaonan over there to ask for the bride. And we'll lasso him for sure. As for Little Boy's Mom, well, I'll just tell her to pay a little visit to her father's house for these two months. We'll say that she and I have gotten divorced. That way, if Sitti Djaoerah knows she won't have to be a second wife, she'll be a bit easier to snare. After all, a man who draws a salary and has high-class blood in him to boot will certainly make her mother and father incline in our direction. Yes, indeed, I think they'll say yes as soon as they get wind of this bit of news—why, folks are willing to pay bribes to get a man who draws a salary as their son-in-law. But how much more so in our case, as I am a great merchant! If all this comes off, Malim, let me tell you 'Alhamdulillah, thanks be to God' quite in advance. So get your stratagems in order, and we'll snag that budding, blooming girl just as fast as possible."

"Now, is all this really true? If we follow this plan, we'll have her father under our control in no more than two or three days, but that woman will be something of a difficult proposition, I'd say. She's a subtle one, knows a lot of riddles, see," said the *malim*.

"Oh, I have the utmost confidence in you, Malim. Just concoct some plan so we can get that girl."

As it got on toward evening Malim Most Hopeful headed off to Awaiting Riches's house. Upon his arrival the Shopkeeper greeted him heartily. Whenever the *malim* would say something he would always follow it with two or three phrases in Arabic. It wouldn't really be time yet, and he would already be up, saying his optional prayers. He would say them faster to speed things up. When it did get to be prayer time, he would say his prayers in the usual way over at the main mosque, and then he'd go on to say his evening prayers. After the prayers and the various other verse recitations he and Awaiting Riches would go home and eat, and then they would chat for a moment. Finally they would crack open the holy texts. They would proceed from one religious law to the next, from the taboos to the things they were allowed to do. The *malim* discussed and investigated the whole lot of them. Finally they got to the laws relating to young maiden girls (that is, to *bujing-bujing*s). Malim Most Hopeful declared: "Whether poor or rich, the fathers and mothers of children bear very heavy responsibilities. Very heavy, indeed! From the time the children are small to the time they are grown, their parents have to take good care of them. And they only become any sort of help to you when they're grown. Now, you do not have to keep a very careful watch on sons, for they can be as freewheeling as they like, but with girls aged fourteen and fifteen, well, you have to watch them like a hen watches her clutch of eggs when a mousedeer hovers nearby. Why, you know, quite frequently, here in this very domain, some folks just let their daughters have totally free rein, going about having a good time, courting all over the countryside. Can you imagine? Think of the magnitude of the sin involved. In the Holy Book does it not say: 'It is a sin for a young girl to meet with a man who is not already designated with certainty to be her future husband.' And it is from that very thing that most sins issue in this domain.

What can guarantee that a person will get his just spiritual due upon this earth? Water buffaloes that have grown up together in a single corral can be watched over by just one person working alone, but we certainly cannot issue any guarantees about humans, can we? About caring for them and keeping them in line? No, indeed! So a certain law has been issued: once female children get to be fourteen or fifteen years old you are allowed to marry them off. In fact, it is really best to do this so that great sins in the hereafter will not result."

"Oh, gosh, is that so, Malim? . . . You know, just yesterday I was despondent, seeing only dark scenes upon this earth, thinking over this situation with my only daughter. You see, it appears that she actually had the nerve to chat with someone out along the riverbank. Why, if her friend had not been my very own womb-child I would have cut that boy in two with a knife. I thought: 'What's the use of increasing the number of sins here upon the earth? Better that we don't have any to deal with at all!' However, since they really were not courting after all I calmed down. I almost made a big mistake," said the shopkeeper.

"Auzubillahi minassyaithonin Rojim," declared Malim Most Hopeful, shaking his head fervently. "What could you have been thinking? Do you want them to do it again before you start worrying? You'd better start keeping a close watch on that child—in fact, you'll protect her behind the walls of the village garrison if you know what's best. When what can happen actually *does* happen, ha! well! Then what can be said? Consequently, it is simply a much better idea to keep a careful watch before-hand, before sins occur. She has already reached the proper age for marriage accord-ing to religious law. So if someone comes along asking for her as a bride it is best that you just marry her off so that you won't have to keep guarding her so closely. Once she's married you're not responsible for her any longer; her husband will be in charge then.

Well, look, it is late at night, so let me go on home. Another time we shall con-tinue our efforts to recite the laws about this matter so that it will all become clear-er for you."

Once the *malim* had left, the shopkeeper had a talk with his wife about their only daughter. "Well, Nandjaoerah, I do think it is best that we get our daughter married if someone happens to come along asking for her as a bride. That way all this won't be such a trial for us, you see. When I think about all the religious laws the *malim* told me about, there really seems to be no safe escape from all these sins except marrying her off. That seems to be the main lesson for folks like us who are protecting young maiden daughters in their houses."

"Oh, for heaven's sake, we cannot follow everything the Holy Book says, you know very well. You must also look to custom and to people's *adat* ways and follow those. Why, consider: even Tuan Syech's daughter has had young guys come court-ing her. Are you going to be more of a *malim* than he is? Now, yes, of course . . . if someone really appropriate happens along and asks for her as a bride, all right, but if it's just any old person we sure don't want to rush into things. Let's just intensify our efforts to raise her well, all right? And, besides, I don't have the heart to see her married yet since she's not of age. Once she's gone off to her new house, well, then she'll be in charge of making a living and looking around for what they lack. Not us!" said the woman.

"Oh, come on, . . . I wouldn't give her to just anyone, you know! He will have to be a nice person," said the shopkeeper piously.

Now, where do you suppose Malim Most Hopeful went after he left the shop-keeper's house? Well! He did not go to his place of residence. No, no, he clambered under the floorboards, back between the houseposts, to hear what Awaiting Riches and his wife might have to say. So he found out everything that Dad and Mom[2] had to say to each other. Only at that point did Malim Most Hopeful finally get a move on and return home.

Next day, at dawn, Sutan Hardwood immediately went off in search of the good *malim* to find out whether there might be some welcome news.

"Well, I discussed and debated the Holy Book with him at length last night, rest assured. Awaiting Riches is beginning to bow his head to us in agreement, I would say, but the woman is stubborn. She keeps upholding *adat*."

"How do you know? Did you ask her when you were in the house?"

"Of course not, but once I saw that the shopkeeper was leaning in our direction I asked permission to go home, and then, when I was about ten steps from the house, I coughed a bit, so they'd figure I was some distance away. Then I came back and crept under the house, up under the floorboards, to listen to what they might have to say. That's how I found out that the woman is big on upholding the *adat* customs of people in this realm."

"Please accept my good wishes and heartfelt thanks, Malim. You have truly discerned what is hidden in my heart; ah—you are truly clever at seeing how many fish I have tucked away in my basket," said Sutan Hardwood.

"Ha, ha, well, just trust me! On the second day I'll come back and crack open the holy texts at the parts that deal with womenfolk who bicker with their husbands and all the sins associated with that. If we strike home a second time with those teachings, well, so much the better for both of us, right? When it gets light we'll tell Djapartaonan to walk disconsolately along the edge of the road, mumbling about all the pain and trials and tribulations suffered by those who have just divorced their wives. Very sad! And he'll do it, too, if he has a tad of affection for us. We'll also tell Naimardjolis to ask for that girl as a bride, to fetch her as a newlywed. That way we'll lasso her for sure," declared the *malim*.

"Your good plans should work. I have great faith that we shall indeed succeed in getting that girl."

"Fine, our good Sutan, but you know, I do believe I shall go back to my own house for a moment. Then, when I get back to town, I can start in on our efforts once again. I am worried about my little kids, who I left behind out there, so destitute what with there being no money for their upkeep and all. If I don't come home, whatever will they do for food? Once I've made a bit of a living out in our village for a week or so, I'll come back here to bring our discussions to a fitting conclusion."

"Oh, but look, your going back home will make things really difficult! How about if we just send them their living expenses from here so we won't have to break off our discussions and cut things short?" said the *sutan*.

"Yeah, right, and what do I have to send them? We all know that I am a most impoverished religious scholar, a fakir who does no more than spread the word of God while the general public occasionally and most kindly provides small alms for my upkeep. That is the only way we survive."

"Oh, but that's an easy matter to take care of—just as long as our discussions stay on track, right? Now, exactly how much do those children need for their expenses? If we send, say, ten rupiah, that won't be any great hardship for us, now will it?"

"One imagines that fifteen rupiah might make it somewhat less difficult for them out there in the farm village," said the *malim*.

"Fine, if you say fifteen rupiah then that is what it will be. Let's send it from the Post Office so it will get there right away," declared the *sutan*.

"Well, I will rest easier once we've sent that money, not having to worry about my children dying of starvation and all, out where we live in the village. So rest assured! I shall be pursuing the shopkeeper like a dog after a deer. I shall chase him out of the forest into the open fields, . . . I will force him back into the foothills. I will hound him out into the wide world. Then he'll get thirsty and seek a water hole, and he'll abjectly surrender to us. And at that point the good gunman will put a bullet in him."

"Whew! If that is the case then do give them their religious lessons! We must get that mother of hers under our thumb," said the *sutan*.

At dusk Malim Most Hopeful strode over to the main marketplace in search of Awaiting Riches. The shopkeeper welcomed him as usual. At first they chatted casually as they waited for evening prayer time, and then, after the drum sounded, they walked over to the main mosque to pray. After saying their Magrib and Isya prayers they returned to the house and ate their meal. Afterward they chatted some more, and finally they got around to their holy text studies.

"Now," said the *malim*, "we shall take up the matter of the laws relating to women—for a great many sins issue from them. Much of what they do is quite incorrect vis-â-vis their husbands, and unfortunately they do tend to wrong these good men. Not only that! Women also tend to leave out a lot when they try to say their prayers, you know. If women commit many sins their menfolk share the reponsibility for that, alas—that is, if the men aren't patient enough to make sure that their wives finally come around and obey their dictates. Very important! So, then, ideally we must take great care that women remain good and friendly toward their *tuans* so that great sins do not result. The worst, the very worst, are women who object to things their husbands say and bicker and take issue with those statements—that is, women who don't follow their husbands' orders and commands. For, after all, a husband is not only an elder lineage companion, quite senior in age to the wife, but he is also the raja of the household. If the woman rebels against the one to whom she must say yes and doesn't follow his good orders, well, on Judgment Day she will cross over into hell via the Jahamnam Bridge. And as a result she will not rise to heaven for, well, decades and decades. In fact, she can't rise from the fires of hell until her husband comes along and offers her a pardon.

So, even though a woman may be adept at finances, see, or expert at making a living, or knowledgeable about *adat* and law, well, if she sins against her husband she's no different from the musician who beats the big bronze drums too loudly— the *tortor* dancers will get worn out following the heavy beat."

But, *then*! A woman who is faithful in the religious sphere, who obeys her husband, and remains friendly and accommodating to the public—ah, now, *she* will secure a very fine spot for herself in the hereafter. Even if she's not well instructed and has not advanced very far in her religious lessons, still, if she knows how to conduct herself respectfully toward her husband, why, that man can take her by the arm and escort her forthwith from the Jahamnam Bridge that leads to hell to the Jannatunain Bridge that leads to paradise. Consequently! Obedience to husbands is the most important thing for womenfolk to learn; it must come before all other lessons! After she's got that one down, she can go on to the other teachings."

"Well, what do you think, Sitti Djaoerah's Mom? I believe you know that women commit a great many sins. If it was just me saying this you'd probably accuse me of just choosing sides."

"Oh, honestly . . . I do object to some of what that Holy Book is saying. Look what happens: you work too hard one day and get totally bushed. So you start cooking dinnner late, and when the rice isn't ready *immediately* the man of the house starts throwing kicks and punches at you. Even though he's been out having a good time! Well, of course, a bad attitude[3] is going to develop from all that. If the man would only do his share of the work then such great sins wouldn't accrue to us womenfolk for disobeying him," declared Nandjaoerah.

"Uh oh, so this is the sort of sweet intelligence this old girl has—she'll be a hard one to subdue, that's for sure," muttered the *malim* to himself. "Oh, but once we've got the man under our control she'll be a cinch."

He went on to say that keeping a woman who refuses to follow religious law is exactly the same thing as keeping unholy tabooed things around the house. Surely the shopkeeper would not want to do that.

Since it was late, the *malim* asked permission to go home. Neither did he neglect to cough a bit when he was about ten steps from the house. And then he snuck back under the floorboards to catch what they were saying.

However much comment Awaiting Riches contributed about the wrongs women do to men, Nandjaoerah shot back just as much in answer to him. She dwelt on men's shortcomings in not teaching their wives how to behave toward their husbands in the first place. If the men act well then the women will respond in kind. But a man who considers it best to stay home and tend to the little kids while ordering his wife to rush out to the rice paddies and do all the work, well, God will make such a fellow slip into hell first! Nandjaoerah averred. And then, too, some men go through all kinds of contortions when there is hard work to be done. Anything, anything to get out of a little effort! They will carefully massage their long leg and arm bones and say how very painful their muscles feel, so their wives give up and just do the work themselves. What woman has the patience to put up with that sort of thing? God may judge who's at fault here, and He will mete out punishments accordingly and give rewards as they are due. No need to fear anything there," Nandjaoerah concluded.

"Oh, good Lord, this woman is too clever by half at answering back," said the *malim* to himself from under the house.

The next day, early in the morning, he told the *sutan* what he had heard that night. "Well, if that's the way it's going, let's have Djapartaonan go over and say that I've gotten a divorce. What would the shopkeeper say to that?"

"Well, all right, I suppose," said the *malim* in a doubtful voice.

The next day Djapartaonan strode on over to the shopkeeper's place. He had a lot of excuses for showing up there, like buying things he didn't need. After Djapartaonan had bought two or three items he had no use for, he finally began to chat. Eventually he got around to the topic of Sutan Hardwood's sad fate, Sutan Hardwood, he who is ashamed to grow old. "Well, it seems that the good *sutan* has divorced his wife, seeing as how she was getting entirely too haughty and was acting high and mighty toward the general public. Of course, the *sutan* himself is quite open and friendly toward folks, but his wife was a stingy, mean-hearted sort. Since the *sutan* is a rich man and held in social regard it is far better anyway for him to have a wife who knows how to respect all the lineage companions, not to mention the general run of family and friends, of course. So the upshot of it all was that he gave her the old Tholak No. 3 and told her to beat it.* Now the good *sutan* keeps himself busy with all of his considerable commercial endeavors, waiting for an appropriate girl to come along to reside in that very fine house of his."

"Oh my, is that so, Djapartaonan?" said Nandjaoerah.

"Yes. . . . Would I tell you lies?"

"Well, gracious, that is such a shame. And the *sutan* is such a friendly, outgoing sort of man. But frankly that woman had more to be jealous and resentful about than he did. Why, I hear tell that sometimes the *sutan* goes out for walks at night— at night! Folks also say that sometimes he will just walk out that front door: at night. And word has it that oftentimes he decides to sleep in the office. Now what woman would put up with that? Honestly . . . one has pity for the *sutan*, but you also can get angry over the way the woman was treated, you know."

"Yes, well, everyone does say that. But a lot of folks sure do want to offer their young daughters to the *sutan* as his new bride. But, you should know, he won't have anything to do with such efforts unless the girl in question has been well instructed in being friendly and truthful to the public," commented Djapartaonan.

"Oh, I do very much agree, that must be the case so that she will be able to get along with the *sutan*, after all. If the man is rich, his wife certainly must also be rich and noble spirited," said Nandjaoerah.

"Oh, yes, that is why folks love the *sutan* so much. But what is to be done? Things aren't going very well. I myself have no family connections with him, unfortunately. Oh well, let me set off on my way," said Djapartaonan.

All that Djapartaonan had observed he reported straightaway to the *sutan*. "Given the good feelings and sympathy Awaiting Riches and his wife have for you, I would wager we could get their girl pretty easily now. Look, they were praising you and finding fault with your wife, weren't they? I'd recommend that we dispatch a bride negotiator to their house as quickly as we can so that our hopes and desires will bear fruit."

"Fine. Tomorrow we'll tell Naimardjolis to get herself over there. Rest assured, that good woman is a very able bride requester," answered the *sutan*[4].

Dawn came. Naimardjolis was indeed told to go over to Awaiting Riches's house. However, she pretended to show up there just like a regular traveler stopping off from a tiring trip—and angry because she hadn't found what she had been seeking.

Normally when women go to someone's house to ask for a bride they will certainly have contacted the occupants beforehand to warn them about what's afoot. After all, that's the *adat* in such cases. And if the visitors have something to say to the man of the house they will work through the woman of the residence so that they will more easily get what they want and all will go well. In this case things did *not* go like that. They figured that Awaiting Riches's wife would be a hard nut to crack, so Naimardjolis just went straight to the shopkeeper himself. As a reason for

---

*That is, he uttered Islam's "I divorce you" sentence.

going to see him she used as her excuse a need to buy an everyday headscarf to wear around the village. As she was making the purchase, Naimardjolis went on and on about how tuckered out she was from searching hither and yon for a new wife for Sutan Hardwood. She had been at it for days and days on end, but she simply couldn't find any fitting ones, any girls who really hit the spot.

"And so, indeed, Awaiting Riches, since I have come here anyway, let me just ask your advice about what the *sutan* should do to get a bride as quickly as possible. What do you think? As for me, I have just worked myself to the bone. Why, I have gone asking for a whole host of girls—rich people's daughters, *ambtenars*' daughters, merchants' daughters, *malims*' daughters, pretty ones, serious and respectable-looking ones, real knockouts, and so forth. But, the *sutan* has not been interested. What *he* wants, it seems, is someone who knows how to write her letters and someone with a generous, gentle heart to whom he can surrender his household. Now, where am I going to find such a person? And then, too, the *sutan* is getting on in years, and a respected gentleman like him must have an educated wife. If he doesn't have such a woman, it doesn't look very good, given his high social position. The *sutan* says it would be far better if she is adept at writing and such, even if she may not be all that pretty or have a high social class background," said Naimardjolis, trying hard to placate and cajole Awaiting Riches.

"Ah, well, he's really set himself some difficult goals to attain, hasn't the *sutan*? I don't really know in what direction to point you to look for a bride. After all, I don't get around the countryside much myself."

"Oh, goodness, now, if someone like yourself talks like that I do not know what I will do, I really don't, I do declare. I am only saying what I know; I can only explain what I see. Could you maybe see your way clear to help me?" asked Naimardjolis.

"Nothing wrong in that, of course. Those of us here upon the earth must always try to come to each other's aid, mustn't we? I'd be willing to offer my help, for I do pity the poor *sutan*."

"Well, then, if that is the case . . . are you, are you, maybe, willing to let Sitti Djaoerah get married? If so, that bride-gift, the gift of Sitti Djaoerah as a bride, would be just perfect, just perfect. She's rich, she's got social position, and she's got enough school knowledge. Why, folks would really fear and respect her in this realm. Let's just put our heads together on this if you can see your way clear to do this, shall we? For I hear tell she's not in school any longer. If you can see yourself agreeing to all this, I shall go and inform the *sutan*."

"Well, true, according to religious law, that child should be married off, I agree. But how could a person like me be family with the likes of the *sutan*? And then, too, this child is too young to know a single thing about anything. Why, she can't even cook a quick meal of papaya leaves and boiled eels yet. So I do not really believe your request can be fulfilled," said Awaiting Riches.

"Ha, ha. . . . Oh, now what are you worried about? After all, the *sutan* pays servants to cook and clean up around the house. There are lots and lots of other people's girls to be had, after all, but isn't it better that we just get to know each other a bit here and become friends? What else are people looking for in life? Isn't it to have folks respect you? Isn't it to make yourself happy and comfortable in both body and mind? And haven't I already said that as soon as folks heard that the *sutan* was divorced they inundated him with girls? But he didn't want to play up to such people. No! The *sutan* insists on having one who can *write*. But he certainly doesn't want this conversation to proceed via nonsequiters.[5] So, what good welcome news may I convey to him?"

She went on: "And you know, of course, that once we are family with the *sutan*, this store's fortunes will shine even more brightly." Naimardjolis was spouting lies to the shopkeeper.

"Well, I am in agreement, for it even says in the religious lessons that we must seek happiness in this life. But, even though I say this, we had better talk things out with her mother first. She is not too keen on being family with folks of high social position, I notice. But, that's *no* problem," said the shopkeeper, standing up and going into the kitchen to call Nandjaoerah. Not long afterward they both came back into the room.

"Come, let us share some folds of betel leaves, shall we, Good Woman-Friend," Naimardjolis said, holding out her metal betel box. Throughout the entire betel-chewing interlude she kept sighing away as if from exhaustion. So Nandjaoerah kindly asked what had made her so tired.

"But that's what I've just been discussing with the shopkeeper here, my Good Woman-Friend. I was just stopping by to get an everyday headscarf when it seems the shopkeeper noticed that I was looking for something, and that started us to chatting about Sutan Hardwood's sad fate—about his being divorced and all by that accursed wife of his."

"Oh my, indeed, Good Woman-Friend. The day before yesterday we did get news of that. But, you know, what is to be done? We can do no more than contribute a bit of sympathy here—surely it's his own close family's prerogative to come to his aid," said Nandjaoerah.

"Oh, gracious, Good Woman-Friend, now as for me, of course, and I am just a solitary woman who is saying this," commented Naimardjolis, "I do notice that your daughter has gotten big and grown up on us of late. Might you be willing to let her go? You rarely get such a person to give a daughter to, after all. Now what do you think is the right thing to do?"

Nandjaoerah remained silent. . . . She thought quietly.

"Well, what do you say, Little Girl's Mom? What do you think about what Naimardjolis has said?"

"Hooooi," went Nandjaoerah's long, slow sigh. Then she said: "Oh, well, as for me that sounds all right, but even though I say that, we can't just do it on my say-so. We'll have to ask the child herself. And what do you think about it?"

"I like the idea, I kind of do. If they mean what they say, let's go ahead and agree to it," said the shopkeeper.

"Well, look, Naimardjolis, would you please ask the *sutan* if he agrees to our asking the child what she thinks first."

The thing that made Nandjaoerah want to ease these negotiations along like this, very slowly, was the fact that she was definitely *not* in agreement with any of it. But she did not reveal the contents of her heart to the other speech makers.

"Well, then, please let me get on back home in that case. If this is what you are thinking I shall just force the *sutan* to agree to your request, rest assured. Marrying some outsider's girl is definitely not always better than marrying someone who's already family.[6] Like the case here."

After Naimardjolis had left, Nandjaoerah spoke to the one to whom she always said yes: "Why in the *world* did you agree to those negotiations? Do you really think that someone like that *sutan* is the right match for our girl? Try not to be so hasty chasing after big money and high social position—isn't it a better idea to see if the man is a fitting match for her? The *sutan* is already topped with a tin roof, he's so old and decrepit. His hair's all gone gray. And our daughter's just a young slip of a thing—do you think they're a good pair? How in the *world*?"

"Oh, you know too much. Come on, lots of folks give their daughters to men of high social position even though the man's so old he's like a knotty tree trunk. You know that—so why are you being so difficult?" said the shopkeeper.

"That's how people who have eyes only for the brideprice gold behave, now isn't it? They forget all about their child's safety and well-being. But it's hard work to find someone who's a really perfect match. Married couples who are truly compatible are happy together, taking delight in getting along so well every day—even though they might not have a single thin rattan mat to their names. They work hard, searching for what they don't yet have, just sort of getting a big kick out of all the chores entailed in economizing. And because they're so much in agreement they're of a single jump, of a single footprint on the ground; they rise together and fall together much like the bunches of fruits on the bulb of the torch ginger.[7] And as a result they enjoy great happiness and contentment. Don't you go thinking that money or wealth makes for happiness, either! It doesn't. Common agreement and compatibility is what does the trick. To try and make people who aren't a natural pair into a married couple, why, you may as well order the child to go hang herself from the hanging rope out on the high tree. It is just as it says in the proverb: 'Unhappiness and pain will surely find a home where folks are at cross purposes, like the upper and lower jaws of a horse chewing its food or like two legs striding in awkward big steps at two separate angles.'[8] Because, even if the man can make coins fall down from the sky like raindrops, if his cashier (that is, his wife) isn't happy there's no way his fortune can be kept in good order. She'll just receive the money with the right hand and toss it away with the left, and she won't give a single serious thought to building up a bit of wealth for the household. She'll let the guy go bankrupt, or even croak—just so she can get free of this living hell. And, when she looks at her husband, ugh! She sees a big earthworm. And then she'll neglect to attend to all the occupants of the house, and she'll start throwing and breaking the everyday dishes—crash!—and all the other household goods will get eaten by the kitchen mice, and the clothes will become torn and frayed and ugly, and, finally, absolutely nothing will look right there in the house. If this happens, well, the invisible beings will just slip into the structure and make off with what livelihood those people have made for themselves.⁹ Now, would this sort of life for your only daughter please you?" asked Nandjaoerah.

"Good grief, you foresee entirely too much happening. If one believes there is a God one simply surrenders oneself to Him. What you've already seen, keep your eye on; what is yet to come, who's to know about that? Don't be such a worrywart."

"Hey, now, one can't be like that. Doesn't it say in the Holy Book: one is not allowed to simply surrender oneself to God; you have to contribute some serious efforts of your own. That is why the Malays say: 'Work hard to make sure you will fulfill your predestined fate.' And then, too: 'Rich people can afford to simply hope for things, but poor people aren't in a position to just surrender to fate.' Believe you me, those sayings are true!"

"Just order the child to do it. What's the use of broadcasting all this news to the whole world," said the shopkeeper.

"Oh, look, cajoling her is no problem. But you have to give it some thought before you go trying it. *I* only raised her. As for the one who's really in control and who really owns her, of course, it's you. But, look, let's give each other good advice so we won't regret things later on, okay? If you've really made up your mind to give that child to him, I'll try urging her to agree," said Nandjaoerah.

"Ah, now, that's the way. That's better than bitterness, better than words that don't go anywhere.¹⁰ Now, go ask the child what sort of gift she might covet, new clothes or gold jewelry or whatever. I'll provide all of that for her. But just don't get into too much of this questioning and answering business," said the shopkeeper.

"Good, all right," said Nandjaoerah, going to look for her daughter in the girl's bedroom.

"Oh . . . Djaoerah, come here, daughter!"

"What is it, Mother?" asked Sitti Djaoerah, coming in and sitting down beside her mother.

"Well, your father has already agreed to initiate the marriage negotiations of Sutan Hardwood for you—the Sutan Ashamed to Grow Old—so will you go marry him, your father asks. It seems he's divorced his wife. Now, daughter, listen, what I say to you is this: are you in agreement with what your father has said? If I order you to do it, or if I make you angry, don't say I am hard hearted. You have only to say that you don't want to go marry him and you won't be matched with the *sutan*. Those are your *ompung*'s orders, you understand?¹¹ And then, too, I see that your father is hot to get a rich son-in-law, one with a high position in life. That's why he agreed to those negotiations in the first place. But you don't have to be stupid and agree to this and enter into some sort of death in life."

"But, but, Father was really that hard hearted? How in the world . . . ? If I don't find it my heart to do it then I just won't. If he comes to fetch me as a bride then he'll just have to try sweeping me away, and if he comes to cut me into strips and set me out to dry, well, so be it," said Sitti Djaoerah with tears pouring down her cheeks.

"Well, then, daughter, just stand up to him when you convey that news to him. If you go there reluctantly it will be as though you are a girl who will not sell well in marriage to anyone, and I could not continue to live upon this earth if that were the case," said her mother.

Once she and her daughter had come to their decision she went in search of the shopkeeper and with great feeling she declared: "I have informed our daughter of these marriage negotiations. I told her she was not allowed to bicker over what her parents tell her to do and that she should continue to be a good, polite, and respectful girl toward her father and mother. I tried enticing her with promises of gifts of clothing or gold jewelry, and I told her she would have lots of servants and that she'd be able to boss people around in the *sutan*'s house. But what is to be said? First she burst into tears, and then she said she didn't want to marry him. She didn't *want* to have a bunch of servants running around the house saying 'yes' to her all the time. And she also said that she didn't want to marry anyone yet. I explained all of the religious laws pertaining to people who have young maiden girls (that is, *bujing-bujing*s) in their houses, about how these girls are not allowed to stay very long with their parents or else great sins would occur, but she still said she didn't want to marry him. So the upshot is that I don't know what to say to that child."

"Oh, you're always doing what the child says for you to do. She thinks she should rule *you*, not vice versa. C'mon, we're not ordering her to go to her death, after all; we're making her happy. So you'll just have to keep on cajoling her. But let's not have this whole thing embarrass us in front of the village.[12] We don't want folks to say we forced her into it," said the shopkeeper.

"It's best that we have someone else cajole her into it, as you say. I think maybe she's embarrassed with me, and that's preventing her from saying yes," said the woman.

"I think you may be right. If Naimardjolis comes back we'll have her try her hand at it."

"All right," said Nandjaoerah.

Well, now . . . as for Naimardjolis, when she got the news from the girl's father and mother she was quite happy and hopeful. She had great hopes of getting a fancy sarong cloth gift from the *sutan* (hmmm, maybe a fancy Morang-style one, no less). So, once she got to his house she twittered along happily and declared: "We've got her lassoed now, Sutan, never fear. Our prey is not even wiggling anymore. I roped in her father and mother with my words and negotiations. Oh, they're much in agreement with the whole thing. Two days from now I'll go back there again, for, as I said a while ago, we've got to do some serious cajoling to get that girl to agree to things."

"What I told them, Sutan" (she continued), "was that people have been coming in trying to bestow their daughters on you but you don't want any of them. That made the shopkeeper more willing to give his daughter to us, I can tell you. He said we'd have to get word back to him right away. But, really, when I started to cajole him the shopkeeper took to those speeches right away. He was a real easy mark. That's why I say we have to get to work cajoling her pretty carefully. That way she'll be snared, right, Sutan? I think we have to play a little game in which each side increases its price so that we hit our target," said Naimardjolis.

"Ha, ha . . . that'll do the trick, all right. That's what we need! Now, I do have great faith in you and feel we shall get what we seek," said Sutan Hardwood, the Sutan Ashamed to Grow Old.

"Rest assured, no one is going to put one over on us. Now let me just get on back home," said Naimardjolis.

"But . . . what sort of gifts are you going to take to that child? Nobody's at home in my house. Here, take this so you'll have something to buy cotton cloth with over at Djapandelianan's shop," said the *sutan*, giving her a *paske* (that is, a ringgit coin).

"Oh, you don't have to do that, our Sutan—as if I'm not expert at carrying along welcoming gifts for that child, to butter her up a bit. Another time, later, later," said Naimardjolis as she left, but her hand still clutched that ringgit.

As she went along her way she remained very hopeful, indeed, of getting that girl—and she was definitely figuring on a Morang sarong as payment for the girl's answer.

When the second day rolled around Naimardjolis returned once more to the *sutan*'s house to announce that she was off to arrange the marriage negotiations at Awaiting Riches's house.

"Well, may your passage proceed by lucky steps so that many happy and fine things will occur. Now, listen, if things do jell be sure to ask how much bridewealth gold they expect, okay? Ask that straight out so that we'll know how much to bring along later. How much Djapartaonan should have ready."

"Yeah, all right . . . we can arrange all that beforehand. And, as for the bride-price negotiation session, if the sums get big, we'll pay big, all right? If they ask for a small amount, we'll pay a little sum. If you trade in water you have to offer a bamboo water-carrying tube, now don't you? If there's a lot of water to haul then your bamboo tube for carrying it also has to be pretty large. And remember: if there's a lot of brideprice gold that means the girl will bring a lot of household goods to the marriage, household furnishings and things."[13]

"What do you say to just eloping with her to make things easier?" asked the *sutan*.

"But the negotiations are going along quite well, Sutan—never fear, never fear. If they are willing to come to terms everything will come out all friendly like, you can bet. . . . Sutan, if we get this girl we'll have a great *big* store. Why, she's their only child; they don't have any sons and no other daughters—just her. Who else would he be leaving all that money to, if not to her? Eloping's always easy, too easy! Girls are always willing to hotfoot it off if the man has a high social position to lure them off with," said Naimardjolis, shoring up the *sutan*'s confidence.

"Ha, ha," said the *sutan*, for he was feeling like quite a youngster by now, quite the cocky teenager. The *sutan*, however, forgot to look in the big mirror hanging on the wall of the house. So he didn't see that his head was already thoroughly tin roofed.

Off went Naimardjolis . . . and all along her way she tried thinking and thinking of a way to get that girl *right away*. It was as if she were deep in a dream. It was only after someone asked her where she wanted to go that she realized she had walked past Awaiting Riches's house. But since she was so very adept at selling hundreds for thousands, at pulling the wool over people's eyes, she just kept on walking so that Awaiting Riches wouldn't know that she was on a brideprice negotiation mission.

One hour later she finally turned back, and, of course, she did stop by Awaiting Riches's house this time. She went in search of Nandjaoerah. As soon as she got to the house Nandjaoerah greeted her very politely so that no living soul would suspect the real agreement she and her daughter had reached. Sitti Djaoerah herself greeted Naimardjolis in a warm and friendly way, and so the woman grew very hopeful, indeed. The shopkeeper himself held out great hope that they had been roped in.

"Well, so let us share some betel leaves, folks, Good Woman-Friend. I felt kind of frustrated when you came here before since you stayed so briefly. It was almost as if you were just passing by," commented Nandjaoerah.

"Oh, yes, indeed. . . . Me, too, I thought the same thing. And my saliva is beginning to flow just thinking about that good betel quid. I had wanted to have some back in Najtarlaboean's house (Tarlaboean's Mom's house), but it seems they didn't have any around."

"Oh, well . . . to bring our little chat to a brief halt, Good Woman-Friend, just let me tell Butet to heat up some water so we'll have something to drink in a bit, so we can converse more comfortably," said Nandjaoerah, telling her daughter to go do the chore.

"Oh, no, no need for that. Another time, another time! We womenfolk do always have to have some coffee together, don't we? Though it's not as if this is the first time I've come here, after all."

"Oh. . . . Now she's stopped boiling the water again! Go ahead, go on, daughter, keep it on," said Nandjaoerah.

"Good Woman-Friend, what you said was rather strange. What made you go over to Naitarlaboean's house? To make you huff and puff this way?"

"Well, you know, because of all the worry and anxiety over what we were discussing yesterday, well, you know, word has it that they have a very nice adolescent girl in their home, too, so. . . ," said Naimardjolis.

"So, do you need one?"

"But that's the thing, Good Woman-Friend. I had no more than noticed that the door to their house was closed than I turned around and came back here. After all, when you're coming to test and investigate a young girl's intentions about marriage there is no point in pursuing closed doors."

"So all of your hard work and exhaustion went for nothing," said Nandjaoerah.

"Oh, well, such can be endured. If a family member is in difficulty, then, of course, one joins in the suffering."

"But, Good Woman-Friend, let me just say, since I did take care to conduct myself rather well toward you folks, what about that matter we discussed last week? Is it possible that it will all come to pass so that I won't have to keep rushing upriver and down? And, I must say, when I cast my eyes upriver and then when I searched downriver, still this spot right here is the very *best* place to set my foot. And that is a sure sign that God is going to shower good luck on us, I will wager! So, Good Woman-Friend, we must be right out in the open with each other, like rice bubbling in the pot, there for all to see. For, after all, it's just the two of us dealing with each other here. I have come here to find out the state of our negotiations, you see. As for the good *sutan*, well, rest assured that I have been pressuring him to agree to take this one young girl. And if he doesn't want to then I won't attend to his marriage negotiation business anymore. So, that subdued him!"

"Oh my, . . . now, whatever can I say, Good Woman-Friend? I did have great hopes, and the same was true of her father, but, you know, when I tried to broach the subject with her, when I told the child about our negotiations, she started in to crying and carrying on something awful. She wouldn't respond with a single intelligible word, either. It was pitiful to see that child because, after all, what can you do? She's my own little baby, the child of my mind and body.[14] If I forced her into a marriage I'd be afraid she'd lose all hope and fall into despair. And so, Good Woman-Friend, you just go ahead and ask her yourself. Maybe she's embarrassed when she deals with me, I don't know," said Nandjaoerah.

"Ha, ha . . . but that's just their nature, you know. When have you ever seen a child willing to get married?[15] But after she sees that her parents mean business of course she'll be willing. Everyone wants to be happy and content and well taken care of, don't they? And rich! And greatly respected by the public, hmmmm?" said Naimardjolis.

"Yes, Good Woman-Friend, I most assuredly agree. I still have hope that you will be able to subdue her will."

"Well, then, call her right over here while you go and make the coffee yourself," said Naimardjolis.

"Okay, but you'd better make a good pitch so she'll want to say yes," answered Nandjaoerah, going back into the kitchen. But she surely managed to tell Sitti Djaoerah not to agree to what the woman said. "Let's just send her packing, this woman who does not yet know her sad fate."[16]

Sitti Djaoerah sidled over to Naimardjolis and plopped herself down gaily.

"Now, then, Little Woman-Friend" (Naimardjolis allowed), "we were just talking with our mother. About you, in fact. Regarding Sutan Hardwood's request that you become his wife since he has already divorced his first wife, you see. We have shown the *sutan* a great many girls, but he only has eyes for you, Young Woman-Friend. Oh yes, indeed, you are a lucky little thing. You're going to get a very important man, you are! Now, since Dad and Mom have already agreed to the *sutan*'s good marriage request, we are only awaiting word from you. And then we can bring these marriage negotiations to a fine conclusion. So, now, Little Woman-Friend, since we are together here surely it's best that we get a close family member for this marriage rather than taking in some outsider. The way I figure it, you're as lucky as a mouse that has landed on top of a big pile of cooked rice—that is, if you *do* get yourself over there as a bride, to that house. This is not an opportunity that comes along every day, no, indeed!"

Sitti Djaoerah kept quiet, her eyes observing Naimardjolis. A moment later she said: "I certainly did not want you to wear yourself out, coming over here like this, and please don't be put out with me, but as to your request my answer can be quite brief: I simply do not want to get married yet. So you're much better off looking for someone else. But also, so you'll know, since the *sutan* is so old that he's got quite a substantial tin roof on top, he needs a woman closer to his own age as his partner. And, as for me, although my father and mother may be poor, I just don't have the heart to go marry such an old guy. Now, we needn't go through this a second time," said Sitti Djaoerah.

"*Torrrrrr*," went Sitti Djaoerah's words as they struck directly at Naimardjolis's heart. The woman sensed that they were true—so consequently she just sat there, dumbstruck. She could do no more than listen.

A moment later Nandjaoerah came back into the room, carrying steaming glasses of hot coffee and their accompaniment of sweets and little cakes. She noticed that Naimardjolis's face was dark and murky. But Nandjaoerah herself was gliding along merrily—she saw what was going on, all right, although she didn't let on.

After she'd stirred the coffee with a spoon and arranged the little treats on a china plate, she said: "Now, do have some coffee, Good Woman-Friend, for you must be thirsty. Here you've come all this way and this is all the food we have to offer you. We do apologize."

"Oh my, you know, I am rather thirsty, arriving here on a visit like this," said Naimardjolis.

"So . . . what answer did the child give?"

"Well, hmmm, she's still holding out. And she says not to try a second time, so I suppose I have lost all hope of succeeding. I guess I'll take my leave of you and the shopkeeper, but, as for the *sutan*, you know, he was very much hoping that I would bring good news from here."

"Djaoerah! Please come here. . . . What did you say to her? Allah, didn't her words strike you as entirely appropriate? *Who* will you listen to if not to me and now not to her? How are we ever to get you married! Isn't it wealth, prosperity, and happiness that people seek here on earth? Now, who are you going to marry?" said Nandjaoerah to her daughter.

"No. . . it is not that I am just being obstinate. When it's a matter of an old guy who is totally tin roofed it is really better that I have no one to marry than to have to settle for him," said Sitti Djaoerah.

"Allah, God above . . . what did you say?! Don't you know how to talk nicely? Is that what they taught you over in that schoolhouse? If so, won't your father be ashamed?"

"So much stuff makes you guys ashamed, honestly! You only make me listen to talk like this because it's coming from her," said Sitti Djaoerah.

"That's enough of such talk, let's just drink some coffee. When her father has a chance to talk to her later she won't be able to utter a peep," declared Nandjaoerah.

"Well, yes, one hopes so," said Naimardjolis, for the girl's mother did seem to be on her side, at least on the outside.

But the fragrant Sipirok coffee and the buffalo milk yogurt (sweetened with store-bought sugar, Quality No. 1) and the cookies (which were trademark Jacob, all the way from Europe)—well, Naimardjolis found that the whole lot of it just tasted bitter.[17] That was because she knew that the *sutan* would be quizzing her harshly on the outcome of all this if they didn't succeed in getting the girl.

"Now, come on, do help yourself, Good Woman-Friend. No need to be shy and hold back. We're all equals here," said Nandjaoerah, glancing out of the corner of her eye at the girl, who was so very adept at stringing words together.[18]

"Oh my, oh my . . ." said Naimardjolis. "Now, we shall just report everything she said to the shopkeeper. No matter what words happen to be said he's the one with the final say."

"Oh, I do agree, Good Woman-Friend. For, after all, I only raised this child. Of course, it is her father who owns her and is really in charge."

"Well, believe me, I shall go right to him," said Naimardjolis.

Once she got to the shopkeeper, she sighed and lamented and declared that the *sutan* had been greatly, greatly shamed. After all, they had already retracted their marriage negotiation offers to other people's daughters, "so I feel, Shopkeeper, as if I am kind of boxed in here and can't do a single thing. I have no room left in which to maneuver; it is as if nothing comes to any good here. What that child said made me believe that there is no hope of a good resolution of these negotiations. So, look, Shopkeeper, it is your affair now. I do not intend to take personal responsibility for this heavy shame—for this embarrassment as heavy as the earth, as heavy as the sky above our heads.[19] I do believe we run the risk of having our good relations totally break down into mutual embarrassment. So I truly, truly hope that you will try to cajole her into it one more time. If she won't listen to her parent, well, I believe that child won't even heed Islamic law, I must say."

"Goodness gracious . . . what kind of answer did she give to make you lose all hope like this? Should we even be asking her opinion? Look, after all, we're just being nice and asking her for her opinion because of *adat*. As for me, I think everything's decided. A done deal! So, look, wait here for a bit while I go and ask her, all right?" said the shopkeeper.

"One certainly hopes that she will change her mind," said Naimardjolis, somewhat happily now, for hope was returning.

The shopkeeper strode into the kitchen to find out what sort of answer Sitti Djaoerah had given to Naimardjolis.

"Well, I just don't know any longer. I tried cajoling her into it. I got angry, in fact. But she just keeps holding out. So you go and ask her. She's so stubborn that it is an embarrassment to us at this point," said Nandjaoerah.

"Djaoerah. . . !!! Why did you refuse their request? Aren't you interested in happiness and wealth? Now, daughter, have some pity on me, you hear? Please don't bring shame down on all our heads, all right? For if you bring shame to me it is exactly the same as if you do not want to have a Dad at all. Do you maybe want some nice new clothes? Or maybe some gold or diamond jewelry? Wouldn't that be nice?[20] Just say the word and I'll get it all for you. *But*, if you say you won't agree to their marriage request, that would directly violate the *adat* of those who have fathers,[21] not to mention running counter to the Syariah law, too," declared the shopkeeper.

"Oh, golly . . . so you go along with them, Father, running the same idea into the ground? Look, as for happiness and people's respect for me: I'm only talking as I do to keep myself safe and healthy. You know I have a healthy, young, vigorous body, Father, yet the *sutan* is long since tin roofed. Do you *really* think he's a fitting match for me? Wouldn't a silver-haired old woman be a more appropriate partner for him? As to money, well, it does have to be sought, of course—but not just anyone turns out to be the sort of guy you like. And that doesn't happen because of wealth or high social position. So, Father, I definitely do *not* want to be sent as a bride to an old geezer like him."

"Don't have so much to say, smart aleck! Is that what that school taught you? And, as to whether you'll say yes or no, I shall be the judge of that. You *must* go to the *sutan*'s house as his bride, you hear?"

"I would rather hang myself. If you're inconvenienced by having me continue to live here in this house, Father, then it's just better that I drown myself in the river rather than go and marry Sutan Hardwood, the Sutan Ashamed to Grow Old."

"Oh . . . if you're going to be stubborn and not do what your parents tell you, then you are just an accursed child. And what need do I have for accursed people? Don't keep bickering and objecting to what we tell you to do. We do not want bad things to happen—most sinful things!" declared Awaiting Riches, going to get Naimardjolis.

When he got to where she was the shopkeeper's brow was still furrowed in anger. His eyes were still as red and fiery as newly plucked ground cherries.

Naimardjolis whispered a soft question to the shopkeeper, asking whether good news had brought him there.

"Go ahead, go ahead with all of it! With all the marriage plans! Go tell the *sutan*! If he is set in his mind about marrying Sitti Djaoerah, he should go ahead and determine an auspicious day for the wedding. Once he has settled on the date you folks can just come over here and fetch her. I can still order her to agree."

Not long afterward, Nandjaoerah came out of the kitchen, wiping away her tears, and saying: "Please, please, don't go so fast! I'll keep on urging her on. We should really go slow here, just so long as we get there safely, now shouldn't we? Isn't that the way? So we won't regret things later on, please."

"So you are just as bad. You don't know how to control your own daughter. Think of how ashamed I feel when I look at the public in this realm—I have only one daughter and I can't even keep her under control. Ah, let's not let her be held up as a bad example by folks around here."

"I don't know what to say. If we force her to go over there as a bride won't that also bring shame to us later on?" asked Nandjaoerah.

"She *must* go . . . ," said the shopkeeper.

"So what do you want me to do?" asked Naimardjolis. "Go tell the *sutan* to consult a *datu*-augurer and chooose an auspicious date for the wedding?"

"Yes! Right! And the sooner the better, too, so the child won't find out too much."

"*Well*, then," said Naimardjolis, mumbling respectful "*horas-horas*" words of leavetaking all around. And then off she scurried to the *sutan's* house.

That whole day long no one moved inside the shopkeeper's house. Everyone kept perfectly silent. Nandjaoerah forgot to cook the meals. Sitti Djaoerah went to sleep without a blanket; she just rolled up haphazardly in a rattan mat. Awaiting Riches went to the rice stall to get something to eat: a *sure* sign things were not going well in that house. After Awaiting Riches left, Nandjaoerah went into her daughter's bedroom and said: "Now, my daughter, I have seen how he is behaving. If you stay here you'll be forced to go to Sutan Hardwood's house as his bride. That's for sure. And if you go there, why, it will be as if you have disappeared! It will be as if I have no trace left of you! And the same will be true for Djahoemarkar: he will have lost you totally. So, Inang, I think it is best that we run away from this realm, all right?"

"Oh, but where can we go?" asked Sitti Djaoerah, a bit perkier now, for she was beginning to see a path toward life here upon this earth.

"Well, if you are willing to follow my lead, I say let's just take off! Your father's words have broken my heart. If you go ahead and move to Sutan Hardwood's house as his bride, I feel it would be better if I no longer continued to live here on this earth. If one's one and only daughter goes and gets married to an old geezer, isn't it as if she doesn't sell well in the marriage market!!??[22] So you just hold on, have a bit of patience! I will think of some way for us to run away to your grandmother's place (that is, to Panyabungan). . . . But once we go there we can never come back. My heart feels as if a needle has been thrust into it to think what your father has done— your father, who is so hot on the trail of a son-in-law with high social position. So take care that our secret doesn't get out, all right? I will arrange for places for us on the night postal cart to Mandailing so that we can travel secretly at night. The mail cart that leaves town at 2 A.M. is pulled by another horse carriage; we can hide inside the big letter box and no one will know."

"Oh, Mother, thank you, thank you! But we'll have to trust the postman, won't we?"

"Yes . . . but don't worry, I know the man well, and they're close family of ours, too, from Siabu. Once he finds out what has happened he'll have a lot of sympathy for us, never fear. He'll want to help us escape from our difficulties."

"Oh, then please arrange it all as quickly as you can—so that we will no longer be beset by a great windstorm that threatens to knock down the house walls, nor by a rain against which umbrellas offer us no protection," declared Sitti Djaoerah.

The next day, once it got light, once the mail cart had arrived from Mandailing, Nandjaoerah went looking for Djabargot (for that was the name of the postman).[23] His vehicle was the one that normally delivered the mail to Mandailing.

Suddenly, without warning, the postman was accosted by Nandjaoerah. They said hello, and then Nandjaoerah whispered to Djabargot that perhaps they could go talk in a secluded spot. She told him about the great trouble that had befallen her and her only daughter. Shocked, Djabargot followed Nandjaoerah's instructions. After all, he was curious to find out exactly what had happened. Once they had reached a quiet spot, away from passersby, Nandjaoerah explained her plan. She also told him about how Awaiting Riches had tried to force Sitti Djaoerah into marriage.

"So we shall enter a living hell if you do not help us. If Sitti Djaoerah is forced to marry the *sutan* it will simply be better for me to die than to live. And the same holds true for the child herself. Because—why, to marry off such a young girl to that old tin-roofed geezer, now, what do you think of that? Doesn't that just say that she would not sell well to regular people? The shopkeeper really means what he says, too, when he orders her to marry the guy."

"Ah, ah, ah, but that's not right! That's terrible. That goes against law. And it doesn't even make sense. The shopkeeper must only be thinking of money and high social position. Apparently he has forgotten that happiness counts for more than hundreds and thousands of rupiah worth of treasure. The whole thing is just inhuman, you know. But, why—why does the *sutan* want to go and bother people like this? He has no *adat* whatsoever, no living person's *adat*.[24] Well, okay, look. . . . What exactly are you asking me to do? Even if it is a matter of life and death, don't worry, I'll help you, of course," said Djabargot.

"I've heard that they've already divined an auspicious date for the wedding but that they don't have a day set to come and fetch this child from the house. The *sutan* is apparently issuing orders right and left to get all the marriage preparations under way. Why, just a bit ago the bridewealth gold payments arrived, the whole lot of them—very, very far ahead of schedule. So when I come looking for you a second time it will mean that the departure day is near. Here, I've got another idea so that people won't find out about our plans: say that your horse has gone lame and that you have to hire someone to carry the post to Panyabungan. But once you get to Siabu, come right back. By eight in the morning, we'll get to Panyabungan and no one will be the wiser. As we start off from Sidimpuan let us stay inside the letter box so that no one will see us. Even if folks living in the houses near the road ask, they won't see us. And once we get to Panyabungan we won't have to care what anybody does. Even if this becomes grounds for divorce from the shopkeeper, well, so be it. I certainly will have no regrets about that," declared Nandjaoerah.

"All right, fine, fine, if that is what you want. I can put the plan into action all right, never fear. But take care that folks don't find out about this secret and no one gets in our way," said Djabargot.

"Now, listen, don't go changing things!"

"Trust me, trust me."

And, as for Awaiting Riches, he was still conducting secret, whispered negotiations, what with all of Sutan Hardwood's brideprice preparations. They were no longer keeping Nandjaoerah informed about any of these goings on; it was as if he didn't take her into account anymore. Even though Sitti Djaoerah's mother knew exactly what was going on, she pretended she was ignorant of all the arrangements. Whenever a man would come to the house, whoever he might happen to be, she would kindly offer him a glass of hot coffee, as politeness demanded. Consequently, Awaiting Riches thought that Sitti Djaoerah and her mother were in a state of fear and respect concerning all these goings on. And he assumed that Sitti Djaoerah had agreed to the whole proposition. They had already accepted the brideprice gold; how much it was, folks didn't know, for the other side had made only token payments as yet.[25] Only after the girl had gone to the *sutan's* house would they go through the whole process of making the additional payments and explain to the public exactly how much brideprice wealth was really at issue.

After they had reached their consensus about the marriage, they tried for an early date, for the *sutan* did not want folks to find out about the whole thing. So he rejected a lot of the later dates. Only after the day had been determined did they tell Nandjaoerah and her only daughter that in three days she'd be fetched as a bride, on that particular evening. "Well, all right, but you'll have to give us some money for new clothes, so that this child will be willing to stride off on her marriage journey. Otherwise she won't want to go, you know."

With evident delight, the shopkeeper handed over the money to Nandjaoerah. In fact, he gave her all the money the *sutan* had turned over to him. Nandjaoerah set off to buy things, but where did she go? Not to the goldsmith nor to the seamstress—no, off she set in search of Djabargot, over near the post office.

"So, what's happened?" asked Djabargot as soon as he saw Nandjaoerah.

"The appointed day's real near now, so we're going to have to set off this evening. Go find a wagon for hire to carry this load of mail. And, listen, pay the guy double, it's okay. Tell him to set off right after you receive the mail at 2 A.M. And between six and seven come over to the house to help us get our things loaded on the wagon. Have the carriage waiting beforehand over near the Ayumi River, all right? We can get on there. Sitti Djaoerah and I and all our things can go into the mail box in the wagon."

"Okay, you folks just get yourselves ready," said Djabargot.

At the appropriate hour Djabargot came to the shopkeeper's house; the shopkeeper happened to be out praying at the main mosque. After they had loaded all the things they needed Nandjaoerah locked the house and the kitchen and they set off toward the bridge over the Ayumi River. They got into the mail box. "Just keep quiet. If anyone asks me anything don't make a peep," said Djabargot, starting the wagon on its journey to Mandailing. When people happened to ask him anything he would say: the post to Mandailing is late today. Since no one was allowed to inspect the contents of the carriage in any event, no one bothered them. Once they had passed the Other-Side Market Djabargot let the horse speed up. Soon they were flying through the wind. They had to move fast to catch up with the wagon that had left at 2 A.M.

Now we'll switch to Padangsidimpuan to see what was happening while all this was occurring with Nandjaoerah and her daughter. Once he had completed his evening prayers, Awaiting Riches went on home, but he found the central part of the house dark and shuttered. He looked into the kitchen: it was also dark. "Now what's all this? Where has Nandjaoerah gotten to?" He knocked on the front door, but no one answered; he rapped on the kitchen door, and the same thing occurred. Shocked, the shopkeeper stormed: "Now where are they? Did somebody come over here ahead of time and fetch Sitti Djaoerah to Sutan Hardwood's house? We hadn't even agreed on a firm date yet. What's with them?"

Tired, finally, from storming around like this, he went over to the neighbors' house, thinking that maybe they had seen where Nandjaoerah and Sitti Djaoerah had gone. Maybe they would know if Nandjaoerah had escorted Sitti Djaoerah to the *sutan*'s house on her marriage journey?

But . . . what was going on? None of the neighbors knew where they might have gone. "By about 5:30 they should be here getting the chickens back into their coops, you know. I think maybe they've gone over to the marketplace. I think I saw them headed that way a while ago. Wait a bit longer before you go asking about them, maybe in the houses of close relatives they habitually visit," said the neighbors.

"Yes . . . all right, we'll wait, all right," said the shopkeeper.

It got to be ten o'clock at night. Very few people were out and about now. But Sitti Djaoerah and her mother still had not come home.

"Things are getting serious here. Where could they have gone!? Go over to Sutan Hardwood's house and ask him what's going on over there," demanded the shopkeeper.

The guy he ordered to go there left. When he got to Sutan Hardwood's house, not a thing was happening. The house was completely dark; no human voices were to be heard—just the buzz of mosquitoes. The guy went back and reported what he had seen and heard: zilch.

When Awaiting Riches heard this he got more exercised than ever. So he ordered someone else to go over to the Other-Side Market to see if maybe they'd gone to Djahoemarkar's house. "But, look, don't say what's happened; we don't want them getting worried this late at night." He went over to the Other-Side Market; he knocked on the door at Djahoemarkar's house and asked what was happening there. Quite surprised, they answered: "But, nothing. No one's come over here."

"Well. Then just go back to sleep, and I'll go on home," said the guy. He returned home and reported what had happened at the Other-Side Market: also zilch.

When he heard this, the shopkeeper flung himself up from where he was sitting and cried: "Take an axe and break down that front door! Maybe somebody's come and murdered them inside the house while I was off praying at the mosque!!"

This scared the two guys, and they broke down the front door with pounding blows. When the door was down they lit the lamps and carried them into the central room, the bedrooms, the kitchen, and all the other rooms. But there was nothing there, no sign of any changes, nothing.

"Okay, okay, let's think for a moment. Let's not sound a general alarm yet and scare everybody," said one of the men, a fairly mature, serious-minded one.

"All right, all right, we'll sit down first," said the shopkeeper.

When they had sat down the older man asked Awaiting Riches if maybe they had had a fight or if something else had made Nandjaoerah or Sitti Djaoerah feel bad.

"Well, we never actually had a fight . . . but I have accepted Sutan Hardwood's marriage proposal and the brideprice gold for Sitti Djaoerah. The *sutan* has just recently gotten divorced, you see. But we are all in agreement on that. Her mother and the child herself both agreed to it. They're getting the wedding supplies ready, in fact, during these last three days before the ceremony. Because, you see, if nothing untoward happens, two nights from now the child will be ordered to go to her new home to be married."

"Oh . . . I see. So that is how it is. . . . But what exactly did Sitti Djaoerah say to all this? Did she like what she saw when she got a good look at the *sutan?*"

"Well, at first she was real stubborn and said she wouldn't go, but after I scared her bit she was pretty much willing."

"Ah. . . . Now, why in the world did you order such a very young girl to marry an old geezer like him, even if folks do say it's great to have a son-in-law of high social position?" he asked.

"But I thought they liked the idea, both the child and her mother! Moreover, religious law says it is appropriate to marry her off."

"Well, look, there's no need to string out this conversation any longer, that's for sure. From what the shopkeeper has said, the child simply could not answer back and say what she really felt. So maybe she felt that rather than suffering the consequences of becoming an old geezer's wife death would be preferable to life. Maybe her mother felt the same way: rather than seeing her daughter enduring great suffering here on earth—why, of course, she would never have the patience for that—maybe she went and killed herself along with her daughter. You must remember the words of the proverb: 'A mother bird will die for her chicks'—and those aren't just words, either. So, look, light the lamps and torches so we can go out to the river's edge and start searching. Maybe that's where they went to hang themselves," said the older man.

"Well, let me just die, then, if they don't want to do what I tell them to," said the shopkeeper, for he was mulling over the immense shame he would feel when approached by the *sutan.* This would end in a court case for sure. The *sutan* wouldn't just take back his money, that's for sure; he'd have to have a girl, too. When you get into court cases with people of high social position you always lose, he said to himself. For, even though the cucumber vine may wind itself around the sticker bush, it will always be the soft, delicate cucumbers that get stuck with thorns.[26]

Once the public heard *this* sort of talk, they saw the shopkeeper's wrongdoing all the more clearly. So they refrained from helping him with his difficulties. But eventually, given living people's basic love for each other, they remembered that a lot of women take off and run away from great pain and suffering. So they took heart again, after all, and thought that the blameless pair might still be aided. So off they went, looking for orange trees, sweet mango trees, *rambutan* bushes, and so on—trees from which the pair might have hung themselves. When they got tired of that search they rushed back to the house and looked under the floorboards to see if they might have hung themselves from the beams under the structure. Then they looked in all the neighbors' houses, in the chicken coops, in the boxes where the chickens laid their eggs, in the big storage boxes in the kitchen, in the salt bins, and up the big bamboo measuring poles—but still, nothing.

Dear Reader, do not laugh at what I have said. That's the way people are: when serious trouble comes, in their anxiety they lay hold of everything. As it says in the proverb: "A lance disappears, but you get flustered and go looking for a salt bin." But, of course, how can such a strategy ever come to anything worthwhile?

They kept working away like this all night long, until dawn, but they did not find them. At that point they finally informed the authorities and the general public; they beat the big, deep gongs for lost persons; they struck the small, lighter gongs, too, and everyone came from all around to help look. Since they did not succeed in finding them some suspected that they might have run away, given all the troubles they had been having. Block the road to Sipirok! Barricade the way to Mandailing! Waylay them along the road to Sibolga! the public clamored.

Just as soon as Sutan Hardwood, the Sutan Ashamed to Grow Old, got word of all this, he felt very sad: well, he wasn't going to get that girl after all! And all that brideprice gold had already been transferred to boot. If the shopkeeper did not see fit to give it back, he'd really be up a creek. "Especially when he figures out that the girl has run off because of me. . . . Allah, my great God," said Sutan Hardwood, throwing himself onto the floor in despair.

Dear Reader, these words shall take a little rest now, and we can turn to the trip Nandjaoerah and her daughter are taking to see how that is turning out.

Once they got to Saromatinggi they switched horses; a tough little work horse was waiting there. So they always had a fresh horse, and this allowed them to move quickly. Once they had crossed the Angkola Bridge in Saromatinggi, Djabargot told them to climb out of the box so they wouldn't get too cramped from being all bent over in there. There were no more big villages along that stretch of the road, and, besides, everyone was asleep. "All right," said Nandjaoerah, since they were aching and tired from keeping their heads bent like water buffaloes ready for the slaughter.

Once they were outside the box and sitting comfortably, they got under way again. When they got to the Simarongit Bridge, Sitti Djaoerah started to sob: "Oh Lord, we're goners, Mother! What sort of evil spirit is that there on the bridge?"

"Now don't you be afraid; those are just monkeys. They live there day and night, and if no one comes along there they stay." And it was true; when they got to the bridge the monkeys scattered.

"Oh, look—all the bridge pillars look like they've been eaten by the mice the monkeys catch. But don't be afraid; they're not man-eaters," said Djabargot.

Djabargot only allowed the horse to trot on freely after Sitti Djaoerah realized that the monkeys weren't going to bother them. Their journey was swift and unimpeded as they passed through the various villages: Sihepeng, Simangambat, Bonandolok, and so forth. But when they got to Siabu they caught sight of a man hobbling along the road all bent over. Djabargot realized immediately that this was a Raja of the Forest—a tiger—who was going to impede their journey most certainly. However, screwing up his courage, he got out of the carriage and rearranged the horse's harness. What he was really doing was fixing some bunches of onions under the horse's nose so that the creature would not sniff the Raja of the Forest and bolt.

"Good boy, good boy, Blossom," he said, walking the horse along gently.

"Who's that walking along so slowly all by himself? Give him a call so we can add a new companion for ourselves. This horse isn't pulling much of a load yet," said Nandjaoerah.

"Oh, there's no way he'd want to join us. He's a jungle guardsman, an *orang kaya*, coming home from the rice paddies, looking for his enemies to kill—that is, all the wild pigs that are marauding in the gardens.[27] He's still hard at work, guarding the crops. Let's not bother him," said Djabargot.

A moment later the fellow vanished, but not long afterward he reappeared. Djabargot was now very much afraid, but his voice was still firm and strong so as not to frighten his two female charges. Well, fear vanishes, bravery arrives, as the Malays say, and Djabargot urged the horse to walk along. "Let's just wait for the *orang kaya* to walk by," he said frequently, so that the ones he was carrying would believe it was a human being there in the middle of the road.

"But that guy's not wearing any clothes - is that a person or maybe a tiger?" said Sitti Djaoerah.

"Oh, well, he's just wearing tight trousers because it is nighttime and cold and so he can go after that prey of his more easily," murmured Djabargot carefully.

"Oh . . . no! For the life of me, that's no human being! Look at his eyes— they're like fire," said Nandjaoerah. Sitti Djaoerah for her part had already insinuated herself between her mother and Djabargot.

"Allah. . . . Don't be such a scaredy cat, Orang Kaya's eyes are just reflecting the light from this cart. That's why they look like fire. Don't be afraid, there's nothing like that in the forest here."

"*Ra-bas* . . ." said the jump of the tiger as he landed on the edge of the road.

"So you got something in your snare, Orang Kaya," called out Djabargot from the top of the carriage, but the fellow remained quiet.

"Come on, let's be on our way. If he snares anything it'll just be a wild pig. If it was a little antelope, well, then we could wait for it so we'd have something to bring the little kids as a present," said Djabargot, putting the whip to the horse. The horse for his part started to canter along in earnest now. After that nothing bothered them along the road, and it was getting on toward dawn.

"Look, we've come to Siabu. Go do whatever you need to so I can change horses. The guy who carried the mail for us is waiting up there. But don't say anything so he won't know." After the horses had been changed, the mail, too, was tranferred from the rented cart to the postal cart. They got right under way again, going just as fast as they could so as not to have daylight overtake them in midjourney in the middle of the road. As for the guy who owned that cart from Sidimpuan, he had no inkling of what had transpired that night.

Noticing how the horse was trotting along at such a fast clip they felt certain they'd arrive quickly in Panyabungan without anyone seeing them. But, what could be done, what can be said, as they were approaching Malintang, as they were going around the twists and turns in the road, as they were going upward toward a nearly grown-over fallow field, as they were coming upon a boggy fen, suddenly, without any warning, a big herd of elephants ambled by—big, big elephants, many, many in number, why, I'd say there were at least fifty of them. They were just sort of milling around there in the middle of the road, not concerned in the least about moving out of the way. Djabargot's *tondi* soul shot right up to the clouds, and Sitti Djaoerah fainted dead away. For as long as she had been a human living on this earth she had never seen anything like *this*! She had heard people talk about elephants, but she had never actually seen one. Nandjaoerah, too, took fright at witnessing all this—what with Djabargot now keeled over unconscious on them, too. The reins had fallen from his hands, and their carriage was veering toward the side of the road.

"Oh—— Gracious, merciful God! Oh—— Beneficent lordly elephants! Elephants filled with magical luck powers! Please open up a way for us, please, please do. We're not out here taking this trip for fun; this journey results from bad fortune, pain, and immense suffering," declared Nandjaoerah, catching hold of the horse's reins.

Slowly the elephants moved to the side and ambled into the rice paddies, acting as if they were going to knock down a thick stand of sugar palms while they were at it. After they were safely past that place, Nandjaoerah nudged Djabargot awake and gave him back the reins. And with her left hand she caught her unconscious daughter so that the girl wouldn't fall off the carriage. Only after Djabargot and Sitti Djaoerah awoke did they make the horse speed up again. What had happened they kept secret, so folks wouldn't know. After they got past Malintang they made the horse go fast again. The owners of the little rice stall at Gunung Tua were already awake and busily cooking breakfast, but they paid the travelers no heed and did not even come outside. The travelers got to Panyabungan by about 5 A.M. They went straight to the house of some close relatives and pounded on the door. And they went right on in once the door was opened.

Of course, the householders were quite taken aback at their arrival, but Djabargot told them not to make a racket so as not to roust everybody out of their houses. The travelers should get some sleep first, so they wouldn't fall ill from their hard journey. After all, they had not slept that night.

"And, as for me, you can believe I'm going to go over to the stable and get myself some shuteye. I'll take the mail to the post office when it gets a bit later in the morning."

"Well, all right," they said. And they rolled out some rattan sleeping mats and fell directly to sleep.

13

At the Marketplace in Panyabungan

Once it got light, in poured all of Nandjaoerah's relatives and acquaintances living there in town. What had made Nandjaoerah and her daughter suddenly show up *at night*? And why were they riding in the *mail cart* for goodness sake? What has happened, what has occurred?[1] We have never seen such a thing! everyone exclaimed.

Nandjaoerah found it quite difficult and painful to explain the whole thing. To tell the truth, she did not want to say much, but since her relatives kept inquiring she went ahead and told them everything, from the beginning up to the part about Sitti Djaoerah being told to go and marry Sutan Hardwood, the Sutan Ashamed to Grow Old.

"Aha . . . so *that* explains it, the way Awaiting Riches wasn't using an ounce of good sense in this whole marriage matter. The guy's incorrigible—it's a good thing you had the smarts to cook up an escape plan so this child wasn't thrust into a living hell. So, look, let us just say thanks be to God . . . Alhamdulillah, and may you continue to remain free of your troubles," they all cried as one.

After they had had their talk, Sitti Djaoerah pestered her mother to come into the kitchen and talk. Once they got there Sitti Djaoerah asked if they could send a letter to Djahoemarkar so that he wouldn't worry—or, rather, so that he wouldn't go hang himself because of their abrupt departure from home.

"Well, fine, my girl, go ahead and write it, and we can have Djabargot himself take the letter back, okay? Otherwise somebody might snatch it in the post office; you just never know how much power people in high social positions can wield. And, if folks find out that we've contacted him, that in itself could harm Djahoemarkar. They'll say he plotted this trip with us. They'll put him in jail; they'll fire him from his job at the school. And then all of us will be in big trouble," said her mother.

"All right, Mother," said Sitti Djaoerah, going to get the paper needed to write the letter she would send, whose words went as follows.

> To My Older Lineage Companion, Djahoemarkar,
> the Place Where I Surrender My *Tondi* Soul,
> back in our old place of residence (Padangsidimpuan)
>
> Older Lineage Companion![2]

First, let me ask formal forgiveness of you. Please forgive all my major and minor sins, which may have recently occurred.[3]

I believe you know that our father has already accepted Sutan Hardwood's bride-price gold as a down payment on the marriage negotiation settlement. And I believe you know that I was slated to go there as his bride two evenings from now. I never told you any of this because it was as if they were keeping me locked away inside a sealed basket. I felt terribly confined and oppressed, not being able to explain any of it. If I had not kept thinking of you I would have gone and hung myself rather than continuing to live. But if I had done such a thing and disappeared from this earth you would have suffered for the rest of your life. And that would certainly have caused a total innocent to suffer.

So our Mother and I came to a consensus: it was better to run away like this than to have me married off to an old man. For if I had gone to Sutan Hardwood as a bride I would not have been your Sitti Djaoerah any longer. I would surely have had to divorce him, and then would you have wanted me back? You would not get a maiden Sitti Djaoerah in that case, but rather a used divorcée.[4] I simply had no heart for this—for I did not want to surrender my body to someone who had no claim on me, who didn't really own me by right. Rest assured, I hold firm to the promise that we made. Rest assured that I shall not change toward you. So, then, that is what I have to say.

Most warm regards from me and our Mother,
Sitti Djaoerah

When the letter was finished Nandjaoerah gave it to Djabargot so that he would give it to Djahoemarkar himself. He would hand it over to him secretly in the middle of the road so that no one would know.

"Oh, I can handle that all right," said Djabargot, taking the letter and then going back home from Mandailing, carrying the mail delivery for Sidimpuan.

Dear Reader, as we await Djabargot's arrival in Sidimpuan, let's see what is going on with the young man himself.

"How's Djahoemarkar doing?" the general public is asking, I'll bet!

Well ... well, he felt as though his heartstrings had snapped when he got word of what had happened, especially since they hadn't let on a thing about it beforehand. But since this young man was an intelligent sort he pretended he did not know what was going on. And, in fact, he helped with the search, running upriver and down and beating the bushes for them. But when he was alone in a secluded spot he saw quite clearly exactly what had happened with Sitti Djaoerah and her mother. He suspected that they were safe, that they were not really in great difficulty. But, even so, he said to himself: "Where have they gone? Have they died? Have the invisible evil spirits[5] made off with them? If they have died, the hour we find their bodies is the very hour I shall kill myself as well. What is the use of living if I cannot be with Sitti Djaoerah? Why would I stay on this earth?" the Young Leaf on the Tree of Life said to himself.

Well, to make a long story short,[6] eventually Djabargot did arrive in Sidimpuan, and he awaited Djahoemarkar's return from school. When Djabargot encountered Djahoemarkar he gave him the letter immediately, surprising him. He took the letter and read it, standing right there on the hanging bridge between the main marketplace and the Other-Side Market. He almost jumped into the river at reading the missive—but his sarong caught on the guardrail and saved him. Once he had recovered his footing he read the letter again, and finally he came to understand everything. Apparently Sitti Djaoerah still loved him; why, she was even willing to run away from home so that she wouldn't have to marry someone else. So hope sprang eternal, although his loneliness and longing for her were almost unbearable.

"Well, fine, rather than having her marry him it is better that they did what they did, I have to admit. We'll cure our longings for each other in the future. But if she had married Sutan Hardwood my loneliness and sorrow would have been immeasurably deep. She would have quit loving me. Well, look, we shall just have to surrender the whole sad situation to God," said the young man, going home so that he would be able to reply to her letter that same day. The words of his letter were as follows.

>To my Younger Lineage Companion,
>the sweet, well-spoken Sitti Djaoerah,
>in the valley lands of Panyabungan,

Iiiile . . . Little Lineage Companion, the kite bobs up and down in the wind, a warning of swordplay, plaything for my love longings, medicine potion to cure my loneliness, rushing and racing me to see who'll grow up first: well, as for the daughter words of your writing script, your letter has come into my hands, and I do understand all of that fine missive's words. Indeed, when I mull over and think of your unspeakable, unutterable leavetaking my heart feels wounded. However, when I consider how very loyal you were to me, to the point that you ran away to escape the hand of that malefactor and murderer—so that you would yet fall into my own hands if God so wills it—well, I simply say thank you, thank you very much.

Well, indeed, then, Younger Lineage Companion, bamboo for conveying ancient messages (1), that isn't a tall enough tube, that isn't a big enough tube (2), (na sundat muse ho Anggi panirinniranan ni tarias hedehede) (3), my sadness exceeds that of the wailing, moaning, Siamang gibbon, pining away in the deep forest lands (4). Oh . . . please do not utter an oath and imprecation, Younger Lineage Companion, on the ill-sharpened cleaver, on the ill-honed knife, on the tools used to gash the ancient message bamboo standing unmolested in the hollow (5), but rather to Toba Silindung you must swear your oath, for from there come these daughter-words of this written script message to this fine valley land (6).*Well, indeed, then, Younger Lineage Companion, happy and well-mannered one, I surely am not very adept at putting words on the tongue. I simply say good luck to you, may we meet again, in happiness and contentment, so that we might support ourselves in our mutual pain and suffering, we who endure loneliness and longing here upon the earth, here far under the sky. So, indeed, alas . . . my father, my mother, who left me a single, lonely, only son.

| Indalu baya pangitean | Our rice pounder used a little bridge |
| Pangitean marponggol ponggol | A bridge all made of segments. |

*Note: This statement says: (1) well, indeed, then, Anggi Tidjaorah; (2) you who have not yet become a full-fledged adolescent, you who have not yet attained full bujing-bujinghood; (3) you who have not yet become the love medicine for this body; (4) you who have not yet become a gladdener of my mind, chasing away all the suffering and pain in the house yards of Sidimpuan; (5) Ois. . . . May you not swear an oath against your father and mother, who have ordered you on your marriage journey; (6) Rather you must swear your imprecation against Sutan Hardwood, for he is the one who caused our father and mother's words to submit to him, so that you'd be seated among the married adults, so that you'd fall into loneliness. (Signed) The Writer.

Mabalu baya so matean	I feel bereaved, though no death's occurred
Paninggalkonmu ma na dangol.	All from your sad departure.

Gari huboto na rere	If I had known there was a mat
Huhadang do hadanghadangan	I would have made a little satchel.
Gari hubobo na kehe	If I had known you were leaving
Huambat do ditongan dalan.	I would have waylaid you on the road.

Muda so tarhadang hadangan	If I couldn't have fashioned a satchel
Pinomat manyusuk simata	At least I could have added a few colored beads.
Muda so tarambat di dalan	If I couldn't have waylaid you on your way
Pinomat hum marsuo mata.	At least our eyes could have met.

Haru landit marpangir unte	Though it's slick to shampoo with citrus fruit
Lumandit do pangir ampolu	It's slicker still to shampoo with ampolu.
Haru hansit na sirang mate	Though it's painful to be parted in death
Humansit do na sirang mangolu.	It's more painful to be parted in life.

Salupak parsamean	One section of the field is sown with seeds
Ditoru ni podompodom	Underneath the podompodom branches.
Ingot au di harianan	Remember me in the daytime
Parnipihon di na modom.	Dream of me when you sleep.

All right, all right, let that suffice, Younger Lineage Companion. . . . Receive my greetings in this loneliness that shackles me, from me, this suffering soul . . . suffering because of untoward fate.

Wg. Djahoemarkar

Once he had finished writing his letter he put it in its envelope and took it to Djabargot so that the man could convey it directly into Sitti Djaoerah's hands.

Dear Reader. . . . Let us go once more to Padangsidimpuan to see how the general public is getting along in its search for the missing persons.

The pair has not been located yet, it seems. The searchers made a number of decisions and issued numerous orders about how to find them—but they surely didn't turn anyone up. So they decided to divide into groups and send search parties out in all the different directions. They also asked people living along all the roadways whether they had seen the two women. But not a single soul had caught even a glimpse of them. A carriage had been seen on the road to Mandailing, but that was just the mail cart; it wasn't carrying anything but the letter box. And no one had seen anything along the Sibolga or Sipirok roads, either. So folks became more puzzled and stunned by the whole situation. What could be going on?

They plunged into the deep forest, looking for them. . . . They looked through all the underbrush, in the small woods in the ravines, in the half-cut stands of trees, in the half-collapsed old field huts, and underneath the torch ginger bushes.[7] Nevertheless, they did not find a sign of them, not even a footprint. That is how it went for days and days on end. The missing persons were never found.

Word got around that many folks were beginning to find fault with the sutan (that is, with Sutan Hardwood) in this whole matter. But the man just pretended that he didn't know anything. He was scared that he might have to take the final blow in the whole mess, afraid of being assigned the final blame. Rather than having all of this rebound negatively on him and ruin his fine high position in society, it occurred to the *sutan* to say: "Oh, what's money for, anyway? I suppose I've lost the brideprice gold I gave them. Well, tomorrow I'll just issue instructions for Uncok's Mom to come on back home so folks won't be too put out with me."

The search parties decided to call a halt to proceedings for a while to see if they could get any news about the two runaway women. After a week, a rumor arrived from Panyabungan: Sitti Djaoerah and her mother had come to that town and were now living in the home of relatives. Once the shopkeeper got word of this he dispatched an underling to Panyabungan to determine whether the news was true.[8]

The underling sped to Panyabungan. He found that the pair was there, all right—and he spoke "*horas-horas*" good luck words to them.

Awaiting Riches finally got a bit of relief when he heard that Nandjaoerah and her daughter were in Panyabungan. But a moment later, a small satan insinuated itself into his heart and said: "Accursed daughter! Unfaithful wife! What are you supposed to do with people like that?" And so, a notion occurred to him: "Ah, well, just let 'em stay there! I don't need to see them again—after all, why should I put up with even more of their sinning?" But a moment later he'd be wanting to dispatch someone to fetch them back home so that things could be drawn to a close in the public eye. If it had not been for that sentiment he would have totally forgotten his wife and daughter by this time.

So one day a guy the shopkeeper had commissioned set off toward Panyabungan to fetch Nandjaoerah and her daughter home. Once the fellow got into town, he went straight to the house of the Nandjaoerah's relatives. Nandjaoerah and her daughter would be there for sure. The day he came he did not convey any important messages except to say "*horas-horas*." He had located them, he thought, so soul returned to body.[9] He felt happy, relieved, and whole once more. Only the next day did he declare how much trouble the lineage mates and the public had incurred, looking all over the place for them. And he informed them that folks' "exhaustion and anxiety lessened only after they got word that you were here. So, well, look, since your journey was wrongheaded in the first place let's not go on being stubborn and refusing to come back. All you have to do is honor the shopkeeper's request—and, of course, that of the lineage mates and the public, too. We must go home to Sidimpuan so that the *tondi* soul will truly return to its proper abode in the body. Now, this isn't said to make you angry or to insult you because this is all a very normal sort of thing. When we're in pain, we know, people sometimes try traversing a road that may not be traversed; we sometimes try doing something like this. But may this simply become an occasion of greater prosperity for you. And the shopkeeper has already forgiven you for all your transgressions against him."

Nandjaoerah came back: "I welcome all of what you say, and we accept it most politely, for that is *adat*, after all. If a friend is in trouble, all the relatives will exhaust themselves trying to lend a hand. But, as for coming back to Sidimpuan, we cannot do so at this time. You must go back home. I do not care what the shopkeeper may happen to think about me or my daughter. Rest assured, we have been thinking about this matter all the while we've been gone."

"Ah . . . now, don't be like that, please. Don't say that. It's not good to cut off negotiations just like that. Don't shut the stream off when the water is following its natural course: surely it's better to just keep going, like we keep breathing, in and out, in and out, without a break. Let's go back to where we were, all right? Just like water in a stream that gets cut off—if it sweeps into a bit of a whirlpool it goes back upriver, right? And that's just how we are!!! Now, I do know and commiserate with how you feel; in fact, I can sit right here and sort of pull those feelings toward me with both hands, in big handfuls. I certainly have great empathy for you! Even though, of course, you didn't see fit to come to me first and explain the situation beforehand. Hmmmmm. Myself, why—I had crossed over the river to go to see you to talk, but you had already taken off and come here. So, look, given everything, I believe we should just go on back home, you know. The shopkeeper has already acknowledged his wrongdoing. So, please, just forget the whole thing."

"Now, how can you say that? We don't want to go home to Sidimpuan. If we die I guess we'll just have to keel over right here. What's the use of living when someone is always trying to stick needles in your heart?!!"

"Just go away, please," said Sitti Djaoerah. "If the governor himself should come here to fetch us we still wouldn't want to go home. Even if a wind that cannot be fended off with walls should come sweeping toward us, or if a rain from which we cannot protect ourselves with umbrellas should pour down from the skies, we really, honestly do not want to live there. You must understand this clearly. It's best this way," said Sitti Djaoerah, wringing her hands.

The man the shopkeeper had dispatched just kept quiet. . . . A moment later he said: "Listen, I ask of you, please, consider going back to Sidimpuan and then returning here. That way, neither one of us will emerge deeply shamed from this whole thing."

"Oh . . . I know poisoned words when I hear them. Get on home with you," said Sitti Djaoerah, bringing the conversation to a close.

The man stood up with a deep sigh, ashamed and weary. But what was to be done? It appeared that he had not drawn his endeavors to a successful conclusion. So he departed dejectedly in the dark, returning home from that realm. All the stuffing had been knocked out of him.[10]

Back in Sidimpuan, he related the response Nandjaoerah and her daughter had given. He told all about the consensus they had reached. They were stubborn, it appeared; they would not budge. The shopkeeper was unbelievably angry at this. His brow furrowed with fury like wrinkled tree bark and his eyes turned fiery red—he was like someone fixing to eat somebody!![11] A moment later a satan insinuated itself into his heart and said: "Daughter from Hell! Mother who doesn't know how to follow *adat* or law! Totally, totally outside of human control! You just wait till I send you your divorce decree. You can bet, there are lots of other women who know their *adat* and law. You just think about how happy and well kept you have been all this long time. But it just made you go and indulge in tabooed things[12] like this adventure. Enough! Good-*bye!*"

Now we'll switch to the house of Sutan Hardwood, the Sutan Ashamed to Grow Old. Once he heard the news that Sitti Djaoerah was in Panyabungan, he regained hope; he felt he had more maneuvering room now. So he dispatched Naimardjolis to go to Panyabungan to try cajoling Nandjaoerah and her daughter into doing his bidding.

Naimardjolis found this to be a heavy, heavy task. But, after all, when she was asked to do this she swallowed her pride and off she set, heavy task or not—all the while, however, making numerous heartfelt requests by means of all sorts of magical spells and charms that she would *not* be made a fool of this second time around. She predicted that Sitti Djaoerah and her mother would not want to come back home, and, of course, that that situation would bring a considerable amount of shame to Naimardjolis herself. And she hadn't gotten her hoped for present of cloth, either. She surely couldn't scrape together the money to pay for it herself.

Off went Naimardjolis and a companion to central Panyabungan, riding in a double horse carriage. When pleasure trippers would venture into Mandailing along that way it would always be a real treat since the road was smooth and well kept and there were fine rows of *kassod* trees planted along the pavement. It was like being in a spacious marketplace, really. But for Naimardjolis, this one time, sitting up on that carriage seat was like being perched on a bed of thorns. Why was that? If you are looking real hard for something but you don't get it, you really feel the loss—and she knew she wouldn't be able to look the *sutan* in the face if something didn't give soon.

After a long, long trip, when it was almost Dusky Dark Evening, she finally arrived in central Panyabungan. She stayed overnight near the marketplace in the house of one of Sutan Hardwood's acquaintances. Next day, she went to the house where Nandjaoerah was staying. When she got there she chuckled to herself a bit, preparing a sneaky strategy for determining the lay of the land. She didn't say straightaway what was on her mind. Rather, she circled around a bit first from a distance.

"Now, gracious, when did you get here, Good Woman-Friend (she asked Nandjaoerah)? We were fixing to go home when we heard to our surprise that you were on a little visit here. So it occurred to me: let's just go home *together*. Wouldn't that be fun? Sharing a carriage together?!!!! I've been away from Sidimpuan for a whole week as a result of the good *sutan*'s pain and worry, don't you know. For I have heard about our daughter here. I didn't have the heart to find out if it was true. I'm over here looking for more girls, see, for the *sutan*. Maybe there's one he'll take to, who knows? If you're going home soon, let me just wait for you."

Nandjaoerah pretended to go along with all this talk, for she said: "So, Good Woman-Friend, how did your search go? Was it a success?"

"Well, there were some nice, friendly ones, and there were also some noble-born ones. I would have no more than said a few playful things and right away they'd submit and agree to the marriage proposal, right on the spot. After all, who doesn't want happiness and satisfaction, you know? But, what can you say? It seems our daughter here is not interested in such things as happiness and a cushy life. But listen! If, say, we turned the whole matter over to the family circle here in Panyabungan, do you think maybe Sitti Djaoerah could be influenced? Really, I'd rather she were the one to get all this happiness rather than some girl we don't even know. I can cancel what I've said to the girl I was just talking about, you know," said Naimardjolis, scratching her head.

"Ha, ha . . . well, frankly, we hardly have it in our hearts to provide Sutan Hardwood with a girl. And so, Good Woman-Friend, if you are going to go home—well, just go! There's nothing more to talk about as far as we are concerned. But, for goodness sake, Good Woman-Friend, why don't you just snatch up the girl you were talking about if she seemed to be a compliant, willing sort and was already agreeing to the marriage proposal? Wouldn't that be a good idea?"

"Uh . . . well, we were just thinking of the future consequences of everything, naturally. As for willing young girls, we do have a good number of them right within the family, of course. Of course! But it's far better to get one with whom you're really happy, you understand. That is why I did not pursue those particular negotiations with any real seriousness, you see. Well, if you are not going home to Sidimpuan I suppose we'll just set off first—so we can bring all these marriage negotiations to a quick conclusion."

"That's fine, just so the *sutan* achieves happiness and satisfaction as soon as possible. We shall remain right here for our part. We can't venture into the main sections of town yet because of the way people are whispering, of course," said Nandjaoerah.

"Well, look, Djaoerah, I suppose I'll be getting on back home. You won't regret things tomorrow—to see some other family's daughter ensconced in the *sutan's* house, bossing all the servants and personal attendants around? It's easy to imagine how rich people live, you know,"[13] declared Naimardjolis.

"Oh, well, as the saying has it: 'It is far better to have torch ginger and not a *halumpang* tree—it is better to have nothing than to encounter anything like that!' I am quite used to having nothing, after all, and living modestly. It has really never crossed my mind to have a flock of servants hanging around saying 'yes' to me all the time," said Sitti Djaoerah.

With an exasperated sigh, Namardjolis went off to the house where she was staying. And she went right home to Sidimpuan as soon as it got to be daylight the next day. Once she got to Sidimpuan she repeated to the *sutan* all that Nandjaoerah and her daughter had said.

"I don't think, Sutan, that it will do a bit of good to pursue these negotiations. We should play up to their father. That's a far better idea. So he'll order his daughter's capture, see. By, um, the Controleur's cops."

Once Sutan Hardwood heard these words he threw himself on the floor in despair, for he had now lost all hope of getting this lovely girl. He silently calculated his losses from the transfer of the brideprice gold, and he discovered that it had totally wiped out all the savings the mother of his little child had amassed. But if he went to court over all this he was afraid the public would find out about the strategy he had used to pursue his goal. So it was like the way an antelope throws a tantrum: lying on his back and kicking his hind legs back and forth but really only managing to rub the skin off his own rump. So, though he might be singing mourning wails inside, he simply had to keep his trap shut.[14]

Now, as for Awaiting Riches, when he heard that Nandjaoerah and her daughter would not come home to Sidimpuan, he took a notion to divorce his wife. He did not want to take her back anyway. He felt that they both had defied him as husband and father. That was sufficient legal grounds for him to press for a divorce for all eternity, he thought.

Dear Reader, may we switch again to the Panyabungan marketplace, to see what is going on with Nandjaoerah and her daughter? The next dawn came, and so, too, day after day, week after week, and month after month—and they were beginning to find it rather wearing to always have their kind relatives feed them for free. They were afraid that the relatives who were giving them bed and board might be inconvenienced, although this really wasn't the case. But they were used to cooking their own pot of rice, after all. They had their own particular tastes in food, which they liked to indulge. Not everyone likes to eat the same sorts of things. Some like lots of salt in their curries, some like hot, spicy sambals, and some like everything to taste pretty much the same, real bland. When you're staying at a relative's house, though, you have to take whatever sort of food they dish out. So an idea occurred to Nandjaoerah: they should try to find some sort of work at the marketplace so that they could earn the means to start cooking their own food. They'd do whatever sort of work was available. So each and every market day in Panyabungan Nandjaoerah would go walking around the market, noting how people seemed to be making a living. She stood to the side of the spot where folks were selling fried cakes and rounds of sticky rice steamed in bamboo tubes. She observed with care how well (or how ineptly) people made such snacks to sell to the passersby in the market. She took note of the fact that the only things they were hawking were these steamed sticky rice treats, some rice flour cupcakes, fried bananas, of course, and a very few other little things. The steamed sticky rice rounds and cupcakes were tasty and heavy and moist, she had to admit. But, after all, the highest quality sticky rice came from this very region and the finest coconuts were native to the area, too, so naturally the sticky rice rounds should be tasty.

Seeing all this, Nandjaoerah decided to sell other types of cakes and sweet treats. "Oh, good, good . . . folks here don't seem to know much about all the different sorts of cakes we have in Sidimpuan. Treats like that will really go fast if we offer 'em for sale since people around here haven't tasted anything like them. Anything that's new always sells."

Once she had made up her mind, Nandjaoerah told her relatives that she was going to go into business over at the marketplace. The whole family had great hopes for the business's success. So they got busy cooking all the different sorts of sweets they would sell at the next market: multilayer cakes, Bugis treats, red sugar snacks, and various other sorts of little cupcakes. Come market day they carried their sales table and everything they had baked and fried the night before over to the marketplace. Their spot was right alongside the tables of the sweets sellers who usually lined up there.

Dear Reader, over toward Mandailing, in Ulu and around Pahantan, adolescent girls are allowed to go to the marketplace on market day to do their shopping. That sort of thing is not taboo at all. That's because this has become the customary practice in that domain. An *adat* custom that has become established as a normal sort of thing does not strike people as bad behavior. So we should not be surprised to find that young girls were quite free to go to the market, to sell things, to shop, or really to do whatever they pleased. Here we witness the freedom girls have over on that side.[15] And we are confirmed in our agreement with what Nandjaoerah said when she was objecting to Malim Most Hopeful's strict religious lessons with the shopkeeper, that is, when she stood so firm in not wanting to destroy all the behaviors folks have established as *adat*.

After all, where we live, men and women are equally rich and equally important. In one or two domains, in fact, some kinds of work are given over entirely to the women. That allows the men to go to other villages to find paid work there—selling goods, working as carpenters, and so on. So because of the freedom that women in Mandailing have it did not strike anyone as strange that girls who had just got married already knew how to shop at the market. But things were definitely not like that in the domains of Angkola and Sipirok and the other areas nearby. Girls there weren't allowed to go to market; that was taboo. As a consequence when they got married they didn't know how to shop. Young wives, dressed up in their lacy jackets for the first time, why, they dissolve in total embarrassment to shop at the marketplace. They don't have the nerve to show their faces in public, much less to haggle energetically over prices with strangers. Sometimes it will have been two or three years since the woman got married, but she still won't have gone shopping in the marketplace because she's so embarrassed and shy around people. She just gets other folks to send her the things she needs. But we should not be surprised at this, for different fields, of course, have their different grasshoppers and different pools different fishes.

Luckily, in this present age, people in the Angkola and Sipirok domains are beginning to understand: even though girls don't join in and go to the market they do at least venture into the little merchandise stalls along the road and the small stands in the villages.[16] They're brave enough to do that and to take a look around for what they want. We needn't discuss this at too great a length, for our story is not going in that direction. That was just a sidelight so we'd have some comparative cases from various other domains in Tapanuli.

Since it was the custom in that domain for girls to shop and even sell things and buy merchandise at the market, Nandjaoerah went right ahead and had her pretty daughter accompany her to the marketplace in Panyabungan and sell cakes and treats there. As soon as the other sellers had their goods arrayed on the tables, Nandjaoerah and her daughter got their various sweets ready, too. They lined them up according to size and shape; the goodies all looked very clean and neatly arranged. In fact, your mouth would start to water when you caught sight of this pretty array.[17]

Early in the morning on market day most folks would just cast their eyes casually back and forth over the cakes and goodies tables because they still had their vegetables and curry fixings to buy, after all. First things first. Some people would have to buy clothes, while others might just be there to see what might be happening at the marketplace. But once it got on toward 11 A.M. folks would start to turn their attention toward the snack tables, to buy sweet cakes, sticky rice treats, and so on. That way they'd have some little treats in leaf packets to take home to the little kids in the villages.[18]

On Sitti Djaoerah's sales table she had red and yellow sugar water drinks set out in glasses along with some plain water. This made passersby thirsty: they simply had to stop and ask for a glass of sugar water. And then they'd go on and ask for some cakes. First one and then another person would come up to gawk at the strange-looking but yummy sweets. "Wrap up five cents worth of red sugar snacks for me, would you?" "A big Bugis cake, please." "A benggol's worth of caramel layer cupcakes, okay?" And their requests just kept coming in. Word got around throughout the marketplace that there were some new sorts of treats to be bought, not to mention brightly colored sugar water. So folks just flocked in, putting in their orders. Not half of them had been served when the cakes and things ran out. Lots of people got sort of put out when they didn't get anything. Nandjaoerah told all of them kindly that they'd be sure to make more for the next market day, so all of the public would get some. Nandjaoerah and her daughter went on home, and it was surely pretty sweet, too, to count up all the profits from their cake and sugar water sales. Ah, this will be enough to buy us our rice and curry fixings, they felt sure. "If this is the way it's going, we won't be left high and dry. We'll be able to live modestly, eking out a nice little existence, with God's mercy, like people who don't have great resources to fall back on."

Word about the cakes and treats that Nandjaoerah was selling got around to all the surrounding villages ringing the town. Many folks praised her exemplary cooking skills. For her part Nandjaoerah just kept improving her merchandise and making more and more of it—near market day, in fact, they were really cooking up a storm. At dawn on Panyabungan market day, they'd be rushing about, hither and yon, picking up trays of cakes and transporting them to the market. However, because Sitti Djaoerah was so assiduous and clever at marking down all the records in account books ("cakes baked," "cakes sold")—and since she was so quick at changing the customers' money—she remained perfectly calm in the midst of all the hubbub as folks crowded around the table. Her mother had enough confidence in her to just leave Sitti Djaoerah there with the sales table duties while she went back to the house to fetch more trays of cakes.

Sitti Djaoerah would not get a single break from wrapping up little cakes and handing them over to the paying customers. She remembered all the *adat* pertaining to speaking politely to the public and all about using just the right kin terms with them. She treated the customers like family. She was always gentle and good humored. So folks were happier than ever to come over to her and buy cakes there. It went on that way from one market day to the next; their cakes always sold well. When a mother would be setting off from the house to go to market and her children would want to be taken along and would start crying and carrying on, she would placate them with: "Now, be quiet, daughter, be quiet, son. Don't worry, I'll remember to bring you some of Nandjaoerah's Bugis cakes or some caramel cupcakes or some red sugar snacks." And the child would hush right up.

Now, Dear Reader, it wasn't just the mamas and the little kids who knew how tasty Nandjaoerah's cakes were: the young men and women in their late teens also knew the score. So it came to pass that the good-looking youths started to flock to the sales table to buy treats. This was especially true of the young merchants, for they figured they could kill two birds with one stone that way. As the saying has it, they'd be eating delicious red ground cherries and all the worms in their bellies would die off, too! That is, they would be able to buy those yummy cakes *and* get to know that blooming, budding girl.

Eventually, buying the little cakes became just an excuse. What they really required was a glimpse of that girl's pretty face and hearing her friendly laugh—that clever girl who was so adept at figuring prices and change.[19] When not many folks happened to be around, some of the young guys would go over and have a try at her. They would walk up and ask for a glass of sugar water. That would normally cost one baru (that is, a pitis coin). But when Sitti Djaoerah would try returning their change they would say: "Oh, keep it, Younger Lineage Companion. Next market day you can just give me another glass of that sugar water, okay?"

"Oh, no, no, Older Lineage Companion. If you don't come and ask for it I'll forget that I owe you the money. Now, wouldn't that just lead me into sin?"

"If you don't give it back or I don't come to ask for it, that's a ticket to the world hereafter for sure."

"Thanks," said Sitti Djaoerah, with a laugh. And just hearing her laugh so lightly would be recompense enough for the young man for the coin he had shelled out.

"Well, everyone has to try to steer his boat to the front of the others, I guess," all the young male merchants would say to themselves. So, they weren't just after cakes now: they were racing each other to see which one could insinuate himself into that pretty girl's good graces before all the others did.

Sometimes one guy would come and get sugar water from her four or five times in a single hour. And others would ask: "Little Lineage Mate! Do me a favor and bring a plateful of those little caramel cakes to my sales stand, all right? I can't come over to you because so many people are crowding around buying my wares. If you carry it over there for me I'll pay you twice the normal price, okay? And I'll throw in a bar of perfumed soap as your tip for being so good and helpful."

"Ha, ha . . . , but I'm busy at my sales table, too, Older Lineage Companion. How in the world am I supposed to find the time to deliver cakes to you at your stand? If a customer comes by, who would help them? But thanks for the offer of the tip, anyway," the girl said, with a tiny chicken smile.

The more time passed the harder the young merchants would press her to deliver cakes to their sales stands. This was not because they lacked the time to pick up the cakes: they just wanted to show that pretty girl how much trade they were enjoying and how much money they were raking in. Maybe that way Sitti Djaoerah would take a fancy to one of them. But, as the saying goes, the roasting spit is still some distance from the hot fire, my friend, young man! Love doesn't come from seeing how prosperous a guy is in commerce nor from observing his big pile of money. Rather, it is a matter of whoever happens to catch your eye—ah, he's the one who'll become your medicine for your love longings and loneliness, the man you surrender your *tondi* soul to, from this world on into the hereafter.

To tell the truth Sitti Djaoerah knew exactly what the young merchants were up to and what they were after, but she had no intention of deflecting her attention from Djahoemarkar—he was the only one she wanted to surrender her sorrows to, here on this earth, that was for sure. So she kept her gaze just exactly the same, no matter who happened to come by the sales stand. She was equally polite and good hearted toward everyone, whether they be rich, wealthy, and aristocratic or dirt poor. She was consistently calm and good humored; after all, she was out there to make money. And, as for wanting a man, well, that one certain guy was the only one for whom she longed. The young guys' hearts spun around and around like tops when they tried to figure out the girl's behavior. But no matter what they did they couldn't get in tight with her.

Now, Nandjaoerah, for her part, also knew what folks were seeing and whispering about her daughter all around the domain. However, she did not give the slightest heed to what other people said, not so much as a rice mill pounder's tip's worth. So, she really didn't feel any great need to remind her girl to remain faithful to Djahoemarkar and not forget him. Of course, she would tell Sitti Djaoerah to send him a letter once in a while or send their beloved husband's sister's son some soap money. Sitti Djaoerah herself had often thought of just the same thing, but she was embarrassed to put such notions into practice. She was especially embarrassed when her mother tagged her as a "pining for your boyfriend" sort of girl. So, as a consequence, she just kept all her true feelings inside. But once her mother had brought the subject up she was willing to remember to do these things. She resented being told that she had forgotten Djahoemarkar; then she would pretend that she didn't want to write the letter. "I've got so much work to do, Mom! Let me write it next week."

Sitti Djaoerah understood what her mother was thinking. The girl herself really didn't like the fact that folks kept falling in love with her. So it occurred to Sitti Djaoerah to make herself look messy and unkempt so that people would think she was really ugly and not pretty like she actually was and the other young girls wouldn't be so jealous of her. So whenever she washed her clothes she would make sure she got lots of blue bleach on some parts of the cloth and none on others so she'd come out in spots. And she'd wear things that were far too large for her. She'd hide under a kind of bulky overcoat or a dull-colored, severely cut jacket. And for her headscarf she'd wear a ratty old mildewed towel—all of this to make out that she was a dispirited old hag, a tired old woman. But none of this funny business detracted a whit from her obvious goodness and beauty. Her face and figure still looked great. After all, even if a diamond falls into a water buffalo's very most favorite wallowing hole and gets buried in the muck, it will still shine brightly. It's always a diamond; that doesn't change.

Now, Dear Reader, as the days went by, Sitti Djaoerah grew taller as she attained her full adult beauty. As she grew her face just got prettier, her figure filled out—and she became just that much more outstanding in comparison with all the other girls in the market.

Nowadays, it seemed, she was as lovely as the tall bamboo shooting straight up skyward, protected from the winds by two surrounding mountain slopes, what with her face as lovely as the round, full moon; her hairbun as big as the weaver woman's huge ball of thread; her eyebrows curved jauntily like the rooster's back claw; her cheeks rosy and round like a ripening mango; her eyelashes thick like fat buzzing black bumblebees; the nape of her neck curved like a bunch of bananas on its stalk, shimmering in the early morning sun; her chin rounded and oval like the honeybees' pendular hive; her fingers long and slim like the quills of a young porcupine; the calves of her legs like rice grains bursting from their husks; the soles of her feet smooth and round like the tender eggs of a hen laying for the first time; her sight so sharp it sends the hillsides cascading down in landslides; her steps so slow and deliberate one thinks she's carrying a burden on her head; her strides swaying like undulant sea waves; her teeth white and even like the grains of sand at Bagan Api-Api; her smile coming and going like the glistening, shining, flying fish as they jump in and out of the water in the radiant moonlight; her manner of speaking as lovely and elegant as the bamboo bending gently over the path; her very cough stirring our feelings of deep love and longing; her gentle throat clearing making whirlpools of our feelings, like hidden eddies in the deepest woods.[20]

But, really, in the opinion of the ones talking about her, such words as these *still* failed to capture her beauty. But when we say passages like these at least that gives us a means of suggesting that she was far beyond the normal sort of human being.

Anyone who has ever passed through the center of Panyabungan knows how the town is laid out, with its marketplace, its roadways, and its intersections. We need not say a great deal about the people there or the residents of the nearby villages. We can just inquire: is it not true that the central part of town is absolutely number one in loveliness? It is only the climate that leaves something to be desired: it is stiflingly hot. The wide roads, all nicely paved with sand, please everyone who has the opportunity to pass over them. This is especially true when visitors see those neat rows of kapok trees lining the right side of the roadway. They continue on until one is far outside the town; why, you think you're still in the settlement, what with that garden look about things. Since the central part of town is so good and level it comes as no surprise that folks there are great, strong walkers. They go striding about with their faces to the wind, leaning forward, moving fast and fluidly. When folks from this town go visiting at other villages everyone immediately knows that they come from level land just from their walk. We can also tell when people live in the mountains from the way they walk: they dive into the wind with their two arms plunging along in front of them as if they were diving into a pool of water, and they walk along swiftly and fluidly.[21]

Even though Panyabungan was a town with a very hot climate, the heat did not hinder Sitti Djaoerah's growth toward adulthood since it was a little less stifling in Panyabungan than in Padangsidimpuan. So the climate just made her skin a bit pale. In fact, it only rendered the skin on her face whiter still. So, because her face was as light and lovely as the skin on a ripe, creamy yellow *lanseh* fruit, the young guys thrust out their muzzles even more forcefully to get a look at her.

Several of the ones who had jobs and drew salaries, as well as all the *leerlingen* from over at the Controleur's office, were simply fixated on her lovely face.* It comes as no surprise that Nandjaoerah was frequently visited by delegations of people asking for her daughter's hand in marriage. However, she rebuffed all these inquiries politely, saying that her daughter wasn't ready to marry yet.

Sitti Djaoerah knew quite well just what was happening, so she tried to think of other ways to make herself look ugly. She would wear the sorts of clothes modest young wives would affect so that people would not find her fetching. One time, she bought a black cloth *kebaya* jacket and put on a cheap old Onion Thread sarong. She went on to cover her head with a long scarf and wore the whole getup to the marketplace so that people wouldn't look at her at all . . .

Next market day, when the sun had risen halfway into the sky, she went off to market in this remarkable costume. She was chewing a wad of betel, just like a real wife, and her hairbun was messy, as if she had just swung her long hair around and slapped it quickly into a knot. But she neglected to secure all her jacket clasps and forgot that she still had her big gold medallion around her neck. And so the glow from the gold clasp pins on her jacket and the medallion contrasted in a breathtakingly gorgeous way with her solid black jacket, and her betel-stained lips were as red as skin punctured by the sharp spines of the *ria-ria* plants as we walk by them in the morning. And her messy hairbun fell into place and began to look like a lovely, full-bodied bun, swung luxuriantly into two generous loops across the back of her head. The gold clasps and the medallion traded radiance sparks with the sheen on the shiny black cloth, and her face shone in the resultant glow.

"*Tapppp*. . . . " And what happened then, the Reader asks? Well, she just got prettier and the young guys were even more beguiled. All her strategies for deflecting attention from herself were a total failure. She had done nothing more than come out of her house, carrying her tray of cakes balanced atop her head, and she was just walking along modestly, putting one foot in front of the other, when what should happen? Unluckily enough, she got sort of dizzy and the road felt as if it were moving up and down in waves. And she started swaying back and forth as if she were walking on soft ground. And all the young guys immediately formed an entourage. One impertinent character couldn't restrain himself and cried out: "Oh, lord . . .[22] that makes all the boats just wash up on shore."

Anyone who has ever been to the Batubara region would have thought she was one of those great-looking *encik* schoolmarms, the ones you see there between Labuan Ruku and Tanjung Tiram, what with her thick, double-looped hairbun and all.[23]

"Good grief, this is killing me. . . . If only she would see her way clear to take my hand sometime," said one of the young guys. "Ha, ha," said his pal, "now, you just have faith! She's the fairest flower of all the *bidadari* angels up in High Heaven.† I guess you'll just have to do some more religious good works so that you'll have a chance of snaring one like that sometime in the future."

Leerlingen is Dutch for pupil.
†Heavenly female angels who beguile human men.

When she arrived at the marketplace, Sitti Djaoerah stood there in front of the sales table with her usual sales activities in mind, but the young merchants were looking at her *real* differently from normal. "Sitti Djaoerah *must* have done that on purpose," they kept thinking. So they were even more attracted to her. And the lovesick ones got more lovesick, and the ones squirming in their seats got even squirmier—and their sales didn't go well at all.

Noticing how folks were looking at her blooming girl, Nandjaoerah asked Sitti Djaoerah once again if she had written that letter to Djahoemarkar. "Now, don't you let that slip or he'll get real worried, not getting any news from us here."

"Yeah, I know. . . . I remember I have to do it. When I get back from the market I'll write it. I've got a lot of work to do, you know," said Sitti Djaoerah.

That particular market day they didn't have to wait long for customers. Everything they had sold right away. People just kept crowding in, one after the other, to buy those delicious cakes. Once everything was sold they went back home where they found that the profits happened to be larger than they had expected.

That evening, Sitti Djaoerah wrote that letter to Djahoemarkar, and its words went like this.

To Djahoemarkar,
Hopefully found in glowing good health
where we live (Padang Sidimpuan)

Kakandaaaaa*

I was just delighted to receive that letter of yours, which Djabargot brought. It did make me feel very bad for you, but, even so, I consider the letter a valuable treasure that I cannot forget day or night.

It has now been four Moonshiny Months[24] since I ran away from our old childhood playground,[25] and I miss you very, very much. If only I could see you—the place where I surrender my body and *tondi* soul!

I am simply unable to describe in writing how bad I feel thinking about your pain and suffering. Suffice it to say, though: if the sea should be all used up to serve as ink for my pen, and if all the leaves on all the trees should be employed as my writing paper, that still would not provide sufficient writing supplies for me to write you how very much I miss you. So you will just have to estimate the situation yourself. And so, Kakanda, we have been hard at work all this time, trying to eke out a living in Panyabungan for as long as we've been in town. Hopefully, with the help and blessings of your good prayers, we shall be able to keep those coins rolling in. I don't just fritter away all the money we make on things I want, either: I put it away for the two of us, for later. So, study hard, so your grades won't slip with the coming exam. If you pass the test, be sure to ask to be *benoemd*† to a school in Panyabungan or Kotanopan, or maybe even Muara Sipongi or Huta Godang, so that together we can try to endure the unendurable. Now, don't you worry: there's no one else for me in this world.

Here's ten florins—for your soap-buying money. If you get one or two free days come for a visit to help cure my love-longing and loneliness for you. Just catch Djabargot's mail cart to Panyabungan and back. Well, let that suffice for now, may

*As noted, this is a flowery Malay salutation used by young women in addressing young men: "Older Brother."
†Dutch for 'appointed', 'nominated'.

both of us remain healthy as we continue to confront our sufferings. May we eventually get what we seek, one fervently hopes. That, then.

Please do accept greetings from your Anggi,
who ceaselessly longs for you.

Wg. Sitti Djaoerah

"All right, Mother, it's finished. I put everything you wanted into this letter," said Sitti Djaoerah, giving her the letter so that it could be sent via Djabargot when he carried the mail to Padangsidimpuan.

"Now, go ahead and read it for me. Maybe you left something out," said her mother.

"No, I put everything in real neatly. I didn't leave anything out. Why do I have to read it?"

"Oh, people do tend to be forgetful creatures, you know. That's their nature. Maybe you left something out and we can add it," said her mother.

"All right, then, have a listen," said Sitti Djaoerah, trying to think how in the world she would repeat what was in the letter. What was really there she didn't want to announce out loud. So she said:

To Djahoemarkar in Padang Sidimpuan

With this letter let me say to you and to our dear mother that we have mercifully remained quite healthy all the time we have been away.[26] May you be the same, certainly, as you receive this letter. Here are ten florins that I am sending you, so you'll have something with which to buy your tobacco. Study hard, so that you will attain your goals. We're not really much worse off than other folks are in terms of making our living—we have enough to buy our rice with, if only a modest amount.

Well, may we all be firm souled, healthy, and hearty, with God as our good companion. Please accept respectful greetings from me and our mother.

SITTI DJAOERAH

"So is there anything I left out that you want to hear in there? Have I forgotten anything I need to add?" asked Sitti Djaoerah.

"Gracious, that's the way, that's the way! That's a very fine letter," said her mother, taking it so she could give it to Djabargot.

After spending some time on its journey the letter got to Djahoemarkar. He did not pay much attention to it at first, but when he saw Sitti Djaoerah's signature on it he read it for real.

The hairs stood up on the back of his neck and his heart thumped loudly— his body was just lifted up into the high clouds. All these four months he had thought Sitti Djaoerah had forgotten about him, for he had not received any news from her except for that first letter. He would sometimes think: maybe she's wasting away from severe malaria.[27] No one suspected that he was thinking this, but his thoughts were always with Sitti Djaoerah, day and night. So his pleasure at getting this letter was immeasurable: a measuring tape simply would not stretch around that huge amount of pleasure. Within a single moment after reading the letter he went and got some paper and ink to write a letter in response to Sitti Djaoerah's. Here are its words.

To the medicine for my love longings and loneliness,
to my sweet, well-spoken, Younger Lineage Companion,
"Sitti Djaoerah," who is hopefully remaining robust and healthy
in Central Panyabungan.[28]

Sweet, well-spoken, Younger Lineage Companion, love medicine for my *tondi* soul and body!

I have indeed received what you wrote and sent via Djabargot, and I understand all that you say.

I say thanks, Syukur Alhamdulillah, to God—so, it seems you have *not* changed the way you think about this poor, unlucky soul. Younger Lineage Companion, I cannot tell you how elated I was to get your letter and your kind blessing words and your sweet requests. Indeed, it will simply have to be to God that we surrender our unhappy, unendurable fate—to God who is so surpassingly well spoken and lovely, to God who created the sky and the earth, who fills our bellies, who first separated our ten fingers. May He continue to support us in our unendurable sufferings here. My God, may You continue to protect us from this unparalleled bad fate.

Now, listen, about that ten rupiah: getting them feels like I have received a gift of solid gold as big as a horse's head that has come falling down on me out of the sky. I was elated, delighted to get it, and I kept hearing your sweet words: apparently you earned this money yourself through the sweat of your brow. If felt just like that time I received that plate of hot rice from you, that time we were standing in the kitchen and your sweat was dripping from all that cooking. Well, Younger Lineage Companion, I won't say anything more about the money you earned: just hearing that you are healthy is actually enough of a gift for you to send me. Your love in thinking about me and keeping me in mind: why, I consider that a veritable cane that I can use to help me over the Sirotholmustakim Bridge, the bridge leading to the hereafter. But, saying this, I ask you not to send me money too often or people will find out about it. You know yourself, Anggi, that water always courses downhill into the valley lands: if we keep sending letters, people will just become maliciously jealous of us and we'll suffer the bad consequences. And then, moreover, I don't particularly need the money. It is quite enough for me if you just don't change the way you think of me from now on into eternity. For, after all, if my pocket is full of money I'll stride off in a lighthearted way toward the marketplace, and then once I get there I'll see all kinds of great things to buy and good things to put into my mouth—and as a result I'll just forget how hard you worked to earn this money. And the upshot of the whole thing will be: I'll just get cocky. So, Lineage Friend, you just remember, as long as this earth's wide land is unfurled like a mat before us, as long as our aims and plans thrive inside us, I shall not forget you, neither day nor night. Now, since we are far apart, you just be sure to look up at the moon at night, and that way each of us can convey our lovesickness, like prayers to each other, via that celestial body.[29]

When it gets to be seven at night, when there's a moon, look up at that bright, shiny globe, and my eyes will be waiting there for your gaze. So, Lineage Companion, accept my warmest regards:

Muda mandurung ho di pahulu	If you should net for fish downriver
Talpokkon simardulangdulang	Make sure to break off the little branches
Muda malungun ho di au	of the castor oil plant.
Tatap sirumondang bulan.	If you get to longing for me

Muda mandurung ho di pahu
Toskon simarbonangbonang
Muda malungun ho di au
Tongoskon di unggas na habang.

Laoenglaoeng ni pining
Launglaung ari manyogot
Horas danggi tondi madingin
Muli mardou do i sogot.

Look up at the Moonlight, Shiny Moon.

If you net for fish downriver
Snap off pieces from the roll of twine.
If you get to longing for me
Send your message on a flying bird.

Taking shelter under the areca leaves
Taking shelter in the dewy morning
May you be healthy and cool souled.
We shall surely meet again tomorrow sometime.

Wg. Djahoemarkar

When the letter was finished he put it in its envelope and gave it to Djabargot so that the man could deliver it directly into Sitti Djaoerah's hands.

What May Never Be Forgotten, 1901-1902: Djahoemarkar's Escape [1]

As we explained earlier in the story, people in Lowland Angkola, it's fair to say, were prosperous and well off.[2] They had quite enough rice paddy fields, garden lands, livestock, and house treasure.[3] Young Djahoemarkar himself had wide rice paddies and expansive garden lands, and moreover his *ompung* had left who knows how many fine, fat water buffalo to his father, and those had all passed from father to son.

Consequently he was not worse off, at all, than most of the general public, even if he had been orphaned while very young. He was counted among the middle class[4] in that domain, you could say. His mother stewarded all their house treasure with considerable care, and so it continued to grow. She was very diligent at this task, when she thought of her beloved child growing up so sturdily, being so handsome, so smart, and so good at accommodating himself to the public at large and winning its heart. She continually gave him lessons and advice, day and night, so that he would be able to deal adeptly and generously with relatives and friends, so that he would be able to speak smoothly and fluently to them.[5]

Nor did Djahoemarkar dismiss his mother's good lessons, advice, and love. No, he possessed no talent whatsoever for repelling her help. Even though he was an assistant schoolteacher who taught pupils in the classroom he still needed lessons from his mother as well as from the general public. He preferred being a listener to being an orator when people made formal *adat* speeches. He would bury all this good advice deeply inside him, one full pole-length down, and holding it two pole-lengths aloft as well: he took it all to heart.

Nor was he the sort to always put himself forward, like Djamonis: that which could be seen he'd fix before he saw it; that which ears could hear he'd take care of before it was heard; that which could be known he'd put in order before you became aware of it.

Still waters run deep was the story with him. He would store all his sufferings and hardships deep down inside; the same was true of other folks' bad deeds, the ones that had separated him from Sitti Djaoerah. He just stored all of these things deep inside him quietly, as if he were tucking them away in small banana-leaf packets. It was to God that he surrendered all his hardship and pain.

There came a time when he did happen to have some time free from work. The rice had been harvested and safely stored away in the granaries. Everyone was just lolling around the villages happy to have a bit of a letup from work. Some people were calculating how much money they would make from selling their surplus rice and how much of these funds they would have to use for everyday living expenses; others went fishing so they'd have some good curry fixings to go along with all that moist, delicious, new rice—always the best of the year—and others just thought about all the lovely new clothes they would buy with their rice proceeds. This way, they'd have something to cheer them up a bit, for sure!

The young guys all strutted about like cocks, searching for likely girlfriends. After they got tired from going on their courtship rounds all over the countryside they would go on back to their villages. If they were thirsty they would drink fresh coconut milk straight from the young green nut, while others would shake dozens of red rose apples down from the trees. Some would make sweet and tangy fruit salad from these, or they'd throw together other treats. In the evenings, they would perform *dikir* recitations or they would beat the *rabano* drum at the mosque.[6] Others would go about making a racket and just generally cutting up and having a good time—they were young guys without a care in the world, after all. Fearless, undaunted, bold.

As for that young leaf Djahoemarkar, who reopens memories of the past, who opens up deep wells of pain and suffering, who opens deep feelings of love-longing and loneliness, well, he didn't join in all the activities in which the other young guys were indulging, for nothing but Sitti Djaoerah could satisfy him. So he thought it best to stay at home and study rather than wearing himself out running around all over the place. When he got tired of studying he would go to the vegetable and fruit garden and chop down the underbrush, or he'd go keep watch on the water buffalo, or he would go catch a snakehead fish out in the paddy ponds. The fish would be so huge that he would have to use a big, heavy hook.

One evening it happened that very suddenly a heavy downpour accompanied by lighter showers fell in central Sidimpuan. It stopped soon afterward, though; in fact, this rain did no more than wet down the dust and cool off the villagers a bit. It provided no more relief than this for the parched plants and trees, which had been roasting in the sun throughout the entire scorching harvest period. And it was not only humankind, the trees, and the plants that rejoiced at the arrival of the rain-drop-sprinkling rain.[7] No, every living creature upon the earth also grew joyful at the brief downpour—especially the birds, which went flitting upriver and down, seeking new food supplies. Why, even the fish in the river grew merry, for swelling streams, of course, meant more food for them. This was particularly true of the golden carp (the little ones about a hand span long) and for Raja Snakehead Fish: they would just float along contentedly and open their mouths wide and swallow their prey. These flooding waters would carry food right to them. Tiny fish, shrimps, and minnows rushed to the riverbanks; they could not withstand the turbid, swelling waters and sought quieter spots, with cleaner water, for safety's sake. But what can you say? It is a small fish's fate to be unlucky. Along would come the wives and scoop them right up with nets. The women had only to reach down and pile the little fishes into their nets. The fishermen would also cast their lines into the turbid water; since the small fish a hand span long would snap at the bait so quickly, they wouldn't remember to watch for enemies. So the fish simply jumped into the fisherman's net in great schools.

Considering all this, the heavy rain's many benefits to the town residents are evident. Some folks, whose rice paddies lay along the Ayumi River, saw some of their fields flooded. It was lucky that it was just past harvest time. Once it got light, the rain pouring down was replaced with a bright, clear day, while the rain clouds and the downpour that had darkened the countryside retreated to the slopes and forested folds of Mount Lubuk Raya. The sun shone its bright light over the domain before going down behind the slope of the big mountain. Since a clear, bright day had replaced a rainy one, all of God's earthly creatures rejoiced—especially the birds, which flitted around happily in search of their food as it got on toward evening. Once they got their bellies full they started hopping about from one branch to another of the trees, singing out their thanks to God, who created the sky and the earth and gave happiness to all his humble servants. Out in the stubble field left abandoned for a year, the warbling voices of the thrushes could be heard (that is, the *baro-baro* birds). They answered the little swallows back and forth in the orange trees. They sang out, do . . . re . . . me . . . pa . . . sol . . . la . . . si . . .

Not long afterward the sun slipped down beneath the horizon and the world darkened. All the birdsong tumult gave way to quieter cricket chirps, a change that said: evening is coming. In the foothill folds of Mount Lubuk Raya the clouds spread out in two directions, shaping themselves into large forms of the sort one might see on the comedy screen.[8] Their figures took various shapes, blown this way and that by the wind as it dissipated the morning mists and fog (the clouds) that had formed into intriguing shapes.

Now, as for Djahoemarkar, he was hard at work memorizing his facts for the geography section on the forthcoming final examination. But he was getting tired, so he went out onto the front porch to look at the pleasant day. His heart grew melancholy!! He was suddenly struck by a poignant feeling of love-longing and loneliness when he heard the birds singing away so merrily in the orange trees. He glanced toward the foothill folds of Mount Lubuk Raya, visible between the tall coconut palms. He caught sight of the clouds shaping themselves into different forms. They changed shape ceaselessly, and this quite took him aback. Unexpectedly, his mother came out onto the porch from inside the house and said: "Now, come on, go ahead and take your bath, son. It's almost evening, and evening prayers are approaching."

"Yes, all right, Mother . . . but look at all the clouds over there on the slopes of Mount Lubuk Raya. They keep forming such wonderful shapes. It couldn't get lovelier."

"Ah, why be amazed at that? That's what always happens. They're called Cloud Shapes. The wealthy aristocrats who own this domain enjoy paying close attention to such clouds, you know. According to custom and to what folks believe, signs of future happiness or suffering will appear in the cloud forms, for instance, the death of a nobleman's wife or the birth of a raja's son. But I say that's all nonsense."

"Golly, folks say that, Mother? But that one over there just has to have a meaning. Look over there . . . beginning over near Mount Sanggarundang the clouds are shaped like cattle and water buffalo standing together in herds. What a pleasure to see. And then look over there. A huge *naga* serpent is emerging from the folds of Mount Lubuk Raya, and his mouth is wide open as he faces all that livestock. And then he gobbles them all up! And then, over in the lower valley lands of the mountain, there is a person who looks very sad and pained. He's casting his gaze on all the livestock the *naga* serpent has eaten. And there's a woman and a young man standing there looking at what is happening. The woman really looks bereft, doesn't she? Her hairbun's come loose as she looks for the livestock the *naga* serpent has gobbled up. She doesn't know where they've gone. And look over there. There's another young man, standing there rubbing his chin and pondering the scene."

His mother stayed quiet as she thought over everything that had happened and what her son had related to her. The young man rubbing his chin seemed to be pondering the situation very sadly. With a deep sigh, very moved, she declared: "Look, son, the young man has flown up into the clouds and where in the sky he has gone we do not know. This is quite amazing, to see all this, I must say. But don't you worry about it too much, now. Many more shapes than those would come if you continued to pay close attention. You're better off just going to take your bath so darkness doesn't overtake you."

"All right, Mother, but . . . after I have said the evening prayers let's eat dinner. But look over there! Now there's a young girl who's come on the scene, an adolescent girl. And someone's bothering her, and now she's rushing here and there looking for something that's lost, and finally her gaze follows the path the young man took toward the higher clouds. Now, how is all this going to come out?"

He went on off to bathe, then went and said his evening prayers, and then they had dinner. What he saw that evening did not disappear from his thoughts. He even dreamed about it.

The days turned one to another and soon became a week, and the weeks turned and became a month, but it wasn't yet a full year since the cloud forms (the Cloud Shapes) had appeared on the slopes of Mount Lubuk Raya when suddenly and without any advance warning a great pestilence (a livestock epidemic), affecting cattle and buffalo, came to Lowland Angkola (in 1901–1902). This epidemic swept down upon all those hundreds and thousands of animals and simply annihilated them. The epidemic's mode of transmission was not like an illness that affects an old *ompung*'s flock of chickens, where only one or two will get sick. No, if it started with one water buffalo or cow the entire corral full of them would fall sick. And that was exactly how it went as the epidemic spread from one village to the next. It got so bad that folks seemed to be standing near the livestock graves all the time, day after day, shoveling in the dead animals. Even though the other villagers would help bury all the dead animals, some of the corpses of the beasts would rot and stink.

Government help came immediately; the veterinarians and medical assistants were on the run the whole time, they were so busy. But what could be done? As the saying goes: "If you have empty gingerroot luck then your salt gets moldy on you, too." Worse luck: the more medicine they employed, the more the pestilence spread.

Consequently, after a year of this epidemic, the grazing fields had been emptied of livestock. What had once been wide grasslands for fine cattle and buffalo were now dry graveyards.

The wealthy aristocrats, the prosperous people, and the rich—who used to have as many water buffalo as grains of sand, as well as great, plentiful stocks of cattle—well, for the most part their great wealth had been tied up in livestock. But to whom could a person complain about the situation? To whom could you lament? No one had caused this pestilence to come. As a result folks would just remain quiet and still and cry silently about all the gorgeous, plump water buffalo that they had lost.

Let us switch to the fate of those whose animals had been destroyed in the epidemic. It wasn't just their accumulated wealth that folks lost: the prices of goods also went up. They felt awful about things, just as it says in the proverb: "First you tumble off the front porch, and that's bad enough, but then you go and bump your head on the steps as well."9 The epidemic just kept raging on, and wherever there was any livestock the plague would sniff it out. People tried hiding their livestock in isolated, faraway fields, far from the villages, but all the animals were wiped out nonetheless. No livestock remained alive.

Dear Reader, let us turn the focus of our storytelling a bit here, and please do not blame the writer if there are excesses or shortcomings. After all, I did not witness these events myself; I am only putting them into a story. It wasn't just the owners of the cattle and the water buffalo who suffered in this epidemic. Rather, all the residents of Tapanuli suffered since the carts weren't running anymore to haul goods from Sibolga to Sidimpuan and from Sidimpuan to other domains. There were no more cart animals to pull the vehicles. The few that were still alive were under quarantine: no livestock were allowed on the roads. So how did people survive? What did they use to carry in the salt and ocean fish and all the other merchandise that we don't have in our own area? Oh . . . Lord have mercy . . . the goods in the stores rose ten times in price. Things that did not sell well at all when the carts were running were in great demand now. "Whatever there is, that's what we'll use!" folks would say.

The animal cart bosses, their drivers, and the common day laborers who had lost their livelihoods because of the epidemic got together and decided to use human labor to pull the vehicles. Word of this quickly got around the countryside, and the labor swiftly appeared. The story has it that thirty to forty people would pull one cart from Sibolga to Sidimpuan; it would take over a week to get there. All the shopkeepers (our own people, and the Chinese, and others as well) were delighted over this strategy.10 So that way they didn't feel overly burdened to have to pay the high fees for these vehicles (the fees were said to run to hundreds of rupiah or even more).

In that way, the residents of the Angkola, Sipirok, Mandailing, and Padang Bolak domains survived and managed to find a bit of salt for their food. The Toba Domain was not affected that much because at that time people generally conveyed their merchandise from Sibolga to Tarutung over the twisting, curving, mountain road that climbed up into the highlands from Sibolga into Toba. (The road that now goes over that route didn't exist as yet. People would just have to work their way through the hills each time they traveled to that destination.)

The sorts of things the cart pullers would do on their trips we will not go into here, but they were young guys, after all! And they would get very tired from their labors—so they would say and do all kinds of things to the folks living along the road. The villagers wouldn't say anything because they knew these guys were having a difficult time. However, there is one incident people will not forget: a fight between the cart laborers working for two different vehicles as they went along the stretch of road that ascends the hill near Siloung. It seems that the fellows started to kid around with each other after they had gotten exhausted from pulling the cart, and their jokes escalated into rough horseplay. Because the day was very hot, and the roadbed sloped upward quite steeply, all sorts of untoward and unanticipated mischief occurred. Their horseplay got way out of hand. The thin-skinned guys got their feelings hurt—and the men started to fight. It escalated quickly into an argument in which everyone peeled off and took sides. They started to throw punches and shout loudly at each other; the blows went "rup-rap! rup-rap!!" and the clubs went "Ra-pak, ra-pak!"[11] Men fell along the sides of the road and toward the center of the path. Some had their heads broken open; others had blood dripping from their wounds. Both sides lost, actually. The fight got out of hand like this because there was nobody there to pull the men apart or arrest them. There were no police forces nearby—none. So, only exhaustion finally caused them to fall back in retreat. Neither side profited in the least from this fight, not even a half-cent's worth. But who can forestall something that is predestined by God?

After this fight the buffalo pestilence disappeared. And the buffalo that were still healthy were once again allowed to pull their carts along the road—so it could fairly be said that that fight drew the final door closed upon that terrible epidemic.

Now we shall look at the truly great suffering this pestilence left in its wake in the Angkola Domain. When it came time for the fields to be hoed for planting, the tough *globulosa* grasses were choking the paddies. They had grown taller than a person. Back before, before the epidemic hit, water buffalo hooves would trample down all the thick coral tree outcroppings ringing the edges of the paddies. And whoever happened to have lots of water buffalo would also have wide paddy lands—because the buffalo could be used to plow all that land. Once the water buffalo had trampled all the land the person doing the hoeing would be able to break up the strips of paddy land into even, plantable ground. And this way they would not have to exhaust themselves preparing the paddies for sowing, like folks in the Sipirok Domain do.[12] Even the people who don't have a buffalo of their own can plow their fields the same way because others will loan them their beasts for the field labor. So, passersby think that everyone in that domain must own buffalo.

But, now, after the epidemic . . . all that thick, tough grass had to be battened down and the strips of paddy fields had to be trampled and broken by foot before they could be planted with rice seedlings. How did the people in the domain feel? the Reader asks. Well, indeed . . . they despaired of the loss of all those fine water buffalo. They just kept ruminating over the situation very sadly, quite despondent.[13] And this is what the folks in that domain found to be the hardest thing to bear: to have to look upon their wide paddy lands, lying there unused—the very source of their livelihood, the wellspring of their money, the fundamental basis of the family wealth of folks in that domain. Consequently, many of these people just went insane. Some of them would go over to their corrals as if they were going out to take care of their buffalo. They'd be holding their switches in their hands; they could be heard saying: "C'mon, get in the corral with ya! . . . Get in, Big Horns! Get in, Droopy Horns. Get in, Young 'Un. Get in, Blossom . . ." But the cane the guy was holding in his hand would just be beating at the high grasses. What they were inviting into the corral no one knew, unless it was the dead water buffaloes' *tondi* souls. When the man would get to the buffalo shed he would start crying mournfully to himself, quietly. One would feel immense pity to see such suffering. But what could be done if this was the will of Almighty God, who controls everything?

Djahoemarkar's mother was counted among those whose mental condition changed after all the buffalo died in the great pestilence. All of her buffalo had died, the whole lot of them—not one buffalo cow was left. So, evening times, she would go out to her buffalo pastures, which didn't have any livestock in them anymore. At dawn she would open up the barn door[14] for them and put them outside; she would do this every day. No matter how Djahoemarkar tried to distract his mother from this, so that she would not ruin her physical health, nothing worked. She did not understand a word of what he was saying. She didn't care if it was the dead of night or rainy and stormy with strong wind shears—no, without his knowing it, quite often she would have stolen out of the house late at night, to shoo the buffalo out of the corral gate, she'd tell him. She didn't want to sleep; she didn't want to eat. She came down with an illness, one carried in by the clouds and cold of the long, dark nights.[15] This illness was really heartsickness brought on by pain.

And so the Adept Spell-Casting *Datu*-Sorcerer found it exceedingly hard to cure this illness with potions.[16] The sickness had spread throughout her entire body, down to her nerves and bones. It got so bad, finally, that she was not able to move her body at all. Since she could not go out of the house, people knew that the illness had become very serious. Many family members came to visit her, and folks offered various sorts of help. Some tried to cheer her up by talking to her, while others tried giving her various sorts of medicine, but the more potions she got the sicker she became.[17] Finally, the end of life came—that gentle, soft-spoken woman breathed her final life's breath and left this world for the hereafter, leaving behind her single little leaf on the Tree of Life, her "Djahoemarkar," who opens up all manner of deep pain.[18]

How much pain did this young man feel at this? the Reader asks. The writer lacks the expertise to relate that.[19] I simply leave this to the Reader's judgment.

In brief, however, we can fairly say that after Taring (Djahoemarkar's mother) was taken to her grave, a *kenduri* communal memorial prayer meal was held, as was appropriate. Djahoemarkar didn't really have the heart to see to all these arrangements, but with the help of the relatives they at least managed to fulfill the letter of the religious law for holding such memorial meals so that there would be some way to aid the departed on her journey to the hereafter. Djahoemarkar simply sat there with his head bowed, like a horse that has lost a match with a rival: he was pondering his unendurably sad fate. After the communal prayer meal the relatives all returned home. That left just Djahoemarkar and his *ompung* there in the house, wiping at their tears. His *ompung* tried diligently to distract him from his cares. But, after all, what could be done, for he was not used to great hardships landing on him in such large numbers, covering him in layer after layer. He suffered a great deal; he felt immense pain.

"My father had already died and left me behind when I had no more than first seen the light of day. And then I found someone to give me sympathy and cheer me up and provide solace, and then Sitti Djaoerah *herself* went and left me, and now my dear mother, whom I shall never forget here on this earth, has died and left me. If not on the Final Judgment Day, then we shall never see each other again. And we don't know how many hundreds of years off the Final Judgment Day is![20] Ah, I am better off dead."

These were his thoughts every night. He would search in different directions, but he would not see anything; he would listen carefully with cocked ears, but he would hear nothing except the soft scurrying of mice under the floorboards. When Djahoemarkar would muse to himself, a voice could be heard saying: "Oh . . . my God, Almighty God, I cannot stand to suffer like this, without letup, to endure the hardships you have handed down. I don't think I can keep fighting all the pain and suffering that have come to me, so please, please, just take me in death . . . my God, so that I will be with Father and Mother and this poor suffering soul can be their little son once again. That is all I ask. Oh . . . my God . . . please show me a path out of this world, for I can no longer bear this heavy burden. Oh . . . it is only thinking of Sitti Djaoerah that stops my hand from yanking taut my hanging rope, killing myself by hanging my body parallel to the hanging tree, from dying in unending, everlasting sorrow and loneliness. . . . Oh . . . my God, I surrender my body and life's breath to you and so, too, the body and breath of my dear *ompung*, that esteemed, respected elder—please, please be our kind companion at every moment, please give us clear thoughts, patient hearts, and easy, unanxious hearts—as easy and unanxious as possible so that I do not go on to commit any more sins against you. . . . Oh . . . my God. Oh . . . Father . . . Mother . . . goodbye, all of you! So what use was all this schooling? I shall just set off and leave this domain. May your *tondi* souls always be my close companions, at every moment . . ."[21]

"*Basssss* . . ." said the voice of his body as it fell in a heap onto a sleeping mat. It seems that he fell right to sleep, accidentally, since he had not slept for who knew how many nights and had been continually mulling over everything that had happened. He began to dream as soon as he fell asleep, and in his dream his mother came up to him and said: "If you go off, Son, and leave this country, do not forget to write a letter to that teacher of yours, asking for permission to take a leave of absence from all those lessons they've been giving you. That way you will not be violating the *adat* of people who have gurus. And then, too, write a letter to Sitti Djaoerah so that she won't worry about you on your journey once they find out that you've run away." As soon as these words were spoken he woke up. He looked out into the central part of the house, but not a thing was stirring. He wiped his forehead, and then he knew: he had been dreaming.

"Well, all right, I'll just do it," he declared, and he went and got some paper to write a letter to the schoolteacher. Its words went as follows.

First, please permit me to offer my apologies to you and then ask for permission to take a leave of absence from my studies. My lord, I simply cannot endure all the suffering and pain that has befallen me. With this letter I ask permission to quit my job as assistant schoolteacher; tommorrow I am going to set off on a journey to who knows where. God will determine things. Please do not try looking for me before I send you my address. I hope your prayers go with me, so that I will remain safe on my journey. That, then.

> Much respect and very best regards from me,
> he of the most unfortunate fate,
> Wg. DJAHOEMARKAR

He also wrote a letter to Sitti Djaoerah, but we won't reveal of the words in that one yet. He took the second letter that very night over to Djabargot's place so that the man would deliver it directly into Sitti Djaoerah's hands.

When he got home from Djabargot's it was getting on toward dawn, and he woke up his *ompung*: "I am leaving you now, Grandmother. Watch the house, all right? And the rice paddies, the garden lands, and all our belongings, you hear? I am going off to assuage all this pain and suffering. Please be happy, all right now? Pray for me often so that perhaps we'll be able to see each other in the future."

On hearing these words, his *ompung* sobbed fiercely: "Don't leave me. Please don't go! Oh, let's just stay right here. I'll look after you. I'll make a living for you. Oh . . . gentle, soft-spoken grandson, please, please, don't leave me . . ."[22]

"Now, yes, yes, Grandmother. . . . I'm not really going anywhere. I am just trying to lessen my pain a bit here. Please, please, don't cry. Please cheer up, please try! Just turn me over to God's care. So, Grandmother, now I am going to set off on my journey. Remain healthy, Ompung . . ."

He carried no more than a modest amount of clothing and money for living expenses. He did not have a set destination; he just headed off toward the Sipirok Road. Once he was walking along that highway he thought about which roads he would take and where he might go. He reached a decision: he would go to the Delilands. But, he knew, the road there was very difficult to traverse. He preferred to travel via Padang Bolak,* but he did not have an official pass to go that way. If he wasn't carrying a pass, the Company's cops would stop him and send him home, for sure.[23] "Well, so, what to do? I'll just go via Toba, I guess. Today I shall head toward Sipirok, and I'll look for a companion or two there to go on with me. Lots of folks from Sipirok are traders doing business in Toba."

Once he got to Sipirok he listened to hear whether anyone was setting off for Toba. By happenstance it was Wednesday, the day before market day in Sipirok. Many people had come from Toba, and a number of the market sellers from that area were staying overnight at the marketplace. Some of the peddlers were even selling right there on Wednesday night so as to get a very early start home. Djahoemarkar listened to all of this without anyone being the wiser. The next day at about 11 A.M. one or two of the peddlers were starting to leave for home, although

---

*This is domain northwest of Padangsidimpuan, a vast plain bounded by rolling hills, which offered an alternative route to the Deli coast.

the big shopkeepers weren't ready to leave yet. So he went very quietly to the road to Toba, and in the village of Purba Tua he waited for a shopkeeper from Sipirok whom he happened to know, the sort of fellow he could trust as a traveling companion.

He had no more than taken a puff on his cigarette at Djaloemandit's fried banana stand when along came the shopkeepr he had in mind as his travel companion. The man stopped there for a glass of hot coffee. After he'd finished, he was about to push off again with a friend he had along. "Please let me go along with you, my good friend, our raja, because I'm going to visit relatives in Aek Botik. Will you be going as far as that?"[24]

"Well, that would be all right, I suppose. But, look, we surely won't get that far today, you know. We'll have to spend the night in Aek Simajambu. Then we'll have to start off real early tomorrow to get to Aek Botik by midday. The second day, it'll be market day in Sarulla." They walked along, and as they did they conversed comfortably about the commerce between Toba and Sipirok. Djahoemarkar effusively praised the shopkeeper's work and expertise at business. And he said, further, that there was no better way of making a living than being a trader. If you're in trade, folks say, you're bound to be a busy man. And then he told them about all that was happening in Sidimpuan and about how clever those Chinese were at making money: why, at first, they had come into that area supporting themselves by carrying loads of goods for other people and hawking roasted peanuts. They had very, very little capital in the beginning. But because they were so exceedingly adept at business it wasn't many years before they had become great traders. Consequently, it is a very good idea to try to mimic their *adat* and life-rules and goals, so that the commercial activities of our own sort of folks will quickly prosper.

The traders took his comments well and felt that his advice did have some considerable truth to it. So, since Djahoemarkar was so polite and expert a talker, they felt right at home with him. As they walked along their way they also found chatting with him such a delicious proposition that their exhaustion dissipated. When they got to Aek Botik, he didn't have to sleep in the little rice stall, to spend the night like he had the night before: rather he went to stay in his friend's own big, comfortable house.

On market day in Sarulla the traders and peddlers from Tarutung flocked in, buying and selling goods. After the market was over, Djahoemarkar asked his kind friend to introduce him to a friend who was going on to Tarutung, for that was really his destination. His companion did so, and off they set for Tarutung. And in that same manner throughout the trip Djahoemarkar would always find an excuse to chat with his traveling companion. Everyone who heard him talk just kept wanting to hear more, and they all simply forgot their feelings of tiredness. When they got to the Padang rest spot they stopped, for it was getting on toward evening. At such times of day it was a lovely sight to look toward Sipirok off in the distance.

The slopes of Mount Sibualbuali were visible and occasionally, in back of that, the slopes of Mount Lubuk Raya. Djahoemarkar found himself enveloped in longing and loneliness at this sight. He looked up at the sky, and the moonlight shone brightly: "Oh . . . later on, at 7 A.M., Sitti Djaoerah will be gazing at the moon. I'll look up, too, so that our eyes will meet." And at 7 P.M. he really did look up at the moon, and he felt that he truly met Sitti Djaoerah there.

It was quite late by the time he went to the rice stall. They all ate their meal, then went to sleep. They set off again at the crack of dawn toward Tarutung so that they'd get there quickly. Once they arrived he went over to a rice stall and asked the proprietor to please introduce him to a trusted acquaintance who might be going to Siborongborong. "Well, fine, I do have a friend who goes there a lot. I'll place you in his hands."

On the evening of the day Djahoemarkar got to Tarutung, he took a good look at the scenery there. Mount Martimbang was visible off to the right, while Mount Siatasbarita could be seen in front of him along with Mount Simanukmanuk. He looked to the left and saw Mount Imun, and he turned around and there was Mount Siborboron. It could be fairly said that these peaks surrounded this good, fertile domain. This realm looked crowded and thriving, with thousands upon thousands of patches of fertile rice paddy and a great many villages jampacked with people. Most of the settlements were surrounded with circles of tough bamboo as protective fences.[25] In the middle of this domain two large rivers flowed—the Sigeaon River and the Situmandi River—both of which greatly benefited this region since they irrigated the aforementioned wide paddy fields.

"Oh, well, these folks have happy lives here in this domain . . ." he said to himself as he went over to his resting spot for the night. After eating his meal that evening he slept soundly. Once it got light again the rice stall owner handed him over to a trusted acquaintance of his from Siborongborong, and off they set on toward that incredibly distant destination. All along the journey Djahoemarkar just kept spinning tales about the lives people led in Angkola, Sipirok, and Toba, all to the continual delight of his traveling companions. Everyone who traveled with him immediately loved him.[26]

When they got to the Siborongborong Domain, Djahoemarkar was quite stunned to see it. He looked upriver and saw the bald-faced Mount Saut, which had no forest covering; past that peak the distant lands of Pangaribuan were visible. Then he looked over toward Mount Imun and the same amazing vistas could be seen: immensely wide fields full of grazing livestock—water buffalo, horses, cattle, and so on. He noticed that folks didn't have too many rice paddies and that what they had sometimes were built atop poor soil; the rice stalks were often only one forearm's length tall. And their grain shafts were only two finger joints long—what there were of them, that is. The villages had large cassava gardens on their outskirts, a clear sign that these folks often didn't have enough food to eat.[27] And that apparently was the case with this land. Livestock thrived, but the people didn't grow much rice, so the livestock served as a means for them to get enough to eat. They'd sell their animals in Tarutung for rice. They also did some selling in Toba Holbung (Balige).

Once they got to Siborongborong things got to looking better. In fact, the scenery made you ache with longing, it was so beautiful. From there the Butar Domain was already visible and also Toba Humbang (that is, Mount Sanggul). Djahoemarkar tried not to pay too much attention to the scenery, for if he had it would have awakened too many strong feelings of deep longing and loneliness. So after they had finished eating something in Siborongborong they set off to Toba Holbung. He had only one companion on this leg of the journey, an older man who was going home to Balige.

Once they got to Sipintupintu (that is, to Tangga Batu) they stopped for a moment, for you could catch sight of Lake Toba from there, laid out all lovely and broad in front of you. Djahoemarkar felt even more lonesome and emotional there. So, when they paused a bit longer, and Djahoemarkar was able to ask questions about what he saw. Off to the left were the high villages, while off to the right were Balige, Lagu Boti, and Siantar Narumonda. And over there was the river leading out of Lake Toba, that is, the river that flowed toward Asahan. And off to the side was Toba Uluan, which the Dutchman had not subdued yet. In front was Samosir Island. And off to the left was the Muara Domain, in Bakkara—that was the ancient tree trunk origin land for the Batak people. That was where you'd find the Ancient First Origin Village, the storied Ancient Creation Times Village, the very place where the land was first separated from the waters. That was the ancestral home village of Si Raja Batak, the one who gave rise to all of us—or so says the storyteller.[28]

"Hoooi!" declared Djahoemarkar. "If only I was here with Sitti Djaoerah I'd be so happy. Even by myself it's wonderful to see this, though it does make me feel lonesome . . ." So before long he called to his companion to set off once again toward Balige. When they got there they asked folks if there was a nice rice stall in which they could spend the night.

"Oh, there is, a nice clean one, Lobe Leman's stall. He's a Balige man, but he lived for a long time off in the *ranto*,* in Sidimpuan."

As soon as they said that the guy had lived in Sidimpuan Djahoemarkar's heart turned over, and he said to himself: "Oh yeah, so it seems I do have a pal here in this far-off land. Well, good! I had just better go affix myself to that *tuan* if I don't want the Red Tobaman to beat me up. I know this Lobe Leman: he was Tuan Syeck Bosar Sidimpuan's pupil in the Muslim school."

Djahoemarkar felt that staying in Lobe Leman's place would be like staying in his own home, so they hurried a bit so they'd get there sooner. The sooner they got there, he figured, the sooner he could start telling this Muslim adept about his trip.

"The *lobe* will help me find some peddlers who work the route into Asahan." When they got there his companion took him to the rice stall straightaway. As soon as he caught sight of Lobe Leman, Djahoemarkar saw that, indeed, he really was Tuan Syech Bosar Sidimpuan's former student. So he immediately reached out and shook the man's hand and wished him good luck and firm-soul greetings. The *lobe* was quite taken back, for he hadn't figured that an Angkola man would ever come to that domain. So he spirited Djahoemarkar off to his house so they could have some coffee.

"Let's have some hot coffee, Djahoemarkar! After traveling a full day I can see you're thirsty," said the *lobe*, setting a steamy mug in front of Djahoemarkar.

"All right with me! We've really been hitting the road today, I can tell you," said Djahoemarkar.

*This is a Batak rendering of the Malay word *rantau* 'the precincts outside the home region'.

"Now, if you can take your mind off all this coffee drinking for a moment, do tell me where you're going! We sure don't see many folks from Angkola in this domain. There's no possibility that you can find a way to make a living for yourself here. And, frankly, you don't really look like you're just passing through on a pleasure trip. So, why would a person from so rich and prosperous a region as Angkola be passing through here? And you being a wealthy man, too," said Lobe Leman.

"Ah, it's not good to remember past wealth in times like these. If I tell you all about it, Lobe, it will hurt a good deal. But if I don't explain things to you you'll just think I'm being willful and doing all this on purpose.

Well, look, it's like this (Djahoemarkar began). Recently a great epidemic struck all the water buffalo down there, and all the beasts were laid to waste along with all the cattle, too. Every single person suffered; it wasn't just me, not at all. But what was so hard to take was the fact that my mother died of heartbreak brought on by thinking about all the livestock that had died. So, when I thought about the situation, I knew without a doubt that I would die, too, if I just hung around and kept thinking about the disaster. So I figured it would be better if I went off to another domain to seek another means of livelihood. . . . So, Lobe, that's what I'm doing, I am migrating to Deli. I ask your help, too. I need you to introduce me to some friend of yours who's going to Asahan. Word has it that lots of people from here go up there to buy merchandise."

"Lahawala walakuattabillah billahi. . . ! Anything can happen if God preordains it, can it not?" said the *lobe* with a deep, sad sigh. "I find I can't say anything at all about the disaster, it sounds so bad. But, look, you rest easy, I can find you a companion who'll go with you to Asahan. In fact, I have an employee who goes there every week, and he'll be here in two days. After market day here he goes back home to Asahan. By introducing you to him I can help you and send you on your way quite safely," said the *lobe*.

"Hey, thanks a lot! I guess we'll just wait for our friend to come, in that case, so we can go the safe and sound route."

Now, Dear Reader, Djahoemarkar's footsteps toward Deli will just have to stop for a moment while we switch over to Panyabungan to see what is happening at Sitti Djaoerah's place.

Djabargot kept close track of Djahoemarkar's letter, which he was carrying, for he knew it contained important news. By dawn he had delivered it. He didn't know many details about what had happened in Djahoemarkar's house or about his mother's death. When it got light, as was usual, Djabargot set off carrying the mail to Mandailing. It took him a half day and a night, and it was near dawn when he finally arrived in Panyabungan. After he had opened the mail box in the cart and delivered the letters to the Post Office, he led his horse into his stable and went right to Sitti Djaoerah's place.

Tek . . . tek . . . tek . . .

"Oh, look, Djaoerah, go open the door, would you? Who could it be? Why would somebody be knocking on the door at dawn like this?"

"It's me, Djabargot, here, look, I've brought you a letter from Sidimpuan. I thought maybe you'd want to send word back."

"Oh, Inang, open the door, open the door—maybe it's a, a letter from Djahoemarkar," said Sitti Djaoerah, lighting the lamp.

"*Rek*," said the voice of door as Nandjaoerah opened it. And Djabargot went in and put the letter in Sitti Djaoerah's hand. "I think this letter says something important because Djahoemarkar gave it to me yesterday early in the day."

"Now, what kind of letter can this be?" Sitti Djaoerah asked herself, opening it and reading it slowly. You could tell from her manner that it hurt her, for her face clouded and she began to cry.[29] Her mother immediately asked her what was the matter. "What's in that letter to make you cry? Read it so we'll see. My good friend, Djabargot, what have you heard that might have happened in Sidimpuan?"

"Oh, gee, well, I don't know. I haven't heard anything because I haven't had the time to go visiting around town you know," said Djabargot.

"Oh, they've all *died*, it's all over. . . . They've dropped dead. They've stopped breathing. . . . Oh, my great God, oh . . . Mother. . . . Oh, this is going to be the death of me," said Sitti Djaoerah with a loud sob.

"God Above. . . . Why are you carrying on like this, Djaoerah? Folks will take fright and won't know what's happened. Read the letter so I can hear what's in it."

"Oh . . . my God . . . oh . . . Mother . . ." said Sitti Djaoerah, going on to read the letter, which went as follows.

To Sitti Djaoerah
in Panyabungan

Younger Lineage Companion Djaoerah!

It is with tears in my eyes that I write this letter to you to tell you that in this brief short while an epidemic has come to Sidimpuan, a pestilence that has wiped out all hope, one that has meant great losses for the residents of that domain—it is a great livestock pestilence, which has killed all the water buffalo and cattle. All of them have been wiped out, the whole lot of them. Not a single tuft of their hair is left. Our two water buffalo, the ones our late father left us, died as well. From heartbreak over this great pestilence our mother went insane; every evening she would go out to put the nonexistent buffalo in their corral. Eventually she contracted additional illnesses, and finally she died. Now both my father and mother have died, and my stores of wealth have also disappeared into the infertile, scorched earth—so what can I do to support myself here upon this earth? I was simply going to hang myself, but, no, I saw your hand stay my movements.

So, Younger Lineage Companion, goodbye to you for a while. I am setting off on a desperate journey, and only God will determine where I end up. I am leaving on my journey, setting out with legs the striders, swinging hands the askers for favors, flying off to unknown places, settling on branches sight unseen, just like *timba laut* tobacco leaves, to the land that is no land, to the sky that is no sky, to a cloud with an unknown edge, to an isolated, faraway land, as isolated and lonely as the spot where *sampilpil* plants grow.[30] Oh, I must have been born in the unlucky extra thirteenth month of the calendar, I have so very much more pain and suffering than all other friends, the two and the three. And so, Anggi, please rest easy. Do not go searching for me before I send you news of my whereabouts. Pray for me constantly, and if we do not meet again in this world then it will have to be in the world hereafter.

Tell your mother everything that has happened, and do not forget me.

Kind regards from me,
Wg. DJAHOEMARKAR

"Lailahaillallah. . . . Oh . . . my God . . . what is going to happen to us now? Who is going to be the person we can depend on in this world? " cried Nandjaoerah, collapsing onto the floor mat. "Why didn't you hold on to him so he couldn't leave?"

"But I didn't know what he was going do! If I had, of course, I would have held on to him. Now, however, are we going to find him? We have no idea where he's going. But, look . . . God is merciful. Don't feel too bad. We'll wait for clear word of him, for surely he will not forget you," said Djabargot, trying to make the sobbing women feel a bit better.

We'll switch over to Djahoemarkar's trip now and go back to the story about the Toba land and the Toba Holbung Domain.

I also must apologize to the Reader for a moment, for we are forced to speak Toba now because this story is taking place there, after all, and that way it'll all be a bit more pleasing and delicious, you see. If there are excesses or shortcomings, I must simply ask forgiveness.[31]

After Djahoemarkar had been in Balige one or two days, the guys did arrive from Asahan. Lobe Leman introduced Djahoemarkar to them and turned him over to them. "Oh, all right, our raja, if it seems that this young fellow is our good lineage mate then we will watch out for him carefully on our journey."

After that, Djahoemarkar said: "Indeed, then, my good elders, the kind *lobe* has turned me over to your care. Now, as for our forthcoming journey to Asahan, permit me to say to you that I am a poor and unfortunate person and don't even have half a cent to my name, but if that's how our *ompung* has arranged things, well, what are we to do? Even if we don't have any money, if the time has come to set off on our journey, then that's what we have to do, isn't it? So let us just set off; I surrender myself to you, come what may. Let me thank you beforehand for taking me kindly by the hand like this and leading me along; our common *ompung* ancestor, I suppose, will just have to be the one to compensate you."

"Oh, well said, young man, well said! But let us ask you what village you might hale from, and what your clan is, so that we might know what kin terms to use with you."

"Oh, why would you need to ask such a thing, our raja? For after all, the fruits never fall far from the tree, do they? Once you've heard me speaking Batak, you know I'm one of Si Raja Batak's descendants, don't you?[32] But, all right, so that you'll know with clarity and definitiveness, let me explain. Our raja, I am from Angkola, and my clan is Hasibuan (this clan Djahoemarkar had actually acquired along the road. His real clan was Harahap).[33]

"Oh, well, that is very fine, indeed, young son—very fitting! That means you're one of our own womb-companions, one of our close lineage mates.[34] So there's no need for you to be afraid of anything happening. I'll carry you along on top of my head if I must, to wherever you please! If you're just going to Asahan, that's a cinch."

"Thank you very much, our raja. May our common *ompung* repay your many kindnesses in doing this for me."

"Well, look, let's eat, son. I'd say you're probably hungry this morning."

"Thank you kindly, our raja, but the shopkeeper already gave me a good meal a while ago."

"Well, all right, if that's the case then let's get ready so we can set off." Once they had stored away all their traveling gear they set off from Balige. Lobe Leman, of course, did not neglect to escort them to the bridge on the edge of town. After they had said their apologies to each other and told each other "*horas, horas*," Djahoemarkar and the peddlers commenced their journey. They went through Lagu Boti, Sigumpar, and various other villages, and from there they arrived in Siantar Narumonda. They spent the night there because the peddlers had kin there. They talked animatedly all along their journey, and they got a big kick out of chatting with Djahoemarkar. But he was still quite uneasy and afraid, even though the *lobe* had turned him over to these peddlers. He said hurriedly: "What will come of this journey anyway? Am I going to be eaten by somebody? Are they going to sell me to the fearsome Red Tobaman? Just look over there . . . all of those villages are totally surrounded by big bamboo fences! Good grief. . . . That's a sure sign that this domain hasn't kowtowed to the Company yet, not by a long shot. And if that's the case there's surely nothing to stop them from killing *me*. I guess we'll just have to turn things over to our *Ompung* Up Above."[35]

But he didn't show any of these thoughts on his face. He kept himself rather aloof from the others, and they thought maybe his feelings were hurt. He already knew the geographical layout of all the villages in this area, since he'd studied it a bit in school.

When they'd stop briefly at rest spots he'd constantly be asking questions about things he needed to know along the way. When it was getting on toward evening they arrived in Siantar Narumonda and slept at the peddlers' house. Djahoemarkar did not forget the words of the saying: "When you go into a water buffalo's mudhole you just have to smell like a water buffalo; then, too, when you root around in the cow's mudhole you have to smell like a cow." And that's how he conducted himself: when he was in a Toba's house he behaved like a Toba.

Without being instructed or told to do so beforehand, just as soon as he got to a house he would introduce himself to the womenfolk inside and present them with small gifts. These would be little rice flour cakes and so on, which he had bought along the road. This caused the householders to accept him readily. When he talked to them he'd make sure to add lots of fancy melodies to his voice, the better to capture their affection; if you do lovely things, they'll treat you well, for sure, after all. Everyone in the house immediately took to him. After eating his fill he fell soundly asleep and no one bothered him.

Early the next morning, after they had said their prayers and blessings and had made their requisite polite apologies to the womenfolk, they set off from the village, headed in the direction of Tutupan. However, they had to cross over the river flowing out of Lake Toba, that is, the headwaters of the Asahan River. There was a certain bridge there, with a man as its watchman. Whoever crossed the river at that point was forced to pay him one etet (that is, a benggol). There was no other route to take to avoid this; there was only the high mountain country. And the water was very deep and swift at that point in the river, so you had to take the bridge or you just wouldn't get over to the other side. As soon as they arrived at the riverbank up came the watchman to ask for his fee, as was his custom. But he asked a higher fee from Djahoemarkar, even though that was the first time he had ever tried to cross that bridge.

As he asked for the fee he said: "Now, kind son of our noble raja, we reside here at this spot without any resources whatsoever. The only means of livelihood available is watching this good bridge for our Ompung Si Raja Batak, you see. He issued a divine decree, back during that time in the past: "Be sure (he ordered me) to keep a tight watch over this bridge! Whenever one of my descendants crosses over, he must give you a small sign of his deep gratitude." So, son of our esteemed raja, let me remind you of this divine decree from our common *ompung*, hmm? We can hardly deviate from the divine order in your case, can we now? And whoever determines not to come to our aid will be charged a higher fee. So give me a ringgit from your bracelet of coins so that our common *ompung* may aid you well."

"Ba! If that is what our *ompung* has decreed then that is what must be done. We would hardly deviate from his orders, but since I am an impoverished, most unfortunate soul, please reduce the fee for me. It's certainly not that I don't want to conform to the divine decree. On the contrary, along with these good escorts of mine, I, of course, concur in turning over the requisite fees to further beautify our common ancestor."

"Oh, now, don't be like that, son of our raja. Since you've never before given a contribution you'll have to chip in a ringgit coin hanging down there on your bracelet or else you can just turn around and go back home."

"Well, if that's the law, who am I to object to it? Here, take this ringgit. It's not much, but then, of course, I am a poor man."

"Thank you, son of our great raja!" said the bridge watchman after he had taken the ringgit.

Then Djahoemarkar said: "Well, look, our esteemed raja! Since this bridge is our ancestor Si Raja Batak's bridge, and he is the common ancestor of all of us descendants, we all own this structure as *pusako*, as our inherited heirloom treasure, right? Isn't that the case, our raja?"

"Ba, that is so, young son," said the bridge watchman.

"Well, if that is so, and if you've been receiving crossing fees for guarding this bridge all this long while, why, then, thank you, Ancient Ompung! You and all of us, too, have surely become quite wealthy from all these small gifts, haven't we? So, since I happen to be crossing over the bridge at this moment, wouldn't you say it's appropriate for you to give me my portion of the fees and gifts for this present year so I'll have some spending money for this trip? Since you're a prompt and loyal sort of man, Good Father should simply give me my money since, after all, this will be the first time I receive any of the wealth of our esteemed distant ancestor."

"Listen, uh, that's not the way it works! You don't get anything back from the bridge watchman. Come on."

"Well, okay, if that's the law. It doesn't hurt to try, does it? Well, so be it. Indeed, then, may you be firm souled, Good Father, and may we remain quite hearty and healthy," said Djahoemarkar, setting off.

After Djahoemarkar was about a hundred fathoms from the bridge he cut off into the forest and cast a powerful sickness curse[36] on the bridge watchman's young daughter. As soon as the potion had found its mark, the girl screamed in pain and her eyes sprang wide open, in shock. Her eyes bulged and darted wildly from side to side, and her teeth started chattering loudly, like those of a crazy person. They tried doctoring her with village medicine, but her illness just kept getting worse and worse.

"Please, go fetch those peddlers who've just passed by! Maybe they can give her some potions that'll work, please! The *begu* spirits have got her now, for sure, the evil ones!" So the peddlers were fetched.

The man who went to get them said: "Oh my good friend, our raja! *Please* come back to the village. Someone has fallen seriously ill in our father's house."

"But we don't know how to make medicinal potions, come on! What would we use to make medicines? You go on back home now," they said.

"No, no, *please*, I implore you to come back with me, our rajas! We are getting desparate because of her awful illness, I tell you."

"Well, if that's the case, all right then," said the peddlers.

"You go on, our raja. I'll just stay here and watch your gear. It won't help for me to go with you, for I don't know anything about doctoring folks."

"Okay, okay, keep a good watch on these things then," they said, and the peddlers went back to the village to take a look at the invalid. Once they got to the house they took a close look at the sick girl, and they could see that the illness was very severe. It was pitiful. They all tried their hands at making potions for her, but none seemed to do a bit of good.

"Oh, all right, look . . . please go and get that Angkola guy. Maybe he has some special store of powerful knowledge."[37]

"Good idea," the bridge watchman's henchman said, and off he went to get Djahoemarkar.

Once the henchman got to him he said: "Oh, Good Friend, our esteemed raja, if you would please come back to the village with me so that Damang* can perhaps make an efficacious healing potion to cure the sick girl. Please."

"But what good would it do for me to go back with you? I don't know how to make potions. Look, I don't even know how to make salve for a mosquito bite! But, all right, if you really want me to go back, I will. Pick up this gear on the ground here, will you?" said Djahoemarkar, setting off.

Just as soon as he got back to the house the watchman caught hold of his arm and implored him: "Oh, please, please, come up into the house, son of our great raja! Please sit down on this rattan mat. Here's some betel quid and some tobacco. Here, let's chew a bit of betel, Good Son."

---

*Damang ("our own dear father"): a respectful term of address.

"Ba! What is going on here, our raja. You seem to be doing things in a different manner than you were before. Maybe if I go into the house you won't even want to receive me," said Djahoemarkar.

"Oh, not at all, not at *all*, son of our esteemed raja. This is how one should behave when one is conversing with noblemen, after all. Please, have some more betel or tobacco, won't you? In no more than a wink of an eye our daughter fell ill here. And we have no idea why! All of a sudden her eyes began to bulge and her lips began to tremble and she tried to bite things, just like a crazy person! So, now, son of our esteemed raja, we have great faith in you, that you can do something to help her, since Angkola people are renowned for their special stocks of most esoteric knowledge. They are famous far and wide, so . . . please, *please*, concoct a potion for her so her illness will go away, please."

"Well, look, I offer my respects to you, our esteemed raja, but I'm no expert in mystical curing lore! I have no idea how to go about healing my little sister here."

"Oh, whatever you do will help, we're sure of it, my son. You Angkola folks are so extraordinary."

"Well, all right, if that's the way it is, our esteemed raja, I'll give it a try, but if she doesn't get better don't be angry with me, okay? When pain and suffering come and beset us we have to determine why that might have happened. So, let's think, Amang: maybe you've done something wrong that angered our distant ancient ancestor, do you think? Who knows, maybe someone in this village violated some rule or divine decree, and the fair and even-handed ancient ancestress Si Boroe Deak Paroedjar is punishing your daughter for it—that ancient ancestress who lives in a lofty place as high as the upper sky, Si Deak, who plays magical musical instruments all day long, who spins and weaves and does elegant handiwork, the adept Si Deak ancestress who created the earth and gave us weaving."[38]

On hearing what the fellow had to say, all the women in the house were deathly afraid, for they *did* have a lot of sins to regret! From the womenfolk could be heard: "Oh, gracious, this misfortune is the fate of our days, the lot of our dreams. Now, who could have broken the customary laws? Who could have disobeyed a divine decree?" And they pinched their cheeks and beat their fists on their bellies, and their tears fell down in sheets.

"Well, look, my son, please go get me one egg from a black chicken and send someone to fetch me some water from a clear spring. And if someone asks you what you are doing, just don't answer," said Djahoemarkar.

After the one who fetched the water had returned he gave it to Djahoemarkar along with the egg.

"Well, we shall concoct this potion, our raja, and we must join together in asking our ancient ancestor for her illness to abate."

"Oh, very fine, very fine," said the householder.

Then Djahoemarkar started to mumble strange laments: "Bitcumillah irrakaman irrakimin" (which is to say, Bismillahir rohman inrohim). And "Now-here-come-the-great-elephants-from-Padang-Bolak-carrying-their-long-tusks-of-ivory! This-sickness-came-upon-the-wind-and-it-should-just-return-to-its-origin-on-the-wind, too! Where did you come from? Why have you come? Just return, go back home! Go home, wind! You, sickness! You came with the wind, go back with the wind! And now I read the egg of the large chicken, which has come my way, the curse and spell of the becrowned woman who can cast back the evil spells of human beings, who can cast back the evil spells of *begus*, who constructs a firm and tough magical fence around this poor sick person to protect her so that all the awful sickness here may be healed . . . hahhhhhhhhhhhhhhhhhhhhhhhhhh."[39]

"Well, now, Father, give this to my little sister to drink and hopefully her illness will be healed."

"Yes, our esteemed raja," said the girl's father, taking the potion and giving it to the invalid.

As soon as the invalid had drunk the potion the sickness simply seemed to fly out of her body.

Djahoemarkar then said: "Well, so it seems our ancient ancestor has come to our aid and my little sister's sickness has been cured. May she continue to remain healthy. So, our raja, we shall just set off on our journey so that darkness does not overtake us," said Djahoemarkar.

"Oh no, there's surely no need to rush right off young man. Please just stay overnight right here. My wife has a couple of young chickens running about the yard. She'll butcher them for our meal, and after that you can go on on your way. . . . For, after all, that is the way we must treat *datu*-diviner-curers. We certainly wouldn't want to violate the rules for dealing appropriately with gurus, now would we?"

"Oh, there's no need to do that, our raja. If you butcher a young chicken I won't eat it anyway, for that's not the sort of thing one can safely pair with my potion. I'm the one who made the vow to the powerful *datu*; let me be the one to pay him," said Djahoemarkar.

"Well, if that's the way you want it let my good son just take along these profits. And, here, take these four ringgits so you'll have some pocket change on your trip. . . . Here, you can buy what you want with this. May you be in good soul-health, and so, too, ourselves as well," said the householder.

"Indeed, good health! My deepest respects to Father, to Mother, and to my sweet little sister, too. We'll just set off, then."

And off they went, repeating their earlier journey—and all the peddlers, the whole lot of them, were quite frightened and respectful toward Djahoemarkar. They said oaths to themselves: "Oh lord, this Angkola guy is a very great and extraordinary *datu*-sorcerer. He must command fear and respect—he's one who knows the laws, who knows the divine decrees, who knows the *begu*'s evil deeds, who knows humanity's evil deeds. Well, I guess we can't go taking *him* too lightly anymore! No, not at all, he is someone to fear, respect, and have faith in."

Well, beginning with that day, they did not ask Djahoemarkar to carry supplies anymore. No, not at all. On the contrary, they catered to him and made sure he didn't get too tired or have any difficulties at all as he walked along on his way.

Beginning in Tutupan and going on to Sugapa and then to Bandarpulo, their trip went very well. No obstacles hindered their way, and after a few days they arrived in Asahan. At that point they split up and went their separate ways. The peddlers restocked their supplies while Djahoemarkar searched for a companion to go with him all the way to Medan. All the peddlers bid Djahoemarkar farewell with effusive statements of thanks: a few of them, that is, gave him a ringgit, while others gave him as much as fifty cents.

After they had separated Djahoemarkar got to thinking about how he could best and most safely resume his dangerous, rough, uncertain journey. Once he had found a friendly, trustworthy companion who was heading toward Medan he left Asahan and traveled on through Kisaran, Labuan Ruku, Indrapura, and Tebing Tinggi, and from the latter he boarded a train for Medan.[40] Between Asahan and Tebing Tinggi Djahoemarkar thought to himself: "Folks say that Deliland is a prosperous land, a land overflowing with ringgits. But then, I think, I look at the residents of all these villages along the side of the road and they don't look that much different from the people back in the villages in Tapanuli. In fact, the poorest ones are worse off than our poor folks back home. So what gives? Where do people get all that money?"

Oh, well . . . Djahoemarkar had not yet seen the city of Medan, so naturally he was surprised and confused by this entire scene. It was, of course, the *maatschappys* themselves, the big companies, that owned all the plantations, not to mention the railroad. If he had actually lived there he would not have been so taken aback by the things that people coming home from Deli had to say.

Once he got to Medan he was amazed by all the beautiful houses and the big, capacious stores. He decided to stop there for a while to drink in the sights and witness all this immense wealth. While he was doing this, of course, he did not forget to keep his ears cocked for job openings so he could maybe go to such places and apply for work. And so, indeed, we shall wait and see what might happen to this young man in this regard.

Cooling Off and
Taking a Break

One or two days after reaching Medan, Djahoemarkar was still left doing nothing more than contemplating other people's piles of money. When he'd go walking about town he'd switch from one worried thought to another, thinking about the residents of the city. Sometimes he'd see himself as being like a very tiny ant—and a jobless ant to boot—in comparison with all the prosperous, rich Medaners. And then at other times he'd think: "Ah, look, there are folks like me here, and in fact there are people who are even worse off than I am. It seems that the prosperous get more prosperous and the wealthy get wealthier around here. But what can I do without an official census number to my name? I'm like the fruits of the *casuari* tree: when they're still on the bush, people can't use them as food, but when the fruits fall to the ground even the birds don't want to eat them. Useless! Given God's control of everything in the world, why are there such differences in wealth? Why hasn't everything been divided up equally so that no one has too much and no one has too little?"

As he was thinking such thoughts he did not neglect to keep an ear cocked for possible news about a job. Word reached his ears that over toward Pangkalan Brandan[1] there happened to be lots of job openings, for the Bataaksche Petroleum Maatschappy was going to expand its operations.

As the old saying has it: "Wherever the *durian* fruit trees are blooming that's where the nighttime hummingbirds will flock." And Djahoemarkar knew that was true, too, and that this sort of thing really did occur out in the villages. That is, when the *durian* fruits were in flower in Angkola the hummingbirds would just pour out of their nests from Sialangan, Simangumban, and Aek Puli (that is, from the Toba Pahae region). Normally by about 5 P.M. the hummingbirds would be whirring their wings, flying over the Sipirok Domain and then pushing on toward Angkola (where the *durian*s were in flower). If you were in Sipirok you could hear them making a lot of noise. Starting about dusk you could hear the little kids cheerfully singing away:

Hummingbird, hummingbird
Please leave your baby bird behind so I can take good care of it.

And the hummingbirds would keep flying overhead, the kids would finally tire of singing, and eventually the birds would arrive in Angkola and start to search for their meals. Some of them would get into fights over which bird would swallow the nectar from those sweet *durian* blossoms. Only after their bellies were full would they think about going back home to Simangumban. Normally it would be about 3 A.M. before they headed back, and some of them would get overtaken by daybreak on their way home. In that case they'd sleep over along the way. Apparently the birds would just sort of crawl along if they got caught by daylight. As it got on toward evening they were going to continue on back home, but their bellies were growling by now so they would turn right around and go back to Angkola to sip all that *durian* flower nectar once again. Some of them would nearly die on their journey, they'd get so tired. We humans are just like that when we hear news of available jobs. When word comes of lots of opportunities for work folks immediately throng into that area.

So, once word got around that there were lots of positions to be had in Pangkalan Brandan people flocked in to see if they could finagle a job. In fact, it was just like a swamp inundated by floods. Djahoemarkar took his place in this crowd, too, and one certain day he boarded a train to go out there to try to find a job. The train trip took almost half a day. Once he arrived in Pangkalan Brandan he went straight to a rice stall like the one he was staying in in Medan, but he was a bit hesitant and worried because the law very definitely said that people who didn't have official passes would be arrested. So he sort of hid out in a lonely spot. "Boy, this is tough," he could be heard to sigh from the place where he was staying. He'd feel especially bad when folks would pass by looking for the *crani*, the hiring clerk, from the Maatschappy. His heartstrings would almost snap in two. There were jobs available, but no one asked for him. If he applied for them he wouldn't get them anyway if he didn't have an official pass or a letter of guarantee. "Rotten, rotten luck! I have the skills, there are jobs available, but I can't touch them. So now exactly where should I go, suffering like this as I seem to be?

Day and night he'd hide. If the Company's cops with their red-striped uniforms just so much as passed by his chest would pump up and down anxiously.

One day he got to thinking about his home territory and the hardships he had recently undergone, about those disasters we are not allowed to forget. He thought of his gentle, soft-spoken mother who was so good to her son, always giving him what he asked for. He thought of the *ompung* he had left behind. And he felt bad when he thought about the letter he had sent to Sitti Djaoerah. Why, it must have reached his beloved by now. "I wonder how bad they feel when they think about my journey here?"

"Oh. . . . my God, Allah . . . if only we could be together in confronting all this pain and hardship, maybe two heads would be better than one." Without his being aware of it a tear fell down his cheek; the wide world felt tight, narrow, and confined.

At this time he happened to hear the voice of a fellow who was out trying to recruit coolie labor for a dredging boat that was deepening the channels out in Aru Baai (that is, the Aru Bay).[2] He sharpened his hearing to catch the news more exactly. Once he had heard definitely, he made up his mind to go over there and try to get a job just as if he had an official pass. Over in that area you didn't really need a pass since not too many folks were willing to go drifting around on the sea, that was for sure.

"Well, fine. I'll just head over there and that way I'll have some way to get a pass. After I've worked there for about six months I'm sure the captain will be willing to issue me my official papers." So as soon as the recruiter had passed by Djahoemarkar immediately started following along behind him, and after they had reached an unfrequented spot Djahoemarkar whispered to the guy: "Hey, help me out, if you would, our Raja. Try to put my name in for that work you're trying to find laborers for so I'll have a way to survive here."

Hearing this request the man seeking coolie labor was delighted. He said: "Well, look, if you don't have a job, then let's just go work at sea together. Each month you'll get a salary of fifteen ringgit dollars or about twenty-two rupiah. And they give you your meals, too, with whatever sorts of curries you want—though, of course, it always has to be fish curry since you're at sea."

"Fine. . . . Sign me up to work on that ship," said Djahoemarkar.

"Well, if that's the case, let's go. Here's your *voorschoi* money (that is, an advance loan) so you'll have something with which to buy all your supplies. Once we get out to sea we can't keep coming back to land," said the guy.

"Hey, thanks a lot. I'll go and get everything I need so we can set off," said Djahoemarkar enthusiastically.

After they had everything packed they walked over to the shore to rent a small boat to go to Aru Bay. Once they got it they got in and loaded all their supplies. They sailed from the Brandan estuary out to sea and then sailed right into Aru Bay.

Even though Djahoemarkar knew how wide and huge the ocean was, due to his geographical studies in school, he had never actually been sailing on the sea. So a thought occurred to him: "Oh, so *this* is what the sea is like; why am I so shocked? Those teachers were lying to us, you know. They said that the sea didn't have an edge to it, but, look, there's some forest, and there're some villages, and people are walking back and forth along the shoreline. The folks who thought up all that fine geographical knowledge are a pack of liars."

Oh well, . . . I think Djahoemarkar just forgot. Even the geography lessons said that Brandan was an estuary, the mouth of a big river, not the open sea, but he forgot that fact and just called geographers big liars.

They set sail from Brandan at 5 P.M. After they'd been sailing for about two hours the land began to disappear and the shoreline wasn't so visible anymore. He looked to the right and to the left and nothing at all was visible except for the sails of other small boats. The young fellow got kind of anxious and hesitant at that point—especially when he saw the sails of all the little boats tacking back and forth. This was a very frightening sight. And the farther out they got the less there was that was visible, there in the extremely bright moonlight, which lit things up as if it were noontime. Nothing at all hindered them as they pressed forward on their passage out there in the middle of the ocean.

"Oh . . . so, *this* is the great, wide, open sea. I guess the teachers and the authors of all those geography books weren't lying after all." (Actually, of course, they weren't really out in the deep sea yet, but since that was as far out in the ocean as he had ever been it was quite enough to surprise and amaze him.)

All the time they were sailing along Djahoemarkar kept wondering what possible sort of *begu* spirit might be hidden down there in the waters. As the sailboat cleaved the waves something down there kept glistening in the moonlight, but he was afraid to ask what it was. The farther out into the middle of the ocean they got the more and more he saw of them. There were more waves for them to jump though, too. Finally he just couldn't hold back, despite his considerable fright, and so he asked his companion what sort of shiny reflecting light that *was*, coming from what sort of *begu*, coursing along in the waves like that?

"So you've never been out to sea before? That's the shiny light from tiny creatures who live in the seawater. They're so small you can't see them during the day. They only show up if you look at them through a Microscope.[3] But they behave like lightening bugs; they turn their lights on once it gets dark."

"Is that what they are? Now I remember what the geography lessons say," said Djahoemarkar.

They chatted on about different things out at sea and only thought of going to sleep once it got late at night. Then they went to bed down inside the sailboat and slept till dawn. Only the guy who owned the boat stayed up to guide the rudder and keep the sails in trim. They got to Nine Islands at dawn.

Djahoemarkar had no idea what had happened during the night since he was sleeping so soundly.

Once it got light they awoke and went ashore to have some coffee in a rice stall along the coastline. After they'd finished that they went walking back toward the settlements and back toward the front yards of all the *maatschappy*s to be found on that island. For instance, they walked past the front lawn of the Padang Longlong Maatschappy, and then they walked over to the Central Telephone Office, and then on to the Office of the Commander of the Sea. Once they got tired they finally decided to go over to the dredging boat, which was being used to dredge the channel for the boats near that island.

"Let's get a move on here, so we can get work. I'll have to play student to find out how to do this job," said Djahoemarkar.

They got back into the sailboat and headed off toward the dredger. Then Djahoemarkar was introduced to the captain of the ship. That first day Djahoemarkar just watched what other people did and followed them in order to learn the job. He'd ask the workers what to do so he wouldn't have to go asking the captain every second or two. The second day they let him guide the long instrument that sliced down through the mud. They let him move it around, and he learned how to make it follow the movements of the ship that was dragging it along. Once they got out into the open sea they showed him how to work the automatic device that ran the ship's scoop, and they showed him how to dispose of the scooped up mud without expending too much energy. But the clumps of mud flowed in by themselves, actually. And then you'd have to shut the hatch real quick so that the water wouldn't get in. Djahoemarkar paid diligent attention to all these orders, and after not too many days he was fully competent in all the different tasks.

The overseer and the shipowner were delighted to see this. He wasn't a braggart and he didn't get into fights; he was just a very hard worker who got along well with all the other guys on the ship. He was also very polite, addressing everyone with the correct kin term. But he didn't let on to them that he knew how to write or that he had worked as an assistant schoolteacher. In fact, when someone would be chatting along about reading and writing he'd pretend he didn't know the first thing about that so that the guys on the ship would not find out that he was a lettered man. After all, his aim here was just to secure an official worker's pass from being on this ship.

And so, as we might say, from day to day and week to week and month to month, eventually he had been working on that dredging ship for a full four months. He saved all of his salary very carefully; after all, he was getting his meals free on board with his choice of curries. When the ship would stop for a while they could fish over the side; they'd be hauling in huge fish one right after the other. The fish they got the most of would be *sinangin* fish, *tarubuk* fish, *karapuh* fish, and some others. If they happened to catch a lot of them they'd cook them in all sorts of different ways. Some they'd fry, some they'd curry, and some they'd just roast over a fire and then toss a bit of ketchup on top with some onions and red peppers. When they'd eat, the whole side of the big roasted carp would be lying there by their side and they'd gouge out a hunk of its flesh with their fingers and dip it in the hot pepper sauce, "*Gap!*" . . . and then stuff it in their mouths, chew it briefly, and dispatch it on its way to the Middle Continent. And a bit of the hot red pepper would sting the tips of their ears, but they wouldn't even be aware of this as they dove back into the big flakes of fish. Sometimes they'd start weeping, it was all so delicious.

That is how it went, good friends . . . though Djahoemarkar never forgot Sitti Djaoerah. In fact, it made him cry when he ate all this delicious food. "If only Sitti Djaoerah was spooning out this rice for us and I was cutting up the fish, I think I'd be pretty darn happy," said the young man to himself. A moment later he thought: "Now, Younger Lineage Companion Djaoerah, I'm not being selfish and eating by myself here on purpose. Here, here's your portion of fish," he said, setting aside a plank steak from the big carp. But where will I send it? Oh, shoot," he said, remembering everything as it really was, then throwing the portion over the side of the boat as if he were offering it to Sitti Djaoerah.

This rice and fish didn't go to waste, either, for as soon as he had thrown it over the side of the ship it was gobbled up by a big sea crocodile. Djahoemarkar kept doing this, every day, until the crocodile developed quite a taste for these meals.[4] Because of this whenever the ship would stop great crowds of crocodiles would mill around, waiting to be fed their rice meals by the sailors. Djahoemarkar usually threw them the most food, so the crocodiles got to know his voice and face and they weren't afraid to come close to the ship. The other sailors loved to see this. It is true that humans and crocodiles are natural enemies, but if one side doesn't bother and plague the other, well, they can get to be friends.

We don't have to go on at too great a length about this friendship of theirs with the crocodiles. Suffice it to say that they usually just didn't bother each other. For as long as Djahoemarkar worked on the dredger nothing untoward happened to hurt his feelings; he was also cheerful in following the orders of the *tuan* or the ship's work gang overseer. On hot days he found it quite pleasant to bob up and down on the waves like a log in the water out there in the open sea, but it was really awful when it rained because the barge did not have a roof over it. You couldn't even use an umbrella because the wind blew so hard. They got soaked in the downpour, caught bad colds, and stood there shivering just like a bunch of monkeys caught in a rainstorm.

It was just a pitiful sight. But to whom could they complain? It was apparently their unavoidable fate to get soaked like that, for, as it says in the words of the song:

Andilan na hinanan	Tree bark in the far past
Hadangkadangan saonnari	But now it has become a basket.
Pangidoan nahinanan	What I asked for in the past
Mananggung badan saonnari.	Is just what I've ended up with now.

Once, when they happened to have some downtime from work, the crop-sprinkling rain was ready to fall and the dredger was full of mud and silt. They were going to haul it out into the open sea and dump it. So they had to depart even though it was surely going to rain. They really didn't want to set off, but they could hardly argue with the ship captain's orders, so they just had to get under way. However, when they got out to sea it didn't rain. It just got real dark. It happened that the ship was pulling four barges filled with mud, so it was just creeping forward slowly, it was so weighted down. Because they were all down with bad colds, they were trying to think of ways to cheer themselves up. Some of them sang *dendang* songs, like the coastal folks do near Sibolga. Some sang Barus-style songs, while others sang songs of sad fate of Hawa Medjelis. Djahoemarkar hummed some *marsitogol* songs, all in the Mandailing style.[5] The words went like this.

Songon dia na so salongon	Whatever cannot be put in verse
Na mulak di golap ni ari	Sad things that occur to you when it gets dark
Songon dia na so taonon	Whatever cannot be withstood
Madung untung dapot na ari.	It will be your fate to have it befall you during the daytime.
Tu Sigama pe so lalu	
Tinggal muse padang garugur	Why, we didn't even get as far as Sigama
Damang maninggalkon aoe	And what's still left to traverse is Padang Garugur.
Dainang pe mago marobur.	My dear Father has gone and died on me
	And my mother too has disappeared from sight.
Na bahat do sipagol	
Sipagol ni Djandjilobi	There are lots of *sipagol* birds
Na bahat do halak na dangol	*Sipagols* from Janjilobi.
Di badan ma na sumurung lumobi.	There are lots of people who are suffering
	But I am suffering most of all.
Satarak satapolan	
Lobilobi ni ampang jual	A double hand span of *satarak* wood
Marsarak baya dohot dongan	Overflows the selling basket.
Baen ganjil ni paruntungan.	I am separated from my friends
	Because I am beset by such an odd, unusual fate.
Hutampul ma singgolom	
Tubu di bona ni galunggung	I chop up the begonia sticks
Hutatap laut manyalonggom	Which grow near the *galunggung* trunk.
Tarsingot au di lambok ni lidung.	I look out over the dark sea
	And I recall the sweet, soft-spoken one.

Jarungjung oburobur	Golden hairpins stuck in hairbuns
Pasangsanggul ni simanjujung	The girl ties her hair back in a knot.
Anggo na so mate marobur	If I do not simply die
Nada tarantak na malungun.	My loneliness and longing will never cease.

"Okay, we'd better be careful in here," said the guy steering the first barge, for a number of large waves had rolled in from the roiling storm out in the ocean.

"Careful now, easy . . . don't get shook or scared. We don't have to get in trouble here. Remember God, remember the prophet Noah, who was driven through the heaving waves in his ark to Mount Ararat."

Once things got to this scary pass, the voices of the Barus-singers and the coastal-style singers petered out. Everyone trembled in fear; they were really shook up, in fact. Not too long afterward a big hailstorm with extremely strong winds blew in, and the winds went "*whoosh! whoosh!*" And "*boor*" went the crashing waves, tossing the barge upside-down with great violence. "Watch out, watch out!" said the voice from up front, from the direction in which they were going. Everything had turned dark and stormy, and when you looked toward the coast you couldn't see land. The rudders of the ship and the barges weren't very effective anymore.

"*Butttt . . .*" said the voice of a very strong wave once again, and then it snapped the tug rope that tied the barges to the ship. "Oh, oh, . . . whatever your fate happens to be on a certain day you shall just have to accept it—"[6] people murmured. All the barges slipped free of the tug ropes and went bobbing up and down in the waves, and all the sailors on the deck were thrown into the sea. The tugboat couldn't help save them because it couldn't turn around in the huge waves. It just slunk off, seeking a safe harbor.

So what happened to Djahoemarkar? . . . When the awful disturbance hit, the steering wheel of the barge went out of control, but even in so terrible and threatening a moment as this he remembered what had happened to Si Djahidin, the guy who got lost over near Papua back in the distant past. Because of this he quickly tied a heavy board to his chest to use as a flotation device so that he wouldn't just sink like a stone down into the seawater. Whatever the case, though, he really didn't think he would live. He just strapped on the board so that his corpse would bob to the surface and when folks read the letter that he had tied to his waist they'd go tell Sitti Djaoerah that he had perished beneath the foamy waves.

Well, these waves got larger and more fearsome still, and all the fishes, crocodiles, and other creatures living in the sea were dashing away just as quickly as they could. As a matter of fact, all of the crocodiles in the vicinity lined up in rows on either side of Djahoemarkar, streaming out of there posthaste, but not a one of them wanted to bother him. Seeing their behavior you would almost think that they had arrived at a village consensus: "Oh, c'mon, let's try helping Djahoemarkar, the good-hearted man who's always feeding us."

The raja of the crocodiles went flitting around, this way and that, issuing orders to his crocodile populace for them to locate Djahoemarkar in the heaving waves. And then, when they'd found him, the raja further ordered that they should guide him toward the shore so he would not drown in the sea. His clothing was totally torn apart; there wasn't a palm's width of good cloth left to his whole suit of clothes—after all, the crocs had kept grabbing his shirt and trousers and pulling him this way and that in the water, trying to save him. But his flesh had not a scratch on it.

The next morning Djahoemarkar was still unconscious, dead to the world, lying there on the shore sprawled out like a corpse. He started to breathe more easily to some extent once it got to be about nine o'clock, after the sun had warmed his skin a bit.

There happened to be a certain sailboat fisherman living there who made his living from the sea. An extremely poor fellow, he'd go out fishing every day to feed his family. He had been close friends with Djahoemarkar all this while, and Djahoemarkar had always been ready to help him out with supplies and small money gifts so that the family would have something with which to buy their rice. Apparently at the time the great waves came the fisherman also got tossed out of his sailboat. But since he was used to being at sea he wasn't thrown into confusion by this—he kept his wits about him and managed to find a safe way back to land. Things were pretty grim once he arrived, though: in the deep darkness of the night he stayed there on the shore, without food, without drinking water, without a dry blanket (since he couldn't build a fire). In short, he was pretty much mosquito bait that whole night long.

Once it got light the guy got back into his sailboat and pushed it carefully along the coastline. Without warning he suddenly saw a man lying sprawled out on the beach. He thought: "This guy must have been drowned in the big waves last night." He felt great pity for the fellow, even though, of course, he had also endured considerable hardships in the same storm. He jumped on shore and took a look, and sure enough it was a human being, albeit an unconscious one. For a moment the fisherman was simply flabbergasted at the sight.

And, as for Djahoemarkar, who opens up all manner of pain and suffering, he was like a person in a dream. He had no idea what was going on in the world, but, because the sun was heating things up a bit, once his body got warm he began to feel a bit stronger and he started to move a little. He opened his eyes and saw that he was on land. He looked in both directions and found that he was on the coastline. "Allah, my God, what carried me here?" Seeing masses of crocodile footprints all around him on the sand it occurred to him: "Why, they didn't bother me a bit last night, it seems. But that's a shame, really—if only they had just swallowed me up I wouldn't be so unhappy; these hardships wouldn't beset me day and night. Oh . . . 'Tidjaoerah, please come and get me here . . ."[7]

"Before I die, before I breathe my last breath, I do hope I shall be able to see Sitti Djaoerah one last time," he thought to himself.

"Is that you, Djahoemarkar?" asked the fisherman, approaching the guy lying on the ground.

"Yeah, but I'm barely alive. You might say I'm more dead than alive, actually."

"Almighty God, I was half dead last night, too. Come on, now, let's get you into the boat so we can go home to the village. Folks must be out with search parties by now," said the fellow.

"Help me along since I can't make it on my own. But let's not go by sea, all right? Let's, let's just go by land, even though I can hardly walk. I'm real weak because I haven't eaten since I got tossed around by the waves."

"I don't have any strength, either, so how can I possibly carry you? But, all right, all right, I'll try. Just as long as I can move I'll see if I can carry you back to the village."

The Nine Islands folks didn't know what had happened to the workers on the dredger's barges. It was morning before they received word that the barges and the sailors had all disappeared. So they got ready to go out and search for the missing. In the wink of an eye they all rushed out of the village, like ants streaming out of an anthill, every one of them carrying his sailboat on his head, rushing down to the sea. The police were dashing around, too. . . . It was a great big crowd, and some of them even took motorboats down to the water. Everyone left behind on the beach was in pain, too, just watching the hullabaloo.

From early morning to noon everyone frantically searched for the missing, all working as hard as they possibly could.

The day was already well advanced, but they had yet to encounter a dead body or, in fact, even the slightest sign of the disaster. The tugboat was listing on its side, and all its occupants were safe, but the barge it had been pulling was in total chaos—parts of it were drifting around on the water's edge. The sailors who had been steering the barge weren't inside anymore. Folks figured that the whole lot of them had died.

People's sailboats went "*serrr*" in one direction and "*serrr*" in the other, scooting around, searching for the missing, but not a single thing was visible. But as it was getting on toward evening the crowd saw someone waving from the shoreline. They rushed over.

It seems that Djahoemarkar and the other guy hadn't been able to budge from that spot of theirs, they were so weak. So folks propped them up, gave them a change of clothes, pumped the water out of their mouths, energetically massaged their bodies, and gave them drops of water that the rice had been cooked in until they finally regained consciousness from all these restorative ministrations. Then they carried them back to Nine Islands so that they could be taken care of properly with the right medications. After a week, Djahoemarkar and the sailor returned to normal.

But the other men never were found, not even their bodies.

Now let us switch over to what happened to Djahoemarkar once he recovered from being tossed about in the waves. All the money he had saved while he was working on the barge he had stored away in a wallet—which was now lying at the bottom of the ocean. He didn't have the heart to start work again, either, because now he got terrified just looking at the ocean. And he didn't have half a cent to his name to go someplace new to look for another job. Also he didn't have any official papers.

So where could he go? He went to the ship's captain to see if the man would provide him with an official letter of introduction and some money for living expenses since he certainly did not want to work at sea anymore. Tuan Captain did take pity on him and wrote him a good letter and gave him twenty-five rupiah—to help out a guy who had gotten into difficulty doing the Company's work out there on the open sea.

Djahoemarkar happily accepted all this from Tuan Captain and thanked him very much, indeed, for all of the *tuan's* help. He was even happier to get the official letter than he was to get all that money—now he had a pass! He could go wherever he wished now, unimpeded, looking for a job in other areas. Before leaving Nine Islands he told all his acquaintances about this and then said goodbye to all of them. Since he had been so generous and friendly to everybody all the time he was on that island, they made sure to send him off with little gifts of living-expenses money. All these little sums added up; Djahoemarkar got much, much more than he had thought he would.

"Syukur Alhamdulillah, thanks be to God, may God repay you for your kind gifts, for I certainly am not equal to the task myself. May you folks all remain healthy and may the same be true of me as I set off toward my distant, unknown destination," he said as he took his leave of the large crowd.

After everybody had apologized to each other for any offenses they might have committed, off he set toward the *maatschappy* pier so that he could catch one of the Company boats returning to Pangkalan Brandan. As soon as he got in the ship he went right to his bedroom so he wouldn't have to catch sight of the open ocean. Once he got to Pangkalan Brandan he stopped at a rice stall briefly and had a glass of hot coffee and a meal since he was famished. After eating he went over to the railway station and bought a ticket to Medan. He got on the train, and at departure time off it went to Medan.

Once he got to Medan he tried applying for jobs in various Dutch offices, but things were still a bit chaotic for him. In fact, things were like the upper and lower jaws of a horse when he yawns: all going in different directions to little effect. Djahoemarkar didn't know anybody in Medan, anyone who could fix things for him behind closed doors.

Often they would have accepted his application to work at a certain office and it was already arranged that he would start his job the next morning, but what would happen? . . . Bad luck! He'd report on time, but they wouldn't take him because some sneaky Indian would have come in and said bad things about him—some Indian,[8] some Keling who had worked in that office before. They'd say all kinds of false things like "I don't know this guy"; "I can't guarantee that he's okay"; and "Well, look, I can't ensure you can put your trust in him." And consequently Djahoemarkar would have to go back home, like a rooster after losing a cockfight, without having gained a single thing from the encounter. And to whom could he complain? After all, he didn't have any acquaintances around there, that was for sure.

"So what did I get out of all that bother? . . . What can a penniless person do? I think it's better that I just go to the outskirts of Medan to try to find work because it won't do me a bit of good to stay here in the city—even when I get a job somebody comes along and tricks me out of it. And I can't ask some friend to come to my aid since I don't know anyone here yet. It looks like if I'm light I'll float, but if I'm heavy, well, I'll just sink to the bottom" he said, leaving the crowded, bustling city behind.

On a certain *onderneming* near town, which we shall call "Onderneming Parsaulian"* in this story, the tobacco leaves had grown wide, thick, and full, but great crowds of worms had come to eat them. There were so many worms that one wondered where they could all be coming from because they could totally wipe out a field of tobacco in one evening and by dawn they'd be back in force. So, the plantation had to add workers to go collect the bugs so that the tobacco crop wouldn't be wiped out. They went looking for extra labor in the nearby villages. People would be paid by piecework, by the worm. At first they'd be paid a cent per worm, but if they kept getting more and more bugs they'd get one cent for two bugs, and so on. But they'd still rake in lots of money; some folks were earning a salary of as much as two rupiah per day.

Djahoemarkar got word of this easy means of making a living, not to mention this big salary. So he thought to himself: "I'll just go there so I can get some money to live on. That sort of work shouldn't be too back-breaking." First he went to find Tandil Padia, who folks had to talk to when they first started work looking for tobacco worms. This man told him all the specifications so that Djahoemarkar could join in and become a tobacco worm coolie.

"Well, okay, because we're still in need of more people, because we're not able to handle all these worms yet," said Tandil Padia, writing Djahoemarkar's name in the coolie registration book. And he told Djahoemarkar to be sure to report for work early the next morning.

At dawn, as they had agreed, Djahoemarkar arrived and got ready to go look for the worms. He got loads and loads of bugs that day; by evening his salary was an entire ringgit.

"Ah, all right, I guess I won't die after all. God indeed provides a means of living," he thought to himself.

When it was time for the laborers to turn in the bugs they had collected, total confusion reigned, Djahoemarkar noticed. At 4 P.M. one of the lesser *tuans*[9] would come to accept the worms, but as soon as he arrived everyone would rush up to show him their bugs. Because there were so many of them to count sometimes it would be 6 P.M. before it was all finished.

With feelings of great pity Djahoemarkar noticed that the mothers and small children were having a real hard time of it, what with getting bitten by mosquitoes and then overtaken by darkness before they could go home to their villages. So Djahoemarkar felt quite sorry for them, and he thought of his late mother: "Ah, my mother worked like this for my benefit, to find me food, but since I stayed home in the village I wasn't aware of all her efforts." He couldn't say what he felt to anyone; he just hid everything inside.

The next morning he told everyone to turn over all their worms to him at three o'clock. "I won't ask any payment from you; let me just help you out by counting how many worms you have, okay? I'll figure out how much each person collected and we'll write it down on a piece of paper, and then, when the *tuan* arrives, we'll just give him this letter. He can look at the different piles of worms and that

*An *onderneming* (in Dutch) is an enterprise, while the Batak word *parsaulian* means 'common good fortune'.

will be that, he won't have to wear himself out counting the worms, and all of us can go home quickly and tend to the little kids who are crying for us to return." Hearing this, they were all delighted. So at 3 o'clock they crowded around Djahoemarkar and turned over all the bugs they had collected, and he counted how many were in each pile. Then he wrote down all the information on a list and stored the bugs away. At 4 P.M. the minor *tuan* arrived. Djahoemarkar showed him his lesson book, pointed toward each of the piles of bugs, and told him who owned which worms.

"Hey, thanks a lot! Now, who made this list?" asked the minor *tuan*.

"Well, I did, Tuan, since I felt so sorry for the women getting caught in the dark on their way home so late at night," said Djahoemarkar.

"So it seems you know how to write, do you? Now, look, I hope you will do this every day! I'll give you five rupiah extra each month for your trouble."

"Thank you, Tuan," said Djahoemarkar politely.

After the worms were all counted up the *tuan* paid each person, and then he went back to the main office to find the big *tuan* of the whole plantation.

"Well, we got this many worms and we had to pay out this much money," said the minor *tuan*, showing the other man the list.

"All right," said Big Tuan, looking at the list but not saying anything.

Djahoemarkar performed the same task day after day on the plantation, never expecting any payment from the people. Often enough, folks would give him a little bit of money so that he'd have some tobacco-buying change, but Djahoemarkar wouldn't take it because he did not hold out any hope of being paid for this service of his. He was doing it all out of kindness. And the minor *tuan* was simply delighted to see this, to notice how good hearted Djahoemarkar was. He decided to help this guy out sometime in the future.

After more and more of Djahoemarkar's lists had piled up on the desk of Big Tuan, one day the man happened to glance over at the big pile. As soon as he had caught sight of it he began to examine the lists carefully.

"Well, my goodness, how nicely formed this guy's handwriting is! Hmm, so clean lined and finely done—I'll bet he's not just any old person. Why, look at these capital letters and how nicely they're slanted—almost as if they are the handiwork of a *begu*![10] This guy is certainly someone who should be cultivated. But what sort of job should we give him? We've already got enough *cranis*," said Big Tuan to himself, pondering the dilemma. "Well, listen . . . later on today, at 3 o'clock, I'll go myself to the worm-counting desk so that I can get a look at this fellow." Once it was 3 o'clock, as he had intended, off he went to locate the minor *tuan*, who was at the desk accepting worms.

As soon as Big Tuan arrived Djahoemarkar saluted him politely. Then Djahoemarkar followed along behind him, pointing out each person's pile of worms.

"So this is the fellow, apparently, who's making these lists?" asked Big Tuan.

"Yes, he's the one, the guy with such good handwriting. Likable sort, huh? Maybe we could help him out."

"Yeah, but you know, I don't know what to do. . . . We've got enough *cranis*, unfortunately. . . . But, you know . . . let's just have him be the one who takes in all the worms every evening. And during the day he can take the tobacco plants to the warehouse. Starting tomorrow he won't have to go collecting worms himself, all right? And make his salary fifteen rupiah per month," said Big Tuan.

"Well, okay. Let's ask him if this will suit him," said the other *tuan*.

"Let me say thank you very much, indeed. I do accept, and I shall try just as hard as I can to do this job diligently," said Djahoemarkar, bowing his head.

At that, the minor *tuan* informed the crowd of folks that Djahoemarkar had been given a new job. "But it'll still be him who takes in all your worms every evening. So keep working hard, all right?"

"Thanks be to Allah," they all said cheerily, happy to hear of Djahoemarkar's promotion.

The next morning the minor *tuan* showed Djahoemarkar how to do all the different parts of the job. And he gave him a room to stay in so he wouldn't have to go back to the village at night. And then he also told Djahoemarkar to come over to his house in the evenings so that he could study the work and learn the job more quickly.

"Thank you, Tuan, whatever you order me to do I shall do it, just as long as it does some good. With God's mercy may this job lead to greater prosperity so that I have a way to support myself in the future." At that time he also thought of Sitti Djaoerah, and he decided to write her a letter. He hadn't had the heart to send her a letter when his luck had been so bad, as it certainly had been until recently. He had not sent news to Sitti Djaoerah since he had left the homeland.

The words of the letter went as follows.

To my kind Lineage Mate,
whom I would never fool,
may you be in good health and strength
in the Panyabungan Domain.

May the strong, fierce-blowing winds send the words of this letter on to my little lineage companion, Sitti Djaoerah. I say thank you, in advance, for letting me present my sad, suffering, painful, fully unendurable fate to you.

I think, Little Lineage Companion, that it has now been five Moonlight-Shimmering Months since I left the home village, striding forth with legs the gallant walkers, swinging my hands, the fervent askers for gifts—as I strode off, throwing my fate to the winds, running off to an unknown, undescribed, untold, far distant land. All this while I have been suffering unendurable hardships. I left home because my mother had passed away. I left behind our *ompung* and the house. I left behind the rice paddies, the garden lands—everything! All because I was in such deep pain. From the time I left my home I had no friends to come to my aid, but since my mind was made up to go on this journey I was able to traverse that hard road wherever it might lead. As I went from village to village I would go from person to person, latching onto whoever might help me, eating whatever was available, grabbing hold of whatever could serve as medicine to cure my hunger pains. Often I'd just have leaves from the trees to eat. This was especially true in Tobaland: I would be forced to eat whatever folks there were eating so that they'd be friendly toward me. If I'd go to a palm toddy stall then I'd just drink palm toddy. And the same was true with places to sleep and so forth. Often I would want to confront them, if I felt insulted after they had tried to trick me, but I had to remember that there was just one of me and I had no friends about. So I'd just put up with everything as long as I got to my destination. Once I got to Deliland I couldn't go looking for work since I had no official letter of permission. Consequently I was forced to go to work on a dredger ship, which was digging the channels in Aru Bay (Aru Baai). After only four months at that job, I did indeed have enough to eat and sufficient clothing—but fate was truly unkind out there on the open sea. And that wasn't all: our barge was turned over in a big storm one day and I was tossed into the ocean and knocked unconscious. Down in the sea I saw many fierce ocean creatures—a few crocodiles pulled me back and forth, and huge sharks were swimming back and forth with their jaws wide open to swallow me. But they didn't; they just went skimming on back into the waters.

I think it was only because I was so skinny that they didn't swallow me. But I didn't perceive any of this clearly; it was all like a dream. The scariest thing was when I encountered a very big fish—I've never seen such a weird fish. It had all these feet and moustaches, like thorns coming out of its body. And its eyes were as big as gongs. At that point, Lineage Companion, I told you my last farewells and got ready to let this fish just swallow me; I felt it was better to die than to live.[11] I couldn't feel a thing—wherever the fish or the crocs would pull and tug me that was where I'd have to go. The next morning by about ten I saw that I had washed up on shore.

"Oh . . . yeah . . ." I said to myself." So I'm still alive it seems," I said to myself, Little Lineage Companion. But I was still only half conscious. The ones who came searching for us carried me back to the village, and I only woke up after they had doctored me up. All the money that I had made over that long while is sitting at the bottom of the ocean. None of my friends' bodies were ever found.

The general populace took pity on me, as did the ship's *tuan*. They gave me enough money to live on, and I was able to quit my job on the ship with good official papers in hand. Nowadays I don't have the nerve to so much as look at the ocean; the moment I catch sight of the sea I get terrified. Once I had my letters I went back to Medan, and that's where I went scratching around, so to speak, for my chicken feed, there in the dust, morning and night. Younger Lineage Companion, let me not spin out stories endlessly about of all my sufferings but simply suffice it to say: I feel as if I have done everything connected with dying except taking that final life's breath.

Well, Lineage Companion, I need not draw this all out or tears will flow without end. May you remain healthy, may I remain hearty, and if we're lucky God will still afford us the chance to meet here in this present world. That, then.

Best regards from me, who suffers and laments,
Wg. DJAHOEMARKAR

When the letter was finished he put it into its envelope and deposited it in the post going to Tapanuli.

To shorten the story a bit, eventually the letter got to Panyabungan after a long time on the road, and at about 9 A.M. on the arrival day the contents of the mail sack were divided up.

As soon as the postman (named Djasipode) caught sight of a letter addressed to Sitti Djaoerah he quickly laid hold of it so that he could get it to her right away. That way, he'd be able to chat with that blooming, budding girl, he figured.

Dear Reader . . . let us switch over for a moment to Sitti Djaoerah's house. It can be fairly said that ever since she got Djahoemarkar's letter, the one he sent from Sidimpuan, she had been gloomy, not knowing where he had gone. The more she thought about the situation the lonelier she felt, and finally her hand found the drum that was lying on the sales table, which they were storing in the house. Her feelings were a delicious mixture of pain and the joy of longing.[12] She sat at the window and beat time on her drum.

Reng, reng, bur . . . bur, reng, reng, bur, burrrr. . . . As soon as these drumbeats sounded out, an old-style pantun escaped her lips, sung so sweetly as to break your heart.*

Singkuang kuala Tabuyung	Tebuyung Bay near Natal
Djauh Siondop kualonyo	Far, far from that bay
Tarbuanglah baden korono untung.	I am cast to the winds because of most rotten
Dengarkan djoeo baritonjo	luck.
	Just sit and listen first to the story.

Reng-reng, bur bur . . . reng-reng, bur bur . . .

Dua nan dake Sidimpuan	Walk two steps up from Sidimpuan
Toga jambatan antaraonjo	There's a barrier on the way in the bridge.
Takonang baden danda oi.	I think sadly of older lineagemate, so unlucky
daparuntungan	And my eyes well up with tears.
Mengilir air dalom mato.	

Cap cap bur bur . . . . .

Taguntagun gunung Kurintji	Tagun-tagun near Mount Kerinci
Pandan bekeliling Panyabungan	Field grasses surround Panyabungan.
Turunlah ombun kanda oi . . .	The clouds sweep in, Lineagemate, and we cry,
kami tangisi	Remembering that Older Lineagemate is off
Mengenang kanda diranto urang.	in other people's lands in the *ranto.*

Reng-reng, bur bur . . . reng-reng, bur, bur . . .

Sakitlah pandan tidak baduri	Even field grasses without thorns hurt
Djika baduri ditobang orang	If someone tries to chop them down.
Sakitlah baden kanda oi . . .	It's tough, Angkang, if you don't have money
tidak baduit	If folks want money from you.
Djika baduit ditegur orang.	

Cap cap, bur, bur . . .

Panjangkan kawet dari Padang	Pull on the wire to lengthen it
Jangan menyusah baropoti	But don't hurt the flying doves.
Tompangkan kami kanda oi . . .	Let me follow you, Angkang, oi, you
sianank dagang	young merchant
Jangan menyusah dinagori.	Don't go suffering in other lands.

Reng-reng bur bur . . . reng-reng bur bur . . .

Pulo Pandan jauh ditonga	Pandan Island's out there in the middle
Dibalik pulu Angsa Dua	Right behind Two Geese Island.
Hancurlah baden kanda oi . . .	My body is destroyed, Angkang, oh, buried
dikandang tanah	in the earth
Budi nan baik takonang jua.	And I think back to when I was happy.

---

*I ask the reader to please sing each of these lines two times. — THE WRITER.

As soon as the girl's verses had come to this point she fainted, as if her *tondi* soul had flown right up into the clouds. The drum slipped from her hands without her knowing it . . .

"Help, help, this will be the death of me," said someone's voice from below the house. It seems that Djasipode had been standing there, open-mouthed in surprise, listening to Sitti Djaoerah's lovely *pantuns*. He hadn't given her the letter yet, either. So, since he was facing upward the drum fell and hit him smack in the face, knocking out the fancy gold filling in his front tooth.

"Now, who in the world is this, dropping in on us without warning?" said Sitti Djaoerah from above.

"It's me, Little Lineage Companion, I'm just delivering a letter to you, which has arrived from Deli. But look what's happened, my filling's been knocked out— and my gold filling is the only thing that makes the girls like me!" One had to laugh at Djasipode; he was hurt and tickled at the same time.

"Give it to me, that letter. . . ! And, listen, that tooth of yours that fell out, that wasn't my fault. You're the one who's wrong for being such a flashy dresser!" said Sitti Djaoerah. With considerable embarrassment, Djasipode went off to put a hot compress of leaves on his sore tooth.

As soon as Sitti Djaoerah saw the letter's address she immediately tore it open, for she knew it must be from Djahoemarkar. She hadn't read the letter but halfway through when she emitted a loud sob and fell over in a faint.

"What's wrong with you, Djaoerah?" asked her mother, catching her on her way down. Sitti Djaoerah's eyes were already turned back, and so her mother started in to crying, too. After a moment she sprinkled her daughter's forehead with drops of cold water. Not long afterward Sitti Djaoerah regained consciousness, and her mother asked her what had happened.

"Oh . . . Mother, oh . . . my God . . . you must know how terrible my luck is. . . . Oh, my God . . ."

"Who's this letter from, girl? Read it so I can hear what it says. And why did you burst into tears right away? Are they still among the living, or is this a death announcement?"

"Oh, but look how painful his luck has been," said Sitti Djaoerah, and then she read her mother the letter.

"Lailahaillallah Mohammadorosurullah. . . . Yes . . . Allah, yes, my God . . . he's really, really had a hard time of it, hasn't he?" said Nandjaoerah upon hearing the words of the letter. Without her being aware of it, tears began to flow down her cheeks.

"Well, now, Mother, at least we've gotten clear word that Djahoemarkar is still alive, and so I think we should just go to Deli ourselves and find him. If he dies at least we'll see his grave, and then I can kill myself so we can be together in the grave. And if he's alive we can be together and try to withstand our life of pain. If we don't go there and he dies we won't even know."

"Well, I think that really is the best idea, my girl. That child's luck is simply unthinkably bad. But who can we get to accompany us to Deli?"

"But, nowadays there are lots of people going there. Just look, people come here every day asking for a travel pass. Sometimes husbands and wives travel together— let's just find us a friendly pair who'll take us there," declared Sitti Djaoerah.

Kitchen Chat*

Djatoeba and Djasiala (Dj. T. and Dj. S.) are at a rice stall at Aek Godang (that is, along the Girl River).[1]†

Dj. S.: *Tok . . . tok . . . tok. . . .* Oh . . . Djatoeba, are you here or not?

Dj. T.: "Who is it? Oh, well, come on up into the house, I'm here all right," he said, opening the door of the house. "Aha . . . so it's you, is it, Djasiala? Come on up and have a seat on the mat right here. Oh . . . Taring's Mom! Get up, look, Djasiala's come for a visit. Get the coffee going, you hear?"

Dj. S.: Oh, now what are you doing? And here you are getting ready to go to sleep. You certainly do keep good *adat*. But I guess this is the sort of thing you have to do when you run a rice stall, isn't it?

Dj. T.: Oh, now what are you thinking of—what's the use of buying a woman as your wife, after all, if she's not here to take care of us and our family, right?

"*Nging*," went the ear of Taring's Mom when she heard what her husband was saying. She felt that what he had said was just too harsh. What was with him, anyway?[2]

Dj. S.: Now what are you going on about, Djatoeba? Haven't you had enough religious recitation lessons poked into you? We're all descendants of Adam and Eve around here, aren't we? God made Adam from the earth, and He made Eve from Adam's left rib. And, it's true, we can compare those modes of creation in an unfavorable light for the womenfolk, but we do have to go together halfsies with them don't we, so that things come out right. That's true when we take a trip, and it's also true in our daily working lives. Why, just think, if there weren't any women around why would you do all this work, huh? Moreover, women are the real diligent, expert workers, especially if we already have two or three kids around the house. Why, they never get to stop working then, do they? Day or night. At dawn, they're already dashing off to fetch buckets of water at the spring, and then they stoke up the fire, and they look to see if there's any rice, and, of course, there's not, so they have to go and pound the husks off some so there'll be something to eat. And after that's done they come back to the house, and the kids are already crying and carrying on. And once the children have been quieted down they still have to wash the dishes, and at that point there's not even enough time to boil the rice. And a punch'll land on 'em if the rice isn't done on time, you can just bet. Whereas the man has only to come in here

Ketjet dopoer, a Malay term.
†*This conversation is related as it would have appeared according to the way the Mandailing language is spoken.*

and do nothing but chat. Well, talk is truly men's wealth, I guess. Do you imagine that women have time to just relax and chatter? Huh, no way!

DJ. S.: Now, look, just think a bit about what sorts of things they might hear you say, so you do them a bit of justice, you know."

Upon hearing what Djasiala had to say, Taring's Mom felt much better, for she always sided with the women. Even though she was a bit put out to hear what her *tuan* had had to say earlier, now she bustled off to get the coffee on and to rustle up some snacks from red sugar and pounded rice.

As soon as Djasiala heard Taring's Mom hard at work in the kitchen he was pleased, especially when he smelled the red sugar–coconut treats. They smelled delicious.

"Oh, honestly . . . to be carrying on about me like that. If you're mad at something don't get mad at me—but if you're longing for someone then make sure it's for me, you hear?" said Djasiala.

DJ. T.: Oh, go on with you, Djasiala, honestly. You have entirely too many snakes in your belly.

DJ. S.: Yeah, well, that's because folks are always talking about me behind my back, since I'm so poor. But to change the subject a bit here, have you heard about the new law that's just been issued?

DJ. T.: What law? You're sure full of information—what, do you get a newspaper or something?

DJ. S.: Oh, come on. . . . That's why I keep my ears open and why I get around the countryside some, you know. So I can find out a bit about what's happening. Earlier today, I went to Pidoli,* and on the way home I stopped over at the mosque to say my prayers. That's where I heard the district chief say that the Controleur has ordered everyone to haul a cubic meter of sand for the government.[3] You're not allowed to have one grain of sand less or more than that—not so much as a little finger's worth over or under. Every time we turn around we have to go and do corvée labor it seems. One time it'll be for the *kuria* district; another time it'll be for the godown. When are we supposed to get time to make a living and grow food and buy clothes for all the kids? Well, pal, what I say is, it's better just to go to Deli. We can't take it much longer here in this realm. Look, last week we got a letter from our younger lineage mate saying that they'd opened up some garden land for new dry fields up there in Deli. He said that we should just to move up there and that way we'd be able to make a living. Surviving's easier up there—why, we can see that from our friends who've come home from Deli. Everyone's always going back and forth. I haven't budged, but here they come, carrying their wooden suitcases, ready to set off again.

DJ. T.: Well . . . I guess all that depends on a person's luck, whether moving to Deli's a success or not. Hard to tell. I'd say folks are luckier right here. It's easy enough to eke out a living.

---

*A town outside of Padangsidimpuan on the way to Mandailing.

DJ. S.: True, true . . . but don't forget, as the saying goes: we have to be the ones to lay down a good, solid roadway so that all that good luck can find its way to us! But how is that supposed to be possible here, when they hit us with corvée labor duties all the time? From now till Judgment Day no one will really take our welfare into account here in this realm. Look what the Malays say: you better work hard at finding a way for your predestined fate to come to you. And what do you think? Will you really be able to put up with hauling all that sand every day, pal? It'll peel the skin right off your backbone! And, look, the kids only have one set of clothes to their name—which will, of course, get ruined. Friend, I think it's better just to move to Deli.

Taring's Mom was delighted to hear what they were talking about. Consequently she quickly laid the sticky rice snacks and the hot coffee in front of them.

DJ. T.: So what did the district chief say? Didn't he try to defend us in some way?

DJ. S.: Well, you know how it is with that raja. . . . He answered by saying that we had just *had* some corvée obligations a little while ago, but that didn't hold any sway with them. I guess they thought it was better for the general public to get hit with the corvée than for them and their friends to. After all, the raja himself was afraid when that proclamation was issued.

DJ. T.: "Ah, well . . . that's the truth," he said, bowing his head. "Let's drink our coffee, eh, or it'll get cold. Taring's Mom, did you remember to put sugar in this coffee?"

"Now, how would I get that? There's no white sugar. But if you want some red palm sugar, all right, I'll bring it."

DJ. S.: God above, now you want to give us sugar, too! When you're having such a hard time of it. We don't need any, don't worry.

And because he couldn't resist the delicious scent of the sticky snacks he pulled the treats toward him and began to eat.

DJ. T.: Hey, bring some of those here, poor excuses for food can still taste pretty good, I guess, just as long as we're still drawing breath.

The woman came in from the kitchen, bringing them the sugar. She laid it down in front of them. "Now, eat your fill, Djasiala. When it's time for the corvée labor you sure won't get anything as delicious as this in your rattan satchel.[4]

DJ. S.: Yeah, that's sure the truth. . . . This really does taste good. Ah, this will fatten me up and maybe give me two more big folds in my belly!" he said, sipping his coffee. "Eerh . . ." he said, clearing his throat. "If I keep getting food like this it'll lengthen my life for sure."

After they'd eaten their fill of rice snacks they laid out their tobacco supplies and had a good smoke. And then, with regard to migrating to Deli, they decided it would be best to take along all their children so that the families wouldn't be split up as they tried to make a living. It was very late at night, so they decided to go to sleep and then later think about what they would do. They would be discussing these things with the women, too.

After Djasiala had gone, Djatoeba asked his wife what she thought about what Djasiala had said. "I think it's a great idea. Let's just hope they don't back out on us."

"Okay, fine, I was real glad to hear what they had to say, too. It's best that we just migrate, so they won't have a chance to put your name on the corvée labor list. That'll be something else to present obstacles," said the woman.

After Djasiala and Djatoeba and the women had made up their minds they went to the office of the Panyabungan Controleur to get their passes, to walk to Deli.

17

Sitti Djaoerah
Goes to Deli

Even after Djahoemarkar's letter arrived Sitti Djaoerah remained downcast. She grew increasingly heartsick, finding that she couldn't sit still nor get a good night's sleep. She would wake up unrested, while Nandjaoerah for her part looked quite the same. Both felt extraordinarily upset and out of sorts.

Early one morning it was almost 9 A.M. but Nandjaoerah and her daughter had not yet got around to cooking their breakfast. In fact, they were pretty much letting everything slide. There weren't very many people in the marketplace yet. The chickens were going "*ko-tek, ko-tek,*" getting ready to lay some eggs, while an occasional young rooster was crowing "*ta-ta-hu-ak!*" And that mournful sound just served to make them think even more morosely and pensively about the one they knew so well, off in Deli.

"*Resss . . .*" said Nandjaoerah, rising to go to the market to buy some vegetables to cook in case they perhaps might feel like fixing a meal. All the way to the market she was in a dream, her feelings dominated by pain. She got to the main road and searched in both directions, but she couldn't turn up any vegetables. She glanced over toward the road near the river, and there she happened to see two men walking along, slowly and laboriously. They were fishmongers, and she figured they'd probably gotten a decent catch from the Girl River. So she waited for them to pass by on their way to market.

Once the men got close, Nandjaoerah called out to them: "Now, where are you two going, I wonder? Oh——Djatoeba? Now, you've never come along this way before. What gives?"

"Oh, well, you know, Older Lineage Companion, life's getting harder and the corvée labor is getting to be such a problem. You'll get one corvée task done and then you'll get socked with another. So we thought over how hard life is here in this realm, and it occurred to us to go to Deli along with all our kids. We'll try to make a living there.[1] Why, right now we're going over to ask for official passes. Djasiala's going along, too."

"Are you serious? No, don't joke around, okay?" said Nandjaoerah.

"Allah, you think we'd try to trick you?"

"Well, in that case, my friend, just come over here a minute so I can say something to you," said Nandjaoerah.

"Now what? If you have a lot to say we'll be late for our office visit for sure."

"Now, my friend, just a little bit ago our dear son sent a letter from Deli, saying that he was having a terribly hard time there. We told him to come home, but he didn't want to. So, I said to myself, we should just go and find him up in Deli. What are we doing *here* if he's in trouble *there*? So, if you're serious about what you say, could you also please ask for passes for me and my daughter, too, so we can go with you? I'd feel more comfortable embarking on such a journey if you had all your little children along."[2]

"Well, I guess so, all right—but look, are you sure there won't be anything to prevent you from leaving at the last moment?"

"But who could stop us? I'm going off to search for my child in Deli, aren't I? Who is better to do that than me? But even though I say that let's keep what I'm saying here a secret. So once you get the passes come right over to the house so we can arrange all the details."

"Well, all right, then, we'll ask for your passes," said Djatoeba.

As Nandjaoerah was going home she bought some sticky rice treats and some fried bananas so the two men would have something to go with their coffee when they came to the house later. Then she went home.

"Oh . . . Djaoerah . . . get the water to boiling, you hear? Two men are coming over later. Right now they've gone over to ask for the Deli passes. I've already asked them to get us ours, all right? If nothing occurs to prevent us, we'll be leaving this week."

"Oh, Mother, really? Really?" said Sitti Djaoerah, but in a carefree way. "It won't be a problem, traveling with just men?"

"Oh, it's all right, their wives and little kids will be coming along, too. So, our trip will be fine," said her mother.

"Well, Mother, all right then! Let's hope nothing gets in the way," said Sitti Djaoerah. At almost 1 P.M. Djatoeba and Djasiala arrived, as they had promised. Once they got inside the house they showed them the full set of passes.

"Where are they? Let me look, okay?" said Sitti Djaoerah, reading them over. "Oh . . . so this is what passes to Deli look like, do they? Well, good, neat! So when do we leave?"

"We're already trying to calculate a lucky day to leave, never fear. If nothing comes up we'll leave in three days. So get all your stuff together. Sell whatever you need to, so you'll have some cash for living expenses. We know you're going on this journey because of the pain and trouble you're in, so we wouldn't want you to be hard up for money on the way," said Djatoeba.

"All right, good idea, but so folks won't suspect that we're going along with you we'll set off at dawn in the carriage and wait for you at Malintang's rice stall. And don't you set off in your carriage too long after we have, all right? Don't worry, I'll pay the transport fees for you all the way to Pargarutan. We mustn't be spending a night between Mandailing and Sidimpuan, you see," said Nandjaoerah.

"Well, all right. If that's the way you want to do it, that's a great idea. And the little kids will surely appreciate not having to walk all that way. Once we get to the Padangbolak Road, we can all go real slow, and we'll just have to get to our destination whenever we arrive, I guess," said Djatoeba.

They went home to Aek Godang after their coffee and told their wives and children about their decision. Everyone had great hopes of not getting too tuckered out once they heard about the pony carriage.

Djasiala and Djatoeba had sold all their things, but Nandjaoerah decided not to so people wouldn't find out that they were going to Deli. They'd just leave their things behind and carry what they could.

To make a long story short, on the appointed day Nandjaoerah paid a carriage driver to leave Panyabungan at dawn, and they made him promise not to tell a soul that they were leaving. "And, look, if anyone asks, just say we're going over to Sigalangan to go visit a new baby who's just arrived.[3] Your carriage is only going that far, after all."

When they got to Malintang's rice stall they stopped and got out of the carriage and ate a meal. At about nine o'clock Djatoeba and Djasiala's own carriage arrived and pulled to a stop. They all ate a meal together. Sitti Djaoerah could rest easy once she caught sight of the men's wives; with companions like these they would have nothing to fear, she was sure.

After they had eaten they hitched up the vehicle again and set off. All along the road Sitti Djaoerah thought how very wild and threatening the deep forest was. She understood how dangerous their trip had been way back in the past once they had gone by the Mosquito Bridge again. She saw all the monkeys hanging from the bridge's crossbeams. "So *that's* what we saw that time; apparently Djabargot wasn't lying after all."

And that is how their trip went that whole day, until finally they got to Sigalangan. Once there, they stopped for a meal at the rice stall near the bridge. While the womenfolk were enjoying their wads of betel Djatoeba and Djasiala went off to find another carriage to take them to Pargarutan, one that would depart that same evening. The driver wouldn't agree to the trip unless they upped the normal fee since they would be traveling at night.

"No problem. Just as long as we set off tonight," said Nandjaoerah.

The guy hitched up the carriage after they had agreed on a price. They put all the kids and the gear up on top, and then Djatoeba and Djasiala got in, followed by Nandjaoerah and her daughter, and finally by the two men's wives. Then they set off.

They got to Sidimpuan at 11 P.M. They pointed the carriage toward the Sipirok Road. There was a good deal of bright moonlight, so everything in the Other-Side Market could easily be seen, although no people were passing by. There was only a night watchman who asked where they were going, but he let them go when he saw their passes. When they saw Djahoemarkar's house Sitti Djaoerah whispered to her mother: "Come on, let's go see if they're there."

"Oh, what's the use, that'll just make us feel bad. Just look, the garden's all overgrown with weeds, and the house is in disorder. That's a sure sign that nobody's there to take care of it," said Nandjaoerah.

"Oh . . . Mother, how, how awful," sobbed Sitti Djaoerah, but her mother muffled her daughter's sobs so no one would hear and try to detain them. They just went on by the house quietly, following the first carriage on toward Pargarutan.

When they got to Djatimboran's rice stall, they knocked on the door to wake folks up. Once they had rousted the householders out of bed they went on into the stall, taking along all their things from the vehicle . . .

"Wouldn't you like to eat a meal? We've still got rice, you know," said the householders.

"That can wait till tomorrow. Just roll out some mats on the floor so the children can get some sleep. They're real tired," said Djasiala.

"Well, all right," said the householder, unfurling some mats. Then everyone fell asleep from exhaustion. They woke up at dawn and went to bathe at Aek Sitorbis, and after that they returned to the rice stall. A fine meal awaited them there, which they proceeded to eat. They divided up the costs afterward and paid the bill. They also paid for the carriage, for the driver was ready to go back to Sigalangan.

After all the bills were paid they walked in the direction of the Padang Bolak Road, for they wanted to be sure to spend the night in Saromatinggi. "Goodbye . . ." said Djatoeba. "May you have a safe journey," said Djatimbor, who took them out to the highway. Getting a good grip on all the gear they were carrying, they set off for Padang Bolak, and finally, at last, it seemed real to them that they were really, actually, going to Deli.

The men carried satchels over their shoulders and balanced other gear on their heads while their wives lugged some of the smaller children in cloth slings on their hips. And Sitti Djaoerah and her mother were weighted down, carrying their things the same way, so they all set off, walking along slowly.

They got to Saromatinggi at 6 P.M. and stayed overnight in a rice stall there. Sitti Djaoerah was unbelievably sore from the trip, for she had never walked so far in her entire life. But that didn't really bother the girl. All of this just made her more diligent at her task, for she was sure that once she got to Deli she would be seeing that love-medicine guy of hers. So she was always ready to get under way when one of them would say: "Okay, let's start walking." She didn't mind whatever sort of work she had to do along the way: carrying a small child in a sling, balancing goods on her head, or slinging a burden on her back and supporting it with straps—she'd do it all happily, whether it was her stuff or someone else's. So people just became even more fond of her.

Nandjaoerah behaved the same way, so nobody had the least bit of resentment against them. Nandjaoerah treated Djatoeba's kids and Djasiala's kids as if they were her own. It was like that every day of the trip. When they'd come to a village they'd stay overnight; after all, there were mothers and little kids on this trip, and, of course, they couldn't go very far. Sitti Djaoerah's feet were swollen and blistered and her forehead was peeling, but she didn't complain to anyone. She just felt that they were not getting to Deli fast enough.

To make a long story short, after they had walked about a month, passing through fields and forests, fording streams and rivers, and traversing swamps with boats and ships, well, finally they got to Balawan, and from there they went straight to Medan.[4]

In Medan they spent the night at Malim Patience's rice stall on Moskeestraat. They stayed there two or three days, in fact, recovering from exhaustion. Sitti Djaoerah wanted nothing but to lay eyes on Djahoemarkar; she didn't pay a bit of attention to how lovely and crowded the city of Medan might be. She needed only one thing: that guy. But they had not heard one word about him all the time they had been in the city. She kept all this inside her, though.

Once they were no longer quite so worn out and their blistered feet and peeling foreheads had returned to normal, Djasiala said: "Well, so what should we do? Should all of us go to Deli Tua to find our younger lineage mate and from there go on to look for your son?"

"It doesn't much matter, but if we go to Deli Tua I think that will make things more difficult for us, not to mention more expensive. So I think it's best that you folks just go on ahead and we shall stay right here in Medan and look for him. Because, after all, the postmark on the letter said Medan. If we don't find him the first month we'll come looking for you, and then we can figure out what to do next," said Nandjaoerah.

"Well, all right. We're not adverse to leaving you right here, for, after all, this rice stall is owned by close family of ours. So we'll just put you in their good hands, and if you don't succeed in finding that son of yours the rice stall owner can bring you to our place in Deli Tua. If you can send a letter to us we'll even come and get you."

"Very fine," said Nandjaoerah, for she was developing more and more trust in Malim Patience and his ability to help them find Djahoemarkar.

So after they had reached their consensus Djatoeba and Djasiala and their wives and kids all went off to Deli Tua to look for their younger lineage mate, leaving Nandjaoerah and her daughter in Medan to plot strategy.

18

In the Delilands

One time it happened that Sitti Djaoerah was sitting there, perched on the windowsill on the street side of the rice stall, gazing out at the busy thoroughfare.[1] Many different sorts of people were passing by, a pleasing sight for contented people. But for Sitti Djaoerah things were not like that. After all, she had yet to encounter the one she sought. She sat there morosely, rubbing her chin, perched on the pillows laid out atop the windowsill. When Nandjaoerah noticed this, tears began to flow down her face. Straightaway she asked her daughter: "Well, now, what do you think, Djaoerah? What can we do to find that guy faster, do you think?"

"You know, Mother, I had a dream last night, and in this dream I climbed up into a big leafy banyan tree. It was full of fruit. I had a terribly hard time climbing up to the top of this banyan, for it had many treacherous, deep folds on its trunk and a multitude of scary biting beasts at its base such as snakes, bees, and stinging wasps. I felt I was surely risking life and limb to scale its heights."[2]

"And so what happened, my girl? Did you make it to the top of the banyan tree?"

"I did, Mother, and once I got up there I sat upon a big branch and I wasn't afraid at all anymore. I felt just perfectly happy and content," said Sitti Djaoerah.

"So what do you suppose that means? What shall be our fate?" asked her mother.

"Well, I don't really know. But I say that from this moment on we must begin to devise a plan so we can locate Djahoemarkar as quickly as possible."

"But what do we know about devising plans like that? Chasing after him upriver and down! Why, we can't do that, being women.[3] And we don't know anyone around here who might help us. So, all told, I must say I simply feel at a loss."

"Well, look, why don't you go downstairs for a moment and just ask the owner of this rice stall if anyone named Djahoemarkar has ever come here? I'll wait here at the front windowsill—though I surely don't want to just give passersby something amusing to look at, I have to admit," declared Sitti Djaoerah.

"You're right, girl. Let's think hard about what to do so as to locate him as quickly as possible."

After her mother had gone on down the steps Sitti Djaoerah looked out the window upon the city of Medan once again. But Djahoemarkar's image did not appear. "Oh——Almighty God, please, please make this man I surrender my *tondi* soul to appear before our eyes so that we may be released from this unceasing suffering."

And "*tap!*" went her hand, as it accidentally fell onto the pillows piled on the windowsill. She lightly rubbed the pillow casing with her hand, and all of a sudden the faint shadow of Djahoemarkar's signature appeared there. It seemed he had signed his name there on the pillow with a pencil. It was very difficult to read what was there, though, because folks had rubbed their hands back and forth on top of it so much.

But employing much patience, Sitti Djaoerah was finally able to read the following words.

To whomever should read this letter

I hope and pray to be freed from my great suffering. If I should die, please convey word of that to Sitti Djaoerah, in Panyabungan.

Wg. Djahoemarkar

The letter cited a day and month six months ago. All this just ended up saddening Sitti Djaoerah more than ever. But even so she did not lose all hope, for here was a sign that he had actually been here. And so she herself wrote out a small message, right below Djahoemarkar's name.

I have come to Deli searching for you. Come and fetch me. Whoever should happen to read this letter, please convey that message to Djahoemarkar if you should happen to meet him.

Wg. SITTI DJAOERAH

After she had finished writing the letter her mother came up from the first story to say: "Well, someone named Djahoemarkar did come by here, but only one time, and since then they haven't encountered him again."

"Oh, that's quite true, Mother, look here: he wrote a letter right here on this windowsill cushion, saying that he came by here on April 10, 1904."

"Where?" asked her mother. "Oh, my goodness . . . but that was so long ago. Who knows where he's gone to now."

"Well, look, Mother, I see that the rice shop owner here subscribes to the newspaper. Let's ask his help in placing an advertisement in *Pertja Timoer*[4] saying that we're looking for Djahoemarkar. That way we can find him fast. And other folks who read the paper will want to help us, too. They'll want to tell us where he's living, and then as soon as he knows where we are he'll come and get us. That's the easiest way to locate missing persons," declared Sitti Djaoerah.

"Well, so what sort of words should we put in our ad?"

"Well, these! 'In search of a man named Djahoemarkar. We ask whomever might happen to encounter him to inform same that his parent has come to Medan. From me, NANDJAOERAH.'"*

"But what if the newspaper owner isn't willing to publish it? What then? What will we do then?"

"Oh, he'll want to. The editor's one of us; he's our sort of folks, after all. He'll take pity on a poor woman—especially one who is willing to put up fifteen cents per word."

"Here, look: here's a copy of *Pertja Timoer*. It says its editor is Mangaradja Silamboee. If he's named Mangaradja, well, that clinches it: he's our sort of folks for sure,[5] especially since it's Silamboee, too. He must be one of the Silamboee people from over in Greater Mandailing."

*The text of this advertisement is in Malay in the original.

"Well, Mother, go fetch the rice shop owner so I can give him the money. How much to you think we should give him?"

"Oh, give him five rupiah to start. If that's too much he'll give you the remainder back."

"All right," said her mother, standing up and then going down the stairs to get Malim Patience. Arriving at the bottom of the steps, she said: "Please help us place this advertisement in *Pertja Timoer*, would you, so we can find the man we're seeking as soon as possible."

"Why are you putting it in the newspaper? What do you say to just telling the police?" asked Malim Patience.

"If we tell the police it will be like we're searching for some big criminal. This way everyone's real friendly. Once the newspaper comes out word will get around. And everyone in Deli who reads the paper will see the ad. Everyone who reads it will take pity on us, and the public will help us search for him."

"Oh, well, true enough," said Malim Patience. Then off he went to the *Pertja Timoer* office, at J. Hallerman Publishers on Kesawan Street (which is called Varekamp nowadays).[6]

As he was on his trip to the newspaper office it occurred to Malim Patience what a very smart girl Sitti Djaoerah was—and what very nice handwriting she had, too. "You know, I do think she's a cut above the average. My gracious, what she's written here is so pretty. Why, she could even be a secretary (a *schrijver*) in the office of the Resident himself, I declare."

Once he reached his destination he went straight to the office of Tuan Administrator. He asked that an ad be placed in the paper, one just like the example he had brought. And he handed over the five-rupiah fee.

"Fine," said Tuan Administrator, "but let me give you a ringgit back. It costs just one ringgit to place an ad."

He gave the advertisement to the newspaper editor so that it would be published that very day.

Once the editor Mangaradja Silamboee caught sight of the name Nandjaoerah immediately he realized that the advertiser had to be a Tapanuli woman—and he thought, with considerable sympathy, that they must already have gone to a great deal of trouble in searching for that son of theirs. He put the advertisement on the front page in very large letters so that people would see it right away. Moreover, he put it into the city news too—in a little story headed "New Advertisement." This said:

Today on page one there is an advertisement that I hope the public will note with care. Please do try to come to the aid of the woman who placed this ad by telling her where the man she seeks is living. —Ed.*

Once the newspapers rolled off the presses, straightaway they were dispatched by the twelve o'clock post from Medan to all four points of the compass and to the eight great village domains all around: the the whole metropolitan area.

---

*This text is in Angkola Batak in the original.

The newspapers dispersed like a huge flock of birds throughout the city of Medan and the surrounding areas, and the public read the ad. However, no one in Medan knew anything, although everyone diligently asked around.

Dear Reader. . . . Let us now turn our attention to the Parsaulian Onderneming, where Djahoemarkar is working. All the while he's been getting one promotion after another. He went from being *crani bangsal* to the *crani* of the godown and from *crani* of the godown to *crani* no. 2 of the whole enterprise. This was simply because everything he did pleased Big Tuan there on the plantation. Everyone else also thought quite well of him, too, most especially the Crani I. The latter made Djahoemarkar his younger brother, his younger lineage companion.

Abdoelmoetolib is what people called Crani I—a popular and well-regarded man on all counts. And on the day the advertisement appeared the newspaper *Pertja Timoer* certainly paid him a visit: for, as it happens, the *crani* always remembered to send in his subscription fees to the newspaper owners on a regular basis. When he got to the office he hadn't yet cracked open his paper since he had been quite busy that day. This was the time when he had to mail in the account books to the *maatschappy*. So he was back home before he read the paper. Then he immediately caught sight of the advertisement. After reading it he mulled over its words and then called for Djahoemarkar. "Now take a look at this ad from your Mother, who's apparently searching for you. Why in the world didn't you send them a letter telling them where you were living? Honestly, they've had to come all the way to Deli, looking for you. Have you gone and forgotten your parents or something?"

"*Sarrrr . . .*" said Djahoemarkar's chest, swelling with surprise. He had not seen the advertisement yet, but he said to himself: "Has Mother come back to life, since the paper says she's come here? Or is someone just playing tricks on me? Never, for as long as I have been here, have I heard of the dead coming back to life. But, if God has fated it to be, anything can happen, I suppose. He created things out of nothingness, so I guess he can make the dead come back to life, too."

"So, Djahoemarkar, why are you still musing to yourself so quietly? Read it so you'll know for certain if they really are in Medan and you can go and get them. Even if it means that things will be crowded and rather difficult here in the house at least they'll be with you," said Abdoelmoetolib.

"*Hoooi . . .*" said Djahoemarkar emotionally, quite moved, as he read the advertisement. As soon as he saw Nandjaoerah's name at the bottom of the notice he realized that it was not his mother come back to life at all but Sitti Djaoerah and her mother who had placed the ad. "It's true that our Mother has come, but it's our Nantulang,* you see, since my own mother has been dead for a long time. That is why I was so quiet a while ago. But it's all the same, anyway, since she's really just like my own mother to me. So, if it is all right, may I have a leave for tomorrow so I can go and get them in Medan? So they won't have to rent lodgings for too long a time? If I knew exactly where they were I'd go and get them right now. But the *Pertja Timoer* office is closed for sure now, so I can't go and ask where they're staying."

"Ah, now why didn't they say where they were so that we'd know? That's a woman for you," said Abdoelmoetolib.

*Our mother's brother's wife, the mother of the woman I should marry.

After they'd finished talking Djahoemarkar went back to his house. What his exact thoughts were we cannot hope to fathom. However, they were about as follows: "Now, why did she come here to Deli? Did Sitti Djaoerah come along, too? Is that child all grown up by now? Or has someone run away with her and married her? Can that be why her mother's come here? To tell me that? What's really going on? If she left that child behind in Panyabungan, wouldn't folks there be able to convince Sitti Djaoerah to go and marry somebody?" He mulled over all this. Tomorrow he would discover the truth.

That night Djahoemarkar had a hard time falling asleep. The one night seemed to last a whole year. Finally he said: "If Sitti Djaoerah came along as well, that shows she really loves me—to throw her life away, coming to Deli, looking for this broken old body." Thanks be to God, Syukur Alhamdulillah, his eyelids finally got heavy and he drifted off to sleep. He did not awaken till dawn.

Once it got light they went over to the main office of the plantation. As soon as Big Tuan came in, Crani Abdoelimoetolib approached him and said: "Tuan. . . . If at all possible, may Djahoemarkar have a day's leave since his parent has come searching for him and is in Medan now. Look at this ad here, Tuan. See how much trouble they have gone to?"

"Why didn't they come over here immediately? They didn't know Djahoemarkar was here?" asked Big Tuan.

"No, apparently Djahoemarkar didn't send them any letters."

"Well, all right, then, go. We wouldn't want them to have too hard a time in Medan. Here's some money for his travel costs. He won't owe me anything; just let this be my way of helping him out."

Djahoemarkar acknowledged his shortcomings immediately: "Just a while ago, Big Tuan, I did send them a letter telling them I was alive—I had no idea they would actually come here. But now that they have arrived I do sincerely hope that Tuan will help provide a living for all of us," said Djahoemarkar, accepting the money Big Tuan was giving him.[7]

He climbed into a horse carriage and headed toward Medan. Once he got there he went straight to the *Pertja Timoer* office. He asked the employee there if he could possibly meet with the editor, Mangaradja Silamboee.

"Well, please wait a moment. What exactly do you need?"

"You just say that the man they were searching for in the advertisement has come in, all right?"

"Oh, fine, so it's you, is it?" said the employee, going up the steps toward the editor's office. Once he got there he said: "Your Honor![8] The man we were looking for in that advertisement has shown up. He's down below right now. If he can, he'd like to talk with you."

"Well, tell him to come in—thank heavens it was so easy to locate him," said the editor.

"Come on up," said the employee.

"All right," said Djahoemarkar, going in to stand in front of the editor. Djahoemarkar had no more than caught sight of him when he lowered his head and offered a respectful greeting.

"So, have you had a chance to see your mother yet?" asked Mangaradja Silamboee.

"Not quite yet, Respected Sir, but after all I have just arrived. That's why I've come, in fact, for I don't know exactly where they're staying."

"Astagafirullah. . . . Yesterday I totally forgot to ask them in whose house they were staying! I forgot because they didn't come here themselves but sent someone to do their bidding. Well, look, what can I say——? What close family do you have here in Medan?"

"I really don't have anyone, Respected Sir. That's why I am in such difficulty now. What in the world can we do to find them? It wouldn't work to just go around paying visits to people's houses. That's why I ask you for advice about what plan to follow."

"Well, let's do this: let's place another advertisement. It can go like this:

To Nandjaoerah, who placed yesterday's advertisement: Please come to the *Pertja Timoer* office tomorrow morning at ten o'clock. Today Djahoemarkar has come, but he does not know where Nandjaoerah is staying. Djahoemarkar, too, will definitely be there at the aforementioned hour. —Djahoemarkar.

When they'd agreed on that Djahoemarkar went home to the Parsaulian Onderneming. His emotions were running high. He passed right in front of that rice shop, but he had no idea that they were there. So he walked right on past. For her part, Sitti Djaoerah was gazing out at the street in front, but she was not paying careful attention to the people passing by, especially since there were so many of them striding back and forth, every which way, in front of her. It did seem to her that she may have caught sight of Djahoemarkar's comely visage. But she didn't really know for sure.

Once Djahoemarkar got back in the Parsaulian Onderneming, the guy embraced him out of worry and pain.

"So, what gives? You didn't see them?" asked Abdoelmoetolib.

"Oh, I don't know, Older Lineage Mate. The editor tells me that they didn't come to the office with that advertisement themselves but sent someone else, and this guy didn't say where they were staying. So I've placed another ad, asking that they come in to the editor's office at ten o'clock tomorrow. So maybe Older Lineage Companion can get me another day's leave so I can meet them as soon as possible."

"Ha, ha, looks like you're just chasing each other around, doesn't it? But, listen, just have patience, you'll get together all right. And don't worry, tomorrow I'll tell Big Tuan about all that's happened," said Abdoelmoetolib.

The next day Crani I conveyed all this to Big Tuan. On hearing it, Big Tuan nodded compassionately and said he was sorry to hear about it all. . . . "They sure show themselves to be women here, don't they? Placing an ad but neglecting to put in the details so that folks end up having to pay twice. Go tell him to be sure to keep his promise on time."

Abdoelmoetolib sent word to Djahoemarkar's house that his leave had come through: "Go on, and be quick about it, so you get there at the time you promised.

Let's not make them hang around like a bunch of bondswomen in the *Pertja Timoer* office."9

And as for Nandjaoerah and her daughter, there they were, still waiting for word from folks about where Djahoemarkar might be living. This was especially true after they saw the editor's special notice in the paper. But it had been two days now, and still no news had come. Because of this they had almost given up hope of finding out where the man was living. At noon the newspaper carrying Djahoemarkar's ad appeared. As soon as the paper came Malim Patience opened it up so that they could see what might have happened with their own advertisement—and suddenly there was Djahoemarkar's own ad, right there.

Malim Patience carried the paper gaily up to the second story. "Look at this ad! It's a response to ours. It seems that our child came into Medan yesterday, but, of course, he didn't meet us. We should have specified where this place was! That was our mistake, and it meant that he just had to go on back home."

Once Sitti Djaoerah had read what was in the newspaper she said: "But tomorrow he'll come back. He's asked that we come to the *Pertja Timoer* office at ten o'clock to meet him. If it's God's will, please don't let him go changing his plans on us! So, what do you say, Mother? Wasn't it easy to find a missing person through the newspaper? We've only had to shell out a ringgit, and now we've found the one we've been seeking. Yesterday, you know, I happened to see a fellow pass in front of this rice shop. His carriage was going so fast, though, that I didn't see exactly who he was. I didn't recognize him, but that must have been him. We'll have to ask him whether or not he passed by this house. Tomorrow, you'll have to get dressed and be ready real early so we can set off. We should be waiting there for him, you know, so we don't overshoot the appointed time. Go ask Malim Patience's help again so he can accompany us on our trip. After all, we don't know where we're supposed to be going."

Nandjaoerah descended to the first story and said: "Perhaps you can help us, Malim, by taking the time to accompany us tomorrow to the newspaper office. We don't know where it is ourselves. Why, we haven't so much as set foot out of this house so far."

"Fine. Why, I'd help anyone in such a case, and, of course, I'll be even more happy to come to your aid. Let me just ask Si Oepi's Mom* to be the one to accompany you there."

It was barely the crack of dawn when Nandjaoerah said: "All right, go change your clothes to something nice so we can leave. Malim's wife will serve as our companion."

"Now, what should I do?" Sitti Djaoerah asked herself. Should she change her clothes? A voice inside her said: "If I get all fancied up, folks will think I'm putting on airs. And then, too, maybe Djahoemarkar is down on his luck these days. What should I wear? If I don't change my clothes from these I have on, maybe folks will ignore me." She didn't know what to do.

"Well, all right, so be it!" she said, and simply stuck on some regular old clothes. They were newly cleaned but certainly nothing fancy.

---

*His wife, referred to here with typical husbandly obliqueness.

"Oh! You know, maybe you could just see your way clear to put on that green outfit, my little woman-friend. C'mon, don't go showing our poverty *too* much!"

"Ha, ha. . . . That's right," said Oepi's Mom.

"Oh, all right," said Sitti Djaoerah, going back in to change her clothes once again. She put on an elegant, flowered Pekalongan sarong, and her *kebaya* jacket was made of fine cloth all the way from Paris. She strung a gold medallion around her neck; it was big and round like her row of gold jacket clasps. She hung gold ornaments from her ears and covered her head with a *gersik* scarf (that is, one from Surabaya). She descended the stairs to the first story. "Well, let's go so we won't be late," she said with a sly little laugh.

"Ha—— so she's got herself all dudded up in the good old style we see back home! Her figure's hard to beat, too. Now, whose girl could *this* be, do you think? Why, even here in Medan one doesn't find teenage girls this good looking. She's light skinned without wearing any face powder, creamy colored without using turmeric on her face, her cheeks are red without the least bit of food coloring—and her figure's the one she was born with. Amazing! Lucky not many folks are about on the roads at the moment or all the *cranis* from the offices would stop dead in their tracks to get a good eyeful, I do believe," said Si Oepi's Mom.

"Well, come on, let's get under way," said Malim Patience, and they started off toward the *Pertja Timoer* office. When they got there Mangaradja Silamboee was standing at the office door.

"Now where exactly might all you be going, walking along together like this, I wonder?" said the distinguished elder.

"Kind Sir, these are the people who placed the advertisement in question. They have come in because they saw Djahoemarkar's ad yesterday, the one that asked them to come. So I have brought them in," said Malim Patience.

"Well, that's just fine. Djahoemarkar will be along in a moment. Please just wait here if you would," said Mangaradja Silamboee.

"Thank you, Respected Sir. I certainly must say I have a great deal of sympathy for her, what with just one son and one daughter. And the son has now been away for over six months and hasn't sent word about where he is. That's why they've gone to the extent of coming here to Deli to look for him."

"Oh, so that's what happened, is it? Well, yes, that's right, he did come in yesterday and he did promise to come in today at ten o'clock. You know, if you had only said where you were staying you'd all have been able to see each other yesterday. Now isn't that right? When I see this child's face I can see Djahoemarkar's face, too, it's no different. It was definitely him who came yesterday," said the editor.

At two minutes before ten a carriage (a horse and buggy) arrived from the direction of the Goldenberg Store. A man was sitting atop the buggy, facing toward the back. In front of Mayor Tjong Apie's house he glanced toward the *Pertja Timoer* office and saw someone there wearing a lacy headscarf, Tapanuli style. He had no doubt: he knew it must be them. He stepped out of the carriage and started walking. It was one minute to ten.

Sitti Djaoerah looked up at the clock on the wall and saw that it was one minute to the promised time. "Oh, let me just go take a peek outside while they're in here chatting. If he's going to keep our promise he must be close by now."

"*Tap!* Their eyes met, and each smiled.

"There he is, Mother! Let's go say hello," said Sitti Djaoerah.

"Where? Where?" asked her mother, looking outside, and as soon as she caught sight of him she sprang forward and caught hold of him. "Yes, yes . . ."

So, young man, apparently we *do* get to meet," she declared, stroking Djahoemarkar's cheeks and chin softly with her hands. Sitti Djaoerah's hand quickly caught hold of Djahoemarkar's. They wept for joy at seeing each other again. After Mangaradja Silamboee had comforted them a bit he said, "*horas, horas.*" They told him to go on back to his work, and he said: "Once you've healed your longings for each other, you all must come over to our house in Sungei Kerah so we can all share a nice meal."[10]

"God will repay your kind thoughtfulness, Respected Sir," they told him as they turned to go back to Malim Patience's rice shop.

When they got there Djahoemarkar said, "Allah! What a pity! I passed right by here yesterday, but I didn't know this is where you were staying. That's why I went straight home."

"And I saw *you*, too, yesterday, but since the buggy was going so fast I couldn't see you clearly. I thought to call out to you, but then I remembered that we're in other people's home territory here, after all, and we have to be a bit cautious," said Sitti Djaoerah.

"You folks go on up to the second story so you can chat more comfortably. People will be coursing back and forth down here," said the *malim.*

"All right," they said, and they went on up.

When they reached the rice stall's upper story Nandjaoerah said: "Oh my, you got pretty tired looking for us yesterday, didn't you, young man? If we hadn't all fulfilled our promise to meet we'd still be in big trouble, wouldn't we, since we forgot to say where we were staying. But, look, now we've succeeded in getting together safely, so you two must eat a meal. Let me go downstairs and fetch the rice."

"No need for that, Mother, I just ate," said Djahoemarkar, but nevertheless Nandjaoerah hurried on off to get the rice.

Actually Nandjaoerah's aim was to leave the two of them alone so that they could satisfy their longings for each other when no one else was around. After her mother had disappeared Sitti Djaoerah threw herself at Djahoemarkar, she had missed him so much. Just talking to him wasn't enough.

"Oh, c'mon, you're behaving like a kid," said Djahoemarkar, catching Sitti Djaoerah in a hug and then sitting her down.

After a bit, Nandjaoerah came back, toting along a big rice meal and coffee. She didn't forget to cough softly at the door, either, so they wouldn't be embarrassed at getting caught kissing.[11] But, what can you say. . . . There never was the least embarrassment between the pair of them, not in the past nor now. So they just pretended that her mother had not seen them.

"Here, now, please have some of this good food, young man. After all, it's been so long since we all shared a meal."

"Come on, then, Older Lineage Companion—our mother's gone to such trouble to fetch a meal for us from the first floor. And, after all, we'll have to pay for it later no matter what," said Sitti Djaoerah.

"So, what are we to do, eat again after we've already had one meal? But, well, okay, so be it. But let's have our mother share this with us so she won't have to just run up and down the stairs bringing us rice. This is surely enough for the three of us," said Djahoemarkar.

"Well, all right," said Nandjaoerah, and all three of them dug in.

As they ate their meal Nandjaoerah intensified her scrutiny of Djahoemarkar's behavior. She scrutinized his feet and his hands, and they were soft and smooth, just like the hands of the Resident's fine clerk. Then she thought back to what Djahoemarkar had said at the *Pertja Timoer* office: that he had a day's leave from work. So, although Djahoemarkar wasn't dressed in a suit like a salaried office worker, still, she suspected that he had managed to find a job. In fact, she had no doubts any longer; just looking at him sitting there her doubts vanished and her soul returned contentedly to her body.[12]

After chatting a bit about things back home Nandjaoerah said: "So, then, young man, let me just say this much! A while back your letter arrived, telling us about your sufferings and difficulties here in Deli, and, well, as soon as we heard that your little lineage companion and I immediately made up our minds to come looking for you here—even if our path had never been trod by human feet before. Thanks to your kind, good prayers, we did indeed succeed in getting here, and we've all found each other. I'm so happy about this, just incalculably happy. Thanks be to God that we have been afforded the chance to meet once again. Now we are all together—but what exactly shall we do to support ourselves?"

"*Sarrr . . .*" said a tear from Djahoemarkar's eye. He was feeling his pain and suffering from before. So he just bowed his head and kept quiet, not giving her an answer. Seeing this, all of them burst into tears, and Sitti Djaoerah immediately scooted over and laid her head on his shoulder again. This as much as said: "Let me simply hand myself over to you now, I have no regrets, my life and death are in your hands."

All was silent. Not a thing stirred at that moment.

"Ohhhh . . . ," said Djahoemarkar, breathing forcefully in and out. Then he said: "Not a thing I said in that letter was a lie, but, well, it did fall short of saying exactly how bad it was so you two wouldn't feel too much pain at thinking about it all. But, c'mon, now that you've come to the Delilands to find me, isn't that all we need, Respected Mother? Doesn't that make things okay?"

"Young man, now, don't you go on about our difficult trip, either. That was simply God's will, after all. You don't need to support us royally, you know—we endured all those hardships so we'd be able to come here to keep you company, so that none of us would die all alone.[13] Whatever can impoverished people do, after all, young man? Even though we may have to pay room and board and live in somebody else's house, like poor folks, don't you go regretting any of this. So, since you're all grown up now and so is your younger lineage mate Sitti Djaoerah—from the time she was in diapers, to the time she went off to school, to the day before yesterday, Sitti Djaoerah has always been the same. Why, look, we took off and ran away from Sidimpuan, throwing our fate to the wind, coming here to Deliland. And we did all of this out of love for you. So, because of that, according to law at least, I don't think there are any obstacles left! I think it's best that we simply make you into an adult, married man so there'll be no obstacle in our way as we try to eke out a living here in other people's land. And here you both are, so what do you say?"

"Allah, most Respected Mother, what you say here strikes me as being as heavy and weighty as the wide earth, as deep and distant as the far sky! What I feel is that my little lineage companion here is still like a sibling to me not a girlfriend."

"Yes, well, listen: siblings will stay siblings, certainly you know better about that than me. But, look, really! What's wrong with what our mother is saying here? After all, what was it you promised me out in the White River that time when you were in there netting fish?" asked Sitti Djaoerah.

"Well, look, even though I really don't have a possession to my name, Respected Mother, let me just try to find us a house with cheap rent so you'll have a place to live. And let me take care of your living expenses. Why, I'll just become a coolie! I'll keep an eye on you here, don't worry," declared Djahoemarkar.

"No, no, young man, I simply cannot agree with what you've said here. If we can't all live together, what good was it that we came all the way to Deli? So, listen, don't worry about it—if we die, at least we'll all die together, won't we? And if we survive, we'll survive together. Even if you don't have any way to make a living we'll just put our heads together and come up with something. Why, even if we just sell fried snacks and little bunches of boiling vegetables at the market, God will still provide for his faithful, poverty-stricken servants, rest assured. But, so matters won't be difficult, we'll still have to get you two officially married first."

"Well, if that's what you have to say, what more is to be done? So, I guess, go call Malim Patience and his wife so we can ask their help and seek their agreement, for it's getting late in the day. And here, here's some money to pay what you owe for staying here all this long time," said Djahoemarkar, counting out a handful of coins.

On hearing Djahoemarkar's words and seeing the coins he was counting out, Sitti Djaoerah lifted her head from his shoulder and said: "So what do we do now?"

Nandjaoerah stood up and called for Malim Patience and his wife, and not long afterward they came up. When they had taken a seat Djahoemarkar declared: "Well, now, Father, and so, too, Mother, since you have helped out the respected elder here for so very long a time, and so, too, come to her aid in finding me, we would like to convey our formal words of thanks to you. I believe I am not able to repay you with labor contributions or fine riches, so let me simply call upon our Almighty God to recompense you properly. May you stay hale and hearty, may your luck continue to be good, may your living expenses be easily met, so we can visit back and forth with you at frequent intervals. Now, then, indeed, Honored Father, since it is getting on toward evening we shall just set off for my home, and, rest assured, when we have the free time we shall immediately return here for a visit."

"Oh, no, I should think it best that all of us just stay put here for a while. Why, we haven't even had a chance to share a simple meal of rice and boiled cassava leaves, and here you are taking off already," said the *malim*.

"Thank you so much, but, as I said a bit ago, Kind Father, when we have the time we shall certainly return for a nice visit, just as long as we all stay healthy!"

"Well, all right, if that's your firm decision, then. But you must come back real soon."

"Now where, exactly, is your residence, young man, so we'll know where you are?" asked the *malim*'s wife.

"Why, it's near here, at the Parsaulian Plantation," said Djahoemarkar.

On hearing what Djahoemarkar said Nandjaoerah rejoiced. So, once Malim and his wife had gone down to the first story Nandjaoerah handed over a big wad of bills to them. No telling exactly how much was in there, but it was over seven hundred guilders. "Here's the money we've earned during all this long time; please just take it, as I can't care for it anymore. We don't want to attract insults; we earned this money to pay for our upkeep."

After Nandjaoerah had concluded her dealings with the *malim*, and after they had all forgiven each other for any and all transgressions, Sitti Djaoerah asked Djahoemarkar: "Do you have a job? If you're just sauntering about aimlessly maybe it's best that we all just stay right here and sell little things from a stand on the street, what do you think?"

"I have a job, Younger Lineage Companion, don't you worry, although I admit my salary isn't all that big yet," he said.

"Well, if that's the case, just why did you keep feeding us all those elaborate answers a while ago? Is it maybe that you're not satisfied to eat what I cook for you? Even though in the past you were the one who told me that just a few drops of my sweat falling onto your pile of rice was enough to make a fine meal for you?"

"Ha . . . that was just harking back to hard times, Lineage Mate," said Djahoemarkar, brushing Sitti Djaoerah gently on the shoulder to shore up her confidence.

"Well, we've got all our bags packed and our debts have been paid, so let's get under way," said Nandjaoerah.

"All right," said Djahoemarkar, going on to call for a horse and buggy. Once all their things had been piled in the carriage they climbed atop the vehicle, too, and set off toward Parsaulian Plantation. What Sitti Djaoerah saw and felt as they made their way along Kesawan Street can hardly be recounted here. We'll just leave that to the Reader's imagination.

After about an hour's trip they arrived.

Crani Abdoelmoetolib and his wife were awaiting the arrival of Djahoemarkar and the ones he had gone to fetch. Djahoemarkar's carriage was no more than barely visible when they all came out to give them hugs. As soon as they got down out of the carriage the *crani*'s wife took them by the arms and tugged them along happily to the house. Once inside, they were offered betel quid so that they'd have a chance to chat about their trip.

"Well, Honored Mother, so that I might know our proper kin terms, who exactly is this blooming young girl that you've brought here?" asked the *crani*'s wife.

"Oh, why, she's my very own daughter: Djahoemarkar's childhood companion and schoolmate. They've been together since they were tiny; that's why they're not the least bit shy around each other."

"Oh, look, it's already time for sunset prayers. Let's go fetch some prayer water for our ablutions. Come on, Little Lineage Mate Djaoerah, let's go and bathe so you don't get too overheated," declared the *crani*'s wife.

They ate dinner after saying their evening prayers, and they did not feel the least bit embarrassed around each other. There was no hesitation, no shyness: it was as if they were already married.

Abdoelmoetolib and his wife were very happy to see the good character, speech, and manner of the pair of them and to see how well they interacted with their children, too. They were just a model of good behavior for Abdoelmoetolib and his wife's children, right from the start.

After they had all chatted awhile Nandjaoerah recounted the details of their journey. "And, well, now that we've located him, now that he's here with us, I must throw myself on your mercy, asking your kind advice about what should most properly be done. I ask you, Mother, and you, Father: I am the mother of a teenage son and I find myself, too, the mother of a pretty teenage daughter. These two have grown up under my guidance; they have been in my hands. And, even though they show no shyness toward each other, let's not have any difficulties here. And so, because of that, what exactly do you advise that we do?"

Abdoelmoetolib answered, "Ha, ha . . . well, now, whatever should I say? If my two little lineage mates have already reached a happy consensus on this, then that's a fine thing now, isn't it? Maybe it's all right that he just came here to Deli, first, before you two did, so you'd have someone here to seek. So, then, indeed, whatever common consensus is reached here to carry us all toward a good end, why, that is the very decision I shall support and balance happily upon my hand!"

"Ah, indeed, to go along with what she has said—why, it is just as your son has said; it's better they do get married so no one takes it all amiss. And even if he's only a mere *malim*, look, let's just call him over to the house here so he can perform their marriage ceremony, all right? So we can make my younger lineage companion here into a grown woman," said the *crani*'s good wife.

"Well, indeed, then, if that is to be our common consensus then let's determine an auspicious date for the ceremony. But since it's late at night let's just get some sleep first." They all slept in the *crani*'s house, but as for Djahoemarkar he went over to the house next door, to Abdoelmoetolib's, to sleep. And that night Sitti Djaoerah and her mother slept soundly, for they had found the one they sought.

As is normal in all *ondernemings*, folks went to work at 5:30 in the morning. So by 4:30 all the people on the plantation had already gathered in a big group. The same, of course, was also true of the *crani*. Drum no. 1 had no more than beat out its first notes when he had gotten up and gone to say his dawn prayers. Then he got dressed, and when it was light enough to barely see the branches on the trees he left the house to report to work. And all the coolies, both the males and the females, and the crew chiefs, and the little *tuans*, and Big Tuan, too: all of them came out of their houses to go along to their jobs. Because everyone had gathered there to start the day, Sitti Djaoerah and her mother woke up, too. They noted how very neatly the *crani* was dressed as he set off to work. Using that as a pretext to say something, Nandjaoerah asked: "So, Honored Father, is this how you dress each day to go to work?"

"Why, yes, Good Mother. It's not like working for the government where you can just go into the office as late as eight o'clock. This is what we have to suffer through to make a living and buy our food, you know—although folks back in our home country think we have it real easy here in Deli."

"*Gap, gap, gap . . .*" said the voice of everyone's shoes, walking along the ground. Not long afterward voices were heard, saying "Come on, Older Lineage Mate! It's almost time. Why did our Mother get up so early?" asked Djahoemarkar.

"Well, it's just that we're so taken aback to see all this. Apparently this is what you do every day here," said Nandjaoerah.

On hearing that, Sitti Djaoerah came out of the house, too, but she didn't join in all the friendly chat since the *crani*s had all gone off to their offices.

"Mother, who was that friend you were talking to?"

"But, that was your Older Brother. Over on the left is the *crani* from this house here, and Djahoemarkar is over on the left."

"So why did they go to the office so early in the morning?"

"That's what's customary here," said her mother.

"Oh, indeed, they probably find it easier to work if they get an early start, I guess." But, as for Sitti Djaoerah's eyes, they just remained fastened on the man she loved. When she looked at his shirt and trousers and his shoes and his jaunty felt cap from far off Johor, she noticed how they all fit Djahoemarkar's body exactly. "Oh . . . Lord, how good looking he is. I'll wager those clothes are in the Cronfield style, you know. Looks to me like this young fellow's job is a pretty darn satisfactory one. A good thing, too! That's what we were hoping for, after all, before, when he was still an assistant schoolteacher. So, then, good morning to you, handsome Older Lineage Mate,* said the girl to herself.

Not long afterward the *crani*'s wife awoke, too. "So, good morning, Mother!" she said. "Let's go bathe so we'll be refreshed when the sun finally comes all the way up."

"Fine, fine," said Nandjaoerah, getting her prayer veil.

After taking her bath and saying her prayers the *crani*'s wife went into the kitchen to start cooking the rice. For her part, Sitti Djaoerah tagged along to help. But the *crani*'s wife prevented her: "There's no need for that, Little Lineage Mate, don't wear yourself out. Why, we don't have anything fancy to cook for curry anyway."

"But, Older Lineage Companion, should I really just sit around when there's work to be done? Should I be acting this way when I need to learn how to cook?" asked Sitti Djaoerah.

"So . . . you're worried because you don't know how to cook yet?"

"Ha, ha . . . I guess you'll have to teach me. Cooking styles are different here from what they are at home," declared Sitti Djaoerah. As they cooked along they

*This is the standard term of address girls use with their boyfriends.

clanked utensils together, as Sitti Djaoerah set her hand to the frying pan, the coconut grater, and the grinding stones for peppers and spices. In fact, she took hold of every sort of utensil they had stored away in the cabinets.

The *crani*'s wife was taken aback by how able and smart the girl was, so she just let her go about her tasks.

"Come over here and chew some betel," said Nandjaoerah to the *crani*'s wife, "until such time as I can rock my little grandchild in his tight cloth sling, all right?[14] I didn't get my fill of seeing you last night when we first got here. I need to see you more to assuage my loneliness and longing for you. Now, why don't you just let your *anggi* attend to the cooking?"

"Oh, gracious . . . you'd have me allow newly arrived guests cook all the meals?" But even though she said this, since Sitti Djaoerah was apparently doing fine, she let her go about the cooking anyway.

Once the rice and curries were done Sitti Djaoerah ladled the food onto big plates and stored them all away carefully. She had prepared everything, the whole meal.

"Well, thank you, Little Lineage Mate! I had no idea you were such an expert cook. I have noticed that many girls who've just arrived from our home country are still unruly and troublesome, but you're really up on things."

"*Gap, gap, gap,*" said the voices of people's shoes, entering the front of the house. "Well, the hearty eaters have arrived. Let's carry the rice and all the fixings out into the central part of the house."

"Everything's ready and stored away in the hutch—come on in and have some coffee," said the *crani*'s wife. And in came Abdoelmoetolib and Djahoemarkar.

"So, Good Mother! This is how folks who live in Deli do things. Let's eat so we can have a good friendly time here all together, shall we? Things taste better this way," declared the *crani*.

"Oh, you go ahead and eat first, before we do, Honored Father," said Nandjaoerah.

"No, no, let's all eat together. After all, don't we still miss each other's company?" said Djahoemarkar.

"Oh, Lord—all right, all right. Let's go, Djaoerah," said the *crani*'s wife.

"Now, don't you be shy, Djaoerah. Make sure to eat a lot, you hear? You got so tuckered out on your long journey," said Djahoemarkar.

"Oh, don't worry, I'll eat a lot, all right. On the journey we just took often we wouldn't get to eat regular meals or rice all that much. Though somehow we stood it," said Sitti Djaoerah.

And so it was that Abdoelmoetolib and his wife simply laughed and laughed to see how well the pair of them got along and how little shyness they seemed to have around each other. So they were all having such a good time chatting happily that they didn't really keep track of the fact that they were getting pretty darn full. Their bellies got stuffed, by accident.

"Well, we sure ate a lot didn't we?" said Abdoelmoetolib, setting his tobacco supplies in front of him.

"I tell you, this rice tastes as good as it does because a young person cooked it," said the *crani*'s wife.

"Wow, so you're already quite a good cook, aren't you, Sitti Djaoerah?" said Djahoemarkar, stealing a quick glance at the girl out of the corners of his eyes.

"Yep, she cooked everything we ate here," declared the *crani*'s wife.

"Oh, golly, you guys would say that a whiff of hearth smoke tasted good. Come on!" said Sitti Djaoerah with a shade of embarrassment.

After they had finished eating Abdoelmoetolib and Djahoemarkar stepped out of the house and went back to the office. However, they had gotten no further than the front yard when the *crani*'s wife said: "But what about what we talked about last night? Have you forgotten it? Our good mother has already got her hair-bun combed and patted down, so if we can find a good free day let's just get them married, all right? Wouldn't that be appropriate, even if they are just like two kids who share the same father and mother?"

"We mulled that over this morning—but we have to wait until tomorrow, you know, to get an auspicious day. We already telephoned[15] all the relatives, so they'll flock here to the wedding tomorrow, and we also called Malim Patience and his wife. So I guess you should get to work rinsing your rice for the big ceremonial meal, and maybe we should go looking for a goat for the ceremonial mound of special blessing foods, too.[16] I didn't tell you all this earlier because we hadn't had a chance to gather all together. And then, too, the ceremony wouldn't be till 11 A.M., so we've still got lots of time to arrange all the festivities."

"Well, okay, okay, if that's the case. Let me just go tell all the relatives here on the plantation, so they won't be caught totally by surprise tomorrow."

When they got back to the house Nandjaoerah asked them how the discussions had gone.

"They have examined all the particulars, Mother, and the ceremony will be held tomorrow, barring obstacles. And they've placed orders for everything we need for the wedding ceremony. And all the kinfolk from Medan have been invited."

Next morning, by about eight o'clock, the guests began to arrive in droves. And so did all the wedding supplies, everything pouring in at once. After the guests had been given some coffee to drink everyone set their hands to their respective tasks. No one got distracted; all the women and menfolk toiled along with great dedication and diligence. After all, they had known Djahoemarkar for a long time by now and everyone wanted to help out at his ceremony as he had at all of theirs. No one took a cigarette break while there was still work to be done, preparing for the wedding.

To put matters briefly, all the festive foods were cooked by eleven o'clock and everything had been ladled out onto the wide serving mats; the elaborate mound of ceremonial foods, which would be presented and read to Djahoemarkar, was also laid out in readiness. The fine ceremonial mound of molded rice, too, had been carefully stored away. All the religion teachers and the village elders had been called to the house to go up into the building and sing Malay *sanji* songs and beat the tambourines. Sitti Djaoerah and Djahoemarkar had been told to put on their wedding finery.

Once they had been sprinkled with holy water, and Arabic prayer phrases had been recited over them, and all the things associated with that had been accomplished, Djahoemarkar was formally given a seat in the front part of the main room so that he could be ceremonially inducted into adulthood and thereafter would sit among the married adults of the village. As was the custom, Sitti Djaoerah was formally questioned about whether she agreed to be presented to the village elders as a newly married person along with Djahoemarkar. Sitti Djaoerah answered this in a polite and comely manner in front of all the witnesses: she announced that she was in perfect accord. At that point Djahoemarkar pronounced the formal marriage phrases, and all the proper prayers were said. After they had prayed Sitti Djaoerah was taken by the arm and escorted into the room and made to sit down next to Djahoemarkar, to his left. The mound of ceremonial food was picked up lovingly like a baby and placed on a mat in front of them, and then the elders spoke all the appropriate words over the special food to the young pair. And, as the eldest honored father in attendance, Malim Patience made the first speech.

"Well . . . what then, indeed, Djahoemarkar, and so, too, *parumaen?** To speak in acknowledgment of my son's bride's fine arrival here from the far home country we have gathered together here in formal congress, according to *adat* and law. Indeed! That has been our *adat* custom, from our grandfathers on to our fathers, when it comes time for sons or daughters to be married. So, indeed, we are not planting new fields of custom here, no, no, indeed: we are just following the time-honored practices. This is the reason we have seated you here in front of the village elders on this fine day; and at the same time we present you with the ceremonial mound of festive food. This is your *tondi* soul's blessing gift, the blessing gift, too, of your bodies, so that you might be prosperous, fertile, and rich. Now, everything on this ceremonial mound of food, from its foot to its head, carries its own special name. So! So that all of us might hear what the fine words have to say, here we have: cooked rice, close-packed carefully into a pyramidal mound, and a hard-boiled chicken's egg, not to mention Arriving Safely Rice. These good foods all ask that riches and wealth might be packed tightly into your union and that your *tondi* souls might stick hard and fast to the inside of your bodies and not go wandering around loose throughout the countryside! And here is Arriving Safely Rice, which hopes that you might be prosperous, wealthy, rich—and may you safely grow into mature, responsible adults, here in front of the village elders as your onlookers! May the two of you be of a single consensus, of a single agreement, so that you may attain whatever you seek. May you go through the air in a single jump and be of a common footstep, too, so that you will get what you are searching for. May you go upriver together as a unit and downriver as a team, rising upward together, falling toward the ground at once, just like the torch ginger's globular fruits, packed together as a ball of tight lumps. May you definitely not be like the horns on a Lopsided-Horns Water Buffalo, which has one horn pointed toward the sky and the other pointed toward the ground![17] And then, too, don't be like the awkward strides of a person walking along with his legs flailing in two directions at once! Neither should you let yourselves argue with each other, like the jaws of a horse when it yawns, the upper set of teeth going to the right, the lower set to the left! So, indeed, I mean to say, may you receive this ceremonial mound of food with both your *tondi* soul and your body.

---

*My son's wife, daughter of my wife's brother.

Palupalu ni mengmeng	Beat the little shimmering gongs
Godangan palupaluna	This little food mound is rather modest in size
Na menet dope pangupa on	as yet, we well realize
Nai godang pasupasuna.	But the blessings it conveys are huge.

Sai tubuan laklak ma hamu jana	May little bits of tree bark flourish,
tubuan singkoru	and Job's Tears grow.
Sai tubuan anak ma hamu jana	May sons be born to you, and daughters, too.
tubuan boru	May we always be able to gather
Sai mamora ma hita lagut anso	in common meetings like this
dalan muli gabe.	so that we all remain prosperous.

Horas . . . horas . . . horas . . . !" said absolutely everyone in the house.

And then the pair ate the ceremonial mound of food and they were joined in this, in consuming the rice mound, by all of the people seated nearby. That is, by Abdoelmoetolib's wife and her children and Malim Patience's wife and her children.

Once those consuming the ritual rice had gotten quite full the family members in attendance were finally given a few old boiled leaves or so to eat—you might say. Well, actually, no one got left out, everyone got to eat their absolute fill of delicious festival foods. Djahoemarkar's wedding feast went off without a hitch, all the attendees went away happy and satisfied, and not a single plate or cup clinked or clanked together noisily. For any excesses or insufficiencies in the relating of this event I most sincerely ask the public's indulgence: remember, I am spinning a tale here.

Sitti Djaoerah Saves Djahoemarkar's Skin ~ And Rescues Him From the Enemy

After Djahoemarkar had sat among the married men and women for about a week Abdoelmoetolib, Djahoemarkar, and all the good wives got together and talked things over. They came to a decision: since the path was clean and clear for the bride to make contact once more with her kinfolk,[1] now was also the time for Djahoemarkar and her to be set up in their own separate household. Actually, they would simply move back to his old house. Abdoelmoetolib, of course, remembered all the particulars of the *adat* customs for setting newlyweds up in their own household: he made sure they moved into the house complete with full sets of dishes, cups, cookpots, and rattan mats.

Nandjaoerah was quite overcome by all this generosity; she had no idea the *crani* would be so very generous. Why, she felt that he was already doing more than enough by simply helping Djahoemarkar to get married. So, given all this kind behavior, she raised her hands to the heavens and asked that Almighty, kindly God might repay Abdoelmoetolib for his many generosities. For she knew she was inadequate to the task herself.

Well, all right, now let's take a look at what kind of life Djahoemarkar, Sitti Djaoerah, and her mother were having. Before the pair got very far into their married life they set themselves a certain challenge and aspiration. This was something they felt they must do if they hoped to be safe and sound on their journey into married adulthood.[2] That is, they made up their minds to heed the words of three old sayings:

1. Be mannerly toward life, resistant of death.
2. Let your eyes be your teachers, but also be sure to read conditions over carefully in your mind.
3. If you walk along with your eyes wide open, pointed toward the sky, a cinder is bound to fall into them, but if you keep your head down, with your eyes carefully fixed on the ground before your feet, you're sure to find something of value along the road.

Djahoemarkar wrote these old sayings in huge letters all around the inside wall of their house. That way they'd be reminded of these three proverbs night and day.

And as for their lifestyle? Well, they didn't live like rich folks, true, but they always got along well with each other, and what little food they happened to have they'd always stretch into big, satisfying meals. When they happened to have lots of food in the house, well, they just feasted and got all fattened up! So everything just went along in a quite moderate and balanced way. Other folks didn't notice them suffering or celebrating one way or the other—no, they were just like a corn stalk growing in poor soil, not too plump and fat but then not too skinny, either.

And, as for Nandjaoerah—the good woman so adept at pleasing her son and daughter-in-law—she didn't go about trying to set the rules of the house. She was not one to lord it over anybody. She realized that they were married now, and if anything needed fixing, well, they'd just fix it themselves. She also didn't want to be too bossy and obstreperous and go about pointing out any faults or mistakes they might make. She'd just set to correcting any mistakes through example, and she always endeavored to speak very frankly to the pair of them, to forestall any hard feelings. So consequently Djahoemarkar and Sitti Djaoerah came to see her as an *adviseur* (that is, someone who shows good ways of doing things) for them there in the household.

As for Abdoelmoetolib, well, even though it was true that Djahoemarkar and Sitti Djaoerah had gone through the formalities of being set up in their own separate household, away from his place, that certainly didn't mean that he had cut all his ties to them. No, indeed, he treated Djahoemarkar like his own younger brother, like his very womb lineage mate.[3] They remained quite close, interacting on a daily basis. In fact, it's fair to say that they shared a common dinner plate, they shared a single meal.

And Sitti Djaoerah, the woman who knew how to take the exact measure of things: she always took care to be polite and observe all the amenities. Even though it was quite true that she was a new person on the plantation (and her social position was modest) she always paid proper respect to folks and caused them to respect her as well. So consequently, if she happened to have some free time from work, she wouldn't just flit off to friends' houses to hang around and chat. No, casual rumors around the community will make people find fault with you. She certainly didn't want to be like the magpie, always flying around the countryside spreading rumors from one branch to another. She was also not the sort to offer false praise to folks who hadn't done anything to deserve it—she didn't go in for empty talk. Whatever she'd say she'd follow up with firm action. She detested the notion of going around currying favor with people or showing off. She fully recognized the fact that that was not the way to behave well.

She considered Abdoelmoetolib's wife a good solid friend in whom she could put her trust. She didn't offer her empty praise just to curry favor with the woman; rather, whatever sort of task she could appropriately perform as a help to her older lineage companion, Sitti Djaoerah would go right ahead and do it. In the morning Sitti Djaoerah would send word over to their older lineage companion's house to send one of her little kids over so that Sitti Djaoerah would have a companion. But her real aim was to give Abdoelmoetolib's wife a bit of peace and quiet so she could have time to prepare her husband's meal.

There was one other important precept that Sitti Djaoerah followed: when in someone else's *adat* domain, do as they do! Follow their *adat* and customs so that you're walking along in step with them. She figured she had better find out about the languages and manner of speaking that folks used there on the plantation so that she'd be able to interact with them. So, since she was so adept at getting along with the people there, she soon learned how to do all the different sorts of work tasks there and she knew how to get along with the Javanese and the Bandung folks as well.[4] Why, she treated them all just as if they were from the same home village. She decided she needed to learn the Javanese and Sundanese languages. So whenever she'd hear something she'd write it down in her notebook, and then when she had some free time she'd memorize the phrases. Soon she would know them all by heart.

And so, because the girl was so smart and diligent at this task of hers, it wasn't too many months before she knew how to speak these languages, albeit just conversational Javanese and Sundanese. She knew how to mimic their precise accents and speaking rhythms, and no one would have suspected that she wasn't a native Javanese or Sundanese woman if they were to hear her chatting away with her Javanese or Bandung woman friends.

And she also emphasized the practice of dressing in the Javanese or Sundanese style and wrapping her sarongs the way they did. So, if she should be going to the big work gang overseer's house, or wherever, she'd always be turned out quite carefully in the appropriate clothing. And Djahoemarkar was the same way: for the entire time he was on the plantation he would always be studying those languages and he'd take considerable pleasure in dressing in the Javanese style. This was especially true when he would attend someone's *kenduri* communal prayer meal.[5] Then he'd get himself outfitted in a short suit coat, a Javanese sarong, and a long formal shoulder cloth. In addition to this, since the plantation didn't have a real religious expert in residence (they just had minor teachers with slapdash knowledge), Djahoemarkar would be the one to say the prayers when folks would have their prayer meals. He would sing the chants and say the recitations in a subtle, smooth form of Arabic, and folks took to calling him Mas Kaji.[6] In sum, they did nothing to displease their circle of friends, there on the plantation.

And so it went, it could be said: as day after day went by, the more she saw, the more she knew. The more diligent she was at studying her surroundings, the more she learned. The nicer she was to people, the more friends she made; the more polite she was to others, the more respect folks had for her. And Djahoemarkar was the same way.

One day, an advertisement appeared in the *Pewarta Deli*[7] newspaper. It read:

Wanted: An experienced *crani*, knowledgeable in all plantation business, who can work in the main office in Medan. Salary starts at fl. 125, house provided. Mature, experienced person preferred. Please submit letters and appropriate certificates and work permits to the *Pewarta Deli administrateur* or simply report in person.

As soon as Abdoelmoetolib caught sight of that ad he knew he had the job in hand. He had everything they were seeking. He was certain he would be their number one candidate for that position. How could he miss? As soon as he got home he explained all this to his wife and told her that he had great hopes of getting that job. "Look, if it comes through it'll be like killing two birds with one stone, for I'll try hard to insure that Djahoemarkar gets chosen as my replacement. He'll get a big promotion, and we'll get a big raise—and get to live in the city and work in the main office."

"That'll be great if it all works out. I guess you'd better go ask for the job as soon as you can, so we can see how it all might turn out," said the woman.

"All right, if you agree, I'll send in the application letter tomorrow. But just keep it a secret, okay? If I don't get the job I'll be embarrassed if people are in on the plan beforehand." So the next morning he wrote out his application and sent it right away to the *Pewarta Deli administrateur*. As soon as the latter received it he showed the application to the *tuan* who had placed the advertisement.

"Well, this certainly came in quick enough. Give it here so I'll know what to think," said the *tuan*. Once he saw the letter and noted how long the guy had been on the job, he sure didn't have to discuss things at length: he knew this was the man. "Oh, this is just fine. Ask him to come in and see me so we can talk, and I can advance him a loan to get started or whatever he might want," said the *tuan*.

The next morning the *Pewarta Deli administrateur* sent an answer to the letter, asking that Abdoelmoetolib come to Medan. If he couldn't make the trip during the daytime he could just come at night.

When Abdoelmoetolib received the letter he read its words and immediately smiled and gave a little laugh. Then he dashed home to tell his rice spooner what was in the letter. "Ha—*got* it! I've got the job, Little Boy's Mom! Later this evening I'll go into Medan to meet the *tuan*. Let's wait till I get back to tell Djahoemarkar about this bit of good luck. So enjoy the news and just have patience for a bit more," said the *crani*, and then he went back to the office.

To make a long story short, as soon as he left the office at 5 P.M. he changed his clothes and set off for Medan. Upon getting to the city he went looking for the *tuan* in the Hotel de Boer, room no. 10.[8] He told the hotel bellboy that he was going to talk with the *tuan* from that certain *maatschappy*. The bellboy conveyed this message to the *tuan*, and as soon as the latter heard that Abdoelmoetolib had arrived he came right out and greeted the *crani* with formality and politeness. Abdoelmoetolib received these greetings with the proper measure of respect. After discussing things and after Abdoelmoetolib had promised to take the job the latter asked to borrow fl. 400.

"Well, all right, I certainly trust you. When do you think you can start work?"

"If Tuan Maatschappy could perhaps give me a lead time of fifteen days before I start that would be good. That way I can find myself a replacement and I won't inconvenience Big Tuan, nor will I inconvenience you, Tuan Maatschappy."

"Fine, fine, do what you need to so we can get things under way as soon as possible," said the Maatschappy.

"Yes, Tuan," said Abdoelmoetolib, bowing his head. Then off he went back to the Parsaulian Plantation.

"So, did you get it?" asked Uncok's Mom.

"Sure did! Here, put this away, it's a loan of fl. 400. Hide it someplace safe so it doesn't disappear. And go call Djahoemarkar and ask him to come over here so we can talk."

"Great!" said the woman, going off to call Djahoemarkar over to their house.

"What do you need, Older Lineage Companion, coming over here so late at night? All right, come on, let's go," said Djahoemarkar, standing up to go. Once he got to Abdoelmoetolib's house he asked the latter what was so pressing that he had to be called over here like this so late at night.

"Younger Lineage Mate, the door of good luck has opened before us. Take a look at this advertisement. I've already checked into the job on the quiet, and hopefully, with your kind prayers, I shall be getting this new position. I've just returned from Medan after talking to the *tuan*. Now, look, Younger Lineage Mate, I would like to turn my job of *crani* on this plantation over to you. I'll tell Big Tuan tomorrow that you should be selected as my replacement. Now, just rest easy; don't get too shook up. I've already seen that you can do the work."

"That's great, wonderful! But do you really have faith in someone as ignorant as I? And then, too, what if Tuan doesn't agree to all this when you tell him tomorrow? What then? But, then, if somebody else replaces you, frankly, well, it will be as if you've set us all loose in the deep dark forest to fend for ourselves among the dangers there."

"Ha, ha, you just let me make that decision myself. I've often talked about you with Big Tuan. So don't be anxious; he'll agree readily enough to whatever I say to him tomorrow. I'll still be here for fifteen days more, and I can teach you the ropes. Now, don't worry; I'll teach you the job."

"Well, all right. If you say I'm up to it, Big Tuan will go along with things," said Djahoemarkar, now with considerable hope.

"Now listen, you don't have to tell your younger lineage companion or her mother, our mother's brother's wife, about our conversation here. Who knows, bad luck might befall us or someone might put a curse on us and all of this might not come off. If they expect something to happen and then it doesn't they'll be peeved for sure. But plans that are in accord with our *tondi* souls, well, it's just like the old saying puts it: 'Big, big dragonfly, even if there's some disagreement folks can still be compatible.'"[9]

"Well, look, we'll just have to put it all in God's hands and hope that our plans come to fruition," said Djahoemarkar. Then he went on back home. As soon as he got there Sitti Djaoerah immediately asked him what had been so important for him to be called out to the *crani*'s house.

"Oh, you know, figuring out how to keep the coolies in line so they don't act up too much tomorrow," said Djahoemarkar.

Djahoemarkar took great care that night going to sleep so that his dreams would tell him what was going to come to pass in the future. The next morning, no later than 5 A.M., when the palm fronds were just starting to unfurl, people started to flock out of their houses to go to work. Djahoemarkar was already dressed and ready to set off for the office.

"Oh . . . Djahoemarkar, come on, pal, the bells are ringing on us here," said Abdoelmoetolib.

"I'm coming," said Djahoemarkar, stepping out of the house.

"So what did you find out about your future in your dreams last night?"

"Ha, ha, I don't know! I have no way of making sense of it because I saw so many things that would occur!" said Djahoemarkar.

"So many things, like what?"

"Well, I dreamed I was out fishing and I was catching a lot of fish. But only big golden carp."

"Ah, well then! You can rest easy in that case. You'll be getting that job for sure. I myself dreamed that I was handing you a great number of logs of wood," said Abdoelmoetolib.

After they got to the office they each began their work, and not too long afterward Big Tuan appeared, looking happy. After a moment or two, after they had gotten all the really pressing business done, Abdoelmoetolib went into Big Tuan's room, greeted him respectfully, and then said: "Big Tuan . . . when you get a moment free I hope we can talk a bit, but let me say that if any of this displeases Tuan I apologize in advance. I hope Tuan will not get angry with me."

"Now what in the world? Tell me what you have to say if it's good news. Why would I get mad at you?"

"Well, all this long time I have been very happy working here alongside Big Tuan. You've given me a lot of valuable lessons, not to mention affection. But, since I have come upon a promising way to make a better living, I hope that with Tuan's help I can succeed in getting that new job. Here, look. . . . Here's an advertisement seeking a mature and experienced *crani* who has worked for a long time on a plantation. Does Tuan feel that it might be a good idea if I go asking for this job, so that I can have a better way of supporting my little kids?" asked Abdoelmoetolib, thrusting out the ad.

"Ha, ha . . . and what would be wrong with that? I'll help you as much as I can. And, in fact, I know this *tuan* who's seeking help. But, look, who's going to replace you?"

"Thank you, Tuan. As for my replacement, what about Djahoemarkar? You don't have anything to worry about in terms of his knowledge of the job, I can guarantee that. He's up to all the various parts of the job. If I can get half a month with him I can show him all the necessary management ins and outs. In short . . . I guarantee it: he will be well up to the task of replacing me."

"Fine, fine. . . . Actually, I think the same thing. Well, look, here, take this letter of recommendation to the *tuan*, so that he gets it on time."

"Thank you, Big Tuan," said Abdoelmoetolib. Once he had the letter in hand he sped back home, and then the both of them went right over to Djahoemarkar's house to tell everyone what had happened that morning.

"Good Mother's Brother's Wife," said Abdoelmoetolib, "now I suppose we don't have to keep hunkering down behind our index fingers nor taking shelter and hiding behind our second fingers: we can just speak frankly and tell you what's been happening. I am going to move to Medan to take a new job there, so I can get a larger salary. And we've already told Big Tuan that my younger lineage mate here must be my replacement. And the upshot of the whole discussion was that he agreed that Djahoemarkar would take over my job. Now, that should please you."

They were quite taken aback to hear all this, especially Sitti Djaoerah. But she didn't have to think long before saying: "Oh Lord, but won't that mean we'll be separated? Who'll keep an eye on us here? Your little lineage companion here looks like a grown woman in a physical sense but she really doesn't have her wits about her, you know. Folks might just neglect us and not care anything about our welfare. What then?

"Now, now, never fear: a *crani*'s luck is like the luck of the great rajas.[10] If Djahoemarkar's able to bear the burdens of the job then his social station in life is high enough. And, listen, I'll be close by in Medan, and I can come and check on you if you get into difficulty. We'll be able to meet all the time, don't you worry."

Well, I guess if that's the situation it's all right then. It's just like the old saying goes: 'One swing of the axe but you hit two trees, two swings at the trunk and two of them fall down.' That's how I feel about your promotion, I do declare."

That morning Sitti Djaoerah carried over the rice she'd already cooked to Abdoelmoetolib's house so that they could all eat together. After they'd finished Djahoemarkar went back to the office and Abdoelmoetolib went on into Medan with Big Tuan's letter of recommendation and also to tell the man that he would be spending the next fifteen days teaching Djahoemarkar the job so that everyone would feel good about the situation. Upon arriving in Medan he showed the letter to Maatschappy Tuan, and he declared what day he intended to start work.

"That'll be fine, but, look, so that your present boss doesn't get mad at you, you just rush on home now and start teaching your replacement the ropes."

And what was Djahoemarkar doing? Once the *crani* had left for Medan he went back to the office. Big Tuan was there, and he called Djahoemarkar into his office to talk. "So what do you say, Djahoemarkar? A door of opportunity has opened up for you, now, hasn't it? All this long while you've been working here I've wanted to do you a good turn and help you out, but there didn't happen to be any available openings. Well, look, I hope my affection for you is not misplaced. Study hard so you can learn the new job. I'm sure you'll move up in the ranks quickly."

"Just as long as Big Tuan is willing to teach me I shall work as hard as I can to learn the job, I assure you. But since I've just been promoted I hope that Big Tuan won't get put out if I happen to make some mistake or other."

At eleven o'clock Djahoemarkar went home and told his mother's brother's wife and his wife all about what he and Big Tuan had discussed.

"Syukur Alhamdulillah, and may the Almighty continue to show His mercy to us in our lives of suffering here. Ah, this new job will be a grand avenue to good luck and good fortune for we who have endured so much pain all this long while," they all said together.

To summarize things, the next morning, after Abdoelmoetolib had returned from Medan, he set to teaching Djahoemarkar his new job right away. Abdoelmoetolib instructed him in everything he didn't know. Djahoemarkar was quite an apt pupil and learned fast. In fact, in about a week he had the job pretty much under control. So Abdoelmoetolib didn't have much to do but stand there and watch Djahoemarkar do his job during that last week. At the end of this period Big Tuan asked Abdoemoetolib if Djahoemarkar seemed to have the work down pat.

"I didn't even have to test him, Tuan. I'd just show him a task once, and he'd get it immediately. Look at how very neat and orderly the entries in this bookkeeping ledger are. The handwriting is so neat and clean lined. Now could Big Tuan find anything lacking at all in this?"

"Zoo, zoo, he's that good, huh?" he declared, patting Djahoemarkar on the shoulder. "Let us simply say thanks be to God for giving the two of you a good means to earn a living," declared Big Tuan.

At the end of the month Djahoemarkar started work at the new job and Abdoelmoetolib officially resigned. Upon taking his leave of the plantation, of course, he did not forget to say his formal goodbyes to all his relatives there, to the main work gang overseers, and so on. They held a big *kenduri* communal prayer meal, in fact, as a leave-taking ceremony and as a way of presenting Djahoemarkar to all of them. Everyone in attendance took great delight in saying *horas* to those who are leaving us, *horas*, too, to those who are staying behind, and may everyone make an easy and very good living, wherever they may be! That's our main wish, on into the future![11]

After Abdoelmoetolib had left, Djahoemarkar moved into the Crani I's house. He was quite delighted at this. His mother's brother's wife and Sitti Djaoerah just kept praising God and saying thank you, thank you, for giving them this wonderful means of making a good living. Their lives and work went along smoothly for several months, but then a great crisis beset them.

It happened in the years 1907–1908. It was all because the government got word of all the hardships of the coolies working on the plantations in Deli. This was especially true after Mr. van de Brand's books were published. These volumes explained conditions on the plantations, for instance, the murders of minor officials, the way the coolies were being harassed, the way salaries were paid, and so on. The government ordered an official commission to mount an investigation in Deli to determine whether these news stories were true or just complaints. Those who were ordered to Deli made their investigations, looked at the situation very carefully, and found that the stories the government had heard were true.

An Arbeidinspectie Commission was formed in Deli to keep watch over labor conditions and make sure that the coolies got paid (and to make sure that the big corporations remained happy, too). One of the rules they issued went as follows: up to now, a coolie's monthly wage was figured as running from the first of the month through to the thirtieth or thirty-first. As the end of the month drew near the books would be closed two or three days from the end of that period so that people's wages could be calculated in time for payday. Oftentimes people who had to go into the hospital at the end of the month or who happened to be in jail wouldn't get paid because they weren't there on payday. Similar difficulties would beset folks who had just returned from the hospital or jail: even if they had worked from the twenty-eighth to the thirtieth, those days wouldn't be counted toward their salary because the books would have been closed for that period. So on payday lots of folks wouldn't get paid or they wouldn't get their full pay. Moreover, often it took till eight o'clock at night to get everyone paid. The coolies really did suffer many severe hardships, especially the women, who had to walk home from the spot where they got their pay. Many of them got robbed or mugged as they walked along the road in the dark, especially when it was raining.

To guard against such things happening an order was issued: the books would be closed on the twenty-fifth or twenty-sixth of each month, and the remaining days of the month would count toward the following pay period. So five days of each month would spill over into the next period. With this system it wouldn't be so hard to calculate people's pay, and payday transactions could be concluded with dispatch.

The first month this system was tried it struck some folks as odd because they seemed to be missing five days of pay. So the commission told the main work gang overseers and the senior officials to be sure to inform the coolies of what was going on so they wouldn't be taken aback by their smaller paychecks. And the new regulation was indeed passed on in announcements to the coolies. But, unfortunately, one particular overseer neglected to inform the workers in one particular *afdeeling* (or section) of a plantation about the change of policy. And so on payday when they got their salaries the coolies were shocked: their salaries had been docked and they hadn't even gone AWOL.

The minor *tuan* explained that that was the way things were going to be handled, and he explained the new order just issued by Tuan Fiscaal (of the Arbeidinspectie). And the main overseer and the minor ones were all brought in to carefully explain to the coolies what was going on, "so that you guys don't get shook up. Your pay hasn't disappeared: you'll just get it next month."

But these explanations didn't do any good. The coolies claimed that the guy who had counted out their pay had cheated them, even though it was Minor Tuan who had counted out their pay. They blamed the Crani I anyway. So off they rushed toward the main office to capture Djahoemarkar and kill him. He was sucking the blood of the coolies, they declared. They set to making a great racket in front of the door to the office, with all of them yelling: "Come on out, Crani, so we can kill you! You cheat folks and suck their blood," they kept shouting. They had their hoes and machetes poised to do Djahoemarkar in if he so much as stepped outside the door. There was no way these guys were going to go home peacefully.

Big Tuan tried explaining the new policy to them, but the message didn't sink in. In fact, they were fixing to run amuck[12] in his direction and kill him as well. So they were forced to barricade themselves inside the office for protection.

Sitti Djaoerah and Big Tuan's wife got word of what was happening, and it frightened them so much that they almost keeled over and fainted. They were terrified, thinking of all those men running amuck right outside the office door with their long knives and adzes at the ready.

"Now, what can we do?" thought Sitti Djaoerah. She ran over to Big Tuan's house, quite surprising his wife. The latter asked: "Whatever's happened? Are they still alive or are they dead already?"

"No one knows as yet, Nyonya,* but the door is still fastened shut. Now, listen, I have a plan, which we must put into execution before the crowd runs amuck and breaks into the office. Here's what we should do. Let's hitch up some horses to

---

*Nyonya is a polite appelation for Mrs. used during colonial times for Dutch women.

a carriage and have it go out to the main road. I'll catch up with it from behind, and the carriage can take me to the plantation. I'll say that I'm the Javanese *fiscaal* officer whom the Raja of Java has delegated to come here. I'll put on men's clothing, just like the *radens*, the Javanese aristocrats. I'm fluent in Javanese, after all," said Sitti Djaoerah.

"All right, sounds good. Go get dressed quickly so I can send the carriage to the road. And the sooner the better, so those Javanese don't start chopping them up into little pieces over at the office."

"Right," said Sitti Djaoerah, running off to her house, where she put on the sort of short jacket and long batik sarong that Javanese noblemen usually wore. The batik cloth was printed with Javanese designs, and she slipped a Javanese *keris* into her waistband, in the middle of her back, just like the *radens* wore. She made sure the dagger's handle was good and visible. She also put on wooden Betawi sandals. Her long hair didn't give her away as a woman either, since the Javanese noblemen kept their hair long, too.

As Sitti Djaoerah was getting dressed the *tuan*'s lady sent him a letter in the office, telling him about Sitti Djaoerah's plan, so that they wouldn't be afraid when they witnessed it.

When she got out onto the road, Sitti Djaoerah hobbled along all covered up in shawls like an invalid so that no one would see what clothes she was wearing underneath. When she got to where the carriage was she threw the shawls from around her shoulders and got into the vehicle.

Soon the horse's hooves were clacking along the roadbed with the Javanese fiscal officer perched on high. If people hadn't known what was going on beforehand they would never have suspected that Sitti Djaoerah was a woman. Why, it was as if . . . as if she had changed into a *raden*! The elegant, swinging, swaying way she handled herself was exactly the comportment of Javanese noblemen.[13] She stepped down out of the carriage and spoke a few words to Big Tuan, and then she turned toward the furious coolies. She told them in Javanese: "I am the fiscal officer whom the Raja of Java has dispatched here to Deli to see what can be done about the hardships the coolies are suffering on the plantations. While I was in Medan, I heard that you were making some kind of a disturbance here. Now, what wrong has been done to you that you want to go running amuck like this? Tell me what the trouble is so that I can mount an investigation. If they're at fault we shall punish the plantation owners. But don't jump right in and go killing people. We surely do not want you getting exiled to prison on the island of Papua![14] Now, look, tell the truth, for the Raja of Java has dispatched me to come here for serious and good reasons."

"My, my Lord . . . Raden Mas," they all said at once, bowing their heads all the way down to their feet to show their respect to Raden Mas.[15] And they explained how they had been shortchanged on their wages by the plantation's *tuan*. And Sitti Djaoerah asked each one of them in turn to make his deposition.

And after that she asked Big Tuan why he would have done such a thing to the coolies.

Big Tuan explained all about the new order just issued by Tuan Inspecteur and how, since this was the first month it was in effect, it might seem to all of them that they were missing five days' salary. "Before payday I told the main overseer to inform all the coolies of what the new rule was, but apparently the message didn't get through to this particular work gang."

"Oh, so! That's why you're carrying on like this, apparently! You think someone cheated you or cut your pay without any reason? But, you should know, this new rule really has been issued; it's the one I brought with me from Java. All this time we've been hearing that oftentimes you'd get paid when it was already dark and that would cause real hardships for you if it was raining or there was no moonlight. And your poor, defenseless womenfolk were always getting mugged in the dark as they were walking back to their cottages. And that situation is exactly what caused me to issue this new order: the account books will henceforth be closed five days before the end of the month. Those five days of pay will be issued during the following month. That way you won't have to be paid after dark and you won't get caught in the rain going home to your cottages. And you won't have to worry about muggings and so on. And if you happen to stop work on the twenty-fifth of a month to go home to Java, well, then the five days' wages still coming to you will be like your savings. So, you mustn't misunderstand what's being done here. All this wasn't the plantation *tuan*'s doing, either. Rather, it was at the instigation of the Raja of Java, who was, of course, working for the good of his people."

"My, my Lord . . . Raden Mas: now that it's been explained that way, we understand. We're fortunate to finally understand what's going on with this new rule and lucky to have had Honored Sir come so quickly to explain things to us. Why, if we had gone ahead and murdered the *crani* and Big Tuan. . . . Indeed, then, we accept the order issued by the Raja of Java and we shall simply go back home to our little cottages," said all the coolies.

Once the *raden mas* saw that the coolies' ardor had cooled a bit he swept his *keris* out of its sheath with a grand gesture and declared: "This is a magical *keris* sent here by the Raja of Java, forged by the master blacksmith of Gunung Jati![16] If any other wrong is done to you, simply say so, so that I might use this dagger to slit the malefactor's throat. There'll be so much blood spurting that all the flies will get their bellies full! He'll croak before you can turn around. Now, you know you can place your trust in me," he said, slipping his magic dagger back into its sheath.

After the coolies started to move off and go on home the *raden mas* solemnly shook the hand of Big Tuan and asked his kind permission to return home. Then he climbed up into the carriage, and the horse trotted off with him toward Medan. However, once the vehicle had gotten to a quiet, secluded spot in the road, away from the eyes of the crowd, he took off his clothes and went back to being Sitti Djaoerah.

Big Tuan, not to mention Djahoemarkar, was simply flabbergasted at Sitti Djaoerah's sharp politics. So, of course, they waited for her to come home from the road. When she arrived they burst into loud guffaws of laughter from relief and happiness at what had happened. Then they went back to Big Tuan's house, for his *nyonya* was going to make a speech.

It seems that as soon as the lady got word that they were safe from danger thanks to Sitti Djaoerah's clever stratagem she asked that glasses of hot tea be prepared for all of them to drink, along with a big spread of fancy cakes and butter cookies.[17]

Once all four of them were seated around a table, the *nyonya* said: "I would like to thank you very, very much, Sitti Djaoerah, and you, too, Djahoemarkar. We have been snatched from the jaws of danger. I never dreamed that a mere woman could think up something so clever, I declare! I never imagined Sitti Djaoerah was so intelligent, so clever at pacifying a madding crowd! So, indeed, I simply hope that God will repay your kind services, and may you be afforded good luck and good fortune so that we might remain safe and sound as we work here on this plantation. Till my very last dying breath, I shall never forget Sitti Djaoerah's kind aid to this plantation and to Big Tuan. Why, if those coolies were still running amuck on us, my little children might be without a father now. So then, Djaoerah, may you remain well and continue to prosper, and may you, too, Djahoemarkar, remain hale and hearty. And don't worry, we shall not forget what you have done here," said the lady.

Tuan Besar added a speech of his own to what his *nyonya* had said, declaring his heartfelt thanks for Sitti Djaoerah's help: "Starting today," he said, "I consider you someone I can really and truly trust. I had so idea there was such a woman! Especially around here—someone like Sitti Djaoerah who could dream up a plan like that. I simply am unable to say how thankful I am to you for all your help."

Sitti Djaoerah responded to the speeches of the *nyonya* and Big Tuan with a nice little declaration of her own. She said that everything that had happened that evening was a result of the beneficence of God and that her part was only to convey those words out there. "So we must all simply say thanks to Almighty God. May Nyonya remain hale and hearty, may Big Tuan reach a fine ripe old age—so that there will still be good mentors for us to guide us along the right path."

They sat and conversed a long while, and then Sitti Djaoerah and Djahoemarkar merrily went on home. And not long afterward Big Tuan's houseboy came running up to Djahoemarkar's house with a big basket of special foods for them—and a big basketful of gifts to boot, the description of which we don't have to go into here.

And that is how, as the storyteller tells the tale, the great coolie commotion ended: resulting in a situation that helped advance the fortunes of Djahoemarkar and Sitti Djaoerah. And, indeed, we shall see just how the whole thing eventually came out.

20

Happiness Gained

After Sitti Djaoerah had demonstrated her cleverness, not to mention her character, in dampening down the big disturbance at the Parsaulian Plantation, Big Tuan decided to place his firm trust in Djahoemarkar. And he also decided to direct his kind attention toward their whole household.

The old proverb of the Latins says: "Voix populier voix dei," which means "the voice of the masses is the same as the voice of God."[1] For God bestows luck-blessings on the same things humans do. And, consequently, once Big Tuan had placed his trust in Djahoemarkar the latter just got luckier and luckier. Big Tuan turned over all the buying and selling decisions on the plantation to Djahoemarkar, and he let Djahoemarkar decide when they needed to make equipment purchases. Djahoemarkar would only have to present Big Tuan with the bills and he would shell out the cash, no questions asked.

And the owners of the equipment stores began to look up to Djahoemarkar more and more, especially once they noticed how polite and respectful he was in answering their questions and accepting the goods. They loved to converse with him—they felt it did them a world of good. Even if some commercial transaction with him didn't happen to come off, they would not feel that they had wasted their time talking to him. Of course, Djahoemarkar was being quite the clever commercial partner here: after all, a duck has to provide its own frying fat if a guy was going to progress in life, he figured! And, indeed, folks were always sending them little gifts, they were so popular and well liked. The gifts came to them in a good, clean, straightforward way; they weren't given to up the price of the merchandise folks were selling to the plantation or to increase the costs of the transactions. In fact, all the while Djahoemarkar was in charge of purchasing equipment and merchandise for the plantation, their expenses were much lower than normal. And so the total outlay of funds on the plantation also went down.

At the end of the year the profits and losses on the plantation were totaled up. The dividends (that is, the profits) had risen considerably because of all the money Djahoemarkar was saving on expenditures. Big Tuan was extremely pleased with Djahoemarkar, and he did not neglect to turn over some of the enterprise's profits to him, too. So it wasn't too many years before the wads of cash grew very thick in Sitti Djaoerah's wallet.

The more Big Tuan believed in Djahoemarkar the easier it became for the latter to earn a good living. However, he kept the same lifestyle, no matter what. It was as if he always remembered the proverb written on the walls of the house.

Be mannerly toward life, resentful toward death.
If you walk along with your eyes wide open, pointed toward the sky, a cinder is bound to fall in them.

And he always made sure to deal with people politely, with just the right measure of respect. Older men he respected like fathers; those younger than him he loved like children.[2] Acquaintances his same age he treated like close lineage mates. For a person without family is a poor man, indeed, here on this earth.

At the very least, if there was no possible family relationship for him to invoke with a person, he would call them "my friend." Consequently, everyone respected Djahoemarkar—in fact, sometimes they paid more respect to him than they really should have. And so, too, other people found they couldn't cut any special deals with him; he treated them all according to the words of the old proverb: "If you borrow some water from somebody, well, then you've got to pay them back with a bucket of water." His behavior simply got better and better. He was never conceited or proud; he was always serious minded and straightforward.

From the example Djahoemarkar set it is already quite clear, surely, that folks respected him very, very highly, although he was not a high government employee. He always enjoyed their full measure of respect, and this was never forced on their part. Forced respect is no more than skin deep; it's just words on your lips—for when a person wants something from you he'll do all sorts of things just to curry favor with you. But after that little transaction is over he vanishes from sight. If you consider the advantages and disadvantages of the situation, well, it's true enough: "Even though the sparrow may be tiny and the elephant huge, both of them have to balance their heads on their necks." So you have to do good deeds for others to reap their thanks. And, most assuredly: "You have to send cigarettes downriver if you want any betel quid to come coursing back upstream to you!"[3]

His relationship with Abdoelmoetolib was close almost beyond telling. If one of them would so much as eat the foot of a grasshopper the other one would be there johnny on the spot to share the meal.[4] Put another way, though they might be physically distant from each other, their *tondi* souls and bodies were always tightly bound together, as if they were being held snugly in a tight fist.

Nandjaoerah, for her part, just kept offering prayers to Almighty God, the creator of the earth and sky. She asked that they all be afforded long lives; that they might enjoy devout, secure faith, perfect in all its particulars; and that they might all continue to live together peacefully.

So it appeared that now it was not just yellow-yellowest, glittering gold that they had managed to get in the distant lands beyond the home villages: no, they also had some sons and daughters born to them. Djahoemarkar's oldest son they named Marah Moedo, after Djahoemarkar's late father.

When Nandjaoerah gazed at her grandchildren, her daughter, and Sitti Djaoerah's husband she was blissful. This was especially the case now that they all shared a common name: Djahoemarkar was Father of Marah Moedo, Sitti Djaoerah was Marah Moedo's Mom, and Nandjaoerah herself was Marah Moedo's Ompung, his grandma. So could they be said to be pretty happy now? You bet they could![5]

Airplane

A nd so, now, how was Djahoemarkar getting along and what was his life like—Djahoemarkar who opens up memories of the deep past, who opens up all manner of deep sadness, Djahoemarkar who opens up feelings of deep longing and loneliness but also Djahoemarkar who opens a way toward happiness?! Well, as more and more days went by things simply got better and better for him. He was thriving. And he got along better and better with acquaintances and friends. Whenever there would be an *adat* ceremony calling for the village elders to be in attendance Djahoemarkar would be summoned. So, too, with any important *adat* congress: he would be called to attend that, as well, as a respected elder.

We can switch now a number of years into the future, so as to advance this story toward its conclusion. That way things will come out right.

Around the beginning of August 1923, all the Eight Adat Domains (that is to say, the regions near Medan) and their general populace were quite agog: the famous and much renowned Toean Chantelouq was coming to the city! Toean Chanteloup, that is, the great airplane pilot.* He was coming to Deli! To Medan, the city that people were calling the Paris of the Indies because it was so lovely, prosperous, and wealthy. He was going to be in Medan for several days, showing off his expertise at flying his plane up into the clouds. Upon hearing this fine bit of news folks from all around the city flocked into Medan to see exactly what the pilot could do. They figured, well, he was really bound to be something! Whoever couldn't come and see the sight for himself would just have to hear about it from others, but, of course, that wouldn't be quite as good as seeing things for yourself. With mere words you wouldn't be able to imagine exactly what the airplane looked like or what Toean Chantelouq's face was like. So you'd regret it for the rest of your life if you didn't come and see for yourself.

Now, before this, Djahoemarkar was never one to put himself out to go see casual entertainments around town if they failed to gain him any particular profit. He was not one to waste money on frivolities. Before Toean Chantelouq came to Medan a number of other shows had come to town: The Queen of India show, the Malay Opera from Selangor, the Harmston Circus, and several others. He hadn't shelled out good money to go and see any of those. However, he felt himself pulled toward Toean Chantelouq, so by the second day the pilot had been in town Djahoemarkar said to Sitti Djaoerah and her mother that they should just go find out what was going on. At first Sitti Djaoerah and her mother felt that this would be a waste of time, not to mention money. They kept dragging their feet; they didn't need to go there.

---

*The author switches the spelling of the pilot's name from Chantelouq to Chanteloup throughout this chapter.

Djahoemarkar understood this behavior, so he said: "But all this will go toward a good practical end, never fear. Going to this show won't be just for fun. Why, seeing someone fly up into the air will afford us the chance to ponder God's greatness, to think about the Almighty Creator's marvelous deeds, the Creator of the natural world and all its contents. Think of it. Isn't it wonderful that one of God's humble servants is able to do such an incredible thing? And think what riches he is earning for the Hereafter. So take your mind off the notion that this will just waste money. Get to cooking our meal as soon as you can so that we can set off at four o'clock. I've already asked for the time off from Big Tuan, and I've arranged for a car to carry us there. Let's take all the children along so they can see, too."

"Well, look, Djaoerah, if *that's* its purpose then let's just go! After what he's said, I do sort of want to go and see it, you know." said Marah Moedo's Ompung (that is, Nandjaoerah).

"All right, all right. Just as soon as your nephew has left for the office let's get to work cooking the daytime meal so that we won't be late leaving," said Sitti Djaoerah.

"Let me go along, Mom!" "Let me go, too, Ompung," piped up Djahoemarkar's children merrily.

"Okay, okay, calm down, calm down, our father's already arranged for a car for us. Now just go get washed so you look decent."[1]

At four o'clock Djahoemarkar left the office and came straight home. He found the car he had chartered from Medan waiting there, pulled up in front of the house. "Hey, so here you are, Bang Roeslan,"[2] he said to the chauffeur.

"Yes, indeed. I came as soon as I could 'cause I was afraid of getting delayed and being late," said Bang Roeslan.

"Well, listen, come up into the house so we can eat before setting off. Oh . . . Marah Moedo's Mom! Go get the food ready so we can eat our meager papaya leaves! I'd wager that Bang Roeslan's pretty hungry by now."

"Oh, now, it's all ready, you know that. Come on up, so we'll be able to leave as soon as possible."

Djahoemarkar and Bang Roeslan came into the house and they all ate their meal, but it didn't taste all that good since they absolutely could not wait to take off see the airplane. The kids barely touched their rice.

"Now, listen, go put on some decent clothes. We won't want folks thinking you just stepped out of the forest," said Djahoemarkar.

"Now, c'mon, they're already done up pretty neatly. If we're going to go, let's go! The old *ompung's* already dressed and rarin' to go," said Sitti Djaoerah.[3]

"Get that old car cranked up, Bang Roeslan, so we can leave." They all piled in and headed off toward the open field out in Djati Oeloe Village, just outside Medan. When they got there they found the field packed with people, and there was also a big crowd standing around outside the fence.

"All right, you folks stay right here and I'll go buy the tickets," said Djahoemarker, plunging into the crowd. He got sweaty fighting his way to the ticket counter. Once he got the tickets he went back and fetched them and they went on into the field through the gate.

"Now, don't get scared and don't let people laugh at you when you catch sight of it, but there's the airplane, over there. You see? And in a moment it's going to fly up into the clouds."

"Yes, but . . . but how does it do that? The plane's so big," asked Sitti Djaoerah.

"Oh, come on, the pilot's not going to flap his wings and carry the thing. Just keep watching and you'll see how he does it," said Djahoemarkar.

Before too long the plane's propellers started to revolve very fast and the whole thing started to move forward gently—and then it just took off into the clouds. It circled the city of Medan, and then after about five minutes it safely returned to the ground. And the crowd sent up a great cheer: "*Horas . . . horas . . .*"

"Now, (said Djahoemarkar), aren't you folks impressed with the greatness of God?"

"Lailahailallah, this does *indeed* prove that folks have quite enough magic snakes in their bellies, I do declare," said Nandjaoerah.

"Oh, so that's the way they do it, is it? And I thought that it was going to be a person who sort of carried it on his back," said Sitti Djaoerah.

"Take another look, folks. In a moment or two he's going to take off again and carry some passengers up into the clouds." Before Djahoemarkar had finished saying this the plane shot up into the sky with two passengers on board. It went way up into the sky and soon looked as small as a hawk up there. Soon the crowd couldn't see it anymore, for the plane had gone all the way to Belawan. After about ten minutes it came back and the crowd let out another big cheer.

After the passengers had disembarked the *tuan* went back up into the clouds again and started turning somersaults up there. Sometimes it seemed he was going to fall straight down to the ground, and then sometimes he would go flipping over upside-down—and then finally he came back down to the earth and landed.

People gulped in surprise to see him flip the plane over like that. Other folks were so taken aback that they began mumbling verses from the Koran.

"So, do you think this was all a waste of money?" joked Djahoemarkar.

"Wow, not any more! We got ten times as much out of it as what we put in. Why, this has really made me believe in God, I do declare," they all said.

Once the leaf-drying sun⁴ had sunk below the horizon the whole crowd went back home. So, too, did Djahoemarkar, Sitti Djaoerah, his mother's brother's wife, and all their children. Still in high spirits they went home to the Parsaulian Plantation.

On the way home they couldn't talk of anything but that airplane. Even the little kids kept relating one story after another about what they had seen out there in the field. They didn't stop till they got back to the house.

"Well, listen, tomorrow we'll go out there again. I saw on the program that he's going to teach all his flying skills to folks, all those amazing things," said Djahoemarkar.

What was Nandjaoerah thinking? Well, while out in the airfield she had noticed a lot of married couples sauntering back and forth together, looking very happy. Her nephew was always knocking himself out, looking after their welfare. So the thought occurred to her that if they went to watch the show again tomorrow:

"Oh, the kids and I don't really have to go along" (she thought to herself). "They should just go by themselves, so no one gets in their way, and that way they'll be able to enjoy themselves out there at the playing field. After all, they endured so many hardships when they were younger. Why, even I, as an old woman, think that it's a very good thing, indeed, for married couples to go walking along hand in hand, especially since Djahoemarkar and Sitti Djaoerah sure don't look any less pretty than the other couples out there! As a matter of fact, I'd say they look first class. They'll look just like a pair of matched male and female ducks, I'll bet.[5] They should just get back at Sutan Hardwood for causing them so much pain in the past."

Early the next morning Djahoemarkar went to ask for another leave to go and see the airplane show a second time.

"Well, all right. Did you take the kids along yesterday?" said Big Tuan.

"Yep, we sure did, but they still want to see more."

It was only three o'clock when Djahoemarkar got home from the office and said to Sitti Djaoerah: "Come on, get ready so we can go again. The car will be here any second."

"Now, Son, we don't need to go along again.[6] I feel sort of dizzy today—let me just stay and watch the kids. In fact, I've already bribed them a little about this. I told them they could have some candy if they stayed behind," said Nandjaoerah.

"Ah, good grief, what's the use of just us going? That would be wasting money. Come on, come on, get dressed. The cost of renting the car is the same whether you all go along or not. So, come on, it makes more sense for you to go with us."

"No, you two go on ahead, there'll be lots of other shows for us to go to in the future," said his *nantulang*.

"Well, if just the two of us are going we should hurry and get ready," said Sitti Djaoerah.

After they had eaten Djahoemarkar got dressed and they set off, but after only about five minutes he said: "Chantelouq won't start his show for a while yet, so let's go tooling around the city of Medan in this car first, all right, while we've got the chance? If we go riding around in Medan by car it'll be quite the sight to see—like a trivet standing on its side, won't it? Now, how much extra will it cost us to go riding around the city?" asked Djahoemarkar.

"Ha, ha, oh, come on, how much could it be? Just the extra gas it takes. But let's stop a second so I can put the top down. Then it will look like we're going on a proper pleasure trip," said Bang Roeslan. And once the car's top was down they set off at a nice slow pace.

"Well, Marah Moedo's Dad, you know, I simply still can't see how Toean Chantelouq managed to go flying up into the clouds like that. It just seems impossible to me," said Sitti Djaoerah.

"But what confuses you so much about that? Didn't you see that the propellers on the front of the plane made it fly? But, you know, the way folks in the Past Age used to fly up into the sky[7] really *was* something. They'd just use their *bailal* *biulul** flying suits to go zipping up to the Upper Spirit World from the ground down here below."

"Ha, ha—what sort of suits did you say?" asked Sitti Djaoerah.

"Well, that's kind of hard to explain because they're *turiturian* words."

"Would you maybe just spin a tale for me about how they used to use those *bailal biulul* flying suits?" said Sitti Djaoerah, still confused and somewhat surprised.

"Now, how in the world could I tell you that tale now? It takes seven full nights to finish it," said Djahoemarkar.

"Just tell me a little of it so I'll be able to compare the way the airplane flies up into the clouds with the way those flying suits you talked about worked."

"All right, all right, have a listen then. But this'll be a real short version, and I'll also eliminate a lot of the little side branches of the story so we just get what we really need."[8]

"Okay," said Sitti Djaoerah, settling into a comfortable sitting position.

"Well, then, indeed . . . it can be rightly said that back in the deep past, back in the far distant, storied past, in the land and valley of Galagala Aeranjung Julu, in the Kuala Batang Muar, in the Batang Muara whirlpool, in the Payapaya Panjolingan, in the captivating pool that never goes dry, in the Tunggar Pangalinom-Linoman, in the flood-soaked woods that folks hide in, there among the *lanseh* trees, with their great masses of ripe yellow fruit, there among the sweet mango trees hung heavy with fruit, there among the jackfruits growing in triple bunches, there amid the red sugar palms with their vats of boiling sap, there in the domain of the most joyful of joyous people, there happened to live a young raja, a young leaf on the tree of life, a young nobleman named Datoek Toeongkoe Adji Malim Leman, the greatest *malim* of all the *malims*, a man who prayed seven times a day, the young son of the honored and revered Soetan Moerik Meden Tinamboran. And this boy had been born of his mother, the well-born Nantjondang Adji Toean Laen Bolon, and he was the grandson of the late Baginda Napal Hatogoean and the *babere* of Soetan Batara Goeroe Doli, who lived far distant in the Upper Spirit Kingdom, in Purba Sinomba Julu."

"Ha, ha, oh, my gracious, such fine names! Now what, I wonder?" said Sitti Djaoerah.

"Well, now, ever since the boy's father, Soetan Moerik Meden Tinamboran, had passed away the great land was quiet, lonely, and still, for it had no one to guide and protect it and make it prosperous. And his dear mother, the well-born Nantjondang Toean Adji Laen Bolon, was sick and ailing, and no one could figure out what her illness was. And so her son Datoek Toeongkoe Adji Malim Leman asked her why she had fallen ill and why things were going along like this, and he also asked her what sort of healing food she might crave so that he could go right out and search for it for her.[9] 'Just tell me what you want, Mother, and I shall go find it straightaway,' said the young son of that fine revered older leaf on the Tree of Life

'Oh, I don't crave anything, my son. You don't have to go wearing yourself out,' said the revered noblewoman.[10]

---

*This playful, alliterative phrase has no meaning at all and is, in fact, not Angkola Batak. Used often in *turiturians* about flying spirit women, it lends a Minangkabau flavor to the proceedings.

'Please tell me, Mother. If you don't tell me what sort of food you crave I cannot rest easy anytime I see you,' said her son.

'But what's the use of my telling you what I want, My Son? Even if I tell you what I have a craving for, you won't be able to get it for me. Why, even when your honored father was alive he wasn't able to obtain this special food for me. So however would you be up to the task?'

'Yes, indeed, My Good Mother, Old Leaf on the Tree of Life, but even so! Just tell me what it is you want. Who knows, maybe I will be able to get it.'

'Well, My Son, if I tell you you'll just wear yourself out trying to find it for me, but what I really, really crave is the liver of a huge Sihatirangga carp, you see,' said the revered great noblewoman.

'Well, that is very fine, Mother,' said Datoek Toeongkoe Adji Malim Leman, going right off to call his dear younger brother, Si Ali Toendjoek Parmanoan.[11] 'Little Brother, Ali Toendjoek Parmanoan! Go spit a magic spell on our fishing net for good luck—on our certain to get a good catch fishnet—so that we can search for that huge big Sihatirangga fish our dear mother craves, our revered, honored mother, that dear old leaf on the Tree of Life.' So Si Ali Toendjoek Parmanoan came on up into the house and cast his magic good luck spell on the fishnet by spitting on it, and off the pair set toward the Whirlpool Fishing Hole of Crashing Thundering Rocks to find their fish.

And then . . .[12]

When they got to the big river they started to cast their net from downstream. However, they did not snare a single thing in their net, although they had passed several rapids by now. They hadn't even had the merest glimpse of a tiny little minnow. All this caused Datoek Toeongkoe Adji Malim Leman to ask: 'Now, why is this happening? I've never had such bad luck at fishing, ever. Well, it looks like we've got just one more whirlpool fishing hole to try. This is all really strange. If we don't get the fish in the Whirlpool Fishing Hole of Crashing Thundering Rocks that's coming up here, we'll really be in trouble: Big Trouble will be our middle name.'[13] So with some small measure of patience he cast his net very widely across the whirlpool—and just as the net hit the bottom of the river Datoek Toeongkoe Adji Malim Leman felt a strong hit on his line: he had caught a huge Sihatirangga fish. 'Here, Little Brother, Ali Toendjoek Parmanoan, hold onto the line from the net so that I can scoop up the big fish.'

And then . . .

Just as soon as Datoek Toeongkoe Adji Malim Leman had stepped into the water to scoop up the fish from the net along came a huge white crocodile as big around as a thriving palm tree. The beast declared: 'Okay, look, Black Haired One— please simply surrender to me so that I may eat you. My, my, my, it's been a long time now since I've had a chance to eat a good juicy Black Haired One,[14] a genuine human being, yum!'

'Oh, please, do not cast me down into defeat. I'm not trying to compete with you here or anything. I'm just trying to fetch what my dear mother has a craving for,' said Datoek Toeongkoe Adji Malim Leman.

'I don't care what you want, I just care what *I* want,' cried the crocodile.

'Oh, all right, if that's the way you are, here, just take your portion then. This is what you deserve!' said Datoek Toeongkoe Adji Malim Leman, unsheathing his mighty Bakisar Bulan *keris* dagger, his *keris* that does its dirty work of its own accord down in its victim's belly, spitting out guts left and right, the mighty, magic *keris* so furious that its teeth grind together noisily, so powerful that it moans *ungut-ungut* laments while still deep inside its sheath, the magic *keris* from which seven drops spill when it is pointed skyward, seven drops more when it is headed earthward, the magic *keris* that lends strength and inviolability when wiped on your body.[15] And then he thrust that magic *keris* right down into the soft belly of the crocodile. Just as soon as he was struck huge gouts of blood spurted out, the flies all got their bellies full, and the crocodile went thrashing his body back and forth both upriver and down. And then he turned to face the big Sihatirangga fish and started to wrestle him in a violent death struggle. The river turned red with the blood spurting out of that fish.

'Oh, my big brother is dead!' thought Si Ali Toendjoek Parmanoan to himself, sobbing loudly as he sat there along the river's sandy bank. But not long afterward Datoek Toeongkoe Adji Malim Leman rose up from out of the water, pulling along the huge Sihatirangga fish.

'Now why are you crying, Little Brother? Don't be afraid, I've killed that vicious white crocodile so he can't hurt you. Come on, let's gut the fish so we can take out its liver.'

But he had only just begun to cut open the fish on its side when he encountered some soggy sugarcane shavings in there. And when he cut into the fish a bit further what should appear but some partially chewed betel quid? He cut a bit further and came up with a single hair. He kept cutting and came upon a golden ring. He slipped it on his finger, and it fit exactly. 'And who was that standing there a little ways upriver?' he asked himself, but he didn't say anything to his little brother. After they had taken the liver of the fish he told Si Ali Toendjoek Parmanoan to carry the fish back home—and ask our mother how she wants it cooked. Tell her I am going off to fulfill a vow, to pursue a promise; I shall go to a land of obstacles I shall knock down, to a land of obstacles I shall overcome. And only when I find that which I so fervently seek shall I return home; if I have not yet found it I shall simply keep on searching.'

And then . . .

Si Ali Toendjoek Parmanoan went back home to the village, carrying the big carp, while Datoek Toeongkoe Adji Malim Leman raced upriver. He used a walking spell to hasten his journey: a distance that would normally have taken him a month he covered in a single day.

And as for Si Ali Toendjoek Parmanoan, eventually he arrived back home at Galagala Aeranjung Julu, right at dinner time, right when the cookpots were being set aside after cooking the meal. He knocked on the door and called out: 'Oh noble-born Mother! Please open the door, for I have brought back a huge Sihatirangga carp for you, its scales glistening gold in the sun!'

'Oh, my goodness,' said Nantjondang Toean Adji Laen Bolon, opening the door. She saw immediately that the carp he was carrying was not the one she had asked for, and she also saw that Datoek Toeongkoe was missing.

'Well, as for Datoek Toeongkoe, he didn't come with me. He made a vow: he would go to the land of obstacles he would knock down, to the land of obstacles he would overcome, he would go in search of what he sought and only come home again if he found it. If he didn't find it he would persist in his quest. That's what his vow was, anyway.'

'Oh Lord, oh Lord, *that's* what this fish has gotten us into. Here, run off immediately and find him. And if you don't find him you're not allowed to come back, you hear?' said Nantjondang Adji Toean Laen Bolon.

So Si Ali Toendjoek Parmanoan retraced his steps, walking along in the dark, walking along in the daylight, following in the very footprints of Datoek Toeongkoe Adji Malim Leman.

And then . . .

Because of his wonderful walking spell Datoek Toeongkoe Adji Malim Leman soon arrived at a place in the path where a tree branch impeded his way. He tried to crawl under it, but it reached out and squeezed and pinched him. He couldn't move past! His head kept running into it. He tried to step over it, but the branch reached out and kicked him. 'Ah, this is a naughty branch, this is,' Datoek Toeongkoe Adji Malim Leman exclaimed, and then he chopped it in two with his magical *keris*, his moonlight-sheen magic dagger. He chopped it into little pieces, and then he was able to go on along his way. After two or three moments it seemed he heard someone calling to him. He stood there and waited. The closer it got the clearer the voice became: why, it sounded like the voice of Si Ali Toendjoek Parmanoan! And not long afterward he did indeed arrive.

'So what are you doing back here again, Little Brother?' asked Datoek Toeongkoe Adji Malim Leman.

'Our mom says that if you don't come home with me she doesn't even want that huge Sihatirangga fish. So come on back with me, please—she's already gone and gotten mad at me.'

Datoek Toeongkoe Adji Malim Leman felt sorry for him, especially since he looked awfully thin and peaked from lack of food. So he said: 'Do you want some of those galagala fruits to eat, Little Brother? If you do, I'll climb up the tree and get them. However, when I kick them down and they fall onto the ground you're not allowed to eat them, all right? If you do you'll die.'

'Okay, okay,' said Si Ali Toendjoek Parmanoan.

As soon as Datoek Toeongkoe Adji Malim Leman got up into the tree he kicked one of the *galagala* fruits down and it fell right in front of Si Ali Toendjoek Parmanoan—and he ate it. He had no more than swallowed half of it when he choked. As soon as Datoek Toeongkoe Adji Malim Leman saw this he slid down the tree trunk and fetched some water, but he hadn't returned with the water yet when his *anggi* breathed his last life's breath and died. And so he cried and wailed *andung* laments and finally went ahead and buried his brother out there in the deep forest. And then he continued on his journey. But he had only walked three strides away when the dead person called to him: 'Wait for me, Big Brother! Please, please don't leave me behind,' he said.

And Datoek Toeongkoe Adji Malim Leman went back and asked: 'Oh Little Brother, what is it that you still want? Look, here are two heirloom treasure objects our dear father left us when he died, a fine metal betel tin and a magic dagger. I'll leave you the betel tin and I'll take the *keris*. And if I come home—if I find what I'm searching for—I promise to visit you right here, okay?'

Datoek Toeongkoe Adji Malim Leman set off, and his little brother no longer called out to him. Eventually he arrived at a wide, lovely garden. Many gorgeous flowers were growing most luxuriantly there, and the garden had many fine houses nearby. He was amazed. He looked around, but not a single person was there, so he called out to see if he could locate anyone. 'Oh my fellow family members! Which one of you owns this garden? Do I have your kind permission to come in?'

An old person answered him from inside the house, saying: 'Well, come on in then. Nothing wrong with that!'

Datoek Toeongkoe Adji Malim Leman did go on in, and they started to chat. They traded clever ripostes, they fought a bit with sly riddles, and so they came to know each other.[16] Apparently this person's mother's sister was Nai Pandan Roemare Boroe, that is, the little sister next in line to Nantiondang Toean Adji Laen Bolon. Datoek Toeongkoe Adji Malim Leman knew of this person's existence beforehand, of course, but he didn't know where she actually lived. And then up spoke Nai Pandan Roemare Boroe, saying: 'Now, where in the world might you be headed, as you loaf so leisurely along the road like this?'

'Oh, Mother's Sister, I don't know. I'm just walking along without any particular destination, shuffling and shambling, and when I hit upon that which I seek I shall finally go back home. And if I don't find what I seek I shall just continue to stay away from home.'

'Well, look, Son, I am aware of what you are looking for, but you got here too late, like flies that show up after the food's been cleared away! The only thing that's left is a few rice grains on the banana leaves strewn about. For only the day before yesterday your mother's brother's daughters got home from the Verdant Orchard,[17] your *boru tulangs*—those seven lovely daughters of a single mother. And, my boy, of course, they only come home here to the Lower World once a year, you know.'

Upon hearing that Datoek Toeongkoe Adji Malim Leman fell silent, and then he went over to the door of the house and paused thoughtfully, rubbing his chin. And there he happened to see some shavings from some sugarcane and some shavings from some betel quid, and a hair that had also been left behind. All of these were lying on the floor before his eyes. And so he compared them with the shavings and the hair he had found in the belly of the fish, and it appeared that they were exactly the same: they all had exactly the same measurements and looked just the same. Because of this he started to cry and began to sing a sad, *ungut-ungut* lament.

Hodong na hutoktok	I chop down the tree for palm fibers.
Hodong muse marporapora	The palm fibers are fragile and brittle.
Ho do anggi na hutopot	You, Little Lineage Mate, are the one I'm seeking
Ho muse ma i marsuada ni roha.	But you don't have anything in your heart for me.

'Now, My Son, Beloved Little Shoot from the Tree, don't you cry and lament. I know a pleasant little entertainment for you; I know an effective little spell. Let's just cast a crafty love spell on her; let's just send a wind spell *dorma** her way! We'll turn her head around with a mystic spell, so that all of them, that whole group of sisters, will come back home to this Verdant Orchard. Son, we shall just have to find a little amulet fence to corral her in, won't we? What we need is some special plants: *Si Rungkari*; *sipabolkas*; *sipillit silindjaung*; the orange branch with seven fruits all on a branch, all pointed toward the light of dawn; and a single solitary palm fiber growing deranged but unperturbed. Then we'll also need some river water swishing around in a circle, not heading upriver or down, and a spurt of Barus incense that came bursting straight out of the tree by itself. Once you've amassed all those things, My Boy, we'll work the spell tomorrow when the sun is standing straight overhead. That's the spell we'll cast tomorrow when it gets on toward noon.'

Once it got light the next morning Datoek Toeongkoe Adji Malim Leman went about seeking all those herbs and potions, and once he had located them he turned them over to his mother's sister, Nai Pandan Roemare Boroe. When it got near noon they cast that secret teachings spell, and Nai Pandan Roemare Boroe mumbled some prayers. And then she cast the spell via a magic single black palm fiber,[18] and as soon as the Barus incense was lit its magical smoke rose up toward the mouth of the sky in a gracefully rounded rainbow."

Dear Reader, let us now switch over to the Upper Spirit World, to Ujung Langit Purba Sinomba Julu, to the great and noble house of the raja, to the windowsill of the Simaninjo opening toward the Purba Sinomba Jube sky, to the cradle made of yellow-yellowest, glittering bridewealth gold, to the joyous continent never beset by clouds of mosquitoes, to the leechless buffalo watering hole—and there sat the daughters of the great raja, weaving away contentedly on their spirit looms.[19]

They were all the comely daughters of the great raja Soetan Batara Goeroe Doli, and these seven daughters of the same mother were called:

1. The Honorable Protective Oceans, Beguiler of the Moon at Night[20]
2. The Honorable Dewdrops in the Sunlight, Fending Off the Wind and Gales
3. The Honorable Moonbeam Girl, Lovely Princess of the Earth and Sky
4. Sitapi Donda Raja, Poetir Elamarelaela
5. Sweet Ripe Bananas Glistening in the Sun
6. The Honorable Lovely Protective Power Spell
7. The Honorable Umbrella Protecting Us from the Sweeping Clouds

And it could be said that as the sun rose to its noonday spot directly overhead, at the time when the decrepit old cows would wander lazily back home, when the bark on the bamboo would begin to loosen into sheets, just when the blacksmith's throat would get dry from thirst and just when the weaver girl would feel faint from hunger: just then, just at that moment, the Barus incense smoke wafting up from the lower world arrived at the golden windowsill of the sky.

---

*A "compell a person to do your bidding" spell.

Just as soon as the noble-born girls smelled the incense smoke their weaving slipped from their hands. They began to pant anxiously, in shock, thirsty, overheated, going up, going down, not knowing *where* they were going. "What's happened? What has occurred? We have *never* experienced anything like this," they said, as one. And finally they simply could not stand it anymore, and off they rushed to find their mother and father, to ask their permission to go back down once more to the lower world, to take a refreshing bath in the special splashing pool. For they just could not stand this heat.

"Well, all right, girls," said Soetan Batara Goeroe Doli and the revered queen, and then their daughters all began putting on their clothes, that is, their fine *bailal biulul* suits, their splendid magic flying suits, their flying suits as effective as hard areca nuts are in betel quid, their flying suits for wafting them all over the wide, wide world.

And then . . .

Off the seven of them flew, and when they arrived at the mouth in the sky, they opened up the door into the firmament, diving down into the huge sky space below with their arms stretched out before them. They zoomed and zipped up and down, this way and that, on the breezes, like hawks diving after prey. And finally they made their lovely way toward the Verdant Orchard with its bathing place of the rajas, set deep inside the blooming, budding trees.

And then . . .

As for the young nobleman, Datoek Toeongkoe Adji Malim Leman, there he sat all this while, pondering his sad and exceptionally unhappy fate and rubbing his chin dejectedly, sitting there in the door frame of the house. And then a second later the sky above the Verdant Orchard darkened and he was quite taken aback, and so he asked his mother's sister: "Why is the bathing pool of the rajas getting so dark all at once, Mother's Sister? I do not understand."

"Ah, that's just a sign that the spell we cast is working now, My Son. Your *boru tulang* will be coming along right away, never fear. So you'd better go on over and hide in that little field hut; if they suspect there's a man here they won't want to land, and they'll go right back home to the Upper Spirit World."

"All right," said Datoek Toeongkoe Adji Malim Leman, and off he went to hide inside an empty grain storage hut. But he opened up a little hole in the rattan mat that covered the sides of the hut so that he could spy on his *boru tulangs*.

One or two moments later down they swooped and landed in the midst of the Verdant Orchard, all seven of them, the seven daughters of a single mother. And, needless to say, they were all so thirsty that they dove right into the water and started to play at whatever games might suit their individual fancies. Some of them set to sucking sugarcane, some munched on slices of ripe papaya, and so on and so forth. After they had eaten their fill Honorable Protective Oceans thought to ask: "Oh, good Father's Sister! Do you happen to be ripening up any good bananas?"

"Yes, Brother's Daughter, I've got a few, though they're not too ripe yet."

"No, I don't want bananas you've got around the house I want the ones out in that field hut over there," said her *parumaen*, her brother's daughter, fit mate for her son.

"Oh my goodness . . . you sure are particular! But if that's what you want you go on over there and look for them yourself," said Nai Pandan Roemare Boroe light-heartedly.

Words need not be strung out too long, for very soon off they went to bathe in the swirling whirlpool swimming hole. As soon as they got there they shucked off their flying suits and dove into the water.

Now, as for Datoek Toeongkoe Adji Malim Leman, the second he caught sight of the lovely Protective Oceans the hairs on the nape of his neck stood up. He called out, more to himself than out loud: "Younger Lineage Companion, *you* are the one I have been looking for! You must become my love medicine, you must be the healing balm for all my pain and suffering," he said to himself. And then he snuck out of the ricefield hut and went and snatched away Protective Oceans' flying suit. Once he had gotten it he went downstream from the bathing hole and covered himself with ashes from the fire till he was absolutely filthy. He looked like someone who had never taken a bath. He started fishing in the stream about three boat-pole lengths from the bathing pool.

And then . . .

When they got tired of swimming and splashing about the noble-born girls moved toward land, and each reached for her set of clothing. But the Honorable Protective Oceans found that her flying suit was not there! She searched in this direction, and she searched in that direction; she couldn't find it! And, now, since it was getting on toward evening her little sisters told her: "Well, Older Sister will just have to stay here with Father's Sister, we guess. Next year when we come again we'll bring you a flying suit to use," they said, and off they flew back to the Upper Spirit World.

And then . . .

Protective Oceans went back to her father's sister's house, and once she got there she related how her clothing had disappeared. She burst into tears just to think about her bad luck.

"Now, don't cry, my son's potential wife. Go back and search for them. Maybe they just got washed away when the wind blew them into the water."

"Oh, maybe so, maybe so, Father's Sister," said Protective Oceans, going off to a spot a bit downriver from the bathing pool. And when she got there three pole-lengths away she caught sight of a man. His face was blackened with ash, but she went ahead and asked him: "Oh, good fisherman! Did you happen to see my clothing float by in the water a while ago?"

The guy answered: "Oh, Daughter of our Great Raja, I surely didn't see anything like that, you can bet. If I had I would have given them to you," he said.

"No, I'm not asking for you to give me fish. I'm asking about my clothing, which got swept along in the river, maybe."

"Ah, I guess your luck's pretty bad here, Daughter of our Great Raja. Normally if I stand here fishing for this long a time I'll get a great big catch. So I guess we'll just have to hope that if I catch two fish here in a bit you can have one and I can have the other. And if I catch three, two are for you and I get one, okay?"

"Don't keep straying off the track of what I'm asking you. It's not as if my father can't provide me with fish! Ash-blackened man, just whose daughter do you imagine I am, the way you keep going on like this?"

"Now don't go getting mad on me, Noble-Born Girl. Just because I haven't caught any fish yet. And, as for all your wealth and your high station, don't throw that up to me, for even though the sparrow is tiny and the elephant is huge both of them have to balance their heads on their necks, you know. And I've never asked you for anything, after all. Look, I always scratch around on the ground for my own chicken feed."

"What did you say? You just like to spout off, don't you? You just wait until I tell my father's sister, the old woman who keeps watch over this Verdant Orchard. She'll punish you, you creep who doesn't know his own fate, who doesn't know his proper social class in life! Huh!" said the noble-born girl.

"Well, you can take me anywhere you want. That old woman is my own Inang Bujing, my mother's sister. And don't you talk coarsely to a good-hearted young fellow like me," said Datoek Toeongkoe Adji Malim Leman.

"This guy simply has no *adat* and follows no rules whatsoever, honestly. That's why I said I'd go tell my father's sister. And here you say she's your mother's sister—so maybe you think I like you? That I'd want you as my boyfriend? You scab-covered creep, think again! Huh, man who doesn't know his own measure!" huffed the noble-born girl.

"Oh, go grate your onions, girl. I have never had the pleasure of eating rice cooked by so fine a daughter of the high nobles. Usually whatever food I can scrape together off the bare ground, that's what I eat; whatever kindling wood I can find, that's what I use to build a fire. Stop being mad at me all the time."

"Oh, *shut* up. Come on, let's go, so you can get your fit punishment."

"I shall go wherever you lead."

"All right, then, let's go. And you go first," said the Honorable Protective Oceans.

"No, I don't want to go first. I'm not going to get myself soaked in the dew by cutting the first path through the forest just to go first toward your father's sister's house," said Datoek Toeongkoe Adji Malim Leman.

"Okay, then, you be in back," said Protective Oceans.

"Nope, I won't do that, either. I'm not some crummy dog."

"Oh, good grief, walk beside me then," said Protective Oceans.

"Nope: not that, either. What if you go fast and I go slow? You'll leave me behind."

"Oh, you are *too* much, you scab-covered creep! What exactly do you want, then?"

"Doesn't matter! I don't even have to go. Look, I don't want to be taken to court. I won't have much luck there. I never expected any of this. And how am I going to find something to eat?"

"Lailahaillallah, come on, then, hurry up. I'll lead you along by the arm, and if you get scared I'll leave you be," said Protective Oceans.

"Okay," said Datoek Toeongkoe Adji Malim Leman, smiling a tiny bit. And when their hands touched he was transported right out of this world. And he said inside: "What's there to be embarrassed about, for you were always my younger lineage companion, weren't you, according to proper kin term talk?"

"Ha, ha . . . this guy is really naughty," said Sitti Djaoerah, and then she spoke the next line:

"And then . . ."

Once they reached Nai Pandan, Protective Oceans said: "Oh, Father's Sister, please mete out some just punishment to this creep. He is just *too* much. I asked him about my clothing and he kept changing the subject and veering off in all different directions. And he went and said all kinds of things he shouldn't have to me."

"So, Creep! Why did you talk that way to the daughter of the great raja?"

"But I didn't, Mother's Sister. . . . She kept hassling me because I hadn't caught any fish. It wasn't that I didn't want to behave in a most refined manner toward the daughter of the raja. I couldn't wrap up any fish for her because I was having a run of bad luck and wasn't catching any."

"Ha, ha . . . yeah, I know, I know. Go on off and bathe, you scab-covered creep, so I can bring this court case to its proper conclusion. If you don't I won't be able to make my decision," said Nai Pandan Roemare Boroe.

"All right," said the creep, going off toward the whirlpool. Once he got to the splashing pool Datoek Toeongkoe Adji Malim Leman gambolled about in the water, making waves, making small ripples, making the crashing thunder rocks push together, making the small stones rustle together, causing the rolling waves to come to the center, causing the roiling ripples to course to the pool's edge, till the great tumult of his splashing echoed back from the mouth of the sky.[21]

When Protective Oceans heard him say this she asked her father's sister: "Who is this guy who's so adept at splashing around? As big as I am I've never heard splashing and swimming like that."

"Oh, what do you need to ask about that for? It's better that you just go off and start cooking so he has something good to eat. Maybe he is family to us, after all. This is the first time a fellow like that has visited here for as long as this farm has been in existence," said Nai Pandan Roemare Boroe.

Once Datoek Toeongkoe Adji Malim Leman had finished bathing he put on the full set of descendants of rajas clothing. He put on the fine-looking *batakat batokit* jacket,* with seven hundred twinkling mirrors in front and seven hundred twinkling mirrors on his back. Once dressed he strode forth and looked just grand. He was perfectly turned out, just like a finely turned handle on the hoe blade: not placed at too sharp an angle, not set down too low. Just right! He was like palm wine made from the first cut of the sugar palm: juicy, very sweet, just right.

As soon as Protective Oceans caught sight of him coming back from the water she asked: "Oh, Father's Sister, who, who is that *great* looking guy? Quick, ask him if he wants to go with me."

"Ah, you are something, always prattling on. Go back to that rice so he'll have

---

*Another exotic-sounding *turiturian* word, similar to the *bailal-builul* of the magic flying suits.

something good to eat. Maybe some son of the great rajas will be coming here for a meal and we sure wouldn't want to be caught out. How embarrassing."

Happily, with some embarrassment mixed with joy, the Honorable Protective Oceans turned back to her rice pot. Once the food was cooked she ladled it up and spread it out in front of Datoek Toeongkoe Adji Malim Leman.

Nai Pandan Roemare Boroe said: "Come here, My Son's Potential Wife, come here so we can talk." And the girl swept right in. "All right now, 'Maen, I'm not going to beat around the bush; this fellow is your father's sister's son. This is Datoek Toeongkoe Adji Malim Leman, the miraculous *malim*, the man who prays a full seven times a day in the Batang Moeara whirlpool, in the captivating pool that never goes dry. So, 'Maen, since it's just us two here, go ask his forgiveness for anything untoward that you might have said. Do that while you're both still young, hear? Now, my son's mother is your father's sister Nantjondang Toean Adji Laen Bolon, and he really came here to find you, you see. Now, 'Maen, since your father's sister is getting on in years I do hope there is some love in your heart for my son here and for me. Please make this man your friend of a single death, your friend of a single life. And tomorrow may you set off for Kualo Batang Muar, for my son has left your father's sister behind there for a very long time."

Protective Oceans answered: "Son of my Father's Sister, I do ask forgiveness of you, but, you know, you also were in the wrong. Why did you behave like that? You should have been frank with me, and then how could I ever have sinned against you?"

"Oh, your sins are easy to forgive, Little Lineage Mate," said Datoek Toeongkoe Adji Malim Leman. "Let's just do everything our mother says."

"All right," they both said.

At dawn the next morning, once Nai Pandan Roemare Boroe had given them her blessings, they set off to go back home to Kualo Batang Muar, retracing Datoek Toeongkoe Adji Malim Leman's original footsteps. After several days they arrived at the grave of Si Ali Toendjoek Parmanoan, and Datoek Toeongkoe Adji Malim Leman declared: "This is where I buried our little brother when I was on the way to search for you. He died because he didn't remember what he should have. Let's open the grave, all right, and see what's inside?" And once they had dug the grave up they saw that his face looked just as it had before, and because of this Datoek Toeongkoe Adji Malim Leman said: "Little Lineage Companion, start pronouncing your secret mantras for contacting the spirits so that we may contact the spirit of our little brother and all of us will be able to go back to the village together."

Just as soon as Datoek Toeongkoe Adji Malim Leman had stopped speaking, the Honorable Protective Oceans took some magic spirit-contacting oil and sprinkled it on the lips of the dead Si Ali Toendjoek Parmanoan—and immediately he woke up, as if he was just rising in confusion from sleep. He was dazed, surprised, but there he was.

"Now, Little Brother, don't be shocked to see this girl in front of you—she's just the older lineage mate I was in search of. So, come on now, let's get back home; our Mom's waiting for us," said Datoek Toeongkoe Adji Malim Leman.

After they had eaten their meal they set on off walking, and eventually they arrived back at the village late at night. They knocked on the door of the Great House, calling out: "Oh . . . Mother, Old Leaf on the Tree of Life! Open this door, please."

Quite taken aback, their mother woke up and opened the door. When she saw it was her sons she immediately kissed them happily, and only at that point did she ask about the friend they had with them. "But, but, it's your *parumean*, Mother, your brother's daughter, the Honorable Protective Oceans!" The girl bowed her head in respect to her father's sister, and the two of them burst into happy tears. And then his mother cooked a hard-boiled egg for them, a hard-boiled egg to firm up the newlyweds' souls, and placed some little fingerfuls of salt in their mouths. Then they all went to sleep, for they were quite tired.

Dawn of the next day came. They struck up the earth-shaking gongs; they beat the sky-rumbling gongs to wake up all the populace from the seven rivers upstream as well as the populace from the seven rivers downstream.[22] People started streaming into the Great House. Bride's betel quid was presented to all the nearby villages, and once everyone had gathered in the home village they held their buffalo sacrifice ceremony to bless the wedding of Datoek Toeongkoe Adji Malim Leman and his mother's brother's daughter. And, starting on that very day, this country gained a raja again. Everyone returned to happiness.

After Datoek Toeongkoe Adji Malim Leman had lived in a married state for some time and had sat among the village elders as a respected married man, the little bird began to call out its happy news, a small sign that Protective Oceans was going to give birth to a baby. The months turned, a year went by, and a child was born there inside the womb, a little boy. His birth was just like that of his father: deep in the middle of the night, on the night of Attian ni Aek, not quite Suma Day by the old calendar, there in the midst of a whirlwind, there in the midst of a fierce tornado, with the chickens safely stashed in their pens to protect them from the gale winds, as the tailless bird beats his wings furiously at the hearth fire from fright . . . and as soon as the baby was introduced to the ground for the first time the ground sloped down out of respect, and then the child was carried around the countryside by the wild animals in procession, and then finally he was brought back up into the house and wrapped gently in a little diaper and a tiny sweet jacket. Once the honored noblewoman had recovered her strength a bit the raja's child was given a blessing ceremony, and they celebrated with a buffalo sacrifice feast and gave the child a name, that is, Porkas Lelo Mandjoloengi, flower of the earth, blossom of the sky— the sweet, pliable, kind, little child who only says yes to family and friends, never never no, the child destined to become the laughter raja of all his little girl admirers.

And then . . .

Once the little noble child had gotten a bit bigger, what do you suppose he did every day? Nothing much, for sure. Actually, he just shot marbles. But he always thought he had to win—according to him he wasn't allowed to lose. And if some little kid tried to quarrel with him he would beat him up. He had thrown things in anger at absolutely all the village chickens, goats, and other livestock. The kid was a holy terror. When he sat down to eat his dinner everything had to be just so, but once he had finished he would throw the dishes and the cups against the wall and break them to bits. He behaved like that every day, till every single plate in the house except the big heirloom treasure procelain serving dish from distant India was in shards on the floor. One time, when Protective Oceans happened to be going out to the stream, Siporkas Lelo waited for her back at the house to ask for something to eat. His *ompung* took a banana leaf, spooned out some rice and fixings onto that, and handed it to him, but the small nobleman did not want that. He declared: "So you think I'm a cat, the way you give me food on leaves?"

"No, no, Ompung,* you are a raja's son, but we don't have any plates left, as you know, so what am I supposed to use as a dish?"

"Well, go and get the big porcelain plate, the big heirloom dish. That's the only way I'll eat anything," he said.

"But we only have that one fancy plate, Little Grandchild, and it's the heirloom dish we inherited from your late *ompung*."

"Well, it has to be off that plate or I won't eat," said the kid.

His grandmother didn't have the heart to refuse him, so she cajolled him sweetly: "Now, please, please don't break this plate, My Little Man, okay?[23] Care for it real well, Child of the Great Raja."

"All right," said Si Porkas Lelo, at least while his *ompung's* eyes were still fixed on him. However, once he had finished eating and his grandmother had deflected her gaze for a moment he immediately threw the big dish down on the floor and broke it into a million pieces along with its cup and side dishes. She shoved him, and then beat him, and then said to him: "I told you not to break that dish! But you went ahead and did it, you oaf! Don't you *know* that your mother did not bring a single plate or cup into this marriage of hers?† She's just a wife who came to us gratis, minus marriage exchange gifts. Oh Lord, she moved in like a chicken with a berth in a henhouse all prepared for her beforehand. Now what are you staring at? Why are you so quiet? Don't you know that we got your mother out of a fishing hole, from a bathing pool? So what do you think you have to be so proud and arrogant about?" said his *ompung*, still stung. Apparently this story struck home with the child, for he began to sob disconsolately. He simply would not be pacified. Not too long afterward Protective Oceans came back from the stream and found her beloved son wailing his lungs out. So she asked: "Little boy, why are you crying? Did you lose at marbles or something? Tell me what's the matter, young man, Mommy's little sweetheart, Mommy's little yes-sayer!" But none of this did any good, and he just cried all the louder and kept getting hoarser and hoarser. So she carried him into one of the Great House's many side rooms[24] and examined him carefully, saying all the while: "Tell me what's wrong, Son, so I can understand." When she cajoled him like this Si Porkas Lelo eventually told her everything that his *ompung* had said. "Mommy, Mommy, she said you didn't bring a single solitary plate into your marriage. She said you're the sort of wife who moves into a house like a chicken with its

---

*Grandparents and grandchildren both call each other *ompung*.
†That is, she did not have a proper *mebat* ceremony in which her family provides her and her new husband with gifts of household goods. The implication here is that she is not a human wife, conforming to orderly human norms.

henhouse all prepared for it! She said you were found in a *fishing hole*! In a bathing pool! That's why I feel so bad, Mommy."

"Yes, yes, little boy, I know, I know, just try to be quiet. Don't cry," whispered Protective Oceans, but inside she felt terrible. She thought to herself: "Oh Lord, to think that Father's Sister would want to say such things about me. Right, Father's Sister—so I'm no one, am I? Well, I'm your own brother's daughter. You're too hard on me, Father's Sister," she kept saying to herself the whole day long. But she didn't let on about any of this; she just behaved as she normally did, there inside the Great House. That was a sign of her high noble breeding, after all. She wasn't like some women, who would flare up in anger and storm out at the least little wrong done them; she wasn't like women who would complain about the quality of the dishes and spoons if she were eating at someone else's house. Starting on that day she just kept bowing her head in dejection, thinking about what her father's sister had said. The whole situation kept bothering her like an aching jawbone, like an aching tooth. But what could she do? It was her own father's sister who had said those things, so who could object? She would just have to remain patient.

And then . . .

Eventually, another great difficulty came to the great raja, Datoek Toeongkoe Adji Malim Leman: for one time, during a severe hailstorm, while he was sitting there in one of the Great House's very many rooms with his wife and son, Datoek Toeongkoe Adji Malim Leman happened to nod off to sleep after they had been chatting a while. While he was asleep Si Porkas Lelo opened all his father's pockets and worked his way all the way to the man's belt and waistband. The child turned out all the contents of his father's shirt pockets. And without any warning suddenly Protective Oceans caught sight of her suit of clothes in there, that is, her flying suit. So she grabbed it. She wrapped an *ulos* blessing blanket securely around the raja so that he'd continue to sleep soundly, and she went off toward the kitchen to cook the meal. After the rice and curry were done she took them into the room where the raja was, and once the food was all safely laid out in little dishes in front of him she donned her splendid magic flying suit. As she was about to go flying up into the air she thought to herself: "Oh Lord, shall I take my little child here along? He'll feel so bad if I just leave him here and go." And so she said a special, powerful prayer out loud and slapped Si Porkas Lelo gently all over his body till he was as tiny as a chip off a hard little areca nut and then she popped him into her hairbun. And then up she flew into an old coconut palm that was standing close to the Great House.

Once there she called out to the bold guardsman standing in front of the house: "Wake up the raja, please, so that he can eat his meal, and tell him I'm up here." So off went the guardsman to wake up the raja, and once the raja had stirred the guardsman declared: "My Lord, the queen says that you should eat now, and, further, right now she is, well, she is way up in that old coconut palm."

On hearing this the raja leapt from the room and ran out to look—and Protective Oceans was already way up at the tippy top of the coconut palm by this point.

"Oh, don't leave me, Lineage Companion! I haven't done anything wrong to you. I still love you very much!"

"Yes . . ." said Protective Oceans, "but I am going to leave you, you see. I'm going to get a set of dishes from my father's village." Then, *purrrrr*!!! And with that she flew up into the deep sky, coursing straight upward.

Datoek Toeongkoe Adji Malim Leman's eyes followed her course upward with tears splashing down his cheeks. He waved desperately at her, but finally she appeared no bigger than a locust and then she disappeared completely.

Then he went into the house and sobbed and howled and moaned *andung* laments in great desperation. He had known that his mother was mad at Siporkas Lelo Mandjoloengi, but he was afraid to get mad at *her*, so he had not done anything at all.

And then . . .

But, my friend, it's impossible to try to ignore that which cannot be ignored, to try to sit when you cannot sit, so finally he decided to fetch his magical Jangga Urere Keris, his piercing the moon *keris*, and off he sped looking for the path upward toward the Upper Spirit World. Off he went, pursuing the dawn and the dusk. When he got tired he would just fall asleep in the folds of the big forest trees.

After a number of days sloughing his way through swamps and marshes, after a month on the road, after a month of hacking his way through the tough rattan grasses, after a month of traversing deep ravines, of going through soggy bogs for a whole month, eventually he arrived at the peak of a certain mountain. He sat there for a while, looked in both directions, and thought to himself: "But there are no more uplands after this! The eye can see no further! So where exactly is the road up into the sky? There aren't even any more mountain peaks," he said to himself. This made him feel terrible, and finally he just fell asleep there, underneath a huge old banyan tree.

"Hey . . . Datoek Toeongkoe Adji Malim Leman, if you're trying to find the road to the sky it won't be from here, you hear? No, you'll have to go on to Toba Silindung Julu, for there you'll find the gluey rock that thrusts into the sky; there you'll find Mount Nanggar Jati, and that will be your fine and fitting way to ascend into the sky."

As soon as the old man said this Datoek Toeongkoe Adji Malim Leman woke up. He looked around, but no one was there, no one at all.

Even so, he decided to follow the fellow's advice, and so off he headed toward Toba Silindung Julu.*[25]

Throughout his journey, all along his way, a great many wild beasts confronted Datoek Toeongkoe Adji Malim Leman. There were huge fierce old tigers, immense elephants, rhinos, prodigious *naga* serpents, crocodiles, and so on, and every last one of them declared: "All right, lookit! Just bow your head down to us, Black Haired One. All this long while we've not been able to snare one of these while he's been out working with his iron spade in the field. But, ha, *now* it seems we've got ourselves one! Great! And he'll taste pretty darn good going down; he'll fill up our bellies right well."

---

*Author's note: Actually, Mount Nanggar Jati is in the Sipirok area, next to Huta Padang. You can still see this peak today, but I don't know if it's the Mount Nanggar Jati in this story. —THE WRITER

"Oh Lord, now they are going to eat me. Well, turnips are better than the caladium plants, better that I just die rather than continue to live,"[26] said Datoek Toeongkoe Adji Malim Leman.

"Oh, no, no, indeed, my honored friend, raja's child. When I hear your voice it is quite like the lovely voice of my *mora*, my wife givers. Are you perhaps the son of Soetan Moerik Medan Tinamboran?"

"I sure am, but a lot of good that does me. Those are just words in a dream, so it's better that you gobble me up rather than letting me suffer like this."

"No, no, no, *no*, Son of our Raja. We are going to help you to the *utmost* of our ability. We shall teach you some secret lore. For when your father was alive I got caught in a trap one time and he freed me. Our rule is that we're only allowed to take dead animals, and if they're still alive we just have to let them go," he said. "So, we're just paying back his kindness here," they all said.

And so they began to teach many, many secrets to Datoek Toeongkoe Adji Malim Leman: some taught him mysterious fencing skills, other beasts taught him how to withstand club and cudgel attacks, others taught him how to magically bound away from danger, while still others gave him amulets and secret-charm lore for warding off mystical attacks. Still others taught him how to use stop them in their tracks spells to paralyze people in their houses and then take what you want from them.[27] And others gave him magic antidotes for warding off military attacks. Ah, all in all, he had a sufficient armamentarium!

Let's switch for a moment to the Upper Spirit World, for just as soon as the Honorable Protective Oceans got to the mouth of the sky the door opened before her and she went into the higher sky.

While she was on her way she thought to herself: "Well, so, should I keep carrying my child with me? But, but, if I carry him along, what can I say, how will I explain things? Maybe folks won't believe that he is a raja's son. Maybe folks will say: 'Water that just swishes around in a whirlpool, going neither upriver nor down, directionless child,' and my good name as well as that of Father and Mother would be besmirched. Oh, it's best that I just leave him here on this blasted heath, in this wasted field, so that he will die here. After all, who'll know he's here? How could his father ever look for him here?"

So once she had made up her mind she left her little child in a big banyan tree. The boy was sobbing all the while, like a motherless field sparrow, totally without food, totally without a blanket wrapped around him to keep him warm. And so she went back to Purba Sinomba Julu, back to the village of her father, back to being an unmarried adolescent girl, back to the weaving looms of the shining Simaninjo windowsill to the sky. Her father welcomed her back most joyfully.

"But, but, this girl's behaving awfully!—and here she is, the daughter of a raja! To just go and leave her child in the middle of the forest like that," cried Sitti Djaoerah, going on to say: "And then . . ."

Djahoemarkar resumed his tale. "Now as for Datoek Toeongkoe Adji Malim Leman, eventually he did arrive in Toba Silindung Julu, to the sticky peak, Mount Nanggar Jati. He looked far up into the highlands, and he looked around the mountain peak, and he saw that it was surrounded with a plot of wide rice paddy land.

There stood Mount Nanggar Jati, gloriously, right in the middle. The base of the mountain was verdant with luxurious orchids and *sahat-sahat* vines. These plants climbed about five arm spans up the peak, so he thought he'd be able to climb that far up on the vines. But once he got that far he could see that the stones beneath his feet had become as slippery as caladium stalks. And it was like that all the way up. He tried to wrap his arms around the rocky face of the mountain but found that that was impossible. And so there he stood, down at the base of the peak, crying and wailing about the whole situation. But then, most happily indeed, along came a big civet cat, which proceeded to say: 'All right, just bow your head down to me in submission, accursed Black Haired One. When I get you in my belly that'll fill me up pretty well.'

'All right, all right, just eat me, I don't care. I can't take all this pain and suffering anymore,' said Datoek Toeongkoe Adji Malim Leman.

'Nope, nope, I guess not! Your voice, it happens, sounds just like the voice of my *mora* wife givers. And so, might you possibly be the son of Soetan Moerik Medan Tinamboran? One time, you see, I snatched one of his chickens. But he didn't kill me, so I shall help you out here, to the very best of my ability. So where exactly are you going?'

'Well, I'm going up into the sky to look for my son, but I can't climb up this rock face,' declared Datoek Toeongkoe Adji Malim Leman.

'Well, look, if you're going up there you just hold onto my tail,' said Civet Cat. So, after Datoek Toeongkoe Adji Malim Leman took hold of the tail, Civet Cat gave him a big, strong pull, and up they went, climbing up the rock until they were halfway up into the sky.

When they got to the upper slopes of the mountain Datoek Toeongkoe Adji Malim Leman had to sit on top of Mount Nanggar Jati, having nowhere else to perch. The big civet cat suddenly retreated from the scene, saying: 'This is all the bother I can take with you. So I guess you'll just have to fend for yourself now, pal.'

So what did Datoek Toeongkoe Adji Malim Leman think of this? He could not budge an inch since he was like a boiled egg stuck onto a water buffalo's horn; and if he tumbled down the peak he'd be totally snuffed out—destroyed completely!

He began to mourn and wail in *andung* laments and to sing a little *ungut-ungut* song.

Indalu pangitean da ina ni Siporkas Lelo	Siporkas Lelo's Mom uses her rice pounder
Pangitean marponggolponggol	as a bridge out in the rice paddies
Mabalu so matean	between the pools
Paninggalkonmu ma na dangol.	A little bridge built in tiny sections
	I'm in mourning without being widowed yet
	Your leaving me has been so very painful.

'Oh——Lord, my soul so lacking in skill for asking needed favors! Why have you behaved this way, Younger Lineage Companion, toward our only son? Toward our own cute little cucumber rootlet?'

Finally, he wore himself out, lamenting like this, and he nodded off to sleep. He started to dream. He saw an elderly man come up to him and say: 'Hey, Datoek

Toeongkoe Adji Malim Leman, tomorrow at about 9 A.M. look upward, and if you happen to see a root from a banyan tree hanging down just catch hold of it. You can use that root to climb up to the mouth of the sky' (the root, that is, of a 'big warfare is coming' banyan tree).

And then . . .

Next morning just at the time the old man had said Datoek Toeongkoe Adji Malim Leman should cast his eyes upward, what should appear but that long tree root. But it was only as big around as a finger. He caught hold of it and climbed upward, rocking and swaying gently in the wind as it blew in different directions."

"And then . . ." said Sitti Djaoerah, breathlessly.

"Well, come on, let's get on out of the car. Here we are at the field," said Bang Roeslan.

"Hey, we're here. Come on, then, Marah Moedo's Mom," said Djahoemarkar.

"We don't have to go see that airplane. Let's just stay right here and finish the story," said Sitti Djaoerah.

"Ha, ha, but folks will laugh at us if we do that, if we announced that we were going to go see an airplane but we ended up telling *turiturians* to each other instead."

"Ah, but I want more," said Sitti Djaoerah, getting out of the car. They walked on over to the field, quite cheerily, actually. After all, no obstacles stood in their path to a good time. They sauntered back and forth like a matched pair of ducks, walking two abreast, and everyone who saw them, everyone who caught sight of them, offered them kind praises.

As it was getting on toward evening, Toean Chantelouq announced: "Whoever wants to go up in the plane can do so now at a cost of no more than twenty-five rupiah." Lots of people did go for rides, especially the Dutch. Some folks got to ride upside-down in the clouds. Some went up into the sky without any extra frills, just hoping to return safely to the ground, which they did.

"Well, what do you say we give it a try, Marah Moedo's Mom? We don't have this chance all the time," said Djahoemarkar jokingly.

But Sitti Djaoerah said very seriously: "Fine, all right. I was just going to say that myself. Ask him if we can go."

"So you've got the nerve?"

"Why not? Go on, ask him. Of course, we don't have much money, as always, but it's not too often we get a chance to go flying."

"All right, let's get a move on," said Djahoemarkar, going over to Toean Chantelouq and buying two tickets. They climbed inside the airplane and flew right up into the sky. Djahoemarkar said: "Now don't look down, you'll get scared . . ."

"Oh, come on, what's wrong with that? 'Cause I feel like I'm just sitting in a car. In fact, I'm happier here because the road's not waving up and down and there aren't any big curves," said Sitti Djaoerah. Djahoemarkar looked down on the city of Medan, and it appeared like a picture below him: why, the roads twisting and turning every which way looked like a big spider's web. But the roads looked no bigger than pieces of thread. He mulled over the amazing expertise people had to have to fly swiftly through the clouds like this.

They were already really high up, but the airplane was still climbing, and finally the houses in the city of Medan were no longer visible. Everything was simply dark, like a steaming jungle. And, as for Sitti Djaoerah, she felt like the daughter of Soetan Batara Goeroe up there in the Upper Spirit World. She thought that they must have come to the mouth in the sky by now. So she asked Djahoemarkar: "Are we going to course on up into the Upper Spirit World in a bit, do you think?"

Djahoemarkar laughed, and then went on: "Yeah, maybe so, maybe so. But how can we get there if that child and his mother don't come along? Because if we get up there, well, a person might forget about life in the Middle Continent, and maybe he couldn't get back home. That's why I kept holding out for the kids to come along with us. But they didn't want to, I guess. Okay, look, let's not neglect them anymore—let's go back down."

"Golly, if you don't know how to get back we surely better go on back down!" said Sitti Djaoerah. And the airplane started to glide down like a hawk homing in on a mouse in the middle of a rice field. When they had returned to the field Sitti Djaoerah felt sort of like her body was still moving. They got in Bang Roeslan's car and went straightaway to the Parsaulian Plantation. Sitti Djaoerah finally came back to herself after they got there. All the time she was in Medan she had thought she was inside a dream because of the turiturian chant. And that is how their trip to Medan came out.

Djahoemarkar's Lezing on the Stage of Medan's Oranje Bioscoop

In past years, as we are all aware, a great number of *syarikats* sprang up among our populace here in the Indies.* Budi Utomo in Java could fairly be said to be the common grandfather of these *syarikat*s, while Syarikat Islam was their father. And Syarikat Insulinde was their father's younger brother, their *amang uda*—and, in fact, these associations also had lots of protective mother's brothers and indulgent husbands of father's sisters.[1] Why, it got so that *syarikat*s were springing up like mushrooms in an open field. And if you happened to visit a town the only thing you'd hear would be that this or that *lezing* was about to be held. Even the women-folk got to know what *lezing* meant. If anyone would just be making some tiny lit-tle speech in an *adat* style, folks would go and call it a *lezing*. It was really something.

In Deli—the land that folks called "millionaire's territory," the land of riches and prosperity—there was certainly no shortage of *syarikat*s. Oftentimes some of the more mature people would get together and decide to establish a *syarikat* for the welfare of the laborers (that is, the workers). Such a committee would decide that its *syarikat* members could perhaps pool their funds and raise some capital. And given the fact that there were so many folks drawing salaries in Deli the founding committee members were pretty confident that their efforts would not go to waste. They would select a spokesman, someone who was adept at stringing words togeth-er and getting an accurate fix on a situation.[2] For this spokesman they'd also need someone who could sway people who were still off to the side, the ones straddling the fence. They knew they needed someone people could trust, someone in whose statements folks could believe. What they didn't need was a magpie, which starts mouthing off at the top of its lungs the second the sun hits it in the morning; with a spokesman like that you certainly could not guarantee that folks would go along with what he said.

After all the available, mature, plausible candidates from throughout Deli were considered, Djahoemarkar himself was chosen as the spokesman for the group's upcoming *lezing*. People trusted him. Whatever he said he would always go ahead and put into practice.

The committee's decision was firm: it would have to be Djahoemarkar as their speaker—if he agreed to it, that is. If he did, they would call him to Medan to dis-cuss what they were going to do. So they sent him a letter, asking him to come

---

*Syarikat*s were social organizations such as the Syarikat Islam, a Muslim merchants' union active in the early nationalist movement in Java. A *lezing* (Dutch) is a lecture.

to Medan if he happened to have the free time. He was to come to the house where they had held their meeting. Djahoemarkar obediently came on into town and they arranged another big meeting of the committee. After they had all shaken hands and passed around the loose tobacco leaves they told Djahoemarkar what sorts of activities their committee hoped to pursue. And they told him that they had selected him to be their speaker at their first *lezing*. He would be the one, they said, to present their good proposals to the assembly at the big public meeting they would hold.

Djahoemarkar responded in good order to what they had said: "I am very proud to hear of your decision about forming the *syarikat*, I must say. Whatever good decisions you have taken about the association's plans, I shall conform to them—I am not one to deviate from a common agreement, of course. However, as for actually becoming your speaker at your *lezing*, well, no, I really cannot do that. I plead with all of you: please don't make it be me. I don't have any expertise in that sort of thing; I won't go thrusting myself in the middle of the public fencing arena like that, believe me. And, besides, I don't know how to make speeches in front of the public. So, really, it's better that you just make me one of the audience members, okay?"

"Now, we're not asking anything inappropriate of you. We ask you to shoulder no burden that you cannot bear. We have made this request because we've noted that you're well up to the task. So we very much hope and pray that you will not refuse the comittee's request."

"Once again, let me say thank you for placing your trust in me, but since I am truly not equal to the task you set before me I must apologize to you all and withdraw from contention."

"Well, so be it. . . . But, listen, since the meeting is still a long way off, please continue to think the offer over carefully. If you refuse our request, why, it's as if you are refusing a solemn request from your close lineage mates, you know. For this is not just our doing—just us, the members of this committee. No, it's the larger public that wants this, too. You being our spokesperson will serve all our common aims and needs."

"Yes, yes . . . I suppose I can think it over, that's possible, but it's best that you folks continue to search for a good spokesperson, someone who will serve you well. And so, if you will excuse me, I will just be getting on back home," said Djahoemarkar, shaking the hands of all the committee elders.

When he got back home Sitti Djaoerah asked him why he had been called to Medan.

"Ah . . . you know, this thing they're asking is really too much. They got together and decided to organize a *syarikat* for all the various groups of laborers, and they want to make *me* their spokesperson, can you believe it? Me, who is clueless about that sort of thing! Now, wouldn't you say that that's simply too much for them to ask of me?"

"Ha, ha . . . but if they sent someone to fetch you wouldn't they already have determined whether or not you were up to the task? Come on!" said Sitti Djaoerah.

"Oh, good grief! I've never even been to a *vergadering**—and now they want

*Dutch for a gathering, a public assembly

me to horse around at *lezing*s. . . . Shouldn't they be picking some brilliant person for that sort of thing, someone with a lot of talent for public speaking?"

"Oh, come on, give it a try, pal![3] If they've gone and reached such a serious consensus it isn't such a good idea to refuse them, you know. If you're not very expert then just say a few words and turn the podium over to someone else. That way you won't be ruining the compact they worked so hard on," said Sitti Djaoerah.

"I don't know. I don't see that I'll be able to do anything for them. But look, okay, however it comes out I'll do what you say."

For the entire time leading up to the first *vergadering* of the organization Djahoemarkar could think of nothing but the words the committee had asked him to convey to the public. He kept searching for a way to avoid stage fright, if only for the beginning part of his speech. So sometimes when there was a good bit of moonlight at night he would go out into the open field on the plantation and practice. There were a great many coconut palms planted out there, lined up in long rows. A plantation worker had left a wooden bench out there, and Djahoemarkar stood up on it and turned to face all the coconut palms. "Well, I'll just pretend that these are the people sitting in rows in the Oranje Bioscoop, okay, and I'm the *lezing* speaker," he said to himself. And then he said: "Honored *tuans*. . . . I come here before you as a kind of helmsman, guiding the ship's rudder . . ." and then he laughed to himself, thinking: "Oh, brother, what if someone hears me. I bet they'll think I'm crazy." And so he got down off the bench and went back home.

The committee for the future *syarikat* had set a date for the big gathering. That is, it would be the tenth of Zoe'lhidjdjah, 1924, when all the salaried workers would be sure to have a day off. That was true of both the folks who worked for private enterprises and the ones who worked for the government—that way there would be no obstacle to anyone's coming to the meeting. They told Djahoemarkar what the date was so he could get ready beforehand. They sent him word of all the details of their plans so he would know what points to be sure to slip into his speech, to sway the public.

As soon as Djahoemarkar got the letter he showed Sitti Djaoerah all the various verses he would have to talk about in his speech. "So, Marah Moedo's Mom, what do you say about all these words they've put in their letter? Look how many points they have here! Even if I memorize them all I won't be able to talk about all of them. This'll all just make me forget some of them and forget what to say, don't you think?"

"Now, don't get shook up, don't get scared. . . . You don't have to say all the words exactly as they've put them down in this letter, you know. This is just a memory aid so you know what you're going to talk about. Whatever occurs to you to say during your speech you just go ahead and say it, all right? The words will come by themselves, never you worry," said Sitti Djaoerah.

"Well, I sure hope so. If I get embarrassed up there and do something stupid don't you go feeling bad. After all, I warned you I was no *lezing* orator, but you just kept on pushing me," said Djahoemarkar.

Before the agreed-upon date invitations were sent to the public and advertisements were placed in all the Medan newspapers. And on the set day folks just flocked in—everyone who did not happen to have a serious time conflict came. Starting that morning, the city of Medan was much busier and more crowded than normal because of all the salaried workers pouring in for the meeting. At eight that morning the crowd was already gathering at the stage of the Oranje Bioscoop, and after no more than half an hour the building was jam-packed. Many folks did not manage to get a seat, and they had to stand outside the stage door.

At nine o'clock the _vergadering_ began. First, the _bestuurs_ of the committee made speeches.* They said: "_Tuan, tuan_, our honored lords, and all of our good friends and close family members who have been fortunate enough to be fleet footed and to have come here to attend this _vergadering_! First, we say thank you very much; we sincerely hope that you will think over very carefully what we have to say. And now we shall turn the floor over to Djahoemarkar to speak to our honored _tuans_, our respected sirs, and our friends and family. Everything that we wish to discuss Djahoemarkar will present to you." And at that point Djahoemarkar climbed up onto the _lezing_ spot on the stage, bowed his head, and paid his respects to everyone who was up there on the stage.

He said: "Now, indeed, in accord with what the committee _bestuurs_ have just said, let me, too, convey my heartfelt thanks to all of you honored _tuans_, respected sirs, lineage mates, close family, and friends for coming here. We are fortunate, indeed, that you have all been fleet footed enough to attend our meeting. Now, then! Let us begin by commenting a bit on things so that we might find our way along a good road toward a verdant grove.† The way the members of the committee view things, well, they have every expectation that those of us living here in Deli will be able to form a cooperative league to further our common interests, the interests of our people. We haven't given this league a name yet, for it is still inside the womb as yet—but we must reach a consensus about it as soon as possible, you see. That way we'll be able to welcome the infant with a proper name, so it won't be embarrassed at birth. As all of us are certainly well aware, many of the _syarikat_s our people have organized eventually just disappeared from the scene. In the beginning, the public always works very diligently to help them out, but then, when things are under way and the _syarikat_ is on its journey, folks go weak in the knees. They sort of nod off to sleep, in fact. Now, why do you think that is the case. . .?"

Well, before you all think of possible answers let me tell you how I see things. The way our kind of folks have been behaving lately, well, they'll have a great deal of energy to carry out some project for a while and then they'll go limp on you and not finish things. If a guy is good at giving a _lezing_ speech then everybody will just close their eyes in delight, listening raptly. And everybody will start shelling out contributions in his direction to boot. . . . 'Now, here, take this _aandeel_, this share, take this little _contributie_, and so forth,' they'll all say.

But after a month they won't have a clue about what sorts of things he was advocating, and they won't care how they behave, either. And the upshot of the whole thing is that the plant dies off while still a stripling!

---

*_Bestuurs_ (Dutch) are the members of the executive committee.
†_The verdant orchard he refers to here is the road to advancement and progress._

Now, I say, if we really intend to help our people advance in the world and progress, it's better that we don't get into endeavors that end up costing us. Now, we have surely seen that if we all work together the burden we bear on our shoulders isn't all that heavy. It's quite light, in fact, and by working together we can reap a profit quickly. Let me ask three things of you members of the public, three things that can serve as our strong houseposts, supporting our work together and holding up the roof of our common endeavors.[4] What I mean to say is that we must have three things.

1. Some capital funds so we can get our business endeavors under way
2. Some good, strong expertise to help support us in our business
3. The basic, raw strength and energy we need to accompany our capital and expertise

Now, the capital we can get from the shares we sell to each other. We've estimated that there must be at least a thousand people here in Deliland who draw a salary. Now, if each of us buys one share for ten florins—why, in a single month we'll have many thousands of florins in capital funds, won't we? And after a year, we won't have to worry: we'll have hundreds of thousands of florins with which to work.

As we have all noted, every day, the *maatschappys* here in Deli are never owned by a single person. Rather, small amounts of stock are combined into a large sum, and then the whole group owns the corporation. Once we've got the capital there are enough of our people who have advanced school training for us to get someone to keep track of the money in an astute, bookkeeping sense. And there are enough coolies for the labor pool, too. Things will work out very well, even though the costs will be relatively small—for, after all, we're the ones who raised the capital and we're the ones who'll reap the profits. Even if we do have to break our backs working to make this thing a success, so be it: all the profits will come to us. Put another way, if we plant vegetable seeds in the ground now we'll be the ones to go plucking the crops tomorrow! Well, look, there's no need for me to go on much longer. I will leave it up to your own good judgment whether or not we can raise this amount of capital. If it's not possible yet, then it's better that we simply keep earning our livings for a while and not pool our resources. So, look, now I ask all of you to give us your views on the situation," said Djahoemarkar, taking his seat.

As soon as he had sat down Dja Pangeldok jumped right up and said: "Everything that Djahoemarkar has told you is quite true, but with all these other *syarikats* around we usually get to read over their statutes of incorporation first. So please explain these to us first, so we can think them over."

"Thank you," said Djahoemarkar.

Raja Turncoat and Traitor sprang up and said: "Now, friends, I really like everything that the good Djahoemarkar has said, but I don't have a huge amount of faith in our own people. So I'm kind of afraid to turn over my share of money to them, you know. For instance, lots of *syarikats* are always getting into internal battles over their funds and squabbling, and it's one's own children who seem to lose out in the scuffle! So perhaps it's best just to be real careful here before jumping into anything."

"And thank you, too," said Djahoemarkar.

And then up stood several others: Raja Swaying in the Wind, and Raja Waylayer of Plans, and Raja I Sure Won't Go Along with *This*. They took turns showing off how very expert they were at pursuing inane details and talking in riddles—finally it got so bad that people's heads just spun. They didn't know who to believe anymore.

So Djahoemarkar got up again and said: "I have heard everything that has been said by our honored *tuans*, by our good noblemen, and by family and friends, and, of course, it is a fine thing for everyone to have his say. Those of us who make speeches up here are sort of like helmsmen on a ship, after all, and we all need to guide the rudder in the proper direction. But, listen, my good friends and relatives: a business without capital, well, that's about as good as someone who goes along as a gambler's sidekick but doesn't have a cent of his own to wager. We're the ones who break our backs, but other folks reap the profits from our labor! I heard people voice the opinion that as long as you've got some investment funds together, well, anyone's smart enough to make a commercial success of that—it doesn't take this *syarikat* to help them out. Anyone can engage in business, in buying and selling things—and who needs capital for that? That's what some clever folks here have said. That's true enough, but businesses like that are just about as good as the folks who own them. And, moreover, not much profit comes of that sort of thing, either. For instance, just consider: if we purchase some merchandise with cash we'll get a discount of 10 percent, but if we buy this stuff on credit the cost goes up by 10 percent. Now, you can all see the difference between buying with cash and buying on credit, I am sure! We reap 20 percent more profit with the cash transaction! Moreover, we won't have to do what other people tell us to do. This way we can light our own kindling wood and start our own cooking fire; that way we can close the door on all that progress from overseas. Most of the people who grow sick and tired of *syarikat*s are just like Pak Instrument Player's way of owning *gondang* gongs: if the gong's sound is good he says he owns the instrument, but if it sounds tinny it's the other guy's gong all right! It's *your* fault. Now, this sort of thing should not happen nowadays, in this present age. Now, what I say is if we're going to form this *syarikat* we need to raise the capital first. And there's no need whatsoever for you to worry. All the money from the shares you buy we'll save safely in a bank in Deli, and no one will be able to touch it unless we all agree to the use of it. And when we take the money out of the bank sometime in the future, that's when we'll give the name to the newborn child, to our new *syarikat*. That's when we'll specify exactly what we're going to do with our enterprise. And by following such a plan we won't just be indulging in pipe dreams; we'll be working with the capital we have at hand. So this is what I ask of all of you, what I've just said. And since, after all, the *bestuur*s of the committee are right here, let me turn the lectern back to them; they are surely the ones most expert at measuring and weighing the situation," said Djahoemarkar.

The chief *bestuur* of the committee declared: "Well, we certainly hope that all of you will think over what we've discussed at this *vergadering* very carefully. Please consider very seriously everything that Djahoemarkar has presented to you. We follow along in seconding exactly what he has told you: folks who work without amassing capital first will have their grand endeavors come to naught. For, after all, if some other capitalist gets mad at us he'll just stop selling things to us, and then where will we be? And, then, if we owe him money he can demand his collateral back. Using money that way is just indulging in daydreams. So please think all this over and then, if you feel it appropriate, send in ten florins for a share. That's per person, but you can also buy a number of shares at once if you want to. And please tell all your friends about us so that they can all send in their money to the committee's *bestuurs*. We *bestuurs* promise that we'll provide receipts before we print up the shares. And if the whole thing doesn't come off (that is, if we can't raise enough capital) we guarantee we will return all your money without prejudice. And now, as a way to close this *vergadering*, we say thank you very much to all of you, Godspeed, and may you have a safe journey home whether you live close by or far away."

23

A Graveside Visit to the Home Village

Ever since the airplane came to town everyone in Djahoemarkar's household had been having a great time, especially the kids. They simply could not stop talking about what had gone on out at the airfield. For her part, Sitti Djaoerah kept thinking about the time she flew up into the clouds, and she especially remembered the Honorable Protective Oceans, the one who flew up to the Upper Spirit World. "Why, we only had a chance to get a little bit into the story," the girl kept saying to herself. And Djahoemarkar's mother was happy to see how healthy and well behaved all her grandchildren were, not to mention her dear children.

One time Djahoemarkar was sitting there with his wife, surrounded by his mother's brother's wife and all their kids. The whole group looked very happy. And it occurred to Marah Moedo's Ompu (that is, to Nandjaoerah) to think back to her origin village and all the hardships they had endured in the past. And a shadowy image appeared in front of the old woman's eyes. So she said to Djahoemarkar: "Son! Well, it appears that I have a couple of sweet grandchildren by now, sweet babies who are golden hairpins in my daughter's shiny hairbun. And you have some sons now, don't you—and I have some little kids who will look up to me and offer their prayers on my behalf. And we're certainly not any worse off financially than other folks are these days. But it has been a long time since we left the home village, so I think it would be a very good idea if we go back home to pay a visit to the graves of Father, Mother, and your *ompung*. While there we can host a small prayer meal and ask the religious teachers to say some prayers for us. When I think back to how folks thought of us back home, and when I think of all the hardships folks have put us through, why, it's just terrible. But surely we are not permitted to simply forget all about our mother and father and about your *ompung*, about whose death we have just found out. If we just forget our elders surely we'd be sinning against them, and we would not want to offend the unseen spirits, now would we?[1] Of course not. So, Son, when you can see your way clear to ask leave from work, let's try to go back home for about ten days. Moreover, according to what the revered gurus say, when you send food, drink, and clothing to the dead you can't simply put it in a postal packet and send it via the post office.[2] No, you have to turn those goods over to the teachers, and they will surrender them to the honored dead along with some prayer recitals."[3]

Djahoemarkar mused quietly about what his mother's brother's wife had said. She was quite right, but the way folks back home had treated them in the past worried him. So he said: "I agree with everything you say, Mother's Brother's Wife. In fact, I have wanted to do just that for a long time now, but because I have been beset with such bad luck all this long while I kept those desires locked up inside me."

Sitti Djaoerah spoke up: "But how can we go back, Mother? Maybe Dad's[4] still got the word out for us to be arrested if we go there. Maybe he'll make things difficult for us. The villain might just take his revenge on us, you know."

"Oh, yes, when you think about it our going back would create something of a crisis, I guess," said Marah Moedo's Grandma.

"Well, look, let's just do this," said Djahoemarkar, making a decision. "First, we'll send some money to the *ompung* out in Sigalangan and she can fix up the gravesites and clean them off. Then we'll come and pay our *ziarah** visit, all right? But we'll have to go into town after dark so no one sees us. We can choose a time when there'll be lots of moonlight. We'll arrange to meet the *ompung* at the turnoff for the cemetery. If she's there along with the old *ompu*, Raja Awaiting Battle, we won't have anything to fear. After we've finished our *ziarah* prayers, we can go straight to Sigalangan and hold the prayer meal there. After that we can go straight home so no one will suspect we were there. There's a fast road these days, and we can just charter a Buick motorcar there and back. Who'll be the wiser?" "Fine . . . that's the way to do it," they all said.

The next morning Djahoemarkar sent off one hundred rupiah to his *ompung* out in Sigalangan. That would go toward cleaning off the graves of his parents and grandparents. With this money he sent along a letter: "When you're finishing fixing up the graves please send word to us immediately so we can come on our *ziarah* visit. We shall come at night so that no one finds out. We're afraid those angry with us might try to exact revenge. After our *ziarah* visit at the graves we'll go straight on to Sigalangan. Keep all this a secret so that no one finds out."

To put things briefly, the letter arrived at Ompung's, along with the money, and she and Raja Awaiting Battle set to their task right away, following Djahoemarkar's directions.

If anyone asked Djaimbaran (Djahoemarkar's *ompung* out in Sigalangan) he just told them he was using his own money to fix up the graves. People believed him, for he was rather well off.

They made the graves look very pretty. The three graves were lined up one right next to the other.

Once they were finished, Djaimbaran sent word to Deli for his grandchild to come right away, and he went on to say: "On the nights of the twelfth, the thirteenth, and the fourteenth we'll be waiting for you at the turnoff to the cemetery. Be sure to come around ten o'clock so no one will know. I'll be waiting there along with Raja Awaiting Battle, right along the side of the road."

As soon as Djahoemarkar got his *ompung*'s letter he told his wife and mother's brother's wife what was in it. They said fine, go ask for a ten-day leave.

The next morning Djahoemarkar explained everything to his boss and said he certainly hoped that Big Tuan could give him the time off.

---

*In Sumatran Muslim practice, a *ziarah* visit is a trip to a dead relative's grave to clean off the tomb, say prayers to the dead, and sprinkle water and oil on the gravesite.

He did give him the leave right away, since Djahoemarkar had been working on the plantation for a long time and had never asked for any time off.

After he got permission for the leave Djahoemarkar wrote a letter to his *ompung*, telling him what day they would leave and reminding him to keep watch at the crossroads just like he had said.

Just about the time the letter was due to arrive they all got their belongings ready, got dressed, and set off on their journey back to the home village. On the second day at about ten at night they pulled into Padang Sidimpuan. All of them were concealed under heavy shawls so that no one would recognize them. Because there was so much bright moonlight they could easily see what was going on in the town, especially since there weren't many folks about at that hour. When they got to Awaiting Riches's store the hairs on the backs of their necks stood up. Even though he had certainly caused them pain, if he had happened to appear from inside the house they would have wanted to talk to him. That was out of loneliness and longing. But everyone was asleep, and no one inside the house saw them. So the visitors just took a careful look at the store from a good distance away. It had changed a great deal from how it used to look. The house was run down from lack of care; old castoff carriage wheels were piled up around the houseposts. That was a sure sign that the shopkeeper had fallen on hard times.

"Yes, that's true enough, because once he married that woman from Natal the only thing they ever did was worry about one religious rule after the other. So the business fell into disrepair. The woman would always be telling him that she wasn't allowed to go outside the house, for if she caught sight of other folks that would break a religious law. And if someone saw *her*, that would also break an Islamic law. 'Why' (she'd say), 'the wealth and riches of this world are nothing more than the fruits of hell, which are the occasion of great sin.' But, frankly, she was just afraid of having to do some hard work. If Awaiting Riches didn't keep buying her beautiful sarongs and new lacy jackets she was none too happy to be doing his bidding, believe you me! And, of course, the food she ate had to be exceedingly fancy and delicious, too."

So the upshot of all this was that Awaiting Riches became her obedient little pack horse, trotting around finding food for her to enjoy. But she surely wasn't allowed to set foot outside the house.

Now, as for Djahoemarkar and his folks . . . once they got a look at the situation in Sidimpuan in the moonlight they turned the automobile toward the Other-Side Market so that Djahoemarkar could get a look at his own house. They all wanted to start sobbing at the sight, but Mara Moedo's Grandma stopped them so that no one would hear them and discover their presence.

There at the crossroads leading to the cemetery were Djaimbaran and Raja Awaiting Battle, waiting patiently for their arrival. After they shook hands and had a short cry they went over to the graves. They sprinkled them with the juice of citrus fruits and scattered some flowers they had brought with them from Deli. They lit some incense and said a few prayers and then went on back. On the way back to the house Djaimbaran and Raja Awaiting Battle made sure they weren't afraid. As soon as they got back to the main road they got right into the car and went off to Sigalangan.

When they got to Sihitang they woke up Boroe Soeti so that she would be sure to come along that night to Sigalangan. Early the next morning they hosted a modest little prayer meal and gave small alms payments to the religious teachers who were helping them out. They also gave alms to the other folks gathered there. After the meal they got dressed to set off on their return journey. Djahoemarkar made sure to leave lots of small gifts for his *ompung* and for Raja Awaiting Battle; Djahoemarkar and his folks also received a great many kind blessing speeches from the people gathered there at the feast, especially from his *ompung*, who had been missing him so very much all this long while.

When it got light they set off toward the *ranto* land. No one bothered them all the way along on their journey, and the same was true till they got back to their workplace.

Dear Reader, this book has now come to its end, but there is one point that is very fitting for us to remember: starting from the time Awaiting Riches ordered his daughter to marry Sutan Hardwood, she would not call him Father anymore. Even though Sitti Djaoerah frequently found herself up against dangerous enemies she would only call on her mother, on God, and on Djahoemarkar for help. This woman had firmly broken all her ties to that father of hers—to that man who lusted after a rich and powerful son-in-law.

So that ends it, then.

—THE WRITER

Notes

CHAPTER 1

1. "Tapian-na-uli," a Toba and Angkola Batak phrase, means "lovely bathing spot." This was a designation created by the colonial administration for the Batak lands around Lake Toba in the Balige area and to the south in Angkola and Mandailing. *Tuan* was the honorific appelation used by members of ethnic societies in the Indies for male Europeans of high social status (e.g., the Resident or chief adminstrator of a province, a school principal, or a Christian missionary preacher). *Tuan besar* means "big *tuan.*" Kuria means a district of a governmental unit such as a province; a huria is a congregation of the Christian church. Sibolga is a commercial town on the Indian Ocean coastline, located below the Batak highlands.

2. The sentence literally reads: "As for the wind-weather of that continent, it was said to be hot . . ."

3. "Commoner Lords, the One and the Many" (situan na torop na jaji) is one of St. Hasoendoetan's favorite ways of referring to "the general populace," the public. He takes this usage from the *adat* oratory of *horja* feasts of honor. There, grandiloquent phrases of this sort are standard usage in the nighttime *alok-alok* political oratory congresses that ceremonial chiefs hold to give their formal permission to the *horja* feast's host household to sacrifice a water buffalo, the "livestock of the rajas, the chicken whose color is glistening white."

4. *Lancat* (*lanseh*) fruits, common throughout Tapanuli, are lycheelike small succulent treats covered with light, buff-colored skins; *lancat* trees growing in the front yard are a stereotypic sign of household prosperity. *Ambasang* mangoes are a special, unusually sweet sort; the Batak languages have many words for varieties of mangoes.

5. Maurasipongi is a large market town in southern Mandailing known for its powerful noble families, its history of mercantile success in the *rantau*, and its cultural closeness to Minangkabau. Rao is a region of Minangkabau, close to the Mandailing border, while Padang is West Sumatra's capital and a thriving commercial port. Bukittinggi is a small mountain city, already well known by the 1920s in the southern and central Batak regions as a major "school town" (the Kweekschool Bukittinggi was there, a famous Dutch-language teacher-training institute).

6. Padang Bolak is the *adat* cheiftaincy domain surrounding the town of Gunung Tua. Rajas in this area have long been respected as superb orators.

7. Literally "kapitein, Luitenant, Officier."

8. A *menteri* was a supervisory official with some technical expertise gained through formal training.

9. ". . . and even some Dutch schools" (sikola Oelando): highly prestigious Dutch-language secondary schools such as Padangsidimpuan's MULO school—a gateway insitution for further schooling in Medan or even on the island of Java. MULO is an acronym for Meer Uitgebreide Lagere Onderwijs.

10. The "Other-Side" Market or Pasar Siborang: a Batak pronunciation of the Malay word *seberang* 'on the other side'. This Other-Side Market figures heavily as a familial home locale throughout the novel.

11. A *naga* is a supernatural, mythical snake mentioned in some Batak oratory.

CHAPTER 2

1. Regarding the title of this chapter, "About the Past" (taringot toe na robian), the Angkola Batak language has a number of mystical, mysterious-sounding ways of referring to the distant past (e.g., "na renci na robi"). By contrast, "na robian" strikes a more mundane tone.

2. Even today many southern Tapanuli people refer to the Minangkabau region, and particularly the area around the city of Padang, as Daret. This reference has an air of exoticism about it: in Angkola, Padang is thought to be the realm of amazingly adept merchants and Muslim sages.

3. The original wording is "Soedena i marsipangido haredjo na toepa tu ibana be." The pronoun *ibana* is not marked for gender (pronouns never are in Angkola Batak), but the sense of this statement seems to imply masculinity.

4. Mr. Thick-Calves (tumbur bitis) is one example of a range of "human body–type" epithets for referring to generic sorts of persons. These names have close connections with the *andung* mourning lament speech used by village women at times of leavetaking (burials of beloved relatives, departures of daughters upon their marriage journeys). In *andung* sob-speech, hands are called Hands the Askers for Favors, fire is Prince Flickerer (one of Van der Tuuk's deft translations), and eyes are Eyes the Peerers. Part 1's last chapter has a lovely, extended example of *andung* speech.

5. "The whole populace" here is put literally as "the Two and the Three"—a usage I sometimes employ in the translation. This is another *adat* oratory convention, rarely used in everyday speech.

6. Little Girl's Mom (Inang ni sitaing): this may be a misspelling of the Mandailing word *sitaring*. Angkola Batak speakers often use teknonyms to refer to adult women or men (Abdullah's Mother, Riana's Father); this is held to be more polite and respectful than bluntly using a person's name (something that is almost never done in polite company). "Inang ni" means "Mother of . . ." while Si Taring (Si Butet in the Padangsidimpuan and Sipirok areas) has the sense of "littlest girl in the family." Later, when a new daughter is born, *she* becomes Si Taring. This is not a personal name but a birth-order name. As we shall see later in the text, girls call their mothers Inang and the mothers use the same word with their daughters in face-to-face address.

7. *Onde-onde* are rounded snacks made of pounded glutinous rice.

8. Throughout the novel, characters are often said to wipe away tears in times of sudden emotional upset. Although this sounds odd in English, I retain the usage here.

9. "The later it got, the longer it got" (murmalamba murmalolot). Wherever possible Soetan Hasoendoetan uses playful, oratorylike phrases of this sort. Usage of this type is associated with joking courtship speech and village storytelling.

10. The author uses the word *huta* for "town" here. *Huta* usually refers to villages.

11. Dear Reader (Ale sipamasa, literally, "Friend the honored reader"): Soetan Hasoendoetan occasionally addresses us in this way, going on sometimes to instruct us to read or sing passages aloud.

12. This playful series of terms for friends invokes a common practice in Angkola speech-about-speech: amused references to the slight linguistic variations found in contiguous regions of Tapanuli.

13. Images of ants are often used in *adat* oratory to connote family luck and prosperity. For instance, when the woven motifs in the *parompa sadun* (baby sling) *ulos* textile is "read" to the infant during his or her birth ceremony, the orator will often refer to the ant design on the cloth and say: "May good luck swarm upon you like armies of ants."

14. Dusky Dark Evening (potang sidumadangari): a *turiturian* chant term almost never employed in everyday speech. Times of the day and night are praised at length in this sort of flowery chant speech in actual *turiturians*.

Chapter 3

1. The images of plentitude evoked here (a spacious house made of stout beams surrounded by trees heavy with succulent fruit) is reminiscent of court chronicles found throughout Sumatra and the wider Malay world about prosperous rajas and their well-stocked larders, livestock corrals, and fishponds. Plump livestock, capacious residences, and so on are taken as signs of noble luck and high standing.
2. This idea of an appointed hour of death is a Muslim concept often invoked in southern Batak areas. In this view, the timing of one's death is not something one may contest.
3. That is, her husband. This funny, affectionate phrase is associated with the formal oratory of weddings as well as folktale speech and proverbs.
4. This image of "breaking open immense stockpiles of grief" recurs throughout the novel, especially in relation to Djahoemarker. *Turiturian* chant speech is said to crack open deep wells of sadness, making listeners feel a poignant mixture of pain and longing.
5. Young Martial Arts Battler: for Angkola readers this name recalls the secret lore of esoteric self-defense knowledge taught by masters to young, subservient protégés. Arcane fencing and judolike knowledge of this sort are often associated with the "sacred power arts of invulnerability" of Minangkabau society in Batak eyes.
6. These praise names are similar to the ones given to princess characters in *turiturian* chants; they are also similar to the eulogistic ways of referring to brides in their wedding oratory.
7. Tu jae tu julu ('both upriver and down'): an extremely common phrase found in *adat* oratory, village folktales, and joking, conversational speech. Areas and people upriver are associated with backwoods regions and rustic ways.
8. They asked him to become their *induk somang*, their protective boss and mentor.
9. Women are sometimes disparaged like this in Angkola, but the overall gender climate is much more benign. Adult married women with several children are held in high regard, as "gifts" from their *mora* (wife givers), thrifty housekeepers, and accomplished orators.
10. The boys are becoming more impervious to mystical attack.
11. "Everything from 'ilmu kasar' to 'ilmu alus'": these are Malay words.
12. Boroe Soeti is a familiar, rather jocular way to refer to this particular woman. It means "daughter of the Nasution clan." Her potential spouses and other joking partners have license to call her Boroe Soeti. The same holds true for the joking partners of Boru Regar, daughters of the Siregar clan; Boru Angin, daughters of the wind clan (the Harahaps); Boru Pane, daughters of the Pane clan; and so on.
13. Angkang, or Older Lineage Companion, is used by younger men to their older lineage brothers; by wives to husbands (companions of a single *kahanggi*, or lineage plus in-marrying wives); and by those women to older women of their same generation who have also married into a lineage. A young women takes her father's clan name and keeps it throughout her life, but when she marries a man from another clan she begins to "carry *kahanggi*," to share in her husband's group identity. They are common *anakboru* (daughters), or wife receivers, to her father's lineage.
14. Southern Batak men greet each other and settle down to formal conversation by sharing the tobacco supplies used for handrolling cigarettes from the area's stringy, rough, pungent mountain tobacco.
15. The exclamation here is, indeed, "Amang inang" ('Father, Mother!').

16. This is a stereotypically luscious, hot peppery meal among southern Batak families. Women in the area are proud of their reputations as fine cooks.
17. This is a formulaic apology, spoken without regard for semantics: women in Angkola who say such things know very well that they have just served up wonderful repasts for their guests.
18. "Domain" here is *banu,* a similar to Malay *benua* 'continent,' 'wide realm'.
19. The original reads "Dalan hamagoan" 'the Path toward Disappearance'.
20. This is another of Soetan Hasoendoetan's jocular character names.
21. Aha na masa na moeba ('what is happening, what might be occurring'): this phrase is often used in both folktales and *adat* oratory.
22. "Lands above the Winds" (Dinagori sabola atas anginanma): a Batak rendering of the Malay "dinegeri sebelah atas angin." This means the European lands.
23. "A young wife" (sada ina ina): *ina ina* is a word used to refer to a young woman, recently married, who does not have any children yet.
24. These two lines read in the original: "Oppas, ning Jaksai / Ku . . . dison paramba taida." *Paramba* refers to a bondsman, while *oppas* refers to minor officials and sometimes the police.
25. The two words used here are *lani* and *onkunami.* The latter is a Padangsidimpuan pro-nunciation of *tuongku,* or *tuanku,* 'my honored Tuan'.
26. "Those skilled at telling tales" (Na marjamita): this seems related to the Malay sense of "yang empunya cerita" ('the one who owns the story'), although *marjamita* is a standard Angkola verb meaning 'to tell a story' or 'to convey news'.
27. In the original, Anggi refers to the young female cook.
28. "I shall consider you Kahanggi to me": part of the same older brother, younger brother lineage within our same clan.
29. Mount Nanggar Jati is a sharp, small mountain jutting up out of the rice paddies near the villages of Hanopan and Hutapadang in the Sipirok area. This mountain plays a leading role in the *turiturian* of Datuk Tuongku Tuan Malim Leman (related later in the novel and published in lengthier form as a separate volume by our writer). The chant's main charac-ters use the peak as their staircase for ascending to the Upper Spirit Kingdom from the earthly realm.
30. This mode of greeting a visitor evokes an image familiar to all who attend *adat* feasts, where honored guests from outside the village are saluted with formal martial arts dances and then escorted into the Great House where the ceremony is being held.
31. Our beloved Dad (our *damang*): adding the d to the basic word for "father" connotes *our* Dad (not simply a classificatory relative we "call Amang" to). The usage connotes warmth.
32. Isarat sarupa poda asa hombar sarupa uhum: literally, 'same rule, same law'.
33. This image evokes the picture of a family accepting a blessing-conveying meal, or *pangu-pa,* at an *adat* feast.
34. *Dongki* ('malicious jealousy and envy') is a pivotal emotion in many southern Batak sto-rytelling narratives. Enemies and detractors seek to ruin fond hopes and plans, for they are jealous.
35. The Black-Haired One (Silomlom Ulu): a human being!

CHAPTER 4

1. The cannon here is called a *lelo.*
2. Desa na walu (Eight *Adat* Domains All Around): these are the surrounding chieftaincies, all of which should send rajas to buffalo sacrifice feasts held anywhere in Angkola.

3. The original wording is "aha na masa na muba di tano rura banua on?!" This is a formulaic query, often used in the *adat* oratory of *horja* feasts when rajas are seeking to determine why a ceremony has been called and convened.

4. Na ulu bulungi (literally, 'that lovely, most highly respected, elderly leaf' on the Tree of Life): an aged raja, one revered enough to serve as a *horja* feast's chief raja.

5. This is a standard eulogistic saying in praise of one's *anakboru*, or wife takers. In *adat* oratory and in proverbs *anakboru* are our cane over the slippery spots, our hardwood plank bolting the door shut against dangers.

6. In the ideal, anyone who attends a *horja* feast should have been approached several days before by two formally dressed representatives of the host family bearing a beaded betel purse. This the two men ceremoniously present to the invitees while asking them to please come to the *horja*.

7. These are the special names for the musical instruments played for *horja* feasts. The rajas are the owners of these ensembles of gongs and drums; only they may give permission for these instruments to be struck (once the blood of the sacrificial water buffalo has been spilt). For a sensitive, ethnographically detailed description of *adat* musical instruments in Mandailing, see Margaret Kartomi's "'Lovely When Heard from Afar': Mandailing Ideas of Musical Beauty" (1981).

8. "Potang sidumadangari."

9. It was like a "pasar malam" (Malay), an all-night fair. Every sizable town will have these: exciting, bustling, nighttime street fairs where people stroll around past innumerable stands selling merchandise and treats.

10. The 1920s was a time of considerable debate in southern Tapanuli Islam over the issue of whether or not the faithful should participate fully in *horja* feasts, which, of course, involved water buffalo sacrifices and much speech making. Some religious teachers considered the latter to be blasphemous praise speeches to ancestor spirits. Modernist Muslims throughout this part of Tapanuli and West Sumatra's Minangkabau society worked to cleanse Islamic life of such "compromises" with local *adat* ceremonial and its spirit-filled worldview.

11. These *tuans* would be the Dutch officials based in Padangsidimpuan.

12. The eye, or essence, of the *horja* (*mata ni horja*) is the most solemn, spiritually portenuous, and dangerous time of the entire event, the time when the water buffalo's throat is slit with a long knife and the ancestor spirits draw near to the assembly to convey their protective blessings.

13. These are standard phrases in *horja* oratory, especially in the nighttime *alok-alok* political oratory congresses where rajas from the Eight Adat Domains All Around gather to give their permission to hold the *horja*.

14. Ankola's slow, elegant, mesmerizing *tortor* dances are performed explicitly to pay homage to the aged rajas in attendance at a *horja*.

15. *Anakboru* dance in a loose circle behind their *mora* (wife givers), protecting them from physical attack. This service is one of the *anakboru's* main contributions to their *mora's* welfare (the latter, in turn, shower spiritual protection on their *anakboru*).

16. The *onang-onang* singer sits by the *gondang* gong and drum ensemble throughout a *horja* feast, singing eulogistic songs in honor of each group of dancers that performs. A good *onang-onang* singer will compose special songs for specific rajas who are scheduled to dance; he will do this by ascertaining biographical details of their lives plus minute points regarding their lineage history and its patterns of marriage alliance.

17. Parsegar caluk kanan i (the ceremonial headcovering, its tie slanted to the right): this is a turbanlike affair, borrowed from Minangkabau.

18. *Horas* is the basic Batak word of greeting, conveying wishes of good luck, approbation, and congratulation. It has a core meaning of good health, and saying the word is thought to have a health-enhancing effect.

19. *Hula-hula* is the Toba Batak word for *mora* (well understood in Angkola). In high *adat* oratory, the *mora* is its *anakboru's* "sun in the sky," always looking after its indebted wife receivers' spiritual health.

20. These noblemen were actual people, well-known rajas in the 1920s.

21. These phrases are taken from *alok-alok* speech and the oratory of *horja* invitations.

22. A person's *tondi* resides within him or her, for life, as a kind of animating force. It can be jarred loose (or, even worse, it can go wandering about the countryside unmoored). *Horja* ceremonies have as one of their principal aims "firming up" the *tondi* souls of all participants, particularly those of the household and *kahanggi* lineage hosting the gathering. For comparative material on Toba, see J. C. Vergouven's classic *The Customary Law of the Toba Bataks of Northern Sumatra* (1933), which has extensive discussions of Toba Batak soul beliefs.

23. *Tua* is a sort of lucky life force, which all households and *kahanggi* lineages need in order to prosper, both in material and agricultural terms and in the sense of producing numerous healthy babies. Ancient ancestors are said to have *tua*; so, too, do a *kahanggi's mora* wife givers, who can convey such magic stores of luck to their beholden wife receivers.

24. Age of Religion (Joman parugamoan): this is a Batak pronunciation of the Malay "jaman peragamaan." A *jaman* is a major era of human time; today "the *jaman* before religion came" (i.e., world religion, Islam or Christianity) and "this present age of religion" are common concepts in Angkola. Islam arrived in this part of Tapanuli in the 1820s and Protestant Christianity in the 1850s and 1860s.

25. Shouting "*horas*" is the general way to close a major *adat* oration. It is a luck-conveying word, often combined with a longer saying, "May all be forever *horas*, may no disasters strike."

26. *Bujing-bujing* is the personhood term used for adolescent, unmarried girls.

27. That is, they had been occupied with serving food to all the men who flowed into the village as honored guests. Angkola young people are worked extremely hard as food servers and cleanup crews throughout the long initial days and nights of a *horja*. Finally, near the end of the ceremony, they are allowed to perform their special dance together (in all other forms of *tortor* except the bridal *tortor* of newlyweds in a wedding *horja*, men and women dance separately).

28. Hum bohaboha ijuk dope: this way of saying "about 5 A.M." is most typically found in *turiturian* chant speech. All major times of the day have indirect references of this sort.

29. That is, they went to the "tanggal batu," a favorite spot, too, for *turiturian* characters to bathe.

30. *Ulubalang*s in Angkola *adat* are swordsmen and military attachés, so to speak, of the village raja. The latter will often draw his *ulubalang* from his *anakboru pusako*, his heirloom-treasure *anakboru* (his *kahanggi's* long-established, traditional, "main" wife-receiver lineage). The word seems to be a borrowing from Acehnese and perhaps Minangkabau court usage.

31. Big Tuan here would be the Dutch Resident himself.

32. Omas sigumorsing: a courtly way to refer to a woman's bridewealth payments. This lovely phrase is used in *turiturian* chants (not surprisingly) but also in all *kobar boru* (negotiating the brideprice) sessions, even those quite modest in scope, which do not involve a *horja*-level wedding. Sometimes the phrase gets extended: "Omas sigumorsing na marlin-

dak marlobi-lobi" ('yellow-yellowest, glittering gold, which overflows its container in swelling waves').

33. *Tarbakta raja* ('glorious time owned by the high rajas').

34. Her mother's brother (her *tulang*), the great merchant from Padang (West Sumatra's capital city in the Minangkabau ethnic area). This is most interesting, since, of course, it refers to a southern Tapanuli family with marriage alliance ties to Minangkabau.

35. Si Taring is the Mandailing birth-order name for the littlest girl in the family. It is a term of indulgence and affection, the equivalent of Angkola and Toba's Si Butet.

36. This evocation of the poignant feeling of *lungun* (longing for times past or personal relationships lost) recurs many times in the novel. It harks back, too, to the raison d'être of chanting *turiturians*: to break open all manner of longing and sadness.

37. This is a sort of dais of honor, similar in form and intention to the textile and pillow-bedecked seating place of a bridal couple in a *horja* wedding. Regular attendees sit on one layer of the rattan mat.

38. Suhut sihabolonan.

39. ". . . patantan simanjojak pagayung alang simangido": this is a recurrent phrase in *horja* oratory, especially when the rajas speak. It alludes not only to gliding motions the rajas supposedly made as they came from their distant home villages to the *horja* but also to the elegant, slow, refined hand, arm, and leg movements of their courtly *tortor* dances in the *horja* at hand.

40. Fathers are said to protect their children in this way, as are the elder members of a *kahanggi* lineage. A noble family's Great House itself is said to hold its occupants tight and safe within its fist. In this passage the "Dutch Raja," or Resident, is flattered with similar protective powers.

41. Tuan Besar is the Dutch Resident, and his Controleur is his representative.

42. "Dear Reader" (ale sipamasa): *ale* here means 'beloved friend'.

43. These various men's games have an air of illicitness in some southern Batak regions, and a faint association with the sort of entertainment indulged in by Indonesian Chinese.

44. That is, "that I'll hightail it back to my natal village (where I lived before I married your father)."

45. This *pangupa* mound of hot rice and a boiled egg is similar to the one presented to newly married couples, whose souls are held to be in dire need of protection and "firming up." Southern Batak *adat* has a number of soul-firming, protective-blessing meals, ranging from special carp dinners for the sick, to *pangupas* of this sort, to truly major restorative efforts such as the huge mound of rice, buffalo meat, stewed jackfruit, boiled eggs, river fish, and tiny shrimp fed to the host family on the eye of the *horja* day at that sort of *adat* feast. Boiled buffalo brains, shared by the assembled noblemen on the same day, are also held to have great "soul enhancement" efficacy.

46. This is another standard *horas* sendoff phrase.

CHAPTER 5

1. Wagering one's *inherited* rice paddies is anathema in *adat* morality: this is one's heirloom treasure from past generations, intended for one's descendants' use and enjoyment.

2. This is a reference to the same shocking idea described in note 1. The words here are *barang pusako*, from the Malay *barang pusaka* 'inherited heirloom treasure goods'.

3. Each major luxury sarong would come with a trademark, usually denoted by a picture on the label.

4. Parents are often thought to be vulnerable to serious illness caused by worry over their young adolescent (unmarried) children. Mothers are thought to be particularly subject to sudden disastrous weight loss from worry of this type. Even having a young daughter or son living far away from the home village can cause such worry sicknesses.

5. Mangamuk kulikuli halak Nias: this phrase employs the Malay verb based on the word *amuk* and the common Batak way of referring to plantation laborers, as coolies. This is a term of abuse.

6. The instrument referred to here is the *sarune*.

7. A clean, unfurrowed brow is a stereotypic sign of an untroubled soul, unbothered by worry or danger.

8. The "plantation owner" here is "nampuna kobun on" ('the one who owns this farm'), using the regular Angkola word for farm.

9. The "Sorceror *Datu*" (bayo datu): *bayo* means "the guy," the *datu*-sorcerer-diviner man. In Angkola, *datus* are spell casters, spell removers, augurers, and village healer-diviners. They can diagnose and cure evil spirit infestations, or (if they are bad *datus*) cause such afflictions in the first place. *Datus* are feared but respected. Families consult them for determining an auspicious day for launching any major undertaking such as a wedding, breaking ground for a new house, or a *horja* ceremony.

10. Utiutian: a customary way of doing things.

11. This long string of "all of us are in this together" sayings is familiar to those who attend *adat* weddings, house-entry *horja* feasts for dedicating new homes, and other ceremonies of thanksgiving. These sentiments are often expressed toward *kahanggi* partners (lineage brothers, their wives, or their male descendants).

12. The sentiments in these two sentences are derived from praise phrases for *anakboru* wife receivers, who act as their *mora's* shield against "the harsh wind and rain."

13. These phrases about flimsy lean-tos figure often in young men's complaint songs, or *ungut-ungut* laments (songs about being ignored by potential girlfriends. *Ungut-ungut* are sung out in the gardens, far from the village).

14. Halalungun: 'deep, poignant longing'.

15. *Marsitogol* singing was an entertainment form performed by young men to lament their hard luck in love. Sung in a low, moaning voice, it is designed to elicit pity and sympathy from young women who may overhear it.

16. Literally, his *roha*, or mind-intelligence, was *rarat*, or scattered about.

17. So that all these distressful sights would *mago* ('disappear, vanish') from his *parnidaan*, from his sight, his vision. The operative focus here is with the eyes, not some "deeper" interpretive mind.

18. In the original, Rangga Balian does not exclaim "Oh, brother!" but first calls out for a magic charm. I have added this to help capture some of the fast-paced fun of the original.

19. This is the same sort of soul-restoring meal as was mentioned in the previous chapter. Health-securing rice is *indahan horas horas*.

CHAPTER 6

1. Awaiting Riches's wife calls "*anggi*" to Pandingkar Moedo, just as her husband does. That is, they speak to him as a junior member of their *kahanggi*, their lineage.

2. In Angkola folktales and *turiturian* chants, married women are often portrayed as sadly musing about lost childhood days (before their marriage, before they had to leave their natal household and, often, their natal village). They lament the loss of their favorite play-

grounds (this sentiment figures heavily, too, in the bride's *andung* laments, her songs of leavetaking sung as she sets off on her marriage journey).

3. In *martandang* courtship speech girls and boys will often refer to potential boyfriends or girlfriends as *mayam-mayaman,* playthings for the heart.

4. These are standardized *martandang* courtship phrases, also used in *osong-osong* contests (verbal duels between a female representative of *mora* and a male representative of *anakboru* at thanksgiving or *siriaon* types of *horja* feasts: wedding *horja* and those for new houses and births). The original phrases read "manyammanyam mi roha do, na tama pasonang ateate, na tupa paria roha . . ."

5. The word here is *kontak,* which people in Angkola use even today to indicate that an electrical circuit has made contact.

6. A young man can only attain full adult status by *mambuat boru,* or taking a bride. The phrase here is "dipatobang mangihutkon adat" ('to be made mature according to *adat*').

7. Light-toned skin is highly prized by Angkola standards of female beauty. This particular phrase occurs in *turiturian* chants as well.

8. Literally, "the public the two and the three."

9. Hadatuon dohot elmu mudo-mudo pe: the last part of this is a borrowing from the Malay *ilmu muda-muda,* the esoteric special lore of young people (the secret courtship arts).

10. These are standard praise phrases used in wedding oratory by village leaders and old women to eulogize the sterling nature of the new bride who has just arrived in their village.

11. According to *tutur,* or proper, polite, accurate, kin term usage. When strangers meet they should first *martutur,* question each other cagily and indirectly about their clan, lineage, and marriage alliance identities, to ascertain what sort of kinspersons they are, so that they might know the proper *tutur*: the right kin terms of address to use.

12. Pandingkar Moedo has all of his *nantulang*'s daughters as his potential wives, so he can speak of this imaginery one as "still living in her father's house" since he wants to declare that he is not yet married.

13. That is, when a father speaks to his son he calls the boy Amang (the word the boy uses for "Father" in direct address). Mothers also call their sons Amang. Additionally, mothers and fathers call their daughters Inang (the same word these adults use to address their own mothers).

14. His honored "*tulang* person," an especially respectful phraseology.

15. This is yet another reference to wedding oratory, especially to speech used to praise brides in their *kobar boru* sessions (the *adat* congresses called to negotiate their bridewealth payments). Good *boru* stereotypically stay inside their parents' houses a good deal of the time, embroidering and sewing away happily (this notion has little connection to reality, even in high-born families).

16. That is, she's asking whether her household has some well-established marriage alliance relationship with these folks—or is her mother making this *tutur* up on the spot to encourage the boiled corn trade?

17. This is a cliché term for "going to market" used even today. In mountainous areas of Angkola, particularly, salt was a precious commodity throughout the colonial era and a major item of long-distance trade. Salt merchants would sometimes walk from village to village, selling this indispensable item for preparing red pepper and fish curries (the village staples).

18. This is another stereotypic reference to a time of life for very young *bujing-bujings.*

19. That is, go and become a bride (subservient to her new mother-in-law).

20. Si Taring uses the Malay word *laku* here, as in a popular food which "sells well" at the market. This is a common way of talking about the marriageability of Angkola girls. "Na man-

gan gaji" (who consumes a formal salary) is also used in this paragraph; men who draw a salary were prime marriage material in the prewar decades, when most young men were penurious farmers. Even the wealthier farmers who had made money on the coffee market apparently felt themselves to be less socially acceptable than salary men. At least they would sometimes talk that way.

21. Toba sirara: the fearsome "Red Toba" is invoked in Angkola speech for its bogeyman potential. The Toba Batak had a reputation at the time of being aggressive, bloodthirsty, and warlike (not to mention pig-eating and Christian). Certainly it is no place for a proper Angkola girl to "marry to"!

22. *Marsitogol* songs, as has been noted, are complaint songs sung by young unmarried men about girlfriends who ignore them, unrequited love, and the like.

23. Note how similar this roundabout courtship statement is to Djahoemarkar's riddle-speech to Sitti Djaoerah in their marriage proposal scene in part 2.

24. This is a standardized *horas-horas* type of signoff, a leavetaking routine.

25. Literally, the initial phrase reads "Pis matamu da baya . . ."

26. "Raja Mousedeer" (Djalandoek): Mousedeer is a beloved animal hero in Sumatran children's folktales. He often bests his larger competitors (such as Tiger) by outwitting them, despite his diminutive size.

27. Klas satu ('first class'): this term combines the Malay word *satu* 'one' with *klas* 'class'.

28. Parbisuk manjuluk tano parakal manorus dolok: a eulogistic praise phrase usually used in *alok-alok* oratory or very formal brideprice negotiation sessions to praise noblewomen.

29. These are ice-breaking gifts meant to get the marriage negotiations going. Every step of the bridewealth negotiation process must be initiated through the exchange of specific types of presents.

30. Ari sidapot-dapot.

31. They are not carrying a *haronduk.*

32. Different types of tobacco have different names in *adat* (just as betel leaves do). Here the women are talking about *timbako tali.*

33. As was noted above, younger women who have a reputation for walking brashly through the village and the countryside are deemed "bad girls," while their opposite numbers are *bujing-bujing*s, those who stay properly inside their parents' houses, sewing, learning to cook, and caring for younger siblings.

34. Your *iboto* 'putative clan mate' in this case.

35. A bride, in wedding oratory and numerous proverbs, is known as the "cane over the slippery spots" (tungkot di na landit) for her new *kahanggi.* She is a boon to them, according to *adat,* in times of familial and financial stress.

36. The cloth is a requirement for a full wedding according to *adat.* Brides put these gifts under their pillows and "dream on them." This provides an augury on the happiness (or problems) of the forthcoming marriage.

37. Djaimbaran is angling for the easiest sort of brideprice negotiation strategy: avoiding a lengthy and expensive *kobar boru* negotiation congress by agreeing on and paying the various sums beforehand.

38. This is a standardized answer, which well brought up young women should give during this early part of their wedding ceremonies. Rajas today say that this statement is necessary so that no one will make a mistake about *which* young man in the village she has come to marry. At issue here also is the idea that the young bride seeks a living mate, not a ghost.

39. These are all standard phrases from wedding oratory.

40. These "moving over the mountain" phrases are taken from *horja* oratory, most specifically *alok-alok* speeches. They represent the gliding motions noblemen make as they stride into a *horja* ceremony.
41. "The birds begin to sing out their glad news" is the standard way in *adat* speech to say that a young wife is in the very early stages of pregnancy.
42. Children are generally said to be born in the womb, in the waters of the amniotic sac.
43. This image seems to have been borrowed from folk Islam, from stories of the Prophet Muhammad's miraculous birth.
44. The village is called Tano Poetih, a Malay phrase.
45. "Sprouting up like a cucumber" is a way of referring to the healthy growth spurts of robust children (in the *adat* oratory of birth ceremonies).
46. *Andung* are sobbed mourning laments of women. The most highly charged genre of Angkola speech in an emotional sense, *andung* routines are moaned at times of major leavetaking (a death, a child's departure for the *rantau*, a daughter's departure from her parental house for her marriage journey). By the 1920s this form of speech was already beginning to die out except in the remotest mountain villages. Only a few old women today know long snatches of *andung*.

CHAPTER 7

1. "Kind women friends" (kele): this is an intimate term of address women use among themselves. It is not a kin term.
2. Pangarkari ni halalungun."
3. These eulogies are reminiscent of the praise phrases for young rajas found in court chronicles throughout the Malay world and in Angkola *turiturian*.
4. Omas sigumorsing.
5. The image of children who lose weight and waste away looms large in Angkola village thought as a prime sign of household and *kahanggi* (lineage) ill luck.
6. "A lump of gold as big as a horse's head" was a cliché phrase throughout the Batak areas and in Minangkabau.
7. Inangna na malo sumalung roha, na pande mangalage hata, na tau dibasobaso: these are standard eulogies for noblewomen, in *horja* oratory, although the last word specifically refers to the secret lore of *sibaso,* female shamans.
8. That is, how to *martutur.*
9. Na tobangtobang: a sign of a well-raised child is his or her ability to sort through all the kin term possibilities and use them appropriately, especially those for high-status, older adults. Controlling the *tutur* in this way is a major part of becoming a fully human person in the sense of *maradat* ('having the *adat*').
10. This is a reference to the way elegant *tortor* dancers should turn their bodies.
11. The Malay words for silver and gold are used here; this may be a borrowed phrase from Malay chronicles or folktales.
12. A *lobe* is an Islamic instructor; *malang* means 'unfortunate' or 'ill starred' in Malay.
13. Si Miskin 'Si Poor Man' (Malay).
14. Young people are supposed to turn over major life decisions to their elders. At least they make a show of saying so in public.

CHAPTER 8

1. In the original the text mistakenly lists this as chapter 7. I have renumbered it here.
2. Even today, married men must be very circumspect in their dealings with young, attractive widows. These women are thought of as sexually experienced, unattached, mature women—an anomaly in polite village or town society.
3. Jagarjagar ni sanggul ni parsondukna (anak dohot boru): this is taken from the oratory of *horja* weddings.
4. The word *tua* is used here.
5. These are the specific type of rice gifts, wrapped in just this way, that *kahanggi* must bring at the birth of a baby.
6. This is a reference to the *parompa sadun ulos* textile, the special baby sling for keeping the child healthy and safe from mystical dangers or attack.
7. The sentiment among Awaiting Riches's clan sisters was: "Let's be sure to keep this pretty little girl with us in the family and have her marry one of our sons. There's no reason for her to marry some outsider since she has all these perfectly good father's sister's sons for potential matches." In anthropological terms, they wish to keep her for a matrilateral cross-cousin marriage, the ideal one in the *adat*.
8. Before this formal naming ceremony, the infant is not deemed a full person.
9. The name is fully capitalized in the original text.
10. These eulogies again recall the praise for young noblemen in Malay world chronicles.
11. In Angkola thought, children do 'replay' the lives and presence of older generations, usu-ally grandparents. Additionally, a perfect matrilateral cross-cousin marriage pair of young children (a boy and his mother's brother's daughter) replay the marriage of their forebears: their father and mother. The brother-sister pair of course cannot marry, for that would break the ultimate Angkola incest taboo, but they arrange for their boy and girl children to be united. This 'forbidden marriage' is always in the conceptual background of perfect matches of young children. Djahoemarkar and Sitti Djaoerah are classificatory matrilateral cross-cousins since Si Taring is considered Awaiting Riches's *iboto* by this point in the story.
12. Five and six year olds sometimes do carry infants on their backs in cloth slings and in fact often serve as prime child minders.
13. This little ditty is in a version of Malay.
14. Hum maralimus.
15. This apparently was a Chinese-owned shop.
16. This is a reference to Minangkabau styles in the city of Padang.
17. Tuan Inspecteur: the Dutch school inspector.
18. This may be a reference to a Javanese-style head covering for men or some kind of Minangkabau-style cloth headgear.
19. The word used here is *huta*, or home village, a reference to their Padangsidimpuan neigh-borhoods.
20. Providing sets of clothing for young relatives is a major point of Angkola *adat*. One main gift obligation of this sort is the one that holds between older brothers (the clothing givers) and their younger sisters.

CHAPTER 9

1. Muslim children throughout Sumatra expect their parents to buy them sets of new clothing for the holiday ending the Fasting Month. Stereotypically they pout if denied their due here.

2. That is, they asked forgiveness of each other "lahir dan bathin," for external as well as spiritual offenses they may have committed over the past year. The phrasing here draws on standardized Muslim southern Batak usage.

3. "Dihatiha na jolo . . ."

4. This staircase metaphor is my own. The novelist says that the girls *marsienekeneki* 'walked along', one after the other, hand in hand.

5. Special fishes are held to have healing, restorative powers in several Batak societies. Some illnesses are even said to be caused by a person's unrequited craving for a certain type of fish (usually a luscious big carp, which the invalid's family then procures).

6. A well brought up person in Angkola will always have access to a betel tin or purse for offering betel quid to guests and inviting them to *mandok hata* or 'say formal words' or speeches. The raja's daughter has truly fallen into poverty, we learn from this detail.

7. This warning is often uttered in *adat* speech-making congresses and also in the proverb-filled speech of village conversations.

8. The word used here is *hurangkurangan*, which indicates that the children felt a loss, a lack of something. The term is borrowed from the Malay word *kurang*.

9. The lesson house: "bagas parsipodaan." This seems to be a self-consciously old-fashioned usage, since "sikola" is the more common term.

10. Djasoerseran.

11. A pair of adolescents with an overt marriageable relationship would have to be more circumspect in their behavior, for otherwise people would mock them.

CHAPTER 10

1. As was noted previously, on the last night of a *horja* for a happy occasion the unmarried teenage girls are allowed to perform *tortor* dances, surrounded by a ring of boys dancing in accompaniment. The girls and boys must be in a marriageable relationship. The movements of the boys' hands and arms "protect" the girls from harm; this is the sense of *ayap-ayapi*.

2. *Syarikat*s were social organizations, leagues, and clubs, which often worked to promote nationalist sentiment. The most famous in the Indies was Syarikat Islam, a Muslim traders' association in Java.

3. The author here uses the Malay phrase "sama rata, sama rasa" ('same level, same feelings').

4. That is, before Islam and Christianity arrived in Tapanuli. The novelist uses the word *ugamo* to mean world religion (*agama* in Malay).

5. This is a reference to the idea that *adat* etiquette governing the behavior of marriagable adolescents is much stricter in villages than it is in the "more cosmopolitan" towns.

6. Parasols were used by young women as a sign of fashion, but in the southern Batak areas they are also major symbols of high noble standing. Rajas at *horja* feasts are shielded from the sun, for example, with yellow fringed parasols. These make up part of the inherited house treasure of noble families, and regular commoners may not use such things.

7. "Bondswomen" (halak gadison): purchased servants. *Hatoban* means slave.

8. Here Nandjaoerah says: "Bia do Apa . . ." ("Now, come on, what about it, Apa . . .") The last word is a Batak rendering of the Malay word *bapak* ('father'), which has been made to conform here with the Angkola usage of the address term *amang*, which a woman would use toward her son. Nandjaoerah is not formally designating Djahoemarkar as son-in-law material yet, it seems.

9. A rosy hue is considered a strong sign of health for adolescents. Eulogistic paeans to a woman's beauty are found in *turiturian* chants, where there are routines for extolling a

woman's loveliness from the top of her head down to her feet. These occur later in the novel, in chapter 13.

10. A properly brought up daughter of the rajas will sport a full set of twenty-four-karat gold ornaments by the time she is a teenager. This set consists of hoop or button earrings, a heavy gold necklace, fancy jacket clasps, and at least one thick, coiled bracelet. She will take this considerable amount of wealth with her into her eventual marriage.

11. Dipasar malam ni surgo jannatun nain.

12. By rights, the Hari Raya guests who came to the house on that day would have polished off all the treats.

CHAPTER 11

1. "Zinc roofed" (martaru seng). Sutan Hardwood is Soetan Hayeo Inggolam, the latter being a particularly hard and tough forest wood.

2. This sentence in the translation draws on American style, of course. The original text reads: Amang inang ('Father and Mother!') sonang ni bayo na posoposo an ('that young guy's happy enough').

3. Here, again, Sutan Hardwood exclaims "Amang inang."

4. Once more, Sutan Hardwood exclaims "Amang inang."

5. Malim Most Hopeful is Malim Mangarop in the original.

6. "Law" is *hukum sia.*

7. In Angkola one always takes care not to induce sudden shocks in other people, particularly relatively vulnerable ones such as teenagers. Unexpected news, sudden harsh words, or a physical shaking can jar the person's *tondi* soul loose from its moorings in the body, leaving the person despondent, confused, and possibly ill. A special soul-enhancing, soul-firming meal would then be called for or an outright consultation with a *datu*-augurer/spell remover.

8. The wording in the original is "anggo di johirna."

9. The wording in the original is "ecet dopur."

10. Small children about age six or seven were often pressed into service as carriers of love letters between adolescent boyfriends and girlfriends. Back before many Batak school-children learned to read and write "the Dutch letters," they would send each other love messages composed of packets of leaves and twigs (*surat katang-katang*). Each leaf or piece of bark (for instance, a sliver of cinnamon bark) would convey a specific sentiment to the boyfriend or girlfriend. One could compose complex messages by mixing several different forest products into the same bundle.

11. "My suicide rope (tali siudoron), which I will yank tight on the hanging tree (kayu sinahi-ton)." This is a highly standardized, familiar image in Angkola. Young people (usually young adolescent girls) sometimes threaten to kill themselves in the forest by hanging themselves from such a tree, often in groups of two to four persons. This seems to be a stereotypical threat rather than a prediction of a real suicide.

12. "A certain promise" (sada janji): This is from the Malay. Elsewhere in this chapter their vow to marry each other is called a *padan janji na togu* ('firm oath-promise'), which is the original novel's subtitle. A *padan* in Angkola is a sacred oath that one simply may not break.

13. This phrase is taken from the *adat* oratory, especially that of marriage negotiation sessions in which lineages haggle over brideprice sums. Frequently they must assure each other that they are not trying to pull a fast one, which, of course, they are.

14. In the courtship verbal duels of *martandang* speech young men often urge their girl-friends to "grow up real fast" so they'll be old enough to marry them. This sentiment seems to lie in the background of boys' gifts of snack foods to their girlfriends.

CHAPTER 12

1. The verb used here is *pasonting*.
2. Ama dohot ina.
3. Roha na so pade ("a state of mind that is not so good").
4. Naimardjolis is being dispatched as the advance force, the one who gets the bridewealth negotiations started.
5. Nipaampalampal in the original.
6. That is, someone whose father's *kahanggi* is already a marriage alliance partner, someone who's already *family*.
7. These phrases are said of happy married couples in *adat* oratory and also of *kahanggi* mates who get along well.
8. This is also derived from wedding oratory: newlyweds must be sure not to work at cross purposes.
9. The wording in the original text is "Mudo ro na songon i marrangkeso ma na i niomo."
10. Hatang-hatang na so marisi sira . . . , a reference to saltiness.
11. Aturan ompungmu do ma i. One may *not* go against one's grandparent's explicit orders or disastrously bad luck will result.
12. Na dua tolu dihuta on ('the public, the two and the three') in the village.
13. That is, at her *mebat* ceremony her father's lineage mates will use much of the bridewealth they have received to set her up in housekeeping (with mattresses, mats, pillows, dishes, cutlery, etc.).
14. The wording here is "danak ni pamatang dohot rohana" ('child of my body and mind-intelligence').
15. Village clichés have it that adolescent girls will normally fight the notion of getting married if their parents are arranging things.
16. Anak boru na so umboto untungna an: a frequent putdown in folktales.
17. Jacob saltines come in big, impressive-looking, tin boxes all the way from Singapore and signal a household's prosperity (even today out in the mountain villages). Store-bought white sugar accomplishes much the same end; most farm families at the time would simply sweeten drinks and foods with red palm sugar.
18. Na baun mangalage hata i: a standardized eulogy for new brides and older married women who are adept at making *adat* speeches.
19. This phrase is used in *kobar boru* oratory (brideprice negotiation speeches) by the young man's family to declare that they have searched high and low for extra funds to meet the "exhorbitant" demands of the bride's side for *boli*, or bridewealth payments.
20. Angkola girls are thought to be vulnerable to offers of jewelry and pretty clothes when an unwelcome marriage offer is afoot.
21. Adat marama.
22. Nandjaoerah uses the word *laku* here (Malay for 'sell well', as in merchandise, but also as in *boru*, or daughters).
23. Djabargot: in other words, Raja Red Palm Tree.
24. Adat ni na mangolu.
25. That is, only a few of the initial payments had been made.

26. This is another proverb often used in *adat* oratory, generally in reference to the *anakboru*'s nature. One must be careful lest one's wife receivers become offended. They are full of thorns.
27. An *orangkaya* in Angkola is a village guardsman, the military attaché, so to speak, of the village raja (*orangkaya* is one of the raja's chief *anakboru*).

CHAPTER 13

1. Dia na masa na muba ('whatever has happened, whatever has changed?'): this is a standard inquiry used in all manner of *adat* ceremonies to inquire why the gathering is taking place (a birth celebration, the arrival of a bride in the village, etc.).
2. Here Sitti Djaoerah uses the flowery Malay salutation "Kakanda" for Djahoemarkar. In Malay it means 'older sibling' and is used in formal letters to boyfriends.
3. Here Sitti Djaoerah is borrowing from Muslim Batak oral speech routines.
4. That is, he would get a *jando*, a Batak pronunciation of the Malay word *janda*, meaning a divorcée or widow. Such women are held in very low repute in southern Tapanuli.
5. The "urang bunian."
6. Pondok jolo hata dohonon ('to simply shorten the words of saying').
7. This is the standard list of places to search for lost love ones.
8. Bulus disuru ia ma halak ('straightaway he ordered a man off'): men who are dispatchable in this sense are *surusuruan*, those you order about to do your bidding. Thus, I have used the word *underling*.
9. Mulak tondi tu badan ('*tondi* soul returned to body'): the word used for "body" here is the Malay *badan* rather than the Angkola Batak *pamatang*.
10. Leham sajo ('just totally tuckered out'): the Malay word *saja* is employed here, for "just."
11. This is a literal translation of "songon halak na giot mangan jolma" ('like someone who is going to eat a human being'). The novelist, of course, knows that many Sumatrans of various ethnic backgrounds fear the Batak societies as (purportedly) recent cannibals.
12. Na haram ('things disallowed in Islam').
13. Here Naimardjolis uses the words *marbabu* ('to have *babus*', or maidservants) and *marrading* ('to have personal attendants').
14. Men are said to be like this: quiet on the outside, crying on the inside.
15. In that area, that region, on that side of the country.
16. That is, they can go to the nearby small markets if not to the big markets in town.
17. Neatness is often taken as a sign of an orderly approach to life in general and is a highly valued trait in Angkola women.
18. Indeed, village children even today clamor for sweet treats brought back from the weekly markets in town. A mother returns to her house empty handed at her peril!
19. In the 1920s the fact that a young girl knew how to do sums quickly and accurately would have been an item of considerable wonderment since few girls had been to school.
20. This rush of lovely phrases is taken directly from *turiturian* speech.
21. This is a standardized way of talking about people from different parts of Angkola and Mandailing.
22. The wording in the original is "Amboi . . . ma . . ."
23. That is, those good-looking Malay schoolmarms who live over that way.
24. "Four Moonshining Months" (opat sirumondang bulan): *rondang bulan* is the moonlight, and *rumondang* has the sense of "shinier moonlight." The infix results in the comparative form, as in *gorsing* 'yellow' and *gumorsing* 'yellower'. The *si* transforms this word into flowery *andung* speech, in which many nouns acquire fancy, indirect forms.

25. A cliché: the favorite playground where I played as a happy, carefree child.
26. Letter writers in southern Tapanuli use *here* to indicate the place where the missive will be read, not where the writers are located.
27. This is a common enough fear in this part of Tapanuli, where severe malaria is endemic.
28. Djahoemarkar uses the words *ubat lungun* here, meaning "medicine for my love longings and loneliness." This is lovers' speech.
29. This is a favorite way for separated friends or lovers to communicate: to meet each other in the moon.

CHAPTER 14

1. "Djahoemarkar's Escape" reads in the original "Dalandalan Djahoemarkar Kehe Mambuang Diri" ('The Road, the Route Djahoemarkar Took to Go Throw Himself Away, to Cast his Fate to the Winds').
2. This is Angkola Lombang, the area around Padangsidimpuan, in contrast to Angkola Dolok, or "Mountain Angkola," the region around Sipirok.
3. The last word is *harto*, from the Malay *harta*.
4. Halak partongaan.
5. A sign of good breeding, this link between speech and good manners is invoked often in *adat* oratory.
6. *Dikir* recitations are hypnotically paced, chanted repetitions of the Muslim confession of faith, often performed in unison in groups.
7. "Si rumondop udan," an *andung* term.
8. "Lajar ni Komidi," a reference perhaps to popular entertainment forms.
9. This is a common proverb.
10. "Our own people" (halak hita): this clearly refers to Angkola people, Mandailing people. The other terms in this sentence are "toketoke Cino" and "bangso na asing" (other ethnic peoples, "bangsa yang lain").
11. The original word is *rapak*, but I have separated the syllables here.
12. This is an accurate point: Sipirok households tend not to use buffaloes to plow their fields.
13. Mulakmulak harkar sidangolan ('their feelings of pain and suffering kept opening up, again and again').
14. This may also have been more in the nature of a corral door.
15. This is a reference to a kind of miasma that chills the bones and leaves the unprotected and vulnerable sick.
16. Datu bonggar ni aji: extremely adept and powerful *datu* healer-diviners.
17. Talking to a soul-sick person is supposed to be a good way to cheer them up.
18. Quotation marks are placed around the name Djahoemarkar in the original.
19. Baritaon patotorkonsa ('to put forward the words of a story'): a reference to oral tale telling.
20. "Ari na parpudi i" is the final day, the Day of Judgment, in a Muslim sense.
21. This heartfelt declaration is of the sort that would be moaned and sobbed rather than simply spoken.
22. This section is an especially heart-wrenching one for Angkola readers since it involves a beloved grandmother holding on to her *paompu* (grandchild) and pleading with him not to leave.
23. "The company's cops" (hupas ni gompomi): the company here is the Dutch state, a reference to the old Dutch East India Company, which predated the establishment of the colo-

nial administration. The Dutch administration (and the Dutch presence in general) were often referred to as the Kompeni far into the 1920s in South Tapanuli.

24. Aek Botik is a small, roadside village on the way north toward Tarutung.

25. Toba villages of the time often consisted of clusters of swoop-backed, thatched houses shaped like boats, surrounded by a tall fance of bamboo as protection from attack by enemies. Toba had been largely pacified by the Dutch by the 1920s, but warfare was still occurring in the 1901–1902 period the novelist is discussing. In fact, this was the period when the warrior-king Si Singamanga Raja XII was still active in his guerrilla insurrection against Dutch military control of Toba.

26. This line is said, too, of great rajas and princes in both *turiturian*s and Malay world court chronicles.

27. The people of Angkola today tend to look down on farm families from parts of Toba as being so poor that they have to mix their rice with cassava or corn.

28. Ninna bayo na marjamita I ('so says the guy who tells the stories'): this throws the veracity of the origin myths into question for the novelist's readers.

29. Her *bohi*, or forehead, became cloudy, troubled.

30. This phraseology is taken from *turiturian* chants.

31. The long passage that follows does have a Toba linguistic flavor, although it is not written in flawless, uninterrupted Toba Batak.

32. According to the origin myths, *all* Batak, of whatever subregion, trace their ancestry to Si Raja Batak.

33. Djahoemarkar, that is, had assumed his Hasibuan clan membership along the road, the better to allow him to fit in with the locally dominant clans in Toba. This clan switching is a common practice. Harahap is the dominant clan in the Padangsidimpuan area.

34. "Womb-companion" (dongan sabutuha): a Toba term for very close lineage mates, essentially brothers.

35. "Ompunta na di ginjang."

36. Tuju golang-golang.

37. "Power knowledge" (botobotoanna): *mamboto* means 'to know'.

38. These phrases are taken from *turiturian* chants.

39. To Angkola readers, this spell-speech would seem garbled and funny.

40. These are all plantation belt commercial towns on the road to Medan.

CHAPTER 15

1. Pangkalan Brandan was an important early oil industry hub on the Straits of Malacca and a magnet for migrants from Tapanuli.

2. Aru Bay is located on the east Sumatran coast of the Straits of Malacca (on the border of present-day Aceh and North Sumatra).

3. The word used in the original text is *microscoop*.

4. Thus begins a Malay-style fish story—similar to the folktales about miraculous crocodiles and princely fishes found throughout the Malay peninsula and along Sumatra's Deli coastline (also an ethnically Malay area).

5. This is one of the novel's many Mandailing song interludes. Mandailing musical styles are fairly recognizable in many parts of Angkola and Sipirok in part because marriage alliance ties link the areas.

6. Oh, oh, . . . untung dapot ni ari nadung dijagit: *untung* ('fate') is a Malay word.

7. This diminutive of Sitti Djaoerah's name is formed with the last syllable of the first word. Diminutives throughout Sumatra work this way: 'Dullah, for Abdullah, and so on.

8. In this passage, Indians are called (derisively) Kelings.

9. The original wording is "tuan kecil" (Malay).

10. A *begu* is an evil spirit. Lovely, well-formed letters were a matter of considerable public interest and commentary in the 1920s according to my Angkola Batak language teacher, who taught in the Hollandse Inlandse school (H.I.S.) in Sipirok at the time.

11. Djahoemarkar uses an unadorned statement of this sentiment here, but in proverbs and *turiturian* chants there are more ornate ways of stating the fact that one would rather die than live.

12. The two feelings described here are "sidangolon" and "riaria malungun" ('pain and suffering' and 'the joy of deep longing').

CHAPTER 16

1. The river referred to is the Batang Gadis.

2. I have added this last sentence.

3. That is, they must perform corvée labor for the Dutch provincial administration to help get the region's paved roads built.

4. People carry their cooked meals in plaited rattan satchels.

CHAPTER 17

1. The exact image here is that they will "look around for food to eat."

2. Nandjaoerah is worried about appearances. It would look bad if two unattached women were to set off on a long journey with unfamiliar men. However, with these men's whole families along everything would be perfectly proper.

3. *Adat* demands that women relatives pay a visit to a household that has just received a new baby.

4. This is a standard device for moving the story along used in both folktales and *turiturian* chants.

CHAPTER 18

1. This chapter begins with a "once upon a time" lead-in phrase: "Dompak di sada hatiha . . ."

2. Big banyan trees with shady, deep folds in their trunks figure heavily in Angkola lore about the forest, for these trees are the abodes of populations of spirits. Additionally, the highest ranking nobles in the region are called the "noblemen of the banyan tree whose leaves all meet in a single cluster" (Haruaya Mardomu Bulung).

3. This is a puzzling phrase, since during my ethnographic fieldwork in Angkola and Sipirok women did not seem particularly self-effacing. Angkola speakers are indirect, however, so perhaps this is an instance of that.

4. *Pertja Timoer* was a real Medan newspaper, and Mangaradja Silamboee was its editor. See H. Mohammad Said's *Sejarah Pers di Sumatera Utara* (1976).

5. Halak hita ('our folks', 'our sort'): an Angkola or Mandailing person. The word *mangaraja* in his honorific title clearly indicates his origins: this is a diagnostically southern Batak appellation.

6. Kesawan was a prosperous shopping and business street, a major center of Chinese-Indonesian trade. Kesawan is located just down the street from the Main Post Office and the mayor's office.

7. Seeking a mentor to provide one with financial support is perfectly respectable in an Angkola worldview. In fact, this is a quite sensible way to ensure that dangerous journeys through unknown lands will come to a good end. For more ethnographic and historical discussion of the wealthy person/bondsperson relationship in Southeast Asia, see Anthony Reid and Jennifer Brewster, eds., *Slavery, Bondage, and Dependence in Southeast Asia* (St. Martin's, 1983).
8. "Your Honor!": "ongku," from Tuanku, my Lord.
9. "A bunch of bondswomen": songon halak gadison.
10. This would doubtless be a meal at which formal "words" will be said.
11. Kissing in public is incredibly risque behavior in the southern Batak cultures, today at least.
12. This is a reference to a feared state in which one's *tondi* soul goes wandering around the countryside, making one sick and despondent. The only cure for this is to put the *tondi* back into the body.
13. Dying alone, without loving kinfolk, is one of the ultimate Angkola tragedies.
14. That is, until you have a baby.
15. The modern instrument of the telephone is meant here, and that word is used in the original.
16. That is, a goat to sacrifice for the wedding *pangupa*. The latter is the big mound of rice, meats, fish, vegetables, and hard-boiled eggs whose "advice to the newlyweds" meaning is "read" to the bridal couple as a series of good luck orations during their wedding ceremony.
17. There really are water buffalo with horns like these, one pointing up and one pointing down.

CHAPTER 19

1. That is, the *pasae robu* ceremony had been held, opening the way for the resumption of normal social relations between the bride and her home-village kin (her father's *kahang-gi*). Immediately after a wedding, a young bride should not visit these relatives; a taboo on easy social familiarity holds until the *pasae robu* ritual "cleanses the path" between the bride's new home and that of her natal kin. After a certain period of time the new couple is *dipajae* ('separated') from the household of the bridegroom's parents.
2. Dalan matobang: the road to maturity, to married, responsible adulthood.
3. Angginja kandung ('womb-anggi'): a true brother, his very own younger brother. The term employs the Malay possessive form for *his* or *her*, and the Malay word *kandung* ('womb').
4. That is, with the Javanese and the Sundanese working there on the plantation.
5. In my interviews on ethnic identity matters in my fieldwork in South Tapanuli, starting the mid 1970s, much the same sentiment was prevalent. In "other people's land," the astute immigrant will quickly take up the local clothing styles.
6. *Mas* is a respectful Javanese term of address for young men, while *kayi* means an Islamic adept, a Muslim teacher.
7. *Pewarta Deli* was another Medan newspaper.
8. The Hotel de Boer (now the Hotel Dharma Deli, right down the street from the Main Post Office) was one of the most prominent and elegant European hotels in Medan. It catered to planters, government officials, and businessmen and had a tropical, colonial air about it.
9. "Sirisiri bongkotol, haru sili laing tongkon," a proverb.
10. The word *tua* ('luck') is used here.
11. These phrases follow the conventions of *adat* speech (the signoff phrases for orations).
12. The Malay word *amuk* is used here.
13. "Javanese noblemen": *radenraden*.

14. Jails in Papua were feared places of political exile.
15. Raden Mas ('the honored, most highly respected Mas'): a young Javanese gentleman.
16. Gunung Jati: a sacred mountain in far-off Java.
17. Eating cakes and butter cookies as opposed to pounded rice-flour snacks was a sign of the European lifestyle often imitated by Batak teachers and plantation clerks in the prewar years.

CHAPTER 20

1. The Latin is used in this sentence in the original.
2. These traits are all signs of a raja's fine, high, refined behavior.
3. This is a familiar proverb from the *adat* oratory: ". . . angkon pahae do sitimpulon anso pahulu simanggurale."
4. This is the sort of closeness men in the same *kahanggi* enjoy.
5. I have taken some license here to capture the tone of the original sentence: "Nada dope he tardokkon na sonang halahi sannari?"

CHAPTER 21

1. The word here is *jeges jeges*, meaning pretty and nice looking.
2. Bang Roeslan: *Bang*, from the Malay *abang* 'older brother', is a term of address one could use toward employees of the same firm. Judging by his name, Roeslan, this driver seems to be a Malay, although that is left undetermined in the text. The Angkola characters in the novel are always identifiable, by their names or by context.
3. I have taken some poetic license with the original text here, which states more simply that Ompung is all dressed and ready.
4. Sidumadang ari.
5. This is a typical way of referring to a handsome couple.
6. Nandjaoerah uses *amang* with Djahoemarkar here, although according to strict *adat* she should call him her *bere* (husband's sister's son).
7. The original text reads "parhabang ni halak na jolo," the mode of flying for folks in the past.
8. A tree motif of the sort used here is often invoked when Angkola talk about the telling of stories (the "shape" of stories).
9. A quest for an elusive special food figures in many *turiturians*.
10. Namora i.
11. Parmanoan, as a name, means that the bearer has been named in memory of a favorite person who has died.
12. "And then" (dungi): regular stories can be paced in this same way.
13. That is, his body will be the *alamat*, the 'address' (in Malay), of all that is painful and unfortunate.
14. Si Lomlom Ulu ('Black Haired One').
15. Magic *keris* daggers that convey invulnerability always have an aura of faraway lands about them in Angkola. Java's and Minangkabau's *keris* lore are, of course, extensive.
16. That is, they sparred a bit as possible *martandang* courtship rhyme partners will do.
17. Porlak parsanggulan.
18. This is a secret move made by *datus* in their curing rituals.
19. That is, now we are switching over to the Upper Continent (these are highly standardized scene-switching phrases).

20. Through about the year 1930, noble families in Angkola and Sipirok would give their daughters fancy, sacred names of this sort.
21. "Mouth of the sky" (Baba pintu langit): from Malay. *Baba* is considered a coarse word for "mouth" in Angkola Batak.
22. This phrasing is also used in *alok-alok* oratory.
23. The plate in question was doubtless part of the family's house treasure, so it should have been treated with great care and fear.
24. Having many side rooms in a house is a sign of immense wealth (probably a Minangkabau motif).
25. Toba Silindung Julu lies to the north, in Toba.
26. This is the standard "better to die than to live" proverb.
27. Many Angkola today believe in the efficacy of this particularly sneaky sort of spell.

CHAPTER 22

1. Talking about the relationship between institutions in a language of clan descent and marriage alliance is a mainstay of Angkola conversation today.
2. The "stringing words together" reference evokes adeptness at *adat* speech.
3. Sitti Djaoerah uses the affectionate address term *le* here, from the Angkola word for friend, *ale.*
4. This reference to houseposts recalls *horja*-level oratory.

CHAPTER 23

1. "Unseen spirits": na so niida.
2. The word *Postpakket* is used in the original text.
3. These *bacobacoan* 'sacred readings' are also gifts offered to the honored dead. The usage is derived from the Malay *bacaan* 'things to read'.
4. Sitti Djaoerah uses the kin term *damang* 'my own father' here (versus *amang*, a less intimate form).

Glossary

adat: 'ancient, inherited custom' in many folk views in southern Tapanuli.

Alhamdulillah: 'Praise be to God', said in thanksgiving.

alok-alok: elaborate oratory delivered by village rajas at nighttime political oratory sessions during *horja* feasts.

amang: kin term used in address and in reference to fathers.

amangboru: the man who married one's father's sister; a woman's husband's father.

amang uda: father's younger brother (often *uda*).

ambtenaar: (Dutch) civil servant, official in the colonial government.

anak: 'son' in the Angkola Batak language; 'children' in Bahasa Indonesia.

anakboru: one's indebted, subservient, wife receivers, one's "girl children"; a lineage's daughters and the men who marry them (and those men's lineage mates).

andung: sobbed lament speech wailed by old women and brides at times of leavetaking (e.g., at funerals over a corpse or when a girl leaves her natal home to be married and move to her husband's home).

anggi: kin term of address older people in a *kahanggi* lineage use toward those younger than themselves, in that group, within the same generation. Older brothers say *anggi* to their younger brothers and to the latters' wives. Women say *anggi* to their husband's younger brothers and those men's wives. Men also say *anggi* to women who stand in a marriageable relationship to them.

angkang: 'older member of my lineage', a kin term used by a man to address his older brothers, older males of his generation within his lineage, and those men's wives. Women say *angkang* to their husbands and older males of their generation within the *kahanggi*. Girls say *angkang* to their boyfriends to denote a marriageable relationship. But girls and women say *ito* ('clan brother') to their brothers in their own home clan.

apa: informal rendition of *bapak*, the Indonesian word for father.

babere: for a man, his sister's child and the young man who marries his daughter; for a woman, her husband's sister's child—and, in the specific incidence of the husband's sister's son, this married couple's *anakboru*, who will apply to them to marry their daughter.

bargot: the sugar palm, the source of red sugar.

Batunadua: major village located several kilometers outside of Padangsidimpuan on the way to Sipirok.

begu: powerful and dangerous evil spirit.

bendi: two-wheeled horse carriage.

benggol: colonial-era coin.

Bismillah: 'In the name of God', said as a sort of grace before meals.

boru: 'daughter', 'daughter of' (as in Boru Lubis, daughter of the Lubis clan).

bujing-bujing: young, unmarried, adolescent girl.

bulu aur tobol: length of bamboo tubing with powerful messages recorded on it in the Batak script.

Butet: 'youngest girl in the family', a term of intimacy and affection.

crani: clerk on a plantation.

damang: particularly intimate kin term of reference for the speaker's own father. The *da* prefix may be attached to numerous Angkola kin terms of address to the same effect.

Daret: reference to West Sumatra and the Minangkabau people who live there.

datu: powerful healer/spell caster.

datuk: honorific title in infrequent use in Angkola but common in Minangkabau.

Dja: shortened form of *raja*.

doli-doli: adolescent, unmarried, young man.

durian: strong-smelling, creamy-fleshed, seasonal fruit.

ende: generic term for "song."

florin: Dutch coin.

gondang: ritual gong ensemble played with the rajas' permission at *horja* feasts.

gordang: special large *gondang* ensemble, from Mandailing, with many drums.

Gunung Tua: town and *adat* domain northeast of Sipirok; Padang Bolak.

guru: teacher.

Hari Raya: the great feast day ending the Muslim Fasting Month.

hikayat: tale, story, history.

horas: 'good luck, good soul-health', spoken as a greeting.

horja: large ceremonial feast involving the sacrifice of water buffalo under the ritual supervision of the rajas.

hula-hula: Toba Batak for *mora* 'wife givers'.

huta: village.

ijeng-ijeng: cleverly phrased songs, probably influenced by Minangkabau styles.

inang: term of reference and address for mothers.

ito: 'clan sister', 'clan brother' in terms of address; also a speaker's own siblings.

jambu: rose apple.

juri: type of horse carriage.

kahanggi: one's close lineage mates (for a man); for a woman, the lineage she "carries" once she gets married (her husband's lineage).

kakanda: 'older lineage companion', address term used by girls with eligible boys.

kebaya: lacy, short jacket worn by married women.

kele: 'kind woman-friend', term of address used between grown women.

kenduri: communal prayer meal in Islam.

keris: magically powerful, curved dagger.

kupia: black felt cap worn by men.

Kweekschool: elite, Dutch-language, teacher-training institute in Bukittinggi and Padangsidimpuan. A *kweekeling* is a student there.

leerlingen: (Dutch) pupil.

lezing: (Dutch) lecture.

lobe: Muslim religious adept.

lomang: sweet treat made of sugar and sticky rice, packed into long bamboo tubes, and steamed.

maatschappy: (Dutch) society, company.

malim: Muslim religious official.

mandur: overseer of a work gang.

mangaraja: honorific title for men.

marah: honorific title for men; rare in Angkola.

marga: patrilineal clan such as the Siregars, the Harahaps, the Lubises, and so on.

martandang: ritualized courtship, with verse speech, often traded in secret at night.

mesjid: mosque.

mera: carp.

Minangkabau: West Sumatra's home ethnic society.

mora: one's holy wife givers.

Nai: 'Mother of . . .' (similar to *nan*).

namboru: one's father's sister; for a woman, her husband's mother.

nantulang: '*tulang*'s wife', 'wife of mother's brother'; for a man, his wife's mother.

Natal: coastal town in southern Mandailing feared for its esoteric lore and knowledge of poison.

nyonya: 'Mrs.', 'married woman', a term of respect for a Dutch woman in colonial times.

ois: term of exclamation thought to be characteristic of older women.

ompung: 'grandmother', 'grandfather'; also the term of address that grandchildren and grandparents use with each other.

onderneming: (Dutch) an enterprise.

orang bunian: dangerous, invisible beings who live in places such as remote mountain ravines and make travelers disappear.

orangkaya: in Angkola, a village raja's main *anakboru* man, his spokesperson in *adat* matters.

pangupa: the ceremonial mound of special ritual foods used in *adat* for blessing a baby or a newlywed couple.

parompa sadun: small *ulos* for carrying babies.

parumaen: 'daughter-in-law'; a woman says *parumaen* to her brother's daughter and her son's wife.

raja: ceremonial chief in *adat*.

ranto: lands beyond the rural home regions in Tapanuli.

rendang: spicy, slow-simmered, meat dish from Minangkabau.

salak: snakefruit.

sarong: wrapped cloth garment worn by both men and women.

sihatirangga: lovely golden carp, whose scales are as red as a new bride's decorated fingernails.

sutan: honorific title for men.

Syariah: Islamic law.

syarikat: organization.

Taring: 'littlest girl in the family' in Mandailing usage.

tondi: soul.

tuan: 'Mr.', a title of respect used with Dutchmen in colonial times.

turiturian: chanted epics.

ulos: sacred woven textiles employed to firm up the souls of wearers. Wife givers bestow *ulos* on their *anakboru* on such occasions as weddings and the birth of a baby.

ummat: members of a religious community, in this case, Islam.

Uncok: Friendly appelation meaning 'littlest boy in the family'.

ungut-ungut: slow-paced lament songs sung by boys.

vergadering: (Dutch) public meeting.

ziarah: a Muslim graveside visit undertaken to clean the grave and pray for the soul of the departed.

Acknowledgements

Translating *Sitti Djaoerah* from Angkola Batak (and its various additional linguistic excursions) has been a long-time endeavor, stretching back to my first Angkola language lessons in 1974 and 1975 with my teacher, Bapak G. W. Siregar, in Sipirok, South Tapanuli. I have amassed many intellectual debts in working on this project: to schoolteachers and ritual orators in the Sipirok region who introduced me (first, as a graduate student) to both conversational-level Angkola Batak and its challenging registers of oratorical speech; to South Tapanuli writers and publishers, who spoke to me at length in 1986 and 1987 about Angkola print literature and the history of southern Batak literacy; and to two American universities and colleges— Ohio University and Holy Cross —which generously supported research leaves in Indonesia, times spent refining the translation and investigating this 1920s novel's original newspaper origins. The Lembaga Ilmu Pengetahuan Indonesia (LIPI, the Indonesian national government's research agency) provided sponsorship for various stages of this research, while the Fulbright program generously awarded me a fellowship in 1992 to return to the Sipirok area (to the village of Bungabondar) for eight months to complete the first draft of the translation. There I was able to check its more difficult passages with Baginda Hasudungan Siregar (now Ompu Raja Oloan), an expert orator of great accomplishment (and sympathy toward his American anthropologist *ito*, or Siregar clan sister). Ohio University's Baker Fund provided support for a summer 1989 trip to Sipirok to begin my intensive collaborative work with Ompu Raja Oloan. Holy Cross went on to afford me a leave in 1992 for the Fulbright project in Bungabondar. The Social Science Research Council and the National Endowment for the Humanities also provided grant support for various fieldwork stays in Sumatra.

Individuals to whom I am most indebted for help in working with this wonderful novel are, first and foremost, Bapak G. W.—his arduous five-days-a-week Angkola language lessons gave me the best possible, early, deep immersion in this language world; Ompu Elpina Boru Regar, one of Bapak G. W.'s fellow retired schoolteachers and my landlady in Sipirok during numerous early fieldwork stays in the 1970s and 1980s; and Ompu Raja Doli Siregar, a prominent raja (or ceremonial chief) from Padangbujur who adopted my early fieldwork efforts concerning Sipirok-area oratory as his own project and helped me gain access to many *horja* feasts where I could tape record and study the types of ritual speeches so integral to the novelist Soetan Hasoendoetan's print aesthetic. All of these fine teachers and protectors of mine have since passed away.

The novelist's daughter, living in retirement in 1992 in a village outside Sipirok, allowed Ompu Raja Doli and me to come to her home several times for long chats about her father's life and work. The staff of the Padangsidimpuan publishing house Pustaka Timur were also generous with interview time in talks about South Tapanuli literary history. The library staff at the National Library in Jakarta and Leiden's KITLV were also unfailingly supportive of this research, especially as it touched on their fine old colonial-era newspaper collections from Sumatra.

My Holy Cross colleagues historian Karen Turner and anthropologist Christine Greenway doggedly and faithfully read through many early awkward versions of both the translation and the introductory essay, and, as always, they cheerily told me to keep plugging away at what often seemed to be too huge a task to ever finish. Holy Cross sociologist Royce Singleton put up with at least three years of complaints along this same line. My department secretary Margaret Post provided superb, unflagging support as well, in helping me prepare drafts of the manuscript. Karl Heider of the University of South Carolina provided sage advice on the whole project in 1994, while three anonymous reviewers for the University of Wisconsin's Center for Southeast Asian Studies monograph series offered on-target commentaries that went far toward producing a more polished final draft. Andrea Canfield, publications editor for the Center for Southeast Asian Studies at Wisconsin, shepherded the project along with patience and much good sense, as did center director Alfred W. McCoy. Finally, Jan Opdyke—copy editor extraordinaire for this uncommonly challenging, multivocal text—earned her spot in Copyeditor's Heaven several times over for her aid in making the English version of *Sitti Djaoerah* as true as we could both to its 1920s Indies, Sumatran linguistic origins and the emotional and literary worlds of its new, English-language readers.

About the Author

M. J. Soetan Hasoendoetan (ca. 1887-1948) was a Sipirok man from the Sipahutar clan who spent most of his work life as a head clerk on a Dutch-owned tea plantation near Pematang Siantar, on Sumatra in Western Indonesia. A largely unknown author today, he wrote numerous Angkola Batak-language works, including a long verse narrative, several novels, and a prose rendition of an epic chant. He often freelanced for Batak-language newspapers, including Sibolga's *Poestaha*, where *Sitti Djaoerah* first appeared. He wrote in relative isolation from more elite Sumatran writers' circles, those associated with Balai Pustaka. As a young man of about 20, Soetan Hasoendoetan and his bride migrated from his home village Pagaranjulu to the Deli coast of northern Sumatra: the same geographical trajectory evoked in his novel translated here into English for the first time.

About the Translator

Susan Rodgers has studied Angkola Batak oratory and print literacy in the Sipirok area of South Tapanuli, North Sumatra, Indonesia since her first fieldwork there in 1974-1977. After undergraduate work at Brown University, she received her Ph.D. in anthropology from the University of Chicago in 1978. She is the co-author, with anthropologist Rita Smith Kipp, of *Indonesian Religions in Transition* (1987), and the author of *Power and Gold: Jewelry from Indonesia, Malaysia, and the Philippines* (1985) and *Telling Lives, Telling History: Autobiography and the Historical Imagination in Modern Indonesia* (1995). She is Professor of Anthropology and Chair of the Department of Sociology and Anthropology at the College of the Holy Cross in Worcester, Massachusetts.

Center for Southeast Asian Studies
University of Wisconsin-Madison
Monograph Series

Sitti Djoaoerah: A Novel of Colonial Indonesia
by M. J. Soetan Hasoendoetan, translated by Susan Rodgers

Face of Empire: United States - Philippines Relations, 1898-1946
by Frank Hindman Golay

Inventing a Hero: The Posthumous Re-Creation of Andres Bonifacio
by Glenn May

The Mekong Delta: Ecology, Economy, and Revolution, 1860-1960
by Pierre Brocheux

Autonomous Histories, Particular Truths: Essays in Honor of John Smail
edited by Laurie J. Sears

An Anarchy of Families: State and Family in the Philippines
edited by Alfred W. McCoy

Salome: A Filipino Filmscript by Ricardo Lee
translated by Rofel Brion

Recalling the Revolution: Memoirs of a Filipino General
by Santiago Alvarez, translated by Paula Carolina S Malay

Anthropology Goes to War: Professional Ethics and Counterinsurgency in Thailand
by Eric Wakin

Voices from the Thai Countryside: The Short Stories of Samruam Singh
edited and translated by Katherine Bowie

Putu Wijaya in Performance: An Approach to Indonesian Theatre
edited by Ellen Rafferty

Gender, Power, and the Construction of the Moral Order
edited by Nancy Eberhardt

Bomb: Indonesian Short Stories by Putu Wijaya
edited Ellen Rafferty and Laurie J. Sears

Aesthetic Tradition and Cultural Transitions in Java and Bali
edited by Stephanie Morgan and Laurie J. Sears

A Complete Account of the Peasant Uprising in the Central Region
by Phan Chu Trinh, translated by Peter Baugher and Vu Ngo Chieu

Publications Committee
Carol J. Compton
Daniel F. Doeppers
Alfred W. McCoy, Chair
R. Anderson Sutton
Thongchai Winichakul
Janet Opdyke, Editor
Andrea Canfield, Editor